THE LAST
GUARDIAN
AND THE KEEPER OF THE MAGI

THE LAST
GUARDIAN
AND THE KEEPER OF THE MAGI

ASHLAND MENSHOUSE

TATE PUBLISHING
AND ENTERPRISES, LLC

Published by Tate Publishing & Enterprises, LLC
127 E. Trade Center Terrace | Mustang, Oklahoma 73064 USA
1.888.361.9473 | www.tatepublishing.com

Tate Publishing is committed to excellence in the publishing industry. The company reflects the philosophy established by the founders, based on Psalm 68:11,
"The Lord gave the word and great was the company of those who published it."

Book design copyright © 2013 by Tate Publishing, LLC. All rights reserved.
Cover design by Jomar Ouano
Interior design by Jomar Ouano

Published in the United States of America

ISBN: 978-1-62746-413-0
1. Fiction / Fantasy / Urban
2. Fiction / Action & Adventure
13.09.27

For my momma.
Except for God, no one have I struggled against more,
But for God, no one has loved me more.

"Are you ready?" Aubrey glanced at Rodriqa to his left.

Rodriqa popped her neck, causing her beaded braids to clink around her shoulders. "Yep."

Aubrey looked to his right. Hidden by a curtain of black hair, Jordana pushed her honey-colored glasses up her nose.

"Good?" asked Aubrey.

Jordana nodded.

The three of them marched up a grassy hill toward a plump man in denim overalls. He shouted, "Hurry it up!" at a dozen men, who were leading a score of horses by their reins away from a two-story barn, which was the size of a football field. Yellow lanterns from inside the stables cast patches of light on the grounds outside that mixed with the moonlight above, projecting an eerie sheen on the dewing grass.

A blast of wind raced across the grounds. Strands of milky clouds stretched across the moon's face. Two mares whinnied and reared upward. Their handlers pulled back, anchoring them in place.

Jordana and Rodriqa's hair swished around their faces as the three friends walked up to the plump man.

"Mr. Creightony?" called Rodriqa.

The man in overalls turned toward them, his right eye twitching as he glared at the three children. "Are you...them?"

Rodriqa nodded. "We're the NeighborGhoul Watch." Rodriqa pointed toward the barn. "Is that where your problem is?"

"Yes." Mr. Creightony rubbed his right eye, trying to press its twitch away. "I thought there were five of you."

"There are," replied Aubrey.

"The other two will be here soon," added Rodriqa.

Mr. Creightony winced. "Can you really do what they say you can do?"

"We've killed three ghosts, two demons, and a witch," said Rodriqa, glancing at Aubrey. He smiled at her halfheartedly. "Sometimes it's a bit messy," continued Rodriqa. "But I think we can help."

"How?" Mr. Creightony squinted to control his twitch.

"Excuse me?" Rodriqa furrowed her brow.

"How do you do it?"

Rodriqa pursed her lips and stretched out her right shoulder. Aubrey scrunched up his cheek and scratched his pale, freckled ear.

Jordana looked up, her eyes peering over the top of her honey-colored glasses. "We're scarier than they are."

Suddenly, the lanterns in the stables flickered. The wind changed direction. More horses bucked against their handlers. Three of the animals yanked themselves free and galloped across the grounds.

Mr. Creightony turned around and shook his fists. "Grab those geldings!"

The door to the hayloft on the second story of the barn slammed open, and clumps of hay spewed across the field.

Rodriqa cracked her knuckles. "Let's get started." She stomped toward the stables.

Aubrey pulled his inhaler out of his pocket, put it in his mouth, and pressed the canister as he inhaled. Jordana nudged him forward. They followed Rodriqa.

"Don't damage anything!" yelled Mr. Creightony.

Aubrey glanced over his shoulder. "We'll try."

Trotting up to the barn, Rodriqa dodged two handlers corralling an edgy mare. A few yards from the barn, she stopped. The door slammed shut.

Aubrey and Jordana stepped up behind Rodriqa.

"Guess we're not welcome," murmured Jordana.

Aubrey rubbed his neck. "Maybe they've heard about us."

Rodriqa balled up her fists and smacked one on top of the other. "Hammer. Nail." She grabbed the handle to the barn door and yanked it open. Slowly stepping inside, she examined the stables.

Bits of hay swirled across the concrete floor. Five paddocks lined each side of the barn's central alley, their doors flapping wildly. Lantern-style electrical lights swung overhead, casting rocking shadows through the railings and stalls. Harnesses and saddles flopped against the walls they hung from.

Walking down the alley and inspecting each paddock, Rodriqa arched her back and shook her fingers. She glanced over her shoulder. "Make it glow, Aub."

Aubrey nodded and stepped inside the stables, his nose crinkling at the bitter smell.

Jordana shimmied around behind him and took off her glasses. "Shouldn't we wait on Buzz and Magnos?"

"We don't have time." Rodriqa held up her hands. Her fingertips glistened a sparkling white, and a ghostly gloss rushed up her arms. "Aubrey. Eyes."

Closing his eyes, Aubrey aimed his face at the end of the stables.

Red and green phosphenes behind his eyelids swirled, merged, and split until darkness wedged in from the periphery. Aubrey squeezed his lids tighter together and focused on pressing his heart outward. In an instant, a small glowing figure appeared in his dark sight. Its long, thin head twitched, and its four limbs scrambled in the air.

"There!" Aubrey pointed up to his left. "Last stall, I think."

"Good." Rodriqa's entire form was now completely transparent. She sprinted down the alley. Jumping up, she grabbed the end rail of the last swinging door and flipped it around. The paddock door slammed shut with her inside. "Now!"

Aubrey snapped open his eyes.

The lanterns shuddered. A green translucent, doll-sized creature with three yellow eyes came into view at the far top corner of the stall.

Rodriqa jumped up and grabbed the creature by its wispy legs. It screeched, and the two of them fell back into the paddock. The stall's walls shuddered. Hay flew into the air.

Jordana yelped and hid behind Aubrey. He grabbed her hand, and she gripped it tightly. His heart fluttered.

Suddenly, the paddock's door slammed open. Rodriqa skidded across the concrete floor and landed against the opposite stall's gate.

Aubrey took several steps forward. "Rodriqa, are you okay?"

"Yep!" Rodriqa hopped up and ran back into the left-hand stall.

Jordana screamed. Aubrey turned toward her. Jordana was scooting along the stable floor on her stomach, her hair standing straight out as if she was being pulled by something invisible.

Aubrey closed his eyes. The phosphenes faded, and the darkness appeared. In his dark sight, he saw the same green, doll-sized creature, floating in midair and hauling Jordana forward.

"Hey!" Rodriqa rounded out of the stall. "It disappeared!"

"It's over here!" Aubrey opened his eyes. The creature pulling Jordana was now physical. Aubrey swatted at it. Squalling, the creature released Jordana and flew straight up, bursting through a lantern. Its glass shattered with a fiery pop. The creature somersaulted through two more lanterns. The fixtures exploded, and sparks showered the stables.

With one arm, Aubrey raised his hand to protect himself and reached for Jordana with the other, helping her off the floor.

Rodriqa raced toward Aubrey and Jordana. In an instant, she was smacked sideways into another paddock door. Rodriqa winced. "Uh-oh!"

She turned to the side and looked at the air around her. "I think there's more than one!"

"Really?" asked Aubrey as he and Jordana backed up against the inside of the barn door. "But I only saw one!"

Rodriqa felt an invisible jab to her stomach. "Check again!" Aubrey closed his eyes. Holding his breath, he tightened all the muscles in his torso and searched his dark sight. In a flash, three green creatures, each with long, thin heads and three yellow eyes, appeared above him, flying in circles.

"Hammer!" shouted Aubrey as he opened his eyes. "Nail!"

The three creatures materialized at the top of the stables, spinning wildly among the sparking lanterns.

With her head down, Jordana tugged at Aubrey's shirt sleeve. He looked down. She pointed over her shoulder. A bale of hay in the corner blazed with fire.

Downhill from the stable grounds, a dark-blue 1970s Volkswagen sped up a dirt road toward the handlers, who were securing horses in a barbed wire pen. The car veered off the road toward the barn, plowing over the field grass.

"Fire!" shouted Mr. Creightony at the handlers as he watched the stables' windows flicker. "Get the hose!"

The Volkswagen pulled past Mr. Creightony and then stopped abruptly. The driver's side door flung open. Magnos, a six-foot-six muscular teenager with shaggy blond hair, jumped out of the car and raced toward the barn.

The passenger's side door opened. Buzz, a chubby boy with dark, curly hair and horn-rimmed glasses, plopped onto the grass. "Wait!" he yelled after Magnos. "I don't have my suit on yet!" Rolling over in the grass, Buzz pulled a blue polyurethane suit, adorned with silver strips up to his waist and pushed himself onto his feet. Grabbing a visor from his seat, he toddled toward the stables.

Inside the barn, smoke diffused along the ceiling. With pitchfork in hand, Aubrey raked strands of burning hay away from the pile in the corner. Jordana ran over to a middle stall. She jerked a shovel off the wall and ran up behind Aubrey. Slamming the shovel's spade against the concrete, she extinguished a patch of fiery straw. Aubrey jumped in the air. Jordana held up her hand so he wouldn't see her eyes. She reared back the shovel and smacked it against another patch of burning chaff.

"Hoaker croaker!" Swallowing against his dry throat, Aubrey raked another patch of smoldering hay across the concrete.

One of the green creatures flew down from the ceiling. It wrapped its wispy arms around Jordana's neck and pressed a pointed finger under her chin. She dropped the shovel.

Kicking off a paddock door, Rodriqa leapt into the air and spun toward the encircling creatures. She caught two by their arms and dropped to the floor. The ensnared creatures screeched and flailed violently in Rodriqa's grip, reeling her apart with outstretched arms.

Aubrey turned around and thrust his pitchfork at the creature holding Jordana's throat. Growling, the green creature's yellow eyes smoldered. It leapt off Jordana and grabbed the tines of the pitchfork. Jordana stumbled backward, clutching her neck.

Wrestling the pitchfork out of Aubrey's grasp, the creature flipped the pitchfork around and pressed its sharp ends against Aubrey's chest. Suddenly, the barn door slid open. Magnos stepped inside. Gripping Aubrey by the shirt collar, Magnos heaved Aubrey off the ground and planted him in the opposite corner. Magnos reached forward and grabbed the pitchfork's pole and wrenched it from the creature's grasp. Seething, the creature flashed tiny sharp teeth at Magnos.

"I got it!" Jordana stepped in front of the green impish beast. She stared at the creature's yellow eyes. Inhaling deeply, she murmured, "Stay. Stay. Stay."

All three of its eyes widened. Bowing its head with its gaze fixed on Jordana, the imp hovered several feet from her. Slowly, she shifted away from the fire. The creature inched back in the air at her bidding.

Magnos and Aubrey looked up. Rodriqa was being lifted off the ground by the other two creatures. She coughed violently as her head rose into the veil of gray smoke along the ceiling. She kicked her ghostly legs, which were dulling into their fleshly form. The two creatures, flying in opposite directions, tried to draw and quarter her.

Aubrey raced toward Rodriqa. He wrapped his arms around her legs. Aubrey's slight frame deterred the creatures' lift only for a moment. Then Rodriqa and Aubrey rose into the air together.

Magnos bounded forward and batted at the creature in Rodriqa's left hand. The creature moaned and dropped to the ground. Magnos stomped it with his size 16 foot. It's spindly extremities wilted and faded away.

Rodriqa and Aubrey fell to the ground and tumbled across the concrete.

With her left hand now free, Rodriqa snapped her palm around the remaining creature's neck. Flexing her shoulders, she ripped the creature in two, and its wispy parts drifted into pieces and disappeared.

Fully dressed in his blue polyurethane suit, Buzz ran inside the stables with haggard breath. He stared at Jordana, the remaining imp floating before her.

"A barnling!" Buzz held up his cell phone and took a picture of it. "We've killed these before."

"A dead barnling." Leaning forward, Magnos grabbed the pitchfork on the floor and speared the creature in front of Jordana. For a few seconds, its eyes flashed brightly. Then the creature evaporated into a fog of green mist.

A stampede of footsteps thundered outside the barn door. Buzz spun around. Three handlers carrying a large white hose charged at the stables.

"There's the fire!" shouted the front handler as he wrenched the nozzle forward.

Buzz held up his hands. "Wait!"

A pressurized spray of water blasted Buzz in the chest and face, knocking him to the concrete. He sputtered and rolled away.

Magnos leaned down and pulled Buzz to his feet. "Glad you hadn't turned on your suit yet."

Gagging and spitting, Buzz ran his hand down his face. "Me too."

The three handlers ran into the barn and aimed the hose at the burning mound of hay, dousing the blaze into sopping embers.

Slowly, smoke billowed out of the windows. The lanterns stopped swinging, and the undamaged ones shined brightly.

While the handlers tugged the hose outside, Mr. Creightony jogged into the barn and inspected the stables. He then glared at Rodriqa. "Did you get them?"

Clearing her throat, Rodriqa stood up. "Yep." She scraped the side of her foot along the concrete, gathering three round, white stones, each with a single point of bright orange light orbiting around it, into a small pile.

Dripping wet, Buzz turned around and pointed at the white stones. "This is how we know they're gone. These stones are a soul remnant of some sort."

"And they don't last long." Aubrey crouched down, hovering his hand over them.

Mr. Creightony crept forward to examine the stones. Each slightly larger than an egg, they sparkled in the lantern light. The orange lights spun around each stone more and more quickly. Suddenly, all three disappeared.

A handler ran up to the barn. "Mr. Creightony, the horses!"

Mr. Creightony stepped toward the door. "What's wrong?"

The handler stopped and shook his head. "Nothing." He pointed toward the barbed wire pen. "They're all sleeping."

Down the hill, mares, colts, and stallions stood still, without a whinny or a twitch.

Looking back at the five friends, Mr. Creightony dug into his pocket and pulled out a wad of hundreds. He slapped it into Rodriqa's hand. "Thank you."

Rodriqa nodded and walked out of the stables. Magnos and Aubrey followed her.

Buzz snapped his arms down to his sides and then saluted Mr. Creightony. "Anytime! If you ever have another spook or phantom, don't hesitate to call us."

Mr. Creightony's right eye twitched.

Buzz sidled up to him and whispered, "And if you know anyone who has a similar problem, make sure to give them our number."

Sliding her honey-colored glasses up her nose, Jordana grabbed Buzz and tugged him outside.

Outside, the handlers stared at the five friends as they walked down the hill.

Magnos blew his hair off his eyes. "At least there was actually something to fight this time."

"And at least it was easier than killing Hovis Trottle," added Jordana.

Rodriqa chuckled. "They've all been easier than Hovis Trottle."

"It would have been a lot easier if I could have used my suit." Buzz stuck out his arms, his blue suit's silver lines flashing in the moonlight.

Aubrey furrowed his brow. "The suit didn't do anything."

"Just wait." Buzz raised his chin. "You'll get your chance to see how uber it is."

In swirling muck between tectonic plates thousands of miles away from Lake Julian, a searing wind rushed over the darkness. Groaning rock dropped into molten ruin as creaking bedrock shook the loam above. Crushed by lightless heat, where the earth's crust broke upon the mantle, boulders of granite and basalt melted into magma, and a sour steam, which would have scorched any flesh that dared enter these depths, simmered upward.

A shrill whisper shattered the shadow of a chasm. "What more have you heard?"

Another voice snapped in reply, "The rumors persist."

"Impossible," seethed the first whisper.

"I've have heard the same warnings," spoke a deep voice.

"How can you be sure?"

"No one can be sure," spoke the second voice.

"Does it have a guardian?"

"No!"

"Yes!"

"The description is unclear."

"Armies are mounting."

"Shade and shinar stand ready."

"How can it be stopped?"

"Some say it can't."

"Anything can be stopped," argued the third voice.

"The end comes too soon."

"The balance must be maintained."

"Could it be the Terminal Prophecy is at hand?"

"The Terminal Prophecy is a myth."

A gray, shimmering light split the darkness of the chasm where three figures stood amidst a whirling tempest of ash and ember.

"Let us go see this seer for ourselves."

CONVOCATION AND PROVOCATION

Wednesday.

Aubrey stood in the doorway at the side entrance to Lake Julian High School. The parking lot was full. He looked back into the hallway behind him. It was empty. He checked his phone. The time was 3:36.

The last bell had rung six minutes ago, and no other kids were leaving the grounds, no cars were speeding out of the lot, and there wasn't a sound to be heard. He withdrew into a tiny foyer as its metal door clicked shut. Aubrey readjusted his backpack on his shoulder and peered down both ends of the hallway. No one was there.

Scuttling next to the lockers, he stretched up onto his toes to peek into several windows of the row of classroom doors down the hall. No students. No teachers. No movement.

His heart skipped a beat, bewildered by the unnerving solitude. *What am I missing?* he thought to himself. He threaded his fingers through his stringy, bright red hair as he decided which way to go next.

Aubrey rounded the corner and sighed with relief. A familiar face was at the opposite end.

Dressed in his forest-green, button-down uniform with an oil-smudged rag dangling from his back pocket, the high school janitor, Griggs, leaned on his mop handle. For Aubrey, Griggs wasn't exactly a close friend, but he had always been helpful, even if Aubrey hadn't wanted his help.

"Hey, Griggs," hollered Aubrey down the hallway. "Where is everybody?"

Griggs didn't move. Aubrey figured with the whitening of his bushy hair and eyebrows, his hearing had most likely faded too. Aubrey trotted halfway down and waved his arms at Griggs. He glanced at Aubrey and then moved into the other hallway, out of sight.

Aubrey grimaced, a little annoyed by his dismissive disappearance. He heard a man with a northeastern accent speaking from around the corner. Aubrey slowed as he approached the end of the hall, listening to the conversation.

"You won't be here long."

"I'll be here as long as there's work to do," bit back Griggs.

"You don't understand the consequences of your actions," replied the man. "Your interference exceeds insubordination. Little tolerance is left for those who repeatedly choose the wrong side."

Griggs snorted. "Isn't it funny how the treacherous always use words that describe themselves?"

Aubrey rounded the corner. Griggs clutched his mop to his side and kept his head straight.

Aubrey had never seen the other man before. Well-groomed, he was dressed in a suit and tie with straight, salt-and-pepper hair cut in bowl style around his crown. His slanting nose turned to the left at the end, and a dark mole dotted the center of his chin.

The man's crystal-blue eyes widened at the sight of Aubrey. Turning quickly, the stranger stormed away with his head high and shoulders back.

Griggs reached his long, lanky fingers across the hall and wrenched Aubrey up by his shirt collar.

"Where is the book?" Griggs demanded, inches from his face.

"The...w-w-w-hat?" sputtered Aubrey, shocked at the janitor's aggressive stance.

"Solluna," Griggs replied. "Is it hidden?"

Aubrey nodded.

"Keep it that way." Griggs dropped Aubrey. "You'll be late."

Aubrey straightened his shirt as Griggs strode forward and opened a metal door across the hall.

"Late for what?" asked Aubrey.

"The convocation." Griggs walked into a utility room, and the door slammed shut.

Aubrey rubbed his freckled temple. *What was he talking about?*

He wandered the halls back toward the cafeteria, looking for anyone, who could tell him what was going on. A murmuring rumble echoed down the next hallway. He picked up his pace and headed for the noise as whispers and chattering escalated into a roar.

Aubrey sped into the gym hall and stopped suddenly. The glass, double doors were propped open. Every member of the student body sat in bleachers or in rows of seats on the gym floor. Aubrey cautiously stepped inside.

Behind the chairs, photographers and well-dressed folks, holding microphones and video cameras, lined the back of the gym. On stage, Principal Lequoia and newly elected city manager, Maximillian Miller, spoke with their heads lowered.

Aubrey's confusion deepened. *Why is everyone here?*

Mr. Vandereff, his physical sciences teacher, waddled up to him, pulling his pants over his gut flab. His moustache wriggling as he glared at Aubrey.

"Is your rump sore?" chomped Mr. Vandereff.

"No," replied Aubrey.

"Then sit," ordered Vandereff. He pointed his finger over the crowd. "The convocation will begin momentarily."

Aubrey scanned the wide, open room. A friendly smile under a mop of black, curly hair popped out of the sea of students' faces. Buzz waved him back toward the rear section. Aubrey rushed toward his row and stumbled over seated students until he reached Buzz.

"What took you so long?" Buzz asked.

"I didn't know there was a convocation today," whispered Aubrey.

A dark-skinned girl with long, beaded braids leaned over Buzz and came nose-to-nose with Aubrey. "Didn't you hear the announcement just before the last bell?"

"I was in the bathroom," said Aubrey.

Rodriqa shook her head and pulled herself back into her seat. "Maybe you weren't listening."

"What's going on?" asked Aubrey. "Some lecture on how to get elected to local government by throwing innocent kids under the bus?"

Rodriqa chortled. "Good one, Aub."

Buzz shrugged. "I don't think so. Seems like a bigger deal than just Mr. Miller's ego."

A curtain of dark, shiny straight hair parted Buzz and Aubrey. "Which is certainly a big topic by itself," chimed Jordana as she grinned at Aubrey. Aubrey smiled broadly, his heart thumping like a tickled dog's leg.

Jordana pulled back into the row behind them. Aubrey looked over his shoulder. She only sat in half of her seat. The broad-shouldered, shaggy -haired Magnos took up her half and the seat next to it. Magnos nodded at Aubrey. Aubrey's smile shrunk slightly as he nodded back.

"I still can't believe he got elected head of the city council by making us look like fools," groaned Rodriqa.

"Seriously," added Magnos. "How did he get so many people to believe that the bigfoot sightings and Hovis's rampage through the power plant was a mass hallucination?"

"Charisma is not just another pretty flower." Buzz crossed his arms and leaned back in his chair. Aubrey and Rodriqa furrowed their eyebrows and glanced at each other curiously. They tacitly decided to let that remark slide.

"People wanted to believe what we experienced last year was a hoax," grumbled Aubrey. "And now he has the whole town's ear like some political puppeteer."

"And yet that snail shucker's neighbor wants us to hunt down a ghost in their neighborhood," added Rodriqa.

"I think it's a trap," said Jordana.

"Regardless," countered Buzz, "it gives us a chance to prove ourselves."

"If only we could get Rodriqa to turn into her Tsul'kalu ghost form in front of Mr. Miller," said Magnos, "then everyone would believe us."

Rodriqa shook her finger at Magnos. "I told you, I don't have any control over it!"

"He'd probably think that was just some trick too." Jordana sighed.

Aubrey looked up at the stage. His eyes widened. The balding Maximillian Miller was shaking the hand of a gentleman with bowl-cut, salt-and-pepper hair, dressed in a suit and tie—the same gentleman Aubrey had seen arguing with Griggs a few minutes earlier. Principal Lequoia handed Mr. Miller a microphone and walked stage right.

Mr. Miller tapped the mic with his finger. Rhythmic thumping pounded over the speakers.

"Quiet, children, quiet," he commanded with patronizing sweetness.

The mumbling din evaporated from the crowd.

"I appreciate everyone's time and attention today. A special thanks to Principal Lequoia for setting up this convocation. I'm proud to have the opportunity to speak to you, the future of our community…the future of Lake Julian." Clicks and lights flashed from cameras in the back. The teachers standing throughout the central foyer clapped halfheartedly. A few of the students moaned. Most were silent.

Mr. Miller gestured over his audience. "Prosperity is growing in Lake Julian. Last year, the Berybomag Mining Corporation began operations here and has flourished, providing many new jobs and an influx of population to our small town. And as many of you already know, another industry opened its doors, the newest part of the business center at Lake Julian Square, State of the Mart!"

Mr. Miller paused, allowing time for the audience's reaction. He heard little more than a few feigned whoops. "This highly innovative megamarket and wholesale supplier procures everything we need for our daily lives, and sells it to us at bargain prices."

"Have you been there yet?" whispered Buzz as he leaned toward Aubrey. Aubrey shook his head.

"It's huge!" remarked Buzz, "and they have everything you can imagine."

"My dad loves it," murmured Rodriqa.

"State of the Mart is the dream of a single man," continued Mr. Miller. "From a single store in rural Connecticut, his chain of omniprovisioned stores expanded exponentially across the country..."

A blond, dreadlocked senior sitting next to Aubrey nudged him. Aubrey sat up straight. The senior handed Aubrey a stack of heavy envelopes without looking at him.

"What are these?" Aubrey whispered.

The senior shrugged. "They passed them down the aisle." He pointed toward the end of the row.

Aubrey searched the end of the seats, but he couldn't see anyone. He flipped through the five envelopes. The beige paper was smooth and slick, and silver-lettered calligraphy had been meticulously scribed on the front of each. Aubrey Taylor. Buzz Reiselstein. Rodriqa Auerbach. Jordana Galilahi. Magnos Strumgarten. He passed the envelopes out to his friends.

"What's this?" Buzz asked.

"Open it, and find out," replied Rodriqa as she took hers.

"Today, this incredible man brings us his next sensational creation." Mr. Miller waved his hands. "But I'm getting ahead of myself. Let me let the man behind the miracle tell you all about it."

Rodriqa tore her envelope open and whispered the words aloud. "As a celebrity of Lake Julian, you have been invited..." She turned the cover over.

"Let's give a big Lake Julian High School welcome to the founder of State of the Mart. Jobe Parotty!" Mr. Miller clapped his hands and handed the microphone to the man standing next to him on stage. Cheering and clapping reverberated off the gym walls.

Aubrey resleeved his invitation. An uneasy twinge of fear gnawed a pit in his stomach. Aubrey knew this was the man Griggs had been talking to earlier, but something was different. *Has he changed clothes?* Aubrey thought to himself. *No. It was the same suit and tie as before. Did he comb his hair? No. It still layered the top of his round head. His blue eyes. His leaning nose. His mole.* Aubrey leaned forward and stared at him. His mole wasn't on his chin anymore! It was on his left cheek, just above his lip.

Mr. Parotty shook Mr. Miller's hand heartily. "Thank you very much," replied the businessman in his thick northeastern accent. He waved at several students in the crowd and lowered his hands, pretending to calm everyone down.

"...to the grand opening of a generation," Jordana continued reading the second page of the invitation. She flipped to the third page. "Tomorrow night, prepare yourself for a night of visionary wonder and intrigue at..."

Jordana turned to the next page. A picture of a robotic hand popped out from the middle of the invitation and waved at her.

"I'm here today not just to let Max brag on me, but I'm here to tell you about the opportunity of a lifetime. Something that will change how you think about your life and the world around it. A glimpse into the future of how your children and your grandchildren will live. And I'm not just gonna tell you about it, you'll experience it firsthand, here in Lake Julian. I present to you…" A black curtain alight with flashing letters dropped down behind Mr. Parotty.

Buzz pulled the hand on his invitation, and glittering letters on a spring popped out at him.

Buzz and Mr. Parotty spoke at the same time, "The Rock-U-Quarium!"

LOST SYMPATHIES

Aubrey was bothered by his own reticent reaction to the Rock-U-Quarium. It was an enchanting prospect to have something so unique so easily available. Yet the more he thought about it, the more his gut rolled with unease, especially since he and his friends had been invited to the opening.

Outside of the high school, Aubrey bicycled the switchback of Asheville Highway uphill. He stood up on his bike, twisting his trunk as he shoved down on the pedals.

He crested the hill and coasted along the edge of the four-lane road atop the dam, allowing the stream of cars backed up behind him to pass. Passing by the dam's observation tower, Aubrey shielded his eyes from the glare of the white sandstone sparkling with sunlight reflected off the choppy blue waters of Lake Julian.

Although the mountainous skyline beyond the lake was plush with snow-covered evergreens, springtime had fully embraced the valley. Water spraying up from the dam's spillway soaked the budding trees with a dewy mist. Emerald ferns pierced the scraggly brush, lining the walls of the deep ravine that plummeted a thousand feet below the dam's face.

Dogwoods and redbuds swayed in meadows around the lake, donning the dross of winter with a fresh coat of color. Cattails and pickerelweed stretched up between the pillowy mosses that carpeted the banks down Wontawanna Creek, which fed the lake. Mr. Osterfeld's white tugboat floated in the middle of the lake while puffy tendrils of smoke curly-cued from its smokestack.

Tents had sprung up along the banks of Lake Julian. The tourist influx usually started around this time every year, but Aubrey was unsure why there was a sizeable increase in this year's tourist population.

At the other end of the dam, Aubrey sped down the road, allowing his wheels to spin freely. A couple more miles and he turned left down Dalton Circle toward his house. At the corner, the doors of Ray Gene's Smart Mart & Finer Diner were propped open, and the small gravel parking lot was vacant.

Aubrey weaved into the lot and hopped off his bike. Swerving to avoid a deep hole in the middle of the handicap spot, he stopped against a concrete bumper and stared down. The sides of the slick hole were damp from water that sprayed upward from a cracked pipe at the bottom.

Aubrey looked up toward the open doors. The store was dark, and he couldn't see anyone inside.

Aubrey shaded his eyes and peered through the store's threshold. Usually stocked full of small electronic equipment, the first row of shelving on the right was now completely bare. The central, wooden countertop at checkout had been flipped up, and the cash register drawer was open.

"Mr. Jennings?" Aubrey stepped inside. His eyes adjusted slowly to the dim light. Stacks of cardboard boxes, wound with mover's tape, were piled in front of the counter.

The pastry display to the left had been cleaned out with only dried icing residue staining portions of the inner shelving. The plastic, highlighted menus, displayed over the kitchen, had been unscrewed from their panels near the ceiling, leaving clean, white rectangles on the dust-stained wall. The dairy refrigerators along the right backside of the store had been shut off, and their fluorescent bulbs leaned against the glass doors, standing ajar.

"We're closed," said a voice from the darkness.

"Hello," Aubrey murmured.

"Aubrey?" asked the voice in a familiar tone. A door toward the front corner of the store opened wide. Mr. Jennings stepped out carrying an empty box.

"Yes, sir." Aubrey smiled.

"Sorry, I couldn't see you in the dark," said Mr. Jennings. "I'd know your red hair and freckles anywhere." He placed the box on the floor and wiped the sweat off his forehead. He combed sprigs of silvery hair back under his royal blue ball cap and turned its bill forward, exposing the embossed white K on the front.

"What's going on?" Aubrey asked.

Mr. Jennings walked past Aubrey, stepped behind the cash register and sat on a barrel-shaped stool. Sighing, he rested his hands on his knees. "Want a soda?"

Aubrey walked toward him and nodded.

Mr. Jennings leaned over and snapped open a cooler underneath the counter. He grabbed two colas and handed one to Aubrey.

"I'm closing the store," Mr. Jennings said as he slurped down his beverage.

"What?" replied Aubrey. "Why?"

"I've only had a handful of customers in two weeks." Mr. Jennings raised his arms in surrender. "Except for a small group who came through this morning, claiming to be bigfoot hunters."

"Bigfoot hunters?" questioned Aubrey.

"Yeah," snorted Mr. Jennings. "Guess they had heard of your antics last fall." He tipped his can toward Aubrey and drank another swig.

Aubrey smuggled a quick grin across his lips. "What about all your regular customers?"

Mr. Jennings shrugged. "I'm just not as busy as I used to be."

Aubrey shook his head, feeling a little guilty that he hadn't stopped by recently. "I can come by more often."

Mr. Jennings smiled. "If you really want to help an old man out, grab one of those boxes for me."

"Sure thing." Leaning over, Aubrey wrapped his arms around the top box and heaved it to his chest. He strained under its weight but stiffened his upper lip so Mr. Jennings wouldn't notice.

Mr. Jennings walked around to the front of the counter and easily hoisted the box below it onto his hip. He led Aubrey toward the door in the corner.

After passing through the threshold, Aubrey kept his eyes on Mr. Jennings to maintain his balance. Hobbling down three flights of narrow stairs, they angled down into a dimly lit room below.

"Over there." Mr. Jennings pointed to a pile of boxes against the wall. He walked to the middle of the room and dropped his box in a different pile.

With an aching sigh, Aubrey plopped the box on the ground and glanced around the room.

A walk-in stainless steel freezer thrummed from the back. Antique family portraits and landscape paintings decorated the cement brick walls. A wooden poker table stood in the center of the room, cluttered with yellowing papers and stacks of open books across its, velvety, green top. On it, a single lamp glowed, providing the room's only light.

The basement's musty smell reminded Aubrey of his great aunt Velda, who hadn't voluntarily left her house in nearly twenty years. The maroon shag carpet under his feet was spotted with dark, matted stains. A few of them appeared to be sticky. He made a mental note to avoid those. Aubrey felt the chill of the freezer as he walked over toward Mr. Jennings. The old man's face was deeply creased, and the skin under his chin drooped lower than Aubrey remembered. The sadness of his forlorn elderly friend nettled Aubrey's stomach.

"It's the State of the Mart, isn't it?" Aubrey asked.

Mr. Jennings pulled out a stool from behind the poker table and rested his hands in his lap. "I can't blame anyone for shopping there," he murmured.

"This is all Mr. Miller's fault," grumbled Aubrey.

"Mr. Miller was elected to office because of his connections. He's just trying to better Lake Julian."

"No," argued Aubrey. "He's simply trying to better himself, and the only reason he won the city manager spot was because he made me look like a delinquent."

"Few people take Max Miller's cockamamie theories to heart," replied Mr. Jennings. "Besides, folks can get everything they need at the State of the Mart and not have to travel all over town. With today's economy, less is more. I'm not gonna take it personally."

Aubrey shook his head. "But they can't just forget about you."

Mr. Jennings picked dirt from underneath his fingernails. "I'm old, Aub. It's time for me to retire."

Aubrey furrowed his brow. "But summer is coming. Business will pick up then."

Mr. Jennings sighed. "I don't think the diner can make it that long." Ray Gene dug in his pocket and pulled out a key. He handed it to Aubrey. "I may not be able to make it up here every day, after I close, and I need someone to look after it. Would you check in on the place for me, every now and again?"

Aubrey's voice thickened. "I can't," he stuttered. "I'm just a kid."

Mr. Jennings smiled. "Best kid I know."

Aubrey looked down.

"Besides," continued Mr. Jennings, "you're close by, and you can call me if there's any trouble."

Aubrey nodded. He reluctantly took the key and slipped it into his pocket.

"Time to look at the damage one more time." Mr. Jennings pulled a piece of paper from underneath one of the books on the poker table, grabbed the lamp, and held it close to his face.

Aubrey's eyes widened. For the first time, Aubrey could see the lamp in full view as Mr. Jennings tipped its shade forward. Its ceramic bottle shape was thin near the top, but it had a bulbous bottom. Below where the light bulb was inserted into a black ring, tiny, bright golden squares encircled its widening girth. Beneath that, two cloudy helices spun within each other. The base of the bottle depicted pastoral scenes and white-capped mountains with the sky merging with the darkness of space, which was speckled with a glowing sun, moon, and stars.

But what caught Aubrey's eye was the symbol that intertwined the helices as they emerged with the rest of the bottle. A symbol with which Aubrey was much too familiar.

"Where did you get that?" Aubrey asked.

Mr. Jennings squinted to read his ledger. "Where did I get what?"

"That lamp," replied Aubrey.

"Oh, this?" He held up the bottle. "My wife inherited it from my mother. She thought it was so ugly she made me stow it away down here." Aubrey nodded. "Do you know what's on it?"

Mr. Jennings glanced at the bottle. "Looks like a fourth grader painted it."

Aubrey rocked his head back and forth, pointing to the symbol of interest.

Mr. Jennings stared at the lamp more closely. "Well, I'll be. I've had this lamp for probably twenty years. Never seen that before."

Mr. Jennings tilted the lamp upside down. An outer thick ring, bearing on its inner side a series of smaller circles, were connected by three wired globes, forming a three-dimensional Venn diagram, which were also united by a central halo. It was the Circle of Circles, an emblem Aubrey had encountered multiple times last autumn.

The Circle of Circles glittered in the light shining down from the bulb like a miniature stained glass window.

"Don't you think that's odd?" asked Aubrey. Mr. Jennings scrunched up his cheeks. "Not really. Not as odd as the hole in my parking lot."

Aubrey thought for a moment. "What happened there?"

"I don't know, but the whole neighborhood is full of them."

Aubrey's forehead wrinkled. Suddenly, his pocket buzzed. He reached in and pulled out his cell phone.

Mr. Jennings arched his eyebrows. "You have service down here?"

Aubrey nodded. "Buzz added a signal amplifier to my phone." Aubrey pointed to a small rectangular attachment that was blinking with a glowing red dot at its center. "So now it works all over Lake Julian."

"Wow," replied the impressed old man.

"Yeah, except he also added his own personal GPS system so we can keep track of each other at all times," replied Aubrey. "Not always fun."

"I guess that comes in handy with your new extracurricular activities."

Aubrey nodded his head and rolled his eyes. He flipped open the phone and a map of Lake Julian flashed across the screen. A round green pin zeroed in Aubrey's location. A small red pin with an R inside it was stationary just up the street. Three other red pins, each labeled B, J, and M were travelling together toward his location.

A text from Buzz flashed across the screen.

Change of plans. Meeting w/ Mt. Camelot client ASAP

"Hoaker croaker," groaned Aubrey. "I've gotta run."

"Duty calls." Mr. Jennings smiled as he patted Aubrey on the shoulder.

"I'll stop by tomorrow, Mr. Jennings, I promise," said Aubrey. "Don't give up yet!"

Mr. Jennings tipped his cap at Aubrey, who raced up the stairs. Aubrey knew he couldn't be late.

HOLEY BLIGHT

With his eyes focused more on the neighborhood than the road, Aubrey pedaled down Dalton Circle. Deeply dug holes peppered every lawn along his street. Several of his neighbors stood in their yards, either gawking at the vandalism or angrily filling in the gaping divots. Lightning arced across the sky. Aubrey glanced upward. Dark clouds, capped with billowy gray thunderheads crowded the horizon.

He sped toward his house. A tall lanky man with wavy blond hair ran out of Aubrey's backyard, carrying a net with a metal pole bent in three places. Aubrey skidded to a stop.

"Mr. Poschyev!" shouted Aubrey. "What's going on?"

Simon Poschyev had arrived in Lake Julian shortly after the crop of bigfoot sightings had erupted last fall. He had been an experienced hunter and tracker in the dense forests of Russia several years prior, and he had hoped for fame and fortune by being the first person to trap a sasquatch. Unfortunately, shortly after he arrived, the elusive creature inexplicably disappeared, but with his skills in trapping animals, he attained the position of Poage county animal control officer.

"Owbrey," spoke Mr. Poschyev in a meaty, Slovakian accent. "That creature is a plague on this country!"

Aubrey knew exactly what he was talking about, but he decided feigning denial was a better tactic. "What creature?"

"That cat!" barked Aubrey's father. He stormed out the front door and marched down the porch steps.

"Whimperfidget?" questioned Aubrey. "He's harmless. All he does is lay under the back porch."

"Today he decided to terrorize the neighborhood." Mr. Taylor ran his hand over his short, receding hair. "I had to leave work early. I had no fewer than ten phone calls from folks complaining about *your* cat tearing up their yards."

"Technically he's not my cat," murmured Aubrey. "He belongs to Rodriqa."

Mr. Taylor glowered at Aubrey. "Fortunately, I was able to get a hold of Mr. Poschyev on short notice." Mr. Taylor glanced at Simon. "Any luck?"

Mr. Poschyev handed Mr. Taylor his mangled hunting net. "What do you think? You shouldn't have called the pound. You should have called the National Guard."

"I really don't think Whimperfidget could have done all this." Aubrey scratched his head. "He's barely more than a kitten."

"Then go catch your kitten, and get rid of it," insisted Mr. Taylor.

Mr. Poschyev chuckled. "Good luck, Owbrey. I've wrangled with bears that are sweeter."

"Aubrey!" shouted a voice from behind him. "Why aren't you in uniform?"

Aubrey turned around. Rodriqa stood outside her front door, dressed from head to toe in a blue polyurethane suit with silver stripes. A visor, wrapped with metal wiring, crowned her head and was clipped to her shoulders, forming an electrical circuit. Rodriqa had one fist planted on her hip, carrying a small black case, and her other hand was pointing up Dalton Circle. The dark-blue 1970s Volkswagen Beetle zipped down the road.

"Dad, we've got a gig tonight," pleaded Aubrey.

"It's not even dark yet," replied Mr. Taylor. "Can't your friends help out with this before you go?"

"Something's up," explained Aubrey. "We've been asked to show up early. We'll come back and clean everything up, I promise."

Mr. Taylor sighed and nodded. After everything he had witnessed last fall, he knew better than to argue with his son over matters of the unexplained.

"Aubrey!" shouted Rodriqa again. The Volkswagen, which held Buzz, Magnos, and Jordana, who were each wearing suits similar to Rodriqa's, was idling on the curb.

Aubrey waved at his friends. "I need two seconds!" He turned toward his father. "I'll check on Whimperfidget real quick, then I have to go." He remembered what Griggs had asked him and wondered if Solluna was safe.

Pulling his bicycle at his side, Aubrey ran around Mr. Poschyev and his dad toward the backyard. The lawn between his and Rodriqa's house was riddled with more holes. The back porch had latticework encasing its dark, damp crawl space underneath. An inconspicuous door had been cut in the wood with its hinges on the inside, allowing access to the crawl space. Today, the gate swung open, with a splintered hole smashed through it. Aubrey leaned over and peered inside.

The afternoon sunlight cast bright beams against the mucky dirt under the porch. Shadows overtook the scant light once he looked deeper under the house.

"Whimperfidget," Aubrey called with a crack in his voice through the rectangular door. More holes cratered the foul-smelling earth. But nothing moved. Everything in the darkness was quiet.

It had been several months since he had been here. Aubrey wanted to stay outside, but he knew he had to check on his golden book first. He decided the quicker he moved, the better. He dropped to his knees and scurried forward, heading for the center of the crawl space.

Bam! Aubrey's head smacked squarely into a plate of aluminum. The house's HVAC unit was contained within a metal enclosure under the kitchen. His dad hadn't been down here in years, so it made the perfect hiding place for Solluna.

Aubrey rubbed his head and slid back a panel on the side of the enclosure. The electric hum from inside murmured through the crawl space, and the sizzling static from the HVAC unit raised bumps on Aubrey's skin. Even his braces sparked from the energetic buzz. Reaching in, he groped for the book. He felt his fingers prickle against rough burlap. Wrapping his fingers around the sack, he pulled it out.

Aubrey's eyes widened. The sack wasn't as heavy as it had been before. He looped the rope entwining the top of the sack through his belt and raced toward the door. He stopped at the first beam of light, tore open the burlap, and stuck his hand inside. It didn't feel like metal but it was cold, and its edges jabbed his fingers with sharp tips. He pulled it into the sunlight. Instead of a golden book, a crystal pyramid gleamed in the sun, casting rainbows across the crawl space. It fit in the palm of his hand, tingling against his skin like Solluna had before. Had someone or something stolen his enchanted book and put this in its place...or was this still Solluna?

Red, glowing eyes bobbed from under the stairs at the front of the crawl space. Aubrey shuffled toward the door. The creature growled, and its bright jagged fangs slipped into the light.

"Whimperfidget!" called Rodriqa from the side yard. The creature whined in pain. Its red eyes darkened, and the beast's fangs and claws shortened.

A furry flail of cream-and-charcoal-colored hair shot out of the small door into the yard. Aubrey perched himself at the edge of the latticework and peeked outside. The cat rolled in Rodriqa's folded arms, rubbing its head against her chin and kneading her chest with its soft paws. "There's no way this sweet little Whimperfidget made all this mess, is there?"

"Put it down, Rodriqa." Aubrey sidled into the yard.

"Why?" she asked. "He's just a precious little baby." The cat purred loudly.

"It growled at me!" Aubrey stepped cautiously toward her.

The cat jerked, leaping out of Rodriqa's arms, and landed with every hair raised on the porch's railing. It craned its head down, eyeing Aubrey, and hissed at him.

Aubrey tripped backward. The cat dove onto the lawn and ran through the backyard, springing out of sight.

Aubrey scowled at Rodriqa.

She dusted the mud-caked cat hair off her suit. "I think he's hungry, and did you forget? We're late!"

Aubrey rushed inside his house, turned through the living room, and raced up the stairs to his bedroom. In his room he pulled the crystal pyramid out of its burlap sack.

Lit only by the afternoon sun, his bedroom was dim, and the crystal appeared to be nothing more than simple glass. The tingling sensation was gone, and the prism didn't refract any light. Aubrey heard a car horn honking the "Battle Hymn of the Republic" from the front of the house. He knew he needed to hurry but decided that leaving this new Solluna unattended wasn't a wise option, especially after what Griggs had said. He opened his closet door where his blue, silver-stripped polyurethane suit occupied center hanger. He unplugged a black lunch box–sized case from the wall at his feet and snapped it into the back of the suit. Clips stiffly flipped around the case, securing it in place. The box thrummed to life.

Aubrey slipped into the suit, cinching the burlap sack holding Solluna tightly around his waist. He strapped his visor over his red hair and turned to run into the hallway.

Aubrey's mother stood there, holding a pair of ironed khakis draped over her forearm. "You'll need these," she said flatly. Aubrey squinted at her and realized she wasn't even looking at him. She was staring out his window. Her curls were matted on one side of her head as if she'd been lying in bed all day. She was dressed in a pink, flannel housecoat, which frayed at the bottom and was sprinkled with coffee stains.

"Not now, Mom." Aubrey rushed past her. "I've got stuff to do." He trotted down the stairs and through the living room, then hurried out the front door.

Rodriqa raised her arm through the window of the Volkswagen, waving him toward the car. Aubrey trotted up to the driver's side window and leaned his head in. He glanced around. "Whoa!"

The hunched-over Magnos grinned at him from the driver's seat.

"Welcome to the Buzz Bug 2.0," announced Buzz from the passenger seat. "Look! No more spatulas!"

Aubrey scanned the inside. The bottom was open, and Aubrey could see the asphalt underneath. Magnos's feet rested on car pedals, suspended from the dash. Below the unicycle seats, the previous gears and pedals had been replaced by thick stainless steel poles, secured to spare tires. A digital alarm clock and a USB port were set in the dashboard. In the back rumple seat, an electric motor was cocooned in a mesh of wires and large batteries.

"It's electric now," gloated Buzz. "See the clips around the windows?"

"Yeah," replied Aubrey.

"Air friction from poor aerodynamics creates static electricity along the outside of the chassis. This device collects that potential charge and stores it in the battery."

"That's crazy," murmured Rodriqa.

"Gets twice as much mileage as the standard electric car," bragged Buzz. "Just wait for the next upgrade."

Aubrey chuckled and rolled his eyes.

"Get in! We're behind schedule!" Rodriqa tapped her watch from the backseat. Sitting next to her, Jordana smiled at Aubrey.

Magnos opened his door and leaned forward. Aubrey crawled in front of Rodriqa to the center seat. Shifting the gear lever forward, Magnos pushed down the pedal, and the motor whirred wildly as the car eased forward.

"Sorry for being late." Aubrey propped his feet up on the edge of Magnos's and Buzz's seats. "Rodriqa's cat decided to ransack the neighborhood today."

"We heard," replied Magnos.

"Time to get that cat neutered," advised Buzz. "He's hit kitty puberty and feels the need to mark his territory."

"We should have taken it back to McCrayden from the get-go," grumbled Magnos.

"That's what I said," agreed Jordana.

"Rodriqa was the one who wanted to keep it," replied Aubrey. "And now it conveniently lives under *my* house."

"Leave poor Whimperfidget alone." Rodriqa crossed her arms. "He can't help it. He's been through a lot."

"Why can't you keep it at your place?" Aubrey asked.

"I told you, my mom is allergic. He's safer under your porch."

"*He's* safer, but apparently no one else is," joked Magnos.

Magnos stopped at Asheville Highway at the top of Dalton Circle and turned left.

"So why are we leaving for the Mount Camelot job so early?" Aubrey asked.

"There's been a new development," replied Buzz. "The woman who hired us left me a message telling me two things. One, if Maximillian Miller finds out we're headed to his subdivision to kill a ghost, he'll have us arrested.

Two, there was something we needed to see, and she said we couldn't appreciate it after dusk, so the sooner we came the better."

"What does she want us to see that's so urgent?" asked Aubrey.

Buzz shrugged. "I'm not sure, but she seems to think it's related to all the hauntings up on Mt. Camelot."

"I still think this might be a trap," murmured Jordana. "Who hired us anyway?"

"Brandy Gungandeep," replied Buzz. "Jafar's mom. Mrs. Gungandeep is good friends with the Creightony family. They spoke highly of us as the NeighborGhoul Watch." Buzz twisted his head, glancing through the windows. "Did everyone do their NGW homework?"

Rodriqa, Aubrey, and Jordana nodded.

"Isn't Jafar in your club?" asked Magnos as he made a right turn.

"Yeah," replied Buzz. "The Torquetum Club. Jafar is a sophomore. He helped pilot Ben-Zing in the Paddling Pumpkin Race last year."

"Is he trustworthy?" questioned Jordana.

Buzz nodded. "I think so. I spoke with a couple other kids who live up there. Sounds like the Homeowner's Association is in a big uproar about what to do about all the hauntings. About half of them think we're as loony as Mr. Miller says we are. The other half want our help."

"Did you talk to McCrayden?" Magnos asked.

Buzz chortled. "No way, dude. That'd be like the gazelle asking the lion's cub the fastest way to the watering hole."

Rodriqa shook her head. "Hamilton asked me if we'd be willing to help out with the ghost sightings. I called him a toad thrower and told him after all his dad had said about us, even if the ghost of Christmas future was after him, I wouldn't twitch a finger."

"Wow, someone's cranky today," remarked Buzz.

Rodriqa rolled her eyes. "I only said that 'cause I was worried he was onto us."

Everyone glanced suspiciously at Rodriqa.

"I meant the toad thrower part," she added.

Aubrey peeped over his shoulder. Jordana had her arms crossed and was staring out the window through her honey-colored glasses, her straight black hair forming a curtain down her cheek. He knew the mention of Hamilton would make her uncomfortable after their encounter at the homecoming dance last year.

"How's your dad?" Aubrey asked, pulling Jordana back into the conversation. She turned toward him and gave him a waifish smile. "Better. He's only in physical therapy three days a week now. Hopefully he'll get to go back to work by summer."

"He had quite a beating," remarked Rodriqa.

"Between the bigfoot...I mean Tsul'kalu and Ms. Thistlewood, he's lucky to be alive," said Buzz.

Jordana dropped her head and nodded.

"So how is it living with the toughest high school principal this side of the eastern continental divide?" Buzz chuckled.

Jordana shrugged. "Uncle doesn't really talk much. He's usually too busy with his own affairs. Father and I keep to our part of the house, but I've enjoyed reading in Uncle's library when he's not around."

"Your uncle has a library in his house?" asked Aubrey.

Jordana nodded. "He used to be the archivist for our tribe before he was principal of Lake Julian. He's accumulated a lot of old literature."

Aubrey smiled at her, her gaze fixed on the green lawns and trees skimming by outside. A glint of sparkling blue caught his eye. Between rolling hills and wooden-slat fences, portions of the banks of Lake Julian peeked through. Hordes of pup tents and pop-up campers lined the edge of the lake, and the further away from the dam they drove, the greater the concentration of campsites grew.

"Wow," muttered Aubrey. "Why are there so many tourists so early in the season?"

"Million moth metamorphosis," replied Rodriqa.

"Huh?" grunted Aubrey.

"It's the million moth metamorphosis," chimed Buzz. "Every thirty-six years, the Southern Appalachian luna moth crawls out of the ground and pupates in the trees. Once they burst from their cocoons, their bioluminescence creates a dazzling display of shimmering lights in the night sky as they fly out to procreate." Buzz wiggled his fingers as he flitted his hands in front of his face.

Aubrey shook his head in confusion.

"I'll translate," moaned Rodriqa. "There's this moth, that for some reason, its eggs only hatch once every three decades or so. It's an endangered species, and supposedly, its last remaining haven is here in Lake Julian. Anyway, after the eggs hatch, hundreds of thousands of these nasty little worms—"

"Larvae," interrupted Buzz.

Rodriqa curled her lip. "Slimy grubs slink up into the tops of the forest around the lake. After they tear out of their cocoons and unfold their wings, they glow all kinds of crazy colors and then fly off to make more eggs."

"Wicked," remarked Magnos.

"How is it that I've lived here my whole life and never heard of it?" questioned the bewildered Aubrey.

"You're not thirty-six years old," replied Magnos.

"It's a twice-in-a-lifetime spectacle," explained Buzz. "Nature enthusiasts and scientists travel from all over the world to see it. It's like an ecological pilgrimage. My dad is already camped out, just waiting for the first moth to light the sky."

Aubrey craned his neck, looking at the tops of the surrounding trees. All he could see were dark, heavy clouds looming overhead. "When will it happen?"

"My dad says sometime within the next week," said Buzz.

"Usually midspring," added Rodriqa. "I only know about it because my dad has had to deal with all the tourists at the dam, and he comes home every night grumbling about it."

Aubrey mused sullenly, feeling slightly left out of his own community.

An evergreen-capped mountain broke through the treetops. Cream- and beige-colored dots haloed its summit amid spindly strings of gray, winding roads.

"What's that?" asked Jordana with a finger pointed toward the windshield.

"That's Mount Camelot," said Buzz. "Where the wealthy and entitled of Lake Julian live."

"No," insisted Jordana as she redirected her finger. "That!"

At the end of the street, before the road hooked to the right up Mount Camelot's base, a large house came into view. The paint of its white siding was peeling, exposing dark rotting boards underneath. The front porch was small with a widening set of stairs that sprawled down from ornately carved doors. A multitude of broad, stained glass windows ringed the first and second levels of the house, and the roof was bordered by a thin wire gate set with a small watchtower atop its dormer. Perched above the watchtower, a dark gray weathervane, sculpted in the form of a man chasing a fish, spun wildly in the wind and a murder of ravens rested on every exposed piece of railing.

"That's Mr. Osterfeld's house," replied Aubrey. "The guy with the tugboat who sounds his horn randomly at night."

"Oh," muttered Jordana. "So unusual."

"Why is that?" Rodriqa asked.

"It looks like a church," mused Jordana.

Magnos, Buzz, Aubrey, and Rodriqa leaned forward and examined Mr. Osterfeld's house.

"It kinda does," whispered Buzz.

Jordana surveyed the house as they drove closer. "It must be the house I read about in Uncle's library. It's one of the oldest buildings in the area. The weathervane was handcrafted by a local apprentice blacksmith, whose father had migrated here from Italy and fought in the Civil War. He was only a kid when he made it and then died shortly after. From something infectious, it sounds like."

"Really?" remarked Aubrey.

"Supposedly, it was one of the first churches in these parts," continued Jordana. "A church that had a priest, who brought new ideas to the area."

The others glanced toward her, unsure what she meant.

"It was Hovis Trottle's church," Jordana uttered reluctantly.

Aubrey turned toward her, his eyes wide, and his mind locked on her words.

Atop Mt. Camelot, the five friends silently gawked at a five-story, white stucco house. Even half buried in a hill, it still towered higher than the neighboring luxury homes. A cylindrical tower rounded the far corner like a castle turret with small rectangular windows stair-stepping their way toward the top floor. Each level above the garage narrowed, distinctly separated by banks of fogged glass windows. A metal balcony surrounded the fourth level of the house, and a wiry staircase led down from the balcony toward the driveway.

Magnos parked the car, and all five teenagers piled out of the Buzz Bug.

"Flustered mustard," muttered Rodriqa, angling her head back so she could take in a full view of the house.

"I didn't know there were homes like this in Lake Julian," murmured Jordana.

"You can't see the really nice ones from the valley," replied Buzz. "Especially since we're on the backside."

Scurrying down the outside stairs, a slim, brown-skinned woman, wrapped in an off-white sarong waved the children up the driveway. "Hurry, children!" she shouted in a thick Indian accent. "Come inside." Holding a small, black box, she pushed a button, and it beeped. The middle garage door slid up. "And park in the garage."

"She's worried about Maximillian Miller," grumbled Buzz.

Magnos got back into the Buzz Bug and drove it inside as the other four walked in.

The woman peeked her head through the door to the garage. "Quickly."

Buzz pulled a black case inscribed with the letters NGW from the vehicle, and everyone lumbered inside.

"Mrs. Gungandeep?" asked Buzz.

She nodded. "Yes, I'm Brandy Gungandeep. Thank you all for coming." The woman held out her hand and greeted each of the teens with a slight bow. Aubrey noticed how fresh and young the woman's face appeared, although there was a tightness to her skin that revealed her true age. "Happy to help," offered Aubrey.

"Even when others chose to ignore the obvious," added Buzz. "I thought Mr. Miller wouldn't be in the neighborhood this evening."

"He's not," replied Mrs. Gungandeep.

"Then why are we hiding?" asked Rodriqa.

Mrs. Gungandeep sighed. "Because you were followed."

"By whom?" asked Buzz.

"Follow me." Mrs. Gungandeep turned the corner and trotted up a set of carpeted steps. The friends followed at a short distance. The walls between the stairs where lined by family portraits of the Gungandeep family, most of which featured Jafar, their only son.

At the top of the stairs, Mrs. Gungandeep walked through her family room, furnished with cushy black leather couches and a large-screen TV. She passed through another doorway to another set of stairs on the opposite side. She advanced quickly, and the children had to quicken their steps to keep pace with her.

The five tread with reverence on to the second stairway, their mouths agape as they took in a full view of the upper room. A gleaming white marble floor, with gray wavy grains, stretched across an expansive formal living room, filled with plush chairs, tables, and three stone fireplaces. Stone columns separated areas of the room into smaller sections. Crumbling at the edges and browned by age, woven papyrus murals covered each of the walls, some depicting scenes of battles between ancient armies and others portraying congregations progressing along a pilgrimage. Suddenly, Aubrey stopped. He reached toward an object on a tiny end table. His fingers came less than an inch from the item of interest before he caught himself.

"What is that?" Aubrey asked. A wide-based jar of thick maroon- and olive-colored glass twisted upward, thinning and diverging into five separate bottlenecks. The tops were sealed with glass stoppers, and a golden Circle of Circles was inscribed on the jar's midsection.

Mrs. Gungandeep turned around and glanced at Aubrey. "An original Aladdin's lamp. It's a called a crucible. Be careful. It's irreplaceable."

Aubrey marveled at the lamp, particularly how similar the glass appeared compared with Mr. Jennings's lamp. He glanced into one of the round openings. Like a tiny mirror, he could see a reflection of his own eye.

"I thought Aladdin's lamp was like those old-timey oil lamps," asked Rodriqa.

Mrs. Gungandeep crossed her arms. "Latter storytellers spoke of lamps similar to those used by nomads at the time of the written manuscripts. Oral tradition purports the lamps were more unique."

"Does it have a genie inside?" asked Magnos.

Buzz snickered. "Can I get three wishes?"

"Not anymore," said Mrs. Gungandeep. "I've already used them all." A corner of her lip curled upward.

Magnos and Buzz looked at each other with furrowed brows.

"How long have you had it?" asked Aubrey, studying the crucible.

"As long as I can remember," recalled Mrs. Gungandeep. "It's been in my mother's family for several generations. It's supposed to bring good luck...if you believe in that sort of thing."

Mrs. Gungandeep ushered them further into the house. At the far end of the formal living room, thresholds led to another set of stairs to the left and into the adjoining dining room, where a large oval glass table stood. An ornate glass chandelier hung above the table, and a hulking mirror occupied the wall next to it.

Brandy Gungandeep stood next to the sheer curtain draped across the large bay window at the front of the room, which overlooked their lushly manicured front yard.

"We're at the top of Mount Camelot." Magnos walked over to the window.

Mrs. Gungandeep nodded. Magnos peered between a break in the curtain. Buried in tall evergreens and budding dogwoods, houses of extraordinary luxury crowded around a wide cul-de-sac. Metal streetlights stood in front of every home. The dark gray sky above wrestled with heavy clouds.

"Who followed us?" Rodriqa asked from behind Magnos.

"Far right corner," whispered Mrs. Gungandeep as she pointed out the window. Everyone but Buzz advanced forward and peered through the corner of the window. Buzz pensively rested the case he had been carrying on the floor and raised his thick dark glasses to his forehead, examining a corner of one of the papyrus wall hangings near the stairs.

Outside, parked in the cul-de-sac, a pale yellow Toyota Prius held a dark figure in the driver's seat, who appeared to be staring back.

"Who is it?" Rodriqa asked, as she took a step backwards and pulled Jordana and Aubrey back by their shirts.

"There are rumors amongst members of the Homeowner's Association that Maximillian Miller has hired a personal investigator to expose the cause of so much supernatural phenomenon in Lake Julian. The investigator has spent a lot of time at Mount Camelot since there have been so many ghost sightings here of late. Mr. Miller feels there must be a scientific explanation, and supposedly this person has a great deal of experience with debunking falsified claims." Mrs. Gungandeep rubbed her nose with her finger. "Of course, Mr. Miller feels there is a straightforward root to the problem, which simply needs to be eradicated."

"What's that?" asked Rodriqa.

Mrs. Gungandeep eyed Rodriqa. "That you all are responsible."

"That's incredible!" shouted Buzz from the back of the room. Everyone turned to stare at him. Buzz's nose was only a few millimeters away from the papyrus.

Thwap! A hand smacked the back of Buzz's head, and his face bounced off the papyrus. Buzz scrambled to catch his glasses as they tumbled off his nose.

"Hey, what's your glamor glitch?" squealed Buzz as he turned around.

Rodriqa met him nose to nose. "We're here to work, not ogle other people's things. Mrs. Gungandeep is telling us important stuff."

Buzz rubbed the back of his head and frowned at her. "I was listening." Buzz walked toward the middle of the room. "I'm not afraid of the investigator because we all know it's real, and there's no way he'll be able to prove anything."

"Proof, one way or the other, seems to be what everyone is searching for," challenged Mrs. Gungandeep.

"I gave Jafar our references," replied Buzz.

"And they checked out," acknowledged Mrs. Gungandeep. "But as many people who appear to agree with what you're doing, there are many who would prefer for you to quietly go away."

Buzz frowned and whimpered, "We haven't destroyed *that* much."

"Because we fight to help others?" argued Aubrey. "Because we've seen ghosts and try to make a difference in people's lives?"

"Because you interfere," concluded Mrs. Gungandeep. "Everyone has an agenda, be they saint, criminal, or in between. And you've made a powerful enemy of Mr. Miller."

"I've never even spoken to Mr. Miller," grumbled Jordana.

"He used to be a nice guy," added Magnos.

"He's already made us look like toad throwers," added Rodriqa. "Why doesn't he just leave us alone? We're not doing anything wrong!"

"Mr. Miller doesn't see it that way," replied Mrs. Gungandeep with a hacky chuckle. "He considers you all a menace. He's forbidden everyone in the Homeowner's Association from speaking with you."

"Then why did you contact us?" countered Aubrey.

Mrs. Gungandeep looked away. "There is too much evidence contrary to Mr. Miller's stance."

"Exactly," pronounced Buzz.

"What have you seen?" asked Jordana.

"Not me," replied Mrs. Gungandeep as she held out her arms, "My son."

Jafar bounded down the stairs from the far side of the room and ran toward the group. His thick black hair sprang from his head in every direction, and his white teeth gleamed like the marble he stood on. He wore a T-shirt that had a crudely painted "3" on it with khakis that were a little long, the cuffs ragged from dragging the ground. His brown skin matched his mother's, but his face was alight with enthusiasm. "Hey, everybody!" Buzz greeted Jafar with a hearty smile. The other friends murmured quiet hellos.

Buzz trotted up to Jafar, and they held their hands out, each palm cupped together with their fingers splayed out toward the other. They inserted their fingers together, like sticking a plug in a socket, and wiggled their digits wildly, while beeping and blurting high-pitched noises.

"What was that?" questioned Rodriqa.

"The official Torquetum Club handshake," replied Buzz.

Rodriqa rolled her eyes.

"Awesome outfit!" remarked Jafar.

"Thanks!" replied Buzz as he stretched out his arms and flexed in full display.

"Is that how you fight ghosts?" asked Jafar.

"Nah," replied Buzz. He pinched his suit at the shoulders and straightened it, then tipped his visor. "This is the Elemag suit." He spun around, exposing the small black box snapped into his lower back. "Short for Electromagnetic. The adjustable current battery in the back can send out a specific pulse charge, creating a magnetic field along these silver lines." Buzz pointed with two fingers to the strips running up and down his legs and arms. "The magnetic field repels most supernatural entities if we get the field values right."

"Mighty sister transistor," remarked Jafar as he inspected Buzz's suit.

"Mighty *what*?" Jordana whispered to Rodriqa.

Rodriqa rolled her eyes. "Wi-chrome speak."

"The polyurethane inlay insulates us," continued Buzz, "and the wavelength of the electrical pulse is adjustable so we can change the magnetic field generated around the pulse lines."

"Can you project charge with this?" asked Jafar.

"No," chuckled Buzz. "The Elemag suits are simply a line of defense. Besides, I'm not gonna share all our trade secrets."

Mrs. Gungandeep turned from staring out the window and licked her lips. Clearing her throat, she addressed the children, "Perhaps we should talk about this more in the dining room."

Buzz picked up the NGW case, and everyone piled into the dining room. Nearly everything was made of crystal-clear glass—from the sculpted table legs and the twelve blown-glass chairs to the plates, silverware, and candle-holders on top of the table. The far wall was a massive sheet of glass with a sliding glass door set into it. Mrs. Gungandeep approached the glass wall and stared outside. "This is why I was worried. This is why I asked you all to come so quickly."

"Because of Mr. Miller?" questioned Magnos.

Mrs. Gungandeep shook her head. "No, because of that."

Jafar walked up to his mom and stared out the window. Magnos, Buzz, Jordana, and Rodriqa looked at each other with puzzled expressions. Aubrey looked beyond the fashionable foliage in the yard and down the hill. More than a mile away, the forest expanded, carpeting mounds of hills in the distance, the budding verdure broken by a wide meadow in the valley below.

Aubrey closed his eyes. Bright lights of phosphenes swirled behind his eyelids. Darkness filled in from the edges of his sight while he concentrated on the invisible world in front of him. No form took shape. Nothing moved. Everything appeared unseen, as it should be.

"I don't understand," muttered Aubrey. "I don't see anything out of the ordinary."

"The tree," mumbled Jafar.

"There's a thousand trees out there," said Jordana.

"The large one in the middle of the meadow," murmured Mrs. Gungandeep. "It wasn't there this morning."

The friends crowded around the Gungandeeps as they scanned the valley floor. With its closest mate several hundred yards away, a solitary aged oak tree stood in the middle of the valley with a flurry of leafy branches stretching upward as if summer had fully embraced it.

"Are you sure?" asked Buzz.

Jafar nodded.

A wave of nausea rolled in Aubrey's stomach. Once before he had seen a vacant lot fill with a stone cottage over the course of a day. He feared a familiar enemy had returned.

"Then we'll need to investigate when the weather is more amenable." Buzz gently rested the case on the glass table and unlocked its latch. He pulled out four TV remote controls and a plastic water gun, which had a miniature satellite dish attached to the end of its barrel. The handle of the gun and the base of the remotes had several yards of wires sprouting from them that met at a central plug. Jafar's eyes widened as he picked up the gun to examine it.

"I've figured out—" started Buzz.

Rodriqa cleared her throat and rested her hands on her hips.

"*We've* figured out," continued Buzz, "that every being, whether living, dead, or otherwise, has an inherent electromagnetic signature."

"How can something that is dead have an electromagnetic signature?" asked Jafar.

"Being dead in this world doesn't necessarily make you dead in the next," whispered Jordana.

Buzz nodded. "For example, our bodies give off heat. Our electromagnetic signature is in the infrared range. The ghosts we've encountered give off signals between the range of infrared and microwaves."

"So every being gives off light, somewhere along the electromagnetic spectrum?" Jafar asked.

"It seems so," concluded Buzz. "But every being is different, and different types of entities exude a specific signature range."

Buzz lifted a remote control and flipped up its plastic end. A small open diode protruded from underneath. "We can sense the wavelength of the entity's signature with these." Buzz pulled a small cartridge fixed with a dial and a red round button out of the box and plugged the wires into the dial. Holding up the remote, Buzz pointed it at Jafar and pressed the remote's power button. The diode flashed red.

A thin wire hand jumped across the cartridge's rotary dial. Buzz leaned over and read it. "Two hundred thirty-four microns. That's the wavelength of your body signature, which is in the far infrared range. That's normal for most humans. To give you an idea, visible light is four hundred to seven hundred nanometers, much shorter than that."

"I know," replied Jafar. "So that's why you can't see my wavelength signature."

"Precisely."

"What's this contraption called?" marveled Jafar.

"ESAU," replied Buzz. "Electromagnetic Signature Analyzer and Usurper."

"Is that your entry for the Poage County Science Fair this year?" Jafar asked.

"Nope." Buzz smiled widely. "I've got something better."

"Usurper?" asked Mrs. Gungandeep. "The analyzer part you've shown us. But what's the usurper part?"

Buzz tapped the satellite dish on the end of the gun. "Once I know the entity's wavelength signature, I dial the number up or down and hold down the trigger. It emits an electromagnetic signal in dissonance with the being, weakening it."

"Dissonance?" questioned Mrs. Gungandeep.

Buzz rubbed his forehead and scanned the dining room. "It would be easier to show you than tell you." Buzz scurried into the kitchen, and everyone watched as he bolted back as quickly as he had left. He approached the ornate mirror with three dry erase markers in hand.

"May I?" he asked.

Mrs. Gungandeep reached forward. "That's eighteenth century—I wouldn't…"

Buzz was already scrawling squiggly marks across the mirror. "Every quantum of energy has a frequency and a wavelength." Buzz turned for everyone to see the red wavy line he had drawn on the mirror. "If another wave comes in contact with it," Buzz drew another squiggly line in blue matching its partner, "and it has similar energy and wavelength, the troughs and peaks line up." Buzz drew a green wave over the blue and red lines, which was double in height. "And the wave becomes stronger. That's consonance."

Buzz scooted backward and drew another red squiggle. "Dissonance is when the energy and wavelengths don't match." He drew a blue wave an inch above and an inch over from the red one. "And the troughs and peaks start to cancel each other out." Buzz pulled out the green marker and made a fine green squiggle, a smaller summation of the blue and red. "Resulting in a distortion or loss of strength.

"ESAU determines the wavelength of an entity and, then with a tiny twist of the dial and a pull of the trigger, blasts them with a pulse of energy in dissonance to its signature."

"So ESAU kills ghosts?" asked Jafar.

"No, but it causes enough of a distraction to let us do our dirty work," replied Buzz.

Everyone was quiet as they thought through Buzz's explanation. Aubrey, Jordana, Magnos, and Rodriqa had used ESAU in action but never really known how it worked.

"Your turn, Gungandeep," challenged Rodriqa. "We've spilled our guts. Now it's time to spill yours."

Jafar looked down, and his mother wrapped her arm around his shoulders. "I'm sure it probably seems silly compared to what you all have seen."

Mrs. Gungandeep wagged her head, licked her lips, and pulled her son closer to her.

Aubrey leaned in. "You can tell us."

"At first, it seemed more like a dream," started Jafar. "I would wake up in the middle of the night and see a really pretty woman in the corner of my bedroom. It was always the same woman with long black hair wearing a white dress." Jafar gulped back against the memories. "She was kneeling in my room with her hands flat together, and her eyes closed. I would look again, and she'd be gone.

"About a month ago, I started waking up to someone grabbing my arm or my ankle. And there she was again in the corner, on her knees and her fingers to her lips, but this time she was muttering to herself."

Jafar's head dropped. "A few nights later, I woke up on the floor, and the woman was leaning over me with her eyes closed and her hair dangling right above my face. I'd blink, and she would be gone." His shoulders slumped. "Then, night after night, I would jerk out of sleep because I felt like I was falling, and I'd wake up on the carpet, and for a split second, I'd see her kneeling in the corner."

Jafar wrapped his arms around his elbows. "Last night, I woke up, and I was hovering in front of my bedroom window, and she walked out of the corner. She slid open my window. I nearly fell out. I screamed, and she disappeared."

"Pretty intense," remarked Buzz.

"I think we'll be able to help," added Aubrey.

"We've done some historical investigation about the origins of Mount Camelot," commented Rodriqa. "We weren't finding much at first, but then I stumbled upon a nursery rhyme that purportedly had its origins in Lake Julian."

Rodriqa placed a yellowed shag of ragged cloth on the glass table. The cloth had been delicately inscribed in calligraphy with a series of stanzas.

> The world turns twice,
> And all seems nice.
> The world turns thrice,
> And her heart's like ice.

> The hand that bathes
> Strikes hard as staves.
> And playful sounds
> Turn upside down.

---※---

She'll give you cake
For a bellyache.
She'll clip your toes
For a bloody nose.

---※---

That's when you know
To walk away.
Before she's smiling
O'er your grave.

---※---

Mayree Krouse seems so lively,
Mayree Krouse don't take kindly,
Mayree Krouse loves the pain,
Mayree Krouse lives again.

Everyone leaned over and read the rhyme. Jafar and Mrs. Gungandeep's lips twisted in consternation.

"So I performed a data search on Mayree Krouse," continued Buzz.

"And *we*," interrupted Rodriqa, "found a Mayree Swanston who had married a John Krouse around 1796 in Asheville. They settled south of Asheville on 'the highest hill within sight of Wontawanna Creek.' That's what the ledger says, and the tallest peak you can see from the head of Lake Julian is Mount Camelot."

"With that lead, we figured out why Mount Camelot might be haunted," said Buzz.

"Mary Swanston was John Krouse's second wife," relayed Rodriqa. "He had five children from his first marriage. After his marriage to Ms. Swanston, one by one, his children died off. One from some rare disease, two from bizarre injuries, the fourth from consumption."

"Mr. Krouse went to the local clergy and asked for help," continued Buzz. "They referred him to the local authorities, who said his children's deaths appeared to be explainable."

"So he consulted a soulmeister," whispered Buzz.

"What's a soulmeister?" asked Jafar.

"Someone who knows a little more than they should about the hereafter. The soulmeister asked him if he really knew his second wife well, but

Mr. Krouse defended her because he loved her so much. As far as he had ever seen, she had treated his children with kindness."

"The soulmeister asked him two more times how well he knew his new wife and refused to answer any more of Mr. Krouse's questions," said Rodriqa.

"Then the soulmeister recited the Bloodrunner anathem," interrupted Jordana, "which states that anyone who refused to return to their Maker once their earthly clay had been broken could be enslaved into the service of another."

"And he told Mr. Krouse to beware of the Preying Mantis," added Rodriqa as she gave Jordana a curious glance.

"The Preying Mantis?" queried Jafar.

Buzz nodded. "That's preying with an *e*, not an *a*."

"Wicked," muttered Jafar.

"Mr. Krouse was unhappy with the soulmeister," continued Rodriqa. "Intent on proving the soothsayer wrong, he asked friends about his wife. No one even knew he had been remarried. He went to the local courthouse to pull up records about his second marriage, but all he could find were documents stating that a Mayree Swanston had died twenty years earlier."

"Mr. Krouse rushed home," spun Buzz, "only to find his ghostly wife holding his youngest and last living child, Jobe, by his ankles, out his bedroom window."

"Desperate to save his only son, he screamed the Bloodrunner anathem at her," muttered Jordana. "She released Jobe and disappeared. Unfortunately, the boy did not survive, and John and his ghostly wife were never heard from again."

"Until now," whispered Aubrey.

Mrs. Gungandeep wrapped her sari more tightly around herself.

"She seems to have something against children," surmised Rodriqa.

"Wow! You all have got this stuff down pat," remarked Jafar.

"We've had a fair bit of practice over the past six months," replied Jordana.

Suddenly, a rapid series of knocks pounded against the front door. Everyone jumped.

"Quickly, children. Downstairs," ordered Mrs. Gungandeep as she licked her lips again.

"Hurry up!" Mrs. Gungandeep darted into the living room.

"What's going on?" Aubrey asked.

Jafar shushed him. "We need to be out of sight," he whispered as he picked up the remote controls and dropped them into the NGW case. Buzz rested the satellite-dish gun in the box and placed ESAU's dial on top of the tangled mess of wiring.

Fervent knocking rapped against the door again.

"We have to hide," urged Jafar. He hurriedly ushered everyone into the living room, and the friends followed him back down the stairs into the family room.

Once downstairs, they leaned up against the wall closest to the steps between the leather couches and listened intently.

Mrs. Gungandeep peeked down the stairs, making sure the children were out of sight, before she scurried into the foyer.

She approached the door and peered through the peephole. All she could see was the front lawn and the cul-de-sac. Another barrage of knocking blasted against the door, and she jerked with a startle.

Mrs. Gungandeep unlocked the door and opened it slightly. On the landing, a short Japanese woman stood. Shiny straight white hair rounded her face, cut precisely shoulder length at the sides with thin strips of bangs cupping her forehead. Adorned in a red pantsuit with a black belt and shoes, she stood barely four feet tall in three-inch heels. Her thin lips curled upward, except for a wrinkle from a cleft lip scar. Her slender eyes peered at an electronic tablet that flashed and blipped with graphs and maps. She tapped the screen with her index finger and various smaller screens flushed to the center. As she looked up from her pad, her narrow eyes burrowed into Mrs. Gungandeep.

"Mrs. Gungandeep?" the woman asked.

"Yes," replied Jafar's mom, licking her lips.

"Brandy Gungandeep?" questioned the diminutive woman.

"Yes," Mrs. Gungandeep responded. "Who are you?"

"I am Dr. Iyashi Gatchiri." Dr. Gatchiri stared back down at her tablet and touched the screen in three different places.

"Can I help you?" asked Mrs. Gungandeep.

"Most likely," replied Dr. Gatchiri. She pulled her pad to her chest and stared around Mrs. Gungandeep. "As I'm sure you've heard, there have been multiple notable events in your small community recently, and the local authorities have contacted the I-5 in the hopes of determining the reason behind these suspicious incidents."

"I-5?" interrupted Mrs. Gungandeep.

"International Institute of Illness Investigation and Intervention," rattled Dr. Gatchiri. "As with any epidemiologic exploration, I am evaluating individual residences around the epicenter of activity. May I come inside?"

"Why?" asked Mrs. Gungandeep.

"I simply need to take an inventory of possible residential contagions, environmental hazards, and other cues that may aid in the discovery of the offending agent, whether microbiological, psychological, or criminal."

Mrs. Gungandeep stared at the ground, unsure of what to say.

"May I come in, please?" reiterated Dr. Gatchiri.

"I don't understand why you need to come inside my house," questioned Mrs. Gungandeep.

"Which part of my explanation was unclear?" asked Dr. Gatchiri.

"I'm really very busy at the moment." Mrs. Gungandeep swung the door, nearly closing it.

Dr. Gatchiri slammed her tablet into the door, holding it open. "I understand that the life of a housewife, can be very...draining, but I really need you to let me do my job."

"I don't think I have any information that can help," asserted Mrs. Gungandeep.

Dr. Gatchiri leaned inward and whispered, "I can assure you the utmost discretion. You can tell me anything."

Mrs. Gungandeep took a step back into the foyer and scowled.

"Why are you scared?" With a click of her heel on the marble, Dr. Gatchiri stepped in.

"What?" Mrs. Gungandeep chirped.

Dr. Gatchiri pulled a penlight out of her pocket and flashed into Mrs. Gungandeep's face, flitting it from eye to eye. "Your pupils are dilated. Your mouth is dry. The temporal artery on your forehead is pulsating at approximately 126 beats per minute. Your respiratory rate has increased from sixteen to twenty-two times per minute during our brief conversation. And," Dr. Gatchiri reached around and felt the doorknob inside, "your palms are sweaty. In short, your sympathetic nervous system is in overdrive. I'm obviously no threat, so tell me, Mrs. Gungandeep"—Dr. Gatchiri took two more steps inside—"what are you afraid of?"

"Nothing," Mrs. Gungandeep blurted.

"Good," replied Dr. Gatchiri. "I'll only be a moment."

❦

Buzz, Rodriqa, Magnos, Aubrey, and Jordana were standing at the bottom of the stairs with open mouths, straining to eavesdrop. Jafar jumped in front of them and pushed them back into the family room as Dr. Gatchiri marched through the living room.

"Who is she?" asked Buzz under his breath.

Jafar shushed him and said, "The woman Mr. Miller hired to expose you all."

"Then let her expose us," insisted Rodriqa.

"Yeah, we don't have anything to hide," agreed Magnos.

Jafar waved his hands, trying to keep them quiet. "I don't think you understand."

"Maybe she's a ghost," surmised Buzz.

Jafar winced and shook his head.

"Aubrey. Eyes," ordered Buzz.

Aubrey frowned and closed his eyes, staring through the wall up to the next floor. Slowly the phosphenes faded. Emptiness was all that remained. Aubrey snapped open his eyes, looked at Buzz, and shook his head.

"Maybe a confirmatory test is in order." Buzz opened the NGW case.

❦

Dr. Gatchiri tromped around the living room, inspecting tables and window curtains, looking behind chairs and examining the svelte sheen of dust on the trim and mantles. She stopped for a moment and admired the papyrus wall hangings, twirling one of the fraying ends between her fingers. "You have impeccable taste, Mrs. Gungandeep."

"Thank you." Mrs. Gungandeep frowned as she trailed after the doctor.

Dr. Gatchiri rubbed her fingers together, grinding up a small strand of the dried antique between them, and then sniffed the residual grains. "These Egyptian tapestries are one of a kind. They must be priceless."

Mrs. Gungandeep wrapped her sari tighter around her arms. "What specifically are you looking for, Doctor?"

Dr. Gatchiri returned to inspecting corners and fine particles of lint on chair throws. "Answers," muttered the tiny Japanese woman as she slid graphs and tables into the corners of her tablet. "You live here with your son and husband. Is that correct?"

"I've already filled out my census questionnaire for this decade, Doctor."

"I'm merely confirming the data I've already collected," smirked Dr. Gatchiri. "Where are your son and your husband?"

Mrs. Gungandeep perched on the nearest sofa, annoyed at the intrusion, and stared into the dining room through the glass wall outside. "My husband is still at work, and Jafar had afterschool activities."

"Really." The doctor tapped on her screen. "I was rather hoping Jafar would be home."

"And why is that?"

Dr. Gatchiri turned around and faced her. "Do you believe in ghosts, Mrs. Gungandeep?"

Mrs. Gungandeep's upper lip quivered. She smiled to hide her shock. "Excuse me?"

"I do not believe the question was a complicated one."

Mrs. Gungandeep sighed deeply and stood up. "Let me give you a piece of advice, Doctor. Lake Julian may be simple and superstitious, but it does not take kindly to outsiders who wish to stir up trouble. We have enough trouble here of our own."

"And yet it is your own who wishes to stamp out the simple and superstitious as you called it." Dr. Gatchiri walked up to Mrs. Gungandeep. "Unlike their parents, children often have an unmitigated view of their community, which is why I was hoping to ask Jafar a few crucial questions."

"Like what?" rang a voice from across the room.

Mrs. Gungandeep hushed a muted gasp as her head jerked upward. Jafar was standing at the top of the stairs with a remote control in hand, held waist high, and aimed at the two women. The remote's cord slipped down into his pants, ran inside his inseam, and exited at the bottom, behind his shoe. The cord snaked down the stairs and rounded the corner into the family room. With the remote's plug snapped into ESAU's dial, Aubrey, Jordana, Rodriqa, and Magnos watched the gauge. Trigger finger ready, Buzz leaned back in the couch with the satellite dish gun aimed upward at the corner of the stairs.

Dr. Gatchiri spun on her heels. "Ah, Jafar. I thought you weren't home."

Jafar shrugged. "I snuck in the back. I've been watching TV." Jafar pushed the button on the remote, and the red light behind the black plastic tab blinked wildly.

"Would you mind if I asked you a few questions?"

"Shoot," blurted out Jafar so the others could hear.

Buzz pushed his thick glasses up his nose, slick with sweat, as he looked at the dial. The tiny hand flitted back and forth and rested on seventeen micrometers.

Dr. Gatchiri walked up to Jafar. "Do you know the children of a Mr. Maximillian Miller?"

Jafar nodded, still pressing the button on the remote.

"What are their names, and how much do you know about them?"

"Hamilton is a senior. All the girls chase after him because he always looks like he just stepped out of a magazine. McCrayden is his sister. She's a mirror image. Only a freshman, but she is quickly overpowering her brother as one of the most popular kids in school."

Buzz flicked the gauge with his middle finger. It popped up to thirty-four meters, but then shuddered and slowly returned to seventeen micrometers. Aubrey, Magnos, Jordana, and Rodriqa divided their attention between watching the gauge and listening to the conversation upstairs.

"And Hamilton and McCrayden are your neighbors?" asked Dr. Gatchiri as she ran her finger across her tablet.

"Yep," replied Jafar, "Ever since we've lived here."

"And is it true that you have a certain fondness for the youngest Miller?"

Jafar scrunched up his nose. "McCrayden?" He wagged his head and licked his lips. "Fondness?"

Dr. Gatchiri took another step toward Jafar. "Would you like for me to repeat the question?"

"B-b-but McCrayden Miller already has a boyfriend. She's dating Teton Bailston."

"But don't you wish it were you instead?" questioned Dr. Gatchiri.

Jafar shook his head again. He could feel his heart pounding in his ears as they blushed red.

"She's asking about school gossip?" Rodriqa whispered.

Buzz turned the dial to fifteen micrometers and pulled the trigger. The satellite dish popped off the front of the gun. Magnos reached for it, but missed. The miniature plastic dish flew through the air and crashed onto the steps, clanking against them with an echoing clamor.

Rodriqa and Jordana both grabbed Buzz and shook him. Buzz shrank down into the couch.

Dr. Gatchiri looked down the stairs, over Jafar's shoulders. She spun on her heels and marched over to Mrs. Gungandeep. "Thank you for your time. I'll be in touch." With administrative haste, her heels snapped against the marble, and she exited the front door.

Jafar turned around and shouted down the stairs, "What's your glamor glitch?"

"Toad thrower here decided to be cute," barked Rodriqa up the stairs as she pinched the back of Buzz's arm. Buzz endured it with a whimpering yelp.

Mrs. Gungandeep raced into the kitchen with her fingers to her lips. She picked up her cell phone and quickly dialed a number. "Hello, Josephine? I need your help."

GRIMMIGRATION

In a patina-hued dress of ruffled stillness, an aged woman stood with stalwart hope over the choppy waters of New York Bay, her ember-forged face fixed against the insidious wear of weather and time. Embracing a tablet of and a torch stretched to the heavens, the Statue of Liberty faced the horizon, guarding the entrance to freedom. Bright square beams of fluorescent light burst with the strength of daylight from her brown stony pedestal, wrapping her in a gleaming cocoon amid the starlit night.

Scuffling across the beach below, a lanky man with disheveled, gray hair and a stubbly beard huddled within an oversized trench coat. He kicked plumes of sand into the air and mumbled unintelligibly at unseen spectators. Exhausted from his excess and chilling in the nighttime breeze, he leaned against the brown-bricked barrier at the monument's base, several yards back from the lolling waters around Liberty Island. He pulled a crinkled brown paper sack out of his pocket and nuzzled it closely to his chest. Sipping from its funneled top, he sunk down along the wall into a crumpled pile.

Plastic wrappers and broken bottles washed up on the beach as the waters pulled further away into the bay. The man nipped at the open end of his sack and nodded off, ignoring the waning waves and calming air.

Without warning, a line of fish popped lifeless to the surface of the water. Hordes of horseshoe crabs scurried out of the receding ocean and buried themselves in holes in the shoreline.

Suddenly, a blast of wind flushed against the brick wall, rattling the man out of his stupor. A swirling tempest of white water and craggy ice exploded out of the churning tide. Crackling light streamed across the foam, peeling out of jagged breaks in the whirlpooling sphere. In an instant, water and ice fell out of the air, like a waterfall, showering the vacant shore below. Tiny jets of ocean sprayed the man's coat and face, and ripples licked at the tattered boots on his feet.

"Water...batter...matter...fatter," blurted the man with slobbered indignation. His eyes widened as stared at the sight in front of him.

Three gray-skinned figures walked out of the ocean shoulder to shoulder as the breaking line of waves resumed their roll away from the island. They looked human but were nearly twice as tall.

The three forms stopped, their gray eyes surveying the tiny island and its statue. The salt-laden breeze returned with full force from the open waters, forcing the man to bury himself in his coat until only his blood-shot eyes were exposed, focusing on the tall, blurry men.

The hunch-backed form on the left appeared elderly, with deeply chasmed jaws under knobby cheeks. His scraggly hair and beard twisted and twirled as it flowed down onto his chest, their braided ends sparking with static between the fraying ends. He wore a red, silky robe, trimmed in gold and copper with bronze pins and loops holding it in place at the shoulders and waist. Electricity arced from wrist to finger, leg to back, and beard to thigh between his robe's metal ornaments, wrapping his body in a perpetual thunderstorm.

Clad in a torn linen tunic that draped over one shoulder and ended above his knees, the bald-headed, sinewy middle form stood a head above the other two. Shreds of cloth rippled in the air around his arms and legs as if the material was being torn away by an unseen force. Aggregates of smooth pebbles and chiseled gemstones glided in perfectly circular orbits about his temple, waist, and ankles. Bleached crustacean shells and grainy fossils spun above his chest like an airy necklace, and unlinked gold and silver chains hovered in a ring around his wrists.

With slim, crescent-shaped eyes straining to stare through the material world around him, the third form on the right craned and popped his neck from side to side. He inhaled deeply, not breathing, but sensing his setting in all its evanescent parts. His black, spiky hair and his smooth skin gave him a youthful appearance. A studded leather belt and a fur-lined hide cloak loosely hung from his shoulders, covering most of his form. With a wave of his hand, the metal studs on the belt enlarged and encapsulated its leather holster, transforming into a shimmering chain-link belt. The cloak shortened. Its inner bristly filaments withdrew. The skins stretched until he was wearing a brown leather flight jacket with pleated wool pants.

Behind the three larger forms, five smaller humanlike creatures lumbered onto the shore. With flap-like ears and three-fingered hands, each appeared with distinct features. One had blond hair, another sparse black hair. One had metallic hands, another long pointy canines, and the last had bushy-green, braided hair.

"We have few allies here," remarked the elderly form on the left.

"It is of little consequence," heaved the middle form. "We only need information. Gaspian, do you sense the warlord?"

The form at the right looked up at the middle figure. "Yes, Thalazzaran, he is here, but we are being watched." He stretched his hand outward and pointed at the base of the Statue of Liberty as his jacket sleeve disintegrated along his arm and reformed into a band of silver rings.

"I am certain our unexpected arrival will be met with wondrous reverence," remarked Thalazzaran as a curt smile curled across his lips.

"Except from the spoiled litter who know no reverence," crowed the elderly form. The air around him snapped with bows of electricity leaping from his arms to his chest.

"Who do you see, Melkyor?" demanded Thalazzaran.

The elderly Melkyor opened his hand. Sparks zapped between his knuckles and shot up the shore.

The man on the beach, hiding in his trench coat, screeched in fright. He flung open his coat and hopped like a barefoot child on a sun-beaten sidewalk. Blue sparks sizzled the matted hair of his head and the bottle in his brown paper sack burst onto the sand.

Gaspian walked up the shore and loomed over the man. He sniffed and snarled his lip at him. The man crouched to the ground and covered his head.

"He reeks of synthesized senescence," Gaspian snapped. "Good," gnashed Thalazzaran, "that should make our job easier." He waved Melkyor forward. "Convince this pud that in his delirium, all he has seen is fantasy. I'll hunt for Magog." He turned behind him, glancing at the five human-oids. "Wait here."

"Yes, master," replied one of the reptilian-skinned creatures.

Melkyor grinned as light crackled between his arched fingertips. Rows of concrete icicles grew down Gaspian's arms, and metal spikes sprouted along his spine. Thalazzaran hovered toward the brick wall. Disappearing through the wall, he ignored any hindrance from physical forms as he passed through mortar, steel, and stone.

On the opposite side of the wall, a vast hollow space, devoid of light, opened up. Thalazzaran halted and closed his eyes, sensing the void. Massive iron beams, latticed together in a puzzle of crosses and polygons, plunged deep through the earth and fastened an upper structure to the bedrock below. Damp dirt caked the inside of the hollow crawlspace. Bundled pipes and insulated wires ran hundreds of yards within the supports in an industrial highway of waste and replenishment.

Thalazzaran examined the stillness. For the elite of the shadow, the untouched cavern created an unequaled home.

Suddenly, the chill in the air steamed with a rumbling wave of heat. At the far end of the crawlspace, smoky yellow eyes flashed alight, glaring at Thalazzaran.

"How dare you!" boomed a voice from underneath the glowing eyes. Lifting its long, bulbous snout from the ground, it exhaled, and gaping round nostrils spewed sulfurous smoke. It stretched its dark, scaly neck, exposing the football-field length of its coiled body and reared its dragon-like head backward, like a snake ready to strike.

Thalazzaran took two steps forward and lifted his arms in greeting. "Hail, mighty Magog."

"You are in my domain now!" screeched the monster as it ground its rows of teeth. Suddenly, dozens of bat-like wings snapped open along its spine and flapped like a hundred cracking whips. In an instant, the creature launched itself across the entire length of the underground chasm toward Thalazzaran.

Thalazzaran's eyes flashed a blinding white, and he flexed his forearms and hands.

The creature stopped in midair. Its jaw craned open, and its eyes widened under the crushing pressure of an unrelenting force. Magog coughed and sputtered, its wings crumpling against its tubular torso.

"Do not threaten me, fallen one." Thalazzaran relaxed his hands, and the creature fell to the ground in a writhing slump. The mammoth beast withdrew upon itself, coiling its broken body into a protective heap.

"Why have you come here, Graviteer?" seethed the beast.

Thalazzaran dropped his arms and raised his chin. "I mean you no disrespect, warlord. There are rumors to which the Magi seek verification. Do you know of the Terminal Prophecy?"

The creature hissed and dove at Thalazzaran. Thalazzaran raised his arms at the beast. It struck its head against an unseen wall.

The creature recoiled and shook off the blow. "There is no such thing as the Terminal Prophecy. Take your fairy tales elsewhere." His scaly tail slinked in reverse toward the far wall.

Thalazzaran closed his hands and raised his arms and shoulders. The colossal serpent rose into the air. "Perhaps you have not been as vigilant as expected. Or else you refuse to share what you know."

"Then ask your concern and leave," hissed Magog as he twisted clumsily in the air.

Gaspian and Melkyor floated through the wall behind Thalazzaran.

Melkyor squinted through the darkness. "Is that Magog?" He held out his hand and a bright pinpoint of light pierced the darkness. "It is Magog." Melkyor giggled in a sinister falsetto. "What has happened to the once great warrior of the rebellion?"

"What does he know?" interrupted Gaspian.

"Where is the seer?" demanded Thalazzaran of Magog.

Magog chuckled hoarsely. "There hasn't been a seer for centuries."

"Word spreads fast amongst the shade. They say the seer is here."

"If there were a seer in my lands, I would know it!"

Thalazzaran sneered at Magog. "Perhaps your control of this territory is not as tight as you think."

Magog snapped his jaws at Thalazzaran. "No seer would dare enter the realm of Magog."

"We have heard otherwise."

"Then you have heard wrong!" Magog flapped his wings in a burst of might, shoving his body out of Thalazzaran's veiled grip. Magog flew upward into the support scaffolding, clambering to escape between I-beams and wooden rafters.

Thalazzaran flexed his broad shoulders and clapped his hands together in a single blow, squeezing his palms together tightly.

Magog screamed in agony. Yellow smoke bellowed from his throat, singeing the metal struts above.

"One...last...chance," grunted Thalazzaran as he crushed Magog.

"*South!*" wheezed Magog.

Thalazzaran dropped his arms to his sides. Magog fell into a lifeless pile on the ground. Slowly, its eyes smoldered into darkness.

"Command the Keepers," commanded Thalazzaran. "They will search the south for this seer."

"The food selection is absolutely fabulous there," remarked Jon Harney, pulling a rack of steaming doughy triangles out of the bottom section of a brick-faced, stainless steel oven. He rested them on the ceramic stove in the middle of the kitchen island behind him. Tall and thin with wavy brown hair, Jon pulled down his ribbed, sea-green tank top, which had ridden above his midriff while he bent over.

"You got all of this from the State of the Mart?" asked Pam Trank, biting off the end of a baby carrot. Pam leaned up against the counter next to Jon and watched him cook, her black pigtails bobbing as she chewed.

"Yes, can you believe it?" Jon angled a pan on the burner, so several patties of cooking meat slid out onto a plate. "And believe me, I never shop sub-bougie."

"I bet if I found an antique Celine Dion LP at the flea market, you'd be there faster than I could say, 'my heart will go on,'" teased Vidalia Arsvine in her sweet, southern drawl. She batted her long curvy eyelashes at Jon from the other side of the island. She smiled and looked down to paint her fingernails with glittery yellow nail polish. Two seats down, Zaniah Jones nodded cheerfully, painting her and Vidalia's toenails, their feet propped on the bar stool between them.

"Too right," agreed Jon with a laugh. "But Celine Dion is not an antique. She's vintage." Jon paused reverentially with his eyes closed out of devotion for his favorite recording artist. Everyone else rolled their eyes. Jon continued, "Seriously though, even the top shelf foodstuffs were selling for bargain prices."

"Where?" McCrayden Miller marched into the room, her golden locks pulled straight back into a tight ponytail on top of her head and a fresh coat of makeup glistening about her cheeks, eyes, and lips.

"State of the Mart," replied Jon. "Have you been there?"

"Uh-huh," McCrayden sat on a stool at the end of the island. She took off her pink cotton bathrobe and hung it on the back of her stool. "That place is way too proletariat for me."

"Is Jon still talking about the State of the Mart?" asked Mesilla Uztek, walking into the kitchen in gym shorts and a plain, white T-shirt.

"Agreed," replied Zaniah, buried in toenail painting.

"Good gravy, man. Give it a rest!" harped Mesilla. She rested her hands on the ceramic tile of the island. "When's the grub ready?"

"Soon." Jon brushed Mesilla's hands away to stack a pile of clean plates.

"I told Teton that if he ever bought me jewelry, it better not be from that place." McCrayden picked up a piece of celery and nibbled at its end. "Jasmine Chordry supposedly bought a beautiful set of diamond and ruby teddy bear pendant earrings, and when I got up close and looked, they were nothing but colored glass."

Gasps echoed from everyone around the kitchen.

"Did you tell her?" asked Jon.

McCrayden shook her head. "If she doesn't know, then it serves her right. No girl should ever wear second-class jewelry."

Everyone in the room nodded.

"Teton knows value, and it's important to have a boyfriend who can see things for what they're really worth."

"I don't understand what you see in Teton." Vidalia adjusted the tissue paper between the rollers in her blonde hair.

"I kinda question your choice as well," agreed Pam. "He's a member of the Mafisito."

McCrayden stared off dreamily. "I don't know. There's something about him that's so...tough. Like he could take care of me if I needed him too."

"But the Mafisito is a gang," interjected Jon. "I don't understand what you see in a thug."

"They don't do anything that's really heinous. They're just shrewd businessmen." McCrayden laughed and shrugged. "Daddy doesn't like it either. He's says it's part of my rebellious phase." She grinned smugly.

"Ta-da," sang Jon. "Hors d'oeuvres are ready." Everyone uttered a collective "mmmmmm" as Jon placed his completed creations on the island in front of them. "We have squeezy-cheesy quesadeezies. Miniature quesadillas with mozzarella, cheddar, and cottage cheese heated and rolled up in a tortilla with salsa and veggies." McCrayden lifted one of the quesadeezies and bit a small piece of the corner, then laid it on her plate.

"There's also jerked turkey sliders and mango hummus with pepper pitas and baked carrot chips." Jon spun around and pulled six champagne glasses from a cabinet above him. "And to drink, I made virgin Mimosas. I call them Mary-mosas." Jon smiled widely.

"It all looks so good," remarked Vidalia. Zaniah, Pam, and Mesilla filled their plates and commenced eating.

McCrayden nipped at another corner of her quesadeezy. "Mmmmmmm," she moaned. "Yummy for my gummy."

"Gummy?" asked Vidalia with a mouth full of food.

"Yummy for her gummy," explained Mesilla, "because she doesn't eat enough for it to make it to her tummy."

Vidalia nodded. McCrayden smirked, tipped her head to her shoulder, and took another nibble.

"It was so cool of your dad to let us have a slumber party in the middle of the week," remarked Zaniah.

McCrayden nodded. "Daddy said I could start spring break early. It's only three days away. Daddy said I deserved it." She dabbed her finger in the corner of her mouth daintily, removing a tiny bit of wayward cheese. "Besides, Daddy and my mom and Hamilton are with Mayor Brackenwright and Mr. Parotty getting ready for the grand opening of the Rock-U-Quarium tomorrow night."

"I'm so excited," hummed Vidalia. "I can't wait to see it."

"Me too," agreed McCrayden. "Daddy's been talking about it for months, but I've had to keep it hush-hush."

Mesilla dropped her food-stained plate in the sink as she finished her last bite. "So what's the plan for tonight?"

"Usually the three Ms." Jon dragged a baked carrot chip through the mango hummus and then swallowed it.

"Three Ms?" questioned Mesilla.

"Movies, muckraking, and makeovers," chortled Jon.

The others laughed in reply.

"Not tonight." McCrayden smiled sternly. "I have another idea."

"What's that?" asked Jon.

"Let's play cards," suggested McCrayden.

"Cards?" huffed Pam. "Talk about proletariat."

"I don't know any card games," said Vidalia. "My parents never let me play. They said it's too much like gamblin'."

"I'm not talking about just any card game." McCrayden stood up and pulled open a drawer on her end of the island. She pulled out a deck of cards and placed them in the middle of the plates.

Everyone leaned over and read the glossy word written on the back of the top card. Everyone's eyes widened. Jon gasped and covered his mouth.

"That's asking for trouble," whispered Pam.

"Ansalem is no joke," whimpered Jon.

"I'm not superstitious, but Pam and Jon are right," agreed Zaniah. "Some things aren't meant to be toyed with."

"It's just a card game," jeered McCrayden. "What harm can there be in it, really?"

"I heard a story one time about some adults who played Ansalem in a cemetery," told Vidalia. "No one ever heard from them again."

"I'm in." Mesilla scooped up the cards. "Whose deal?"

"Just like a true rowdy," cheered McCrayden. "Who's game?"

Pam, Vidalia, and Zaniah stared at the food on the island. Jon shoved another chip in his mouth and crunched down on it.

"Oh, come on, you bunch of sissies," insisted McCrayden. "What are you afraid of?"

Zaniah rocked her head back and forth. "There's a lot of rumors floating around these days."

"Yeah," said Pam. "And most of it's probably nonsense, but isn't there some ancient proverb about not tempting fate, or something like that?"

"Don't tell me you all believe in ghosts," chided McCrayden.

No one responded.

"Like Daddy says, believing in something you can't see or prove is like flying first class without a miles card. You may enjoy the trip, but you're not getting anything out of it."

Jon smiled. "So you think Aubrey and all his friends are just pulling the wool over everyone's eyes?"

"Exactly," concluded McCrayden. "It's just a big show."

"I have computer class with that tub of grub, Buzz Reiselstein," groaned Mesilla. "I swear, if he goes off on another tangent about connectionism in artificial intelligence networks again, I'm gonna poison his cafeteria food."

"Doesn't Magnos hang out with them now?" asked Vidalia.

McCrayden nodded. "Magnos is a has-been. Glad I figured that out a long time ago." She stood up and, pulling Mesilla's T-shirt, walked out of the kitchen. "Anyone who wants to be invited to another slumber party needs to walk with me. Oh, and bring the food."

The other four reluctantly stood up, lifted up their plates, and followed McCrayden down a long hall covered with oil prints. She stepped through a doorway at the end of the hall, and everyone tiptoed after her.

"This is the formal dining room," said McCrayden. "It'll give us plenty of room to play." Outside, thunder crashed and lightning flashed through the story-tall windows. Heavy droplets of rain pelted the glass while McCrayden walked up to each of the oak slat blinds and closed them.

In the center of the rectangular room, rolling leather chairs lined an oval mahogany banquet table that was a half-dozen yards long.

McCrayden pulled out a chair and slid into the seat. She unfolded a piece of paper and tossed it to Jon. "Read the rules while I deal."

Thunder rattled the entire house.

THE PREYING MANTIS

Fully dressed in his Elemag suit, Aubrey sat on the curb atop Mount Camelot with his head in his hands. The streetlight above him had burned out, leaving him to sit alone in the dark.

Looking up at the night sky, he knew the clouds tumbling by wouldn't hold back for long. He pushed a small, round button on his earpiece. "It's gonna start raining soon."

"You know the drill," replied Buzz through Aubrey's earpiece. "The ghosts always come after you first. It's better that you're out in the open. That way you can see them first too."

"Yeah, I know," pouted Aubrey. "Picking on the freckle-faced, metal-mouthed, cherry top is standard."

"It's a tough job," consoled Rodriqa through the radio snow. "So you can toughen up."

"Thanks," muttered Aubrey.

"Mrs. Gungandeep must be the woman to know on Mount Camelot because she has set us up with some cush digs," gloated Rodriqa.

"Seriously," said Magnos. "I'm watching TV right now on an eighty-three-inch screen in Sly Bollard's bedroom."

"Tasha Tremtouche gave me the key to her girl's room," bragged Jordana. "I'm snacking on chocolate éclairs under tanning lights."

"Alysteene Corlstand's parents put me up in the spare room over their garage. And it has a soda fountain and a sauna," crooned Rodriqa.

"Not fair!" griped Buzz. "I'm in the garbage hamper underneath Andre Prevermach's porch!"

Chuckles mumbled through Aubrey's earpiece.

Several heavy raindrops splashed on top of Aubrey's head. "And I'm outside in the rain," he said without pushing his earpiece's button. He covered his ear to keep it dry.

Lightning streaked across the sky, and thunder shook Mount Camelot. Aubrey scooted away from the streetlight, and a heavy rain blanketed the cul-de-sac. Aubrey scrunched his forehead, pulled his knees to his chest and wiped his brow.

"Aubrey, are your eyes closed?" sputtered Buzz across the bandwidth.

"Yes," lied Aubrey as he held his head down, water streaming through his hair and down his face.

"Okay, good," reported Buzz. "Time for radio silence."

Everyone else moaned over their headsets.

"So boring," complained Magnos.

Aubrey heard scraping on the asphalt in front of him. He looked up. A raven stood only a few feet in front of him, raking its talons against rocks in the road. Aubrey paused as a memory of last fall flooded back. He had seen this raven before, with its gray eye and another black eye, which matched its midnight-stained feathers.

Its long, curved sabre-like beak bowed three times before him.

Aubrey shook his head. "What do you want?"

The raven crowed at Aubrey and hopped forward. Instinctively, Aubrey kicked his feet, and the raven unfurled its wings and flitted back. It cawed again.

Aubrey leaned forward. The raven glared at Aubrey with its black eye.

Aubrey furrowed his brow. *Maybe it's trying to help*, he thought. "What is it?" he whispered. The raven bowed its head again twice and then burst into flight over the cul-de-sac. Within moments, the bird's inky form disappeared into the darkness above.

The streetlight above Aubrey fluttered alight. Aubrey looked up, and the light flashed and burnt out again. Suddenly, every streetlight in the cul-de-sac brightened quickly then dimmed to a mere flicker. Every house on the street darkened.

"Brownout," Aubrey mumbled to himself. Aubrey closed his eyes. Lightning flashed again, and for a moment, it brightened the darkness behind his eyelids. Green and red phosphenes swirled and merged, then split apart and drifted into darkness. Figures formed and faded. Complete blackness painted the field of view in his mind.

The rain fell harder. Water dripped into his suit and dampened his clothes. A shiver tingled down Aubrey's back.

"Nooo," groaned Magnos, "The electricity went out! The ball game was almost over!"

"Radio silence," Buzz reminded him.

"I wonder how much time we have until Mr. Miller gets back?" asked Jordana.

"Mrs. Gungandeep promised us four hours. We've got one hour left," chimed Buzz. "We shouldn't be perturbing the electrical ether."

"What's the plan if we don't see anything tonight?" asked Rodriqa. Aubrey pushed the button on his earpiece. "That won't be an issue."

Several overlapping whys echoed through the headsets.

"Because I see something." Aubrey stood up with his eyes closed. A small pink pinpoint of light pierced the darkness behind his eyelids.

"Really?" asked Jordana.

"Are you sure?" asked Rodriqa.

"Does it look ghostly?" asked Buzz.

Aubrey angled his body so the pink light was in the center of his view. "Yes. I'm walking toward the manifestation now." He took a slow step forward, and the pink light brightened.

"Move out, troops," ordered Buzz.

Heel to toe, Aubrey stepped forward, keeping the pink glow in the middle of the darkness behind his eyelids.

"Aubrey, is the bogey still in sight?" Buzz asked.

"Yep, tracking it now," said Aubrey into his headset.

"Don't open your eyes," ordered Buzz.

Feeling patronized, Aubrey grumbled under his breath. He had done this before. He knew what happened when he opened his eyes.

"Someone drank too much bossy sauce this morning," replied Rodriqa. "Leave Aubrey alone. He knows what he's doing."

Aubrey grinned, slowly stepping bit by bit into the middle of the cul-de-sac.

"I was just trying to help," said Buzz. "Sometimes it's hard to keep track of everything, especially in high anxiety situations."

As Aubrey walked closer, the pink dot behind his eyelids took shape. He could now clearly see that it had taken the form of a woman with long hair; she was kneeling with her hands pressed together in front of her.

"High anxiety is being told what to do all the time and how to do it, especially when you already know what you're doing," continued Rodriqa.

Jordana, Magnos, Buzz, and Rodriqa walked out of the houses in which they'd been. With flashlights skittering bands of light across the yards, they approached Aubrey, who was walking toward the far end of the street's entrance. Buzz waddled with the NGW case at his side.

"Why are you picking on me?" squalled Buzz. "There's nothing wrong with keeping us organized."

"Organized is fine, but condescending is obnoxious," bantered Rodriqa.

Aubrey could now hear them arguing both over his earpiece and in the cul-de-sac as they neared him.

"Obnoxious is you blasting your mouth off all the time," countered Buzz.

Rodriqa balled up her fists. "Look here, you little…."

"Enough," yelled Aubrey as he stopped. "Something's wrong."

"What?" Jordana huddled up next to Aubrey, almost trying to see through his eyes.

"I'm not sure." Aubrey concentrated on the pink-radiating woman as she stood up and outstretched her arms.

Magnos held out his hand. "The rain stopped."

"Good! Now we can use our suits." Buzz pressed a button on the side of the black box locked to his lower back. The suit popped and crackled to life. Buzz grinned proudly.

Magnos grinned back. Jordana and Rodriqa rolled their eyes as everyone else flipped on their Elemag suits' power buttons.

"This suit will be more comfortable once I get my braces off." Aubrey switched on his suit and winced as the electricity coursed around the outside of his body. Blue sparks jumped between the wires of his braces and his mouth glowed in the night.

"Most of the ghosts we've stopped have a pink glow around them, right?" asked Aubrey.

"Yeah," agreed Rodriqa.

"Well, this one just changed from pink to green, and now it's filling up my entire field of view."

"Which house?" asked Buzz.

Everyone looked in the direction Aubrey was facing. The massive four-story colonial home creaked loudly as the siding of its front walls bulged in and out.

"That's McCrayden's house," murmured Magnos.

"Come on. We need to hurry," urged Aubrey.

"We can't go in there," argued Jordana. "That's the Millers' house."

"We have to," said Magnos. "That's where the ghost is."

"What if he calls the police?" asked Jordana.

Magnos raised his hands. "What if McCrayden is in there?"

Jordana scowled at Magnos. "Or Hamilton?"

"It doesn't matter whose house it is," said Aubrey. "They're in danger."

Jordana bit her lip and turned away from Magnos.

"We were hired for this job," said Rodriqa. "And we're wasting time."

"Agreed," said Buzz. He rested the NGW case on the asphalt and handed Jordana, Rodriqa, and Magnos each a remote control. Snapping the dial into the front of his belt, Buzz grasped the satellite-dish gun and gave the trigger a practice squeeze. With Aubrey in front, the others were tethered together by loops of wire from ESAU.

Eyes still closed, Aubrey held out his hand, and Rodriqa grabbed it, guiding him.

The five of them walked up to the Miller house. Rodriqa warned Aubrey of the step up to the sidewalk. Magnos moved forward and opened the front gate underneath the trellis. Banded together, they shuffled along the stone walkway.

"I hear screams," muttered Rodriqa.

Everyone stopped for a moment and listened. The windows were dark, and the walls swelled as they cracked and split. A distant, muffled wail echoed from inside the house.

Magnos dropped his remote control and bounded up the rest of the walkway, landing on the front porch steps. He pulled and twisted the ornate brass doorknob. It was locked.

"McCrayden! Let me in!" Magnos hollered, pounding on the heavy wooden door.

The other four friends plodded up the steps together and stood behind Magnos, with Aubreytrailing the pack.

"Guys, the green glow is now swirling inside the house," Aubrey stammered.

"That sounds familiar," grumbled Rodriqa.

"We've not encountered another specter like Hovis Trottle," surmised Buzz. "They've all been a little wimpier."

"Maybe being cursed makes you tougher," guessed Jordana.

More screams reverberated from inside. Magnos beat the front door again. "McCrayden! What's happening!"

Moaning under pressure, the door bowed outward and nearly touched Magnos's face. Everyone moved back. Rodriqa bumped into Aubrey, knocking him to the top step.

"Hey!" chirped Aubrey, grabbing Rodriqa's arm.

"Sorry, boo," said Rodriqa, pulling him up by his shirt.

"What's going on?" asked Aubrey.

"The whole house looks like it's about to explode," explained Buzz.

Magnos punched the front door with his fist. The door creaked loudly but remained intact. "It's insanely hard. Is it still wood?"

Buzz shone his flashlight close to the door and examined it. "I think so."

"Help us!" yelled voices from inside.

"It's McCrayden. We have to get in there," insisted Magnos.

"Maybe we can take the door off its hinges," said Buzz.

"That'll take too long." Magnos ran around the others and jumped down the steps into the yard. He raced down the stone walkway, into the cul-de-sac, and into a yard on the opposite side in only a few moments.

"Where's he going?" Rodriqa asked.

Jordana shrugged with furrowed brow.

Gripping his flashlight in his teeth, Buzz picked up Magnos's remote control and held it to the door. He took a reading. The dial didn't register. He dropped the remote. "Aubrey, what do you see now?"

"It's the same. It's huge," replied Aubrey.

Cautiously, Rodriqa reached out her hand and touched the door. A tingling chill crept up her fingers and forearm, and they faded to transparent, giving them a ghostly appearance.

Buzz shook his head and grinned. "Watching you take on the spirit of the bigfoot never gets old."

"Tsul'kalu," reminded Jordana.

"Oh, yeah, right," uttered Buzz.

"At least one of us is ready for a fight." Jordana wrapped her long hair in a ponytail and slid her honey-colored glasses to the end of her nose.

"What's that?" Rodriqa pointed at the front yard.

"What's what?" replied Buzz and Jordana in unison.

"There." Rodriqa's finger darted at the stone walkway. "There's a raven with a gray eye watching us."

Aubrey snorted. "It's just this bird that keeps following me around. Don't worry about it. It'll fly off eventually."

Rodriqa sneered. "How long have you had a raven following you around?"

Aubrey shrugged. "Since the first time I visited the Circle of Circles cemetery last fall."

"Don't you think that's kinda odd?" asked Buzz.

"What's odd anymore?" murmured Aubrey.

"Good point," agreed Buzz. Buzz's eyes widened. "Look out!" He shoved Jordana and Rodriqa apart. Buzz dove across the porch, landing with a thud on his belly.

The two girls looked up across the cul-de-sac. Rodriqa yanked Aubrey out of the way.

A flashlight bobbed in the darkness of the yard across the street as Magnos barreled with gazelle-like speed between houses, over the sidewalk, and across the cul-de-sac. In a couple of seconds, he reached the Miller's. He galloped across the yard and launched himself over the front porch steps. Turning his shoulder forward and rolling his head to his chest, Magnos collided with the front door.

The door exploded, blasting across the porch. Jordana and Rodriqa hunkered down and covered their heads with their arms. Aubrey felt sharp points nettle his skin. He slapped his hands to his face and opened his eyes.

Instantly, the interior of the house came into view for all to see. A green light flooded the outside, and Magnos was sucked into the house's foyer.

Like a released pressure valve, once the doorframe opened and the inside exposed, the house sighed and retook its former cuboidal shape. Suddenly, Buzz, Jordana, Rodriqa, and Aubrey were sucked inside.

Rodriqa grabbed the doorframe and held on tightly, her legs pulled horizontally into the foyer. Now transparent from head to toe, she looked like an apparition, caught in between the realms of the wordly and unworldly.

Rodriqa looked down into the house. Jordana held to both of Rodriqa's ankles, her fingers slipping.

Inside the two-story foyer of the Miller home, Magnos rolled and bumped across the floor, swept around by a wind that circled from ceiling to floor. He grabbed the bottom banister of the right-hand staircase and glanced up.

Grasping to the rungs of the handrails lining the double-sided curved staircase, McCrayden, Pam, Mesilla, Vidalia, and Zaniah screeched and yelled in desperation. They ducked to avoid debris, which was flung through the air by the whirling tempest.

Toward the back of the foyer, in a small hallway that led into the living room, a woman with long black hair and a white dress on knelt with her hands clasped together and her eyes closed over the pale, still body of Jon Harney, who lay prone on the floor.

A green hue blazed around the woman. Her eyes slowly opened, and she looked at the intruders.

Aubrey and Buzz dangled from the crystal chandelier that hung at the top of the foyer. Aubrey pulled himself into the tangled hive of glass to protect himself. Buzz locked his elbow around its bottom metal frame. ESAU was wrapped around the top of the chandelier, and its TV remotes flapped in the breeze.

Aubrey and Buzz glanced down. They both caught sight of the lifeless Jon Harney.

Buzz hollered, "Mayree Krouse! Stop!"

The kneeling woman glared at Buzz. She opened her hands and stood up.

Slowly, the wind died, and the debris dropped onto the floor. Rodriqa and Jordana fell against the hardwoods in the doorway, and Aubrey and Buzz swung from the chandelier. Magnos righted himself and ran over to Jordana.

"Where are you going?" asked the woman, her hollow voice echoing in the foyer.

Magnos froze just behind Jordana.

"Don't answer her!" hollered Aubrey. "It's a trap."

The woman craned her head upward and glared at Aubrey, who was struggling to climb the chandelier. "I knew you would come, Nawbey. Now you will give me what you have kept hidden for so long."

In her ethereal form, Rodriqa jumped up and turned toward the woman. "Ain't nothing for you here, lady. Time for you to go!"

The woman sneered. Her jaw dropped, and she emitted a guttural growl. She snapped her arms above her head. Twisting and stretching, her arms expanded into jointed insect-like legs, with long bristly hairs and a single sharp claw at the end.

Screams blared from the girls along the stairs. More tentacles erupted from her body as her torso cracked open with bright glowing green crevices. She rocked her head from shoulder to shoulder, and two bulbous eyes and a small jaw broke free from her skin. In a few moments, the woman's new wraithish bug form filled the hallway, tripling in size.

The preying mantis scurried forward. Her carapaced arms swung at the chandelier. Buzz and Aubrey were knocked off, and they fell to the ground. Magnos jumped forward and caught Buzz. Rodriqa lunged and slid her ghostly self underneath Aubrey, breaking his fall. Rodriqa rolled Aubrey onto the floor, and she regained her feet. One of the giant arms knocked Rodriqa to the floor; she skidded along her back to the edge of the wall. Magnos tackled another arm, which dove at him, and he gripped it tightly. The jaws of the bulbous-eyed head squealed, and the mantis jerked her arm away, trying to shake off Magnos.

Buzz scurried back to where Jordana was standing near the front door and batted at a third arm that chased him.

The claw of the fourth arm shot at Aubrey, who was lying face down on the floor.

"Aubrey! Watch out!" cried Rodriqa as she pushed herself up.

Aubrey flipped over. The arm came down. He could feel the arm hit his chest. It knocked the wind out of him. Aubrey struggled to catch his breath. The claw had torn his suit and pinned him to the ground.

"Aubrey! No!" hollered Jordana. Rodriqa raced toward the center of the foyer. Aubrey struggled against the large tentacle. It wouldn't budge. The arm raked Aubrey and his suit along the floor, pulling him into the hallway.

Aubrey looked down. The claw had ripped his suit, but missed his skin. Instead, the claw had pierced the burlap sack holding Solluna, which he had tied around his waist. He slipped his hand in the burlap bag and pulled out the crystal pyramid.

Suddenly, the jaws of the mantis lunged at Aubrey. He held Solluna in both hands and pulled it toward his neck, fending off the jaws with his elbows.

"Give it to me!" seethed the mantis.

Buzz and Jordana turned around, startled by a loud flapping noise behind them. They crouched down. A large, black raven with a saber-like beak flew through the open door, cawing loudly. It landed next to Aubrey's head on the floor, then spread its wings wide, its long sable feathers stretching several yards from tip to tip.

A blinding flash filled the room. Aubrey closed his eyes, but as quickly the phosphenes swirled behind his eyelids, they melted away, washed out by the light.

Suddenly, Aubrey felt dizzy, and his thoughts and movements were slow, as if his arms and legs were weighted with lead bricks. He could see the bright light recede, and Aubrey thought it was odd that he could watch the edge of the light drift away from the center of the room.

The pincer jaws and bulging eyes of the mantis loomed above Aubrey, but the creature was frozen. Even its phantasmal green skin undulated more slowly.

Aubrey glanced around the foyer and noticed everyone in the room was motionless. From the girls along the stairs to Magnos clinging to the ghost's arm, to Rodriqa stuck in midstride as she bolted toward him. Everything was quiet and still, as if time had nearly halted.

The foyer steadily dimmed. In place of the large raven, a lanky, bald-headed man stooped over Aubrey. The man's skin was gray, and loose strips of cloth hung from his tall, thin frame. His right eye was gray and seemed dysfunctional, but the right one was dark, absorbing light, and it peered straight down at Aubrey.

Aubrey had seen this man before in the magma pit of Hovis Trottle's house under the Circle of Circles cemetery. Aubrey wanted to be afraid, but his mind couldn't find the energy.

"You must stop with these parlor tricks," said the man. His mouth didn't move, but Aubrey heard the words. His voice was soft, like a whisper.

Aubrey didn't understand what he meant, and the man seemed to sense Aubrey's confusion.

"Your gifts are for a grander purpose," continued the gray man, "and you must cease using them thoughtlessly."

Who are you? Aubrey thought to himself. He tried to speak, but his throat and tongue moved too slowly.

"My name is Zaks. Heed my warning. You have exposed yourself unnecessarily by chasing after ghosts. These spirits are of no consequence, and their fate is already determined. The pyramid will draw the shadow."

Zaks bent down closer to Aubrey so that all Aubrey could see was the gray man's face. "A great threat is coming, and you must be prepared. A recent enemy has new allies. An ancient master hunts for a means to restore his glory."

What does that mean? asked Aubrey.

Zaks shifted his gaze forward at the mantis's head, hovering in complete stillness over Aubrey's body. With a single swift lunge, Zaks clapped his hands together, catching the bulbous eyes of the mantis between his gangly fingers. The jaws let out a screech as it was pulled forward. The ghostly insect imploded toward the space between Zaks's palms, tearing her limbs and torso apart until every writhing green bit of the overgrown bug had disappeared into the middle of Zaks's grasp.

In place of the collapsed specter, a single white stone glowed faintly with a single spinning point of orange light orbiting around it. Zaks's fingers curled around the white stone, and its radiance faded.

In less than a moment, Aubrey glanced up, and the raven stood over him with its wings fully unfurled. Zaks was gone. The edge of the slowly moving, blinding flash of light dispersed into the walls of the foyer.

Time returned to its normal pace. And the preying mantis was gone. Aubrey could move, breath, and think as before.

The lights flickered back on. The raven crowed and flew out the front door. Jordana and Buzz ducked to avoid it. Its black body dissolved into the night behind them.

Magnos dropped several feet to the floor and landed with a thud on the tile. He shook his head and scrambled his arms and legs to force himself up.

Rodriqa, in Tsul'kalu form, dove on top of Aubrey. "Are you okay?" she panted as her transparent sheen dematerialized into her rich, dark skin. She dug through his torn Elemag suit, looking for signs of injury. Aubrey grunted as she accidentally elbowed him in the stomach.

"Are you hurt?" she asked.

"No," replied Aubrey.

"Where did she go?" hollered Buzz, blinking and rubbing his eyes.

Jordana took a few calculated steps toward Magnos, leery of the foyer's new atmosphere. "I think she's gone," Jordana muttered as she walked over to help Magnos stand.

A jaw-grinding scream bellowed from above. Pam Trank bolted down the stairs with her pigtails waving behind her. She rounded the bottom bannister and raced toward Jon Harney, who lay lifeless on the floor in the hallway. Falling beside him on her knees, Pam shook his shoulders. "Jon, wake up!"

Aubrey lifted his head off the floor and watched Pam lean down to listen to Jon's chest.

"What's this?" asked Rodriqa as she pulled the crystal pyramid out from his suit.

Aubrey frowned at her and grabbed the pyramid. "Nothing," he mumbled as he shoved it back in the ripped burlap sack.

Vidalia Arsvine, Zaniah Jones, and Mesilla Uztek trotted down the stairs.

"Is he alive?" Zaniah looked at the ceiling but glanced out of the corner of her eye at Pam and Jon.

"Somebody call nine-one-one," blurted out Vidalia as she covered her mouth with her hands.

"Where did the ghost go?" Buzz wandered around the foyer, scanning the wreckage.

McCrayden marched down several steps. "You tell us!" she demanded as she frowned, her golden locks flattened to one side of her head, with bits of dirt and wood dangling off the end of her curls. "Look at this mess!" She pointed around the room with an outstretched hand. Many of the wooden supports of the railing and bannisters were cracked or shattered, lying in pieces along the steps and hardwoods. Most of the glass ornaments of the chandelier were missing, and the remaining had pelted the wallpaper, leaving a graffiti of dents and scrapes along the walls. A mangled desk lay crumpled in the far corner, with its accouterments spilled across the hallway.

"How are you going to explain all this when Daddy gets home?" yelled McCrayden.

"You can't be serious," said Magnos.

"We tried to save you," replied Jordana.

"No, this is *all* your fault," charged McCrayden. "You misfits are notorious for tricking people to believe that some ghost has created some sort of havoc. And then you *step in* and play the hero. When, in truth, you are the ghosts and the reason for all this mayhem."

Aubrey shook his head. "You're wrong," he shouted, but his voice cracked. He couldn't keep himself from mulling the slow-motion events over in his mind.

"Am I?" McCrayden clucked derisively. "Then prove to me a ghost was here."

"Jon is *dead*!" squealed Pam as she gripped her pigtails and pulled them down to her shoulders.

Buzz took two more steps toward the hallway and looked around Pam at Jon. He curled his lip and shook his head. "No, he's not. I can see him breathing."

Pam cocked her head to the side and loosened up on her pigtails.

Buzz turned toward McCrayden. "That's not fair! You know what you saw. We all saw it." He glared at Zaniah, Mesilla, and Vidalia. They lowered their heads and focused on Pam and Jon.

"Who do *you* think Daddy will believe when I tell him what happened?" McCrayden raised her head.

Buzz's jaw dropped, realizing their precarious position and paucity of proof.

Rodriqa stood up. "You toad thrower! There's a special place in time-out for you, and it's *not* the corner." Rodriqa shook her finger at McCrayden. "Let me tell you something, if you think for a single minute we're gonna stand by and let you vilify us, when we saved your precious little—"

Jordana marched over to Rodriqa and jerked on her arm. "You're not helping.""Don't preach to me," chided McCrayden. "I'm not the one who needs to learn a lesson."

Suddenly, Jon Harney sat straight up, turned green and vomited partially digested cheese, hummus, and turkey across the hallway floor. Pinching her nose, Pam jerked herself to her feet and took a couple of steps back.

Buzz stormed over to Jon. "What were you all doing before all this happened?"

Jon wiped off his mouth, furrowed his brow, and thought for a moment. "We were playing cards."

"Which game?" asked Buzz.

"Jon! No!" roared McCrayden.

Jon turned toward Buzz and muttered, "Ansalem."

Buzz's eyes widened. He spun around and pointed at Vidalia, Zaniah, and Mesilla. "That's why the ghost was here," indicted Buzz. "That's why your house is a mess. If it wasn't for us, you'd all be—"

"What's going on here?" bellowed a voice from the front door.

All the friends turned toward the entrance and shuddered. A tall, wiry man stood in the threshold. Except for the small ringlet of gray hair around his temples, the shiny, smooth top of his head reflected the dwindling light from the chandelier. His nostrils flared as his eyes darted from child to child.

"Daddy!" squalled McCrayden as she fled toward the door. Mr. Miller caught her as she embraced him.

Mrs. Miller appeared out of the night and knelt down beside Mr. Miller. She pulled McCrayden to her, and the girl cried on her mother's shoulder. McCrayden's brother, Hamilton, peeked over his father's shoulder to view the inside of their house.

Aubrey rolled over and looked up toward the door. He covered his forehead and eyes with his hands and moaned.

Buzz lumbered across the foyer. "Mr. Miller, you had a ghost in your house!"

Magnos shushed Buzz and walked up to McCrayden's dad. "Mr. Miller, I know this looks bad, but please let us explain. A lot has happened in the past few minutes."

Mr. Miller glowered at Magnos. "Was this an attempt to regain my daughter's affections?"

Magnos tilted his head to the side. "Huh?"

Jordana scowled at Mr. Miller.

"We came to help," insisted Rodriqa. "Your house was under attack!"

Mr. Miller shifted his gaze from Magnos to Rodriqa, to the damage in the foyer, and then to his daughter. He leaned over and rubbed his daughter's head gently. "What happened, pumpkin cakes?"

McCrayden sniffled back several deep, stuttering sobs. She raised up her head and looked at her father. "Oh, Daddy, it was awful." She dropped her face back into her mother's shoulder and wailed like a frightened toddler.

Mr. Miller looked over his shoulder at Hamilton. "Go call the police."

Hamilton grinned. "With pleasure." He slid between his father and the doorframe and strutted through the foyer. He glared at Jordana as he walked past her. Jordana lowered her head.

"We haven't done anything wrong," pleaded Buzz.

Mr. Miller ignored Buzz and cradled his wife and daughter.

Aubrey sat up. "Why won't you believe us?" he mumbled to Hamilton. Hamilton ignored Aubrey.

Magnos's shoulders slumped. He glanced at Jordana, whose eyes were distant, staring at the floor.

Hamilton stepped over Jon and disappeared into the hallway.

Rodriqa clenched her fists. "We did everything we could to help your daughter, and you repay us by treating us like criminals."

Mr. Miller turned his head and glared at Rodriqa with a malicious grin. "Time to pay the proverbial piper, honey."

DARKNESS'S APPRENTICE

The near full moon gleamed though breaks in the clouds overhead, casting Lake Julian's meadows and hilltops in a wavering amber glaze. The springtime air cooled quickly, winter's touch lingering.

Several floors above a grassy field, a shapely silhouette darkened the glow of a high-arched open window that had been cut into a mammoth oak tree. The figure positioned a red-wax candle and a small burlap sack on the curved windowsill. Slender, pale fingers untied the sack and pulled out a bundle of dried sassafras twigs, a toadstool mushroom, and crumpled-up scraps of a plastic grocery bag. The figure leaned to the side and reached for a long pipe of bamboo skewered with a bleached white squirrel skull at one end. The delicate hand and wrist, adorned with a brown sandstone sundial watch, twisted the pipe, exposing the hole at the base of the rodent's skull, and rested the sassafras twigs in the tiny cranium.

The form turned abruptly, her red, wavy hair cascading down her shoulders and her hollow green eyes examining the dimly lit room.

"Matsinstrus!" snapped Magnolia Thistlewood. "Don't touch that!"

A smoky, charred skeleton jerked its hand back from a porcelain jar that held the prime position on a crystalline marble mantle above the fireplace. A tiny, cream-colored cat with charcoal patches leapt upon the skeleton and raked its paws down its face, then plopped on the hearth and rolled around on a straw mat in front of the fire. "Sorry, my queen," hissed the skeleton as wisps of ash twirled away from its shifting frame.

Ms. Thistlewood acknowledged his apology with a terse nod. "There is another lesson you need to learn, Matsinstrus." Her lips curled as she spoke. The skeleton cowered away from the fireplace. It peered at the gnarled wooden ceiling above, where a white skeleton frozen into the warped timber intensified his fear.

The woman wrapped the crinkling plastic bits of bag around the twigs in the skull and crumbled the edges of the toadstool over it. "How to preserve your corpse." She turned the pipe on its edge, lighting the tip of the skull's contents in the candle flame. Closing her eyes, the woman placed the pipe to her lips and inhaled deeply.

"How can I do that?" asked the skeleton.

Ms. Thistlewood's eyes snapped open. She took several quick steps to the center of the round, wooden room and handed the pipe to the skeleton.

The skeleton's red glowing eyes darted around the room. Its phalangic fingers quivered as it griped the pipe.

She spun gracefully on her heels and walked back to the window, her translucent, violet gown flowing behind her. The beautiful woman sat gingerly in a carved oak chair and crossed her legs, staring at Matsinstrus. "In your previous form, the dioxins and formaldehyde from the burning plastic would have been toxic. But for us, it quickens the life force within us and fixes it to its earthly enclosure."

The skeleton nodded. It sucked on the end of the pipe, and gray smoke oozed from its blackened ribcage and sank down into its pelvis.

"Our objectives must be clear." The woman took another pipe from a drawer in the small wicker table next to her. "You must provide me with the stone I require."

"Tomorrow night I will have the stone of the keeper."

Ms. Thistlewood nodded. "And since Whimperfidget has been unable to locate Solluna," she waved her hand at the cat rolling on the floor, "it will be up to you to obtain it."

The skeleton inhaled greedily on the pipe. "Yes, and those children have it."

"No," chided the woman. "Only one of them has it. Aubrey Taylor. He must remain your main focus. Without their seer, they're nothing more than an uncoordinated gang of misfits."

"Do not worry. My plan is already in motion." The skeleton's jaw and rotting teeth contorted in an attempt to form a grin.

"Do not underestimate them. Many have already made that mistake." Ms. Thistlewood sighed. "Besides I have other plans for their undoing."

"As you wish." The skeleton puffed on the pipe again.

The woman glanced out the window, appraising the moon's approach to fullness. "I will provide you with something I should have had when trying to open the Tomb of Enoch."

"We are powerful! What more do we need?" Gray and black smoke fumed from every bone of the skeleton.

The woman sneered at him. "An army." She stood up and glided over to the fireplace. She reached her hand in through the searing fire and pulled out a white sandstone sundial, her skin remained as pale and unblemished as before. She wrapped the watch around his wrist and secured its leather clasp.

The woman turned the arm of the sundial and took a step back. The smoke in the room whirled and gathered around the skeleton, congealing to flesh over the skeleton's bones.

"A new phylactery for my favorite prodigy."

CAGE QUARREL

Facing the window, Aubrey sat quietly in the backseat of the Poage County police sedan. He hoped that by staring at the yards and woods they passed by, he could avoid the officer driving the car for as long as possible.

Criss-crossing strips of metal separated the front and back compartments, yet there was enough space in between the gray steel barrier for Aubrey to see the road ahead. Humiliated and frightened, he replayed the evening's events over in his mind, deciding what he should have done differently and regretting his participation in the Mount Camelot job.

But for the raven and the baldheaded, gray man, this job was similar to all the others. Aubrey wondered if anyone else had seen what he had witnessed in slow motion.

Aubrey trembled with a cool chill that prickled the hairs on the back of his neck. Aubrey bundled his arms around his stomach and dug his cold nose into his shoulder.

White and orange fluorescent lights illuminated Lake Julian High and flashed inside the police car as they drove past. Out of the corner of his eye, Aubrey glimpsed the side of the officer's face. The brim of his flat-topped police cap covered most of his wrinkled brow. His chubby cheeks sagged, which melded seamlessly into his stout neck below. He saw the officer was mumbling quietly to himself.

The lights of the high school twinkled away within the forest behind them while they headed up the switch-backed curve that led to the Lake Julian dam. A heavy darkness shrouded the cab of the police car. Aubrey knew there'd only be one more stop tonight.

"This is bad business, Aub." Sergeant Van Zenny's voice from the driver's seat startled Aubrey. Van Zenny glanced over his shoulder to make sure the boy was listening. "I's not gonna be able to let this time go." The sergeant's gruff accent was a mix of Guido and hillbilly.

Aubrey leaned forward. "But you know what we're dealing with at the Miller's place. You saw Hovis Trottle last year. You were in the power plant. You know that these…these…these whatever they are…aren't make-believe. They're real! And if we don't stop them, who knows what will happen?"

Van Zenny squinted his eyes as the car drove over the dam, the lights from the observation tower nearly blinding him. "Tha's just it, Aub. Ya's don't knows what'll happen if you don't stop messing with these...these spirits. Maybe they just wants to be left alone."

Aubrey furrowed his brow. "How many calls do you get about spooks and unexplained sightings?"

The sergeant waved him off. "Crackpots mostly. Mr. Miller has a point. Once one person sees something weird, everyone else thinks they're seeing it too. It's called mass hallucination."

Aubrey fell back into his seat. "Mr. Miller isn't nearly as smart as he thinks he is."

The sergeant shrugged. "The fact of the matter is ya's and ya's friends haven't got a clue whats you're doin'. And each time ya's get involved, I'm left cleaning up the mess."

Aubrey huffed and stared out over Lake Julian.

"When does it stop, Aubrey?" asked Van Zenny.

Aubrey ignored him. Honestly, Aubrey thought it was a fair question, but he had no idea how to answer, and he wasn't about to give the sergeant the satisfaction of fumbling through it.

"If ya's keep stirrin' up this kind of grief and pokin' folks with worry, the whole town is gonna be in ruins, and ya's will still have more monsters to chase."

"How about the Creightonys? They're glad we stepped in. And Mrs. Kapodopholous. Without us, she'd still be trapped in that well," insisted Aubrey.

Sergeant Van Zenny cut him off. "Simply put, ya's have chosen the wrong enemies. Mr. Miller bends a lot of ears in Lake Julian. Ya's need to let it be for a while."

Aubrey twisted his lips, considering his predicament. The car turned down Dalton Circle, passed the Ray Gene's Smart Mart & Finer Diner, and pulled in front of Aubrey's house. A single small yellow lamp shone in his living room window. Aubrey glanced at Rodriqa's house next door. All the lights were out. Rodriqa's dad had come to get her before the sergeant had shown up.

Van Zenny shifted the car into park and turned his head over his shoulder. "I suspect Mr. Miller won't be kind. Expect some serious consequences."

Aubrey sulked a bitter nod. Sergeant Van Zenny waddled out of the driver seat and opened the car door for Aubrey; then he turned back around to face the road. Aubrey pulled himself out of his seat and looked up at the sergeant. Van Zenny looked away. Aubrey swung the heavy door shut. Van Zenny sat back in the car and drove off.

Aubrey stood on the side of the road with his hands in his pockets as he watched the red taillights of the police car disappear around the bend. The deep red lights almost looked like red eyes, taunting him through the darkness. It reminded him of a time when he knew the world, both seen and unseen, was against him. A lump welled in his throat. He feared that time had returned.

ORNERY ORRERY

Thursday.

Jerking open a heavy metal door on the side of Lake Julian High School, Aubrey barreled through corridors and turned several corners before bolting straight for a closing classroom door. Aubrey slapped his hand against the cool metal just before its latch caught the frame as the last bell rang overhead. Aubrey felt the door's weight give way, and he leaned clumsily into it.

Opening wide, the door revealed a pudgy balding man, with chalk dust powdering his plaid shirt, which had been tucked haphazardly into his brown slacks. The man wrinkled his lip, and his bushy mustache shuddered as he glared at Aubrey. "How many days should I let you cut it this close before I start marking tardies in your attendance ledger, Mr. Taylor?"

Aubrey skulked around the doorframe and fiddled with his book. "Sorry, Mr. Vandereff. I won't let it happen again." Although Mr. Vandereff had been strict and steadfast, physical sciences had become Aubrey's favorite class, and Mr. Vandereff his favorite teacher.

Mr. Vandereff harrumphed as he closed the door and hobbled back toward the chalkboard.

Aubrey walked around the outer edge of the classroom. His foot caught the corner of a desk, and he stumbled, nearly tossing his backpack. Aubrey caught himself and regained his balance. The chubby Lenny Van Zenny sneered up at him from his desk. "Watch it, Taylor," Lenny grumbled under his breath.

Aubrey looked around the room and everything was out of place. Instead of rows, the desks formed a horseshoe shape around the classroom's perimeter. In the center of the room, a tall, thin wooden box, riddled with knots and deep grooves, sat upright, nearly grazing the ceiling. Each side was no wider than a foot, and about halfway up, there was a division in the box's frame, forming upper and lower panels around its four sides.

"Mr. Taylor," bellowed Mr. Vandereff from behind his black lab bench.

"Yes, sir," replied Aubrey as he spun around toward the front.

"Due to your lack of preparatory time, you have failed to read the directions, which everyone else seems to have mastered with little guidance. Would you mind?" Mr. Vandereff tapped his knuckle against the blackboard. Aubrey nodded and read the three chalky sentences.

Pick either an apple or a pear.

Find your seat in the horseshoe.

Don't touch the box in the middle.

On the black lab bench across the front of the class, two aluminum platters held several green pears with the letters O and G written on them in red marker and a single yellow apple with the letter G marked on its peel.

Aubrey wove his way between the desks toward the lab bench, carefully avoiding the unusual box in the middle. He picked up the lonely apple and turned around. Buzz, Magnos, and Jordana sat together in a small arch of desks in the back. Buzz waved at Aubrey and pointed to an empty seat between him and Magnos.

Aubrey smiled and hurried to his friends. He squeezed his slender torso between the empty desk and Magnos and slid into his seat.

"What's up with the fruit?" asked Aubrey.

"Old man's finally lost it," uttered Magnos as he tapped his apple to make sure it was real.

"It's part of the lesson," corrected Buzz. He marveled at his juicy pear. "I hope we get to eat it afterwards."

"Me too," agreed Jordana quietly as she rubbed her pear on her sleeve to a shiny gloss.

Mr. Vandereff cleared his throat. "Now that we're all here, who can tell me what this coming Friday is?"

Buzz's hand shot straight up.

"Anyone except for Mr. Reiselstein," grumped Mr. Vandereff.

Buzz frowned, and his hand dropped limply to his desk. Mr. Vandereff's repeated denial of Buzz's overly eager and resolute desire to answer every question had turned into a daily competition of wits between the two. For everyone else, it was amusing to watch. Benny Van Zenny, Lenny's twin brother, oftentimes kept score.

McCrayden Miller raised her arm on the right side of the class and genteelly wiggled her fingers. Jordana curled her lip. Magnos glanced up but quickly redirected his attention back to his apple.

"Ms. Miller," called Mr. Vandereff.

"It's the first day of spring break," she replied.

Mr. Vandereff nodded and sighed. "Yes, but today we're still in class, specifically science class, and I was looking for something related to our subject of study."

McCrayden snarled slightly and murmured mockingly to herself as she wiped the red OG off her pear.

Lenny Van Zenny and several other students put their hands in the air.

"Mr. Van Zenny," chose Mr. Vandereff.

"Friday is when our weekly element assignments are due," stated Lenny.

"Yes, and it's been that way for every Friday, all school year. I'm talking about *this* Friday," replied Mr. Vandereff. "Anyone else have a guess?"

"Good Friday?" said Celia Blyers, sitting at the front, left-hand side of the class.

"No, no, that's in two weeks," grumbled the frustrated science teacher.

"Baseball game against the Cullowhee Caribou," hollered out Paul Jamsen, next to Jordana.

"Nah, that got moved to Sunday," corrected Benny Van Zenny.

Mr. Vandereff wagged his head.

"It's the total solar eclipse!" blurted out Buzz.

Mr. Vandereff froze. Buzz gasped and covered his mouth.

"Wrong!" barked Mr. Vandereff.

Buzz's eyebrows crumpled together.

"It's an annular solar eclipse," continued Mr. Vandereff, as a sly grin curved under his mustache.

Buzz rolled his eyes.

"What's the difference?" asked Celia Blyers.

"Let me show you," replied Mr. Vandereff. He walked toward the tall, thin box. He unfastened several brass latches at the front and the top and then slid the front panel down. With three sudden snaps, the other three upper panels released, swung down, and smacked against their lower panel counterparts.

Buzz's eyes widened. Everyone else looked at Mr. Vandereff curiously.

Mr. Vandereff grasped a series of straight, thick wires, which stood upright. Scattered throughout the miniature forest of tall metal tines were small spheres of various shapes and colors.

"Everyone, watch yourselves," said Mr. Vandereff. The students scooted back slightly in their desks. Mr. Vandereff released his hold on the wires and lumbered quickly back.

At first, the long wires fell slowly at odd angles. Then, in a final rapid succession, the entire gadget unfolded, and all the wires bounced to the horizontal, coming to rest. Previously hidden in the middle section of the box, just above halfway, a bright yellow globe glowed brightly, like an oversized light bulb.

"What is it?" asked Aubrey.

"It's an orrery," replied Buzz.

"A what?" questioned Aubrey.

Mr. Vandereff cleared his throat while he walked around his lab bench to the chalkboard. "Does every planet in our solar system experience a total *solar* eclipse?"

"Yes," busted out Paul Jamsen.

"No," scolded Buzz.

Mr. Vandereff glowered at Buzz. Buzz shrank into his seat.

"Let me rephrase the question," redirected Mr. Vandereff. "How many planets in our solar system experience a total solar eclipse?"

Most everyone in the class shook their heads. "One," replied Mr. Vandereff. "And only one. In fact, it may be one of the rarest occurrences in the entire universe."

Mr. Vandereff grabbed a piece of chalk and drew three circles, a large one on the left side of the board, a smaller circle to the right side, and a tiny one next to the second circle. "It just so happens that in our time, not millions of years in the past nor millions of years in the future, but in our tiny blink of the universal moment, the sun is about four hundred times further away from the earth than our moon, and the sun is about four hundred times larger than the moon. Which means...."

"In relative terms, the sun and the moon appear to be exactly the same size from our position here on earth," concluded Buzz as he poked the tiny purple ball sitting lopsided on the wire in front of him.

"Yes," grumbled Mr. Vandereff. He drew crisscrossing lines across the chalkboard connecting the spheres, demonstrating paths of light. "Thus anywhere from two to five times every year, somewhere on our planet, it appears that the moon blocks out the sun...that the heavenly bodies lighting our world collide, turning day into night." The teacher walked around his lab bench and into the mesh of wires, radiating outward from the open box. He flipped a switch underneath the glowing globe. With a shuddering grind, the box trembled, and the wires with their tiny balls sputtered as they glided clockwise around the middle of the room.

"This is an orrery," announced Mr. Vandereff. "A physical representation of our sun's planets and their moons as they move through space. It's not to scale, but hopefully it gives you a clearer understanding of planetary motion."

Buzz murmured to Aubrey pointing out the discreet, yet finely detailed exactness of the miniature solar system. Mercury, closest to the glowing globe, spun hurriedly around the mock sun, completing a full revolution in only a few seconds. Just out from there, Venus and Earth orbited more slowly, with the moon twirling quickly around Earth. Between the petite maroon Mars and the basketball-sized Jupiter, which was covered with orange and cream swirls and a single, red oval dot, a craggy field of asteroids, represented by gravel glued to clear cellophane, undulated in a wide circle, dividing the inner solid planets from the outer gas giants. Spaced much further out and moving even more slowly, Saturn spun erratically with its yellow rings and tiny moons. Blue-hued Uranus and Neptune sat nearly still, near the edge of the filamentous disc. Finally, the minuscule Pluto gradually swung in a catawampus ellipse that grazed the floor at one point and then angled high above the other planets on the opposite side.

"But look," whispered Buzz. He stuck his hand out as Neptune approached. "Even the wires adjust while the planets move. The orbits are mathematically correct." The wire holding Neptune shortened and missed Buzz's hand. Aubrey eyed Buzz with a bewildered stare.

"Now back to Ms. Blyers's question," continued Mr. Vandereff. "What's the difference between an annular and a total eclipse?

"Anything with mass has gravity. The greater the mass of the object, the greater its pull on other objects." Mr. Vandereff drew a wide, rounded ellipse on the board. "Planets and moons travel in ellipses, not circles in their orbits. Just as the sun pulls on each of its planets, so the planets pull back a little bit with their own gravity as well, causing the path of any satellite to be more oval than circular."

Mr. Vandereff dusted off his hands on his khaki pants. "Fruit time." He raised his hands. "Everyone with an apple scoot back. Everyone with a pear scoot forward."

Aubrey and Magnos shuffled their feet against the floor, and their desks slid backward. Jordana stood up and pulled her desk forward a few feet and then resumed her seat. Buzz lunged his body outward, and the desk warbled in agony as it edged slightly forward.

Mr. Vandereff scribbled a hefty round dot in the center of the ellipse. "Since orbits are elliptical and not circular, there are times when the planets are closer to the sun and the moons closer to their planets in their orbits."

McCrayden reared back in her seat as Neptune swung in front of her and grazed the tip of her nose. She batted at the planet with her pear and shot her hand in the air. "Mr. Vandereff, I think we're a little too close."

Mr. Vandereff guffawed. "Thank you, Ms. Miller, for proving my point." He tapped either side of the ellipse with his chalk on the board. "What is the astronomical term for when the heavenly bodies are closer to their respective partners?"

"I get it! I get it!" hollered Buzz as he swung his pear over his head and kicked his heels into the bottom of his desk.

Aubrey nudged him and muttered, "Dude, calm down."

Mr. Vandereff glowered at Buzz. Buzz covered his mouth and knocked Pluto with the edge of his shoe as it raked along the floor.

"Does it have something to do with our fruit?" asked Paul Jamsen as he spun his apple on top of his desk.

"Exactly," replied Mr. Vandereff with a twitch in his mustache. "Whenever two bodies are closest in their orbits to each other it's called perigee. When they're at their farthest points, it's called apogee."

"Ah! Now I get it!" shouted Paul. "I have an 'apple-G', and I'm further away. Buzz has a 'pear-O-G', and he is closer. Apogee. Perigee." Paul turned toward Buzz with an enlightened smile. But Buzz wasn't in his desk. Paul looked down. Buzz was slinking underneath the twirling wires.

Aubrey was leaning forward over the top of his desk, nearly tipping out of it, reaching for Buzz. "What are you doing?"

"Something's wrong with the orrery," replied Buzz as he brushed Aubrey's fingers off his shirt. Buzz pointed up. "Look at Venus. It's not rotating retrograde like it should."

"Who cares?" reprimanded Aubrey. "Get back up here, or you're gonna get in trouble."

"Buzz, listen to Aubrey," scolded Jordana.

Buzz waved her off. "I'll be right back."

Jordana slunk down in her chair, trying to be invisible. Magnos covered his eyes and rubbed his face.

Mr. Vandereff continued drawing on the blackboard. "So when the moon is near apogee to the earth and the earth is in perigee to the sun, the relative sizes change. Thus a solar eclipse still has a ring of sun visible around the outside. This is an annular eclipse."

Buzz scooted forward on all fours to the box in the middle. Turning around on his haunches, he leaned against the box and waited for Venus to pass by overhead.

Lenny lurched forward in his desk, clutched the turquoise-colored orb of Uranus in his hand and pulled it back high out of its orbit, holding it in place.

Buzz popped up and tapped Venus on its underside, forcing it to spin in the opposite direction. Every eye in the horseshoe focused on Buzz and Lenny as Mr. Vandereff droned on with his lesson.

Grating grinds and moans spasmed from within the thin wooden box. Buzz spun his head around, and a tiny crack etched down the side of the wood. A bright light filtered through from inside. Buzz squinted and leaned sideways to get a better view of the box's innards.

Mr. Vandereff turned around.

Lenny released Uranus. Like a tetherball wound too tightly, Uranus hurdled across the room, bouncing across the wires that held Jupiter and Saturn.

Pop! Uranus hit Buzz's bulbous gut and ricocheted off his flab. Uranus's wire warbled and convulsed outward. Cracked like the end of a whip, Uranus split from its hold and flew toward the back of the room, straight at Aubrey's head.

Buzz howled and wrapped his right arm around his stomach. With his left hand, he reached back and touched the crack in the box. A spark of electricity flashed between Buzz's index finger and the gears inside. Buzz jerked, surprised by the jolt that tingled down his arm, instead of up it. Aubrey ducked Uranus. Suddenly, Magnos's arm snapped in front of Aubrey's face. Fingers spread, Magnos's beefy palm stopped the turquoise ball. Magnos clamped down on the ball and flung it toward Lenny. Lenny squirmed to move out of the way, but he was too slow. Uranus pelted him in the forehead, then flew across the room and bounced across the lab bench. A red welt quickly rose on Lenny's brow.

Mr. Vandereff slammed his hands on the bench. "Enough!" Each student still seated in a desk sat up straight with wide eyes. Buzz crawled on his wounded stomach toward his desk.

A white light grew from inside the thin wooden box. Within it, gears revved to an ear-searing pitch. The wires holding the planets and moons in place flailed up and down, smacking against the floor and each other. The sun flickered and rose high up out of the center on a click-locking set of growing racks and pinions.

McCrayden pointed at the box and wiggled her finger. "Mr. Vandereff, look at what Buzz did to your thingamabobber."

Buzz scrambled into his desk. "No, I didn't!"

In an instant, the entire asteroid field dropped to the floor. Spontaneously, the entire box shifted its weight against the asteroids and pushed itself upward as if it were alive. Spinning ninety degrees to the left, the orrery leaned forward and dropped to the ground several feet closer to the ring of students.

Everyone watched, stunned. The sun, now towering on its clockwork pedestal only inches from the ceiling, leaned toward Lenny, meeting him globe to face. Lenny slid his desk back. The earth and its wire slid under the top of Lenny's desk and pulled him back into the middle of the room.

"What's happening?" asked Lenny. He batted at the sun. It pitched backward, avoiding Lenny's swing, and then slid forward as if challenging Lenny to swing again.

McCrayden flapped her arm at the machinated armature supporting the sun. From her left, Jupiter spun recklessly toward her, spiking her hand with a twirling flurry of its moon.

"Ouch!" she cried. "It's out of control!"

Mr. Vandereff tottered hurriedly toward the middle of the classroom, dodging a sideswiping Mars and Venus, which jabbed at his thigh. He flipped the switch on top of the wooden box. The light within the box dimmed, and the orrery's wires dropped limply to the floor. The sun whined and crackled at Lenny, before its light dulled out.

Mr. Vandereff sighed as he dusted off his chalk-caked hands on his pants. "Mr. Van Zenny. Mr. Strumgarten. Mr. Reiselstein." He nodded at each of them in succession. "Detention this afternoon will not be nearly as tolerant of your foolishness as I am."

Columns of ragged, gray rock rose to sharpening pillars atop a mountain overlooking Lake Julian. Flaky, pale-green lichen pockmarked the aging stones' faces, invading crevices that sprouted with grasses in scanty bloom. At the base of the chimney-like stacks of rocks, several gaps in the mountain exposed the darkness of the winding bedrock-bound tunnels beneath.

Between escarpments and fissures, the series of caves sketched a profile of a man sleeping with his mouth open, the largest cave gaping vertically as it dropped into the earth's interior.

The surrounding forest canopy of sparsely leaved twigs bore burgeoning flowers and stems as if the trees were stretching their winter-starched branches out of last season's melting wake. The woodland floor, scattered with fledgling vines and blossoms sifting upward through last fall's dying spray, coated the landscape like smeared pigments on a painter's palette.

A few yards from the opening of the caves, at the edge of a trail, a pewter historical marker read:

Crannynook Caves

Early mining operations, which opened in the early 1700s, unearthed a lucrative load of precious minerals and metals, drawing many prospectors and pioneers to the region. The influx of industry and population provided a fertile start to Lake Julian. An unfortunate series of unusual accidents forced the camp to close in the last part of the eighteenth century. Several decades later, the balmy caves housed Consumption Dome, Appalachia's first communal convalescent facility for tuberculosis and other chronic infectious diseases. Renowned for its unrivaled cure rates, Consumption Dome cared for more than 10,000 patients over a century, many of whom reported odd noises and tiny ghostlike figures in the countless recesses of the cavern. Now notorious for its mysterious lights, the Crannynook Caves are frequently visited by spelunkers and amateur diggers, looking for a supernatural edge to their subterranean sport.

A tiny ray of sunlight broke through the sky and raced along the forest floor, glinting across the historical marker's face. The pewter placard sparkled. Quickly, the weathery gloom returned, the clouds above battling to blot out the sun.

The cave mouth groaned. Screeches echoed from deep inside. A bellowing roar rumbled through the mountain. Trees shook, and their leaves trembled. Birds burst into flight, and squirrels buried themselves in their nests.

From the cave shot hordes of wispy green barnlings. Their spindly limps crumpled as they flew out of the mountain, and their triplet sets of yellow eyes bulged from their long thin heads.

With heavy breath, a hulky humanoid form climbed out of the mouth of the largest cave, ripping the fleeing barnlings from the air and pressing them into its torso. Squalling in a final plea, the barnlings were dissolved into the form's blackness, pulled into oblivion.

As curls of fading vapor twisted off its frame, the humanoid figure's midnight coloring slowly tinged green as it absorbed more of the barnlings. Its amorphous form slowly sharpened. A vast grin spread across its pointed jaw.

Relishing a surge of renewed strength, the humanoid toppled out of the cave's mouth onto the forest floor and rested on its back. Heaving with anguished relief, its chest and limbs shuddered as its skin tightened.

A gale blasted across the forest floor. Dead leaves rippled into tiny whirlwinds, and tree limbs bowed under the wind's weight.

Two creatures with reptilian skin raced on all fours up the mountain's face, their triangular heads bobbing as they sniffed the air. In a few bounds, they leapt from the rise at the base of the cliff to the rocky shelf at the cave's opening.

The dark humanoid regained its feet. Immediately, the form fell backward against the ground, landing with a harsh thud. Each of the reptilian creatures held an arm of the figure in its grasp, pinning it to the forest floor. Their flap-like ears flitted against their bald heads as their narrow tails swished feverishly behind them.

The form opened its eyes, and golden orbs glowed from their sockets set above a pointy, long noise. The greenish black humanoid looked up and met the large, round green eyes of its captors.

"Keepers," he said with a chuckle. "Have you missed me?"

The keepers growled, exposing a rack of fangs. "You have not been missed," came a voice up the mountain slope.

The figure looked down at its feet.

Floating through the underbrush, a tall man with a bald head, sinewy thin arms and legs, and a darkened left eye and a gray, foggy right one, hovered toward them. The luster of his gray skin partially absorbed the light around him. Dried bits of bark and pebbles orbited the fringe of his frayed tunic. "And more importantly, you should not have escaped.".

The greenish black form grinned. "Zaks." It paused for a moment, forming its words. "It's been ages. Is this how you greet an ancient compatriot?"

The man's black eye squeezed slit-thin. "I've *never* been a compatriot of the shadow." Zaks glanced at the keepers. "Tartan. Shway Shway. Stand down."

The two keepers bowed before Zaks. They released the form and took several steps backward on their hooved feet.

The greenish black form rose and arched its back. "At least you remember reason."

Zaks raised his right hand and spread his fingers wide. A wave of invisible weight thrust the figure back against the forest floor. It groaned as it shook its head. "Why do Graviteers always have to use their muscle?"

Zaks floated toward the form. "You freed Mayree Krouse."

The form nodded and replied wheezily, "And I would have absorbed her if I hadn't been so weak from my imprisonment."

"Have you been freeing other wayward spirits?"

The greenish form pursed his thin lips. "I don't like your question."

Zaks held out both of his arms and scooped the air in front of him. The form lifted off the ground and buoyed in midair. "Your lawlessness is not permissible here. Rules must be maintained. The balance cannot be compromised. And it is my job to ensure it."

"I know what your job is." The form's arms and legs swam in the air. "Was it also your job to free me?"

Zaks paused, angling his head to the side. "You are mistaken. I have never been untoward in my role as Magi."

The form cackled. "You are responsible for all of these events, Zaks. *You* moved Enoch's tomb to the surface. *You* allowed me to escape.""

Zaks pressed his hands together. "Who are you?"

The form gritted its teeth and grunted against pressure collapsing its trunk. Arching its back and legs backward, the form wailed under the pain. It flashed its golden eyes at Zaks, and then suddenly the darkness of its sharpening figure flushed an olive green. As if gripping the field Zaks held upon it, the form shoved it away from him. Leaves and debris blasted off the forest floor. The keepers and Zaks were blasted to the ground.

The figure jumped on top of Zaks and leaned toward Zaks's black eye. Suddenly, Zaks recognized the pointy, long nose and chin.

The shade squeezed Zaks's cheeks. "I am the Watcher who imprisoned you." Bat-like wings unfurled behind the Watcher and he lifted skyward.

Quickly, the Keepers scrambled to right themselves and ran over to Zaks. Tartan yanked Zaks by the arms. Zaks sat forward.

"Who was that, my lord?" Tartan glanced from Zaks to the figure fading through the clouds.

"Azrynon," murmured Zaks. "I have freed Azrynon."

CAFETERIA COUPS

With her gym bag hanging from her shoulder and her arms loosely folded, Rodriqa stood outside of Mrs. Makelroy's classroom, awaiting Jordana's emergence from their advanced algebra midterm. Rodriqa had finished the exam early, her mind preoccupied with last night's events. Despite Mr. Miller's reaction, her own father's chastisement on the way home, and the unusual end to the ghost that had plagued Mount Camelot for months, there was one question that pricked her mind more than any other.

Glancing at her watch, Rodriqa drummed her fingers inside her elbow. The door opened, and several other students walked into the hallway. Rodriqa flashed them a smile and looked away. None of them were Jordana. She knew she had to catch Jordana before lunch, or else she'd have no other chance to speak to her alone any time soon.

The door clicked closed in front of Rodriqa. Her eyes snapped forward. Jordana was standing in the hallway, clutching her books to her chest. Her head was down, and her straight black hair shrouded her face.

Rodriqa took a step toward her.

"I don't think I did very well," murmured Jordana.

"I rushed through it," commiserated Rodriqa. She waited for Jordana to start walking down the hallway and then matched Jordana's pace.

"You always finish early though," replied Jordana. "You're good at math." She glanced at Rodriqa through her honey-colored glasses.

"Not that good," said Rodriqa.

Jordana lowered her head again as they turned a corner. "We've not been studying like we used to."

Rodriqa sighed. "Ngw."

Jordana looked over at Rodriqa. "What did your dad say last night?"

Rodriqa peered at the floor. "Not much. We have a family meeting tomorrow night, and I'm sure I'm the main subject."

Jordana pursed her lips sympathetically.

"And your uncle? What did he say?" asked Rodriqa.

Jordana shook her head. "I don't think he has heard about last night yet. My dad was still up when I got home. I told him about the preying mantis and our run-in with Mr. Miller. Of course, after everything that happened last fall, he's on our side."

"Have you talked to Buzz or Aubrey?"

"Not really. I saw them in first period, but Mr. Vandereff had this crazy contraption trying to explain the solar eclipse this week."

"I bet Buzz was all over that."

Jordana snickered. "A little too much. I think Buzz did something to it and made it go haywire. He got detention for it."

Rodriqa feigned a swoon. "Buzz's first detention. I'm so proud."

Jordana giggled. "You should have seen the look on his face."

Rodriqa laughed. "So no insight from them on what really happened last night?"

Jordana bit her lip. "Weird, wasn't it? One second, Aubrey's about to be swallowed whole, and then the next…there's nothing there. And not like the ghost ran away, but like she simply didn't exist any more."

"Pretty weird," murmured Rodriqa. She lowered her voice as they turned down the hallway toward the cafeteria. More students walked close by.

Rodriqa glared at Jordana. "I expected you would know what happened."

Jordana straightened up. "I saw what you saw. Why would I know anything more?"

"You knew an awful lot about the Bloodrunner anathem at the Gungandeep's."

Jordana stopped and turned sharply toward Rodriqa. Rodriqa swiveled on her heels to face her. Several pairs of students sidestepped them.

"It was my research assignment for NGW. We all had assignments," countered Jordana, "which is why I haven't had time to study Algebra."

"An awful lot of information you found out in such a short period of time, don't you think?"

Jordana rolled her eyes. "You can find out anything on the Internet."

Rodriqa stiffened her lip. "There are some books and some knowledge that will never make it to the Internet. And you know it."

Jordana dropped her textbooks to her waist. "What are you trying to say, Rodriqa?"

Rodriqa's neck swiveled. Her beaded braids swished around her neck. "You're not being free-lipped with me."

Jordana raised an eyebrow. "Free-lipped?"

"Honest," replied Rodriqa.

"Why would you think that?"

Shouting echoed down the hallway from the central foyer. Jordana and Rodriqa turned toward the ruckus. A flurry of students raced from the central foyer into the cafeteria.

Rodriqa and Jordana walked swiftly toward the cafeteria doors and filed in behind the students hurrying inside.

Threaded between chairs and round Formica tables, a crowd of students huddled in a circle at the center of the cafeteria. Shouting bellowed from the middle of the circle, and more students rushed toward it.

Rodriqa and Jordana slipped through the crowd. The shouting loudened. Rodriqa pointed toward the shaggy blond hair of Magnos's head, above every other head in the crowd.

"What's going on?" Rodriqa asked Magnos as she squeezed in front of him and rose up on her tiptoes.

"The Mafisito is teaching Jon Harney a lesson," replied Magnos.

Half a dozen of the Mafisito, each identifiable by their slicked-back hair, oversized tank tops, baggy khakis, and designer sunglasses, held the crowd back with outstretched arms, forming a tiny protected ring around their leader, Teton Bailston. Teton held the fashionably dressed Jon Harney off the ground by the back of his belt. Jon swung in Teton's grip with his head down and feet flailing in the air.

Teton scowled, and both of his biceps bulged as he struggled to keep Jon suspended. "This will teach you, lily britches! You don't crow about another man's woman!"

"Teton! Let him down!" shouted McCrayden, who was being held back by one of Teton's gang brothers.

"Jon! Throw a left hook," yelled Vidalia Arsvine.

A spectating student held up his cell phone at Jon and Teton and hit the video. One of the Mafistio ripped the phone out of his hands and threw it across the cafeteria.

"He can't be serious," chuckled Rodriqa. "Teton thinks Jon is trying to steal McCrayden from him?"

Magnos scrunched up his face. "Not exactly."

Jordana leaned into Magnos and didn't bother to look over the huddled mass. Rodriqa's words were lingering in her mind.

"We should help," said Rodriqa. She pushed her way forward.

Magnos's broad, meaty hand wrapped around her arm and pulled her back. He leaned down and whispered, "This isn't our fight."

Rodriqa curled her nose and nodded.

"Enough!" commanded a voice from the entrance of the cafeteria. Principal Lequoia stood in the threshold of the set of double swing doors leading into the cafeteria. The middle-aged, tan-skinned man's barrel chest, high forehead, and downward wrinkle in the corner of his mouth pronounced a confident tyranny.

Each student turned toward his voice. The commotion quieted as the principal marched toward the chaos.

"Time to split," mumbled Magnos. Magnos, Rodriqa, and Jordana walked away.

The din of the bully ring softened into a scattering of harsh whispers. Students spread across the cafeteria. The Mafisito gang members dropped their hands and sifted leisurely through the crowd.

Startled by Principal Lequoia's sudden appearance, Teton lost his grip on Jon's belt. Jon fell face down onto the floor. A tiny red stream of blood gushed from Jon's nose. He clawed against the tile and scrambled himself upright.

Lequoia was nose to nose with Teton in only a few seconds. Keeping his gaze set on Teton's sunglasses, he leaned over and helped Jon up. Jon cupped his hand around the middle of his face.

"My shirt," he squalled in a muffled tone as he dabbed at the splatters of red soaking into his linen polo.

"This is a high school! Not a prison yard!" barked Lequoia at Teton. "Fighting brings serious consequences."

"We weren't fighting," insisted Teton. "We were having a discussion."

"I didn't do anything!" screeched Jon, his fingers clamped down tight on his nose.

"I didn't do anything either," mocked Teton.

"Did he hit you?" questioned Lequoia to Jon, the principal's eyes locked on Teton.

Jon wagged his head and then looked down. "He didn't have to."

Teton rolled his eyes behind his sunglasses and crossed his arms. "He dissed my girl. He's got more coming to him."

"Suspension would only be a gift." Principal Lequoia curled his lip. "Two weeks detention, Mr. Bailston. To start today."

Principal Lequoia scanned the cafeteria. Rubbernecking eavesdroppers sharply turned away. Lequoia grabbed Jon Harney's elbow and led him out of the cafeteria.

Aubrey scuttled up to his lunch table where Magnos, Jordana, Buzz, and Rodriqa sat on one side elbow to elbow, leaning forward and whispering to each other.

Aubrey laid his book bag on the table and sat down opposite his friends. "What's going on?"

"Jon Harney narced," replied Magnos.

Aubrey pulled himself up tighter to the table. "You mean…"

"Jon Harney told several people who weren't rowdies about what really happened last night," clarified Rodriqa. "McCrayden and her crew were trying to keep everything secret, act like we had vandalized her house. Jon Harney let the tiger out of the cage."

"And Vidalia Arsvine found out," continued Magnos. "Vidalia acts all sweet on the outside, but inside, she's full of venom."

"Just like her dad," scoffed Rodriqa.

"Who's her dad?" asked Jordana.

"Judge Arsvine," replied Rodriqa. "Crooked as a dog's hind leg. So I've heard."

"What did Vidalia do?" asked Aubrey.

"Vidalia told Teton," replied Magnos. "And Teton took care of the rest."

"Ah," said Aubrey, "hence the bloody nose."

"Exactly," agreed Rodriqa.

"And all Teton got out of it was detention," grumbled Magnos.

"Sounds like he'll be in good company," jeered Rodriqa as she poked Buzz's chubby gut with her finger.

Buzz sat in between Magnos and Rodriqa with his hands in his lap, his shoulders slumping. "I've never had detention before."

"I think I spent more time in detention than actual class last year." Magnos laughed and then quieted as he thought for a moment. "Come to think of it, a lot of those times were for things I did to you two." He pointed to Aubrey and Buzz.

"Probably so." Aubrey rolled his eyes. "What all did Jon Harney say to folks before he got smatterwhacked?"

"I'm pretty sure he spilled the whole crate of onions," replied Magnos.

"That's awesome!" Aubrey cheered. "That'll make it harder for them to hide what really happened last night."

"Doubtful," countered Magnos. "You know the rowdies. They keep together."

"And popularity is power," added Jordana.

"Only to the powerless," mumbled Buzz.

"That's my Buzz." Rodriqa wrapped her arm around him. "Speaking about what happened last night, what happened last night?"

All four of her friends looked at her with furrowed brows.

"What do you mean?" Aubrey asked.

"I mean, what happened?" replied Rodriqa.

Buzz ran his sleeve across his nose. "We went to Jafar's house. We staked out Mount Camelot. McCrayden's house was haunted. We busted in—"

"I'm not looking for a play-by-play," chided Rodriqa. "I was there! One minute we're gettin' our salami handed to us, and the next minute, Mayree Krouse is like a quail at a gun show. What happened?"

"Rodriqa's right," replied Magnos. "Aubrey, I thought Mayree Krouse was gonna eat you."

"Yeah," agreed Buzz. "She had her teeth dug into you."

"And what's up with the raven?" said Jordana.

Aubrey sighed, looked down at the table, and collected his thoughts. "Remember in Hovis Trottle's house, under the cemetery, in the pit of magma where Hovis, Ms. Thistlewood, and your dad were?"

Jordana's gaze drifted downward. "How could I forget."

"There was another man...or ghost or something. The one who freed Hovis and then disappeared."

Jordana nodded.

Aubrey gulped. "He's the raven that's been following me. And last night he destroyed Mayree Krouse."

"Why didn't we see any of it?" asked Rodriqa. "I didn't see anyone help you. I just saw a large phantom bug about to eat an Aubrey dumpling."

"Because it happened faster than the blink of an eye." Aubrey scratched his head. "But at the same time, it felt like it lasted much longer."

"Aub, man, you're talkin' gibberish." Magnos rubbed his forehead.

"I can't explain it exactly. But he was there, and he warned me about us chasing after ghosts. He said something bigger was coming, and we needed to get ready."

"What something?" asked Rodriqa.

Aubrey shrugged. "He also warned me about this." Aubrey untucked his shirt, loosened his belt and slipped a burlap bag out from his pants. Glancing around for onlookers, he reached into the bag and placed the clear crystal pyramid in the middle of the lunch table.

"What's that?" asked Rodriqa.

"It's Solluna."

"I thought Solluna was that golden box-book thing that had metal pages and wrote its own nursery rhymes."

"Poems," corrected Aubrey.

"Whatever," grumbled Rodriqa.

"When exposed to sunlight or moonlight, verse scrawled across its pages. At least, that's what it used to be. Now, as of yesterday, this is Solluna."

"Looks like a nice ornament you could hang from your rearview mirror," commented Jordana.

"Are you sure that's Solluna?" asked Buzz.

"Yep," said Aubrey, and then he rethought his certitude. "Well, I wasn't before last night, but now I am."

"I sure as wampum hope that's not what I think it is." A gruff voice tumbled down over them.

Startled, all five of them looked up. Dressed in his forest-green, button-down uniform, Griggs stood next to the table his white wooly-worm eyebrows scrunched together.

Aubrey scooped up Solluna and wrapped it in the burlap bag.

His jaw grinding, Griggs leaned down and poked his crooked index finger into Aubrey's chest. "I told you to keep it hidden!"

Aubrey slid the bag back into his pants. "It is hidden!"

"This is not some measly trinket you're carrying around! It's dangerous!"

"I know that," argued Aubrey.

"Would you strap a nuclear warhead to your chest?" asked Griggs.

"Of course not," replied Aubrey.

Griggs straightened up and snarled, "Then you have no idea just how dangerous Solluna is if you're keeping it tied around your waist." He turned and walked out of the cafeteria.

"Dude, that janitor is off the scale on the creep-o-meter," mumbled Buzz. "Maybe I need to use ESAU on him."

"Ya know, I don't understand a lot of things around Lake Julian," thought Rodriqa out loud, "least of which why our janitor seems to know more about what's going on than we do." Rodriqa tapped her finger on the table. "Regardless, at this point, I have to agree with Griggs. You shouldn't be carrying that thing around. I don't get what it does or even why you have it, but it's bad juju, Aub. You need to put it someplace where no one can get it."

Aubrey sighed. "I had it buried under my house, but I just don't think it's safe there anymore."

"Who would look for it under your house?" asked Buzz. "That crawl-space is so dark, even the shadows are scared to go down there."

Aubrey bit his lip. "It's the things scaring the shadows that worry me."

DEGRAVED SLAVE

Spindly black fingers pinched a loose opener tab on a rusting, half-squashed soda can. Spinning it on its base, one finger pushed the edge of the tab, while two other fingers searched the mangled opening. Three more fingers caressed the rim of the can's bottom, two fingers peeled the painted label off, and the remaining fingers turned the can.

Bulging yellow eyes inspected the can. Perched atop an arching nose, the eyes never blinked, but simply darted from side to side. The fingers, set on the end of the creature's stubby handless arms, twirled the can faster.

The shadowy misshapen creature grunted angrily. It flung the can into the distance. The can splashed into the middle of a moldy black tire, its inner hull half-full of stagnant rainwater.

Mountains of rancid food, shriveled plant cuttings, shredded plastic, and tarnished metal rose and fell in great swathes of foaming, putrid waste. Black vultures, crows, and gulls swarmed above, hunting for the tastiest dross and battling one another for prime roosting sites. House-sized dump trucks dropped more trash on the edge of the landfill. The shadowy creature hobbled to a smaller mound full of fast-food wrappers and egg crates. Jawless and with a pointed head, its globular torso bobbled on stick-thin legs. Light-starved skin robbed every glint of sun that passed near its body. A single, bat-like wing flapped clumsily atop its back, propelling it awkwardly forward in a zigzag direction.

The shade pulled a battery from a garbage bag. A black, mealy tongue twisted out from under its nose and slobbered the battery's metal nub. It felt the tingle of electricity and moaned in unfulfilled satisfaction.

A seagull dove past the creature and snapped at the shade's ragged wing. The shade slashed its fingers at the bird, which squeaked as it flew away. Wobbling, the shade flapped its wing, trying to fly, but the most it could do was bounce.

One of its scrawny legs slipped on a piece of festering eggplant. The creature skidded and then tumbled down the slope of trash.

In an instant, a gaping hole opened in the middle of the trash heap. A massive, bouldered face lunged forward, and its mouth collapsed down on the shade. The creature had been swallowed, and the bouldered form buried itself back within the mound.

"There you are!" Gaspian appeared out of a dark cleft of trash a hundred yards from where the shade had fallen. His spiky black hair was unmoving and his leather jacket and boots pristinely clean amid the garbage. "Melkyor! Thalazzaran! I've found him!" The bald Thalazzaran hovered down from above with the white-haired Melkyor, floating next to him. "Where?" asked Thalazzaran, searching the debris.

"There!" said Melkyor as he pointed toward the mound. His arm shuddered, and a jagged bolt of electricity flashed from his fingers toward the mound. The energy exploded as it slammed into the heap of trash.

"Yaw!" an earthshaking scream bellowed from the rocky mouth that opened in the trash. Two large craggy arms breeched the trash line and reached into the air.

"Rise, slave!" commanded Thalazzaran. His muscular forearms twitched as he lifted the creature up with an unseen force.

Out of the mound of refuse, a titanic humanoid creature, bouldered in form, gravitated upward. Its brawny arms and legs spun wildly.

Two stories in height, its entire physique resembled darkened stones pressed together in a neckless, but jointed mass of living mountain. Its rough-hewn surface was blanketed with bits of moldy food, oily cardboard, and half-burnt wood chips. Grinding against one another, burly limbs clunked with each movement. Its flat eyes blinked repeatedly.

"No!" shouted the creature as it flailed in the air.

"Let it go," chuckled Gaspian.

"As you wish." Thalazzaran relaxed his arms. The creature dropped face first into the filth below.

"What a disgusting creature," mused Melkyor.

With a single massive push-up, the creature launched itself upward, spun around, and sprinted away from them.

Gaspian lifted his hand and stretched out his fingers. Squinting his eyes, he concentrated on the creature. The garbage littering the creature's body melted into a liquid gray mass and congealed together in a band around its chest.

Suddenly, the creature stopped running. It turned around and raised its hands. "Please, no, Quarkherder!"

"It knows my name," bragged Gaspian. Melkyor rolled his electric blue eyes.

Gaspian contracted his fingers. The steel band wrapping around the rocky creature's torso shrank.

The creature dropped to its knees and groaned, "It hurts, Quarkherder! It hurts!"

"Enough," commanded Thalazzaran.

Gaspian scoffed at Thalazzaran and dropped his hands.

Relief washed across the creature's face as the band loosened.

Gaspian flipped his fingers in circles. The trash below the creature transformed into cords of heavy chain links that fused together and then melded into the band around its chest.

"What's your name, slave?" Gaspian asked.

"Astham," said the creature.

"Where is the seer?" questioned Thalazzaran.

Astham shook his head.

"Many have heard," said Melkyor, raising his bony hand. Sparks jolted between his fingers. "I know you've heard."

"South," gasped Astham.

"We are south," insisted Thalazzaran.

"Not south," choked Astham. "Further south."

"What is the place?" asked Gaspian as he looked around.

"West Virginia," replied Astham.

"This trash heap is West Virginia?" asked Gaspian.

"Here is West Virginia." Astham pointed to the ground. "This area is in the state of West Virginia."

"Then where is the seer?" demanded Thalazzaran. "I won't ask a third time."

Astham flinched. "North Carolina, western North Carolina."

"Very good." Thalazzaran nodded.

Gaspian waved his hands. The chains dissolved into slivers of metal and sprinkled against the garbage below.

"Tell no one we were here," commanded Thalazzaran.

Astham nodded as he pulled at the metal plate around his chest.

"And tell no one who we were looking for," added Gaspian. "For soon, the seer will be no more."

DUELING DETENTIONS

With feet dragging, Buzz moped down the hallway from his last class toward the blind end of a windowless corridor. Students rushed past him, leaving school. Buzz kept his head down, hoping no one would notice which way he was walking.

Covered in a grimy lace of dust and cobwebs, the fluorescent lights above flickered. Buzz's backpack hung lopsided on his back, and he twiddled his cell phone in his hands, trying to find some way to avoid thinking about his impending punishment.

He stopped at the end of the corridor, where a darkened corner held a single inset door with the word *detention* marked on a yellowing scrap of paper, taped to a small wooden plank. Buzz stared at it. His throat cramped as he swallowed back his tears, and he felt his palms moistening his phone with sweat.

A thought popped in Buzz's head. He flipped open his cell phone and typed a text.

The door snapped open. Mr. Vandereff stood in the threshold. "Welcome, Mr. Reiselstein. Take a seat." His bushy mustache twitched as he spoke.

Buzz sighed and waddled forward. His backpack slipped off his shoulders.

Out of the corner of his eye, Buzz spotted Magnos sitting at the forward-most table. Lurching over to Magnos, Buzz flopped his bag on the table and dropped in the seat. He crossed his arms and rested his head in the cradle of his elbows.

Magnos shifted his weight in his cracked plastic seat and flipped through his pre-algebra textbook, staring at the scrawl on each page. "Are you okay?" he whispered to Buzz.

Buzz rolled his head to the side, just enough for one eye to peek out over his sleeve. The eye glared at Magnos. Then Buzz buried his face again against the table.

Magnos chuckled under his breath and flipped another page.

Mr. Vandereff counted heads and scowled at his roster. "Seems like we're missing a couple students." He held up his index finger. "No one speaks. No one moves."

"Breathing is moving. Can I breathe?" mumbled a voice from the back.

A faint trickle of snickers bounced around the room.

"Another comment like that and I'll seriously consider discontinuing that option," grumbled Mr. Vandereff. "I'll be back more quickly than you think." He lumbered toward the entrance of the room and slammed the door as he left.

"Buzz! Buzz!" whispered someone harshly from the rear of the room.

Buzz didn't move.

"Buzz! Buzz! We can't find them!"

Magnos looked over his shoulder and then turned back around.

"Buzz! Where are they? Come on, man! Tell us!"

Magnos nudged Buzz. "Are you gonna answer him?"

Buzz sat straight up, his arms dropping to his sides. He turned toward Magnos and glowered at him. "Didn't you hear Mr. Vandereff?" hissed Buzz. "He said no talking!"

Magnos shrugged. "He can't hear us now."

"He could walk through the door any minute! I have no intention of ever tarnishing my record, ever again!"

Buzz pounded his elbows on the table and buried his head in his hands.

"Buzz! Buzz!" insisted the voice. "You've gotta tell us where the bigfoot are!"

Magnos looked around and frowned at the back row.

Buzz wrenched around in his seat. "I told you last week. They're gone!"

Wearing camouflage, Stew Parsons leaned over the last table in the room, pulling at its front edge. Next to Stew, Snakes McWhorter, with his brunette diamond swathes of hair layering his temples, polished his compass with a bright orange handkerchief.

"Bigfoot just don't disappear, dude!" charged Stew. "You're hiding them, and we're gonna find out where!"

Buzz laughed. "How could I hide a bigfoot? I've told you, they're gone, and besides, you couldn't catch one anyway."

Stew smacked Snakes in the chest, and Snakes grinned at Buzz.

"We can hunt anything," grumbled Stew.

"Hunt, maybe. Capture…no way."

The door slammed shut. Buzz froze. He slowly turned around, searching the front of the room out of the corner of his eye.

"Isn't this skinny? I didn't know I was going to have the privilege of sharing detention with half the school's dork squad." Teton Bailston strutted into the room, his grin as wide as his sunglasses.

Buzz sighed, grateful it wasn't Mr. Vandereff. Magnos kept his head forward as Teton slid by him.

Teton stopped and glared at Stew and Snakes at the rear table. "Aim your peepers that way, Poncho," ordered Teton. Snakes crinkled his forehead and continued polishing his compass. Stew crossed his arms and turned his head to the side.

Teton dropped into a seat at the second table, propped his feet up, and rested his hands at the back of his head.

"What did you two misfits get detention for?" asked Teton to the forward table. Buzz rolled his eyes and pulled out his physical sciences textbook. Magnos didn't move.

"I hear you all have more than detention to worry about," jeered Teton. "McCrayden's dad has plans for you two and your little group."

Buzz snapped his textbook against the table. "If we hadn't been at the Millers' house last night, McCrayden wouldn't be alive."

Magnos glared at Buzz out of the corner of his eye and shook his head.

"That's not how Mr. Miller tells it," scoffed Teton. "Man, is that crony powerful. You wouldn't believe what he can make happen in this town." Teton paused for a moment. "No, wait. I bet you do know, don't ya, Mag, and I bet you miss it."

Magnos clenched his jaw, and his cheeks flushed cherry red. A hint of a smile broke Teton's lips.

"In fact, I bet you miss a lot of things," continued Teton, "like your old girlfriend." Teton crossed his right ankle on top of his left foot. "McCrayden is clearly the hottest girl in school, and I love that little pouty-look she gives me every time I wink at her. Bet you miss having her as your girlfriend, don't ya, Strumgarten?"

Magnos's lip twitched. "I have a girlfriend."

"Yeah, that little four-eyed freak, Jordana," chortled Teton. "I bet you two sit up late at night concocting these bizarro ghost stories you have half the town sucked into."

"We don't concoct anything," said Buzz. "These ghosts are real, and if it wasn't for us, McCrayden and her friends would've—"

"Would've been just fine," interrupted Teton. "They were playing a card game, and you all ransacked her house."

Magnos leaned back in his chair, the frail plastic creaking under his shifting weight. "You're clueless, Bailston. You'd better open your eyes, or you're gonna be sorry."

"Take your threats elsewhere, Maggie," replied Teton. "You're not a bully anymore. Your rep is done. Everyone else knows it. Time for you to realize it."

In a single swipe, Magnos raked his hand behind his chair. His palm smacked the leg of the table behind him, torqueing it skyward. The table flipped. Teton was flung backward to the floor.

The table twisted backward in the air as it arced and then fell. Magnos jumped up and caught the table, just before its edge landed near Teton's face. Magnos returned the table to its upright position. "I may not be cool anymore, but I'll always be bigger than you."

Stew and Snakes chuckled as they watched Teton squirm.

Teton mumbled as he adjusted his sunglasses on his face and clambered off the floor.

"And better," mumbled Buzz.

"Sure thing, Reisel-stimmy." Teton stood up and lifted his chair. "Weirdos."

Magnos brushed his hair off his eyes and sat down. Buzz smirked at him and then flashed him an upright thumb. Magnos grinned.

With a deep sigh, Buzz stared outside at the sun beaming above the trees in the afternoon sky. Ideas ransacked his brain…one…then two…then five…faster, more complex, like shuttles at a train station zipping at light speed from track to hub and back again.

His eyes darted back and forth. His eyelids flittered. His arms and legs stiffened, and Buzz shook in his seat. It lasted a few seconds, and then Buzz grabbed onto the table as he slunk into his seat.

Magnos leaned over and grabbed Buzz's arm. "You okay?"

Buzz's curly hair trembled, his head turning from the window to Magnos and back again. "Yeah, never been better." Buzz's crossed eyes realigned themselves, and he smiled.

CHIN MUSIC

Pedaling down Dalton Circle, Aubrey's backpack vibrated against his back. He stood up on his bike and reached inside. He pulled out his cell phone, flipped it open, and read a text from Buzz.

> Can u get a ride to Rock-U-Quarium tonight? Magnos will pick up Buzz Bug & meet us there. He can take us home after.

Aubrey thumb-typed into his phone while he balanced the crossbar of his bike between his knees.

> Sure. I'll ask my dad.

———❈———

Drawing near to his house, Aubrey closed his phone and focused on the road ahead. After cornering into the gravel driveway, Aubrey hopped off his bike, careful to avoid Whimperfidget's holes.

At the back of the house, Aubrey dropped his bike and sidled up against the edge of the porch. Finally, he had a moment, without friends, without foes, without family, to do something he'd been waiting to do for nearly twenty-four hours.

Aubrey angled himself next to a small patch of sunlight that broke through the trees in the yard. Pulling the crumpled bottom of his shirt from jeans, he dug in between the denim and his underwear. Removing the crystal pyramid, Aubrey held it out in front of his face. Clear and flawless, each edge and plate were smooth and cool to the touch. If held more than a few feet from his eyes, it might even be invisible, but it felt harder than stone and weighed nearly as much for being only as wide as his palm.

Watchfully, Aubrey inched Solluna into the sunlight. Yellow beams twinkled through the crystal's faces, appearing brighter on the exiting side than where they entered. His fingers tingled as if he had slept on his hand. He angled the pyramid up and out, still holding it in way of the light. He looked down, hoping to see a rainbow, but Aubrey could only see a spot of light on his shirt, where the light passed through the pyramid. His skin warmed underneath the gleam.

A steady etch scrawled in cursive along the face of the pyramid. Aubrey watched the word form in the crystal.

Open.

"Open?" Aubrey rubbed his index finger against the word. The crystal felt flush even though he could see the word written in its face.

He turned the pyramid ninety degrees to the left. Another word was etched in the crystal.

The.

Aubrey turned the pyramid again.

Sealed.

Once more he turned it.

To.

Aubrey twirled the pyramid full circle and read the words together, "To open the sealed."

"Aubrey!" hollered a voice from the back porch.

Aubrey jumped, and the pyramid popped out of his hand and tumbled across the lawn into the tree shade. Light escaped the pyramid. The words disappeared.

Mr. Taylor walked forward and stood at the edge of the porch with a baseball bat perched on his shoulder. "When did you get home?"

Aubrey scurried forward and bent over, picking up Solluna and jamming it in his pocket. "Just now."

Mr. Taylor rubbed his hand across the widow's peak on his forehead. His lean, sideburn-drizzled cheeks tightened. "We need to talk."

"If it's about Whimperfidget, I'm working on it." Aubrey turned away from his father and adjusted Solluna through his jeans.

"No," said Mr. Taylor. "It's about last night."

"Oh." Aubrey straightened up, turned around, and faced his dad. "I can explain."

"I think I should do the talking." Mr. Taylor walked away from the edge of the porch. Aubrey sighed and plodded toward his father.

"With all the crazy stuff that's been happening lately, I think you need a new hobby." Mr. Taylor stomped down the stairs. "And I figured I could help out with that."

Aubrey looked up. Mr. Taylor walked into the backyard and threw a catcher's mitt to his son.

Flinching, Aubrey held his hands straight out. The mitt bounced off Aubrey's right shoulder and plopped to the ground. "But, Dad, I'm not good at sports."

"How do you know?" Mr. Taylor trotted over and picked up the mitt. "You've never tried to be."

Aubrey raised his hands, hoping to accentuate his thin frame. "Look at me."

"That's just puberty, Aub." Mr. Taylor smiled at him. "Once the hair starts growing, you'll be stronger than you think."

Aubrey blushed.

Mr. Taylor pulled a baseball from his pocket and tossed it in his hand. "Let's give it a try."

Wrinkling his forehead, Aubrey nodded.

Mr. Taylor handed his son the baseball bat. "Stand over there by the first tree." His father pointed toward the nearest clump of large oak trees. Aubrey scuttled over, dragging the bat behind him. Mr. Taylor jogged toward a white aluminum shed on the opposite end of the yard.

"Ready?" Mr. Taylor pounded his mitt.

"I don't have much time," whined Aubrey. "I got an invitation to the opening of the Rock-U-Quarium tonight. I need to get ready."

"Really? The Rock-U-Quarium?" Mr. Taylor tilted his head. "Who invited you?"

Aubrey shrugged. "I'm not sure. But they invited Buzz, Rodriqa, Jordana, and Magnos too. We're supposed to go together."

"Okay," said his dad, "but I'm sure we have a few minutes before you need to go."

Staring at the grass, Aubrey kicked the bat with the instep of his shoe. "Can you take me to the Rock-U-Quarium tonight? I can get a ride home after."

"Gaetan can take you," said Mr. Taylor. "He's going too."

Aubrey groaned. "Are you sure I can't ride with you instead?"

"There's no sense in taking two cars, and I know Gaetan doesn't want me to take him." Mr. Taylor twirled the baseball in his hand. "Now let's play some ball."

Aubrey sighed and plopped the bat onto his limp shoulder.

Mr. Taylor put his head down and chuckled. "First things first. Face the house."

Aubrey turned toward the porch and rolled his eyes.

"Spread your feet about shoulder width apart."

Aubrey looked down and wiggled his feet sideways.

"Bend your knees a little bit. You look like a statue."

Aubrey sneered at his dad and crouched a little.

"Grip the bat with both hands and hold it just out from your ear."

Wrapping his fingers around the bat's base, he raised it close to his face.

"Looks good." Mr. Taylor gave Aubrey a thumbs-up. "Now this is the most important thing. No matter what you do, never take your eye off the ball. Understand?"

Aubrey nodded and furrowed his brow, focusing on his father.

"Here it comes!" Mr. Taylor wound up the pitch and threw it toward Aubrey.

Aubrey gripped the bat tightly, his eyes following the ball. Aubrey kicked up his left leg and swung. *Whoosh!* Aubrey spun in a complete circle. The baseball smacked a tree and bounced to Aubrey's feet.

"Not bad," said Mr. Taylor with raised eyebrows.

"But I missed," muttered Aubrey.

"Yeah, but had you hit it, you probably would've knocked out one of the Auerbach's windows." Mr. Taylor walked several yards to his right and held out his mitt. "Throw me the ball."

Aubrey leaned down, picked up the baseball, and tossed it to his dad.

"Okay. This time, pull your shoulders back and keep the bat in motion."

Aubrey nodded and looked down. He spread his feet apart, bent his knees, and pushed out his elbows as he swirled the bat out from his neck.

Mr. Taylor pitched the ball. It flew straight toward the tree. Aubrey swung. The bat slipped out of his hands and soared across the yard. It toppled end over end against the lawn before rolling to a stop.

"Oops," said Aubrey.

Running over to the bat, Mr. Taylor picked it up. "You've got a pretty good arm." He lobbed the bat back to Aubrey. "Just need to focus it."

"Thanks." Aubrey dodged the spinning bat as it bounced next to him and threw the ball back to his dad.

"Keep the edges of your hands touching on the bat. Don't let them overlap," instructed Mr. Taylor. "And arch your back a bit."

Aubrey nodded and adjusted his waist and feet. Mr. Taylor threw the ball.

"Eyes," said his father. Aubrey torqued his head up and squinted.

Aubrey swung. *Crack!* Aubrey spun around. The baseball sailed up and over the shed.

"Pretty good." Mr. Taylor followed the ball.

Aubrey smiled. They both listened as the ball thudded along the ground on the other side of the shed. Aubrey's cheeks bunched up tightly.

"I got a call from Maximillian Miller today," Mr. Taylor said as he trotted around the shed.

Aubrey's face flattened. Last night's events flooded his mind. "It wasn't our fault. There was a ghost in their house. Mrs. Gungandeep said there was something haunting Jafar, but then it appeared in the Millers' house, and there were kids inside, and we had to help them."

Walking from behind the shed, Mr. Taylor held up his hand. "Get in your stance."

Aubrey bit his lip. He widened his feet and bent his elbows with his bat up. Mr. Taylor threw the pitch. Aubrey swung, and the bat shot the ball across the yard toward the back fence.

"Explaining it to me doesn't matter, Aubrey." Mr. Taylor watched the ball bounce a hundred yards away. "I know what happened last fall. I know you're trying to do something good. Something I don't completely understand." Mr. Taylor turned toward Aubrey. "The problem is there are people who don't believe you. And unfortunately, these people don't want to understand or give you the benefit of the doubt." Mr. Taylor pulled another ball from his pocket and motioned with his hand for Aubrey to hold up the bat. "They see you and your friends as troublemakers. They plan on putting you in your place, regardless of your intentions."

Aubrey held up the bat and shrugged his shoulders with his elbows angled outward. "I don't know what to do. It's not like I'm asking these ghosts to appear. They just keep coming. And folks keep asking for our help."

"I suspect they won't be asking much longer." Mr. Taylor threw the ball. Aubrey swung. The ball snapped against the wood of the bat and rocketed forward, slamming against the metal shed.

"Why?"

Mr. Taylor scrunched up his face as he chased after the ball. "Mr. Miller is finding ways to undermine the NeighborGhoul Watch. The money you all have earned will go to fix the Millers' house."

"How much of it?" Aubrey sulked.

"Mr. Miller told me how much damage there was. Sounds like we'll be lucky if we don't have to pay anything out of pocket." Mr. Taylor threw the ball. "And there's more."

"What are you two girls doing?" Gaetan launched himself off the front porch and in two bounds, intercepted Aubrey's ball barehanded with his large, boney fingers. "You shouldn't be playin' a man's game." Gaetan flipped his muscular arm from his shoulder to his wrist and hurled the baseball at Aubrey.

The ball pelted Aubrey's thigh, in the same spot where he had hidden Solluna. Sharp pains pierced Aubrey's skin. He dropped to the ground and gripped his leg. Rocking in the dirt, he bit his tongue to keep himself from screaming.

"Gaetan!" shouted Mr. Taylor. "Why did you do that?" He ran toward Aubrey.

"He shoulda' kept his eye on the ball," chortled Gaetan.

Mr. Taylor glowered at Gaetan as he leaned over Aubrey. "You know better! You're stronger than he is!"

"Aww, is poor little *Brianna* hurt?" Gaetan balled his fists and twisted them next to his cheeks. "Serves you right, you little snail shucker."

"What has gotten into you?" Mr. Taylor tried to examine Aubrey's leg, but Aubrey pushed him away.

Gaetan grabbed the bat and tossed it in the air. "Well, maybe if he wasn't always causing so much trouble, he wouldn't make so many people angry." Mr. Taylor reached for Aubrey's leg, but Aubrey rolled away from him.

"I'm fine," squeaked Aubrey. He perched himself up on his knees.

"You can't act like this, Gaetan," scolded Mr. Taylor.

"Oh, and he can tear up the entire neighborhood, and no one bats an eye. I threw a ball at him, and you're glamor glitchin'?" Gaetan grunted. He turned and walked toward the porch.

Mr. Taylor straightened his posture. "I don't think your behavior is conducive to you attending the Rock-U-Quarium this evening."

Gaetan stopped and looked over his shoulder. "Are you grounding me?"

"That depends on you," asserted Mr. Taylor.

Gaetan steadily wheeled around to face his father and took several steps toward him.

"No, it depends on you," scorned Gaetan. "You're the parent. For a few more months anyway."

Mr. Taylor clenched his jaw. "Tell your brother you're sorry."

Gaetan curled his lip and took several more steps toward his father until their faces were only inches apart, except for the half a foot of height Gaetan had over his father.

Gaetan searched his father's eyes. Mr. Taylor had never realized how much taller his son had grown. He lifted his jaw to match his son.

"Sorry," muttered Gaetan.

Aubrey pushed himself to his feet and hobbled toward the porch.

Gaetan spun around and hurried past his brother.

"Aubrey needs a ride tonight," hollered Mr. Taylor after Gaetan.

Gaetan jogged onto the porch and wrenched open the back door. "Can't. I've got plans." Gaetan stepped inside.

"Aubrey's headed to where you're headed," yelled Mr. Taylor as he marched forward.

Gaetan rocked a step backward. "The Rock-U-Quarium?"

"Yep," said Mr. Taylor. "And you're gonna take him." He caught up with Aubrey and supported him as he plodded up the stairs.

"No way! I'm not having him tag along." Gaetan pointed at his brother. "My invitation is for me and Fayla, and that's who I'm taking!" Gaetan bolted inside. The door slammed behind him.

Mr. Taylor jumped forward and caught the door's rebound. He raced inside. Aubrey limped after them. He pulled Solluna out of his pocket and returned it to its burlap sack inside his waistline.

"Aubrey has his own invitation." Mr. Taylor stormed inside the house.

"Great! Then he can find his own ride." Gaetan charged down the hallway into the living room.

"Don't walk away from me!" ordered Mr. Taylor.

Gaetan spun around. "Don't treat me like a child!"

"Don't act like one!"

"Why are you babying him?" Gaetan motioned toward Aubrey, who was walking inside. "He needs to man up!"

"Maybe, if his big brother was nicer to him, he'd be tougher."

"Maybe, if his father wasn't such a wuss!"

"That's not fair!" Mr. Taylor charged forward. "You know he's been through a lot!"

"Yeah! Because it's been a fairy ride for the rest of us, and he's the only one who deserves special treatment!"

"Your mother and I have done the best we can!"

"Your best isn't good enough!"

"Tanny." The soft, tremulous word drifted over the bannister, halting the conversation. "Tanny, I'm sorry."

Mr. Taylor and Gaetan looked up. Aubrey shuffled forward to the edge of the hallway's ceiling. Leaning against the bannister stood his mother, her half-curled hair matted on the left side of her head. Pitted wrinkles sagged under her dark eyes. Her worn and unwashed flannel nightgown draped her body, with its unraveling ends dangling around her ankles.

"It's all my fault." Mrs. Taylor stared at Gaetan. "Please forgive me."

Gaetan's lips parted. His jaw locked. He turned and looked down.

"Take Aubrey with you," spoke Mrs. Taylor softly. "For me?"

"Then it's settled!"

Maximillian Miller racked his gavel against the long cherrywood council table at which he sat in room 34D of Lake Julian's city hall. "City ordinance number 32-47-16 passes unanimously, thus declaring any use of an industrial or electronic suit employed to perform a function of an extricating, eliminating, exterminating, enhancing, or examining nature, without a permit, illegal." Mr. Miller rubbed his bald head and smiled. "I'd like to thank each of the city council members for clearing their schedules for this emergency meeting. Lake Julian is now a safer place."

"Certainly," spoke an elderly woman as she stood up next to Mr. Miller and slid her rose-colored glasses up her nose. "Children shouldn't play with such dangerous devices."

"Agreed, Freyma." Mr. Miller winked at her.

Freyma Spindergrath pulled her silk coat snug around her shoulders as she walked around the table and glided toward the door. "Now it's time to prepare for the festivities."

"See you tonight," said Mr. Miller, shuffling together a stack of papers and jamming them in his briefcase.

"I'm still not exactly clear why we simply can't speak with the parents of the children involved and have them confiscate the suits in question." Earlyan Gungandeep shifted in his seat opposite Mr. Miller and massaged his wrinkling forehead.

"Because these vagrants need to be taught a lesson," replied Mr. Miller. He dropped his briefcase on the floor. "We need to make an example of them. And the only way to do that is to demonstrate a solid front, both politically and legally."

Mr. Gungandeep raised his hands. "Kids will be kids. I don't think they mean any harm."

"Harm!" shouted Mr. Miller as he snapped to a standing position. "Have you seen my house?"

Mr. Gungandeep leaned on the table. "Max, we've all been hit hard lately." He sighed deeply. "Something is happening in Lake Julian, and it's nothing good."

"Which is why this ordinance is so important." Mr. Miller bent over and grabbed his briefcase. "Either you're with us or against us on this one, Earlyan."

Mr. Gungandeep licked his lips and bit the inside of his cheek.

"I, for one, applaud you," said a man next to Mr. Gungandeep in a hoarse voice. The man's aged body hung in the chair like a doll. "The Harneys will always agree with reason."

"Thank you, Cyrus," said Mr. Miller. "Sense and practicality must prevail." He walked around the table and strode toward the door.

"Anyone who thinks they're above the process needs a little needling." Cyrus Harney coughed through his sentence.

"Too right," said Mr. Miller with a chuckle. He hurried through the threshold and turned into the hallway. Looking at his watch, he hummed an upbeat tune and focused his attention on his evening plans.

"Who can fight the arm of justice?" the steely sweet voice from behind stopped Mr. Miller a few feet from the exit. He glanced over his shoulder. A woman with pale green eyes and long bright red hair approached him.

"No one," he grunted, "as long as I'm on city council."

Her thin lips smiled. "That's why I voted for you. You always have everything under control." She walked up to Mr. Miller, arching her back to show off all of her curves.

Mr. Miller faced the woman and stretched out his open hand. "And you are?"

The woman chuckled as she clasped her hands. "My name isn't important, but I know the opportunity I'm about to offer you will be." Tactfully denying his handshake, she caressed her neck slowly. The light from the windows glinted off the brown sandstone watch clasped around her wrist.

Feeling slightly dizzy, Mr. Miller squinted his eyes to refocus. "I know everyone in Lake Julian, but I don't know you."

"Then we shall have to change that." Ms. Thistlewood leaned in and whispered, "We have a common enemy."

"Who might that be?" asked Mr. Miller, his stance wobbling.

"Those children," whispered Ms. Thistlewood. "The ones who damaged your house."

Mr. Miller felt like he was falling. He couldn't look away. He couldn't even blink. "Quite right. They're a menace. They have to be stopped."

"I have a plan."

"Wonderful," he murmured in a hazy euphoria.

"In the next seventy-two hours, I will call you. You will do what I say and bring whom I ask. Understood?"

"Absolutely."

Ms. Thistlewood pulled away and twisted her neck. "And then we'll both have what we want." Quickly, she strode around Mr. Miller, down the hallway and out of the building.

Slowly Mr. Miller's senses returned. He shook his head and spun on his heels. "Wait!" Mr. Miller called after her. "I didn't give you my number!"

Ms. Thistlewood was already gone.

THE ROCK-U-QUARIUM

Aubrey slid off the slick leather seat of his brother's car onto the sidewalk and cranked the door shut. The Pontiac GTO's tires screeched as the vehicle roared down Main Street along Lake Julian Square.

Aubrey pulled out his inhaler and pressed it in his mouth. He stumbled backward slightly, dazzled by the flashing lights and murmuring crowds filling the central cobblestone road.

Both the historical and civic core of Poage County, Lake Julian Square was lined with restored nineteenth-century brick buildings that housed the bureaucratic heart of Lake Julian. Centuries-old houses, now converted into trendy boutique shops, huddled in between commercial and governmental offices. Tonight, Lake Julian Square could have rivaled Times Square. The cobblestone road was blocked off to traffic, yet on either side, the street was lined for valet parking. Kettledrum-like spotlights beamed columns of blinding white, sweeping circles in the sky and dotting the clouds. Tall streetlamps, garnished with crowns of tiny white lights, sparkled above droves of couples, walking up and down the square.

Aubrey brushed down the front of his blazer as he inspected himself from chest to toe. A frown flickered across his face. His oversized shirt and khakis were already wrinkled from the ride into town. Pulling up his pants, he stuffed the flap of his shirttails down his inseam and adjusted the position of the burlap sack holding Solluna.

Aubrey brushed his fingers through his scraggly red hair and, with a deep sigh, plodded forward.

After walking several hundred yards while searching for his friends, he noticed a throng of kids huddled together in a line, herded between two red velvet ropes. Looking up at the warehouse-sized building beside him, Aubrey could see the entrance sign to the Rock-U-Quarium.

Above a bank of tinted windows, each letter of the sign glowed yellow and shook on small metal rods, jutting in and out from the building. Speakers on either side of the sign shuddered as the latest hip-hop release thundered over the crowd.

"Aubrey!"

Aubrey turned toward the road. He heard his name through the din of the fanfare but wasn't sure where it had come from. Across the street, the lights from the State of the Mart shone like daylight, and it was hard to see faces in the crowd from the glare. A gleam glinting against metal caught his eye.

Old Widow Wizenblatt was waving her walker on the sidewalk opposite the cobblestone road. Her white, matted curls shook nearly as much as the flab wiggling at the underside of her arms as she rocked on her bare feet. Her oil-and-mud-stained floral-print dress flitted in early spring's breeze exposing the wrinkly skin of her thighs.

Aubrey could see the widow's mouth move, but he couldn't hear what she was saying. As if she were a stone in a rapid, everyone created a wide path around her on the busy sidewalk.

Slowly, Mrs. Wizenblatt turned her head in Aubrey's direction and glared at him. Aubrey's throat tightened. He slipped sideways behind the edge of the waiting line of people.

"Aubrey!"

The voice sounded next to him, and he jerked backward.

Jordana chuckled as she grabbed his hand. "Why are you always so jumpy?" A smile brightened her face. Aubrey gawked at her. Dressed in a mint-colored, shoulderless silk dress, Jordana's feminine curves were drawn in by the garment's tight fit, and its pastel shades highlighted the rich tone of her tan skin. Her heels lifted her to Aubrey's height. Her tiny ruby earrings glistened in the streetlight.

"Wow!" Aubrey whispered. "You look amazing!"

"Thanks," she murmured as she looked down, her honey-colored glasses resting at the tip of her slender nose. Her straight, dark hair fell forward, covering most of her blushing sorrel face. "We're over here. We don't have to wait in line."

"Oh," Aubrey said.

She spun away and, linked by their intertwined fingers, Jordana pulled Aubrey down the sidewalk.

Jordana's snug grip around Aubrey's palm warmed his chilled hand. Her lavender perfume wafted back, and the sweet fragrance tingled in his nose, flushing his face.

As they darted left and swerved right through tourists and visitors, Aubrey's mind wandered, and for a moment, he dizzyingly forgot where they were. Aubrey had no idea where she was leading them. And he didn't care.

From the folks ahead emerged a moppy crop of blond hair a full head above the crowd. Magnos was easy to pick out.

As they moved closer, Aubrey groaned. He could see most of Magnos, and he was dressed just like Aubrey: navy blazer, white shirt, khakis, and no tie. Jordana directed Aubrey around a lamppost and between two parked cars, and they popped out onto the cobblestone street in front of their friends.

"Where have you been?" questioned Rodriqa.

"Did you two plan your outfits?" asked Jordana as she waved her hand between Aubrey and Magnos.

Aubrey hung his head and sighed.

Pulling at his lapels, Magnos puffed out his chest and smiled. "Yep!"

"You kinda look like twins." Jordana grinned.

"Yeah," blabbered Buzz. "Except it looks like Magnos stole all of your blood supply while you were in the womb."

"I must have gotten a fairer share of the uterus," gloated Magnos.

"The grass is always green on the other side of the placenta," giggled Buzz.

"That's completely disgusting," moaned Rodriqa.

Aubrey rolled his eyes and changed the subject by pointing directly at Buzz's waistline. "*What* is that?"

Rodriqa smacked Aubrey's hand. "Don't point at Buzz's fat. It's rude."

"I'm not!" Aubrey pulled back his hand. "I'm talking about his belt buckle."

The other three glanced down and marveled at Buzz's protruding rectangular silver buckle, embossed at the front with a pearly blue, cursive B. Smooshed behind it, his chubby gut bulged around the buckle's edges.

"Is that your attempt at a girdle?" Rodriqa's left eyebrow curled upward.

Buzz shook his head. "It matches my bowtie." Buzz tugged at the ends of his blue, paisley bowtie, which was stiff and crinkled. "And my cufflinks." Elbows bent, he held up his wrists to show off the studded sodalite gemstones carved with the letter B.

"You're a blue paisley mess," muttered Rodriqa, crossing her arms. "Detention must have pushed you over the edge."

Buzz smirked, rolling his eyes.

"What are these for?" asked Jordana, looking at his elbows. She slid her fingers under one of a pair of metal rings clasped around his upper arms.

"They're garters." Buzz lifted up his ankles, showing off a matching pair of metal rings pinching his slacks around his calves. "Snazzes up the outfit."

"I think I would have gone inside already if I was dressed like that," mused Aubrey.

"I wanted to," grumped Rodriqa. "But she wouldn't let us." Rodriqa nodded toward Jordana.

Aubrey glanced at Jordana and bit his lip, hoping he wouldn't blush.

"We were waiting on you," Jordana said as she looked down at the cobblestones. "We figured it would be best to go in as a group."

"Why's that?" asked Aubrey.

Magnos pointed toward the entrance of the Rock-U-Quarium.

Aubrey turned around. "Oh," he replied flatly.

Next to the front of the line of expectant patrons, Ned and Fred Kluggard stood on either side of the doors to the Rock-U-Quarium. Dressed in navy uniforms with bright golden buttons and flat-topped caps, the brothers greeted invited guests and inspected their invitations.

"I haven't seen them since last fall," murmured Aubrey, "since the Paddling Pumpkin Parade. I wonder where they've been?"

"And why aren't they wearing their police outfits?" added Buzz.

"I overheard Lenny and Benny talking one day at school," replied Magnos. "Supposedly they were kicked off the force for suspicious behavior. I guess this is their new gig."

"Well, we shouldn't dawdle." Rodriqa lifted her chin. "We have nothing to be afraid of here." She pulled her invitation out of her tiny, square handbag and marched through the crowd toward the entrance. Her friends followed.

<hr />

Across the street in front of the State of the Mart, Griggs strolled along the sidewalk in his forest-green, button-down uniform. He pulled out an oily rag from his back pocket and wiped off his forehead and walked up to Old Widow Wizenblatt.

"I'm not convinced this will work." Griggs's white, wooly eyebrows wriggled across his forehead.

The widow dropped her walker. "It has to. If Aubrey Taylor is the last seer, then there isn't much choice." She scowled as her eyes remained fixed on the front of the Rock-U-Quarium.

"We're still not sure," grumbled Griggs.

"We'll find out shortly," replied the widow, scratching her neck. "Magnolia Thistlewood has a plan, and a sacrifice may be the only way to stop it."

THE HAND THAT ROCKS
THE WORLD RULES THE CRADLE

Aubrey barely noticed the tourists he weeded through as he kept his eyes on Ned and Fred Kluggard, who flanked the tinted glass entrance to the Rock-U-Quarium.

Tall and lanky, with dark hair so well groomed you could seen the tines of the comb he had, Fred stood on the right straight and stiff, like he was carved from the brick building behind him. On the left, Ned, whose uniform was in a tug of war between his blubbery frame and his buttons, flashed his pocket light at anyone who approached the door.

A few feet from Fred, Aubrey pulled out his invitation. A chubby hand ripped it out Aubrey's fingers.

"Who invited you?" accused Ned in a shrill tone.

Aubrey examined Ned and then looked up at Fred, unsettled by Ned's voice. Fred didn't move. His eyes looked blankly forward over the crowd.

"I'm not sure," murmured Aubrey. "We got the invitations at school." His four friends walked up behind him.

"You *all* were invited?" Ned flashed his police light in Aubrey's eyes.

Aubrey squinted and held up his hand.

"Yep," said Buzz. "And we've all got the same invi."

Rodriqa smirked at Buzz and then stepped up to Ned. "Is there a problem?" She flashed him her invitation.

Ned dropped Aubrey's invitation on the ground, grabbed the handle of the door and yanked it open. "When it comes to the five of you, there's always a problem."

Aubrey leaned over to pick up his invitation. Rodriqa pushed Aubrey inside, and the other three friends followed. Ned dropped the door closed as Magnos cleared the threshold.

"Guess they weren't glad to see us," said Magnos as he jumped forward.

"Can't blame them," bragged Buzz. "Since we made them look bad."

"Didn't that seem odd to you all?" asked Aubrey.

"They've always seemed odd to me," replied Rodriqa.

"Yeah, but Fred was always the one who used to do all the talking," said Aubrey. "Now it's like Ned's in charge."

Jordana nodded as she thought about what Aubrey said. Rodriqa eyed him warily. Magnos edged them deeper into the foyer.

The closing doors muffled the roaring din outside. Clumped together inside, all five friends gawked at the interior.

Five curved marble steps led up to the spacious main level, where a series of mobile-like chandeliers composed of glass, carved stones, and intricately inlaid silver turned, lighting the room.

"Wind chimes?" asked Aubrey.

"Probably," murmured Magnos.

"Invitations, please."

The five friends jumped, unaware of the four-and-a-half-foot tall girl standing in front of them with her hands out. Her wavy black hair was tied back with a ponytail, wrapped to one side, and her glasses were so thick it made her eyes appear twice the size as expected for her small round head. She wore a bright red blazer with a rectangular nametag pinned to her lapel that read "Xiomena Kontrearo: Press."

"Oh, hey, Mena. You startled us," said Rodriqa.

"Amazing isn't it?" said Mena with a crooked smile as she turned to the small flight of stairs. "I can't wait to get to see it all."

"How did you get an invitation?" Buzz pulled out his invitation and handed it to Mena.

Mena's lip curled and she scratched her scalp under her ponytail. "Mr. McElory said if I'd work the front door, I could get a sneak peek. He even said he'd let me write an expose on whatever I wanted."

"Nice," said Rodriqa as she handed Mena her invitation.

"I read your last one." Buzz snapped his fingers. "What was it called?" Buzz tapped his forehead. "Oh, yeah…'Genetically Engineered Trout: The Attrition of Fishin'". It was very, uh, mouth-watering."

Magnos and Aubrey stifled a chuckle.

"Gracias, *hongo mojado*," said Mena, snatching Jordana, Magnos, and Aubrey's invitations out of their hands. "I'd ask how you all got invitations, but I've already seen how criminals are given benefits in this town."

Rodriqa rolled her eyes. Buzz stuck out his tongue at her.

Magnos sighed. "Where do we go?"

"Up the stairs," said Mena. "I'm sure you'll find your place quite easily."

"Thanks." Magnos herded the other four up the stairs and into the center of the main ballroom.

"Who was that?" asked Jordana.

"Remember Jaime, the security guard at the dam who's good friends with my brother?" replied Rodriqa.

"Yeah," acknowledged Jordana.

"That's his younger sister, Mena. She's in eighth grade."

"Is she always that friendly?"

Rodriqa rocked her head. "Depends on what her glamor glitch is that day."

"Usually less so," added Buzz. "Ever since she got that junior beat job at the *Lake Julian Mountain Lyre.*"

"She writes for the newspaper?" asked Jordana.

Rodriqa nodded.

The five of them stopped next to a cloverleaf-shaped table and stared.

Like trees in a forest of contemporary décor, marble pillars, inset with numbers and letters racing in digital fluorescence down the column's grooves, displayed stock market prices and professional and college ball game scores, with video highlights glowing from screens anchored to the ceiling above. Tables of various shapes and sizes, from shallow colanders to horizontal windmills, were placed around the room with invited guests marveling at the room's unique features. In the back corner, a wide, circular food and drink bar with leather stools, secured underneath a granite counter, spun slowly as servers from within delivered drinks and appetizers to patrons riding the rotating island of refreshment.

A gleam of light from behind the bar caught Aubrey's attention. Men and women, dressed in tuxedo-styled serving outfits, bustled in and out of a swinging red door, behind which a light sporadically escaped. Aubrey squinted to see inside but then felt foolish. He was peering into the kitchen.

Aubrey glanced to the right of the red door. Just behind the hinge, sitting in a row of benches, two very short men hunched over a table, facing each other. Both were dressed in fedoras and beige dusters, one with his back to Aubrey, the other had large, round green eyes that rolled under the brim of his hat.

Aubrey leaned forward and blinked his eyes to clear his sight. Suddenly, he realized the large green eyes were staring at him.

"Wow," mused Magnos. "All the high and mighty of Lake Julian are here."

Aubrey faced Magnos, eager to look away from the diminutive men.

"Jobe Parotty is here," agreed Jordana.

"Duh," blurted Buzz. "He's the owner."

"That doctor woman is here too," added Magnos.

"Who?" asked Jordana.

"Dr. Gatchiri," replied Buzz. "The woman from Jafar's house."

Jordana acknowledged his answer with a long, murmuring moan.

"Yeah," said Rodriqa, "and now I'm starting to wonder why they invited us."

"Because we're local celebrities," touted Buzz as he straightened his bowtie. Suddenly, Buzz pointed across the room. "Oh, look!"

"Don't…" Rodriqa smacked his arm. "Embarrass us."

"But it's Freyma Spindergrath!" exclaimed Buzz. "And she's wearing her famous satellite pearls."

"Only you would notice that," remarked Rodriqa.

Jordana searched where Buzz had pointed. Several men and women stood talking and snacking on hors d'oeuvres. But one woman in an elegant, white lace-trimmed ball gown stood distinguished above the rest. A string of pearly black stones, polished into perfect spheres, decorated her neckline. Jordana turned her head, mesmerized by the older woman, who wore pink-tinted glasses that rested at the end of her long nose. Her silvery gray hair was wound into a perfectly sculpted coif, and her long willowy arms gripped a crystal glass.

"What are satellite pearls?" asked Jordana.

"They're pearls made of meteorites," explained Buzz. "Her particular strand of satellite pearls is said to be worth over forty million dollars."

"Really," said Jordana.

"That's an expensive rack of old burnt-up rocks," remarked Magnos.

Rodriqa snorted. "Fagin McElory is here. I'm sure this event will bring him headlines for days."

Aubrey's eyes widened, and he felt his throat tighten as three figures walked around a far corner into the main ballroom.

"Maybe we should leave," suggested Aubrey as he turned away.

⋘⋙

Maximillian Miller, Mayor Obsidian Brackenwright, and Judge Rakeman Arsvine rounded a curved hallway out of the center of the Rock-U-Quarium into the main ballroom. All three men were dressed in tuxedos with short coats and metal pins tacked to their lapels, which read, "Lake Julian: Where Prosperities Meet."

Judge Arsvine raised his hand to allow his eyes to adjust to the change of light. "I'm still not sure we can trust him."

"My people have checked him out," said the corpulent mayor, out of breath as he lagged behind the other two men. "I think he's good for Lake Julian."

"He's a gift," replied Mr. Miller. "Jobe Parotty will help propel Lake Julian into the twenty-second century and bring dozens of Fortune 500 companies to our doorstep."

"I've heard different opinions from a few of my constituents," spoke the judge under his breath.

"Opinions are like eyelashes, Rakeman," replied Mr. Miller. "We may not realize they're there, but we all see the world through the ones we have."

The judge narrowed his eyes and thought for a moment. "I'm not convinced."

"Jobe Parotty could be Lake Julian's next golden boy," affirmed Mr. Miller.

"I hope you're right," grumbled the judge. He slid his hand along his greased black hair, realigning several strands that had fallen out of place.

The three men approached Jobe Parotty as he raced up to them. Mr. Parotty's salt-and-pepper, bowl-shaped hair bounced, and his dark mole rode high on his left cheek as he grinned.

"Simply marvelous, Jobe." The mayor thrust his hand forward and shook Mr. Parotty's hand. "This place should bring tourists to Lake Julian from all across the continent. I can only begin to predict the revenue you'll generate."

"Thank you, sir." Mr. Parotty wrenched his hand free from the mayor's tight grip. "Tonight should be very exciting. Both for myself and Lake Julian."

Judge Arsvine leaned forward, strands of his oily black hair falling forward, and grabbed Mr. Parotty's hand. "We're all eager to see what you can do for our community, and we're grateful you've chosen Lake Julian as your new home."

Mr. Parotty smiled. "Lake Julian has the perfect potential for growth. Commercially, it is truly a diamond in the rough, which hopefully we can carve into a bounteous stone together."

Mr. Miller took Mr. Parotty's hand. "Well said, my friend. I look forward to years of partnership and success."

"I can only hope we won't have any trouble tonight…of all nights," prickled a raspy voice from behind the men. "We certainly wouldn't want anyone upsetting the apple cart."

The four men turned as Freyma Spindergrath walked up to their circle.

Mr. Miller sneered. "Freyma, I'd like you to meet the Rock-U-Quarium's proprietor, Jobe Parotty."

"Good evening, Ms. Spindergrath." Mr. Parotty extended his hand.

Ms. Spindergrath daintily squeezed his fingers. "Charmed." She turned back to Mr. Miller. "Max, I hope you're not backpedalling."

Mr. Miller furrowed his brow. "What do you mean, Freyma?"

"The children regarding whom we held an emergency council meeting earlier today." Ms. Spindergrath looked over the top of her pink-tinted glasses. "They're here."

"What?" Mr. Miller's head twisted from side to side, searching for them.

"Do you mean the five children who've started such unrest recently?" asked Mr. Parotty.

Mr. Miller continued searching the ballroom. Mayor Brackenwright fidgeted with his watch.

"Yes," grunted the judge.

"I invited them," spoke Mr. Parotty.

Mr. Miller and Ms. Spindergrath faced Mr. Parotty and scowled. The judge and the mayor winced.

"You did what?" scoffed Ms. Spindergrath, swishing her drink in her hand.

"Keep your friends close and your enemies closer," whistled Mr. Parotty.

"Agreed," said the mayor. "Besides, we've already dealt them a legal blow."

Judge Arsvine bowed his head. "Thanks to Max and Freyma."

"Shrewd." Ms. Spindergrath said as she scrutinized Mr. Parotty's face. "At least if something goes wrong, we know who to blame."

Mr. Parotty smiled politely.

"Brush the dust outta your ditches." Rodriqa crossed her arms and turned toward the front. "Look who's coming." She nodded toward the foyer while her eyes glared up at the ceiling. Her four friends followed her nod.

Walking up the marble stairs with a glistening smile and dressed for an awards banquet, McCrayden Miller crested the top step and slid her see-through shawl off her shoulders. She glanced around the room to see who had noticed her.

Quickly from behind, Pam Trank, Zaniah Jones, Vidalia Arsvine, Mesilla Uztek, and Jon Harney joined McCrayden. Each child was dressed in top-line formalwear. Jon took McCrayden's shawl and threw it down to Mena. The others spread out around McCrayden and staked out the ballroom in various poises of allure.

McCrayden spotted her father and trotted toward him.

Jordana glanced up at Magnos, who was staring at McCrayden. Jordana twisted her lips.

Magnos noticed Jordana out of the corner of his eye. "Uh, rowdies travel in herds," he commented. "You'd rarely see a group of joxsters like that."

"Unless the joxster is dating a rowdy," argued Rodriqa.

Glaring at the foyer, Aubrey's heart sank, and he turned around. "We need to find another place to stand."

From the foyer, Gaetan walked up the marble stairs with Fayla Strumgarten, her arm wreathed around his. Gaetan's muscular shoulders and chest bulged under his powder-blue shirt. Fayla's aqua silk dress embraced her long legs as she walked. Gaetan dug his heels into the marble floor and feigned falling. Fayla laughed at him, her long neck cradled in a bouquet of silvery-blonde hair as she threw her head back.

"Hi, Daddy." McCrayden sidled up next to her father.

"Sweetheart! Are you enjoying the party?" he asked as he wrapped his arms around her.

"Definitely," she said with a sumptuous smile. "But you know what would make the night grander?"

"What?" whispered her father.

"If you'd let me tell the misfits the news."

Maximillian Miller straightened up and pinched her nose softly. "Have at it."

Aubrey glanced back at the table near the kitchen. Both gentlemen were staring back at him. A form intercepted Aubrey's view. "I guess this is where the losers hang out," said Bates Hindenberg in his high-pitched, prepubescent voice.

Aubrey flashed a half-smile at Bates; although a junior, he was Aubrey's height. Aubrey glanced over Bates's shoulder at the two short men near the kitchen.

Buzz took two steps forward and faced Bates nose to nose. The boys could have been twins, had Buzz not been twice as wide as Bates. Both had thick, black glasses that made deep impressions across their noses and cheeks"Ready for tomorrow, Hindenberg?" The cheek of Buzz's haughty grin raised his glasses nearly to his forehead.

"Ready for your reign as County Science Fair champion to come to an end," challenged Bates.

"I wouldn't count on it, Bates. Tomorrow I'll be unveiling my finest invention yet."

"It won't be grand enough," scoffed Bates.

"Bates, what are you doing here?" Rodriqa asked. "I thought this shindig was by invi only."

"Oh, I was invited," chuckled Bates. "I helped construct one of the rooms in the back. So I'm a special guest of Mr. Parotty's."

Buzz's mouth gaped open. "They asked you? And not me?"

"Chew on that," said Bates as he turned away. "Hopefully the sting will prepare you for tomorrow's defeat."

—◆≫◆—

Jobe Parotty strode to the center of the ballroom. He placed a halolike headset on his head and raised his hands.

"Ladies and gentlemen!"

The ballroom shook with the sound of Mr. Parotty's voice, and the lights from the mobile chandeliers brightened and turned, casting a bright glow around him. A hip-hopified country ballad blared from the speakers above.

"Welcome to the Rock-U-Quarium!"

Everyone in the main ballroom applauded. Jobe Parotty swung his arms in front of his chest like the conductor of a symphony as the music roared overhead. "Let the procession begin!"

Rodriqa leaned forward and whispered to Aubrey, "Did you bring your wax?"

Aubrey touched the braces in his mouth. "No, why?"

"I have a feeling…we're about to catch a bunch of cheese."

Jobe Parotty trotted toward the curving hallway. Everyone on the main ballroom gathered around him. The mayor, the judge, and Mr. Miller moved to the edge. Mr. Parotty herded the some fifty-odd individuals together into a tight ball, and then he took a single step backward.

"With these steps, you walk into a new epoch of entertainment. There will be no more couch potatoes. There will be no more gaming recluses. Today, humanity takes a marvelous step forward. A melding of mind and body, a union of sport and fun, kinetics will unravel potential, and there will be no discernible distinction between work and play."

Mr. Parotty took several more steps backward into the dark, curved hallway. Bunching together, everyone moved forward after him.

McCrayden sidled up next to Magnos. "Exciting, isn't it?" she whispered as she lifted her chest and brushed her golden, curled locks off her neckline.

"Yep," stuttered Magnos as he struggled to keep his head forward.

On the opposite side of Magnos, Jordana glared at McCrayden and then grimaced at Magnos as they marched through the rounding corridor.

"You know, you don't have to be a misfit forever," McCrayden said. "You could always be a rowdy again someday, if you tried."

Jordana snapped her head away from them and took several quick steps forward.

Magnos cleared his throat. "I like my new friends."

McCrayden laughed. "I'm sure they're fun to play with, but at some point, you have to take life more seriously."

Magnos scrunched up his face. "Where's Teton?"

McCrayden looked away and ran her fingers across her neck. "He had other plans tonight."

"So he wasn't invited," said Magnos.

"He wasn't interested," she replied. "He doesn't care for these sorts of things."

"And I'm guessing your dad doesn't care much for him."

McCrayden's eyes narrowed. "At least he offered to help clean up my house after you and your friends nearly destroyed it."

"Would your dad have let us help if we'd offered?"

"But you didn't," replied McCrayden. "You skidded off like scared puppies." She pulled a lock of hair forward, twirling the strands between her fingers. "And that's why you deserve to have your little electrical suits outlawed."

Magnos stopped and looked down at McCrayden. "What?"

McCrayden kept walking. "Daddy had an emergency meeting with the city council this morning. They made it illegal to wear your little suits in Lake Julian without a permit. Enjoy your night."

"Our first stop! Gymanergy!" Jobe Parotty stopped in the middle of the rounded hallway and pressed a blinking light on the outer black wall. Slowly the darkness lightened as the tint on the wall disappeared pixel by pixel, revealing a series of clear fiberglass panels, through which beams of white fluorescence washed the corridor alight.

Most of the guests held up their hands to shade their eyes and cooed in awe. A few steps behind, the friends wheeled their heads around to view the spectacle.

"*Gymanergy*. Human energy from a gym! It is the health club of the future, available now in Lake Julian!"

Behind the clear walls, an expansive three-story room was exposed, fit with rows of stationary bicycles, stair-climbing machines, bench presses and weights, each tethered to the floor by a series of joints and gears.

"Not only will individuals come to *Gymanergy* to stay in shape, but they'll use the energy they generate to fuel their community. Each aerobic apparatus and all the free weight sets are equipped with an electromagnetic dynamo, thus turning more than fifty percent of their fat-burning, cardio-pumping workout into electricity that will be fed back to Lake Julian."

Whispered wonder rustled through the crowd.

"And don't forget about the carbon," interrupted Mr. Miller.

"Thank you, Max," laughed Mr. Parotty. "And all that carbon dioxide we exhale as we're burning those calories will be turned back into food we can eat." He pointed up through the wall to the ceiling of the gym. Everyone's eyes followed. Above the third story, a canopy of broad green leaves, spiraling vines and cascading tendrils spilled out from a trellis suspended within a circular walkway.

"All the fruits and vegetables grown here are featured in our restaurant."

"The cycle of life all in one room," commented Mr. Miller. Several guests chuckled.

Mr. Parotty nodded. "That's the plan!" He waved everyone forward. "On to the next stop."

———✦———

With his face only millimeters away from the clear wall, Buzz grazed his fingers along the surface, examining the intricacies of the curved fiberglass.

"Fascinating use of technology, but it's not new. Gyms like these already exist in a few major cities," remarked a voice next to Buzz.

"Who cares about the gym," balked Buzz. "The chromatophoric design of these fiberoptic panels is beyond cutting-edge. I never knew anything like this existed." Buzz caressed the wall and leaned in to smell it.

A finger tapped against the wall. "Looks standard to me."

Buzz scoffed and turned toward the voice. He stumbled a step back. He wasn't sure what unnerved him the most: that Iyashi Gatchiri was shoulder to shoulder with him or that she was wearing a hot pink pantsuit with matching lipstick.

Dr. Gatchiri's lip creased at her cleft scar as she looked more closely at Buzz. Instantly, her hand jerked to his face, and she squinted as she closed in on Buzz. Buzz's eyes widened. He held his breath.

Her index finger and thumb jabbed at the corner of Buzz's glasses.

Buzz fell back against the wall. He felt like he'd been shot.

Dr. Gatchiri mused at the wispy strand of aged fibrous thread she had plucked from the hinge of Buzz's eyewear. "This looks like papyrus."

Buzz slid to the floor, watching her as the ambling guests shot the two of them curious glances.

She twirled the thread between her fingers. "From an Egyptian tapestry." She ground the fiber in the pads of her fingertips and smelled the grains. A snarl rippled across her lips. Pulling her electronic tablet from her suit jacket pocket, she tapped it several times, and it flashed alight. "Where were you yesterday, Mr. Reiselstein?"

"With me," snapped Rodriqa. She yanked Buzz to his feet by his shoulder and pulled him into the crowd. Dr. Gatchiri tapped the camera on her tablet and grinned.

———✦———

Another blinking light appeared on the outer wall as the group rounded another curve. Mr. Parotty playfully trotted up to the panel and drummed a quick beat on it with his thumbs. A semicircle of black panels cleared.

"The Parkourium!"

Behind the fiberoptic panels, two- and three-story windowed buildings and stair-step alleys abutted dipping arroyos and short bridges like a miniature city block, wrapped in foam and padding. A network of metal tubing tracked above the contours of the obstacles.

"Now you and your loved ones can practice the newest of extreme sports while eliminating the risk of injury." Mr. Parotty opened one of the panels and reached into the Parkourium. He removed a padded suit that was connected to the metal track above by wires and displayed it to the crowd. "Wearing one of these, you can vault, roll, and jump over, on and through a cityscape...and even fly." Mr. Parotty wrenched the suit to the floor and then released it. The wires whirred and jerked the suit through the open panel into the room, stopping a few feet below the metal tubing. "The retractable safety cord provides mobility and security. And the track it rides upon has multiple intersections, to provide the avid traceur a new experience every visit."

Lined up against the panels, everyone marveled at the inside.

"If parkour is ever an Olympic sport, the Parkourium will help Lake Julian supply a competitor," touted Mr. Miller.

"I bet you're right," replied Mr. Parotty. "Who wants to be the first to try this bad boy out?"

Gaetan jumped out of the crowd, into the room, and had a padded suit in hand before anyone else could answer.

Mr. Parotty laughed. "Go for it, my eager friend."

Gaetan unvelcroed the suit and pulled it on. He crouched, activating the snap back of the wires, and leapt. Gaetan soared upward and landed agilely on top of a bridge. Many of the guests outside clapped.

After jumping up to another level, Gaetan scaled the outside of a building, climbed in a top window, swung out another window, and sailed with a back flip onto the top of the next building.

"I'm a superhero!" shouted Gaetan from inside. Most of the crowd laughed and cheered. Fayla clapped her hands. Aubrey rolled his eyes.

"So what's it like being the leader of the most notorious gang to run rampant through the streets of Lake Julian since prohibition?" Aubrey winced at the sound of the voice and looked over his shoulder. Mena Kontrearo stood with her face even to his shoulder blade, her bespectacled eyes fixed on him.

"What are you talking about?" asked Aubrey as he leaned away from her.

"You're the leader of the NeighborGhoul Watch, right?"

Aubrey shook his head. "I'm a part of it, but I'm not the leader."

"That's funny, because they all say you're their leader." Mena pointed with her thumb over her shoulder.

Leaning against the opposite wall several yards down, Jordana, Rodriqa, Buzz, and Magnos, quickly turned from looking at Aubrey toward Gaetan, who was running upside down underneath a breezeway in the Parkourium.

Aubrey sighed. "It doesn't matter who the leader is, we all play our part."

"And what part do you play?" Mena pulled out a purple pen. It was husky in width and held an assortment of clicky buttons at its top. She removed a small pad of paper from her purse and wrote several sentences across the top of its exposed page.

Aubrey felt his insides quiver and his back stiffen. "That's, uh...really, not uh...I'm not really supposed to say."

Mena raised her eyebrows and pursed her lips. "Oh, I love secrets! This is gonna be my best story yet."

"You're not writing a story about me," insisted Aubrey.

Mena waved him off. "It's not about you, silly." She continued to scribble on her pad.

Aubrey's shoulders loosened. "Oh, good."

"I'm doing a story on the destruction and chaos that the five of you have brought to this town over the past six months and how unchecked adolescent behavior represents a spinning maelstrom that's tearing our country apart."

Aubrey's breath stopped mid-inhale. He thought for a moment and then said, "Are you serious?"

Mena smiled and nodded her head, still writing. Aubrey walked around Mena toward his friends.

"By saying nothing, you've given me everything," she said as he walked away.

"While Gaetan breaks in the Parkourium, let's move onto the next section, the Re-Reality Room!" Mr. Parotty patted Aubrey on the shoulder as they passed each other. Aubrey stopped, startled by the friendly gesture and looked up at him. Mr. Parotty winked and then waved everyone forward.

Around the corridor up from the Parkourium, Mr. Parotty touched another blinking button on the wall. The walls here didn't transform. Instead a door clicked open. Mr. Parotty waved folks forward. "Everyone inside!"

One by one, the guests filed into the room. The friends huddled together inside, a little uneasy at what they saw.

Every surface in the room was black. Several small recessed bulbs shone dim cones of light onto the room's center.

An army of robotic men filled the space. Placed at regular intervals, ten abreast and ten deep, the eight-foot tall, white-and-gray polyvinyl figures held their arms bent at their sides and their legs frozen in midstride on a glossy hemisphere, rising up from the floor. Their heads were shaped like overgrown fighter pilot helmets, and their husk-like torsos bulged out front and back.

"The Re-Reality Room provides a full virtual reality experience. Each Cyber Rudder, which you see here," Mr. Parotty pointed toward one of the robotic suits, "can be connected to the Internet for a full-bodied gaming adventure where you and your friends can share times in an imaginary world."

Mr. Parotty walked up to the nearest Cyber Rudder and pulled down a small lever under its arm. The trunk shifted forward, and its side opened up, revealing a hull of armbands and leggings that a person could slide into.

"You four. Come up and look inside!" Mr. Parotty pointed to Magnos, Buzz, Aubrey, and Rodriqa. Buzz raced up to a Cyber Rudder. The other three looked at each other warily and crept forward.

<hr />

"Dreadfully cumbersome." The raspy voice tumbled down from behind Jordana.

Jordana looked over her shoulder. Freyma Spindergrath stood behind her, carefully swishing the last sips of her drink. She peered over her rose-colored glasses at Jordana's friends as they examined the open Cyber Rudder.

Jordana smiled at her and then took a step away.

Ms. Spindergrath took a firm step toward Jordana. "I'll never understand why boys never get tired of toys." She took another sip and then nodded forward. "Are they your friends?"

Jordana nodded but kept her head forward with a curtain of her dark hair hanging between them.

Ms. Spindergrath leaned down. "My dear, you really are quite striking."

"Thank you," answered Jordana, more embarrassed than flattered.

"You have beautiful eyes, and your cheek bones are nothing short of elegant."

"Thanks." Jordana's face flushed.

"And you look so familiar."

"I haven't been in Lake Julian long."

"Still, there's something about you…" Ms. Spindergrath twirled a satellite pearl between her fingers. "Are you from Nashville?"

"Yes."

"I think I remember who you remind me of."

Jordana smiled weakly.

"Although if I tell you, you won't know who it is." She rested her drinking glass on a small ledge on the black wall. "A not-very-well-known country singer I met several years ago. Come to think of it, I believe she passed away not too long ago."

A lump throbbed in Jordana's throat, and she could feel her heart racing. "Really?" she asked, trying to sound uninterested.

"Never mind, dear. I'm just an old woman rambling on."

"Who?"

"Excuse me?"

"Who do I remind you of?"

Ms. Spindergrath lifted her head up to think. "If I remember correctly, her stage name was Lilliana. I'm not sure if that was her real name or not. Really, it's not important. It was simply a passing thought."

Ms. Spindergrath grimaced as Buzz squeezed his chunky lower half into the Cyber Rudder.

"Lilliana was my mother." Jordana could barely breathe enough to make another sound.

"Fascinating!" murmured Ms. Spindergrath. "Your mother was truly an outstanding performer and talented in so many ways."

"Yes, she was." Jordana hung her head.

"Such a terrible death. I'm so sorry, dear, you must be devastated."

Jordana nodded. Her lip trembled.

"You seem so much like her." Ms. Spindergrath touched Jordana gently on her shoulder and leaned forward again. "An enchanting beauty such as yours should always be careful. You never know who may want more from you than you're willing to give."

Jordana stared at Ms. Spindergrath. "What do you mean?"

Ms. Spindergrath whispered in Jordana's ear. "Don't ever let anyone hurt you for what they want. Only you can dissuade the incorrigible." She peered at Jordana over her eyeglasses. Jordana felt a rush of overwhelming emotion burst in her heart. She opened her mouth, but she didn't have any words to speak.

Ms. Spindergrath straightened up and walked away.

—◆◆◆—

Buzz hobbled forward, rubbing his right thigh and wincing with every step.

"Guess they don't make Buzz-sized Cyber Rudders," smirked Rodriqa.

"One more stop before refreshments!" Mr. Parotty bound from the middle of the room and into the curved corridor. The guests filtered out of the Re-Reality Room after him.

With his hands clasping the lapels of his blazer, Bates Hindenberg walked past Buzz with his head held high and said, "Hope you enjoyed the preview of the pain I'm gonna bring you tomorrow at the science fair."

Buzz mumbled at Bates under his breath as he limped forward.

The crowd angled through the last leg of the long circular hallway. Everyone could now glimpse the rotating bar and the main ballroom.

A glimmer of multicolored lights flashed out of an open room and spilled into the corridor. Everyone stopped.

Mr. Parotty peeked his head around the corner. "Don't be shy! Come on in to the Break-n-Shake!"

The guests moved forward into the flashing lights. Glitter balls rotated on the ceiling, reflecting light from a myriad of rotating, rainbow-colored stage lights next to them. Computer screens lined the walls, running lists of singers and songwriters like miniaturized digital jukeboxes.

"Download the music you want to hear, and play your favorite selection from your smartphone in our computerized danceteria!"

Mr. Miller pulled McCrayden out of the crowd, and they walked to the edge of the dance floor. He bowed to McCrayden, and she curtsied with a smile. Mr. Miller tapped a computer screen beside him, and the speakers embedded in the walls resounded the latest pop hit.

"What did I miss?" hollered Gaetan from behind the crowd. He sprinted around the corner, grabbed Fayla and spun her around the dance floor.

Buzz rubbed his hands together. "I was counting on this."

"You were hoping there would be a dance floor?" asked Rodriqa with a raised eyebrow.

Buzz nodded. "Now I can show Bates a thing or two...or ten." He snapped open his rectangular belt buckle and pulled out five wires each with hooked ends.

"What is that?" Rodriqa asked.

Buzz lifted his chin. "I call it the White Man's Best Friend." He hooked one wire to his bowtie and wound the other four individually through a garter on each of his extremities. Finally, he hooked the other end of each of the four wires to either a cufflink or a shoe. "With this, I won't just cut the proverbial rug, I'll give it a mani' and pedi'."

Rodriqa's mouth gaped open. Aubrey and Jordana laughed.

"That's awesome!" announced Magnos.

"How does it work?" asked Aubrey.

"There are microreceivers in the belt buckle that sense the beat and rhythm of the music. Rotors within the buckle wind and unwind the wires, forcing my body to dance." Buzz swished his hips from side to side and clapped his hands. "I've programmed a ton of dance moves, like the dizzy crankshaft, the spastic marionette, and, my fav, the drunken puppet."

"Drunken puppet!" asked Rodriqa. "What in your snail shuckin' world is the drunken puppet?"

"You'll just have to watch and find out." Buzz pressed a sodalite button on top of his buckle. "Time to grind."

The belt buckle whirred and vibrated, shaking Buzz's pudge. The wires yanked his limbs. Quicker than the blink of an eye, Buzz was holding his hip in his right hand, his left hand was behind his neck with his elbow gyrating, and his feet were stepping knee-high to the beat of the music.

Buzz shuttled out on the dance floor, prancing, flailing, and twirling to the music.

Magnos guffawed until his shirt came untucked.

"I need a soda," murmured Rodriqa. She walked off toward the rotating bar.

"Wanna dance?" Magnos asked Jordana as he extended his meaty hand. She smiled and placed her slender fingers in his palm.

Aubrey watched as they walked out to the dance floor hand in hand. He didn't want to be jealous, but Aubrey wished Jordana would like him the way she liked Magnos. His heart soured, and he sighed. If only he could show her how he felt, but Aubrey knew it wouldn't be fair to Magnos. A year ago, Aubrey wouldn't have cared how Magnos felt. But now, with all they had been through together, Magnos was one of his closest friends.

Magnos bounced from foot to foot and snapped his fingers with Jordana matching his rhythm in front of him. They tried to mimic Buzz, but they couldn't match how quickly he moved under the influence of his contraption. Bates Hindenberg's chin dropped to his chest as he watched Buzz's moves. Vidalia Arsvine spun around the dance floor, hovering close to Buzz and cheering admiringly.

Aubrey smiled as he watched the action. It wasn't often that he and his friends simply had fun together. Aubrey took a step forward onto the dance floor.

A hand caught his shoulder. "Aubrey, can I talk to you?" Jobe Parotty stood next to him. Aubrey looked up, taking a moment to process what Mr. Parotty had said over the music.

Aubrey nodded. "Sure."

"How about some place a little quieter?"

Aubrey nodded again. Aubrey stared at Mr. Parotty's face. Something was off.

Mr. Parotty walked across the room, through an opening next to the rotating bar and into the restaurant. Aubrey followed, looking at Mr. Parotty's bowl-shaped, salt-and-pepper hair bounce as he trotted forward.

Mr. Parotty stopped next to the cloverleaf-shaped table. Aubrey scanned the corner next to the kitchen door out of the corner of his eye. The two short men were still there, both of them glancing at Aubrey as he walked up to Mr. Parotty.

"Aubrey, I bet you and your friends are wondering why I invited you."

Aubrey stared at his face, unsettled by it; he couldn't figure out what had changed. "To be honest, sir, I'm surprised you even know my name."

Mr. Parotty snickered. "My boy, I doubt there is anyone in these parts who doesn't know who you are."

Aubrey frowned at him.

Mr. Parotty winked to lighten the mood. "Things aren't easy for people like you and me."

"What do you mean?" Aubrey concentrated, searching for what was bothering him.

"We both are playing very special roles in Lake Julian. Sometimes we can be distracted by things that aren't important, and we need people on our side to help keep us on the straight and narrow."

Aubrey shook his head.

Mr. Parotty's grin limped at the edge. "I know it's confusing, but I wanted to be clear about one thing in particular."

"What's that?" asked Aubrey.

"If you ever need anything, you can count on me. Understand?"

"Yes, sir."

"And I'm hoping I can count on you as well."

Aubrey cocked his head to the side. "What could I do for you?"

Mr. Parotty laughed. "Funny you should ask. There's one tiny little thing I could use your help with." Mr. Parotty looked over toward the kitchen. "But tonight's not the night to discuss it."

Mr. Parotty glanced into the Break-n-Shake and then back over to the kitchen. Suddenly, Aubrey realized what was different. Mr. Parotty's mole was in a different position on his face, yet again.

"I want you to enjoy the rest of your evening." Mr. Parotty's forehead creased. "Enjoy being a kid for a change." He looked over his shoulder toward the entrance and then stared at the kitchen. "You'll have to excuse me. I have some business to attend to." Mr. Parotty sauntered past Aubrey toward the kitchen door.

Aubrey turned around. Only one of the short men sat at the benches next to the door. And his round green eyes were glaring straight at Aubrey.

HERE-SAY

Thalazzaran, Gaspian, and Melkyor drifted up the steep, leaf-littered hillside below Crannynook Caves. A white orb gleamed in Melkyor's open palm, lighting their way through the darkness.

"I sense little here," scoffed Gaspian.

"I've been here before." Electricity arced between Melkyor's beard and head. "I know what I'm looking for."

"Melkyor is right," spoke Thalazzaran. "We are getting close."

The three gray forms hovered closer to the largest opening of craggy rock near the top of the mountain.

"I don't understand." Melkyor's head turned, searching the entrance to the caves. "There used to be so many."

"So many *what?*" grumbled Gaspian.

Melkyor floated into the cave. He raised his arm and extended his fingers. A jolt of lightning flashed from his index finger into the cave.

A shrill scream echoed from within. A green barnling clambered out of a nook behind a stalactite, hurling itself deeper into the darkness.

Thalazzaran raised his hands and curled his fingers. The creature stopped in midflight, grasped by an unseen force. Thalazzaran yanked his arm to his chest, and the creature sped toward the Magi.

"Barnlings." Melkyor caught the creature.

The barnling wailed, stretching its head between Melkyor's fingers. Its three eyes darted in different directions as it wiggled its arms.

"Where are your friends?" Melkyor pulled his hand close to his face.

"No more!" squalled the barnling. "No more!"

Melkyor turned the barnling in his palm. "Are you sure?" Melkyor released a snap of energy from his hand.

The creature's green form crackled. The barnling screamed. "Yes, Magneleckticist! No more! No more!"

"How cute." Melkyor glanced at Gaspian. "It knows what I am."

Gaspian grimaced.

"What happened to your colony?" asked Thalazzaran.

"Watcher!" The barnling's eyes twitched. "Watcher was here! Consumed so many of us!"

"So it's true," said Gaspian.

"A Watcher has been released." Thalazzaran bowed his head. "Who released the Watcher?"

"No trouble," bawled the barnling. "No more trouble!"

Thalazzaran raised his hands and pinched his thumb and index finger together.

"Zaks!" wheezed the barnling under the Graviteer's pressure.

"A Magi?" questioned Thalazzaran as he lowered his hand.

The barnling coughed harshly and nodded.

"Have you heard of the seer?" questioned Melkyor.

"Here." The barnling spat at Melkyor. "The seer is here."

"And where is the Magi?" asked Thalazzaran.

"Lake Julian," replied the barnling.

"We have confirmed the rumors."

"Our duty is clear," said Gaspian.

Melkyor nodded with a wispy grin. "You've been most helpful, little barnling." Melkyor squeezed the creature. Sheets of electricity engulfed Melkyor's hand in a ball of jagged light.

The barnling stiffened. Its three yellow eyes dimmed into darkness.

A wedge of white light spread across a cobblestone alleyway behind the Rock-U-Quarium. Jobe Parotty stepped out and careened his head, searching the sliver of space between buildings. To his left, he saw the silhouette of a fedora hat atop a figure in a duster, standing near the edge of the street.

Mr. Parotty cleared his throat. The figure at the end of the corridor stood still.

Mr. Parotty pushed the door forward and trotted down the small set of brick stairs in front of him. The door behind him closed with a loud crash. Darkness flooded the alleyway. Pulling a pack of cigarettes from his slacks' pocket, he tapped the end of the box on his sandstone watch.

The silhouette's head turned to the side. "How long did it take you?" The creature's tongue snapped within its jowls and it inhaled as it spoke.

Mr. Parotty pulled a cigarette from the pack and flicked a bright flame from a small lighter. "Take me what, Tartan?" He took several slow strides forward.

"How long did it take you to figure out that you were simply a pawn in this lavish game?"

"A few months." Mr. Parotty puffed on the glowing cigarette. "But I figured out what was going on pretty quickly. Thought I'd hedge my bets."

"Pretty dangerous bet," remarked Tartan. "But it looks like it's paid off."

"Pretty much." Mr. Parotty blew a stream of smoke into the air. "I can't complain."

"And you've done well." Tartan turned back toward the street, musing at the crowd lining up along Lake Julian Square.

"Besides, the reward was in the gift," added Mr. Parotty, stopping just behind Tartan's shoulder.

"One being's gift is another being's curse," scorned Tartan.

"Both are relative."

"Clearly," replied Tartan. "But what you've done is truly astounding. You've drawn the crowds, just as you needed."

Mr. Parotty drew another drag on his cigarette. "I learned how to do that with the State of the Mart. Guess that's why I was chosen."

"Most certainly. But what I can't understand is why you and your master haven't chosen to act."

Mr. Parotty chuckled. "In time. Now, the Rock-U-Quarium is the main bait."

Tartan stroked his chin with his three-fingered hand. "For the children?"

Mr. Parotty nodded. "My master is eager to bring them into her fold."

The cool air misted from the Tartan's flat nose. "My master has a sort of sentimental inkling for these children. It's rather odd, really. Considering his previous disdain for puds." Tartan turned to face Mr. Parotty. "That's why we're here tonight. To warn you. Stay away from them."

Mr. Parotty sized up the three-and-a-half foot tall creature in front of him, its pale reptilian skin glistening in the streetlights flickering from the square. "You weren't invited." He looked up over Tartan's hat.

"We didn't need to be," scowled Tartan as it blinked repeatedly and flashed its round, green eyes.

Mr. Parotty sucked down a chestful of smoke and then blew it in Tartan's face. "Isn't your master supposed to maintain the balance…or something?"

"I don't question my master, and neither should you."

"Well, I'm not disrupting the balance, so why do you care?"

Tartan pointed at Mr. Parotty. "You plan to take the children's divinoi."

Mr. Parotty frowned. "Not at all. We don't need them."

Tartan's flap-like ears crested under its fedora. "Then you plan to eliminate them?"

"Yep." Mr. Parotty dropped his cigarette and snuffed it out. "Right after I eliminate you." He snapped open the top of his sandstone watch and grabbed Tartan by the shoulder.

Arching his back, Tartan turned away and flipped off his trench coat, freeing himself from Jobe Parotty's grip. It was too late.

A dozen shimmering black, tube-shaped shadows sprung from the open portion of Mr. Parotty's watch. They wrapped themselves around Tartan's upper arms and torso. Their oily skins writhed as they absorbed the light glinting into the alleyway. The spirit shards' circular rows of fangs latched onto the reptilian skin. Tartan spun in circles, trying to shake them.

Tartan clawed off one of the spirit shards. He flung it to the ground and stomped on it with his hooves. The shade squealed and then clamped onto his thigh.

Tartan gritted his teeth and concentrated. For a brief moment, Tartan's body became translucent as he tried to fade from this world, but the spirit shards clamped down more fiercely, drawing the life from the creature. Tartan dropped to the knees of his backward-bent legs. Slowly, he closed his eyes and fell forward flatly onto the cobblestone.

The spirit shards consumed Tartan and all that remained was a wriggling, shimmering mass of fattened black snakes.

Jobe Parotty smiled. "Keepers can be so simple." He reached down into the crawling murk of spirit shards and turned his sandstone watch again. Quickly, they scurried into the watch's innards. He snapped it closed.

Mr. Parotty crouched down and marveled at a glowing white stone, orbited by a single ball of orange light that hovered a few inches above the ground. Gently, he reached down and scooped up the stone, its light quickly fading behind his closing fingers.

"If you only knew the army, your sacrifice will reap, my friend."

AND THE CAT
RAN AWAY WITH THE LOON

The Buzz Bug pulled to a stop in between Rodriqa and Aubrey's house under a streetlight illuminating the sidewalk.

Rodriqa slipped out of the backseat, her dress swirling around her. "See you toad throwers tomorrow!" She smiled and waved before turning toward her house.

Aubrey tumbled out of the middle seat. "Thanks for the ride, guys. Be careful driving home."

"We will." Buzz moved into the middle seat and waved. Magnos and Jordana smiled at Aubrey. "Night, Aub," hollered Rodriqa, opening her front door.

"Night," replied Aubrey. But she had already disappeared through the threshold.

The Volkswagen turned a sharp semicircle in the middle of the road and puttered away.

Aubrey stared up at the night sky while he felt for Solluna to reassure himself it was still there. The sky seemed darker tonight, which Aubrey thought was unusual since the nearly full moon was at the top of the sky. The shadows that crossed inside his front porch seemed deeper than before, but there was also a lack of light from inside the house. Despite the streetlight, the side yard between his and Rodriqa's house was filled with an empty blackness. Even the distant glow of the city lights from Asheville seemed dimmer than usual.

Thoughts of last fall crept into Aubrey's mind. When Solluna had been a metal encyclopedia of gold and silver, it had read differently in the moonlight and the sunlight. Today, as a crystal pyramid, the words "To open the sealed" were scribed in the sunlight. He wondered what it would read in the moonlight.

Aubrey took several quick steps toward his house. He glanced around as he loosened his belt. He angled his back away from the road and pulled Solluna out of his pants and into the moonlight.

The crystal pyramid prickled his fingers with electricity. Black smoke billowed from within it, and every portion of crystal darkened, as if it had transformed from a diamond to onyx in a few moments. To Aubrey, it looked like a geometric shadow. He could feel it, but it no longer looked real.

Thin gray curves swirled in the pyramid's face.

Opened.

Excitedly, Aubrey turned the pyramid.

The.

He turned it again.

Seal.

And again.

To.

Aubrey grunted. "Another riddle."

He read the words together. "To seal the opened."

Aubrey tapped on the edge of the pyramid. It was still hard as stone. "But what's opened...and what's sealed?" A breeze tickled Aubrey's nose. The dying chill of winter raised goose bumps on his arms. Aubrey shoved Solluna back into its burlap sack and folded his arms around his chest.

Focusing his thoughts on happier notions, he avoided the shadows and walked briskly toward his front porch. Overall, tonight had been a good night. Although he and his friends weren't completely out of trouble, he felt like they had made a good impression at the Rock-U-Quarium. And good press was exactly what they needed right now. If only they could make a few more things right, they might get Mr. Miller off their backs.

Crash!

Aubrey stopped and looked down the street. A clanging echoed off the surrounding houses.

Rolling on the asphalt, a metal trash can spewed garbage out of its top.

"Whimperfidget," murmured Aubrey. An idea flashed through his mind. His eyes lightened, and his cheeks lifted in a smile.

Aubrey tiptoed back out onto the street. He flitted down the road, and picking up his pace, Aubrey leaned down with his hands and rushed toward the bottom of the trashcan.

In a single motion, Aubrey flipped the bottom of the trashcan, hopped up, and landed rear down on top of the overturned bin.

The trashcan scooted and shifted underneath him. Aubrey clutched the body of the can with his ankles. Bellowing from within, the cat squalled and hissed. It smacked at the insides of its enclosure, popping out dents in the can's hull.

"Got ya!" Aubrey cheered. He dug in his pocket and pulled out his cell phone. He opened and viewed the three dots, representing his friends in the Buzz Bug, moving along the Asheville Highway.

"Bit of the bully, aren't we?"

Startled, Aubrey jumped at the sound of the voice and tossed his cell phone onto the asphalt. He turned to look around behind him. Old Widow Wizenblatt stood in his neighbor's yard, resting herself against her walker, which was sinking into the dew-damp soil. Crusted with dirt, her silvery curls draped her wrinkled face, like a Spanish moss over a gnarled tree limb. Her tattered floral dress, pockmarked with holes and stained with watermarks, waved lazily in the cool night's breeze.

Aubrey swallowed a lump in his throat. "Can you help me?" Aubrey tried to look at her as he spoke, but her dark eyes unnerved him. "I need to keep this cat contained until I can get someone out here to haul it away."

"Help you?" grunted the widow. "You think because you have defeated ghosts, you can prey on other defenseless creatures of darkness!"

"Defenseless!" Aubrey twisted his body to face her. "This monster has torn up the entire neighborhood!"

The old widow snickered. "Maybe it's searching for something." She curled her lip as she glared at Aubrey. "Something you shouldn't have."

Reflexively, Aubrey reached for the pyramid at his hip. He squeezed his eyebrows together. "What do you mean?"

"You know what I mean." She pointed to his thigh.

Aubrey looked away. "But, but...what would it want with Solluna?"

Mrs. Wizenblatt clicked her tongue against the roof of her mouth. "The important question is why do you want it?"

"I don't," he replied. "Not really."

Mrs. Wizenblatt sneered as she nodded her head. "If you treat it like a toy, someone will take it under the guise of play. If you treat it like a treasure, it will be pilfered when you sleep. You do not own Solluna. It belongs only to one. And if you're not careful, it will betray you as it has so many others."

Aubrey shook his head. Fiddling with his belt, he reached into the burlap sack and pulled out the blackened pyramid. He perched it on his fingertips, so she could easily see it.

"Do you want it?" accused Aubrey. "Is this what you're after?"

Old Widow Wizenblatt cackled. "Boy, do you still know so little? Only someone dull to the future would cling to such a thing." The widow focused on the shadowy pyramid in Aubrey's hands. Her eyes glistened in the streetlights, and the corners of her craggy mouth upturned. "And yet hope never flees too far from danger." She sighed and rested her body back on her heels. "It has not been a pyramid for quite some time. Luck favors the foolish." She rubbed her hands together. "You may be meant to have it. For now."

Aubrey scowled, and then he stared at the pyramid. Bile rumbled in his gut as he bitterly reminded himself that he never asked for any of this. He never wanted to see ghosts. He never wanted to battle specters. All he ever wanted was to be normal. And Solluna was nothing more than another reminder of his undesirable freakishness.

"How cruel life can be," he murmured.

"Cruel to the near-sighted," said the widow. "Many wait for you to fail in hopes of taking your place."

"They can have it," grumbled Aubrey. "I don't see the point to all this."

Mrs. Wizenblatt shook a pointed finger at him. "Everything has a point. Everything has a purpose. The universe is knit together by reason. There is no such thing as coincidence."

Aubrey slid the pyramid back into the burlap sack. "How would you know?"

The widow yanked her walker from the dirt and stamped it a pace forward.

Suddenly, the metal trashcan launched off the ground, ringing like a bell. Aubrey fell onto the sidewalk, landing on his elbow and thigh. Solluna jabbed his scrawny leg. Aubrey nearly lost his breath from the pain.

The can clanged and shuddered, bouncing down the asphalt. A whirling blur of wet fur and pointed claws ran in circles around the widow and Aubrey. Aubrey rolled off his side and rubbed away the pain from the pointy Solluna. The widow's head bobbled as she watched the cat run loopty-loops.

In an instant, the cat stopped in the middle of the road and glared at Aubrey. With its back arched and tail stiffened straight, Whimperfidget growled at him and raked its paws fitfully against the asphalt. Its eyes, red like glowing marbles, smoldered as its body swelled, its skin and fur expanding further with each heave of its torso.

Aubrey scrambled on all fours, scurrying away.

"Now you've done it," chuckled the Widow. "You made it mad."

"Help!" squealed Aubrey.

Suddenly, the cat screeched and, shrinking into a ball of matted hair, bolted down Dalton Circle, racing out of sight. The widow's jaw dropped. She pulled her walker from the ground and raised it over her head. She swung the walker through the air, batting at the night air. A fearful squeal escaped from her mouth, and she hurriedly toddled off the lawn and ducked into the backyard.

Aubrey stopped in the middle of his neighbor's yard and leaned up onto his knees. His eyes darted between the road and the backyard. He frowned in confusion. Angling his head upward, he watched the stars twinkle close to the moon. For a moment, they seemed brighter than they had been before. Aubrey raised his hand. The air was still. Everything was quiet. A shiver trembled down his back.

He wiped his hands on his khakis and scuttled forward toward his cell phone. "Dumb cat."

Without warning, the trashcan flew up into the air, arced over the yard, and landed with its open end on top of Aubrey. Sharp pains shot up Aubrey's right arm and leg as the lid of the can pressed hard against his wrist and ankle.

"Ow!" squalled Aubrey as he pulled in his extremities. The can thudded against the sidewalk.

Stunned, Aubrey pushed against the barrel of the can with his shoulder. It wouldn't budge. He smacked the dented metal with his hands. It didn't move. He tried to stand up, but the can wouldn't give way.

"Let me out!" he cried, his voice echoing.

Wheezy breaths seethed above the trashcan. Aubrey flinched backward and closed his eyes.

The darkness behind his eyelids swirled with flashes of green and red hazy blobs, some coalescing into larger clumps and others tearing apart and fading away. Slowly, the phosphenes dissolved into the inky background.

Aubrey couldn't see anything behind his eyelids. Nothing moved, and nothing glowed. He pushed against the inside of the can. It inched forward, and then he heard something grunt as it pushed back against the can.

Aubrey pivoted his body, bracing his back to the ground, and edged his feet upward toward the top of the can. Like a reverse pounce, he shoved his legs skyward.

Popping straight off the ground like a rocket, the trashcan clanged with the force of his shoes against the metal.

The moonlight and streetlights streamed across Aubrey. Wearing a fedora and a duster, a triangular face with round, green eyes, set wide below a bald crown, glowered down at Aubrey. Its flat nostrils flared, and sharp canines peeked out from underneath its curled lip. Tiny, thin arms stretched out from its scaly, tapering trunk. Three broad fingers fanned out from each hand, where it had been holding the trashcan.

Aubrey gasped and pulled his arms and legs into a ball. The trashcan bounced next to him and rolled away. The creature's eyes widened. It hopped backward twice and vanished as if its body had melted into the night. The duster and fedora dropped to the ground.

Aubrey rolled over and hunkered up on his hands and knees. He twisted his head, scanning the road and nearby lawns for the creature.

The trashcan jumped off the ground and soared through the air, falling toward Aubrey. Aubrey leapt to his feet and dodged the spiraling can as it landed top down on the sidewalk next to him. Aubrey kicked the can. It skidded out into the street. He swung his arms, flailing them through the air, and closed his eyes. The phosphenes swirled and faded. The creature glowed behind his eyelids, running straight toward him.

Aubrey opened his eyes and scampered backward. Out of the ether, the three-foot tall creature reappeared in plain sight. Aubrey cringed at its oddly shaped body. Large flap-like ears layered the sides of its head. Its thighs were muscular and backward-bent, but its thin lower legs funneled down into hooves. It more limped than ran as its legs galloped toward Aubrey with a narrow tail swinging behind it.

The creature leapt at Aubrey. Aubrey spun on his heels and bolted into a sprint. Two steps later, he was face down on the grass.

Aubrey flipped over and raised his hands. He squinted through his eye-lashes. The creature was gone.

Aubrey could hear clanging along the asphalt again. He pushed himself up and glanced at the street. The trashcan rolled up the road and lifted off the ground, hovering through the air.

Aubrey rolled forward onto his feet. The can bounced on its own several feet off the ground. Aubrey squeezed his eyelids together. The phosphenes filtered through the darkness and quickly disappeared, leaving a green out-line of the creature racing at him with his short arms above his shoulders.

Aubrey opened his eyes. Below the bobbing trashcan, the creature appeared with his three-fingered hands gripping it tightly.

"Ayy!" squalled the creature, flinging the trashcan at Aubrey. Aubrey leaned to the side. The trash can whizzed by him and bounced along the grass.

The creature stomped its hooves against the ground. "Stop it! Stop it!" The creature flagged its tiny arms at Aubrey, and it inhaled its speech.

Aubrey took a step forward. Aubrey blinked. The creature stopped in midstride and raised its upper lip, exposing fangs. It vanished into the air again.

Aubrey chuckled to himself as he closed his eyes, except he couldn't close them all the way. He contracted his cheeks and forehead, hoping to force them together, but something was holding them apart.

Suddenly, Aubrey lost his breath as a sharp stabbing pain pierced his gut. Rows of points poked at his eyelids like a tiny needles. And something pulled at his lids by the lashes, stretching them out over his cheeks.

"Ow!" screamed Aubrey. He reached for his eyes but something unseen smacked them away. He twirled and batted at the air, trying to push the pain away. He zigzagged across the lawn. Dropping to the ground, Aubrey buried his face in the grass. He slid his hand up to his eyelids and closed them.

As soon as the phosphenes faded, he turned his head to the side and opened his eyes. The creature was on top of him, pulling at his belt.

"Give it! Give it!" squealed the creature. "You shouldn't have it! You shouldn't have it!"

With its muscular legs wrapped around Aubrey's midsection, the creature raked at his back, its fingernails shredding his shirt. Aubrey flipped his body over, pinning the creature underneath him.

The creature hollered out in muffled agony, "Get off me!"

Aubrey sat up, squishing the creature under his rump and shoved himself onto his feet.

He quickly searched the road and sidewalk near him. A red glint caught his eye. He bolted for the rhythmic flash.

The creature stood up with a single stretch of its legs and looked down at itself. "No! No! No!" it shouted and then vanished again.

Aubrey was only a few yards from his cell phone. In an instant, his feet were behind him and moving upward faster than they were moving forward, his face plummeting toward the asphalt. Aubrey closed his eyes and stretched his hands out in front of him.

Thud!

Aubrey crashed onto the street, his chin and chest taking the brunt of the fall. He could feel warm liquid dripping from his nose. Aubrey kept his eyes closed, and quickly the creature came in to view behind his eyelids.

He opened his eyes. The creature stood above him on the street. Aubrey wrenched his arm forward, grabbed a hoof, and pulled it back. The creature catapulted backward onto the road.

"Ayy!" it screamed, its tail crumpling beneath it.

Aubrey reached for his cell phone, flipped it open, and hit the alarm button next to the pound sign.

The phone's numbers lit up, and the screen flashed like a beacon in the night.

Aubrey turned himself over just as the creature vanished. He could see his house down Dalton Circle. Measuring the distance, he pushed himself onto his feet, aimed his torso for his front porch, and ran.

The night spun around him as he focused on his front door. He felt pressure on his ankles and hurtled through the unseen force. He felt a jab to his chest. Aubrey swatted at the air around him. Prickles scratched at his thigh. He rotated into the pain, hobbling off the sting as he pressed forward.

Aubrey sensed pressure at his temples. He brushed at his ears. A puncturing ache stabbed his head. He dropped to the ground in a moaning heap.

Tucking his legs against his chest, Aubrey grunted against the pressure squeezing his skull. The world twisted around him, and he felt himself falling, even though he knew he was lying flat on the ground. With his eyes closed, the darkness behind his eyelids was pierced by a single green light that enveloped his entire ethereal view. Aubrey gripped his head and tried to pull away the pressure grappling his mind.

His movements slowed. The green light in his vision darkened. Aubrey felt control of his senses loosen as if he was being pinched away from his consciousness.

A raucous scream squelched from behind Aubrey. The pressure released from Aubrey's head. The spinning stopped. He snapped his eyes open.

Dressed in a gray sweat pants and an oversized baseball shirt, Rodriqa stood a few yards away from him.

The creature had vanished.

"What was that thing?" shouted Rodriqa.

Aubrey wiggled his fingers in his ear canals and shook his head. "I don't know." Aubrey stretched out his aching legs. "Whatever it was, it scared Whimperfidget and the old widow away."

"What was he doing to you?"

Aubrey shook his head again as he leaned forward. "Not sure, but I think he wanted Solluna." He pointed to the burlap sack hanging out of his khakis.

Rodriqa frowned. "I thought we agreed you shouldn't be carrying it around."

Aubrey shrugged. "I haven't had time to hide it."

Rodriqa felt something tug at the bottom of her shirt. She swatted at her stomach, but she could only touch air.

Crumpling into a wrinkled ball, the bottom of her baseball shirt lifted up and jumped into her mouth. Rodriqa inhaled to scream. The shirt went further back down her throat. She gagged and fell backward.

"Rodriqa!" Aubrey stood up and closed his eyes. The phosphenes faded from behind his eyelids. Aubrey could see the creature's green glow run toward him.

Aubrey opened his eyes. The creature melded into view. It lunged toward him. Aubrey jerked backward. The creature's teeth grazed his hand.

Aubrey looked down. Solluna was gone. Aubrey looked up. The creature extended its neck and swallowed the glass pyramid with a hard gulp. Aubrey watched the creature's cheeks and throat bulge from Solluna's triangular corners, like a snake swallowing a rat.

Aubrey jumped forward. "Give it back!"

The creature swept a foot under Aubrey's ankle. Aubrey tripped forward onto the grass. The creature leapt onto Aubrey's back. "I wasn't finished," it seethed, wheezing inward as it spoke.

"Help!" wailed Aubrey, but his breath left him suddenly.

The creature opened its jaws and clamped its teeth down tightly around Aubrey's neck.

Aubrey's limbs writhed haphazardly. He held his eyes open, but his need to resist waned as he fought to hold on to consciousness.

Screech!

The Buzz Bug fishtailed in the middle of the road and spun 180 degrees. The driver's side door flew open. Magnos vaulted out of the car. In two bounds, he cleared the road and sidewalk and then pounced from the lawn toward Aubrey.

The creature released Aubrey and turned toward the road. Magnos tackled the creature. The two rolled across the yard. The creature snapped at Magnos with its sharp fangs. Magnos dodged its teeth and jerked its head back by its flap-like ears.

With his head on the ground, Aubrey watched the scuffle, forcing himself to keep his eyes open. He took a deep breath. He could feel his energy returning.

Buzz and Jordana jumped out of the Buzz Bug. Jordana stood in the street, watching the melee with her fingers curled up to her face. With ESAU's remote control in one hand, Buzz raced toward Magnos and the creature.

"Hold it still!" shouted Buzz. "Let me get a reading!"

Jordana surveyed the scene and noticed Rodriqa squirming on the ground a few yards away. She ran over to her and helped Rodriqa pull her shirt down.

Rodriqa coughed and sputtered as she cleared her throat. Jordana helped her forward and patted her on the back.

Magnos flipped over onto his back and held the creature high in his arms, its neck clutched in his right hand, its hands bound in his left, and its hooves tucked between Magnos's locked knees.

Aubrey sat up, his eyes tearing up as he refused to blink.

"What is that thing?" asked Jordana.

Aubrey could feel darkness squeeze in from his peripheral vision. "I don't know! It just attacked me on my way home!" Aubrey leaned forward. "But it's trying to disappear and as long as I focus on it and keep my eyes open, it can't!"

"Let me go! Let me go!" bawled the creature as it shuddered in Magnos's grip.

Buzz aimed ESAU at the creature and watched the meter. "Got it!"

"Who cares?" hollered Rodriqa. "Just kill it!"

Buzz nodded and looked at Magnos. "Finish it."

Aubrey held out his hands. "Wait! It has Solluna!"

"We'll get Solluna after we kill it!" Rodriqa pulled cotton threads out of her mouth.

"But who knows if it'll still be there?" insisted Aubrey, his eyes focused on the creature.

"I have an idea." Buzz took another look at the meter on ESAU's handset and dashed back toward the Buzz Bug. Leaning through the driver's side, he rummaged through the back, pulling out his balled-up Elemag suit with its black battery.

"I brought it, just in case." Buzz closed the car door and walked back across the street.

"Wait!" grunted Magnos. "The Elemag suit is illegal now."

"What?" asked Rodriqa.

Magnos struggled against the creature. "McCrayden told me. Her dad held an emergency council meeting. They made our suits illegal."

Rodriqa grimaced. "You're kidding."

Magnos shook his head. The creature freed its hand, and Magnos locked it in his elbow.

"Well, it may be illegal, if a human wears it. But what will Mr. Miller say if this *thing* is wearing it?" Buzz pointed at the creature.

"Let me go! Let me go!" squalled the creature.

Jordana's eyes widened. "That's a great idea! We can trap it and take it to the mayor!"

"They wouldn't let us get near the town square," retorted Rodriqa. "They'd take the creature, arrest us, and we'd never hear another thing about it."

Aubrey clambered onto his feet. "But I'm not supposed to let anyone else have Solluna."

"Who says?" questioned Rodriqa. "The raven?"

"No! Griggs!" Aubrey strained to hold his eyes open; they were burning from his refusal to blink.

"The janitor?" asked Buzz.

"Yes." Aubrey sighed. "He's the one who helped me figure out what it does last year. He knows all about it. And he made me promise not to lose track of it."

"Good going, sneeze cheese," said Rodriqa.

Aubrey dropped his hands to his sides. "It wasn't my fault. I didn't know I was going to be attacked by this thing."

"You shouldn't have been carrying it around," scolded Rodriqa.

"Wait a sec," interrupted Buzz. "Are we all talking about the same Griggs? The guy that mops the floor at the high school? I thought you said the raven told you about Solluna."

"No! You don't understand!" Aubrey wiped the tears trickling down his cheek.

"Could someone do something?" grunted Magnos, his arms and legs shaking under the pull of the writhing creature. "I don't think I can hold it much longer."

"Here! Help me!" said Buzz waving Rodriqa, Jordana, and Aubrey toward Magnos. "The meter on ESAU reads 54 centimeters. I'm gonna set the suit to pulse at 53 centimeters and see if we can trap it inside." Buzz turned a dial along the side of the black box attached to the suit.

"You and your crazy ideas." Rodriqa wound her fingers around one of the creature's wrists. Magnos release the creature's hand, and Rodriqa's arm stiffened.

"Leave me be! Leave me be!" The creature snapped its sharp teeth.

Buzz unzipped the suit and held it open. Jordana and Aubrey each grappled with one of the creature's thighs. Rodriqa sleeved the thin arm, holding its wrist on top of the suit so it couldn't pull back out. She placed the suited arm back in Magnos's clamped palm and repeated her previous steps, sleeving the creature's other arm.

Rodriqa turned toward Jordana and Aubrey. "One at a time," she directed. They both nodded. Rodriqa walked around behind them and cupped the creature's ankles as Jordana and Aubrey secured each leg in the suit.

"Great ready." Buzz pulled the suit's visor out of its pocket. He flipped the black battery's switch and set the visor on top of the creature's squirming head. Jordana, Aubrey, and Rodriqa jumped back. Magnos dropped the creature's arms and rolled away.

Zap! Electricity sparked through the suit's silver wiring. The creature dropped to the ground, still as a stone.

Aubrey rubbed his eyes, relieved by the opportunity to close them.

"It hasn't disappeared," remarked Jordana.

"Maybe it's dead," said Magnos.

Aubrey closed his eyes and stared at the creature.

"Maybe it's not a ghost," said Buzz.

"I can't see it behind my eyelids now," said Aubrey.

"Look." Jordana pointed at it. "It's shaking."

"No, it's not." Buzz leaned over the battery. "The suit seems to be working just fine."

"Look at its head," insisted Jordana.

Everyone looked at the back of the creature's bald head, now ringed with the electric visor. The head trembled, and the flap-like ears wiggled against its temples.

"Is the suit electrocuting it?" Jordana leaned away and cringed.

Buzz shook his head, staring at the prone beast. "Shouldn't be."

"She's right." Magnos crouched down. "It is shaking." Magnos edged his index finger toward its fan-like ear. With a quick jab, he poked it.

The creature flung its arm next to its head, and then the arm dropped flatly into the grass.

"See! It's still alive," reported Buzz.

"I'm not sure *alive* is the right word," remarked Rodriqa.

Aubrey opened his eyes. Annoyed by everyone's trepidation, he marched around Buzz toward the head of the beast. Kneeling down in front of it, he looked at Magnos and said, "Help me flip it over."

Aubrey slid his hands underneath the creature's shoulders, Magnos gripped it around its waist, and Buzz circled each hand around a hoof.

"On the count of three," said Aubrey. Magnos tightened his hold. Buzz leaned back and said, "Mind the battery." Rodriqa stepped forward to watch, and Jordana spun around and faced the road.

"One. Two. Three."

The three boys flipped the creature over. Magnos and Buzz jumped out of the way. Aubrey hovered over its face.

The creature lay still on its back, its torso arched upward with the battery underneath it. Its eyes were shut, and its head quivered. Its nostrils flared as air moved in short bursts, and its mouth was crinkled closed.

"Are you okay?" Aubrey placed his hand on the creature's temple.

The creature opened his eyes and glared up at Aubrey. Aubrey marveled at its large, green irises, which held pinpoint black pupils.

"I'm stuck," whined the creature.

"What did it say?" Rodriqa peered over top of it.

"I'm not sure." Buzz scratched his head. "I can't tell if it's speaking or just breathing loudly."

Aubrey thought for a moment with his head turned to the side. "I think he said, 'I'm stuck.'"

Jordana turned back around. The five friends studied each other's faces.

Buzz shot his arms into the air victoriously. "We did it!"

"Did what?" asked Rodriqa.

"It can't vanish…like it was doing before. The suit is containing it here in reality." Buzz puffed out his chest and rubbed his hands together. "I'm so brilliant, I even surprise myself sometimes."

Rodriqa rolled her eyes. "I just hope your brilliance doesn't get us killed someday."

"Um, we need to move," shuddered Jordana.

"Why?" asked Buzz.

"Because we're gonna have company soon." Jordana pointed to the house on whose lawn they we're standing. Every window of the second story lit up. "We need to move," said Magnos.

"We can't just leave it here," demanded Rodriqa.

"Where are we gonna put it?" asked Jordana.

"I'm not bringing that thing in the house," insisted Rodriqa.

The front porch light of the house flashed on.

"Shhh," sputtered Jordana.

Aubrey put his finger to his mouth. "I've got an idea."

Trembling under a halo of light, Aubrey fiddled with a ring of keys, jiggling one after another into the lock of the front double doors to Ray Gene's Smart Mart & Finer Diner. The nighttime seemed even darker with his four friends pressing him from behind.

"Are you sure those are the right keys?" asked Rodriqa over her shoulder. She and Jordana stood in front of Aubrey, Magnos, and Buzz, keeping a lookout.

"Yes," muttered Aubrey.

"Why do you have keys to Mr. Jennings's store?" Buzz shone a flashlight over Aubrey's shoulder.

"He asked me to watch the store since he was closing it." Aubrey hobbled back and forth to stay in the beam.

"Why couldn't he watch it himself?" grunted Magnos. He clamped the creature, wrapped in the Elemag suit, to his chest as it tried to wriggle free.

"I don't know." Aubrey wiggled another key in and out of the lock. "He retired, I think."

"This is a bad idea," whispered Rodriqa.

"Then you think of something," snapped Aubrey.

Rodriqa crossed her arms and tapped her flashlight against her chin.

"It's not a bad plan," said Buzz. "If we can just get inside."

"But what if Mr. Jennings comes back?" asked Jordana.

"Car!" shouted Rodriqa.

"Got it!" said Aubrey. The key clicked, and the door snapped open.

The five of them barreled inside. Buzz pulled the door closed and locked it.

Rodriqa handed Aubrey her flashlight. Aubrey directed them to the right-hand corner. Opening a small door, he angled the flashlight down into the staircase. A lump swelled in his throat as he stepped toward the basement. Warily, Aubrey looked back at his friends. Every eye, including the creature's, was glaring at him.

Aubrey sighed and raced to the bottom. A herd of footsteps followed him down. He searched the room with his flashlight. Everything was unchanged from yesterday. One by one his friends walked into the basement.

"Yuck," murmured Jordana. "What died down here?"

Rodriqa waved her hand in front of her nose. "It smells like old people."

"Be nice," said Aubrey. "I think Mr. Jennings used to stay down here a lot when the store was open."

"Rhizopus," commented Buzz.

"Rye-what-us?" asked Rodriqa.

Buzz sneered at her. "It smells like rhizopus. Common bread mold."

"Gross." Jordana pinched her nose.

Buzz raked his shoes through the shag carpet. "I'm digging this floor." He stretched out his finger. A lightning-blue spark shot from his hand to Rodriqa's arm.

Rodriqa squealed. She smacked Buzz's hand. "If you *ever* do that again…"

"Guys, I don't think I can hold this thing much longer." Sweat had moistened Magnos's sideburns, and rivulets trailed down his cheeks. Aubrey trotted over toward the poker table in the middle of the room. Searching across papers and books, he found the bottle-shaped lamp. He reached underneath it and flipped on the light. A dim, orange glow flushed throughout the room. Aubrey took a second glance at the Circle of Circles on the lamp's bottom and then refocused on Magnos and the creature. "There's a freezer in the back." Aubrey pointed toward the stainless steel wall. "I think we can store it in there for now."

Magnos scuttled up to the freezer. Aubrey followed him and yanked on the large metal handle. The door snapped open and a blast of frigid air filled the room. Magnos rushed inside. The creature clawed at him. Magnos balled up its torso and launched it into the corner.

The creature crashed into a wire shelf. The shelf overturned, and several large pots and cardboard boxes dropped from the shelving and scattered across the frostbitten floor.

Magnos spun around, dashed out of the freezer, swung into Aubrey, and they both fell on the door. The door slammed with a loud clank.

The creature burst upward, almost instantly, was at the door, its head bobbing up and down behind the slim window above the handle.

"Let me out! Let me out!" The creature shook the handle from inside. The door shimmied wildly, but didn't open.

Magnos pulled up himself and Aubrey. "Good," murmured Magnos. "It's locked in."

Buzz, Jordana, and Rodriqa cautiously crept behind Magnos and Aubrey.

The creature backed up in the freezer and spun in circles as if it was chasing its tail, stretching to reach the battery on its lower back with its short arms.

"Now what do we do with it?" asked Rodriqa.

"We should sleep on it," answered Buzz. "We'll come up with a plan in the morning."

"What if someone else finds it?" asked Rodriqa.

"Hopefully, they'll leave it alone," muttered Aubrey.

They huddled around the door and peered through the window. The creature dropped to its back and was scraping the battery along the icy floor.

"Look," said Buzz. "It made a snow angel."

"I wonder if it'll freeze to death," asked Jordana.

"It's obviously not of this world," chuckled Buzz. "I doubt temperature is much of a concern."

Suddenly, the creature hopped up on its backward haunches, wrapped its arms around its torso, and shivered. "It's so cold. It's so cold. It's so cold."

Jordana's hand covered her mouth. She wrapped her hand around Magnos. "See? It is cold!"

Aubrey shook its head. "I don't think so. I think it can hear us."

The creature curled its lip at Aubrey and stopped shivering. It looked around the room. It saw one of the cooking pots and lunged for it.

"It's kinda cute," said Jordana.

Aubrey furrowed his brow. "Yeah, it's cute…until it tries to kill you."

The creature beat its back with the cooking pot.

"Hope that battery holds," said Magnos.

"Oh, it will," said Buzz. "It has a miniature double carabineer-type lock. It won't come out without someone lifting it out. And it'll take two or three tries at that."

Aubrey closed his eyes. The phosphenes swam behind his eyelids. The colors faded and darkness dimmed his view.

"We should go," whispered Rodriqa.

Aubrey's eyes popped open, and he stared at the creature. "We can't. I have to get Solluna back."

"We can," replied Rodriqa. "We know where Solluna is. So we'll get it back."

"Maybe it'll poop it out," said Buzz.

Rodriqa grabbed Aubrey by the arm and turned him around. "Besides, I have a feeling if Mr. Miller has outlawed our suits, we have bigger worries."

"Where is it!" demanded Ms. Thistlewood, her bright red hair tussling in the breeze from outside. She turned away from the window atop the massive, hollow oak tree and scowled at Matsinstrus. Marching toward her crystalline marble fireplace, her shapely figure swayed with each pointed step.

"But I-I-I brought you the stone," wheezed the blackened skeleton, lying prostrate on the wooden floor. Trembling, he stretched out his arm and opened his palm. The bright orange glow from Tartan's white stone seeped between his boney fingers.

"That wasn't your only task!" The woman glowered at Matsinstrus. The fire in the hearth raged. The firelight glinted in her pale greens eyes.

"But it was the most important," protested the skeleton. "The eclipse is tomorrow!"

Ms. Thistlewood leaned over and ripped the white stone from his hands. Examining its glow while the small light orbited around it, her tight face relaxed at its marvel.

"Where is Solluna?"

Matsinstrus scurried away from her. "Aubrey has it. I just didn't have the opportunity—"

"You've only fulfilled *half* of your purpose!" Ms. Thistlewood stormed into the middle of the room. "So you shall be treated with only half of the kindness you deserve."

"I can get it," insisted Matsinstrus. "I need more time."

"Time is not an option."

The skeleton choked up vapors of smoke, which billowed from its ribcage. "I can't blow my cover. The time has to be right, and it will be right. I will get Solluna."

"Yes, you will, or I will not suffer you any further." Thistlewood sat down in her wooden chair.

Scratching echoed from outside the window.

"You are not my only alternative," grumbled Ms. Thistlewood.

Brawny paws with sharpened claws emerged from outside and gripped the windowsill. Whimperfidget crested the ledge of the window, his cream-and-charcoal-colored fur twisted and spiked from his inflated torso. His tail flopped wildly from side to side. His eyes gleamed bright red.

Ms. Thistlewood waved the cat toward her. Whimperfidget leapt from the window onto her lap.

"That's a good kitty." She caressed his fur, and the cat purred through a hollow growl. "I bet my sweet is hungry."

Whimperfidget howled, and his tail straightened.

Ms. Thistlewood reached for her wrist and turned the dial on her brown sandstone watch. The watch opened with a hiss. The blackest hues of writhing midnight spewed from inside it as shimmering serpents wiggled into the air. With a jolt, a dozen spirit shards jumped from the watch into Whimperfidget's eyes, disappearing into the cat. Ms. Thistlewood closed her watch.

Whimperfidget squeezed his eyes together, and his head shuddered. The feline uttered a truncated screech and trembled violently. Within moments, the skin of the cat stretched, and his hair lengthened. He dropped to the floor, fitfully writhing.

Ms. Thistlewood scratched the cat under its chin. Now the size of a bobcat, Whimperfidget heaved haggardly.

"Teach my prodigy a lesson he won't forget." Ms. Thistlewood stood up and walked across the room.

A brightened red glow flashed from the cat's eyes. Whimperfidget rolled onto all fours and hunkered down its shoulders, ready to pounce.

Matsinstrus raised his boney arms to shield himself.

Ms. Thistlewood glared at the skeleton on the floor as she strode by him. "I have given you a gift, Matsinstrus. Hopefully, my trust in you won't be wasted." She stepped onto a spiral staircase at the end of the room. Whimperfidget leapt toward Matsinstrus. Matsinstrus cried in agony.

Stepping down the gnarled wooden rungs, Ms. Thistlewood relished the sounds of his pain, a grin creasing her lips.

Hurried plodding scampered up the stairs toward her. She stopped, and her smile flattened. She glanced over the railing. Two familiar forms raced up the steps.

"Ms. Thistlewood! Ms. Thistlewood!" cried Ned Kluggard as he ran up the spiral staircase, clutching the top of his baggy uniform pants. Fred was right behind, his lanky frame nudging his brother forward. They stopped, out of breath, meeting Ms. Thistlewood with their eyes to her knees.

"Yes," she replied.

"Don't be mad," Ned Kluggard begged. "Please, don't be mad."

"Why would I be mad?" She raised her chin, motioning for the brothers to address her face, not her legs.

"Someone is here," replied Ned. He flinched as he spoke.

Ms. Thistlewood pursed her lips. "What's the point of having guards if they don't *guard* me!"

"But wait," stammered Ned. "This person wants your help and says they can help you."

"Person?" she questioned.

Ned glanced at Fred. Fred looked down.

"I don't know if it's a man or a woman," whimpered Ned.

"And why not?"

Ned cupped his hand to his mouth and whispered, "They're in disguise."

Ms. Thistlewood rolled her eyes. "Remind me to have you bathe Whimperfidget later."

Ned and Fred nodded eagerly.

She placed her hands together and then parted them. Ned and Fred broke apart, both leaning over the balcony as she stepped through them down the stairs.

The staircase ended at a large room inside the bottom of the massive oak tree. Several wooden chairs and two small tables rested on a dirt floor. Mud-caked roots lined the walls, and another crystalline marble fireplace burned with a small orange blaze.

Ms. Thistlewood gazed at the figure standing in front of her red front door. The individual was concealed in a black hooded cloak, which only allowed exposure of the person's fingertips and boots. The person stood quietly, head down, feet together, hands crossed.

"May I help you?" Ms. Thistlewood crossed her arms over her chest.

The figure nodded. Raising a hand to their mouth, the figure spoke through a small round device. "I know who you are." The voice was warped and electronic, barely distinguishable as human.

Ms. Thistlewood smirked. "Magnolia Thistlewood. Pleasure." She nodded. "And who are you?"

The device clicked. "I know what you're after."

Ms. Thistlewood squinted her eyes. "Please don't waste my time. My patience has been worn mightily thin today."

"Solluna is no longer a book."

Ms. Thistlewood's eyes widened. She glared at the hooded figure and popped her neck. "What do you want?"

"To be like you. To be your servant." The person knelt on one knee and bowed.

Ms. Thistlewood strode toward the cloaked person. She examined the figure's features. Placing her fingers under the individual's chin, she tilted the person's head upward, pulling the figure's face toward the firelight. The head jerked backward as if shocked by a spark.

Ms. Thistlewood sighed. "Finally, someone with some sense in this Clockmaker-forsaken town." She tapped her tongue against her teeth. "This just might work." Ms. Thistlewood walked away and stood in front of the fireplace. "Hope you're not afraid of the dark."

"No," the device clicked. "I love the shadow."

"Wonderful," she replied. "But I have a favor to ask first."

THE DOCTOR IS IN

Friday.

The electronic bell chimed overhead. Shirt untucked and flapping behind him, Aubrey raced down the Lake Julian High School hallway with his book bag swinging off his shoulder.

He rounded a corner. Mr. Vandereff's door edged into view. It was closed. Aubrey sprinted. Mr. Vandereff had a habit of locking his door once class had started.

Falling against the door, Aubrey clutched the handle and yanked it counterclockwise. It turned. Aubrey sighed. He pulled open the door and rushed into class.

Aubrey stopped and looked around. The desks had returned to their usual gridded arrangement. All his classmates were seated, but many of the students were turned toward a single person in the classroom. At the front, the lab bench and blackboard were empty. The orrery was gone.

McCrayden Miller sat in her desk, head high and blonde curls bouncing as she spoke. "You simply must see it for yourself. The Rock-U-Quarium will quickly become the most popular spot in Lake Julian." Murmuring whispers cascaded across the room.

Aubrey lowered his head and grimaced. He pulled his book bag around to his chest and walked to his desk.

"Is it still there?" whispered Buzz.

Aubrey dropped in his desk to the right of Buzz and pulled out his textbook. "Yeah. I checked the freezer before I came."

"What do you think it is?" asked Buzz.

Aubrey shrugged. "It's not a ghost."

"Are you okay?" asked Jordana to his left.

Aubrey glanced over. She was staring at him with a wispy smile.

Aubrey's heart lightened. He could stare at her face forever. "I'm good."

"I was worried about you," replied Jordana, her honey-colored glasses teetering at the end of her slender nose. "You'd looked pretty beaten up last night."

"Nah," Aubrey said. "I'm all right."

"You simply must go!" crooned McCrayden over the din of the class-room. "You'll never have as much fun anywhere else ever again. It opens to the general public tonight!"

"She won't stop talking," grumbled Jordana.

"I wish someone would shove a sock in her craw," groaned Buzz.

Magnos turned around from the seat in front of Aubrey. "That's McCrayden. Center of attention, even when the center is someplace else."

Jordana smirked. "Center of obnoxious."

Aubrey laughed.

McCrayden overheard him, turned, and scowled.

Aubrey sunk into his seat. "Something's not right."

"I agree," said Buzz. "Mr. Vandereff is never late."

Aubrey wagged his head. "I mean with everything that happened last night."

"What do you mean?" asked Jordana.

Aubrey stared at his desk. "That creature isn't a ghost, but when it attacked me, it felt like it was sucking the life out of me."

"We've run into that before," scoffed Buzz.

"But only from Ms. Thistlewood. No one else." Aubrey rubbed his chin. "And why was I able to keep it from vanishing into the spirit world? I've never been able to do that before."

"Maybe your eye thingy is getting stronger," replied Jordana.

Aubrey blushed. "And why did it nearly kill me for Solluna?"

"It's a freak of nature," muttered Magnos.

"I think it's doing you a favor," whispered Jordana. "Solluna has always been problematic."

"Even more problematic," interjected Buzz. "What happens when Mr. Jennings finds the creature?"

The door creaked open. The schoolroom banter hushed. Everyone faced forward.

Principal Lequoia stepped into the classroom. He scanned the desks and then walked toward the front of the blackboard.

He placed his crossed hands on the lab bench as he cleared his throat. "Children, Mr. Vandereff is unexpectedly absent this morning. However, I have found an eager adjunct, who is willing to enrich your learning time."

Principal Lequoia cleared his throat again and looked down at the lab bench. "Your substitute this morning will be Dr. Gatchiri from the International Institute of Illness Investigation and Intervention."

With her white, straight hair bobbing as she walked, Dr. Gatchiri marched through the door, carrying a large suitcase. She was dressed in an olive green pantsuit and matching stiletto heels. Her tiny frame swung the suitcase onto the lab bench. Principal Lequoia flinched and took a step backward.

"I'm here to teach you a valuable lesson." Only Dr. Gatchiri's head appeared above the case on the bench. "Skills every person should know. A tool set no growing mind should be without."

She snapped open the case. Out lurched a plastic, flesh-colored manne-quin. Every student in the class jumped in their seats. Dr. Gatchiri grabbed a piece of chalk and scrawled three letters on the blackboard as she said them aloud.

"C. P. R."

Jordana slid her tray onto the lunch table. "You should have heard McCrayden gloating about he Rock-U-Quarium this morning." She sat in her chair and scooted forward. "You would have thought she owned it."

Rodriqa plopped her tray on the table and sat down. "What a glamor glitch."

"I know." Jordana peeled open her yogurt. "Someone needs to bring her down a notch."

"Her and her whole family." Aubrey walked up to the table and dropped into the seat next to Jordana.

Rodriqa leaned in. "What about that thing we caught last night? Is it still in Mr. Jennings's freezer?"

Aubrey slumped his elbows on the table. "It was this morning."

"How long do you think we can keep it down there?" Rodriqa asked.

Aubrey shrugged. "Until it breaks free. The freezer is a mess. We have to get it out of there before Mr. Jennings stops by."

"Where did it come from?" Magnos pulled a chair to the table and sat next to Aubrey.

Aubrey rubbed his temples. "Wanna hear something strange?"

"What's strange at this point?" replied Rodriqa. Aubrey sighed through a nod. "I think I saw it at the Rock-U-Quarium last night."

"What?" Rodriqa snapped her beaded braids. "Why didn't you tell us?"

Aubrey raised his hands. "I didn't know it was going to attack me."

Jordana slid her honey-colored glasses up her nose. "Where in the Rock-U-Quarium?"

Aubrey scanned the cafeteria, searching for eavesdroppers. He noticed McCrayden and several other rowdies talking at their usual table in the middle of the room. "Remember the two gentlemen sitting next to the entrance to the kitchen, on the benches?"

"Whatever you saw last night, it was no gentleman," scoffed Rodriqa.

Jordana and Magnos thought to themselves and shook their heads.

Aubrey dropped his hands in his lap. "Anyway, that's where I think I saw it for the first time."

Jordana nudged Rodriqa. "Guess who we saw this morning!"

Rodriqa took a bite of her sandwich. "Who?"

Jordana eyed Magnos and Aubrey knowingly.

Magnos laughed. "Dr. Gatchiri."

Rodriqa's eyes widened. "Here? In school?"

Magnos nodded. "Mr. Vandereff was out. So Principal Lequoia brought in Dr. Gatchiri to teach us CPR."

"That's some serious creepitude," said Rodriqa, chewing her food slowly.

"I don't think it was a coincidence she came to our class," added Jordana.

"She had us and Buzz grouped together," said Aubrey, "and she kept asking us questions while everyone else was doing their skill stations."

"Like what?" asked Rodriqa.

"She wanted to know our spring break plans," smirked Jordana.

"And what our childhoods were like," grumbled Magnos.

Jordana smiled. "Fortunately, Buzz kept blathering on about the million moth metamorphosis."

"No matter what she asked, he kept going back to that." Magnos chuckled. "She got so frustrated."

Rodriqa straightened up. "Speak of the devil."

The other three looked forward. Buzz approached the table, trembling from head to toe.

"What's wrong?" asked Jordana.

"Did you see something?" asked Magnos.

Aubrey stood up and raced around the table. "I think he's about to have a seizure."

Rodriqa looked him up and down. "Nah, I think he's just excited."

Aubrey grabbed Buzz by the arm. "Are you okay?"

Shivering like a puppy at the vet, Buzz turned toward Aubrey. "I am so pumped!"

"See, I told ya." Rodriqa crunched on a carrot. "He's overjoyed. Spring break is just a few hours away."

Buzz immediately stopped shaking and frowned at Rodriqa. "The Poage County Science Fair starts in five hours, forty-six minutes, and twenty-six seconds!" Buzz fell into a seat, opposite his friends.

"Oh," mumbled Jordana and Magnos.

Aubrey snickered and walked back to his seat. "That's right. How could we forget?"

"Yeah," scoffed Rodriqa. "How could we possibly forget? Not like there's much else on our plates."

"You don't understand," said Buzz. "Everything is working out perfectly!"

"You finally settled on the best invention to enter?" Aubrey sat back down between Jordana and Magnos.

"Not only that," replied Buzz. "But with the annular solar eclipse occurring at the exact same time as my ten-minute presentation, it's gonna be epic!"

Magnos's eyes darted from side to side. "I don't get it."

"You'll have to come to see." Buzz reached over and grabbed half of Rodriqa's sandwich. "I haven't lost a science fair yet." He bit a mouthful from her sandwich.

Rodriqa gritted her teeth. "That's because you've only won the *only* fair you've ever entered."

Buzz shrugged. "Still counts." He gulped down his half-chewed food and took another bite. "You all are gonna be there, right?"

Magnos, Jordana, and Rodriqa glanced at each other.

Aubrey grinned. "Wouldn't miss it. Besides, watching Bates Hindenberg go all green after you won last year was definitely worth seeing."

"Sure," said Magnos. "I'll come."

Rodriqa sighed. "I'll be there. But I might be a little late. I have a family meeting. My brother is back in town from college, and my dad wants us to all 'regroup.' Whatever that means."

"Yeah, me too," said Jordana. "My dad wanted to speak to me after school."

Crash!

The lunch table shuddered. All five friends wrenched backward in their seats. Teton Bailston landed with his face on the table, scuttling Rodriqa's lunch tray off onto the floor.

"You won't believe," said Teton, spastically pushing himself up. "You won't believe it!"

"Oh, I believe it," scowled Rodriqa. "You just ruined my lunch!"

Regaining his posture, Teton brushed down his tank top. "No! What I saw at the Circle of Circles cemetery last night."

Aubrey's searched Teton's face. "What?"

Teton reset his sunglasses on his nose. "I was at McCrayden's place last night, and I stayed a little too late, if you know what I'm sayin'. I tried callin' a few of my Mafisito bros to come get me, but it was too late." He chuckled arrogantly.

Rodriqa rolled her eyes. Magnos clenched his jaw.

Teton cleared his throat. "Anyway, I was walking home, and I decided to take a shortcut after I had passed the dam. So I walked across the hill toward school."

Aubrey and Buzz leaned in.

Teton popped his neck. "Once I got to the top of the hill, everything got really dark. Like all the stars had blacked out." He squatted and whispered. "And I started hearing all these bizarre noises."

Teton rested his hands on the table. "I thought someone was playin' a trick so I hid in the woods. You know, planning to scare them before they scared me."

"What did you see?" asked Buzz.

"Some…some creature." Teton grappled air as he attempted to describe it. "It looked like a cross between a dog and a bat."

"What?" asked Rodriqa with a smirk on her face.

"I'm serious," insisted Teton. "I've never seen anything like it before. It was crawling around on all fours like it was stalking something."

"Did it come from one of the graves?" Aubrey asked.

Teton shook his head. "The graves aren't there anymore. It's a giant pit filled with sand."

Aubrey's eyes widened.

"Was it after you?" asked Jordana.

Teton stood up. "I didn't stay to find out. I've seen all the horror movies. I know what happens to guys like me who go investigating." Teton slid his sunglasses down a bit and winked at Jordana. "I'll leave the investigating to you all." He turned and walked away.

Buzz scrunched up next to Rodriqa. "What do you think he saw?"

"Don't know. Don't care," replied Rodriqa. "We've got our own problems."

"But what if what he saw is related to the creature from last night?" Aubrey asked.

"There's no way to know," said Jordana.

"Unless we investigate," added Buzz with a wily grin.

"I think we're already in deep," returned Rodriqa, frowning at Buzz.

"Especially with our parents on our backs," agreed Aubrey.

"But in a few hours, we'll be on spring break." Buzz propped his arms up behind his head. "And after I win the science fair tonight, we'll have an entire week to figure it all out."

⬥

"It's okay, Jon. I forgive you."

Across the cafeteria, McCrayden Miller patted Jon Harney on the shoulder. She rearranged the food on her tray, pushing her apple away and separating her broccoli from her carrots.

Jon smiled crookedly at her, his bloated and bruised upper lip straining to curve against its own swelling. His left eyelid was black and swollen so tightly that only a sliver of eyeball was exposed. "Thank you," he muttered hoarsely.

"You're such a sweet soul," said Vidalia Arsvine, who was sitting next to McCrayden. "So kind and generous."

"I know how hard peer pressure can be." McCrayden chewed on a sprig of broccoli. "Daddy says we all face moments of weakness, but it's only the weak who take more than a moment to get over it."

Jon nodded. He lifted a spoonful of applesauce to his mouth and took a bite. Half of the applesauce dribbled onto his tray.

"Hey, babe." Teton slid a chair from the next table and pulled it in between McCrayden and Jon. "What's up?" He plopped down. Jon leaned away from Teton.

"Jon and I were just making up," McCrayden replied.

"Good deal," replied Teton. He turned toward Jon and flexed his biceps. "Don't worry, little guy. I'm not gonna hit ya." Teton smiled and then jerked his hands toward Jon's face. Jon flinched. A tear dripped from his bruised eye. "Not today anyway," mumbled Teton.

Teton turned toward McCrayden and whispered in her ear. "I put the lox in the hen's croup."

McCrayden rolled her eyes and continued eating. "You mean the fox in the chicken coop."

"Whatever," said Teton. He grabbed her apple and bit into it. "I did what you asked."

McCrayden smiled. "Good boy."

FAMILY TIDE

Rodriqa raced her bicycle down Dalton Circle and coasted into her driveway. She unfastened her helmet as she pedaled the last few yards into the garage. Hopping off her seat, she propped up her bike on its kickstand and rushed toward the back porch with her gym bag over her shoulder.

She trotted up the back steps, and the door opened.

"What's up, sprout?" A tall young man with a shaved head and dark skin stood in the doorway.

"Robert!" Rodriqa dropped her gym bag as she reached up and hugged her older brother. He leaned down and squeezed her. "How's life?"

"I'm so glad you're home!"

"It's good to be here." He nuzzled his chin on top of her head. "You're getting taller."

Rodriqa took a step back and straightened her shoulders. "I'm gonna catch you some day."

Robert smiled. "You just might." He turned around and walked into the house. Rodriqa launched herself after him, and he clumsily caught her in a piggyback.

"You might catch me in weight too," Robert grunted.

Rodriqa slapped him lightly on the cheek. "Hasn't college taught you anything? Never mention a girl's weight!"

Robert laughed. Bobbing through a small hallway, they lumbered into a well-lit kitchen, furnished with stainless steel appliances, granite countertops, maple cabinets, and hardwood floors.

A slender woman with a green silk scarf tied around her neck, stood in front of the sink, skinning carrots. Braided tightly, her dark hair draped down her back. She hummed quietly as she glanced between the sink and the window in front of her.

"Hi, Mom." Rodriqa hopped off Robert's back.

"How was school?" Mrs. Auerbach waved at Rodriqa with peeler in hand.

Rodriqa walked over, picked up an unskinned carrot, and chomped at its end. "The usual. Heinous and exciting all at the same time."

Mrs. Auerbach chuckled.

"Dinner smells amazing." Robert leaned over the stove and smelled the aromas steaming from several boiling pots.

"It's your favorite," replied Mrs. Auerbach. "I bet you haven't eaten a meal that didn't consist of french fries or pizza since Christmas."

Robert and Rodriqa glanced at each other and grinned.

"So when's this family meeting?" Rodriqa asked. "I promised Buzz I'd go support him at the science fair this evening."

"What's Buzz invented this year?" asked Robert.

"Who knows?" Rodriqa rolled her eyes. "Something crazy, I'm sure. All I know, if he doesn't beat Bates Hindenburg, I'm gonna have to hear about it till next year."

"Make sure you stay inside this evening," directed Mrs. Auerbach.

"Why?" Rodriqa bit down on her carrot again.

Mrs. Auerbach edged her shoulder toward the end of the counter. "Because of the solar flare today."

Rodriqa examined to where her mother pointed. A copy of the *Lake Julian Mountain Lyre* lay rumpled Bolded headlines read: "Solar Flare during a Solar Eclipse: How to Avoid the Tan of the Century."

Robert shuffled over to the corner, picked up the newspaper, and summarized bits of the article aloud. "They're predicting a coronal mass ejection."

Rodriqa sneered. "A what?"

"A coronal mass ejection," continued Robert. "It's a huge blast of energy from the sun. The paper says it might hit the earth today during the eclipse." He scanned several more paragraphs. "Says people should stay indoors."

Rodriqa rolled her eyes. "I wasn't planning on being outside anyway. The science fair is in the high school gym."

"Good," said a deep voice from the back of the kitchen. Mr. Auerbach ducked as he passed through the threshold.

Rodriqa waved at him and smiled. "Hi, Dad."

Mr. Auerbach walked up to his daughter and kissed her on the cheek. "We've been monitoring the atmospheric changes at the dam. The solar flare is bound to upset a few things for a couple days."

Rodriqa hugged her father. "How do they know a solar flare is coming?"

Robert dropped the newspaper back on the counter. "Satellites have been monitoring sun spot activity." He opened the pantry and looked inside. "They watch for twisting magnetic fields in the sun's corona. When the fields are wound too tight, they snap, releasing tons of energy and gas, i.e. a coronal mass ejection." He pulled out an opened bag of potato chips and scraped the bottom for a few stragglers.

Mr. Auerbach looked at his son and winked. "Good to know all that money for tuition is paying off."

Mrs. Auerbach laughed as she dropped the last of the carrots into a steamer.

Mr. Auerbach ambled over to the sink and looked at Mrs. Auerbach. "Should we talk now?"

"Now's probably good." Mrs. Auerbach dried off her hands. "Dinner should be ready in half an hour or so."

Mr. Auerbach nodded and glanced at Robert. Robert rested the potato chips on the counter and looked down at the floor.

"So what are we talking about?" Rodriqa looked between her mom and dad.

Mrs. Auerbach turned around, crossed her arms, and sighed. "Babe, we need to talk about you."

Rodriqa's jaw halted in midchew. "Why?"

"I got a call from Mr. Miller today." Mr. Auerbach rubbed his forehead. "Did you and your friends really cause fifty thousand dollars in damage to his house?"

"No way!" Rodriqa swallowed her partially chewed carrot. "It was just the foyer that was damaged, and it wasn't our fault!"

Veins popped out of Mr. Auerbach's temple. "It was more than the foyer."

Mrs. Auerbach touched her husband's shoulder. "Jamison, we all know Mr. Miller is prone to exaggeration." She focused on Rodriqa. "Honey, what happened the other night?"

"What always happens." Rodriqa shook her head and looked down. "We were hired to find a ghost and get rid of it. There was a little collateral damage, but in the end, we did what we were asked to do."

"A little?" Mr. Auerbach raised his voice. "You nearly destroyed a house."

"No, we didn't," insisted Rodriqa. "The ghost did."

Mr. Auerbach clenched his jaw. Mrs. Auerbach gently touched his chest, and he turned around and walked to the other side of the kitchen.

Mrs. Auerbach took a few steps toward her daughter and squeezed her arm. "Why do you think it was a ghost?"

Rodriqa furrowed her brow. "Because it was huge and transparent, and it tried to kill us."

"No one believes you." Robert looked up and glared at Rodriqa.

Taking a step backward, Rodriqa cocked her hands on her hips. "You're in on this too?"

"The family meeting was his idea," gruffed their father.

Rodriqa popped her neck. "I don't understand why, all of a sudden, me fighting ghosts is a problem."

"Because before two nights ago, I thought it was a silly game." Mr. Auerbach pounded his fist against the counter top and turned around. "Now I can see it's civilly disruptive and a flagrant disregard for the law!"

Rodriqa bit her lip. "Why are you all picking on me?"

"Because you're too old to be playing make-believe." Robert walked over to his sister. "You're in high school now. You can't keep acting like this."

"Acting like what?" snapped Rodriqa, the beaded braids in her hair swishing about her neck. "Like I'm the only one in this family who can really see what's going on?" Rodriqa turned back to her mother. "Ask the Creightonys! Ask Mrs. Gungandeep! They'll tell you. There are ghosts in Lake Julian!"

"No one believes them either," grumbled Mr. Auerbach.

"Then…then ask Mr. Taylor," stammered Rodriqa. "He'll tell you exactly what we're fighting! He saw it last fall! He believes Aubrey!"

"Everyone knows that whole family is crazy," murmured Mr. Auerbach.

Mrs. Auerbach gave her husband a stern glance. "The Taylors are having a tough time right now. Things aren't going well for Mr. Taylor at the plant ever since the incident. Mrs. Taylor hasn't shown signs of improving in quite sometime."

"And Gaetan is a grade A toad thrower," added Robert.

Mrs. Auerbach frowned at Robert. "Aubrey's probably the most stable one of them all right now."

"Stable, no," returned Rodriqa. "Keenly insightful, yes."

"Even if Aubrey is the normal one," said Mr. Auerbach. "He's probably just doing all of this for attention." He scratched his palm as he glared at Rodriqa. "What I don't understand is why you got sucked into all this insanity."

Rodriqa stomped her foot. "Because it's real! Because there are things in this world no one can explain. There are creatures out there who mean to harm us, and if we don't stop it, who knows what will happen?"

"That's exactly right," said Robert. "If you all just stopped what you're doing, who knows what would happen."

Rodriqa huffed and stared at the ceiling.

"Maybe you wouldn't be a vandal anymore," Robert continued.

Their father crossed his arms and turned sideways, away from Rodriqa. "Maybe you'd be the daughter I raised you to be."

Mrs. Auerbach sighed and took a step forward. "Driqa, this has to stop. You're better than this."

Rodriqa looked down. Her eyelids swelled with tears. She desperately wanted to turn into her ghostly appearance, but the spirit of the Tsul'kalu was dormant. She wasn't in danger. Her guardian form never awakened on command, and that made her even angrier. "I am the daughter you raised me to be." She raked her tears away with the back of her hand. "If you could only be there to see what we do."

"That will never happen." Mr. Auerbach glanced at his wife.

Mrs. Auerbach turned toward her husband and walked to his side. "Except for school, you will no longer be allowed to see your friends."

"What?" Rodriqa raised her hands. "That's not fair!"

"You need some time away from them," Robert said.

"You're punishing me for standing by my friends?" Rodriqa clenched her fists. "You're punishing me for standing up for what's right?"

Mr. Auerbach glowered at his daughter. "Repeatedly attracting the attention of the police and destruction of personal property are not values I taught you."

Rodriqa shook her head. "Maybe not. But you did teach me to fight for what I believe in." Rodriqa twisted her beaded braids into a large knot. "I believe in what I've seen. I believe in my friends." She turned and ran out of the kitchen.

"Rodriqa! We're not finished!" hollered Mr. Auerbach.

"You might not be, but I am." Rodriqa ran down the small hallway toward the back door.

Mrs. Auerbach raced after her. "Driqa, where are you going?"

"To be with those who judge me for what I do." Rodriqa flung open the backdoor and scrambled outside. "Not what they see." She slammed the door behind her.

BLOOD IS THICKER THAN BARTER

With several books pulled to her chest and her book bag draped over her shoulder, Jordana raced into her uncle's empty garage. Carefully wrapping her fingers around a doorknob on the right-hand wall, she eased it open and leaned her ear to the crack. Distantly, she heard her father and another man, whom she didn't recognize, talking upstairs.

Jordana slunk through the door and nudged it shut. Touching the steps with the ends of her toes, she snuck up a set of carpeted stairs, still eavesdropping on the louder portions of her father's conversation.

Several steps from the top, she stopped and leaned forward, peering around the corner into her father's bedroom. She could see the visitor standing in front of her dad, who sat in his wheelchair, next to his bed.

At the top of the stairs, Jordana leaned against the opposite wall and edged her thin frame into the hallway. She looked out into the front yard. She couldn't see her uncle's car. Quickly, she spun around and headed for the back of the house.

Jordana drifted around another corner to a door, inset with a window. Looking inside, she examined her uncle's small library. Books of varying colors and sizes lined the shelves on all four walls, and a varnished wooden desk occupied most of the center of the room. Except for the library's accouterments, the room was empty. Most importantly, her uncle wasn't there.

She placed her book bag on the floor and rested the books in her arms on top of her bag. Using her books as a stepping stool, Jordana reached to the top of the door's frame. She ran the tips of her fingers along the trim. A tiny brass key tumbled to the floor.

Jordana hopped down. She listened for noises down the hall. The conversation from her father's bedroom continued undisturbed. She picked up the key, unlocked her uncle's library, and opened the door.

Nudging her schoolbooks inside with her feet, Jordana walked inside and pulled the door closed.

She trotted to the desk and plopped down in the leather swivel chair. Lifting her foot out of her shoe, she raked the ends of her toes along the bottom of the lowest, left-hand drawer.

A small lever in the space between the drawer and the edge of the ledge flipped out. Another drawer dropped out from under the desktop above her legs.

Jordana grinned. Inside the secret drawer lay a wide, aged leather-bound tome with the word *Anathagraphia* scratched diagonally in golden letters across its face.

Cautiously, Jordana pulled the book onto her lap. As she touched the book's spine, she found a small back string and pulled it taut.

She lifted the cover and thumbed through the yellowed pages until she stopped where the black string was wedged next to the spine. Wrenching the book fully open, she skimmed the words.

THE BLOODRUNNER ANATHEM

Earthly spirits rent, expelled, or released from their terrestrial enclosures are protected and secured to the Clockmaker by the Potter's Covenant. The Potter's Covenant indemnifies a physically untethered individual with a timely return to the Clockmaker unless precedent cause for immediate condemnation betides the fallen. If the spirit chooses not to return, whether by intentional action or external intervention, the covenant is breached, exposing the spirit to risk of anathema induction, including, but not restricted to, the Bloodrunner anathem.

The Bloodrunner anathem enslaves the formerly loosed spirit to another soul of the inducer's choice. Servitude, potentially eternal, remains incontestable until the subject's master confers ownership by this anathem or itself returns to the Clockmaker. Because of the insidious nature of this anathem, status inculcation can only be interred with a significant, personal, and damaging sacrifice by the declaimer. Also, the anathem can be invoked in series, forming a predatory lineage of masters and slaves, each subservient to the former.

The originator of this anathem purportedly spoke the following words to execrate its account.

You should not exist,
Lest death never desist
By All Law, be dismissed,
Or else as a slave persist.

In suffering, you shall subsist,
Rended will, from freedom's twist.
Through my gift and by this curse,
May your soul never resist.

Jordana pulled her cell phone out of her pocket and angled its lens to focus on the page. She took a picture and turned to the next page. Several ghostly figures had been drawn, each bowing before a spirit above it, forming a spiraling series of masters and slaves down the paper. She turned several more pages, hunting for a particular word. She didn't see it.

Clumping together several sections, she flipped the corners between her thumbs, scanning each paper's title. Suddenly, she slapped her hand between two pages. She had found her word of interest. *Divinoi.*

She hefted back the bulk of text to the page with the words "The Clockmaker's Divided Divinoi" written at the top. Numbers one through five were staggered down the page with highlighted words written next to each number.

1. Seeing
2. Might
3. Healing
4. Protection
5. Confession

Jordana stopped at number five and read the explanation after the word.

Confession draws emotion, experienced by another, to the surface, exposing an inner truth that had not been otherwise expressed…. The abuse of this ability, whereby the confessor compels another individual to feel something contrarily unnatural to their subconscious, is termed *coercion*. The nefarious and unbridled employment of coercion can place the user at risk of anathema and can permanently alter how a coercing individual manifests their divinoi.

Jordana gasped. After taking another picture with her cell phone, she read the three sentences again, wondering if they spoke of something she could do.

"Jordana!"

She slammed the book shut with a loud thud, and her entire body jerked forward to the edge of the chair. Glancing over the top of her eyeglasses, she looked toward the door.

Principal Lequoia stood inside the library, the door partly open and his flank facing the desk. His eyes were directed down the hallway with his hand gripping the doorknob.

"I'm sorry, Uncle." Jordana's heart throbbed, and she felt her pulse pound in her ears.

"This is *my* house!" shouted Lequoia. "And you will follow *my* rules!"

Jordana rested *Anathagraphia* on the desk and furtively pocketed her cell phone. "I'm sorry. I was just curious."

"My library is off limits! I've been very clear about that!"

"But there is something I desperately need to know!"

"That is no excuse!" Lequoia's eyes darted toward Jordana, and then he looked up at the ceiling as he stepped inside the library. "I know what you and your friends are up to. It has led you down a grim path. A path which ends in infirmity, misfortune, and tragedy, a tragedy you will not escape, unless you abandon your abilities."

"How can I just stop?" whimpered Jordana.

"If you don't use them, they will fade away," asserted Lequoia.

Jordana dropped her hands at her sides. "But it's difficult to do. I can't simply turn it off!"

"If you tried harder, then it wouldn't seem so difficult." Lequoia swallowed a mouthful of spit. "You're as stubborn and reckless as your mother."

"I don't care what you think." Jordana gritted her teeth. "I am *not* my mother."

"You will *not* speak to me in that tone, young lady!" Lequoia glared at her.

Jordana lifted her head as a scowl squirmed across her face. "Yes, sir."

"Don't look at me." Lequoia held up his hand to block his eyes from her view.

Gall rose in her throat, and her fists tightened. "Maybe if I knew more, I wouldn't be so dangerous."

"That's exactly the stance the darkness of this world wants you to take. Then that darkness will consume you. What more of an example do you need? Is the death of your mother not enough for you?"

Jordana marched toward the door and glared at her uncle. Closing his eyes, Lequoia took a single careful step out of her way.

Bending over to grab her books, Jordana rounded the door and stormed into the hallway.

"Your father wants to see you!" shouted her uncle behind her.

Jordana flung her book bag over her shoulder as she turned another corner. Her high, sorrel cheeks flushed red. She tossed her books onto a chair in the living room and rushed toward the middle of the house.

"What?" announced Jordana, shoving open the door to her father's bedroom.

Her father sat in his wheelchair, facing the window. He turned his disfigured and pitted face toward her and smiled.

Scarred skin contracted across missing caverns of flesh in his cheeks and jaw, and the tissue remaining from his absent left ear was partially covered by a few tufts of dark hair combed over his scalp.

Jordana's anger softened as she viewed her father. His waifish arms rested in his lap and his bony legs only filled a fraction of his seat and footrests.

She could easily remember how handsome he had been: rugged forehead, high, slanting cheeks, a firm jaw, and a full head of thick, black hair. Between the mine explosion several years ago and the battle with the Tsul'kalu last fall, he was barely more than half a man now.

"There she is," said her father. "Isn't she beautiful, Galyon?"

"More beautiful than her mother, if that's possible," replied a man standing next to the bed.

Jordana's angry demeanor washed away. She lowered her chin, slightly embarrassed. "Hello, Mr. Tweever."

Galyon Tweever took two steps forward and bowed his head. The light from the window glinted off his smooth, almond-brown scalp. Polished, golden loops swung from his earlobes. Fitted tightly against his lean frame, he wore a mud-stained, yellow sleeveless vest that exposed most of his tan chest. An octagonal blue gem hung from his neck. Branching veins coursed within muscles in his arms, and gemmed bracelets encircled both his wrists.

"Arturo, do you have any aspirin?" asked Mr. Tweever.

Mr. Galilahi wheeled himself around in his chair. "I think so. Are you okay?"

"I'm not sure." Mr. Tweever placed his hand on his chest. "I believe your daughter is making my heart ache."

Jordana smiled at him.

"Galyon, I think it's time for you to go," said Jordana's father with a stern smirk.

"How's the mine?" Jordana asked.

Mr. Tweever rubbed his bald head. "Busy. Which means business is good, but we're all eager to get your father back in the foreman's saddle."

"Soon," commented Mr. Galilahi. "Very soon."

"Your father's made a remarkable recovery," admired Mr. Tweever. "Hopefully those monsters won't ever return."

Mr. Galilahi sighed. "I think they've moved on."

Jordana stiffened her lip. "They have. I'm sure of it."

"What I don't get is the lack of interest by the local government," replied Mr. Tweever. "Those things almost shut us down and nearly killed you. How could they turn a blind eye?"

"Mr. Miller has his own agenda," mumbled Arturo. "And keeping Lake Julian looking neat and clean is his top priority." Arturo caught Jordana's eye. "Speaking of which, I need to speak with Jordana."

Jordana looked away.

"Understood," replied Mr. Tweever. "I should get back." He stepped forward and shook Arturo's hand. "Stay well."

Mr. Galilahi returned his smile. "Take care, Galyon."

Mr. Tweever bowed at Jordana again and stepped through the bedroom threshold. Jordana stepped inside and closed the door.

"Uncle has already scolded me," grumbled Jordana. "I don't think I'm up for another lecture."

"Who said anything about a lecture?" Her father wheeled himself over to his desk.

"Then what do you need to speak to me about?" Jordana crossed her arms.

"Well, I think one thing you already know about." Mr. Arturo pulled open a drawer and lifted a box into his lap.

"Yes," she muttered.

"Then I guess you've already heard?" Her dad spun his chair around and faced her.

"The suits we were using were outlawed."

Mr. Galilahi cocked his head to the side. "What suits?"

Jordana waved him off. "Nothing. Just one of Buzz's silly inventions. It's not like they did much anyway."

Mr. Galilahi shrugged and wheeled forward. "I was talking about my doctor's appointment today." He shifted the chair's brakes and lifted each of his legs, planting his feet on the floor. "Hold this." He handed the box to Jordana.

"What's this?" Rotating the gray cardboard box, she examined the outside and shook it, feeling the loose contents rattle inside.

Jordana gasped and dropped the box. Covering her mouth with her hand, she stared forward in amazement. Her father had pushed himself up out of the wheelchair and was standing on his legs, unaided.

Jordana raced toward her father. They embraced each other tightly. Mr. Galilahi laughed and stumbled backward. Jordana tried to hold him up, but he sunk back into his wheelchair.

"I can't believe it!" squealed Jordana.

"The doctor said I can go back to work in a few weeks." Mr. Galilahi shifted in his seat. "The mine says I can have my old job back."

"That's wonderful!" Jordana squeezed her father's hand.

"It's been a long six months, but the worst is behind us." Arturo reached up and patted his daughter's cheek.

Jordana leaned into his hand and whispered, "And we can get our own place away from Uncle."

Mr. Galilahi sighed. "Hopefully. We'll have to see." He pointed toward the floor. "Now the box."

Jordana bent over and picked it up. "What is it?"

"Something I should have given you a long time ago, but honestly I had forgotten about it." Mr. Galilahi rubbed his scarred cheek. "Maybe I wanted to forget."

"Galyon found this in my desk at the mine and brought them over. Considering everything that's happened lately, I figured this might give you a little pick-me-up." Mr. Galilahi leaned forward and oriented the box in Jordana's hands.

Jordana flashed her father a skeptical eye as she ran her fingers along the seam in the middle.

"Go ahead," urged Arturo. "Open it up."

Jordana flipped the brass latch and pressed open the lid. Nestled in wads of cotton, a pair of eyeglasses glinted in the light from the window.

Jordana looked up at her father. "Thanks, Dad"—she pushed her own honey-colored glasses up on her nose—"but I already have plenty of replacement glasses."

"These aren't replacement glasses," replied her father. "These were your mother's. The last pair she ever owned." Her father reached around the box and slipped them out of the cotton "They were her favorite."

Jordana inspected the glasses. The arms and bridge were crystal clear and sparkled like diamonds. The frames were octagonal, and the lenses were rose-tinted, lightly hued near the top and darker at the bottom.

"Can I?" asked Jordana.

"Of course," her father replied.

Her father closed his eyes. Jordana slid her glasses off her nose and placed them in the box. With her fingers straight, she cupped the arms of her mother's glasses, careful not to smudge the crystal. Slowly, Jordana rested the arms around her ears and pressed the bridge to her nose.

"Okay," she said.

Mr. Galilahi opened his eyes. "Beautiful."

Jordana smiled and combed a lock of hair behind her ear.

"I've gotta see!" Jordana trotted out of her father's bedroom and around the corner. She ducked into the bathroom in the hallway.

Flipping on the light, she leaned over the sink and peered into the mirror. The glasses gleamed, and the rose coloring painted her sorrel cheeks with a hint of rouge.

She laughed quietly, proud to be wearing her mother's glasses. She studied her eyes behind the lenses. Emptiness gnawed at her gut. She bit her lip. Maybe her uncle was right. For she knew, behind the glasses, she was becoming more like her mother every day.

THE POAGE COUNTY SCIENCE FAIR, PART 1

Aubrey suddenly realized he was drooling. He closed his mouth and wiped off his chin. He wasn't sure how long he had been standing inside the doors to the gym. Time seemed to slip by seamlessly; so fascinating was the spectacle within.

Every empty space on the gym floor was occupied. The bleachers were fully retracted, forming a wall of slatted wood, which, with the lacquered floor under foot, cradled everything in the gym like a varnished ark. Students, teachers, judges, and parents meandered elbow to elbow between tables. Each table held a colorful triptych poster, ensconcing a project's model. Aubrey took a step forward. The placard below the first table read:

THE PRESSURE OF PLASMA
Dralia Dorsty
Mountain Cove High School

Aubrey touched the edge of the table. But what he really wanted to feel was the objects lying on the table. Three long, spindly Mylar balloons, rested, like elongated silvery raisins, in the middle of the presentation. A tall, thin girl with tightly wound french braids stood behind the table and pointed to her poster as she spoke to the passing crowd.

"Helium is used in today's dirigibles to keep them afloat in the sky since this element is both lighter than air and nonreactive." She pointed to another section of the poster. "However, larger airships require immense stores of helium to remain aloft and require frequent replenishment due to the inevitable escape of gas from their compartments. This can make using these aircrafts prohibitively expensive."

Dralia Dorsty pulled a lever connected to the wrinkled middle balloon. Its Mylar crackled and sparked. The balloon glowed pink and expanded into a rotund oval. Slowly, the energized balloon rose off the table and floated over the spectators.

Dralia Dorsty smiled. "When noble gases are ionized with an electric or magnetic field, the gas turns into a plasma, exerting a greater force on its surroundings, thus occupying a greater space than the few gas molecules trapped within the vacuum did before. The high-pressure, low-density plasma rises."

Dralia Dorsty snapped down two more levers. The two other balloons hummed and brightened, lighting up with blues and purples. They floated upward, meeting their counterpart. "Such that even heavier noble gases, such as krypton and xenon, could be used for lighter than air flight."

Magnos walked up and nudged Aubrey's shoulder. "I feel like I'm at the circus." Magnos's head swiveled, surveying the congregation of competitors and onlookers.

"Circus of genius," mumbled Aubrey.

Magnos pointed across the crowd. "Look at that!"

Aubrey followed Magnos's line of sight. Several rows back, a white, fuzzy globe, resembling a supersized snowball, towered over the fair. A wedge of its cross section had been removed, exposing various colored layers.

Jordana walked up to Magnos and Aubrey. "What are you looking at?"

Aubrey chuckled. "Everything." He glanced over at Jordana and then leaned toward her, staring at her face.

"I like your new glasses." Aubrey smiled.

Jordana flashed a quick smile in return. "Thanks." Pushing her rose-tinted glasses up her nose, she looked away and gazed around the gym. "There are tons of people here. Who would have thought a science fair was so popular?"

"Seriously," agreed Magnos. "I've never been before. Now I feel like I've been missing out."

"What is that huge, round thing?" asked Jordana, discovering what the boys had been looking at.

"Let's go check it out." Aubrey threaded his way through the tables. Magnos and Jordana followed.

Examining a presentation demonstrating the migratory patterns of honeybees in North America, an elderly gentleman, wearing a brown derby scribbled on a pad while a petite woman peered at a triptych poster displaying the specific gravity disparities of semiprecious alloys. Both wore nametags on their lapels that read "Judge."

Dressed in a Lycra tank top and gym shorts, the Lake Julian football coach, Mr. Kaniffy, wore a nametag with the same moniker pinned to his elastic waistband. He gawked at the expansive white ball towering above him. Mr. Kaniffy reminded himself to close his mouth as he stared upward.

Aubrey, Magnos and Jordana, edged their way in front of the judges.

The placard at the table read:

EXPLORING EUROPA

Charyn Harolsted
Chimney Falls High School

Directing a laser pointer, Charyn Harolsted walked away from her table as she spoke to the crowd. The pointer's red dot of light bounced between sections of the exposed portions of the globe. "Here you can see the various layers of Europa, Jupiter's fourth largest moon. As predicted by data taken by NASA's *Galileo* spacecraft in the mid 1990s, Europa has an icy surface and a rocky inner core, but in between lays a pan-planetary mega-ocean of liquid water."

"Another planet exhibit." Rodriqa nudged Aubrey from behind.

Aubrey turned his head to his shoulder and whispered, "But I've never seen one so...elaborate."

Rodriqa chewed the inside of her check. "Eh, bigger is the new better."

Jordana leaned in toward Rodriqa. "How was the family meeting?"

"Could've been worse." Rodriqa curled her lip. "Not by much, but still could've been."

"Sorry," mumbled Jordana.

Rodriqa took a closer look at Jordana. "Nice glasses."

"Thank you. My dad gave them to me." Jordana touched one of the glass arms. "They were my mom's."

Rodriqa nodded. "Sounds like your family powwow went better than mine then."

Jordana grinned at Rodriqa quickly, then turned back to the Europa exhibit.

Charyn Harolsted cleared her throat. "Due to Europa's suspected high water content, it may be capable of supporting multicellular life. However, one of the biggest obstacles our scientists have is physically examining a planet without contaminating it microbiologically. So here is my proposal for exploring Europa."

Pop!

Everyone around the table jumped. Above them, dozens of gray metal cones extruded from the globe's fuzzy surface.

"An orbiting capsule drops probes on the surface." Tiny metal springs with glowing red tips burrowed through the layers of the cross section. "Spiral titanium excavators, with diamond-tipped bits, which will be heated to a thousand degrees centigrade, will mine through Europa's frozen crust. While extracting frozen methane for fuel, the heated excavator will corkscrew through miles of ice and sterilize any potential terrestrial microorganisms that may have traveled with the probe from earth."

"It looks like an alien invasion," murmured Aubrey. Magnos and Jordana nodded.

"Yeah, except we're the aliens," added Rodriqa.

"How droll," spoke a voice from behind them.

The four friends turned around. With his arms crossed, the shrill-voiced Bates Hindenberg scoffed at the globe.

"Ready to lose again?" jeered Rodriqa.

Bates smirked. "I don't think so, Driqa." Bates looked around him. "All of these simpleton exhibits lack practicality or ingenuity. They have no true vision for advancing our society. No hope in propelling us to grander means. My project has it all. Creativity. Distinctiveness. Brilliance."

"And hopefully a tuner to dial down your arrogance," grumbled Rodriqa.

Aubrey and Jordana chuckled.

"Joke on," continued Bates. "Your laughter is passion fodder. First place is already mine." Bates brushed lint off his sleeves. "But I have my sights set on a bigger prize. Like a grant from the National Science Foundation."

"Dream on, toad thrower." Rodriqa popped her neck, and her beaded braids swirled around her neck. "If anyone around here is winning a grant, it's Buzz."

"Doubtful," scorned Bates. "Have you seen the mess he's made out front? It's a hideous debacle of chop shop parts." Bates walked away. "After I reveal my project, no one will give Buzz Reiselstein a second look."

Rodriqa rolled her eyes.

"Buzz is out front?" asked Jordana.

"I didn't see him when I walked in," replied Rodriqa.

"Ladies and gentlemen!" roared the gym's speakers overhead. The din of the crowd softened as the announcement echoed. "The solar eclipse will begin in three minutes. Everyone *outside!*"

A stream of people shifted toward the outer doors. Several teachers grimaced, unsure of who was using the press box during the science fair. The judges stopped looking at what they were evaluating and headed outside.

"Why does that voice sound so familiar?" asked Magnos.

Aubrey pointed up to the press box as a smile filled his face. "Because it's Buzz."

With his black curls bobbing up and down, Buzz raced across a concrete walkway out of the press box and hobbled down a set of stairs at the end of the bleachers. He rounded the corner at the bottom and shot outside through the doors.

"Let's go!" Rodriqa sped into the crowd. The other three friends followed.

Outside, a standing circle of people occupied a large swathe of the asphalt next to the high school. The sun beamed from above the treeline. The wind blew harshly. Jordana held her hair back to keep her black wispy strands off her face as all four of them advanced toward the middle of the ring of onlookers.

"We're not supposed to be outside," said Rodriqa.

"Why not?" asked Magnos.

"The *Lake Julian Mountain Lyre* said something about a solar flare during the eclipse," Rodriqa replied.

"How much of the *Lake Julian Mountain Lyre* do you believe?" Magnos plowed his way to the front of the crowd.

"Sixty seconds!"

Beep!

Standing on top of a crate, Buzz lowered a megaphone from his mouth and shouted over the crowd. "Grab some sunglasses and a piece of paper with a hole in it!" Buzz pointed to an open cardboard box next to him. It was packed with dozens of black, plastic glasses and a manila folder full of white sheets of paper with tiny central holes. A small line formed next to the box.

"What's Buzz standing in the middle of?" asked Magnos as Rodriqa, Aubrey, and Jordana gathered around him.

"What are you talking about?" Rodriqa pulled a pair of sunglasses out of her pocket and put them on.

"The metal things," replied Magnos.

Aubrey trotted over to the box and grabbed a handful of glasses, examining Buzz and his contraption. Surrounding Buzz, a ring of metal wires emerged from the bottom of the crate on which he was standing and then curved upward seven feet. To Aubrey, it looked like a massive metallic spider flipped on its back with its legs reaching skyward.

"Put these on." Aubrey handed a pair of sunglasses to Jordana. With her eyes closed, she switched her glasses with the pair Aubrey had given her.

Aubrey offered Magnos sunglasses. Magnos waved him off. Aubrey shrugged and put on a pair.

"It's starting!" Buzz flipped his snap-on shades down over his glasses as he pointed toward the sun. "Don't stare at the sun. Watch the eclipse's shadow with the paper."

A sliver of the sun's edge darkened. The afternoon light dimmed. A murmur flitted through the crowd as they held up their pieces of paper and watched the ball of light darken underneath it.

MIDDAY DUSK

"Quickly!" shouted Magnolia Thistlewood. "We're losing time!"

Ms. Thistlewood crouched over a porcelain jar, glancing between the rocks below her and the sun low in the sky, whose edge darkened with the moon's curve.

"Yes," replied Matsinstrus. "Almost there." His blackened skeletal form crept up stacks of dolomite above Crannynook Caves, wheezing as his limbs struggled against the crumbly rock.

Blasts of wind beat against the mountain's summit. Ms. Thistlewood's bright red hair whipped around her face. The lightness of day dimmed. The sun's face grew black.

"Hurry!" yelled Ms. Thistlewood. Her pale green eyes quivered. She stretched her arms to the sky and arched her back as if basking in the light's demise.

Matsinstrus peaked the ledge of the cliff face and skidded down the opposite side, racing on all fours toward his master.

Ms. Thistlewood stood up. "Take the jar! Don't open it until I tell you!"

Matsinstrus crawled up to her with his head low. "Are there enough?"

"See for yourself." Ms. Thistlewood loomed over him, daring him to open the jar. Matsinstrus nodded and gripped the jar.

Turning away Ms. Thistlewood caressed her neck and swallowed the rolling air. Within moments, midafternoon had dwindled to dusk.

"How easily the light is destroyed." Ms. Thistlewood raised her chin. "How quickly the shadow wins. Our time is here. No one will stand against us!"

Matsinstrus shuddered at her words. "It is as you have seen. Your army awaits, my queen."

Magnolia Thistlewood marched toward the edge of the summit. She planted a foot on the edge of a knoll and leaned on her knee, viewing the town of Lake Julian in the valley below.

Quickly, she turned back toward Matsinstrus. "Here it began! Here it ends!"

Matsinstrus lifted the porcelain jar toward the disappearing sun. "On your mark!"

Ms. Thistlewood watched the sun, nearly engulfed by the lunar disc. Turning the dial on her brown sandstone sundial watch, she released a spray of dust. Her bright red hair vibrated. Her milky skin blurred. The curves of her chest and thighs disintegrated, swirling into a horde of squirming worms that slipped from her frame and disappeared into the watch. The army of spirit shards that created the façade of Ms. Thistlewood wriggled into her phylactery.

Fully exposed, a black skeleton with a yellow mist seething from her jaw and thorax stood with her right arm reaching toward the fading sun and her left stretched out at Matsinstrus.

"It is time!"

CORONATION

Thousands of miles above Lake Julian in the void of outer space, the dusty gray moon glides silently in orbit over western North Carolina, casting its shadow on the sunlit earth and draping a round swathe of southern Appalachia in darkness.

Behind the moon, less than nine minutes away as the photon travels, the sun, swaddled by a near perfect vacuum, blasts its mixture of life-giving warmth and scathing radiation in every direction as it has for a billenia. Masterful powerhouse at the center of our galactic neighborhood, this yellow ball burns a third of a ton of hydrogen every time a human heart beats. Its core compressed to fuse, the sun slowly seeps light toward its surface, and its flailing exterior whips searing energy across the universe.

Aimed at the earth, a dark blemish on the star's face widens. Cooler than its surrounding plasma, the sunspot winks. Tightening bands of magnetic fields snap. A portion of the sun's mass is released. From the sun's crown, a soaring soup of ions is hurled toward the earth, its moon, and the tiny town of Lake Julian.

Within minutes, a year's worth of radiationreaches our moon. Its gravity funnels the excited milieu of protons and photons into a scorching corkscrew, which singe orbiting asteroids and flimsy metal satellites in its path. Our planet's protective shell, the magnetosphere, bends, a minuscule dyke against the colossal wave.

A billion gigatons of slung flame pierces the sky, the fury of this coronal mass ejection unstoppable by anything natural.

THE POAGE COUNTY SCIENCE FAIR, PART 2

The moon crossed the sun's midline. Afternoon looked like evening. Warm air breezed through the alleyway behind the high school as the gathering crowd grew around Buzz and his upward-reaching ring of wire tentacles.

Buzz raised a box switch in his hand. "It seems impossible that a single invention might provide the world's population with all of its energy needs while simultaneously preventing continued global warming. But not after today." Buzz pressed the switch. Four vacuum compressors near the edge of the box sputtered. "And I'm not simply speaking of eliminating greenhouse gases. I'm proposing regulation of global temperatures with the touch of a button."

Perched on the crate in the middle of the ring of wires, Buzz slowly lifted off the ground. "Today, destiny is upon us!" A large crack forked up one side of the crate. "For not only is there a solar eclipse. Not only is a solar flare aimed directly at our planet." The crate cracked again. Buzz jumped down. "But today in Lake Julian, we are predicted to be at the center of the eclipse as a coronal mass ejection plows through our magnetosphere and hurls to the earth's surface!"

The crate shattered into several pieces. The forward members of the surrounding crowd, including Buzz's four friends, stepped backward "Behold!" shouted Buzz. "The Superterrestrial Solar Panel!"

Large, black garbage bags, knitted together to form-fit in the spaces between the metal wires, inflated with a congealing foam that forced the bags to flatten out and track up the wires into a warped satellite dish configuration. Now the contraption reminded Aubrey of a monstrous black flower.

"With squadrons of these energy-converting cells in high-earth orbit, no longer will so much of the sun's energy be lost! My proprietary silicon foam not only converts light into electricity but also changes ionizing radiation, such as positrons and gamma rays, into useable energy that can be beamed back to earth!"

The judges scribbled feverishly in their notebooks.

Buzz raised his arms to the disappearing sun. The sky was nearly dark as night. "All our energy needs can be met! Fossil fuels will be extinct once more! And the sun's rays will finally be tamed!"

Buzz pointed to a small computer monitor, connected with a large cable to the solar panel. The monitor displayed a stack of empty bars, highlighted with red at the bottom, yellow in the middle, and green at the top. "Watch the Superterrestrial Solar Panel's battery as the solar flare fills the sky!" The bottom red bar filled in. "And let us all marvel at the power of light!"

Except for a small halo of light at its periphery, the disc of the sun had been completely blotted out. The air was calm. Day had become night. Everyone in the crowd stared between Buzz's invention and the projection of the sun on the ground through their hole-pricked paper.

Jordana gasped.

"What's wrong?" whispered Aubrey.

"Look." She pointed at the eclipse. "It's changing."

Suddenly, the thin white light around the shadow of the moon expanded, doubling the size of the disc. Arcs of orange and yellow reached further into the sky, like an army of wispy tendrils fleeing from the sun. Aubrey felt his face flush from the heat.

The coronal mass ejection was here.

ETHEREAL INDIGESTION

Shway Shway pushed off against the rear metal wall of the freezer, leapt two steps, bounded over sections of mangled shelving, and plowed sideways into the door. The battery, clamped into the back of the Elemag suit, crackled but held its position. Shway Shway bounced off the door and crashed into the shelving. The pale, reptilian-skinned creature spit and cursed under his breath. He kicked at the bent wires around him and pushed several frozen cardboard boxes away. He wrenched forward onto the floor, scraping off icy shavings as he squirmed. Shway Shway pushed himself up in the oversized, blue Elemag blue suit.

Twisting in circles, he clawed at his back for the battery. Shway Shway tripped over a flap of the suit. He spun and dropped to the ground. Groaning, he flipped himself over and sat up. He wagged his head, and slobber seeped from his mouth.

Suddenly, his eyelids swelled. His large, round, green eyes twitched. His legs stiffened, and he arched his back. His three-fingered hands dug at his stomach. He felt the crystal pyramid spark and shock inside him.

Shway Shway screamed as he fell backward and writhed in agony.

THE ARMY'S DAWN

In her blackened skeleton form, Magnolia Thistlewood trained her yellow-orbed eyes on the fully eclipsed sun. The rim of light around the moon's shadow dilated to twice its size, and veiny eruptions of fiery light ripped through the black sky as the solar flare hurdled toward the earth.

"Now!" shouted Ms. Thistlewood. "Open the jar!"

Matsinstrus wrenched the top of the porcelain jar open, and it spouted black fumes. More than a hundred shimmering serpentine shadows with rings of sharp teeth erupted from the jar and snaked across the field. Matsinstrus dashed away. The spirit shards, each nearly three-feet long and a foot in girth, scurried through the grass, hunting for something to bite or swallow.

Holding her left hand out in front of her, Ms. Thistlewood opened her fingers. Tartan's stolen white stone glimmered in her palm as a tiny orange light orbited it. She examined it briefly and then squeezed the white stone with a crushing force.

Ms. Thistlewood stretched her right hand toward the sun, her phalanges splayed open as if she might grip the eclipsing disc. She closed her eyes and concentrated on the heavenly bodies above.

The air shuddered, and slowly the wind calmed.

In a sudden flash, lightning streaked up from her hand toward the sky. Clouds evaporated. The stratosphere moaned. A whirlwind of ions and energy funneled like a tornado toward the ground. The arcing strands of sunlight swirled downward.

Siphoning the colossal explosion of the earth's star, Ms. Thistlewood drew the solar flare through the atmosphere into her open palm. Her blackened skeletal frame shimmered until it appeared out of focus. Gigatons of energy coursed from her right hand, down her arm, across her chest, and out her left hand. The white stone in her palm simmered and cracked under the heated pressure. Thousands of jagged jolts of electricity exploded from her left hand. Coursing across the field, the bolts electrified the myriad of spirit shards crawling along the ground.

Their shimmering skins stretched and warped. The shadows squealed and convulsed, their glistening bodies tearing and buckling. A deeper darkness grew from within each of them, transforming the serpentine shards into quadruped forms with triangular heads and spiny tails.

The maelstrom of particles and photons subsided. The air was still. The light twinkling around the moon softened and retracted. The moon moved away from the sun. Sunlight returned to the valley.

No longer squirming tubes of blackness only a few feet long, the developing shadows sniffed the grass and stared at the world through large green eyes as they pushed themselves off the ground onto three-fingered hands and hind hooves.

Ms. Thistlewood opened her left hand and turned it upright. Where the glowing white stone once was, a pile of dust sifted between her fingers, falling to the rock beneath her.

Unable to hold herself up, she dropped to her knees. Yellow vapor wheezed from between her ribs. She pulled herself to the ledge of the mountain and glared at Lake Julian. Ms. Thistlewood limply waved the growing shadows forward to her. Slowly, more than a hundred creatures of darkness, which Ms. Thistlewood had created, gathered around her.

Magnolia Thistlewood pointed to Lake Julian.

"Feed, my children. Feed."

THE POAGE COUNTY SCIENCE FAIR, PART 3

The fringe of the sun peeked beyond the edge of the moon's globe. The solar flare's arcs dissipated into the reemerging blue of the sky. The fullness of afternoon returned to Lake Julian.

Aubrey touched his face. It no longer felt warm. Buzz sat cross-legged in front of the small computer monitor attached to his Superterrestrial Solar Panel. He rocked on the asphalt. Only half of the second lowest red bar had filled on the lower part of the screen.

Two of the judges turned and walked inside. Coach Kaniffy walked toward Buzz and tapped him on his shoulder with his closed fist.

Mr. Kaniffy cleared his throat. "Nice display, little man. Shame it didn't turn out like you planned." Coach Kaniffy gave the display a second look, grimaced, and then walked inside.

Buzz typed manically on the keyboard. A projection of the sun, the orbiting moon, and his satellite dish flashed across the screen.

Aubrey walked up to Buzz and knelt next to him. "What happened?"

Buzz typed and rocked more quickly. "I don't know."

Magnos walked up behind Buzz and Aubrey. "Buzz, I don't care what happened. You're the coolest geek I know."

Buzz rubbed his forehead. "Who cares about cool? The solar panel should have absorbed terawatts of energy by now." Buzz smacked the side of his computer several times. The monitor snowed and then flashed back to its previous image.

Jordana ambled over to Aubrey as she held up her hand to view the sky. "I wonder what happened to the strands of light around the eclipse."

Rodriqa bit her lip, watching Buzz splice together a pair of wires connected to the computer. "Sometimes things don't always work as planned."

"I think you'll still win," said Magnos.

"Of course, he will," agreed Aubrey.

Rodriqa wiggled her fingers in Buzz's curly hair. "Come on, big guy. The award ceremony will be starting soon."

Inside the gymnasium, students were breaking down their posters and dioramas as most of the crowd mingled toward the stage. Aubrey, Magnos,

Jordana, and Rodriqa stood behind Buzz, who sat in a chair unscrewing the casing plates to the Superterrestrial Solar Panel's battery while he mumbled to himself.

Standing behind the podium, the bookish woman judge held up a silver badge and announced into a microphone. "And in second place, 'The Pressure of Plasma.' Dralia Dorsty from Mountain Cove High School."

The crowd applauded. Dralia Dorsty threaded through the spectators, climbed the small stairs next to the stage, and bowed as she accepted her award. The man wearing the derby, Coach Kaniffy, and Principal Lequoia shook her hand as she crossed the stage.

The bookish woman approached the microphone again. "And this year's winner of the Poage County Science Fair..."

"Here we go," whispered Rodriqa.

"You got this," muttered Magnos as he rubbed Buzz's shoulders.

The bookish woman held up a gold medal. "Lake Julian High takes it again!"

"Yes!" Aubrey stifled a shout.

"Bates Hindenberg!" continued the bookish woman. "For his project 'Couture de Force: harnessing the static electrical energy of objects in motion.'"

Applause erupted from the crowd.

"Ah, nah," moaned Rodriqa.

Buzz dropped the casing plates on the gym floor. Aubrey and Magnos's shoulders slumped.

"Buzz didn't win," said Jordana.

"He didn't even place," sighed Rodriqa.

Bates Hindenberg rounded the edge of the curtains from the back of the stage. The bookish woman handed him his gold medal and shook his hand.

The man wearing the derby walked up to the podium. "We were particularly impressed, not only with Bates's ingenuity, but also how he was able to apply his idea practically." The man shook Bates's hand. "Can you show us your project, Bates?"

Bates nodded eagerly. The black curtain behind him parted. An empty car chassis, with its wheels on a conveyer belt, was connected to several wires along the car's hull. The wires ran below the conveyer belt and were plugged into a boxy voltage meter alighted with the numbers 00.0 at the front of the stage.

Bates cupped his hands together and shouted in his high-pitched voice from the stage. "Watch how much static electricity can be recouped from a low-velocity car ride!" Bates ran over to a wide fan in front of the chassis and flipped it on. The fan's blades spun. Air rushed over the surface of the chassis.

The crowd gasped and cheered as the voltmeter's digital face quickly tumbled to 16.7. Bates bowed deeply.

"That's my idea," whimpered Buzz.

"You have the same thing on the Buzz Bug," remarked Aubrey.

"He stole your idea," said Jordana.

"How did that happen?" asked Magnos.

Buzz covered his face with his hand. "I was bragging about it at our last Torquetum club meeting."

"He still shouldn't be allowed to steal it," Jordana grumbled.

"It's not fair," blubbered Buzz.

"Is there any way to protest?" Jordana searched her friends' faces.

Rodriqa shook her head. "Not unless there's proof that Buzz came up with it first."

"But we have it on the Buzz Bug," insisted Jordana.

"Witnesses don't count," whined Buzz. "The idea has to be documented."

Aubrey and Rodriqa glanced at each other and frowned.

Aubrey grabbed Buzz's shoulder. "Come on, bud." He pulled him out of the chair. "I know how we can forget about all this."

ENCROACHING DARKNESS

Ray Gene Jennings stooped over the passenger seat inside his sedan, rummaging through the glove box under the dim light of the dashboard. Faded receipts, expired insurance cards, and pens tumbled onto the floorboard as he dug deeper into the compartment.

He flipped over a thick leather-bound owner's manual and freed a small silver cylinder from underneath it. Muttering "Aha!" under his breath, Mr. Jennings pulled the small flashlight out and twisted the top. Nothing happened.

He leaned down and examined the bulb under the dashboard light. Mr. Jennings smacked the bottom of the flashlight and shook it. Its bulb flickered. Pulling his royal blue ball cap down on his head, he stood up and slammed the door shut.

A cool nighttime breeze gusted through the parking lot of his Smart Mart & Finer Diner. Mr. Jennings bundled his jacket close around his neck and aimed the flashlight onto the gravel, scanning the ground as he trudged toward the front door. Loose, damp rocks crunched under his feet. The cloudless night sky wrapped the store in shadow. Neither glinting stars nor the reflecting lights from the dam provided much illumination.

Mr. Jennings glanced at the extinguished neon sign in the window and grimaced. With each passing day since he closed his shop, the finality of its foreclosure solidified the emptiness he felt. His life's work obsolete, his purpose past, he had graduated to uselessness. Holding despair away was more difficult with every sunrise.

At the door, he grabbed the rectangular handle and jostled it. It was securely locked. Mr. Jennings slid the flashlight into the crook of his elbow and patted his jacket for his keys. He found the jagged lump in his right pants pocket. Fishing out the tangled fray of scored metal, Mr. Jennings pointed the flashlight toward the keys and hunted for the right one.

Hisss!

Mr. Jennings jerked. The keys clanked to the ground. Pulling the flashlight from his elbow, he turned toward the source of the noise.

A small cloud of dust wafted over the parking lot, the flashlight's fuzzy cone of light bouncing off the small particles hovering in the air.

"Who's there?" called Mr. Jennings. He jerked the flashlight, searching the dark lot.

A tiny pair of red, iridescent eyes flashed underneath the gritty smoke.

Mr. Jennings stomped his feet. "Go away, you nasty critter!"

The eyes ducked down. Scrapes raked along the gravel. Mr. Jennings aimed his flashlight and crept forward.

"Scat!" he yelled, tromping forward and shaking the flashlight at the eyes. Advancing a few more feet, Mr. Jennings could see a crater dug in the gravel underneath the fog of dirt. He angled his flashlight down into the pit. Gnarly twines of beige and cream hair spiked upward around a fuzzy ball of spinning claws digging feverishly at the ground.

Whimperfidget hissed again, its reddish eyes glinting out of the middle of the crater.

"Get on outta here!" Mr. Jennings waved his flashlight.

Suddenly, Whimperfidget stopped scratching, and his glowing red eyes widened as he glared up at Mr. Jennings.

Mr. Jennings kicked a mound of gravel into the pit. "Go on! Git!"

The cat squalled, leapt backward, and scurried off into the night.

Mr. Jennings sighed. "Dumb cat." He pushed some of the unearthed dirt back into the crater.

Mr. Jennings felt the breeze to his back change. Warm, moist air blew against his neck. He turned around and gasped.

A large pale green eye met his, only a few inches away from his face. He spun around and whimpered, "No." Mr. Jennings tripped backward into the crater.

He only saw two more things before everything went dark: a long black face, and a pair of sharp white canines glistening in the beam of his flashlight.

Saturday.

Daytime streamed through a widening crack in a weathered warehouse's face as a sliding door's rusting wheels squealed against grinding metal, slicing a break in the enclosed night of the steel barn's expansive interior.

A man stepped into the rectangular doorway's threshold, his shadow stretching across the floor. Salt-and-pepper curls swathing out from his temples were projected as a surly crown of horns on the dirt below.

He was dressed in a plaid, button-down shirt with opalescent buttons and cut-off carpenter shorts. He raised a hand and surveyed the darkness. Glowing bits of dust flitted through the air, highlighted by the sunlight from behind, but there were no other signs of movement.

He took a step inside. Daylight glinted against rows of cut and polished hubcaps on the far wall about a hundred feet in front of him, which took the shape of a shiny, angular Vitruvian man. Several partially disassembled motorcycles lay in a mangled heap in the far right-hand corner underneath three unicycles that hung upside down on the wall. A forest of computer cords and telephone wire coiled on rusting nails set in the left-hand wall, which had been painted with a mural of yellow sunflowers amid a decoupage of human faces and fish, flying between clouds aloft in a baby-blue sky.

Like a postapocalyptic war zone between armies of mechanized scrap, the dusty floor was strewn with doorless minirefrigerators, oil-oozing lawn mower motors, tiny cracked springs, greasy pistons, and fog-stained diodes.

The man tilted his head upward to look over the edge of a second-story loft in the back right corner of the building. Supported by a scaffolding of timber stilts, a corrugated metal ledge jutted out from the wall and occupied a quarter of the upper space of the barn.

The man walked over to an extension ladder that was tied with nylon string to the floor of the loft. Rattling the ladder, he trudged clumsily up the wobbly, substitute stairs.

Atop the loft, Aubrey rubbed his eyes and yawned widely. He pulled a sheet up around his neck and rolled over to face the loft's ledge. Lying on a bare twin-sized mattress, which rested directly on the corrugated, metal floor, Aubrey shifted his rump off a lump in the bedding and rubbed his backside where a spring had poked him for most of the night.

The twittering squeak of the extension ladder rattled the metal underneath Aubrey. He pushed himself up to see who was coming.

Aubrey grinned as the man breached the edge of the loft's horizon. "Good morning, Mr. Reiselstein." Aubrey yawned again and swallowed the sticky taff, which lined his mouth.

"Good *afternoon*, Aub," returned Arvel Reiselstein with a wink.

Aubrey sat up on the mattress and crossed his legs, glancing around the loft as Mr. Reiselstein stepped onto the loft's landing.

Magnos lay sprawled on another naked mattress behind Aubrey, his arms out to his sides, his legs dangling off the bottom, and his head cocked backward against the floor. Magnos's mouth gaped open, and drool streamed down his right cheek.

Beside Magnos and swaddled in a thick curry of blankets, Buzz slept in front of a black wire stand that held three dull brown televisions, which dimly reflected the light from the door below. Set in tandem, each screen had its casing removed and their inward jumble of wiring spliced, interspersed, and woven together into a masking-tape wrapped bundle, leading to a myriad of video game consoles in the shelving underneath. It reminded Aubrey of a makeshift mission control for an underfunded moon landing.

Behind the television screens, three cattle prods leaned against the wall, each handle strapped with a computer motherboard. Aubrey remembered that these were the battle prods they had used last fall to try and subdue Jordana's sasquatch.

Mr. Reiselstein tiptoed over to Buzz's mattress with a wily grin on his face. Aubrey shivered as sleep left him. He rolled around and punched Magnos in the shoulder.

Magnos snorted and choked out several coughs as he wiped the drool off his face. His eyes blinked open, and he looked over at Aubrey. Aubrey pointed to Mr. Reiselstein. Magnos sat up.

Crouching over Buzz, Mr. Reiselstein held his index finger to his pursed lips and glanced at Aubrey and Magnos. They took the hint.

Mr. Reiselstein leaned down, and his finger drifted slowly back and forth above Buzz's textile chrysalis.

Quickly, his index finger dropped. It dug between the sheets. Buzz's hand swatted haphazardly, but Mr. Reiselstein's finger only bored more vigorously downward.

Magnos and Aubrey glanced at each other and smiled.

A muffled, "Stawp et," whined from inside Buzz's mummy-tight linens.

Mr. Reiselstein whipped out his other index finger and plunged it into another opening in the sheets.

Maniacal guffaws erupted from the blankets. Buzz's arms and legs bicycled against the mattress. "No more!"

"Where's Virgie? Virgie?" squawked Mr. Reiselstein. "I can't find Virgie!"

"Virgie?" mouthed Magnos to Aubrey.

Aubrey snickered. "Virgil is Buzz's real name."

Magnos smirked.

"I'm right *here*!" screeched Buzz. In a single motion, he jerked his covers from around his face, and his torso sprouted vertically off his mattress. Buzz shoved his dad and his index fingers away.

Mr. Reiselstein chuckled. "Wake up, little Virgie!"

"I'm awake," groaned Buzz, his dark curly locks splayed straight out from his temples. "Dad, I'm not ten anymore." Buzz crossed his arms. "I deserve a little more respect than to be woken up by tickle torture."

Mr. Reiselstein grinned. "I agree. At the ripe old age of fourteen, I should be dowsing you with cold water instead, preparing you for the kind of treatment you'll get at college."

Buzz frowned at his father and then his lip quivered. "They really do that to each other in college?"

Mr. Reiselstein smiled and looked over at Aubrey and Magnos. "What time did you all go to bed last night?"

"We didn't go to bed last night," grumped Buzz. "It was daylight before we fell asleep."

Mr. Reiselstein scratched his head. "I didn't even hear you all come in last night. I thought you were going to spend the night at Aubrey's."

Buzz shook his head and looked down.

Aubrey shuffled forward on his mattress. "We took our time getting everything back from the science fair and then just decided to stay here since it was so late."

"Oh, that's right!" With brightened eyes, Mr. Reiselstein raised his arms. "How did the fair go? Where's your ribbon?"

Buzz glared at his father flatly. "I didn't win."

"What?" replied Mr. Reiselstein. "Which project did you enter?"

Buzz nodded to the back corner of the loft and then flopped back on his mattress.

Like a wilted metal flower, the Superterrestrial Solar Panel's wire antennae slouched, still hooked to the central body of the battery and the trash-bag gel sacs had been deflated.

Mr. Reiselstein crumpled his lips. "Honestly not your most inspiring idea."

Buzz harrumphed.

His father walked over to the corner and examined it. "It's certainly got potential though. I would have thought the judges would have liked it. What happened?"

"It didn't work," grumbled Buzz.

Mr. Reiselstein cocked his head to the side. "That doesn't happen very often."

Buzz's lower lip slid outward as he glowered at his father.

Mr. Reiselstein held up a finger in thought. "Well, we can have a look at it while were staying at the lake."

Buzz shook his head. "I don't want to."

"You can't stay inside the Screever's Lair all day," protested Mr. Reiselstein. "It's the first day of spring break. We have to do something fun."

"Yes, we can, and no, we don't." Buzz wrapped his blankets around his head and rolled away from his dad.

Magnos frowned. "What's a shiver slayer?"

Aubrey turned toward Magnos and cranked an eyebrow skyward. "Screever's Lair," he articulated.

Mr. Reiselstein smiled. "It's what we call this old metal barn." He stretched his arms out. "When I bought this land in the mideighties, it had been an old hippie compound, and the hippies were growing up and moving on, so they sold me the land cheap, including this stopgap depot. As you can see, they practiced their art on the walls, so we started calling it the Screever's Lair."

Mr. Reiselstein sat down on Buzz's mattress. "Buzz's mom and I let him use it for his workshop when he was little. And now he scrounges in my junkyard for parts and makes his contraptions here."

"Contraptions that don't work," moaned Buzz.

"Come on." Mr. Reiselstein shook Buzz's shoulders. "Let's go. You boys can come too." He nodded at Aubrey and Magnos. "It'll be like a campout. Just us guys. Besides, you don't want to miss the insect spectacle of a generation."

"That sounds fun." Aubrey stood up. "I had forgotten about the moth thing."

"Yeah," agreed Magnos. "I don't have any plans for spring break, and I'd rather not watch Gaetan and Fayla mack out on the couch all week."

Aubrey grunted. "Me neither."

"Then it's settled," affirmed Mr. Reiselstein.

"Where's your mom?" Aubrey asked Buzz.

"Molly is out of town for a couple weeks," replied Mr. Reiselstein. "Rodeo Convention."

Aubrey nodded knowingly. Magnos decided not to ask.

Mr. Reiselstein stood up and stepped over Buzz. He grabbed a steel-mesh sack off the wall and stretched open its wire drawstring. He grabbed a battle prod from behind the television screens and examined it in his hand. "What were these for again?"

Magnos's eyes widened. He shivered at the sight of the battle prod. "Last time I saw that, I crashed into the back of a house."

Mr. Reiselstein furrowed his brow and then nodded with recollection of the events of last fall.

Aubrey thought a moment, staring at the battle prod. "We can use them to zap bugs."

"Perfect." Mr. Reiselstein dropped it in the sack. He walked over to the middle of the loft and spun around, hunting open spaces between boxes and shelves. "Where's the Mole-Pole tent?"

"Oh, don't take that old thing." Buzz rolled over and planted his face in his mattress.

"Why not?" asked Mr. Reiselstein. "It was your very first invention, and it's perfect for camping."

"It's stupid," insisted Buzz, his voice muffled through his bed, "and I'm not even sure it still works."

"Ah! Found it." Mr. Reiselstein waved Magnos over. "Help me lift the Solar Panel and the Mole-Pole tent into the sack."

Magnos nodded and lurched off his mattress.

"If we're gonna see the million moth metamorphosis, we need lots of room, and there's no harm in showing off just a little bit too."

MOTH-ERS

Aubrey clung to the roll bar in the back seat of Mr. Reiselstein's jeep as the car swerved into a parking lot above the eastern bank of Lake Julian. Sooty dust unfurled from the gravel and twirled through the air like a miniature sandstorm. Aubrey wiped the grit from his eyes and blinked sticky tears from his lashes as the jeep braked to a stop at the end of the lot.

Aubrey stood up and stared over Mr. Reiselstein's seat. Shading his eyes from the late afternoon sun, Aubrey stared at the grassy areas down the hill.

In a mere couple of days, the banks of Lake Julian had transformed from a scattering of campsites and wandering travellers to a swarming city of tents, RV caravans, and concession stands, filling nearly every open space from the dam to the mouth of Wontawanna Creek. A cool spring breeze cleared the dust from the lot but exchanged it with campfire smoke and the smell of portable toilets.

"Whoa," exclaimed Magnos as he leapt onto the gravel lot. "This place is packed."

"Any natural event that happens only once every thirty-six years, regardless of what it is, is bound to draw a crowd." Mr. Reiselstein stepped out of the jeep. "The moth-ers have arrived."

"Whose mothers?" Aubrey climbed into the jeep's trunk space with an eyebrow scrunched up his forehead.

"*Maw*thers," said Buzz, while he lumbered out of the front passenger seat. "Not *muu*thers."

Mr. Reiselstein walked around to the back of the jeep and swung open the rear gate. "Moth-ers are what they call those folks who chase unusual butterfly and moth species around the globe. Mostly, it's an eclectic group of retired scientists and natural history buffs, but some think they're just a crowd of overly educated hippies." He pulled the steel-mesh sack out of the back and with a grunt flung it over his shoulder.

"Boys, grab the cooler. Magnos, would you mind carrying the tent?"

"Not a prob." Magnos trotted to the rear of the jeep. Magnos eyed the green, spiral-bound tarp with flaps, which contained a screw-shaped metal pole the size of a tree trunk within it. To Aubrey, it looked more like giant umbrella than a tent. Magnos heaved the Mole-Pole tent onto his shoulder and stumbled a couple steps before steadying the weight.

Standing in the rear of the jeep, Aubrey scooted the cooler toward the ledge. Buzz grabbed a handle. Aubrey hopped down and clutched the opposite handle. In unison, they slid the cooler off the rear. It dropped like a lead weight to the ground.

Magnos chuckled. "Need help?"

Buzz bent over and squeezed the handle on his side of the cooler with all ten of his chubby fingers. "We got this." He nodded at Aubrey. Aubrey sighed and reached down for the cooler.

"One…two…*three*."

Aubrey and Buzz struggled against the plastic handles. The cooler slowly lifted off the ground. Buzz shifted his feet backward, skidding his heels through the rocks and dirt. Aubrey shuffled forward, matching his speed.

Mr. Reiselstein turned around and looked through the crowd. "Let's find a spot." He strode down the hill toward the lake. Magnos followed closely behind. Buzz peeked over his shoulder, directed his rump toward his dad and tottered backward with cooler and Aubrey in tow.

Aubrey strained to carry his end of the cooler, switching his grip around the handle every few seconds to keep his hands from going numb. He glimpsed the crowd as they passed by.

Sets of smoldering campfire rings separated rows of port-a-potties pressed together like barricades. With red carpet flare, the marshy banks were lined with photographers securing their tripods into the mud of the banks, checking the lighting with handheld gauges and focusing their lens at various focal points across the lake.

Billowy charcoal clouds of smoke puffed from a single smokestack, striped red and black, on Mr. Osterfeld's tugboat as it chugged through circles in the middle of the lake.

Like overachieving door-to-door salesmen, young ladies and gents, dressed in white button-downs and slacks and strapped with shallow boxes that read State of the Mart, yelled over the din about their purchasable wares as they roamed the crowds. Quickly, the workers sold most of what they carried, from bottles of water, protein bars, chips, and snacks to ready-made meals. As soon as they were empty, they rushed back to a white circus tent, flying a banner with the SotM logo, to refill their bins and cash out their fanny packs.

"How…much…further?" grunted Buzz. Aubrey looked at him. Streams of sweat rolled off his forehead and dripped off his chin. His thick black glasses had slid to the very tip of his nose, and tiny beads of perspiration sloshed at the bottom of his lenses. Aubrey glanced up ahead. Mr. Reiselstein had stopped, and Magnos had planted the Mole-Pole tent upright into the ground.

"Almost there," heaved Aubrey.

Suddenly, Buzz dropped the cooler. Aubrey stumbled forward and caught himself on the cooler's lid. "What gives?"

Buzz took off his glasses and wiped his face with the bottom of his shirt. "We can drag it…the rest of the way."

Aubrey nodded.

Magnos walked over to Aubrey and Buzz and shook his head as he grinned. Magnos reached down and grabbed the cooler, lifting it with ease to his chest. Buzz ducked as Magnos swung the cooler around and marched over toward Mr. Reiselstein.

"Even better," sighed Buzz.

"Buzz!" hollered Mr. Reiselstein as he rummaged between the flaps of the tent, "Which switch do I flip first?"

Buzz hobbled over toward his dad. "There are three switches. The order is bottom-up."

Mr. Reiselstein nodded as he felt for the switches along the trunk while balancing the pole against his shoulder.

Magnos dropped the cooler next to the steel-mesh sack that lay a few yards behind the tent. He walked over to Mr. Reiselstein and grasped the top of the Mole-Pole tent between his meaty hands, steadying it.

Buzz lifted up several of the tent flaps and ducked underneath, disappearing within the folds.

Aubrey stood back and watched the two of them wrestle with the overgrown umbrella.

"*Ack!*"

The din of the crowds softly hushed as most who were nearby turned to look for the disturbance. Aubrey's arms and legs tightened. He jerked his head toward the source of the scream near the lake.

With wide eyes and gaping mouth, a pudgy woman, squeezed into a frilly tube top and a pair of jean shorts, stood in the open doorway of a cream-colored Winnebago with her hands pressed firmly against her cheeks.

"Stan! Come look! We've got neighbors!" squealed the woman. She bounced down the RV's steps and hurried across the grass toward Aubrey.

Aubrey looked behind him, hoping to find the folks to whom the chubby lady was referring, but all he could see was a troop of Boy Scouts, setting up tents and hanging tarps in trees.

Aubrey turned back, and leaning backward, he winced. The woman and her foul, spicy breath were inches from his face.

She pulled his hand from beside him and shook it like she was trying to beat lint off a rug.

"How are you, young man?" squalled the woman with a beefy smile of yellow teeth and cherry red lipstick. Old-fashioned curlers, wrapped around her blonde hair, bobbled up and down, exposing her dark roots.

Aubrey took a step back. "I'm okay, I guess." He reeled in his arm slightly, but the woman's grip was too tight for him to regain possession.

"Are you here for the million moth metamorphosis? Stan and I are so excited. We've been talking about this for months. We drove in this morning. Heard the bugs are almost ready to pop."

Aubrey yanked his arm free. "That's funny. I've lived here my whole life and just found out about it four days ago." Aubrey took a step backward. The woman matched his step.

"There we go!" cheered Mr. Reiselstein. The woman looked over her shoulder. Aubrey took advantage of the distraction. He trotted around her and shuttled quickly toward the tent.

The Mole-Pole tent groaned and warbled. Magnos and Mr. Reiselstein jumped back as the flaps unfurled. The central trunk spiraled down into the earth, its screw furrowing soil onto the grass and driving its unwinding core into the ground. The top portion of the trunk elongated as it unscrewed, and the tent grew two stories in height.

"Wow!" crooned the woman, ogling the tent. "It's *huge!*"

Aubrey rolled his eyes and joined Magnos behind the growing tent.

"Who's that?" Magnos whispered to Aubrey.

"No idea," replied Aubrey.

"Stan!" hollered the woman. "Stan! Come here!"

The Winnebago rocked back and forth. A bald, stocky man, wearing a tank top, bounded into the RV's doorway. He gripped a razor in his right hand, and a lathery coat of shaving cream blanketed his left cheek and neck.

"Franny!" screamed the man. "I'm busy!"

"Your two o'clock shadow can wait!" insisted the woman. "You have to see this!"

The man stormed out of the Winnebago, muttering unmentionables under his breath. With a heaving chest and fists clenched tight, he walked up to the woman. "What do I need to see right this minute?"

The woman pointed indignantly in front of her. The man turned around and dropped his jaw and his razor.

"Whoa." He marched up to the tent and stuck his head through the flaps. "Nice tent!"

Inside, leaning over the bottom of the central shaft, Buzz looked up and furrowed his brow. "Thanks," he said uneasily. "Dad! Come here!"

Mr. Reiselstein wormed his way through the flaps. His face appeared next to Stan's. Mr. Reiselstein gave Stan a curious glance. "Yes, son."

Buzz tapped a black-and-red-painted bolt on top of a small box connected to the base of the central trunk. "I think the battery is dying. The tent poles won't stiffen without more juice."

Mr. Reiselstein thought for a moment. "I think there are some car batteries behind the Screever's Lair."

"Your tent runs on batteries?" asked the man.

Buzz scowled at the man. "It doesn't *run* on batteries. The electromagnetic fields in the tent poles keep them in place."

The man crossed his eyes and grunted, "Huh?"

Buzz rolled his eyes and pushed through his dad and the man. When he stood up outside, the pudgy woman met him face-to-face. Buzz took a step back.

"Is this yours?" asked the woman, a roller dangling midforehead.

Buzz scrunched up his cheeks as if he had just bitten into something sour. Unsure of what to say, he eyed Aubrey over the woman's shoulder. Aubrey shrugged his shoulders.

The woman reached for Buzz's hand. Buzz quickly shoved his hands into his pockets.

"My gracious. How rude of me," said the woman. She reached around Buzz and yanked her husband out of the tent. "I'm Fran Losepkee." She wiped the shaving cream off the man's face. "And this is my husband, Stan."

Buzz wormed his way several feet away from the entrance of the tent. "Hello, Mr. and Mrs. Losepkee." Buzz scratched the back of his head and looked at the ground. "You wouldn't happen to have an extra car battery with you, would you?"

Fran Losepkee straightened her husband's shirt and tucked it in his pants, stretching it over his round belly. Stan Losepkee pulled his shirt back out and smacked his wife's fastidiously nimble hands.

"Naw, son. I wish I could help you," said Stan as he ended the couture war by gripping his wife's hands tightly.

"No worries," said Mr. Reiselstein, emerging from the tent with the dead car battery. "We can run home and get another."

Mr. Losepkee grimaced at Buzz's dad. "You keep spare car batteries at your house?"

"It's not your average house," chuckled Mr. Reiselstein. "Arvel Reiselstein. Thanks for coming over."

Stan thrust his hand forward, but Mr. Reiselstein raised the car battery and grinned.

Mr. Losepkee took the hint. "Good to meet you." He looked at Fran and thought for a moment. "I just replaced our battery last year, and I don't have a spare, but I have some jumper cables."

Buzz squinted his eyes at the mention of jumper cables. "I don't think that will work."

Stan pondered Buzz's comment. "Yeah, probably not. Guess the tent isn't the same as a car." Stan snickered. Fran rolled her eyes. Buzz tapped the leads of the battery in his dad's hands and sighed.

Brushing his sweat-drenched bangs off his forehead, Magnos stepped out from behind the tent. "Why wouldn't jumper cables work?"

Buzz glared at Magnos. "Because in a car, the alternator helps recharge the battery. The jumper cables just give it the jolt it needs to get it going. We need more than a spark to keep the Mole-Pole tent aloft."

"Aloft?" questioned Magnos and Mr. Losepkee simultaneously.

A scowl scrawled across Buzz's face. "It's easier to show you than to tell you."

At the sight of Magnos, Mrs. Losepkee elongated her posture and, arching her shoulders, lifted her chest. "H-e-double L-ooohhhooo," she murmured. "Where have *you* been hiding?"

"Uh, over there," stammered Magnos, pointing behind the tent.

Mrs. Losepkee strutted up to Magnos, her head at the height of his chest. She grasped his beefy forearm and pulled him toward her. "I'm Fran Losepkee. Pleasure to meet you."

Magnos stepped back and frowned. "Hi, Mrs. Losepkee. I'm Magnos."

"Oh, fiddle faddle! Call me Fran." She winked at Magnos and softened her tone. "You can even call me Franny if you want to."

"Franny, behave!" scorned Mr. Losepkee. He pulled her away from Magnos.

"Excuse me, but did someone mention needing a car battery?" The question wafted over their conversation from outside the camp.

Aubrey and Buzz turned around.

With a three-fingered salute, a tall gangly young man with a blond, high-and-tight crew cut and arms that nearly reached his knees, gazed at them. With a slouch to his neck and back, he stood amid a crowd of middle and high school kids, all of them dressed in the same uniform: tan button-downs adorned with bright red ascots knotted over their collars and forest-green shorts, which nearly met their matching knee-high socks.

Aubrey, Buzz, Magnos, Mr. Reiselstein, and Mr. and Mrs. Losepkee stared at the cadre of Boy Scouts, all looking back at them with curious expressions.

The young man unshielded his eyes and straightened his stance. "I didn't mean to eavesdrop, but it sounded like you all needed some help setting up your…your tent." His Adam's apple pointed out so far it looked like a second chin in the middle of his long neck.

"We do," hollered back Mr. Reiselstein. "Do you have an extra car battery?"

The young man smiled gleefully. "I've got a couple extra batteries for my four-wheeler. I bet one of them will work."

Mr. Reiselstein nodded. "Probably." He waved the group over.

The clump of tweens broke rank and trotted over toward the Mole-Pole tent. Buzz puffed out his chest and grinned widely. He shoved himself under the draping door and hollered to the crowd behind him. "Come on in! Let me show you how it works."

One by one, the younger Scouts pulled open a nylon fold and scuttled in.

"Hey, Magnos!" shouted Buzz. "Get in here! I need someone to hold up the flaps."

Magnos grumbled. Out of the corner of his eye, he caught Mrs. Losepkee eyeing him up and down. Magnos escaped under the tent. Mrs. and Mr. Losepkee followed close behind.

The gangly young man walked up to Mr. Reiselstein and saluted him. "Coren Belward, senior Scout leader. Troop 254. St. Pinnetakwah Council of northeast Georgia."

Mr. Reiselstein returned Coren's salute. "Hello, Coren. Welcome to Lake Julian." Mr. Reiselstein laughed as he watched the younger Scouts marvel at the tent and how quickly Buzz's demeanor changed with his new audience. "Hopefully the million moth metamorphosis and all its wonder will be a huge hit with your troop."

"We're definitely excited about it, sir," replied Coren. "But we're also here on official Scout business."

"Oh, really?" replied Mr. Reiselstein. "What kind of business?"

"We're providing first aid and basic immediate care for anyone injured during the festival. We have roving centers, anything from a small wagon to a trailer bed full of medical supplies, helping folks out when they need it."

"That sounds like a very thoughtful plan." Mr. Reiselstein leaned over and placed the car battery on the ground, wiping the grease from the battery on the grass.

"It's for my Eagle Scout project. But we're available to help in other ways too." Coren scratched his chin and looked at the dead battery. "I've think I've got just the replacement for you."

Coren spun on his heels, and with his long chicken-like legs, sprinted back toward his campsite.

Mr. Reiselstein smirked at Aubrey. "He seems like an eager fellow."

"No kidding," remarked Aubrey.

Holding up a flap, Aubrey peered into Mole-Pole tent.

"Pay close attention," said Buzz.

With his arms fully outstretched, Magnos grunted as he held up a portion of the tent in his wide wingspan.

A half dozen eager Boy Scouts, Buzz's dad, and Mr. and Mrs. Losepkee crowded around the central screwlike shaft, focused on Buzz. Aubrey leaned back to escape the suffocating warmth accumulating under the tent.

A glint of white from the corner of his eye caught his attention. He turned toward the lake and looked beyond the campsites and photographers. Usually Mr. Osterfeld's tugboat only bobbed lazily around the lake. Today, it was racing in tight, controlled circles. Charcoal gray smoke erupted from the tugboat's red-and-white-striped smokestack while white, foamy wake sloshed at the boat's bow and stern.

"Each nylon sleeve contains a hundred or so small rectangular-shaped electromagnets placed end to end," continued Buzz. He cranked a tiny wheel several revolutions on the tent's trunk, and a thin, white tube coursed out of a tiny hole and snaked across Buzz's open palm.

Mr. Reiselstein held apart two ends of a black and red wire connected to the ATV battery Coren had brought from his campsite. Coren kneeled next to the battery, securing the protective flaps on the terminals where the wires made contact. Mr. Reiselstein tapped the exposed ends of the wires together.

Zap!

Electricity snapped between the wires, filling the tent with the smell of ozone.

Buzz peeled back part of the nylon sleeve. "When the electromagnets are energized…" He held up the exposed circuit to his dad. Mr. Reiselstein touched it with the wires.

Instantly the white tube straightened. "They line up." Buzz flicked it with his finger. The nylon tube warbled but maintained its newly linear configuration. "Tense as a metal pole."

The Scouts and Losepkees cooed. Buzz glanced up at Aubrey, who was looking away from the opening of the tent.

"Better come in for the main event," declared Buzz to Aubrey. "We're about to open this baby up!"

"I've seen it before." Aubrey smiled at Buzz. "And I've heard the spiel. Besides, there's something I want to check out real quick." Aubrey dropped the tent flap and looked at the lake again.

"Okay, then," chimed Buzz to his attentive audience. "Let's feed the nylon sleeves into the tent." Buzz cranked the wheel. The tent purred as it filled with nylon tubes.

Aubrey marched toward the bank as he watched Mr. Osterfeld's tug-boat. The tugboat was now plowing through the lake in figure eights.

Swoosh! Snap!

Aubrey turned around to look at the noise behind him. Fully expanded, the Mole-Pole tent towered over the grounds like an overgrown teepee. Muffled applause cheered from inside. Aubrey grinned, knowing Buzz was enjoying his moment of celebrity.

"Aubrey!" shouted a voice from the bank.

Aubrey spun around, and his grin squirreled into a frown.

Dodging campers and his own scurrying mobile sales clerks, Jobe Parotty charged up the bank with a broad wave and a hefty grin. Salt-and-pepper strands of the man's bowl-shaped hair flitted in the lakeside breeze, and his round mole rested in the center of his forehead.

"Aubrey," greeted Mr. Parotty in his northeastern accent. "I'm so glad I found you. I felt terrible about ending our conversation so early the other evening. You're such a pleasant young man." Aubrey feigned a grin. "Thanks," he blurted out. Fidgeting with his fingers, his eyes darted between Mr. Parotty and the ground. Aubrey noticed his mole had moved again, but he didn't want to stare.

"Did you have a memorable first night at the Rock-U-Quarium?"

"Oh, yeah," Aubrey glanced at Mr. Parotty's mole again. Aubrey decided either his memory was faulty or Mr. Parotty's beauty mark was more of a facial toupee.

"Good, I'm glad to hear it." Mr. Parotty wiped the sweat from his brow and squinted as he glanced at the sky, awaiting more enthusiasm from Aubrey. Aubrey nodded and bit his thumbnail to keep from staring.

"Well, I hope you'll be joining us regularly," continued Mr. Parotty. "We should be offering season passes soon, so you can drop by whenever you'd like."

"That'll be great." Aubrey kicked his shoe in the dirt.

Mr. Parotty lowered his voice and leaned in toward Aubrey. "But there is something a little more important I want to speak with you about."

Aubrey leaned back, and lines creased across his forehead. His eyes stared behind Mr. Parotty. "What's that?"

Mr. Parotty gazed around him. "I think we should speak in a more private setting." He scratched the back of his head and snickered a short, wry snort. "Outside the range of so many wandering ears, if you get my meaning."

Aubrey furrowed his brow. "Hmm," he muttered with concentration.

Mr. Parotty held his hands up. "Now, I know what you're thinking, and I don't want anything to be awkward. So if you'd like to ask one of your friends to be there, that's fine by me."

Aubrey took a step back as his eyes widened. "But, uh, I…"

Mr. Parotty shrugged his shoulders and crinkled his eyebrows. "I'm talking about the opportunity of a lifetime here."

Aubrey shook his head and stepped back again.

"No," asserted Mr. Parotty. "An opportunity of a thousand lifetimes," he whispered. "An opportunity of *mythical* proportions."

Aubrey's eyes quivered. Suddenly, he reached forward and grabbed Mr. Parotty by the shirt. "We can talk about whatever you want, but right now we gotta move!" Aubrey spun Mr. Parotty around to face the lake.

Mr. Parotty gazed at the water. His jaw dropped.

Wrumph! Crash!

Photographers bolted up the bankside. Campers grabbed coolers and children and ran. And Parotty's employees dropped their fare and fled.

Aubrey turned and dashed for the Mole-Pole tent.

Mr. Osterfeld's tugboat had risen out of the water and raced inland. The boat plowed into the grassy bank, its bow cutting through muck and moss. Cameras and tents crumpled under the steel hull. Campers screamed. Onlookers shouted warnings at those in the ship's way. The tugboat raged onto the shore, bringing waves of water with it.

Metal ground against rock, squealing in high-pitched moans. The tugboat barreled across the land, dredging a ditch in the earth.

Mr. Parotty gawked at the scene, frozen by the rapid approach of the steel vessel and its field of destruction.

Slowly, the tugboat slid to a halt a few feet from Mr. Parotty. The engine choked and sputtered, spewing out a few final sprays of lake water. The smokestack blasted a mushroom cloud of sooty, black char toward the sky.

Marveling at the wreckage, Aubrey trotted up toward Mr. Parotty. "Are you okay, sir?" Aubrey's eyes darted between Mr. Parotty and the tugboat.

Mr. Parotty nodded slowly, swallowing hard against his dry throat. He took a calculated step back.

Cautiously curious, the surrounding crowd edged their way toward the boat, murmuring to one another with pointed gestures and covering their mouths with awe-filled expressions. Buzz, Magnos, and Mr. Reiselstein filtered through the tourists, quickening their pace when they saw Aubrey.

Aubrey examined the boat more closely. The tugboat, named *Derelict Dolly*, appeared much larger than he expected once it was out of the water, and he couldn't see over the railing. Craning his neck for a better view, he stepped back and walked alongside the boat.

Aubrey eyes widened. Phineas Osterfeld lay limp against the tug's large round wheel. His back was stained with sweat. His protuberant belly rested against the wheel with his head slumped over it. His eyes were closed, and his skin and lips were chalky gray.

Aubrey's stomach rolled with a sour quease. He turned away and closed his eyes.

A single scream echoed from the crowd. "That man is hurt!" shouted a voice from the back.

Ringing needled Aubrey's ears, and he felt the world tumble around him. He dropped to his knees to regain his balance. A hand gripped his shoulder. "What happened?"

Aubrey opened his eyes. Rodriqa stood over him, keeping him from falling. Beads of sweat dotted the rich, dark skin of her forehead as she searched his eyes for answers.

Aubrey shook his head. "What are you doing here?"

She rattled her cell phone in her hand. "I've been looking for you for hours. I called and texted, but you didn't answer."

"Sorry." Aubrey sighed. "I left my cell phone at the Screever's Lair."

Rodriqa frowned. She looked down away from Aubrey.

Aubrey furrowed his brow and stared at her. "What is it?"

Rodriqa's eyebrows twisted. "Mr. Jennings went back to his store last night."

"Oh no," murmured Aubrey. "Is everything okay?"

Rodriqa shuddered. "They found him in the parking lot this morning. Comatose."

GAUGING TRIAGE

Aydria Auerbach walked through sliding doors with her daughter, Rodriqa, and her friends, Aubrey, Magnos, Jordana, and Buzz, following close behind. As the fluorescent lights in the Lake Julian Regional Hospital foyer gleamed off the marble floors, Mrs. Auerbach slid her sunglasses off her nose and pulled her forest-green silk scarf down from her head to her shoulders.

"Your father is going to kill me if he knows I have you out with your friends," Mrs. Auerbach whispered to Rodriqa.

Rodriqa frowned. "Personal tragedy trumps grounding." She dropped back to be closer to her friends.

Buzz pulled at Rodriqa's sleeve. "Does your mom know which floor Mr. Jennings is on?"

"I'm not sure," she whispered back, "but it shouldn't be too hard to find out."

"I hope he's okay," murmured Jordana. Aubrey hung his head. "I just hope it wasn't that creature's fault."

Pausing for a moment in the sterile glow, Mrs. Auerbach placed a handle from her sunglasses in her mouth and examined the entrance. To her left, a spacious carpeted area filled with dark brown couches opened up to several stories above, revealing a row of administrative offices behind a split-level balcony.

To her right, prospective patients of all ages sat in a panel of cubicles lining the wall. Nurses dressed in scrubs took blood pressures and temperatures, asked questions, and typed into computers next to them.

Directly in front of Mrs. Auerbach, a middle-aged woman with a flat nose and wrinkled frown sat behind a curved counter. A small placard to the right marked Information in smaller-than-expected letters.

Mrs. Auerbach took several strides forward, her skirt rippling around her ankles. Folding her sunglasses, she slid them into her purse. She stopped at the counter and stood above the woman behind it, whose eyes were fixed on a computer screen in front of her.

Mrs. Auerbach cleared her throat.

The woman's eyes didn't move, but she cleared her throat in return and said in a flat, mumbling tone, "Can I help you?"

"Yes, thank you," replied Mrs. Auerbach. "I'm looking for Ray Jennings. Do you know where he is located?"

The woman behind the counter typed on the keyboard. "That information is restricted."

Mrs. Auerbach jerked her head backward. "Restricted?"

The friends huddled around her.

"He's not allowed to receive visitors at this time," mumbled the woman, her eyes unmoving.

"Is there somewhere we can wait until visiting hours?"

"Not really," snorted the woman. "Doesn't look like he'll be having visitors for quite some time."

Mrs. Auerbach frowned and leaned forward. "What do you mean?"

The woman's fingers chattered against the keyboard, and then with, a final tap of the return key, she glared up at Mrs. Auerbach. "He's been quarantined. That's all I can tell you."

"Quarantined," murmured Mrs. Auerbach. The five friends glanced at each other.

"Are family members allowed to see him?" questioned Mrs. Auerbach. The woman didn't move and made no attempt to reply.

Mrs. Auerbach sighed.

"What do we do now?" Rodriqa asked her mom.

Mrs. Auerbach turned to face the children and placed her hand on her hip. "We try a different approach."

Aubrey bit his lip and scanned the hospital entranceway. He noticed someone familiar on the far side of the lobby. "Mrs. Auerbach, maybe she can help." Aubrey pointed across the chairs in the lounge.

"Good eyes, Aubrey," said Mrs. Auerbach. She stepped away from the counter and walked through the lobby into the lounge.

The friends followed. From their perspective, it was easy to see where she was heading. In the far corner, in front of a glass window with a small circular hole, a tiny woman with silvery white hair, wound tightly above her head, leaned toward the glass with both hands planted on the counter below.

"But I'm his *wife*," she declared into the hole in the glass. "I have a right to see him!"

As Mrs. Auerbach approached the woman, she opened her arms. "Elma, are you okay?"

The woman turned, and her shoulders slumped. "Oh, Aydry!" She leaned up, and the two women hugged each other tightly.

"This has been so awful. He was outside all night, supposedly. I didn't know where he was this morning. Then I got a call from the police, telling me they've taken him to the hospital, and now they won't even let me see him!" Mrs. Jennings's eyes glistened with tears.

"Is he okay?" Mrs. Auerbach took a step back to look at Mrs. Jennings.

"I don't know." Mrs. Jennings dotted her cheeks with a folded tissue. "They won't tell me anything. They just keep saying he's been quarantined."

"Yeah, we heard that too," said Aubrey, walking up behind them.

Mrs. Jennings held out her arms and hugged Aubrey. "Oh my! Look how you've grown. You'll be as big as your brother before you know it."

Aubrey smiled and wiggled out of her grasp. "Doubtful," he murmured.

"How's your mother?" Mrs. Jennings asked.

"About the same," replied Aubrey. "I hope Mr. Jennings is okay."

"Me too, dear." Mrs. Jennings sighed.

Mrs. Auerbach leaned over Mrs. Jennings and placed her mouth over the hole in the glass. "Not only is this hospital's behavior utterly unconscionable, but it is also morally and ethically derelict. You cannot separate loved ones, no matter what the reason."

"Actually, ma'am, we can," reported a voice from a chair below. A receptionist with a thin face and glasses, wearing an overly ironed shirt and a thin tie, looked up from his desk.

"Excuse me?" Mrs. Auerbach glared down at him.

"According to hospital policy, next of kin are almost always allowed in, but this is an exceptional circumstance."

"Exceptional," she barked. "You better bet it's exceptional. Exceptional that you are denying Mrs. Jennings her rights!"

"Go, Mom!" whispered Rodriqa with a wily grin. Magnos and Jordana smiled at her.

The man shook his head. "There's nothing I can do. The quarantine is enforced to protect the public, and I can't override it."

"On whose authority?" questioned Mrs. Auerbach.

"Mr. Miller and Mayor Brackenwright."

Mrs. Auerbach straightened her neck. "If Mrs. Jennings is not allowed to talk to her husband immediately, then the next person she'll be speaking with is her lawyer!"

The man shifted in his chair. "It would take a miracle to get you in at this point," murmured the receptionist. "There's nothing I can do."

Mrs. Jennings patted Mrs. Auerbach on the arm. "It's okay, Aydry. Maybe I can visit the Millers tonight and ask for their help."

"Maybe's a cop can help," said a twangy Italian voice from behind them.

SPRING BROKEN

Sergeant Van Zenny ushered Mrs. Auerbach, Mrs. Jennings, and the five friends into a stainless steel elevator. The doors closed as everyone turned around to face the front.

A stuffy silence squeezed their ears. The sergeant fastidiously pulled up his belt, shoving the loose bunches of his uniform shirt into his pants. Mrs. Auerbach drummed her fingers against her forearm while she glanced at the sergeant from the corner of her eye. Mrs. Jennings glanced down at her watch and twirled the ends of her purse straps.

An electronic beep dinged overhead with the passing of the floors.

Mrs. Auerbach sighed. "Alec, what's going on?"

The sergeant curled his lip. "Bad business, Aydry. Things ain't quite what they used to be in Lake Julian."

"Why has Ray Jennings been quarantined?" insisted Mrs. Auerbach.

"He's not well." He tipped his cap to Mrs. Jennings. "I'm sorry, Elma. But they've got a team of doctors looking after him as well as that lady from the I-5."

"The what?" questioned Mrs. Jennings.

"Oh," replied the sergeant. "That woman doctor from the International Institute of Illness Investigation and Intervention."

"What do they think happened?" asked Mrs. Auerbach.

"I's got no idea, but Mr. Jennings isn't the only one affected. The town leadership is in a tizzy. And I don't think I's have to tell ya's who's he thinks is responsible."

"Hence the police escort," said Buzz.

"Well, it's not our fault." Rodriqa popped her neck. "We love Mr. Jennings! We'd never—"

Mrs. Auerbach glared at Rodriqa. Rodriqa clenched her jaw, crossed her arms, and looked away.

"Who else has been quarantined?" asked Aubrey.

The electronic beep chimed overhead, and the doors slid open.

"Go see for ya'selves," said the sergeant. He waved them forward and held the door open.

Elma Jennings hurried out of the elevator. She walked through the middle of a room, jacketed from corner-to-corner in white and brightened by rows of fluorescent lights lining the ceiling. Ahead, in the center, a semi-circular series of curtains were drawn closed.

Sergeant Van Zenny waited for Mrs. Auerbach and the children to exit into the room and then followed them out of the elevator.

"What is this place?" Jordana asked.

Aubrey and Magnos shrugged as they gawked at the room's sterile nakedness. Ceramic tile layered the floor and waist-high walls, and rows of glass had been taped over with linen coverings. A soft hum from the ventilation vibrated from the back of the room, nearly masking a few rhythmic beeps pinging from behind the semicircle of curtains.

"Looks like they converted one of the old nurseries into a clean room," surmised Buzz, examining every angle. "They've rigged a negative-pressure system and sealed it tight with caulking."

"They's limitin' the air exchange around here," reiterated the sergeant.

With a quick shiver, Rodriqa crossed her arms. "It's creepy. Like B-rated, slasher-movie creepy."

Jordana nodded.

Mrs. Jennings peeked around a curtain but then quickly pulled back.

"You're not allowed to be running around the ward unattended," barked a sharp voice from behind the curtain. The curtain screeched open along its metal rod. Mrs. Jennings placed her hand on her chest and took a step back. Iyashi Gatchiri marched up to Mrs. Jennings. Nose-to-nose, the doctor glared at the elderly woman through straight, white bangs.

"Who are you?" demanded Dr. Gatchiri.

"Elma-ma Jennin-nings." The elderly woman backed away. "I'm...I'm looking for my husband."

"Who authorized your entry?" Dr. Gatchiri pressed forward.

Mrs. Jennings eyes twitched as she glared back at the tiny Asian woman.

"She's Ray Gene Jennings's wife." Mrs. Auerbach marched forward. "She can see him whenever she likes."

Sergeant Van Zenny sauntered toward them. "Doctor, I'm afraid she's right."

Mrs. Jennings stiffened her lower lip. Dr. Gatchiri didn't move. Mrs. Jennings looked down behind Dr. Gatchiri and gasped. She covered her mouth and darted forward. "Ray!"

Dressed in a hospital gown and covered from his chest to his feet in a white sheet, Mr. Jennings lay on a hospital bed behind Dr. Gatchiri. The friends raced forward to see him, but Dr. Gatchiri raised her hand at them. They halted and leaned around her to look.

Mr. Jennings's eyes were closed, his arms and legs limp at his side. Ashen gray, his skin appeared more like unkilned clay than flesh. With loss of muscle tone, his wrinkles on his putty-like face and cheeks sagged around his ears and neck. An oxygen cannula rested in his nose. Assorted clear, plastic tubes ran from his arms to various colored liquids in half-empty bags hanging above him. Aubrey never realized how little hair Mr. Jennings had since he was rarely without his royal blue ball cap.

Three small LED screens hung from the ceiling above Mr. Jennings's headboard, with blue, red, and green numbers flashing and changing next to squiggly waveforms.

Sitting next to her husband's still body, Mrs. Jennings clutched his hand and rubbed his fingers gently. Tears rolled down her cheeks and dripped tiny, round watermarks on his sheet.

"Is he okay?" Mrs. Jennings choked out the words.

Dr. Gatchiri turned around and faced the monitors over Mr. Jennings. She walked over to the head of the bed and lifted her electronic tablet off a small table. She tapped the device's screen. "I don't think that's the right question."

Mrs. Jennings tightened her lips and cleared her throat. "Can you help him?"

"I hope so," said Dr. Gatchiri.

"What's wrong with him?" Mrs. Jennings brushed a few sprigs of hair in line across the elderly man's forehead.

"All his tests are normal," reported Dr. Gatchiri in a flat tone as she looked at her electronic tablet.

Mrs. Jennings smacked the bed and stood up. "*This* is not *normal*!"

Dr. Gatchiri looked up and turned her head to the side. "Hysterics won't help us figure out what's going on with your husband, and it *won't* make him better."

Trembling with astonishment, her mouth opened wide with a retort, but Mrs. Jennings turned back toward the bed with her wet cheeks bunched up tightly.

Buzz took a step forward and looked behind the curtain next to Dr. Gatchiri. "Hoaker croaker," he murmured as he pulled it open.

Jordana jerked her head away and closed her eyes. Rodriqa pulled her hands to her mouth. Magnos scrunched up his face, and his upper lip drew away from his teeth as he cringed. Unable to draw breath, Aubrey dropped his jaw.

Two more hospital beds stood next to Mr. Jennings. Both were with a patient as still and apparently lifeless as Mr. Jennings, both gray in color and connected by plastic and wiring to a bank of computer screens, digitally shimmering with numbers and letters above them.

Mrs. Auerbach covered her mouth and took a step back.

The children easily recognized Mr. Vandereff and Brandy Gungandeep, despite their pale and departed appearance.

"You shouldn't be here!" Dr. Gatchiri yanked the curtain closed. "Why did you bring them here, Van Zenny?"

Sergeant Van Zenny plodded forward, holding his belt. "These kids are uh…good with the unusual. Thought they might have some insight as to what's goin' on."

Dr. Gatchiri's lips curled, creasing her cleft lip scar. "Are you insinuating I need *help*, Sergeant?"

"Oh, no, ma'am." Van Zenny looked at the ground, but kept his chin up. "The more heads workin' on this thing, the better."

Behind the patients, a set of swinging double doors hurled open. Several men and women dressed in blue scrubs pushed a gurney into the room, holding another gray patient, attached to a series of tubes and wires.

Dr. Gatchiri trotted toward them. A man with a paper mask and a maroon stethoscope hanging from his neck raced ahead of the gurney and approached Dr. Gatchiri. "There's another one," he said, panting, as he handed Dr. Gatchiri a clipboard thick with papers. "*Everything* is normal. Blood counts, inflammatory markers, electrolytes, arterial blood gas are all unremarkable."

Dr. Gatchiri flipped through the clipboard. "Drug screens? MRI? Echocardiogram? Is your workup complete?"

The man nodded. "Brain MRI and MRA are normal. There are no signs of hemorrhage or ischemia. Urine and serum drug screens are negative. Chest X-ray and EKG are also normal. I haven't gotten in touch with the cardiologist yet to get an echo."

"Infection?" charged Dr. Gatchiri.

"C-reactive protein, lactic acid levels, and sedimentation rate are normal. White count is seven thousand with a normal differential. Blood cultures and viral titers are pending."

Dr. Gatchiri squinted her eyes at the man and plopped the clipboard down on the passing gurney. She glanced at the new patient and rubbed her fingers across his damp, gray arm. "He's not anemic?"

The man shook his head. "His hemoglobin is 13. Renal, liver, and pancreatic functions are normal. There are no signs of trauma on exam. I thought about doing a spinal tap because of his altered mental status, but—"

"Psshh!" Dr. Gatchiri held up her hand. "I'll take it from here. Make sure the doors are sealed on your way out."

Wiping the sweat from his forehead, the man nodded and turned away.

The other medical staff wheeled the new patient next to the other three and attached his lines and electrodes to monitors on the rack above them.

"Vitals?" Dr. Gatchiri surveyed the numbers of the flickering screen.

A nurse pulled a pad from her pocket and read off several numbers. "Temperature 35 degrees centigrade. Heart rate 52 and regular. Blood pressure 100 over 55 and stable. Respirations 11 per minute. Oxygen sats 95 percent on room air."

"Are you sure?" grunted Dr. Gatchiri. "Those are the exact numbers of the other patients. Could you have transcribed them incorrectly?"

The nurse shook her head. "I triple checked them manually. They haven't changed since he's been here."

Dr. Gatchiri rubbed her nose with the back of her hand. Pulling a short, black stethoscope out of her pocket, she inserted the rubber ends into her ears and placed the bell on the new patient's chest. "You're dismissed," said Dr. Gatchiri, her eyes fixed on his quiet thorax.

As quickly as they had entered, the medical staff scurried out of the quarantine bay and exited through the back doors.

Aubrey looked at the new patient with widened eyes. Everyone recognized the old man on the gurney, who lay unconscious and pale, swaddled in white sheets.

"Mr. Osterfeld too?" asked Rodriqa.

"Guess so," mused Buzz. Aubrey felt a sudden tug on the back of his shirt. He stumbled backward.

The sergeant leaned down over him and met Aubrey face-to-face.

"What's goin' on?" Van Zenny asked.

Aubrey shrugged and shook his head.

"Look, I's trying to be the good guy here, but if ya's can't help me, then I's can't help you," said the sergeant.

"I don't know," stammered Aubrey. "We've never seen anything like this before."

"Did you all do this?" questioned Van Zenny.

Aubrey looked up at him. "N-n-n-no." Aubrey swallowed hard against the sticky mucus congealing in his throat. At first, he was hurt by the sergeant's accusation, but then doubt crept into Aubrey's heart. *At least I don't think so*, he thought to himself.

"You're really saltin' my celery here, Aubrey. I brought ya's up here so you could tell me sumpin'. 'Cuz without an explanation, Mr. Miller's gonna be comin' after ya's."

Aubrey looked down. "Do we have time to think about it?"

The sergeant released Aubrey and mumbled under his breath.

Buzz stepped in between the beds and turned in circles. "Wait a second! If this is a quarantine room, why aren't you wearing suits or something to protect yourselves?" accused Buzz, raising a pointed finger at Dr. Gatchiri. "And why would you allow us to be exposed to...to...whatever is going on!"

Dr. Gatchiri stuck her index finger into Buzz's chest and pushed him away from the beds. "Very clever." Dr. Gatchiri smirked. "The quarantine was a ruse to keep unwanted visitors and the media away until we knew more about the situation."

"Then what is going on?" asked Mrs. Auerbach.

"I'm certain the children already know," countered a gruff voice from behind.

Everyone turned around. Maximillian Miller and Mayor Brackenwright stepped out of the elevator at the entrance of the quarantine bay.

"Who let *them* up here?" roared Mr. Miller, pointing at the five friends.

"I thought they's might know what happened," explained Van Zenny with a tremble to his tone.

"Brilliant, Sergeant," seethed Mr. Miller. "Bringing the coyotes into the barn isn't exactly the best way to protect the flock."

Mayor Brackenwright shook his head. "If you really think they're responsible, then they need to be at the police station, not the hospital."

"Yes, sir," grumbled Van Zenny.

"And what proof do you have that any of these children were involved?" demanded Mrs. Auerbach.

Mr. Miller scoffed. "How much truancy, delinquency, and infidelity to the law can any gang participate in before their obvious guilt and lack of remorse is undeniable and worthy of the fullest penalty?"

"Excuse me?" retorted Mrs. Auerbach with a twist to her torso.

"They've hypnotized most of the people in this town, endangered scores of lives at the Paddling Pumpkin Raft race and parade, ransacked the power plant, and destroyed my house!"

"None of that was our fault!" yelled Rodriqa.

Mrs. Auerbach shot her daughter an icy glance. Rodriqa bunched up her lips and looked down.

"Baseless accusations will not stand up in a court of law." Mrs. Auerbach placed her hands on her hips.

"We'll see if a jury of their peers will see it the same way." Mr. Miller turned toward the mayor and raised his hands. "How much longer must we procrastinate justice?"

Sighing, the mayor rubbed his forehead and stepped up to Mrs. Auerbach. "A lawyer might not be a bad idea, Aydry."

"In lights of recent events, I'm afraid I'm gonna have to ask ya's to not leave Lake Julian until further notice," Van Zenny said with his left hand on his handcuffs and his right hand on his holster.

"There goes our spring break," grumbled Rodriqa.

"Show them out," grumbled Mr. Miller to Sergeant Van Zenny.

"We know the way," bit Mrs. Auerbach. "But Mrs. Jennings has a right to stay with her husband." She ushered the children toward the elevator.

Mr. Miller curled his lip and motioned Dr. Gatchiri toward him. He pulled out a red paisley handkerchief from his back pocket and covered his mouth and nose.

Dr. Gatchiri walked up to Mr. Miller and the mayor. They huddled together in a corner away from the row of patients.

Dr. Gatchiri eyed his handkerchief. "There's no evidence that it's infectious."

"Then why are they in a coma?" asked the mayor.

"They're not in a coma."

"Then what do you call *that*?" Mr. Miller pointed at Mr. Jennings.

"They're in torpor," replied Dr. Gatchiri.

"What?" asked the mayor and Mr. Miller in synchrony.

"*Torpor*." Dr. Gatchiri articulated the word. "It's a state of hibernation."

"What caused it?" whispered Mr. Miller.

Dr. Gatchiri thought for a moment and then tapped her fingers on her electronic tablet. "Could be toxin mediated. The comprehensive toxin screens haven't returned from the lab yet. Could be related to seizure activity, but the neurologist hasn't had enough time to fully evaluate their EEGs."

"I never knew humans could hibernate," replied the mayor.

"They can't," said Dr. Gatchiri. "It isn't physiologically possible for our species to arrest our metabolism sufficiently for torpor."

"Then how is this happening to them?" Mr. Miller glanced between the doctor and the pale, stone-still patients.

Dr. Gatchiri wrestled the bitter words across her sharp tongue. "I don't know."

Mrs. Auerbach stood in front of the open elevator with her hand against the door. "I'm going to make sure Mrs. Jennings is okay. I'll be down in a minute. Wait for me downstairs in the lobby."

Bunched together in the middle of the elevator, the five friends silently nodded. Mrs. Auerbach moved her hand, and the doors closed with a quiet clink of metal.

With the floors chiming by overhead, Magnos pulled his friends into a circle and leaned in. "Okay, we need a plan."

"Magnos is right." Buzz rubbed his chin. "Something strange is going on. And unless we figure out what it is, they're gonna pin it on us."

"Definitely." Rodriqa cracked her knuckles. "We should check out Mr. Osterfeld's tugboat. If he got ill on his boat, there might be some clues up there as to what's going on."

"We should visit his house too," said Magnos. "Doesn't his niece live there? She might know something."

Aubrey shuddered at the thought of visiting Mr. Osterfeld's house, Hovis Trottle's old church. "What if the creature in Mr. Jennings's store basement got out? It still has Solluna. We have to check out the Smart Mart first."

Buzz nodded. "We need to talk to Jafar. Find out if he knows anything."

"Maybe run by Mr. Vandereff's place," added Magnos.

"And if Teton Bailston really did see something nasty at the Circle of Circles cemetery," recalled Rodriqa, "we'll need to look around up there too."

"What about that massive tree behind Mount Camelot?" Jordana pushed her rose-tinted glasses up her nose. "Its sudden appearance can't be coincidence."

Magnos, Buzz, Aubrey, and Rodriqa nodded.

"Looks like we suddenly have a full spring break ahead of us." Buzz rubbed his hands together.

Rodriqa's shoulders slumped forward. "I've got a problem." The other four looked at her. Rodriqa sighed. "I've been grounded."

"What?" replied Magnos, Aubrey, and Buzz.

"Why?" asked Jordana.

"The Miller incident."

"Oh," replied Aubrey. "I figured your parents would understand."

Rodriqa grimaced. "Yeah, me too."

"But you're out of the house now," said Buzz.

"It's not that kind of grounding," murmured Rodriqa.

"What do you mean?" Aubrey asked.

Rodriqa lowered her head. "I'm not allowed to hang out with you all anymore."

Her four friends stared at Rodriqa, her words rolling around in their minds.

"Not funny," said Buzz. "Clearly, you're with us, and your mom knows about it. You're gonna have to do better than that."

"My mom gave me special dispensation because of the circumstances."

Aubrey's mouth slowly opened. "Are you serious?"

Rodriqa nodded. "My dad thinks I've strayed from the path. He feels I need a new direction and new peers."

Aubrey tilted his head. "That's not fair."

"That's what I said." Rodriqa wrapped her arms around her chest. "Honestly, the punishment is my dad's. I don't think my mom is backing him a hundred percent."

"So we'll never see you again," asked Magnos.

Rodriqa held up her hand. "I'm not unfriending anyone. I'm just making you aware of my circumstances."

Buzz crossed his arms. "Well, that puts a damper on investigating."

"Not really," said Jordana. "It just means we have to make sure Rodriqa spends spring break away from home and out of sight."

"But with us," added Buzz with a grin.

Rodriqa smiled at him.

"I wish we were better at staying out of sight." Aubrey wrinkled his eyebrows.

"That'll be our goal this week," said Jordana with an authoritative nod. "Prove we're all on the straight and narrow."

Magnos nodded.

Buzz danced a quick jig. "Spring break in Lake Julian it is."

"A trip to the beach would have been much nicer," replied Rodriqa.

"Why?" Buzz chuckled. "So you could work on your tan?"

Rodriqa scowled and smacked Buzz's arm.

Buzz hunkered down, preparing for more retaliation.

"Your pasty white toad thrower could use some sun." Rodriqa smirked.

Aubrey looked at his watch. "It's gonna be dark soon. Should we start investigating tonight?"

"Who's gonna want to talk to us at night?" said Magnos. "We're the enemy, remember?"

"Ah, yeah, good point," mumbled Aubrey.

"First thing in the morning then," said Buzz with his eyebrows high. "I'll bring the Buzz Bug."

A Ruse Between Two Thorns

Sunday.

Kneeling at the edge of his bedroom closet, Aubrey dug through several mounds of clothes on the floor. He pulled a T-shirt from the middle of the leftmost pile. He took a whiff and sneered as he dropped it back on the rightmost pile.

His cell phone buzzed on the floor next to him. He opened it. He read the text from Buzz.

> Aubrey & Rodriqa, check out the Finer Diner. Magnos, Jordana &
> I are gonna check out the tree & we'll meet up after.

Aubrey glanced at the alarm clock on his nightstand. It read 7:12. Leaning into his closet, he grabbed the first shirt he saw on the top of the middle pile. Aubrey smelled it. Thinking for a moment, he cocked his head from side to side. *It'll do*, Aubrey thought to himself and slid on the shirt.

Shoving his phone in his pocket, he trotted over to his desk and opened the drawer. He pocketed the Finer Diner key and a crinkly wrapped candy bar and then held still, listening for other noises in the house.

Aubrey heard a popping sound echo from the hallway. Slinking toward his doorless threshold, he angled his head, ear out, to listen more intently. The popping noise was coming from downstairs.

Aubrey stepped to the top of the stairs and looked down into the living room. Gaetan sat on the edge of the couch, hunched forward with his long legs bent, almost as if he was crouching against the floor. He threw a baseball from his left hand into his mitted right hand over and over again.

Aubrey couldn't see Gaetan's face. The living room was dark except for the dull light from outside filtering through the curtained window behind Gaetan. Something wasn't right. Aubrey took a deep breath and stepped down the stairs. He relaxed his shoulders and decided to ignore Gaetan.

Aubrey sauntered through the living room and kept his face forward as headed for the front door on the other side of the dining room.

Gaetan's catcher's mitt snapped sharply with a fast pitch into the leather. Aubrey shuddered but kept walking.

"What are you doing up so early?" Gaetan rolled his head down and glared at Aubrey from the top of his eye sockets.

Aubrey stopped, just a few feet from the dining room table, and turned toward Gaetan. "I'm headed to the million moth metamorphosis. Buzz and his dad are there." Aubrey took a step toward the front door.

"But it's spring break," replied Gaetan. "Shouldn't you be sleeping in like most of the other runts your age?"

Aubrey swallowed the lump rising in his throat. He considered running for the door, but he knew Gaetan could easily catch him if he wanted to. Aubrey decided to play Gaetan's game.

"How about you? It's your spring break too," countered Aubrey.

Gaetan lifted his head. "Practice." Gaetan coughed hoarsely, covering his mouth with the back of his empty hand. "I have a baseball game later."

Chills prickled Aubrey's spine. "Looks like we both have a busy week." Aubrey didn't wait for a reply. "See ya." He marched for the front door.

"Where are you going?" demanded a voice from the top of the stairs.

Aubrey's stomach flipped. He turned from the foyer and slipped into the dining room. His father stood at the top of the stairs in a white T-shirt and boxers, his short, receding hair flared up into twirly spikes at his temples.

"Mrs. Jennings asked Rodriqa and I to check on the store this morning," said Aubrey.

"How is Mr. Jennings?" Mr. Taylor's face softened slightly.

Aubrey shrugged. "Haven't heard anything new. I'm gonna go check on him after while."

"I thought you were on your way to the lake," questioned Gaetan.

"I am," replied Aubrey, "after."

Mr. Taylor brushed his hand through his thin hair. "Just be careful out there. You and your friends are already in the hot seat. Don't be stirring up any more trouble."

"Good advice," added Gaetan.

"I'll do my best," echoed Aubrey's voice as he disappeared out the front door.

"I called Jafar last night, but he wasn't really eager to talk." Buzz squeezed out of the passenger side of the Buzz Bug while Jordana held the door open for him.

"Probably has a lot on his mind," remarked Magnos over the top of the car.

"Probably pretty scared too," added Jordana. "I would be. He's been haunted by a ghost for months, and now his mom is comatose. And he only lives a few doors down from Mr. Miller."

"Mr. Miller is scary enough by himself." Magnos glanced up at the distant houses atop Mount Camelot behind him.

"I guess so." Buzz straightened up. "I'm kinda surprised he wouldn't say much. Just that he didn't hear about his mother until after she had already been taken to the hospital, and nothing unusual had happened that day."

Jordana pushed her rose-tinted glasses up her nose. "Can't blame him for being lock-lipped."

Buzz nodded. "He asked me something curious though."

"What's that?" asked Magnos.

Buzz walked around to the front of the car. "He wanted to know if we really had eliminated his ghost or just freed it from him to haunt somebody else."

Magnos frowned in thought.

"Did he see something?" Jordana joined Buzz at the front of the car.

Buzz shrugged. "He must have."

The three of them looked up and surveyed the land next to the asphalt road. The midmorning sun warmed a field of green and golden waist-high grasses that blanketed a flat plain between Mount Camelot and the distant forest-covered mountains of the Pisgah highlands. Far in back of the field sat a lightwood tree the size of a small skyscraper, its wide trunk gently tapering toward the top. Its gnarly branches curled in spirals with sprays of foliage fanning out at their twisted ends.

"Is this as close as we can get?" Jordana shaded her eyes and gauged the distance to the tree.

"'Fraid so," replied Buzz. "Except for Mount Camelot, this is the closest road."

"I wonder why no one's said anything about it." Magnos scrunched his face and tried to recall if he'd seen the tree before.

"Maybe no one else has seen it." Buzz examined the edges of the valley and judged the distance between the two.

"Who could miss it? It's huge!" remarked Jordana.

"If you're looking for it," commented Buzz.

They stepped off the road. Jordana held her hands out, parting her way through the briary stalks of weeds, whose oat-like tassels occasionally scraped her chin. Buzz sidestepped through the tall weeds, figuring he was thinner from flank on. Magnos marched ahead, his large feet plodding swatches of grass to the ground. He purposefully stomped hard to scare away any hungry snakes writhing from their winter hibernation.

After a few yards, the other two decided to follow Magnos's path.

Buzz smacked his forearm. Magnos smacked the back of his leg.

Jordana frowned at them. "What is it?"

"Black flies," commented Magnos. "They'll bite the fire outta you."

A hum tickled Jordana's ear. She jerked her head away and swatted at the air near her head. The hum prickled against her ear lobe. She squealed and batted harder at the noise. Sharp needles dug into the scalp behind her ear.

"It's in my hair!" screamed Jordana. She clawed feverishly at her long, dark locks as the straight strands wound into clumps.

Buzz twisted his head around to search for her assailant, while maintaining his distance. Something green with numerous appendages wriggled violently between nests of hair at the back of her head.

Magnos turned around and gripped her shoulder. "Hold still."

"I can't!" She shimmied her body and swung her head.

Magnos took a step forward. His beefy hands smacked together next to her head with a clutch of hair caught between his palms.

Jordana froze, her head locked into place by Magnos's grip. She felt the stinging sensation fade. Nothing moved or buzzed around her.

With her head cocked to the side, Jordana looked up at Magnos and sighed with relief.

Magnos opened his hands and examined the offender. "It's just a katydid." He chuckled as he pulled the dead green bug from her hair.

Jordana's lips trembled. Magnos dropped the lifeless insect on the ground. She yanked her hair from between Magnos's fingers. "I don't know if I should thank you or hit you." She raked her fingers frantically through her hair.

"Thank me. Hitting me would only hurt you." A smile crept across Magnos's face, and he winked at her.

"I think a katydid is the least of our worries," snickered Buzz.

"You wouldn't think so if it was in *your* hair," bit Jordana.

"At least it's something we can see…and kill," remarked Buzz.

Curling her fingers up to her mouth, Jordana pondered what he said. "Do you think there might be those snake things in here too?"

"You mean spirit shards?" Buzz asked.

"Yeah." Jordana nodded.

Buzz thought for a moment. "If they are, we can't see them without Aubrey. So if you start feeling funny, holler."

Magnos nodded. Turning back around, he mowed down more clumps of grass into squashed bails as he moved forward.

Buzz glanced around Magnos and took in a view of the lush meadow. "Look at that," murmured Buzz.

"What?" Magnos stopped abruptly and looked around his feet.

Jordana squeaked a shrill scream and jumped back, dancing in place to keep moving.

"No, the tree." Buzz pointed out in front of him. "It's full of holes."

Magnos squinted and leaned forward. "Those aren't holes." He turned his head to the side. "They're windows." Magnos's eyes widened, and the color drained from his face. "I think we should go."

"Windows?" questioned Buzz as he pounced several paces forward "Are you sure?"

"This is bad." Magnos stiffened.

Buzz shaded his eyes. "Maybe they're just bird nests."

"I see someone standing in one of the windows," whimpered Magnos. "And she has red hair."

Buzz's jaw slowly dropped.

Jordana slipped up behind Magnos and peered around him. "We should turn around." She tugged at Magnos's shirt

"I'm beginning to think you're right," muttered Buzz.

Magnos clenched his jaw. "Too late."

"Whimperfidget! No!"

Aubrey tripped down the stairs of his front porch, startled by the yelling. In the side yard between the Taylor and Auerbach homes, Rodriqa crouched over a flowerbed, her beaded braids dangling forward around her neck. She jiggled a large branch, sticking out of a rose bush in the middle of the plot. A low throaty hiss seethed from between the branches.

Aubrey walked over to Rodriqa. "What's he done now?"

"My mother's ceramic gnomes." Rodriqa stood up. "He's eaten all of them. And now he's eating bits of siding off the house!"

Aubrey sidled up next to her and leaned over the smooth rock border of the flowerbed. Cracked pieces of painted ceramic littered the soil in the plot. One gnome had only its feet left in the soil. Several red pointy cone hats lay in a row of hosta with the many of the plants stripped of their leaves. "There's a name for that," said Aubrey.

"Yeah, vandalism."

"No, what's that called?" Aubrey snapped his fingers and looked up.

Rodriqa frowned at him. "What's *what* called?"

"You know, when someone eats things that don't have nutrition. *Pica!* That's it, yeah, pica."

"Great, now we have a name for it." Rodriqa placed her hands on her hips. "That'll make it all better. Are you sure you and Buzz aren't related?"

Aubrey chuckled. "I remember reading one time that when someone has pica, they're lacking something they need. Sometimes it can be associated with anemia. You know, like an iron deficiency."

Rodriqa pointed at Whimperfidget. "Does this cat look anemic to you?"

Buried in a twisted mane of cream-and-charcoal-colored tangled mats, tiny red eyes flashed at them from the interior of the rose bush.

"Guess not," said Aubrey, "but maybe he's craving something. Maybe he's hungry for something he can't find."

"He's telling me he's hungry for some time at the pound."

Aubrey shrugged. "What can we do? No one can get near him."

Rodriqa tapped her foot. "Maybe Buzz could make a contraption to catch him."

"Maybe," said Aubrey. "I was kind of hoping he'd just run away. Or get run over by a truck."

Rodriqa scowled at him. "That's not nice."

"Neither is your cat," mumbled Aubrey.

"He's *our* cat."

Aubrey rolled his eyes. "Let's go check on our other pet."

"Bad Whimperfidget!" scolded Rodriqa. The cat hissed again and huddled deeper under the rose bush. Rodriqa stuck out her tongue; then she and Aubrey headed for the sidewalk along Dalton Circle.

Aubrey glanced at Rodriqa curiously. "Aren't you supposed to be grounded?"

Rodriqa shrugged and kept her head forward. "My parents are at work. They won't know. Besides, my grounding, in my opinion, is inappropriate and unfounded."

Aubrey nodded. "Have you heard anything about Mr. Jennings?"

"My mom called Mrs. Jennings this morning. She said he's exactly the same. Pale and asleep. He came to for a few brief moments. Sounded more like he was dreaming. He groaned and mumbled something about a horse with green eyes, then went right back to the way he was."

"A horse?" questioned Aubrey.

"Yeah," replied Rodriqa. "Weird, huh?"

"The green eyes could be the creature, but who could mistake him for a horse?"

Rodriqa shrugged. "Doesn't make much sense to me. Hopefully it's right where he's supposed to be."

Aubrey furrowed his brow. "What if it's playin' possum? It can get in and out of the freezer, and we just don't know it?"

"That's possible," replied Rodriqa. "But if that's the case, then there should be some sort of clue. I doubt it would remember to cover its tracks."

"Good point," said Aubrey.

Rodriqa snorted.

"What?" Aubrey asked.

"It might not be the only one playin' possum."

Squinting his eyes, Aubrey faced her as they walked next to each other along the road. "What do you mean?"

Rodriqa looked around for anyone listening. "Promise me you won't say anything?"

"Promise," said Aubrey.

"I'm serious," insisted Rodriqa. "I don't want to spread rumors...or talk bad about a good friend."

"But," urged Aubrey.

"I wouldn't even be saying anything if I wasn't worried about her," muttered Rodriqa.

"Spit it out."

Rodriqa frowned. "Jordana is hiding something."

Aubrey toggled his head from side to side. "She's been through a lot with her mom and dad. She has a reason to be a little quiet at times."

"No," continued Rodriqa. "She knows more about some things than any of us could ever figure out. And to be honest, I think oftentimes she knows more than she's telling us."

"Why would she do that? She works just as hard as the rest of us do at researching stuff for our clients. And she takes the same risks. Just like all of us do."

"I know," said Rodriqa, "but she knew about the Bloodrunner anathem." Rodriqa held up her hands. "How could she find that out?"

"You sure you're not being too hard on her?"

"Probably." Rodriqa looked down. "But I'm calling her out the next time it happens. Friend or not."

"Four."

"I only see two."

"There's four. Two of them are low to the ground." Magnos peered at several spots in the tall grass ahead. They were shifting through the weeds in the distance, moving directly toward Jordana, Magnos, and Buzz.

"It's the Kluggards." Jordana stood on her tiptoes and stared at two men stomping through the weeds.

"Those jokers." Buzz guffawed. "Why did we stop? They're harmless. Not to mention less competent than a kindergartener without crayons."

"Yeah," grumbled Magnos. "But whenever they're around, so is she."

"You mean Ms. Thistlewood?" asked Jordana.

Magnos looked down at Jordana, who had her arm wrapped around his waist. He nodded without looking her in the eye.

"I'm heading to the tree." Buzz tromped two steps forward. Magnos thrust his arm out in front of Buzz, catching him in the chest. Buzz looked up at Magnos. Magnos's jaw flexed, the artery in his neck pulsing vigorously.

"I want to leave," grumbled Magnos.

Buzz rolled his eyes. "And I want to pick a fight."

Grinding his teeth, Magnos furrowed his brow at Buzz.

"I didn't know it was recess!" hollered Ned Kluggard from across the meadow. Dressed in his navy blue uniform, his round body trudged through the grass like a bulldozer. His smile beamed cheek to cheek with his flat-topped cap set far back on his head. "We would have come out sooner if we'd known there was a daycare field trip. Isn't that right, Fred?" Fred followed next to him quietly, his face vacant, and his lanky frame limply wobbling across the field.

"Well, yodel my clover!" replied Buzz. "If it isn't the dropsy twins! How's the security business, boys?"

Ned chuckled. "Hey, Fred! Lemme ask you a question." Fred's oblong head nodded like a bobble, and a squiggly smile wandered across his lips. "What happens when the cream at the bottom of the barrel tries to mix with the cream at the top?"

Fred's head teetered from side to side.

"The cream at the bottom turns to curd." Ned's wide grin transformed into a sinister snarl, and he marched faster through the grass.

"Something feels wrong," whispered Jordana. "We should go get Aubrey and Rodriqa."

"This is just how they are," said Buzz. "Trust me. They're total posers. We can take them if we have to." Buzz cupped his hands around his mouth and shouted, "You obviously know nothing about organic chemistry!"

"Nice comeback, geekwad," mumbled Magnos.

Buzz dropped his hands and crinkled his eyebrows together. "Well," his voice cracked at the end, "they don't!"

"You runts ready to get what's coming to you?" shouted Ned.

Buzz put his hands to his face. "Define runt!"

"Those who choose to fight on the wrong side," crowed Ned.

Magnos took a step back. "They're too close."

Jordana stepped forward and pulled her glasses off her face. She focused her gaze on Ned.

Ned and Fred pulled sunglasses over their eyes. "We're onto your little trick, princess," said Ned. "And you're not fooling anybody."

Buzz strode forward. "Then if you're not fools, you should realize, we beat you once, and we'll do it again!"

Ned scoffed. "You won round one. This is round two. And we've upped the ante."

Buzz raised his hands. "We're not playing poker, so we don't care!"

Ned waved his arms forward around his sides. "Neither are we. Poker is for bluffers. We're not bluffing."

The green and golden grasses for a hundred yards around Ned and Fred twisted violently. Buzz looked up at the sky, searching for a storm, but the sky was clear. He held up his hand to capture the wind, but the air was still.

"Oh no," murmured Jordana.

Buzz stood still and watched the shuddering vegetation squirm forward.

"Run!" cried Magnos.

"Do you think it got out?" Aubrey asked.

"How could it?" Rodriqa replied.

Both of them pivoted their heads from side to side as they peered through the square window to Mr. Jennings's storage freezer in the basement of the Smart Mart & Finer Diner.

"Besides, the freezer door seems pretty solid." Rodriqa shook the heavy metal door. It barely trembled in its frame. "And there's no signs of damage."

"It has to be in there." Aubrey stuck his nose to the glass and searched the freezer's innards. Three banks of wire shelving were toppled over into a metal lattice heap in the middle of the room. Iced cardboard boxes, shredded into small strips, littered the frost-laced floor between dented and bent pots and pans. "But then how did it hurt Mr. Jennings?"

Rodriqa shrugged and slid her face next to Aubrey's.

Aubrey pressed his forehead against the glass. "I have to get Solluna back."

"No, you don't," replied Rodriqa. "Maybe this thing is supposed to have it."

"Yeah, but Solluna gave me another riddle to solve."

Rodriqa glanced at him with a bent brow.

"Remember last fall when Solluna was a golden book and it had two sets of verses? One that it showed in the sunlight, and another in the moonlight?"

"Yeah, I remember. And I remember those poems being quirky and weird. And I think they got us in more trouble than they were helpful."

"This time was different though."

"How so?"

"In the sunlight, it read, 'To open the sealed.' In the moonlight, it said, 'To seal the opened.'"

Rodriqa pulled away from the glass. "What does that mean?"

"I don't know."

"Well, if you don't know what it means, then it's not helpful."

Aubrey sighed. "I just need more time to figure it out."

"We got bigger worries, Aub."

Aubrey nodded. A dry lump rose in his throat. "I guess we should go in."

"Yeah." Rodriqa leaned forward, her eyes reexamining every corner inside the freezer.

Aubrey pushed down the handle. A cool blast rushed past them.

Rodriqa touched Aubrey's hand. "Wait. I should be the one to go in."

"But I'm the guy. I should go first."

Rodriqa sneered. "And I'm the guardian, remember?"

Aubrey dropped his head. "Guess you're right. Can you do your ghost thing?"

Rodriqa chuckled nervously. "I tried." She swept her beaded braids back behind her shoulders. "The spirit of the Tsul'kalu doesn't seem to be at home right now. I'm not scared enough."

Aubrey nodded.

Rodriqa tapped her finger against the door.

"What?" Aubrey asked.

"Aren't you gonna look?"

"Oh yeah." Aubrey turned, gazed through the window, and closed his eyes.

Phosphenes swirled on a black backgroundand passed out of his view until all that remained was darkness. No lights, no movement, no shadows.

"Nothing there," said Aubrey as he opened his eyes.

Rodriqa nodded. She took a deep breath, stretched her shoulders back and popped her knuckles. "Close the door behind me, in case it tries to get out."

Aubrey nodded, his palms dampening with sweat.

Rodriqa swung the door open, flung herself inside, and closed the door behind her. She looked over her shoulder and glanced at Aubrey through the window. Aubrey's heart pounded in his chest.

Surveying the chilled wreckage of wire and cardboard, Rodriqa took a step forward. "Hello?" Her quiet tone echoed softly in the stainless steel room. She kicked the downed section of shelving in front of her. It rocked stiffly against the floor.

"I don't think it's here." Rodriqa took another step forward.

Suddenly, a blur dropped from the ceiling. Rodriqa fell to the ground. Flailing arms and legs wrestled into the near corner. Scuffling hands and feet scraped against the frosty floor.

"Rodriqa?" Aubrey leaned in, standing on his tiptoes to gain a better view of the melee.

A raspy scream resounded from the room. A comet of flailing blue hurtled across the room and fell against the far wall.

Sparkling and ghostly transparent, Rodriqa jumped to her feet, and bits of ice danced to the floor from her clothes. Bracing her stance with out-stretched arms, she shouted, "You never touch a woman like that!"

With its flap-like ears unfurled, the pale green creature, still dressed in the Elemag suit, clumsily regained its feet and growled at Rodriqa.

"Bring it, shorty!" Rodriqa took a step forward, fully enveloped in the spirit of the Tsul'kalu.

"Let me go!" squalled the creature, its large green eyes glaring at her.

"This place is a mess!" Rodriqa shouted. "You need to clean it up!"

The creature stretched its arm and pointed at Rodriqa. "You do not command me!"

"Oh, I'll command you all right!" Rodriqa jumped on top of the toppled shelving and steadied herself. "What did you do to Mr. Jennings?"

"You do not question me!" The creature stuck out its neck and exposed its sharp teeth.

"How 'bout if I question you with my fist?" Rodriqa leapt forward.

The creature snapped at her. Rodriqa grabbed its ear and yanked it to the floor.

The creature screeched as it fell. It curled its legs around and swept them against Rodriqa's ankles. Rodriqa stumbled backward onto the wire shelving.

Rodriqa rolled over onto her side. The creature hopped to its feet and lunged toward Rodriqa. Rodriqa kicked her feet upward, pounding the creature in its chest. It dropped with a loud thud. Rodriqa righted herself and landed on top of the creature. Her knees pinned its arms to the ground, and she planted her rump on its chest.

"What did you do to Mr. Jennings?" asked Rodriqa.

"I don't know this Mr. Jennings!" The creature squirmed underneath her.

Rodriqa examined the creature's pale-green reptilian skin, bald head, and flat nose more closely. "Dude!" she exclaimed, scrunching up her face. "You are one ugly toad thrower!"

"I am Shway Shway! Release me!" The creature convulsed its hips.

"You're a shway shway?" She snickered, holding it in place. "What's a shway shway?"

"That's my name, miserable pud!"

"What did you call me?" Rodriqa raised her closed fist.

Shway Shway flinched and stopped moving. "Enough! Torture me if you must. You don't deserve it!"

"Deserve what?" asked Rodriqa.

The creature clamped its mouth shut, and its round, green eyes rolled around in their sockets.

"What happened to Mr. Jennings?" Rodriqa squeezed its torso between her feet.

The creature's eyes squinted, leaving only a slit of green between its lids. "Who is Mr. Jennings?"

"The gray-headed old man who owns this store…wears a blue ball cap with a white K on it…the old man you attacked two nights ago."

"I attack only those who need be." Shway Shway smacked his lips.

"What did Mr. Jennings do?" Rodriqa shook her head. "Why did Mr. Jennings need be?"

"I never attacked Mr. Jennings."

"Then who did?"

The creature shut its mouth and rolled its eyes.

Rodriqa shook Shway Shway by the shoulders. "Tell me!"

Shway Shway snarled at her. "You speak in riddled nonsense. The old man here is of no interest."

"Then why did some creature with large green eyes attack him two nights ago?"

Shway Shway furrowed his brow and searched Rodriqa's eyes. Suddenly, he shook his body violently. "Trick!" Shway Shway tossed his head back and forth. "This is a trick!"

In her ghostly form, Rodriqa hunkered down, clamping its body between hers and the icy floor. "Aubrey! Help!"

Heaving his weight against the handle, Aubrey wrenched open the door and bolted inside. He leapt onto the wire shelving and landed on its edge. The ice under his foot gave way. Aubrey tumbled forward. His face and chest plummeted against the grating, and his braces clinked against the aluminum lattice.

Rodriqa winced as she watched Aubrey fall. "Are you okay?"

"Yeah," Aubrey grunted and pushed himself up.

Shway Shway lifted his head. "Where did *he* come from?"

Aubrey leaned back and wiped his face. "If it didn't attack Mr. Jennings," he pointed toward the creature, "what did?"

Rodriqa glared back at Shway Shway. "What attacked Mr. Jennings?"

Shway Shway looked back and forth between Rodriqa and Aubrey. "How long has he been here?

"Answer the question!" roared Rodriqa.

"Did he hear my name?" murmured Shway Shway.

Rodriqa sneered. "We don't care that your weird name is Shway Shway."

"The seer cannot know my name!" screeched Shway Shway.

"Why not?" asked Rodriqa.

Aubrey shuffled off the wire shelving and planted himself upright on the floor. "Does it still have Solluna?"

"Oh, yeah." Rodriqa shook Shway Shway. "You need to give Aubrey his little doodad back."

"You do not deserve it!" shouted Shway Shway.

Rodriqa glanced at Aubrey. "I don't think we're getting anywhere."

Aubrey sighed. His breath fogged in front of his face. He took a step to his left into a clearing surrounded by ladles and colanders.

"Hey!" Rodriqa leaned back. "I have an idea."

"What's that?" replied Aubrey.

"Why don't you look for its stone? Like you did to Hovis in the power plant. Maybe you'll see Solluna." Rodriqa pressed on Shway Shway's stomach. "Then we'll force it out if we have to."

Shway Shway grimaced, flashing the edge of his top teeth.

Aubrey nodded. "I can try."

Rodriqa moored her hold on Shway Shway. "Do it!"

Aubrey closed his eyes and inhaled deeply. He squeezed his eyelids tightly, focusing on Shway Shway in the darkness. The maroon- and olive-colored phosphenes swirled and split away from the center of his vision. Blackness engulfed his sight. Aubrey held his breath and tightened his chest, mustering all his strength, searching for his own stone inside him. Aubrey felt the blood vessels in his head pulse. He balled up his fists, straining to see the darkness with all his might.

Suddenly, the white stone within Aubrey gleamed with an orange glow, and the single tiny point of light orbiting his stone spun in quickened circles. With his eyes closed, Aubrey searched the room. He saw the pink shimmering outlines of Rodriqa and Shway Shway several yards away. Aubrey groaned as the pressure inside him forced him to tremble.

"It's working!" shouted Rodriqa. She looked down. She saw both her and Shway Shway's white stones, glowing orange in each of their chests.

"*Ack!*" screamed Shway Shway, squirming under Rodriqa.

Rodriqa examined Shway Shway. "Keep going!"

Heaving his gut upward, Aubrey focused on the two forms behind his eyelids.

A smoky mist steamed off Shway Shway's baldhead. Shway Shway screeched.

Rodriqa ruffled the Shway Shway's Elemag suit. More smoke rolled out from within the suit.

"Something's wrong," muttered Rodriqa.

Aubrey bent his knees. Spittle dripped from his mouth. A glint of the crystal pyramid flashed in Shway Shway's stomach.

Shway Shway convulsed and then suddenly went limp, his head flopping to the side.

"Stop!" hollered Rodriqa.

Aubrey flicked open his eyelids and rocked backward, moaning as he wrapped his arms around his stomach.

Rodriqa disappeared. With flaccid limbs, Shway Shway lay on the frozen floor alone.

Aubrey wiped his mouth with the back of his hand and blinked repeatedly, unsure of what he saw.

"Rodriqa?" Aubrey searched the room with his normal vision. "Rodriqa? Where are you?" Aubrey closed his eyes. The phosphenes swirled and slowly faded. In the darkness, Rodriqa stood, in full ghostly form, directly in front of him.

Aubrey felt pressure plow into his stomach, knocking him to the ground. Aubrey grunted and rolled onto his side. His eyes flashed open.

Aubrey looked up. Galloping clumsily on all fours in the Elemag suit, Shway Shway bolted out of the freezer and into the basement.

"What happened?" Rodriqa reached down and pulled Aubrey forward. The spirit of the Tsul'kalu faded, and she returned to her normal self.

Aubrey shook his head. "I don't know. Where did you go?"

"I was right here!" said Rodriqa. "Get up! Shway Shway escaped!" Rodriqa yanked Aubrey up to his feet. Rodriqa and Aubrey ran into the basement. They could hear footsteps bounding up the stairs. At the threshold, Rodriqa suddenly stopped and backed away.

Magnos turned the corner with his beefy arms clamped down on the writhing Shway Shway.

Buzz popped around Magnos into the basement. "You can't be serious! We can't let this thing go!"

"We didn't let it go!" Rodriqa set her hands on her hips. "It got away!"

"A dozen plus two of one, a fortnight of another," said Buzz, waving his hand in the air.

Aubrey took a thankful breath. "I'm glad to see you all."

"Looks like you needed to see us sooner," scoffed Buzz. Magnos walked over to the freezer. He heaved Shway Shway into the freezer. Shway Shway bounced off the far wall and crashed into the wire shelving in the center. Buzz slammed the freezer door shut and shook it to make sure it was securely closed.

Jordana trotted over to Aubrey. "Are you okay?"

Aubrey smiled weakly, and his heart flipped. "Yeah, I think so."

"You won't believe what just happened," said Rodriqa.

"Tell us on the way," said Buzz. "We've got bigger news."

Rodriqa twisted her neck. "And just what is that?"

"Ms. Thistlewood is back."

"We need to get rid of that thing!" Rodriqa slammed the passenger door to the Buzz Bug and buckled herself in the front seat.

"Did it hurt Mr. Jennings?" Buzz squeezed his rear in the center seat.

Rodriqa shrugged. "I don't think so."

"H-h-how do you know Ms. Thistlewood's back?" questioned Aubrey. He pushed his head around Buzz's belly and plopped into the back seat.

"I saw her." Magnos climbed into the driver's seat.

"Where?" asked Aubrey.

Jordana touched Aubrey on the shoulder. "She was in the large tree in the empty field below Mount Camelot."

"That's no tree," said Buzz. "It's a tree *house*. Maybe even a tree mansion. And just like she created a stone cottage out of nothing last fall, she's taken up residence in that previously empty field."

"Are you sure?" Aubrey glanced between Jordana and Buzz.

"Trust me. I'm sure." Magnos pulled his door closed.

Aubrey pushed against Buzz and pulled himself forward. "But that's not possible."

"Why not?" Buzz twisted in the middle seat to face Aubrey. "Actually I've been waiting for her to show up. She simply disappeared before. We don't know what happened after Hovis's house collapsed. She could've gotten out."

"How does someone escape a house buried under a cemetery that exploded like a volcano?" Rodriqa crossed her arms.

"Yeah, but she's one tough chick." Buzz wrenched around to face Rodriqa. "She could have gotten out any number of ways."

"Here's hoping you're wrong." Rodriqa turned her head and looked out the window.

"There's more." Magnos shifted the car's gear lever forward and pushed the accelerator pedal down. The Buzz Bug's electric motor hummed as the vehicle advanced out of the Smart Mart & Finer Diner's parking lot and onto Asheville Highway.

Jordana lifted her feet, watching the asphalt slide by underneath.

"Not only are the Kluggards with her," continued Magnos, "but she has something else fighting on her side."

"What?" asked Aubrey, his voice cracking.

Buzz scrunched up his face and twisted his fingers in the air. "It looked like some sort of dog with a really long tail."

"No," said Magnos. "It was a bat with a long snout."

"A what?" asked Rodriqa and Aubrey simultaneously.

"Actually, I thought it looked more like a goat with a really wide back." Rodriqa sneered. "Who got the best look at it?"

Magnos kept his eyes on the road. Buzz was still rolling his fingers in the air. Jordana rocked her head as she thought.

"Well, did you all see something or not?" asked Aubrey.

"We're not exactly sure," said Buzz. "Whatever it was, it was hidden in the grass. We couldn't get a good look at it."

"But it looked like a dog, a bat, and a goat?" Rodriqa furrowed her eyebrows.

Jordana and Buzz looked away. Rodriqa leaned her head forward to catch Magnos's eye.

"What are you all not telling us?" Aubrey pushed harder against Buzz.

"We ran," said Magnos.

"It was hidden, and we ran," countered Buzz.

"*They* were hidden, and we ran," corrected Jordana.

"They?" asked Rodriqa and Aubrey simultaneously.

"I think there was more than one," said Buzz.

"There was definitely more than one." Jordana nodded authoritatively.

Aubrey rubbed his chin. "Then is what you saw the thing attacked Mr. Jennings, Mrs. Gungandeep, Mr. Vandereff, and Mr. Osterfeld?"

"Maybe," muttered Buzz. "But there's no way to know. Did you learn anything from the creature in the store basement?"

"That it's a total toad thrower." Rodriqa dropped back in her seat.

"I don't think it got out though." Aubrey leaned back. "And it has green eyes, but it doesn't look anything like a horse. I don't think it's interested in Mr. Jennings. Did what you all saw look like a horse?"

Buzz shook his head. Jordana rubbed her temple. Magnos kept quiet.

Aubrey sighed and leaned back. "Anyway, Shway Shway still has Solluna, so we can't get rid of it."

"Shway Shway?" asked Buzz and Jordana simultaneously.

"Shway Shway," replied Aubrey. "That's its name."

"Wait," said Rodriqa. "I thought we were heading to Mr. Osterfeld's place."

"Later," said Buzz. "If Ms. Thistlewood is back, we need to check out the last place we saw her."

"It's not centered!" Mr. Miller yelled at the half-dozen workmen precariously balancing on metal scaffolding in the middle of his foyer. Swinging from a multitiered system of ropes and pulleys, a sparkling crystal chandelier dangled several yards from the floor.

"That chandelier is worth more than you make in a year!" Mr. Miller shouted. "You have to be more careful!"

"Yes, Mr. Miller," grunted one of the workmen who was pulling at the ropes. "We're trying."

Another workman shuffled toward the edge of the top platform. A rope loosened. The chandelier jerked to the side. All the workmen shifted to catch the massive glassworks. The veins in Mr. Miller's bald head bulged under his skin. "Try harder!" With digital bleating, the phone rang from the kitchen. Mr. Miller stormed after it. He yanked the phone off its receiver. "Hello!"

"Do you remember me?" trilled a sweet voice over the receiver.

Mr. Miller's anger and frustration melted into an unsteady calm. "Of... of...of course."

"Do you remember what I told you?"

"Yes." Mr. Miller lied as his eyes darted back and forth, trying to recall from whence he knew the tone.

"Good," spoke the voice. "Are you ready for revenge?"

Suddenly, his mind cleared, and he remembered the beautifully enchanting woman from the hallway at city hall.

"Absolutely."

THE WADING WEARY

The Buzz Bug peeled through the gravel lot next to the eastern shoreline of Lake Julian. Magnos slid the tiny Volkswagen into a parking spot and wrenched the gear lever upward, shuddering the car to a stop and, from its open floor, filling its cabin with gravely dust.

Rodriqa waved her hand in front of her face "I wonder if Mr. Osterfeld's tugboat is still beached on the shore?"

"Nope." Buzz scrambled out the passenger door with Rodriqa. "The city had it hauled back to his house before sundown yesterday."

"I thought we were going to the Circle of Circles Cemetery," Aubrey asked with his hands over his face.

"I need to get something out of the Mole-Pole tent first, then we can walk up from here." Buzz pushed Rodriqa forward, and they slipped onto the lot. "Besides, this will be a good central point to work from."

Magnos snapped open his door and helped Jordana and Aubrey out of his side. "Wow," he murmured. "The Moth-ers are multiplying."

The four others stumbled up to the edge of the knoll and peered down toward the lake. Part circus, part roadshow, every previously green portion around the lake had been filled in by the reds, blues, whites, and blacks of tens of thousands of spectators and tourists.

"Flustered mustard." Aubrey's jaw dropped. "I had no idea there'd be so many people here."

"Mr. Miller's been promoting the Rock-U-Quarium and the million moth metamorphosis like crazy." Magnos scanned the crowds. "I'd bet even Lake Julian Square is full today."

"I can't even see where the Mole-Pole tent is." Aubrey surveyed the shoreline with his hand shading his eyes.

More than a head taller than his friends, Magnos and searched the mass of tents, RVs, and roving people for Buzz's contraption. He pointed into the distance. "It's over there."

"I don't see it," said Rodriqa.

Aubrey, Buzz, and Jordana kept looking.

"Let's just stay together," said Magnos. "I can get us there."

The other four nodded and huddled behind Magnos's bulky frame. With him in the lead, they plowed through the crowd together.

Brightly dressed State of the Mart retailers weaved through the swarms, selling cameras and posters depicting the life stages of the Southern Appalachian luna moth. Local vendors sold large balloon moths and candies shaped like moths, bartering for the wandering mob's attention.

Magnos held his hands out as they crossed the countercurrent stream of folks walking toward them.

"What's that beeping?" complained Rodriqa.

Suddenly, the masses opened up ahead. Magnos took advantage of the break and scuttled forward.

A four-wheeler hitched with a plywood flatbed sped into the opening. Magnos braced his hands against the handlebars as the four-wheeler squealed to a stop.

Coren Belward looked up at Magnos, his Adam's apple bouncing up and down above his scout tie.

"I've been looking for you all." Coren hopped off the scooter.

"Hey, Coren," said Buzz, peering around Magnos. "Have you seen my dad?"

"Yes. He's with your tent." Coren pressed in closely to the group. "Something's not right."

Magnos leaned backward, uncomfortable with the lack of space between them. "What do you mean?"

Coren leaned in. "There's way more sick people around here than there should be."

Buzz waved him off. "It's an older community. It's to be expected."

"No." Coren's eyes widened, his lanky arms hanging at his sides. "Most of the tourists are younger. I've gone through a week's worth of medical supplies in a day."

"Maybe you just underestimated how many people would be here," said Aubrey.

Coren shook his head. "There's more to it than that." Coren leaned in further. "One of my younger Scouts wouldn't wake up this morning. They had to take him to the hospital."

The five friends looked at him intently.

"Maybe he just wanted to go home," said Rodriqa.

Coren stared at her. "I heard you all were the people to talk to if there's something unexplained going on."

Magnos grumbled, Aubrey rubbed his forehead, and Jordana dropped her head, so her long black hair covered her face.

"Coren, we would love to help you." Buzz nudged Magnos forward. "But our plate is a little full right now."

"Plus, we're not really allowed to help folks out that way anymore," added Aubrey.

"You're not allowed to *help* people?" questioned Coren.

"It's not that simple," muttered Rodriqa.

Coren wagged his head. "It's always that simple."

"There's nothing we can do," said Jordana. She helped Buzz shove Magnos.

"I've got a troop of kids I'm supposed to watch out for, and we're more than a hundred miles away from home." Coren's Adam's apple trembled. "Isn't there something you can tell me?"

"Look," offered Buzz, "give us a few hours to figure a few things out, and we'll come find you."

Magnos looked over his shoulder and glowered at Buzz.

"Okay." Coren nodded. "Then I'll meet you back at your tent."

"Sure," said Buzz. "But it may take a while."

"No problem, boss!" Coren leapt backward. "I'll let you get back to work." Hopping on his four-wheeler, he cranked it and pumped the horn with his fist t.

"Who was that?" asked Rodriqa, a smirk snaking across her lips.

"Long story," mumbled Aubrey.

The five friends struggled through the zigzagging flow of folks until they reached the Mole-Pole tent. Mr. Reiselstein stood on the far side of the tent, facing the water. His curly black hair lolled in the breeze.

"Hey, Dad!" Buzz rushed inside and hurried back out, carrying a white backpack. "Just came by to grab something."

Mr. Reiselstein didn't answer. He didn't move.

"Mr. Reiselstein, are you okay?" Aubrey asked.

Buzz stopped. He turned toward his father. "Dad?"

Mr. Reiselstein kept completely still.

Buzz walked over to his father and grabbed his elbow. "What's wrong?"

Gripping his steaming cup of coffee, Mr. Reiselstein jerked out of his daze. "Oh, Buzz, hi! I didn't know you were here."

Buzz glanced in the direction of his father's gaze. "What are you staring at?"

"I'm not sure." Mr. Reiselstein spun around and waved hello to the other children.

They waved in reply, their faces tight with consternation.

"Did you see some moths?" asked Buzz.

"No." Mr. Reiselstein returned his attention to the water. "Not yet."

"Then what are you looking at?" insisted Buzz.

"The Losepkees," muttered Mr. Reiselstein.

"The Losepkees?" Buzz looked over at their RV. "Why are you staring at the Losepkees?"

"They're gone," murmured Mr. Reiselstein.

"No, they're not," chuckled Buzz. "Their RV is still here."

"Yeah," agreed Mr. Reiselstein. "But I'm not sure where they are."

"They're probably out hunting for moths."

Mr. Reiselstein shrugged. "Their door was wide open this morning. Water was running in the shower, and the gas burner was alight on the stove. It's like something took them right in the middle of their morning routine."

Buzz frowned at his father. "Did you turn off the stove?"

Mr. Reiselstein nodded. "And the water."

"Maybe they had an emergency."

Mr. Reiselstein rubbed his chin. "Maybe."

Buzz felt his father's fog of thought infecting him. He shook it off. "Dad, we need to check on a few things. We'll be back later." He trotted back to his friends. Mr. Reiselstein turned around. "Hey, Aubrey!"

"Yeah," hollered Aubrey.

"The man from the Rock-U-Quarium stopped by today. You know, the guy with the mole. He came by looking for you."

Aubrey moaned. "Jobe Parotty?"

"Yep! That's him," replied Mr. Reiselstein. "Said it was important he sees you."

Aubrey looked down.

Rodriqa followed his expression. "Tell him we're on spring break," she shouted to Mr. Reiselstein.

"Will do," he replied.

Rodriqa patted Aubrey on the arm, and the five of them turned and headed into the thickening crowd.

"Be careful!" Mr. Reiselstein shouted. "Don't get in any trouble!"

"Who are the Losepkees?" Rodriqa stepped ahead of her friends as they exited the herd of tourists mingling along the lake.

"This loud couple who are staying in the RV next to the Mole-Pole tent." Aubrey pulled out his inhaler and pressed it in his mouth.

"And they're hard to miss, never mind lose," huffed Buzz, sweat rolling down his cheeks.

The five of them entered the tree line and traipsed through dead leaves and twigs as they wound their way up the hill next to the dam.

"I wonder why your dad was so lost in thought over them," Aubrey asked.

"He does that sometimes." Buzz shrugged and wiped his forehead. "He's kind of weird, I guess."

Rodriqa and Aubrey shared an amused glance.

"I wonder if the Losepkees are in the hospital." Magnos ducked a tree limb.

"Along with Coren's Scout," mused Buzz.

"Who was the tall, skinny, blond guy who looked like he had a tumor for an Adam's apple?" asked Rodriqa.

Jordana giggled and moved over to follow Magnos's path.

"Coren Belward," replied Aubrey.

"He's up here from north Georgia with his Scout troop, working on some project," added Buzz.

"There's a bunch of them," said Aubrey.

"Coren seems a little intense," assessed Jordana.

"Yeah," agreed Buzz. "But he's a nice guy. Helped us out with the Mole-Pole tent yesterday."

Rodriqa picked up a stick and twirled it between her fingers. "I would think if he's already used up all his medical supplies, he should take his Scouts and head back home."

"He might not be finished with his project," said Buzz.

"If I'd used up all my stuff, I'd be done." Rodriqa threw the stick far into the distance. "Especially with all the crazy stuff that goes on here."

"Guess he needs to wait for his Scout to get better," said Aubrey.

"So we have four local adults with the same problem in the hospital, a visiting kid there too, and now two missing adults." Buzz counted on his fingers. "I don't like how this is adding up."

"I can only imagine what's next," grumbled Aubrey.

The five friends topped the hill's summit and walked out of the woods into a large oval-shaped patch of grasses and weeds surrounded by a garrison of tall white pines. Sunlight suffused the opening in the canopy, brightening the hilltop and warming the air.

"This is it," said Buzz.

"Or used to be it," added Rodriqa.

Jordana shuddered. "This place brings back bad memories."

"Amen," agreed Aubrey and Magnos.

The five of them stepped gingerly through the mossy grass, careful not to disturb anything.

"Whoa," said Buzz. "It's all filled in."

The other four stopped and looked at Buzz, who was pointing forward with his head up. They turned to look at the declining hill a hundred yards ahead. Where the grass ended, dark brown dirt, neatly tilled into lines, layered most of the ground in the center of the large clearing.

"Where's the crater?" asked Aubrey.

"Where are all the graves?" Rodriqa shook her head in disbelief. "Did they move all the markers too?"

"I think they got fill dirt from the mine," said Jordana. "Mr. Miller had a crew out here shortly after the explosion last fall."

"He'd do anything to cover up what happened," added Magnos.

"And I bet my dad helped," continued Jordana. "He wanted to forget about it too."

"The gate around the cemetery is gone." Aubrey felt his throat dry out.

"I can't believe it," said Buzz. "You'd never even know there was a house here...under the ground."

Buzz and Magnos edged closer to the line of dirt.

"What do you think Teton saw up here?" Jordana looked over her rose-tinted glasses.

"It's got to be responsible for everyone going to the hospital," said Rodriqa.

Buzz stopped. "Whatever it was, it wasn't a ghost."

Magnos leaned over to look where Buzz was. Buzz waved everyone over. Dropping to his knees, he pointed to the dirt. The other four rushed toward him and stared at the ground.

"Footprints," said Buzz.

In the compacted fill, a series of two crescent-shaped impressions, each facing the other, were stamped facing various directions along the old cemetery's edge, as if something had trampled through the area.

"Hoof prints," said Rodriqa.

"That's the horse we're looking for!" exclaimed Aubrey.

Buzz leaned down. "I don't think it's exactly a horse."

"Well, why not?" asked Rodriqa.

"Because they don't look like hoof prints."

"Since when are you the authority on hoof prints?" questioned Rodriqa.

"I think it's quite obvious I know more about biology than anyone else here," said Buzz.

"Since when?" replied Rodriqa.

"Since about the second grade," rebutted Buzz.

"Buzz does know a lot about nature stuff," said Aubrey.

"But it's not like he's an outdoorsman," argued Jordana.

Rodriqa's neck twisted and the beads in her braided hair swooshed around her shoulders. "Look here, just because you invent garbage, doesn't make you the almighty on anything scientific."

"Uh, yes, it does," replied Buzz. "I'm clearly a scientific expert."

"Expert's a bit extreme," said Magnos.

"Ego doesn't compensate for knowledge," mused Jordana.

"I don't have an *ego*!" squalled Buzz.

"When it comes to science, your ego is bigger than Mr. Miller's," added Rodriqa.

"That's a bit unfair," said Aubrey.

"I think she has a good point," replied Jordana.

"Hay-lo!" The meaty Slovakian accent jolted the friends out of their argument.

The Poage County Animal Control officer, Simon Poschyev, stood a few yards in front of them, panting heavily, with his double-barreled shotgun resting against his shoulder and pointing toward the ground. The bottom of his shirt was bloody and shredded.

"Where did it go?" asked Mr. Poschyev, eyeing each of the children.

"Where did *what* go?" asked Buzz.

Simon Poschyev lowered his shotgun. His disheveled blond hair swayed in the breeze. "The beast."

"What beast?" asked Rodriqa.

Mr. Poschyev looked up from under his brow. "The beast that just ran through here."

"What is he talking about?" whispered Rodriqa to her friends.

Jordana, Aubrey, and Magnos shrugged.

"We're not causing any trouble, sir," announced Buzz with overly articulated syllables. "We're just checking out the area."

"Hey, are you hurt?" Rodriqa pointed to the bottom of Mr. Poschyev's shirt.

Mr. Poschyev waved her off. Dropping to the ground, he scooped up a handful of dirt and lifted it to his nose. Snorting violently, he flung the dirt over his shoulder. "I'm afraid you are all in trouble."

Ca-caw!

The five friends looked up at the edge of the forest. At the end of a thick limb of white pine, a large raven flapped its wings as it crowed loudly over the clearing.

"It's that raven," whispered Aubrey. "The one that was in the Miller house. The one I was telling you all about."

"How do you know?" asked Jordana.

"Its eyes," replied Aubrey.

The friends watched the raven carefully as it shook the limb in its talons and squawked its piercing cry. It bowed its head repetitively, driving its saber-like beak into the bark. The bird's left eye was as black as its feathers. Its right eye was opaque.

Mr. Poschyev glanced at the raven over his shoulder. "Do you know this bird?"

The friends glanced between Mr. Poschyev and the raven but didn't say anything.

"That infernal bird has followed me all day." Mr. Poschyev lifted his shotgun to his shoulder and took aim at the raven.

Before he could fire, a loud crack from a tree sounded behind him.

Mr. Poschyev and the children turned toward the noise at the edge of the clearing. The raven soared out of the tree.

Splintering into bits of timber, a thick white pine toppled into the dense foliage in the forest. Thin reptilian-skinned limbs with three-fingered hands receded from around the falling tree, and a pair of large green eyes disappeared behind another tree.

"There it is!" shouted Mr. Poschyev. He launched himself upward and bolted across the dirt toward the creature.

"What was *that*?" asked Rodriqa.

"That's our target," murmured Buzz.

Shouts echoed from the hill below. The friends' heads volleyed between the running Mr. Poschyev and the sounds crescendoing up from in front of them.

Dressed in camouflage and bright orange vests, Stew Parsons and Snakes McWhorter ran up the hill, carrying rifles at their sides.

"Where did it go?" Stew stumbled as he heaved haggardly. Snakes matched his pace and clicked the safety on his rifle.

"What are you guys doing?" Buzz stood up.

Stew leaned over and propped himself on the butt of his rifle. "We found something." Snakes nodded. He looked over Stew's back at the cloud of dirt filling the air where the pine had fallen.

"What something?" asked Magnos.

Stew smirked. "Something more wicked than a bigfoot."

Buzz curled his lip. "What did it look like?"

"Like nothing I've ever seen before."

Snakes patted Stew's shoulder and pointed toward the ground.

"Prints," muttered Stew.

Snakes bent his head, examining the patterns. He held up two fingers and then pointed toward the forest's edge.

Stew and Snakes raced out of the clearing in Mr. Poschyev's direction.

"Hey!" hollered Buzz. "You've got to tell us what you saw!"

"Come find out for yourselves, toad throwers," yelled Stew over his shoulder.

Magnos ground his teeth. Rodriqa clenched her fists. They looked at each other and rocketed into a sprint after Stew and Snakes.

Within a dozen seconds, they had all vanished into the forest. Buzz, Aubrey, and Jordana glanced back and forth at each other.

"Are we really gonna run down this hill again?" asked Aubrey with a crinkle in his eyebrows.

"Look at it this way." Jordana pushed her glasses up on her nose. "At least it's daylight this time."

THE MEETING OF THE MAGI

The black, saber-beaked raven rose out of the clearing on the hill and soared above the forest canopy next to the Lake Julian dam. The bird flattened its tail and spread wide its wingtip feathers, pitching back toward the lake as it glided above the quarry of the Berybomag Mine. Angling its left black eye at the ground, the raven watched the train of humans chasing after two shadowy creatures slinking through the woods. The raven flapped its wings harder, soaring further ahead and surveying possible routes the pursuit could take.

Suddenly, the wind around the bird churned, and it fluttered its feathers to stabilize itself. Low-lying clouds swirled down from above like a new-born tornado, with the tip of its funnel spinning toward the raven. It cawed in protest and flapped fervently to escape.

In an instant, the bird's wings crumpled, and its legs and beak curled to its chest. The raven tried to cry out, but it couldn't move. Its tail furled. The bird dropped through the air like a heavy rock.

Plummeting toward the ground like a feathery comet, the raven struggled within its balled-up body, but the unseen cage gripping it was too strong. With a resounding thud, the raven crashed into the earth, forming a divot in the dirt.

"It's disgusting." Electric sparks jumped from Melkyor's long, white beard to the tendrils of curly hair swirling at his temples.

"He's taken on the form of earthly vermin," exclaimed Gaspian, his leather jacket transforming into a long black cloak. "So crude."

Squawking and screeching, the crow lifted its head from the small crater. With extended wings, it limped out of the mud and onto dry ground.

"Filthy. Why would you give up your true form?" asked Thalazzaran as he watched the disheveled crow hobble.

The wind howled along the creek. The water rippled, and pebbles scrambled along the bank and then lifted into flight, orbiting the raven. The grass bent in toward the bird, pulled prone by an unseen force. The air bent outward and then shook as if the ether was being twisted in two.

The raven buried its beak under its wing, and one by one, strands of its long, ebony plumage escaped from its body and whipped around its head like a feathery, black hurricane. The dark, rotating mass drew dirt and dead leaves into it. The center of the turbulence grew in size, matching the height of the Magi.

Slowly, the wind relented. The grass returned upright, and the water calmed. The swirling darkness materialized into a dull gray humanoid with long spindly arms and a bald head, clothed in flowing robes that draped the ground. Transformed from the raven, Zaks stood among his Magi brethren.

The sunlight was both partially absorbed and reflected by Zaks's translucent skin. His right was eye was flat and gray, but his left eye took the shape of a dark oval. Several bits of rock and broken twigs slowly turned in orbit around his torso, ignoring earth's gravity.

"We all gave up our true form," replied Zaks, "when we made our choice."

"Then in remembering your choice, Zaks, have you forgotten your obligation?" asked Gaspian

"No, Master Magi." Zaks bowed. "I maintain the balance as is my duty."

"We have heard of the nearly opened Tomb of Enoch," accused Melkyor.

"Without a Graviteer, the tomb would not have been moved from its place in the earth's crust so easily," agreed Thalazzaran.

"I nudged the involved parties." Zaks nodded. "But I did not help either the Tsul'kalu nor the witch and her ghost."

Melkyor cackled. Gaspian curled his lip.

"We will judge later," said Thalazzaran. "There are more pressing matters to attend to."

"The seer," seethed Melkyor.

"You know him," charged Gaspian.

"Yes, masters," replied Zaks, "I know the seer, and I've seen what he is capable of."

"Then it's true!" Melkyor cried.

"Did we come too late?" questioned Gaspian.

"Does he have a guardian?"

"And a teacher?"

"A guardian, yes, one fights at his side, but I have not seen a teacher. His friends are as ignorant as he is."

"Then you have taken great pains to know this seer," surmised Thalazzaran.

Zaks nodded. "He is not what I expected. Nor as one would expect from what the Terminal Prophecy foretells."

"You must bring this seer to us," commanded Thalazzaran.

"Why not go see him yourself?" asked Zaks.

"We cannot interfere!" insisted Gaspian.

"He must be brought to us," said Melkyor.

"Bring him to us, or we will not judge your previous indiscretions as kindly as we do now." Thalazzaran raised his hand.

"As you wish. Zaks bowed deeply and then slowly raised his hands, with his index fingers extended. "However, if he passes your test and you decide him to be true, you must no longer seek him out. You will leave him undisturbed and allow whatever course has been set to come to pass."

"Of course," said Gaspian. "We can do no more, no less."

"It is necessary to maintain the balance," added Melkyor.

"Agreed," said Thalazzaran. "Let it be as you say, Zaks."

"But he is a pud. What pud could resist us?"

"What pud could pass our tests? The greedy mongrels never know what is best."

"What you speak is mostly true." Zaks folded his arms. "But this seer will surprise you."

"We shall judge," said Gaspian.

"No pud has ever surprised me," said Thalazzaran.

Zaks bowed his head. "In three days, the seer will meet you."

"Bring him to where the water falls," said Thalazzaran. "There he shall see our power and agree to be a seer no more."

FIELD OF SCHEMES

Aubrey's chest heaved as he jogged through the woods. Clearing the final clump of trees, Aubrey dropped to his knees. His heart pounded hard enough in his thin trunk that he could feel it beat against his shirt. He pulled his inhaler from his pants pocket and pressed it several times as he breathed in.

Buzz ran up to Aubrey from behind and slumped down next to him.

"Do...you...see...them?" asked Buzz between haggard breaths.

Aubrey shook his head as he recapped his inhaler.

Jordana trotted out of the forest. She stopped next to the boys, holding her long, straight back hair behind her head in a makeshift ponytail. "Where are we?" Jordana stared over an empty asphalt parking lot.

"Baseball...field," heaved Buzz.

Aubrey looked up. He could see a turnstile and the back of several stands of bleachers on the opposite side of the parking lot, which was encircled by a six-foot-high chain-link fence. Adorning the wooden entrance, a gray and blue sign read Home of the Lake Julian Belugas.

"Why would the creatures flee to the baseball field?" Jordana asked.

Aubrey and Buzz shrugged as their breathing slowed.

Buzz pointed toward the edge of the stands. "There's Magnos and Rodriqa. They're inside."

Magnos and Rodriqa were running down the top row of bleachers and quickly disappeared below the horizon of the parking lot.

"Let's go!" Jordana wiped the sweat from her forehead and stepped onto the asphalt. Aubrey and Buzz pushed themselves off the ground.

The three of them jogged across the parking lot toward the baseball field's entrance. They landed against the turnstile. It shuddered against its frame. They gave the turnstile another hard push.

"It's locked," said Jordana.

Buzz stumbled to the side and surveyed the entrance. "We could climb over the fence."

Jordana wedged herself against the turnstile and pulled herself between the teeth and the frame. "Or we can slip through."

"Good idea." Aubrey sidled up next to Jordana and followed her.

Jordana sprinted toward the end of the bleachers.

Buzz's shoulders slumped. He glared between them and his chubby belly. "Ah, come on, guys. That's not fair."

"Run around to the other side." Aubrey popped through the turnstile. "There's gotta be a break in the fence somewhere."

Buzz pouted. With his arms dangling at his sides, he traipsed along the fence.

Aubrey chased after Jordana. She stopped at the end of the bleachers and looked down into the empty field. The green diamond had been freshly trimmed, and the brown foul lines in front of the concrete dugouts had been recently dusted with chalk. Magnos and Rodriqa stood with their backs to the bleachers, where several stationary objects lay on the ground in front of them. Magnos and Rodriqa were speaking to each other.

"What are they doing?" Jordana tilted her head for a better view.

Aubrey clutched her elbow and pulled her forward. "Let's go find out."

Aubrey and Jordana ran across the bleachers. They turned and stepped quickly down the flimsy metal staircase. Once on the yard of the field, they hurried toward the pitcher's mound.

"Hey!" hollered Aubrey. "What did you find?"

Magnos and Rodriqa didn't move, and they didn't answer. Aubrey and Jordana glanced at each other as they ran.

Suddenly, Jordana stopped a few yards behind Rodriqa and Magnos. She covered her mouth and gasped. Aubrey slowed his pace as he approached the mound, scanning the ground over and over again, unsure of what he was seeing.

At the edge of pitcher's mound, Simon Poschyev, Stew Parsons, and Snakes McWhorter lay face up on the ground, their eyes closed and mouths gaping open. Their arms and legs were limply splayed out at their sides, and their skin pale gray.

"What happened?" Aubrey stepped up between Rodriqa and Magnos. "Was it those things they were chasing?"

Magnos shook his head. "Don't know. They were like this when we got here."

Aubrey felt his throat scratch with dryness. "Are they...?"

Rodriqa nodded. "They're breathing...barely."

"And they have a pulse," added Magnos. "But they look—"

"Hey, guys! You won't believe what I found!" Buzz yelled from the back of the field as he hobbled with a limp up to the pitcher's mound.

"We found something too," replied Magnos.

"No way!" Buzz slowly approached the bodies on the ground. "Did you guys do this?"

Rodriqa scowled at Buzz. "No, numb knuckle. We found them this way."

"So cool." Buzz kneeled down next to Stew and grabbed his wrist to feel for a pulse. "They look just like Mrs. Gungandeep, Mr. Jennings, and Mr. Osterfeld!" He leaned his ear over Stew's mouth. "And they're alive."

Jordana peered around Magnos, looking up at the sky to avoid the sight. "What did you find, Buzz?"

"Oh," replied Buzz. "Sergeant Van Zenny is here."

"What?" asked Aubrey.

"Where?" asked Magnos.

Buzz shrugged. "I don't know, but his police car was parked behind the field."

"See, Officer? I told you these little toad throwers were the worst kind of trouble."

All five friends twisted around, startled by the voice behind them. Dressed in a light-gray suit, Maximillian Miller stood next to Sergeant Van Zenny, who had one hand on his belt and another on his holster.

"More victims of the NeighborGhoul Watch." Mr. Miller lifted his chin high. "And this time, there's no one else to blame."

"This isn't our fault," insisted Aubrey.

"The evidence shows otherwise." Mr. Miller crossed his wiry arms, the late afternoon sun glinting off his bald head.

"I's sorry, Aub." Van Zenny pulled five pairs of handcuffs off the side of his belt. "This don' look good."

"They were like this when we got here," crowed Rodriqa.

Mr. Miller chuckled. "Denial is the weakest form of protest, and the strongest staple of conviction." A thin grin scrawled between his concave cheeks. "Book 'em, Van Zenny."

HARD TIME

"Ya's sit here and don't touch anything!" Sergeant Van Zenny looked at each of the five friends as he adjusted his holster. "I've called ya's parents. They's on their way."

"Does that mean we can go home?" Aubrey asked, his voice cracking.

Sergeant Van Zenny shook his head. "This mess may be more than I's can get ya's out of."

The five friends sat on a wooden bench behind a series of computers atop unoccupied desks in the center of the Poage County Police Department's back office. Each of the friends leaned forward with their heads hung low. Their hands, resting in their laps, were each enclosed in handcuffs.

"I'll be back." The sergeant shuffled sideways between desks. He opened the glass office door and stepped into the hallway. The door slammed behind him, rattling a framed picture of a map of Lake Julian on the wall.

Separated by a large pane of reinforced glass, the sergeant glanced warily at the children in the office. He walked up to Judge Arsvine and Mr. Miller, who were waiting to speak with him.

A single tear slipped under Jordana's glasses and dripped off her cheek. She leaned into Magnos and rubbed her face dry against his arm.

"I can't believe we're in jail," muttered Rodriqa. "And I'm supposed to be grounded."

"Technically, we're not in jail," replied Buzz. "We're just in holding."

Rodriqa turned her head and glowered at Buzz. The veins in her forehead throbbed as she clenched her jaw.

"But close enough." Buzz looked away.

"This can't be happening," whimpered Jordana. "I'm gonna be in so much trouble."

"That's the truth," agreed Rodriqa. "We've been in hot water before, but this is bad mustard."

Jordana choked back her tears. Magnos spread his elbows apart and raised his cuffed hands. Jordana slid her head between his arms, and he hugged her. She buried her face in his chest and cried.

Muffled yelling reverberated through the glass window at the front of the office. The friends looked up and watched Mr. Miller, Judge Arsvine, and the sergeant gesture angrily at each other in the outer hallway.

Buzz's leg twitched. He leaned on it with his arms to hold it still.

Aubrey sighed. He knew Rodriqa was right. They had been in some tight places and had some near misses with the police, but the risk of being convicted of committing a crime had never been so real before. Aubrey knew his father would be angry. His dad might even threaten again to send him to military school. Maybe they would all have to go away. And to make matters worse, the one person he liked the most sought solace elsewhere.

Mr. Miller, Judge Arsvine, and Sergeant Van Zenny stormed out of sight.

"What did you see?" Aubrey asked Rodriqa.

Rodriqa shrugged. "Mag and I chased Mr. Poschyev and Stew and Snakes into the baseball stadium. At first we couldn't find them. Then Mag noticed something on the field. We ran down there." Rodriqa inhaled deeply. "They were just laying there, lifeless. We yelled at them. They wouldn't move."

"Any sight of the creatures?" Buzz rolled his head around.

Rodriqa shook her head. "I never saw them again after we ran into the forest."

"Me neither," added Magnos.

"And where did Mr. Miller and Sergeant Van Zenny come from?" asked Aubrey.

Rodriqa sighed. Buzz shivered and pulled his shoulders in.

"We were set up," grumbled Magnos.

"But how?" Aubrey asked.

"It's not like it would be that hard," said Jordana. "Everyone has it out for us. They all think we're delinquents." Jordana unthreaded herself from Magnos's arms. "And who can blame them? We go around acting like we can beat something nobody can see, and all we do is destroy stuff!"

Rodriqa and Aubrey hung their heads. With his head forward, Magnos shifted his body toward the edge of the bench. "But we saw it."

Rodriqa, Buzz, Aubrey, and Jordana looked up at him.

Magnos turned toward them. "We all saw it."

The five friends shared knowing glances, each one calmed a bit by the fact that, although the rest of the world was clueless, they had shared this unseen struggle together.

Suddenly, Buzz's head flopped back against the wall abutting the bench. His legs stiffened and then convulsed. His arms jerked spastically in their handcuffs, and he slid to the floor.

Aubrey pressed his hands into Buzz's belly and pushed Buzz into the bench. "Help me," Aubrey said to Rodriqa.

Rodriqa leaned in and cupped her arms under his knees, rocking him back onto the bench.

Jordana gasped and covered her mouth. "What's wrong?"

"He's having a seizure." Aubrey leaned against Buzz harder as his seizure intensified. "It happens every so often."

Buzz sighed deeply. His limbs relaxed. He shook his head. "Am I okay?"

"Yep," said Rodriqa, scooting back in the bench. "You're fine. Just don't drool on me."

Buzz smacked his handcuffs on the bench. The other four jerked at the loud crack.

"I've got it!" Buzz hollered.

Sergeant Van Zenny closed the door to the office. Taking several steps forward in the hallway, he glanced through the window at the five friends, seated on the wooden bench along the office's back wall.

"Alec! Why aren't you booking them?" Maximillian Miller squeezed his forehead with his hand.

Sergeant Van Zenny placed his hands on his belt and walked over to Mr. Miller and Judge Arsvine. "Don't ya's think we's need some more investigation into all this?"

Mr. Miller dropped his hand and squinted his eyes. "Don't tell me you're on their side, Van Zenny."

Van Zenny shook his head, and the flab under his chin wobbled. "No, sir. The only side I's on is the law's side."

"Good!" Mr. Miller lifted his chin. "Then there's only one appropriate course of action. Don't you agree, Rakeman?"

"These kids have represented themselves as a danger to our community long enough," said Judge Arsvine. "I think it's time for them to feel the legal ramifications of their actions."

"Insinuation is one thing," replied the sergeant. "Proof's another."

"What do you mean, insinuation?" Mr. Miller's nostrils flared. "You were there! You saw what happened!"

The sergeant nodded. "Yes, but I's not convinced they's as guilty as ya's think they's are."

"Why not?" Towering over the sergeant, Mr. Miller leaned forward.

"I's seen…"

"I don't care about what you've seen, officer. I care about the facts!"

The sergeant cleared his throat. "Then I's has some facts you should know about."

"What facts, Sergeant?" asked the judge.

"Freyma Spindergrath's ranch was broken into and ransacked yesterday. I's at her place investigating the scene when you called me to come get the kids at the baseball field."

Mr. Miller's jaw dropped. "More destruction! More irreverence for the law." He turned toward the judge. "What more do we need?"

"The problem is," interjected Van Zenny, "it occurred yesterday."

"So?" snapped Mr. Miller. "They're on spring break. They have free reign—"

"Except," interrupted the sergeant, "it occurred yesterday while we were all at the hospital."

Judge Arsvine eyed Mr. Miller.

"Are you sure?" asked Mr. Miller.

The sergeant nodded. "Absolutely's. The only times Ms. Spindergrath was gone from the ranch was the precise times we were assessin' the quarantine." Van Zenny rubbed his chin. "And the kids was at the hospital that whole time."

"That doesn't clear them of other charges," huffed Mr. Miller.

"No," sighed Van Zenny, "but it don' make it a clear-cut case either."

"Is Ms. Spindergrath all right?" asked Judge Arsvine.

"She's unharmed," replied Van Zenny. "A bit shaken, but nothin' hurt. Perhaps ya's like to see her. She's stayin' at my place."

"Yes, of course," replied the judge. "I can't believe I hadn't heard sooner."

The sergeant looked down. "Ya's know Freyma. Likes to keep to herself."

"I'm glad she's okay, but we can't ignore what these children have done." Mr. Miller pointed a finger into Van Zenny's chest.

The sergeant took a step back. "I's promise there will be a full investigation."

Mr. Miller straightened his shoulders and glared at Van Zenny. "An empty promise is like a colander full of ants. You can shake it out any way you want, but there's always a nest of biting annoyances left to clean up afterwards."

The judge sighed. "We should check on Freyma. Certainly, a shock like this at her age can't be a good thing."

"I 's can take you to her now." The sergeant raised his hand toward the door behind the men.

Mr. Miller and Judge Arsvine turned and walked away. Sergeant Van Zenny followed.

Buzz lurched off the bench and dropped to his knees, his muscles still weak from his seizure. Holding his handcuffed hands up, he shuffled forward along the floorinches at a time.

"I don't think we're supposed to leave the bench," said Rodriqa.

"What are you doing?" Aubrey asked.

"Is he still having a seizure?" Jordana asked.

"I have an idea," said Buzz. "I need to look something up." He crept up to the closest desk and slumped into the chair. Sliding upward, Buzz pulled himself chin level to the keyboard. He raised his bound hands and tapped on the space bar. The computer screen flickered on as the hard drive hummed.

"Now is not the time to play computer games," groaned Rodriqa.

Buzz smirked at her. "Any time is the time to play computer games." He twisted his torso up further up in the chair and rested his hands on the desk. "But I think I know what we're up against."

"Besides the entire Lake Julian City Council and half the town's population?" Jordana rubbed her eyes under her glasses.

"We all know there are scarier things than Mr. Miller," asserted Buzz.

He typed on the keyboard. The Lake Julian city seal appeared in the middle of the screen. At the bottom, a blank line blinked with a cursor above a request for a password.

"You can't hack the computer," grumbled Rodriqa. "We're in a police station."

"I'm not hacking," replied Buzz, "I'm borrowing."

Rodriqa rolled her eyes. Buzz typed in short bursts. After each burst, he hit the Return key. Each time, the computer flashed, "Denied." Buzz stuck his tongue out at the computer. "I need a password."

"Try 1-2-3-4," replied Magnos. He stood up and looked at the computer screen.

"Yep." Buzz pushed himself up. "I tried the four most common passwords. 1-2-3-4-5. Q-W-E-R-T-Y. Q-A-Z-W-S-X. I-L-O-V-E-Y-O-U."

Magnos nodded. He walked over behind Buzz and rested his handcuffed hands on the back of the desk chair. Buzz surveyed the desktop around the computer.

A small planter sprouted with a violet, which also held a small plastic tag explaining how best to care for the plant. Three pictures hinged together in a single frame portrayed a family photo in the middle with smaller pictures of a young boy and a Yorkshire terrier on either side.

"Let's see," mumbled Buzz. "Looks like this computer belongs to Belry Kayston."

"Doesn't she live up by Warsh and Wrench Cleaners?" Aubrey bent forward off the bench and walked over to the computer.

"Yeah," agreed Magnos as he leaned down to examine the picture. "But I thought she worked as a receptionist at the vet."

"She used to." Buzz held up a finger. "Until her dog died last spring." Buzz squinted at the dog bone-shaped tag hanging from the Yorkshire's collar in the photo. "What was her dog's name?"

Aubrey leaned down next to Magnos as they both attempted to read the name from the picture.

"Boodlebop?" said Magnos.

"No," replied Aubrey. "Bundlebust."

"That's it." Buzz nodded as he typed. "Anybody know how old Ms. Kayston is?"

"This is ridiculous," mumbled Rodriqa.

Aubrey spun around and pointed at Rodriqa. "Didn't she go to school with your dad?"

Rodriqa turned up her lip. "Yes."

"What year was your dad born?" asked Buzz.

"1963."

Buzz typed again and tapped the Return key. The Lake Julian city seal faded, and Belry Kayston's main screen filled in.

Jordana slipped off the bench and stepped up to Buzz. "Good work."

"Sharp," remarked Magnos. He and Aubrey high-fived clumsily with their handcuffs.

Buzz clicked on the web browser. "Pet name and year of birth are the most common personal items used for passwords." Buzz typed in a web address for his favorite search engine. "Now down to business." Buzz tabbed through several blank fields. "Aubrey, how did you feel when Shway Shway was attacking you the night after the Rock-U-Quarium?"

"Uh." Aubrey furrowed his brow. "I don't know. It was sorta like my life was being sucked away."

Buzz nodded. "And what are the most common symptoms of the victims we've seen thus far?"

Rodriqa stood up and stomped her foot. "Shway Shway is the easy answer for all this. We already know that."

Buzz shook his head. "Answer the question."

Rodriqa folded her arms and marched over to the desk. "They're all pale and lifeless."

Magnos chuckled. "Sounds like Lake Julian has a vampire."

Rodriqa nudged him. "Everyone knows there's no such thing as vampires."

"Agreed," replied Buzz. Buzz typed in a single word and held his index finger over the Return key. "What's it called when one being steals another being's life force?"

The other four glanced at each other. Rodriqa huffed. Jordana tapped her finger against her cheek. "Parasitism?" Aubrey mumbled.

"Yes!" exclaimed Buzz. "But it was called something else before there was science." Buzz smacked the Return key.

A dark page loaded on the screen. Blue cursive lines scrolled across it. The friends behind Buzz leaned in and read the web page.

"Ranching?" asked Jordana.

"Yep," said Buzz.

Aubrey's eyes rolled from side to side, scanning the lines of the page. "This is one weird website."

"Are we really gonna have a conversation about weird right now?" Buzz cleared his throat and read from the page.

> In a time when spirits were lost in darkness and light had spared the lost, the shadows learned to share, or better, steal, what they needed to propagate their power and influence. The most ruthless and enduring of souls would ranch, or absorb, the abilities or energies of lesser entities and assume use of both their skills and vitality. Often, ranching left the weaker victim defenseless and vulnerable, and thus the offending spirit would have to ranch multiple victims in order to maintain their newly obtained power.

"It's a divinoi," said Jordana.

"Huh?" snorted Rodriqa.

"Ranching. It's one of the divinoi," repeated Jordana. "We heard the term *divinoi* last fall. It's why we're different. It's what we can do. It's how we affect the world."

"I remember that," agreed Magnos. "Divinoi. It's why I'm strong, and why Aubrey sees stuff."

"Oh, yeah," said Aubrey. "I remember now."

Rodriqa searched Jordana up and down. "How do you know?"

Jordana looked back toward the computer screen. "I read about it in Uncle's library."

"Uh-huh." Rodriqa turned back to Buzz. "So you think Shway Shway is running around Lake Julian *ranching* the life out of people?"

"Probably not," replied Buzz. "But if there's one deviant creature of the shadows lurking around, then there's bound to be more."

Magnos scratched his temple. "Which is what Mr. Poschyev, Snakes, and Stew were chasing."

Rodriqa thought for a moment. "Maybe."

Aubrey rubbed his chin. "If there are more and they're responsible for everyone falling ill, then where did they come from?"

Buzz rested his handcuffed hands on the desk. "That, I don't know."

The faces of Mr. Jennings, Mrs. Gungandeep, and Mr. Vandereff threaded through Aubrey's thoughts. He considered how Shway Shway or something like him could attack a random group of people. As he recalled the night of Shway Shway's appearance, something the widow said echoed in his mind. *The universe is knit together by reason. There is no such thing as coincidence.*

Aubrey looked up. An object caught his attention. "I think I might know."

"What?" questioned Buzz.

Aubrey bent over and opened the desk's top drawer. He rummaged through sticky notes, paper clips, and letter openers and grabbed a dry-erase marker. Weaving around his friends, Aubrey scuttled to the opposite side of the jail's office.

Standing in front of the framed map of Lake Julian, Aubrey drew four circles on the glass. His friends followed Aubrey and peered over Aubrey's shoulder at the map.

Aubrey pointed to the first circle. "Here's where Mr. Jennings was attacked." Aubrey pointed to the other two circles in succession. "Here's where Mr. Vandereff and Mrs. Gungandeep live." Then he pointed to a circle in the middle of the lake. "And here is where I'm guessing Mr. Osterfeld was on his tugboat."

Aubrey drew four straight lines north of the circles toward a single intersecting point. He tapped the end of the marker at the intersection. "I bet we'll find something here."

His friends leaned in to look at the map.

"Crannynook Caves," read Buzz. "Not a bad place to start."

"That place is spooky," murmured Magnos.

Jordana examined one of the lines Aubrey had drawn more closely. She pointed to the map. "See this line from the Gungandeep's house? It passes straight through where that massive bizarre tree would be."

"Magnolia Thistlewood," said Buzz. "Crannynook Caves. That's gotta be it." Buzz smiled. "Nice, Aub."

Rodriqa stepped back and looked at her friends. "Only problem is when are we getting outta here to go check it out?"

Screeetch!

The noise scraped from the back of the office. All five of them jerked around.

"Aubrey, eyes," whispered Buzz.

"Already ahead of you." Upon hearing the sound, Aubrey had shut his eyes and faced the other side of the room. The phosphenes behind his eyelids swirled and merged, then slowly faded.

Aubrey opened his eyes. "It's clean."

Rodriqa pointed to a desk in the far corner. "That chair just moved."

Benny and Lenny Van Zenny peered around the corner into their tiny kitchen, their eyes wide as they listened to every barely audible word.

Freyma Spindergrath pulled her brown shawl around her shoulders. Pointing at the tile backsplash with her pink-tinted glasses in hand, she was mumbling into the sink.

"Can't believe…who would…why that…do they know…." Her head bobbed, and her hand jerked from side to side.

Their stout frames pressed against the wall, Lenny and Benny leaned forward, straining to catch more of her monologue.

"But why that…" Freyma spun around, her eyes down.

Benny and Lenny hoisted their heads back behind the corner.

Suddenly, Ms. Spindergrath stopped talking. The twins looked at each other. Lenny pointed around the corner toward the kitchen, urging his brother to look. Benny shook his head. Lenny lifted his hand and shoved the side of his brother's head toward the doorway. Benny brushed Lenny off and popped him in the gut with the back of his hand. Lenny pushed Benny away from the wall.

Now in clear view of the tiny kitchen, Benny glanced in. With her glasses off, Ms. Spindergrath glared at him, her gaze latching on to his.

Benny stopped. He couldn't move or look away. His stomach dropped with growing dread, and the hair straightened on his arms and the back of his neck. Freyma lowered her head and squinted as she stared at Benny. He had only felt this way once before, when he had stolen Jordana Galilahi's glasses last fall.

A sharp pain grazed the back of Benny's skull. He jerked out of his fearful daze.

"Stop gawkin'!" Sergeant Van Zenny scowled at his sons. "Go's play video games or sumthin'!"

Lenny ducked a swipe from his dad and bolted into the living room. Benny stumbled after his brother.

Van Zenny turned as Mr. Miller and Judge Arsvine walked into the kitchen. "Ms. Spindergrath is in the kitchen." He ushered them forward.

Ms. Spindergrath slid on her pink-colored spectacles.

"Rakeman. Max," she greeted them. "So good to see you."

They both gently hugged her.

"Are you all right?" Mr. Miller kissed her on the cheek.

"Did someone try to hurt you?" asked Judge Arsvine. "The state plans to prosecute with the swiftest justice."

Ms. Spindergrath smiled softly. "Thank you. I'm no worse for wear. Fortunately, I wasn't home when the vandals came."

"Are you tired?" asked the judge.

"Have you eaten?" asked Mr. Miller.

"Gentlemen, I'm fine." Ms. Spindergrath tenderly pushed them away. "The sergeant has been very gracious and accommodating."

Mr. Miller glanced around the tiny kitchen with a wrinkled nose. "Well, if you need another place to stay until your place is settled, you're welcome at my home any time."

"That goes for me and my family as well," added the judge.

The sergeant cleared his throat. "Freyma, I have my deputy working on several leads. When I's know something, I'll let ya's know."

"Thank you, Alec."

The sergeant tipped his cap. "I's need to head back to the station. Lots of paperwork left to do."

Ms. Spindergrath took a step forward. "Sergeant, a moment before you go." She nodded at both Mr. Miller and Judge Arsvine. "Excuse me, gentlemen."

"Of course, Freyma." Mr. Miller bowed slightly.

Ms. Spindergrath walked up to the sergeant and followed him out of the kitchen with her arm wrapped in his. "Before I left yesterday, I realized there was one item in particular that was missing." She pulled the sergeant close to her.

"Do you think it was stolen?" whispered Van Zenny.

"Most likely," replied Ms. Spindergrath. "It's a family heirloom. Priceless to those who know what it is."

"What is it?"

Ms. Spindergrath pulled a faded photograph from a pocket in her long dress. "It's a lamp."

The sergeant examined the picture. A multicolored glass jar rested on the top shelf of a set of bookcases. Its bulbous bottom funneled upward into a twisting neck, where glistening gems were inset.

"It looks more likes a bottle." The sergeant turned the photo to view it from several angles.

"Don't be deceived by it's unusual appearance. It's an ancient lamp. Middle Eastern. Perhaps from the cradle of civilization itself. It's more than three thousand years old. I've had it carbon-dated."

"Wow," said the sergeant. "That's amazing. Like sumthin' out of a museum."

Ms. Spindergrath grinned. "It's very important to me. Everything else can be replaced. I'd like this back."

Van Zenny nodded. "I's on it." He slipped the picture into his uniform shirt pocket.

Ms. Spindergrath stared at him from over top of her pink-tinted glasses. "Thank you, Sergeant."

Holding her pocketbook close to her side, Aydria Auerbach slipped through the front entrance of the Poage County Police Department past several deputies, who were leaving the station. She pulled her translucent, green scarf down to her shoulders and peered into the reception area.

Since it was the weekend, she hoped there would be little activity at the police station. Unfortunately, increased constabulary need from the recent plague of illness and the minor crimes stirring at the million moth metamorphosis had levied every available employee to work overtime.

The reception area swarmed with activity. Mrs. Auerbach held her head down as she searched for someone she might know. Typing behind keyboards at their desks, several clerks took reports from tourists, who sat in nearby chairs. A couple of assistants darted between filing cabinets and the clerks' desks. Mrs. Auerbach didn't recognize anyone. However, she also didn't see Rodriqa.

Mrs. Auerbach lifted her head and walked up to the counter.

Leaning on the front reception desk, a familiar face was bowed into an open encyclopedia.

Mrs. Auerbach leaned down to catch his eye. "Jaime?"

A young man with wavy black hair glanced up at her. "Hi, Mrs. Auerbach. Can I help you?"

Mrs. Auerbach leaned down and whispered, "What are you doing here?"

"I work here on the weekends." Jaime turned a page in his book. "I'm applying for the police academy this summer, and I thought this part-time job might help me out." Jaime lowered his head back into his book.

"That's exciting." Mrs. Auerbach straightened up and looked around. "We'd hate to lose you at the dam."

"Thanks," replied Jaime. "But I don't want to work security forever."

"I understand." Mrs. Auerbach smiled at him. She leaned down to catch his eyes. "Jaime, can you help me with something?"

He sighed and leaned back in his seat. "Sure."

"Do you know if Rodriqa is here?"

Jaime shrugged. "No, why?"

Mrs. Auerbach leaned forward. "I got a call from Sergeant Van Zenny. He told me to meet him here immediately."

Jaime rubbed his cheek. "I'm not really in the know when it comes to police business. I'm just the receptionist."

Mrs. Auerbach nodded. "I thought you might have heard something."

"Not really." Jaime looked up and pointed to the front doors behind her. "But I guess if he's here and you're looking for Rodriqa, then she probably is here."

Mrs. Auerbach turned around. Dan Taylor pulled open one of the front doors and walked into the foyer.

"Thanks, Jaime," whispered Mrs. Auerbach.

Jaime nodded and lowered his head into his book.

Mrs. Auerbach strode up to Mr. Taylor as he looked around the waiting area.

"Hi, Aydry." Mr. Taylor shook her hand and sighed.

Mrs. Auerbach folded her arms. "Dan, I'm worried about our kids."

"Me too." Mr. Taylor rubbed his widow-peaked forehead. "If it wasn't for everything I saw at the power plant last fall, I'd never have agreed to let Aubrey chase more ghosts."

"Regardless of what you saw, it doesn't give them a license to do as they please." She glanced around to see if anyone was listening. "This has gotten out of hand."

"I know," replied Mr. Taylor. "But what if they really are doing something good in Lake Julian? What if this is more than just hyperactive imaginations?"

Mrs. Auerbach closed her eyes and shook her head. "Dan, I know you've been through a lot. Especially with Sarabelle being sick for so long—"

"This has nothing to do with my wife," interrupted Mr. Taylor. "It has everything to do with something our children believe in."

Mrs. Auerbach pressed her tongue into her cheek. "Did you know Jamison and I grounded Rodriqa three days ago?"

"No." Mr. Taylor lowered his voice. "Aubrey hadn't mentioned it."

"We tried anyway," sighed Mrs. Auerbach. "Lot of good it did. Now she's in jail."

"They're in jail?"

Several secretaries behind the reception desk looked up to see who was speaking in the foyer.

Mrs. Auerbach shushed Mr. Taylor. "Why else do you think we were called here?"

"Who's in jail?"

Mr. Taylor and Mrs. Auerbach turned toward the front doors. Dressed in his plaid shirt with opalescent buttons and cut-off cargo shorts, Arvel Reiselstein walked up to them.

"Did you get a phone call too?" Dan Taylor pointed at Arvel.

Mr. Reiselstein nodded. "Sergeant Van Zenny called me like half an hour ago." He shook Aydria Auerbach's hand. "Where are the kids?"

Mrs. Auerbach sighed. "We're not sure yet."

Mr. Reiselstein whistled. "This can't be good if we're all here."

"Clearly," resounded a voice from behind Mrs. Auerbach.

The three of them turned to face the deep voice coming from a sorrel-skinned, barrel-chested man.

"Quetam?" Mrs. Auerbach stretched out her hand. "Why are you here?"

"I'm here to bail Jordana out of jail," huffed Principal Lequoia.

"So they are in jail." Mr. Reiselstein rubbed his temple. "What happened?"

"We're not sure yet," replied Mr. Taylor.

"What have you heard?" asked Mrs. Auerbach, directing all her attention toward Principal Lequoia.

"It's not good." With wrinkled brow, Principal Lequoia glared at the other three. "Neither for us nor them."

"Well, whatever is going on, it needs to be wrapped up by five because I have a tanning appointment."

The four adults faced the intruding voice. Mrs. Auerbach took a step forward and stretched out her neck. "Excuse me?"

With her silvery-blonde hair wrapped into a ponytail, Fayla Strumgarten rolled her eyes and crossed one ankle over another. "My mom sent me to pick up Magnos. It's no wonder he's in jail considering who he's with."

Mrs. Auerbach crossed her arms. "Say that again."

"Let me make this perfectly clear." Fayla crossed her arms and stretched her neck toward Mrs. Auerbach. "Your children are all ingrates."

Rodriqa raised her index finger to her pursed lips as she pressed her handcuffs together to keep them quiet. She motioned Magnos and Buzz toward the left-hand edge of the desk in the far corner and pointed for Jordana and Aubrey to walk toward the right-hand side. Rodriqa tiptoed down the middle of the office. Following her lead, her friends quietly weaved between the desks toward the chair in the back.

A few feet from the desk in the corner, Rodriqa leaned down and examined the seam between the desk and the floor. A dark shape blocked light from under the desk. Rodriqa straightened up and jabbed her finger in the air toward the bottom of the desk.

Buzz and Jordana nodded in acknowledgement.

Buzz pulled a mouse from a nearby computer and gripped it in his handcuffed hands. Magnos stationed himself at the desk's corner with his arms forward, ready to catch the intruder.

Jordana grabbed Aubrey's hand and pointed toward his eyes. Aubrey's stomach flipped as Jordana's soft, slender fingers warmed his clammy palm. He could feel the fingers from her other handcuffed hand brush against his. He held his breath and felt his throat tighten.

Jordana furrowed her brow and angled her head to the side, her eyes darting back and forth as she searched Aubrey's eyes. Aubrey's heart pounded, and his mouth went dry. Jordana released his hands and raised her hands toward his face. Aubrey felt dizzy. Slowly, Jordana placed the pad of her thumb and index finger on his eyelids and closed them.

Aubrey took a deep breath, relieved and disappointed at the same time. He understood what she wanted. The phosphenes swirled behind his eyelids. Aubrey looked down toward the desk. Jordana lifted her handcuffed hands and slid her rosy pink glasses off her nose.

With calculated movement, Rodriqa stepped onto the top of the desk. Inching forward over its monitor, she leveled her body upright while balancing each quiet step.

Aligned with the back edge of the desk, Rodriqa held up her hands as Buzz sidled next to Magnos on the left, and Jordana led Aubrey up to the right.

Rodriqa extended three fingers in succession. *One. Two. Three.*

Rodriqa lurched forward and yanked the chair upward. Magnos lunged down into the desk's foot well.

"Ack!" echoed a voice from below. "Let go of me!"

Buzz swung the mouse above his head in the air. The cord slipped through his fingers. The mouse sailed across the room and crashed against the wall.

"I don't see anything," said Aubrey.

Jordana peered around the desk into the foot well.

Magnos scurried backward against the floor.

"What is it?" asked Rodriqa, searching Magnos and Jordana's faces.

Jordana slid her glasses back on her nose. "A snoop."

Aubrey opened his eyes. "A what?"

Jordana pointed toward the desk's foot well. From underneath the desk, a familiar bespectacled figure with a headful of dark hair wrapped in a pony-tail and tied to one side, emerged on all fours with her purple pen and writing pad gripped in her hands.

"Mena?" Rodriqa leaned over the front of the desk. "What are you doing here?"

Mena Kontrearo batted her pad at Magnos as she pushed herself up to standing. "Helping to keep Lake Julian in the know, *perdedores*."

Aubrey frowned. "How did you get in?"

"A journalist never betrays her sources." A grin scrawled across Mena's face, and she scratched the scalp under her ponytail. "Or her accomplices."

Rodriqa stepped onto the floor and met Mena face-to-face. "Have you been listening to our conversation?"

Mena held up her writing pad. "I have it all right here." Rodriqa reached for her pad. Mena twisted away. "Eh, eh. This is public domain now."

Magnos pulled Mena's pad out of her hands. "No, it's not."

Mena scowled at him. She snatched at her pad, attempting several times to pull it from Magnos's grasp.

Magnos held her pad high above his head in his handcuffed hands.

Mena smirked. "That's okay." She tapped her husky purple pen against her temple. "I have it all right here."

"Why are you doing this?" asked Aubrey, stepping forward.

Mena turned around and glared at Aubrey. "I don't know why you all are worried about me. Seems like you need to worry more about spending your spring break in jail."

"Why you little—"

"Aydry!" Principal Lequoia stepped between Mrs. Auerbach and Fayla Strumgarten in the police station's foyer. He turned toward Fayla. "Your words are unbefitting a sophisticated young woman."

Fayla lifted her chin. "I never knew honesty went out of style."

"Honest is fine." Mr. Taylor stepped between Lequoia and Fayla. "Rude isn't."

Fayla scoffed. "Rude is allowing wayward children to run rampant vandalizing their community."

"I think you're being a little unfair," said Mr. Reiselstein. "Our kids just want to help."

"Help?" Fayla chortled. "Help what? Help destroy lives? Help foster fear? Help Lake Julian look like it's full of crazies?"

"You're out of line," demanded Mr. Taylor.

"Coming from the maestro of crazy himself." Fayla tapped her finger on her cheek. "Tell me something. Do you charge to run that loony bin you call a house or does the state pay you to keep the crazy inside?"

Mr. Taylor gritted his teeth. "Listen here!"

"Don't even." Fayla held her finger out. "If you all had been better parents, none of this would have happened."

"This little missy needs her mouth cleaned out." Mrs. Auerbach shoved past Principal Lequoia. "And I've got just the fist for the job."

"Hold it!" Sergeant Van Zenny barreled through the front door, his gut lumbering over his belt.

Mrs. Auerbach clenched her jaw and took a step back.

"That's enough." Taking several deep breaths, he stopped in front of Fayla. "Do I's have to arrest the parents too?"

Mrs. Auerbach's eyes widened. "Is Rodriqa in jail?"

"What about Aubrey?" asked Mr. Taylor.

"Is Buzz okay?" Mr. Reiselstein rubbed the back of his neck.

Sergeant Van Zenny held up his hand. "They's just in holding. Everybody's fine. I'm not chargin' them with anything for nows. But there's an investigation."

"What did they do?" Mr. Taylor squeezed his forehead.

"Mr. Miller found them standing over the bodies of Simon Poschyev, Snakes McWhorter, and Stew Parsons at the high school baseball field."

Mrs. Auerbach gasped and covered her mouth.

"Is anybody…dead?" Mr. Reiselstein closed his eyes as he asked.

"No, but they's appear to be very ill." The sergeant rested his hands on his belt.

"What did our kids do?" asked Mr. Taylor.

Van Zenny shook his head. "It's unclear if they's did anything. Maybe just wrong place, wrong time. But I's not sure yet." Sergeant Van Zenny gathered the five of them closer to him. "But if I's were ya's, I'd wouldn't let 'em outta sight, and I's certainly wouldn't let 'em outta the house. Not 'til I's figure out what's goin' on."

Mrs. Auerbach, Mr. Taylor, and Mr. Reiselstein nodded.

Principal Lequoia sighed. "Are they being released this afternoon?"

"Yeah." Sergeant Van Zenny glanced at the clock on the wall. "I's need to speak with 'em first."

Principal Lequoia pursed his lips and looked down.

Van Zenny frowned at Lequoia. "Ya's look disappointed, sir."

The principal nodded. "Honestly, Sergeant, a night in jail might do Jordana some good."

"Well, maybe, but not tonight." Van Zenny rubbed the pocket of his uniform shirt. "Let me finish processin' 'em, and I's bring them out to ya's."

"Thank you, Alec." Mrs. Auerbach she smiled at him.

"Yes, thank you, sir," replied Mr. Reiselstein and Mr. Taylor in tandem.

Sergeant Van Zenny tipped his cap and flashed them a wispy grin. He turned and walked through the reception area. Passing through a wooden turnstile, he nodded at Jaime as he opened the door that led to a hallway behind the reception desk.

Fayla clicked her tongue. "You need to hurry. I'm already late for my pre-tan spray treatment."

"You were trying to frame us?" Rodriqa pressed her nose toward Mena's face.

Mena took a step back. "*Frame* isn't the word I would use."

"Then what do you call it?" asked Aubrey.

"Frame implies innocence." Mena held her head up and took several steps away from the desk. "And none of you are innocent."

Buzz walked up to her and reached for her pen. "What is this?"

Mena gripped the pen tightly. Both of them held it. With his handcuffed hands, Buzz raised the husky purple pen in front of their faces, examining it closely.

Mena smiled. "It was a gift."

Buzz angled his thumb to press one of the multiple clicky buttons at the pen's top. "From whom?"

Mena wrenched her hand away. "Bates Hindenberg. He calls it a Spooly Pen."

"Spooly Pen?" questioned Buzz.

"Yeah." Mena walked toward the office door.

Rodriqa stomped forward. "You're not leaving."

Mena scampered away. "Yes, I am. You all have visitors."

The office door opened.

"Have a good evening, officer." Mena slipped between the doorframe and Sergeant Van Zenny.

Aubrey, Buzz, Jordana, Magnos, and Rodriqa slinked backward toward the bench.

Van Zenny glanced at Mena several times as she jogged down the hallway.

"Wha's she doin' here?" asked Van Zenny.

Aubrey looked down and shrugged. Van Zenny shook his head. "Trouble." He lumbered up to the bench. "Ya's are all lucky." The sergeant pulled a ring of keys from belt. "I's not chargin' ya's with anything."

"Really?" Aubrey looked up at Van Zenny.

"Not today anyways." The sergeant unlocked Aubrey's handcuffs.

"That's great news!" Buzz rattled his handcuffs in the air. "Then we're free!"

"Not exactly." Van Zenny unlocked more handcuffs. "Your parents are out front. I's asked them to keep you inside until we figure out what's going on."

"What?" Buzz slid off the bench. "But, Sergeant, if anyone in Lake Julian can figure out what's going on, we can."

"I'm already on house arrest." Rodriqa stood up and rubbed her wrists. "But I agree with Buzz."

Aubrey slid off the bench. "If we can't help, then we can't clear our name."

Rodriqa twisted her neck, and her braided beads swished around her head. "We didn't hurt Mr. Poschyev, Snakes McWhorter, or Stew Parsons, and you know it."

"But we might know who did," added Buzz.

Sergeant Van Zenny gathered the opened handcuffs together and laid them on the desk behind him. He sighed and riffled through his front uniform pocket. "There's one small thing ya's might be able to help me with." The sergeant pulled out Ms. Spindergrath's picture and showed it to Buzz. "Does this mean anything to ya's?"

Buzz touched the picture. "Beautiful built-in cabinetry."

"The lamp," huffed Van Zenny.

Magnos, Jordana, and Rodriqa gathered around to examine the picture.

"Are you sure that's a lamp?" Rodriqa squinted at the photograph.

"Let me see." Aubrey squeezed between his friends. His eyes widened as he saw the gem-encrusted multicolored jar. "Yes! It is a lamp!" Aubrey pointed at the picture. "It's just like the one in the Gungandeep's house."

Buzz looked at the picture more closely. "No, it's not."

"And it's like the one in Mr. Jennings's basement with the Circle of Circles emblem on it."

"Are you sure?" Rodriqa looked at the picture from a different angle.

"Yes!" insisted Aubrey.

"Why would someone want it?" asked Van Zenny.

Aubrey searched his mind. "I'm...I'm not sure."

Van Zenny frowned. "Is it special or just another piece of baked clay?"

Aubrey shrugged.

"I's looking for a reason someone might want it." Van Zenny shoved the picture back in his pocket. "I guess it doesn't mean anything to ya's. Now, ya's can help me by staying out of sight."

"Wait," replied Aubrey. "Where is this lamp?"

"It was at Ms. Spindergrath's ranch." Van Zenny rubbed his chin. "But not as of yesterday."

"Someone stole it?" Buzz asked.

"Seems so, but nothing else," replied the sergeant.

"Weird," mused Rodriqa.

"Is Ms. Spindergrath okay?" Jordana asked.

"Yep," replied Van Zenny.

Aubrey snapped his fingers. "That's it!" He ran over to the map of Lake Julian on the wall and rubbed off the criss-crossing marks they had drawn. "Everyone who has one of the lamps has turned up sick. Mr. Jennings. Mrs. Gungandeep."

"Except Ms. Spindergrath is okay," countered Rodriqa.

"Yeah," said Aubrey. "But her lamp is gone."

"What about Mr. Osterfeld and Mr. Vandereff?" Buzz asked.

Aubrey chewed the inside of his cheek.

"What about Simon Poschyev, Stew Parsons, and Snakes McWhorter?" added Magnos.

"And what about the couple from the million moth metamorphosis?" asked Van Zenny.

"Who?" Aubrey raised his eyebrows.

Van Zenny sighed and pulled up his belt. "There's a couple of tourists stayin' in town that have reportedly gone missin'."

"The Losepkees?" asked Aubrey.

Van Zenny frowned. "How did ya's know?"

Buzz stepped in front of Van Zenny. "So the creatures are after the lamps. And they take out anyone who gets in their way."

"What creatures?" Van Zenny asked.

Rodriqa crossed her arms. "The creatures Simon Poschyev, Snakes McWhorter, and Stew Parsons were chasing before they were ranched."

"Before they were *what*?" Van Zenny turned, glancing at the children.

"Do you think it's Shway Shway?" Jordana asked.

"Who's Shway Shway?" asked Van Zenny.

"No way," replied Rodriqa. "There's gotta be more than one."

"Maybe even an army," muttered Magnos.

"Who's got an army?" huffed the sergeant.

A grin stretched across Aubrey's face. "Looks like we have a plan."

"*No!*" Sergeant Van Zenny pounded his fist against the desk. "No plans! No more silliness! Ya's are all on house arrest. If ya's go outside, ya's goin' to jail!"

Her back against the handle, Mena Kontrearo pushed open the door at the end of the hallway. She stepped through, and the door slammed shut behind her. She examined her Spooly Pen and pressed the red clicky button.

A static-laced recording of Jordana's voice detailing the meaning of the word *divinoi* buzzed from a tiny speaker near the end of the pen. Mena grinned.

Feeling someone watching her, Mena looked up. Across the police department's reception desk, Dan Taylor, Aydria Auerbach, Arvel Reiselstein, and Quetam Lequoia glared at Mena from the foyer. Fayla Strumgarten tapped her foot and glanced repeatedly at her watch.

Mena scurried up to her brother, Jaime, who, with his face down in his book, turned a page. Mena nudged her brother. "Thanks. I owe you."

Jaime grunted. "How about you owe me a billion."

Mena sneered. She shoved the Spooly Pen in her pocket, slipped through the wooden turnstile and, with her head up, strutted through the foyer and out the front door.

A few minutes later, Sergeant Van Zenny appeared through the hallway door, herding Aubrey, Magnos, Buzz, Jordana, and Rodriqa. All five stared at the floor as they trudged through the reception area.

Jaime raised his head. "Hey, Rodriqa. Tell Robert 'hi' for me."

Rodriqa nodded, keeping her face down.

Slowly, they wound their way through the turnstile and into the foyer, each child standing next to their relative.

Sergeant Van Zenny shook the hands of the parents. "Theys know the rules. Ya's know the rules. I don't want to hear anything outta ya's."

"We won't let them out of our sights," said Mr. Taylor.

The sergeant wiped his brow. "For their sakes, I hope not."

"It's empty!" Magnolia Thistlewood threw Ms. Spindergrath's jewel-encrusted lamp across the room. Matsinstrus winced as the dense glass of the lamp pelted his charred ribcage before it dropped to the wooden floor and bounced down the double spiral staircase.

"I need a crucible with a Magi in it!" Ms. Thistlewood stormed toward the window of her oak house, her red hair reflecting the gleam from the flickering flames in the crystalline marble fireplace.

Matsinstrus bowed. "I'm sorry, my queen, but that's the only other crucible the keepers have been able to find."

Ms. Thistlewood sighed. She peered over the ledge and examined the horde of black, winged creatures milling through the high grass at the base of the oak, their large round eyes scurrying through the field at dusk. A couple of the shadowy creatures scuffed at the ground with their hind hooves. Others pulled up roots with their three-fingered hands.

Ms. Thistlewood smiled at her creation. "Then the keepers will have to look harder."

"Yes, of course. They will." Matsinstrus rubbed his bony fingers together. "They need to feed again. One of them nearly ate my hand."

Ms. Thistlewood smirked and crossed her arms. "It's good that they're hungry. I want them unstoppable."

"They're already an army. Just as you've wanted." Matsinstrus smiled and yellow vapor oozed from his jaw.

Ms. Thistlewood turned. "Let them loose on the Moth-ers. Let's see how big they get." Matsinstrus bowed and walked toward the staircase. "And don't let them huddle around the valley anymore. They're too exposed here."

Matsinstrus stopped at the top step. "Where should I keep them?"

Ms. Thistlewood rubbed her index finger across her lips. "The Crannynook Caves. They'll be well-hidden there."

Matsinstrus nodded and walked down the stairs. Ms. Thistlewood walked over to her wooden rocking chair and sat down. She pulled her squirrel-skull pipe out of the drawer in the table next to her and filled its end with sand. Waving her hand over the sand, it transformed into a dark powder and then flashed with a small flame and smoldered.

She puffed on the pipe and blew smoke into the air. Tapping her fingers on the chair, she considered her plan. She had her army. Now she needed to grow it, shape it, and then wield it. She took another drag on her pipe. She knew she needed more help. Matsinstrus wouldn't last much longer. He was weaker than she had anticipated. Ned and Fred Kluggard were, at best, helpful only with menial tasks. Soon the keepers would be mature, but without more hands, the beasts could turn on her. Ms. Thistlewood took another puff on her pipe and blew out through her nose. She decided she would be patient as she had been for so very long. A face formed in the smoke and grinned at her.

Ms. Thistlewood fanned the smoke with her hand. Most of it dispersed, except for the face. The mouth spoke. "Such an apathetic crutch."

"What?" Dropping her squirrel-skull pipe, Ms. Thistlewood leapt to her feet. She clenched her fingers. All the smoke in the room fell to the floor in a rain of pebbles.

"Patience." The voice from the smoke echoed in the wooden room. "You've settled on patience."

Ms. Thistlewood turned her head from side to side. "Show yourself, demon."

The voice laughed. "The great Magnolia has settled on patience."

Ms. Thistlewood held up her hands. A wave of static electricity dispersed in a quick snap throughout the room. "Who are you?"

"You should know me. You released me." Out of the burning fire, an olive green humanoid with golden orb-like eyes stood up from the hearth. Akin to a darkened shadow, the creature more floated than walked toward her. His pointy, long nose nearly touched his pointed chin as he smiled.

Magnolia Thistlewood angled her head and examined the emerging shade. Her pale green eyes quivered, a distant memory flashing across her mind. "Azrynon?"

The shadow stood in front of her. "You remember." Only a few inches separated their faces. "Such a sweet little girl you used to be. You've matured perfectly." Azrynon's hand caressed her forearm.

A single tear dripped from Magnolia's left eye. "It worked." Her voice cracked. Her lower lip trembled. "I freed you from Enoch's tomb."

Azrynon nodded. "My strength grows." Azrynon choked down a cough. "Slowly." He turned away and basked before the fireplace. "I've been watching you."

Magnolia smiled. She stepped forward. She wanted to embrace him, but fear outweighed her longing.

Azrynon glanced over his shoulder. "Why are you so fixed on these children? They are dust among soldiers' feet."

Ms. Thistlewood squinted her eyes. "Don't you remember?"

Azrynon scoffed. "I remember everything."

"But," Ms. Thistlewood shook her head, "the Terminal Prophecy."

Azrynon turned around and slammed his fist into his opposite palm. "The Terminal Prophecy is a nursery rhyme meant to terrorize the universe into submission." He moved toward her. "The first rebellion took a toll on the Clockmaker. One more good hit and he'll no longer be sovereign."

Holding up her chin, Ms. Thistlewood nodded. "I agree. That's why I've created an army."

"What you've created," Azrynon raised his hand and pinched her chin in his fingers, "is a circus of mindless ants."

Ms. Thistlewood closed her eyes and imagined his ethereal touch. She sighed as a host of forgotten feelings flooded her heart. "A man may seem like a god…to an ant," Ms. Thistlewood took a step backward, "but even an army of ants can take down a man."

Azrynon grinned. "But your keepers are will-less and inept."

"They are growing." Magnolia turned around and faced the darkened window. "They don't need will, only power."

"Clever." Azrynon floated around her and sat on the open window-sill, his olive green coloring and golden orb-like eyes the only portions of him visible with the background of night. "But an army of experienced and trained shade would be more formidable."

"The darkness is too disorganized." Ms. Thistlewood shook her head. "Too many warlords rule too many sects. They would war more among each other than against the shinar."

Azrynon nodded. "I agree, but there is good news."

Ms. Thistlewood frowned at him.

Azrynon lifted her squirrel-skull pipe off the floor and twirled it in his fingers. "Magog is dead."

"The Warlord to the North?"

"That opens a hole in power." Azrynon stood up. "If a few more warlords were disengaged, a melding of sects might create a vast army, capable of once again challenging the Clockmaker's might."

Ms. Thistlewood bit the inside of her cheek.

"But I'll rest for now and regain my strength." Azrynon moved toward her. "I'm curious to watch your plan unfold."

Ms. Thistlewood curled her lip. "Once these children are out of my way, I won't be stopped."

Azrynon slipped her pipe between her fingers. "I'll be happy to see you succeed." His rested his hand on her shoulder. "But if you don't, I'll be there to pick up the pieces." Azrynon closed his eyes, and the golden orbs disappeared. His shadowy form faded, like wafting smoke in a breeze.

Magnolia raised her hand to her shoulder, but his hand was already gone. Her brow furrowed. Tears fell like stones on her cheeks. She grabbed her chest and inhaled deeply, as if she had never breathed before. Clutching the squirrel-skull pipe, she stepped forward. Her legs wobbled. She dropped to her knees and wept.

VEXTING

Monday.

A ray of light peeping through a flap in the Mole-Pole tent, flooded Buzz's closed eyes while he lay in his sleeping bag. He flopped his hand over his face. Glints of sunlight continued to flash through his fingers, stabbing his eyelids with brightness.

Buzz grunted. Rolling over in his sleeping bag, he pressed his cheek into the bag. Another, flicker of light cut through the darkness. Buzz winced as the pulsing glow intruded his slumber. Angrily, he snapped open his eyes. Next to him on the floor of the tent, a red light on his cell phone was blinking. Buzz sat up. He grabbed his phone and flipped it open. An application, called Cliqcom, was highlighted with a number 2 in its upper right hand corner. Buzz opened the application.

R: (Rodriqa Auerbach): I feel like a prisoner in my own home. My dad is so mad at me.

A: (Aubrey Taylor): My dad didn't say much last night. But he left another pamphlet for St. Pinnetackwah's Military School for Boys on my bed. :/

Buzz typed in Cliqcom.

B: (Buzz Reiselstein): My dad made me stay at Lake Julian with him. He grounded me from video games for a month.:')

R: At least you're out of your house. My dad said I wasn't to leave my room all week.

Jordana and Magnos joined Cliqcom.

J: (Jordana Galilahi): Uncle is giving me the silent treatment. He and my dad yelled at each other for an hour last night.

M: (Magnos Strumgarten): Fayla told me I have to do all the chores while my mom was gone. She screamed at me and then threw a lamp at me.

B: Speaking of lamps, why is Ms. Spindergrath's so important?

R: Probably because she's rich and that lamp is expensive.

B: I overheard my dad speaking with one of the deputies last night. Apparently that lamp was the only thing stolen from Ms. Spindergrath's ranch.

R: That's odd.

B: You know, Ms. Spindergrath has some phat lewtz in that ranch of hers. Why would someone want just that lamp?

R: Maybe the creatures stole the lamp?

A: It's not a lamp, it's a crucible.

R: Huh :@

A: Remember. That's what Ms. Gungandeep called that bizarro lamp in her house. A crucible.

R: Ah, yeah, but her crucible doesn't look like Ms. Spindergrath's lamp.

A: Not exactly, but they're both oddly shaped and unusual.

B: Who else has a crucible?

A: I think Mr. Jennings has one in his basement.

B: So if the other folks who fell ill, like Mr. Osterfeld and Mr. Vandereff, have one, then most likely the creatures are after the lamps.

A: It would seem so.

R: Too bad we can't find out if they have one.

B: Wouldn't it be creepy if we found Ms. Spindergrath's lamp in the Crannynook Caves?

J: We should check it out.

M: I agree.

R: Which word of the phrase "house arrest" is confusing to you?

J: That part where the adults have no clue what's going on and we're the only ones who can figure this out.

A: Go, Jordana!

R: Excuse me! We've already ruined our spring break. Should we ruin our futures too?

J: Mr. Miller is gonna make sure that happens regardless, unless we prove him wrong.

A: Jordana's right.

R: Cheese Louise! Am I the only rational one? Ghost hunting has driven you all crazy. Buzz, back me up.

B: We know what the creatures are doing. We know what they're after. Now all we have to do is figure out why, and we can defeat them and save the town!

R: Are you serious?

A: We've been in tough spots before. If we stick together, we can school the adults on the darkness. :)

J: I wonder if there have been any more attacks since yesterday.

A: Maybe we should go after Ms. Thistlewood. If she's back, then she's gotta be behind all this.

B: We can't attack her head on. She'll be expecting that. Besides, if the Kluggards and those creatures are guarding her, we'll be shucking snails for sure.

A: Good point.

M: I don't want to face her. She scares me

A: Sorry, Mag. :(

B: Who can get out?

A: My dad and Gaetan are gone. They won't be back till later. I can sneak out.

R: My mom and dad went to work. They told Robert to keep an eye on me. I'm stuck.

B: I'm at the million moth metamorphosis with my dad. I'm sure I could invent a reason to get out.

M: My mom's still out of town, and Fayla and Gaetan went somewhere. I can get out.

B: Here's the plan. We all tuck out. Driqa and Aub, check out the Osterfeld place. Mag, Jordana, and I will search Vandereff's place. Then we meet up at the Crannynook Caves.

J: Too late.

A: Why?

B: What happened?

M: Huh?

J: Uncle had to go to school early this morning. I'm already at Ms. Spindergrath's. I'm about to have a word with her. :D

B: Rock on!

A: You go!

M: Awesome!

B: Mag, meet me at Vandereff's. We'll be back before our parents know we're gone.

M: K.

A: How should we travel?

B: No Buzz Bug, no bikes. We hotfoot it, so we can't be spotted.

M: Good deal.

A: I'm gonna check on Shway Shway and Mr. Jennings's crucible while Rodriqa finds a way out.

B: Meet at Crannynook at high noon.

R: Ugh. :/

Buzz rolled out of his sleeping bag, grabbed his book bag, and shoved several items in it from around the floor of the Mole-Pole tent. He bounced over to the cooler on his dad's side of the tent, flipped open the lid, took out a pimento cheese sandwich, and thrust it into his mouth. With cheeks engorged ith a mash of orange cheese and soggy bread, he lifted another sandwich into his book bag and raced out the tent's front flap.

Crash!

Arvel Reiselstein fell backward onto the grass. He grunted while he gripped his stomach. Buzz rubbed his head and stumbled forward, squinting in the morning sunlight.

"Where are you going?" Mr. Reiselstein grimaced as he leaned forward.

Buzz glanced between his dad and his bag. "Hmm…I'm gonna go bug hunting. See if there are any moths ready to break out of their pupa."

Mr. Reiselstein rolled up to his knees. "Not sure that's a good idea."

Buzz's arms fell slack. "Why not?"

"You know why."

"But it's not like I'm going far. Just around the lake."

"Too far."

"So I have to sit in the tent all day?" whined Buzz.

Mr. Reiselstein stood up. "No, but you need to be where I can keep an eye on you."

"It's not like I'm taking the Buzz Bug somewhere."

Mr. Reiselstein grinned. "I know."

Buzz frowned. "Huh?"

"I took the battery out of the Buzz Bug this morning. It's not going anywhere."

Buzz's jaw dropped. "You didn't dismantle the electric rotor, did you? It took me forever to balance the distributor."

"Don't worry. I didn't injure your baby."

"Where did you put the battery?"

Mr. Reiselstein chuckled. "Buzz, I'm not telling you."

"Fine. What do you want me to do while I'm grounded? Sit in the tent and eat all day long?"

Mr. Reiselstein shook his head and stifled a grin. "Why don't you go help out the Scouts?"

Buzz turned around and groaned. Then suddenly, he thought twice about his dad's idea. "Okay," moaned Buzz. Swinging his book bag over his shoulder, Buzz marched toward the scout camp.

Once Buzz was sure his dad was no longer watching him, he weaved between several tents until he saw Coren Belward stocking medical supplies on the trailer bed hitched to his four-wheeler.

Buzz ran up to him. "Coren, I need to ask a favor."

"Anything. The Scouts are here to help." Coren nodded eagerly as his Adam's apple bobbed along his neck. "Did you all find out anything yet?"

Buzz lowered his voice. "We have a few more leads, but we're still investigating."

Coren leaned in toward Buzz. "When do you think you'll know what's going on?"

"Soon." Buzz smiled. "That's why I need you to cover for me."

THE EYES HAVE IT

Jordana flipped her cell phone close and slid it in her pocket. Sighing, she pressed her rose-tinted glasses to the top of her nose and viewed the landscaped grounds from the bottom of Freyma Spindergrath's meandering concrete driveway.

A blurry fog of thoughts doused Jordana's mind. What was the lamp? How long had Ms. Spindergrath had it? Had anyone or anything attacked her? Were Ms. Spindergrath's eyeglasses similar to hers? Did she wear them for the same purpose? But a single question nettled her heart as well as her mind: what did Ms. Spindergrath really know about her mother?

When Jordana was twelve years old, her mother had been murdered by a few of her closest associates. The consequential scandal had resulted in huge financial losses for her family. With little money and a new job, her father had brought them to Lake Julian last fall for a new start.

Her newly minted friends and their unusual adventures had provided her with a new hope and some distraction, but whenever she was alone, whenever everything was dark, whenever life was jumbled and upended, her thoughts returned to her mother. Today, her mother's presence was as vivid as it had been the last day of her life.

Jordana brushed wayward locks of her hair behind her ear. Quickly, she arranged her thoughts as to how she would approach Ms. Spindergrath and strode forward.

Several yards along the concrete driveway, the front gate was ajar, and her thin frame slipped through the ornately framed wrought iron bars. Jordana trotted along the edge of the driveway with her head down.

Passing a row of sculpted trees, Jordana skipped a few steps faster as a swoosh of water from a stone fountain in the middle of the yard startled her. A few yards beyond a bend in the driveway, Jordana reached an expansive woodwork porch that wrapped around most of the ranch-style home.

She wavered at the bottom of the steps, staring at the frosted glass front door. The front door creaked a high-pitch whine. Jordana took a step back. The left-hand portion of the front door swung open.

With her white hair wound tightly on top of her head, Freyma Spindergrath glared at Jordana. "Have you come to steal from me too?"

Jordana rubbed her fingers together. "Uh, no, ma'am." She softly cleared her throat. "Would you have a few moments that I may ask you a couple questions?"

"No." Ms. Spindergrath stepped into the threshold. "Now is a bad time."

Brushing her hair behind her ears, Jordana looked up at her from the bottom of the porch. "Don't you remember me?"

Ms. Spindergrath squinted her eyes and shook her head. "I'm neither in the mood for games nor properly presentable for visitors. Good day." She slipped back inside, and the glass door closed.

"Wait!" Jordana raced up several steps and slid her rosy pink glasses off her nose. Holding her breath, she stared at Ms. Spindergrath. "You have to remember me."

Ms. Spindergrath peeked her head back out the door. Her eyes locked with Jordana. For a brief instant, Ms. Spindergrath felt dizzy. Her eyes widened. Her memory returned. "Oh! Yes, of course! From the Rock-U-Quarium." She lifted her spectacles, which hung by a thin chain about her neck, onto her nose and re-examined Jordana.

Jordana smiled. "Yes, ma'am." She folded her glasses and held them in her hand. "Could we talk?"

Ms. Spindergrath's gaze bounced between the porch and the foyer inside. "We might be able to share a few moments." She waved Jordana forward. "Come in."

Taking a step back, Ms. Spindergrath widened the opening in the door. Jordana bowed her head and walked inside. Ms. Spindergrath surveyed her front lawn for other unwanted guests as Jordana passed by her.

Ms. Spindergrath closed the door and turned to face Jordana. Jordana focused her stare at Ms. Spindergrath's eyes.

"I won't take much of your time." Jordana took a step toward her host. "There are only a handful of things I need to know."

Ms. Spindergrath peered down at Jordana through her pink-colored glasses. "You are such a beautiful girl." She touched Jordana's shoulder. "Remarkable, really."

Jordana's focus waned as her cheeks blushed. She gritted her teeth. "Tell me about your missing lamp."

Ms. Spindergrath nodded and folded her hands. "Crucible."

Jordana's shoulders slumped. "That's right, the crucible."

Ms. Spindergrath angled her head. "Dear, did you really come here to ask me about my lamp? I sense you have a more personal question you'd like to ask."

Jordana pursed her lips. "Take off your glasses."

"Really." Ms. Spindergrath cackled. "Do you think I'd willingly dismiss my best defense?" Ms. Spindergrath slipped her glasses to the end of her nose and peered over their rims. "I don't think you're ready for the consequences."

Jordana wrinkled her forehead. A glazed fog seeped into her mind, slowing her thoughts. She tried to inhale, but couldn't. She wanted to turn her head, but her body would no longer obey her.

"Sit," commanded Ms. Spindergrath. Jordana shuffled backward and dropped into a chair in the corner.

Ms. Spindergrath pressed her glasses back to the top of her nose. Jordana's fog lifted. Her senses returned, and she sighed.

"The crucible has been a family heirloom for several generations." Ms. Spindergrath paced around the foyer. "My great grandmother received it as a present from an Ottoman sultan in the early nineteenth century. Crucibles like mine were the origins of the genie in the lamp folk tales. By legend, the crucible was once home to a being of great power. But either that being has left or, as myths tend to be, the influence of the crucible has been substantially exaggerated."

Jordana stood up. "How did you do that to me?"

"Do what, dear?" Ms. Spindergrath faced Jordana. "Don't you want to hear more about my lamp?"

Jordana shook her head. She looked at her own rose-tinted glasses and then stared back at Ms. Spindergrath and her pink spectacles. "You did to me what I've been doing..."

"Yes," interrupted Ms. Spindergrath, "but undoubtedly, you've been only able to use it when your emotions flare, making the results of your demands erratic and destructive."

Jordana's mouth opened. Ms. Spindergrath looked away. Jordana slid her glasses back on. "What is it?"

"What is what?" asked Ms. Spindergrath.

"This thing we do that...overwhelms others with our own emotions."

Ms. Spindergrath pressed her glasses against her face. "It is a gift." She approached Jordana. "Not unlike a sixth sense or a deeply honed intuition. Except our ability allows us to search for the truth in others." Ms. Spindergrath pursed her lips. "We enable others to disclose veracity, even when their own consciousness tries to prevent it." She waved her hand in circles. "At least that's how it's meant to be used. Surely, you've already discovered that it can be manipulated to control as well as to reveal reality from another's eyes."

"Confessor," mumbled Jordana.

Ms. Spindergrath nodded. "That's right." She pointed her finger at Jordana's eyes. "And when it's used irresponsibly, its called coercion."

"My mother." Jordana's mind raced. "She...she could do it too."

Ms. Spindergrath smiled. "My dear, who do you think helped your mother develop her abilities?"

Jordana clenched her jaw.

Ms. Spindergrath grabbed Jordana's hands. "And now daughter dearest, with the same raw talent, has shown up at my doorstep, seeking the same advice." Leaning in, Ms. Spindergrath squeezed Jordana's nose. "Isn't it fascinating how delightfully well-woven the fabric of the universe is knit."

"Show me." Jordana's voice trembled.

Ms. Spindergrath took a step back and stared at Jordana. "Are you sure?"

"Yes." Jordana nodded. "Show me everything."

"But your mother." Ms. Spindergrath held up a finger. "What happened to her was no accident."

Jordana bit her lip. "I don't care."

Rodriqa leaned back on her bed, staring at her open cell phone lying next to her. Texts, misgivings, and possibilities rolled in her mind as she mulled over what she should do next.

Robert was downstairs. She knew it would be difficult to leave without him knowing. However, her friends needed her, and she knew that only they could really figure out what was happening in Lake Julian.

She stared at a picture on her mirror. It had been taken nearly a decade ago. Her brother was swinging Rodriqa in the yard by her arms. How simple things were not so long ago. Her stomach soured at how quickly she had been forced to face things greater, stronger, and more hidden than most adults had ever known. She inhaled deeply, discouraged by her predicament and her inability to fix it.

Through the muddled fog of mental tumult, a new idea presented itself. She would tell her brother the truth. Everything. From beginning to end. No embellishment. No filter. No opinion. Every detail. Every crime. Every victory. She would tell her brother the honest-to-goodness truth about all that had happened over the past six months.

Honesty to the frankest degree would be difficult, but once she had told him everything, he would have to believe her. Then he would let her help her friends.

Rodriqa bit her lip and leaned forward. She listened for movement downstairs. She could hear her brother walking through the kitchen. Popping her neck and cracking her knuckles, Rodriqa stood up and marched out of her bedroom.

Rodriqa heard the front door open. Robert was speaking to someone, but she couldn't make out what they were saying. She glided down the hallway and took several steps down the stairs, staying out of sight.

At the third step, she stopped and listened.

"But it's my only day off this week," entreated a voice from outside.

"I can't go anywhere," replied Robert. "My parents asked me to watch Rodriqa."

"Are you babysitting?" The voice loudened. The visitor walked inside. "Rodriqa's too old for a babysitter."

"It's not that," said Robert. "She's kind of in trouble. She isn't supposed to go anywhere."

"Are you in trouble too?" asked the voice.

"No."

"Then why do you have to be stuck here?"

Robert mumbled something Rodriqa couldn't make out.

"Dude, I've got free tickets to the Rock-U-Quarium. I haven't been yet. Have you?"

"No."

"I hear it's awesome!"

"Yeah, but I can't go today. Couldn't we go another day?"

"I have to work at the dam the rest of the week."

With this, Rodriqa realized the visitor was Jaime Kontrearo, security officer at the dam, Mena's older brother, and Robert's best friend from high school.

"Come on! We haven't hung out in ages," continued Jaime. "Tell Rodriqa to stay put, and we'll be back before your parents get home."

Robert mumbled again.

"I hear the Parkourium is unbelievable. You're a daredevil and a super-hero for half an hour."

Rodriqa hovered at the top of the steps, straining to hear the whispering between her brother and Jaime.

"Rodriqa!" Robert yelled up the stairs.

Rodriqa took a step back. Suddenly, she realized that if she answered, Robert would know she was eavesdropping. If she ran back to her room, Robert might hear her footsteps. Quickly, she covered her mouth and hollered back, "Yeah!"

The muffled reply carried into the living room.

"I'm stepping out for just a few minutes." Robert shouted up the stairs. "Don't go anywhere!"

"Okay!" Rodriqa's muted response resonated down the stairwell.

Rodriqa heard hurried footsteps scamper across the living room. Then the front door closed. Rodriqa bounded back to her room and peered out the lower edge of her window down at the street. Jaime and Robert climbed into Jaime's car and drove up Dalton Circle. Rodriqa ran out of her room, down the stairs, and opened the front door. She peeked outside. The road was clear. No neighbors were outside. All was quiet. Rodriqa slipped outside and raced up the street.

<hr />

Mena Kontrearo grinned. Holding up the Spooly Pen to her eye, she pressed the blue clicky button several times as she aimed it at the running Rodriqa.

Squeezed between an oak tree and a prickly holly bush in a neighbor's front yard several dozen yards up Dalton Circle, Mena mumbled to herself, "Muy bueno, big bro."

Aubrey angled himself next to the window in the stainless steel door in the basement of Mr. Jennings's Smart Mart & Finer Diner. Slowly, he slid his left eye into view of the freezer.

Broken and dismantled, the banks of wire shelving lay in crumpled pipe and twisted metal along the floor. Frosted shavings and ripped peels of cardboard papered every surface like vellum snow. Iced chunks of meat and vegetables and warped crockery peppered all the frosty metal.

Mr. Jennings's freezer had become a frozen, industrial battlefield with a creature of darkness warring against the inanimate. And he was losing.

Festooned in his oversized blue NGW suit, Shway Shway heaved sobs in the far corner of the freezer. With his head down, he raked his hands along the steel floor.

Aubrey jerked his head back out of sight. Now was the time to test something. Aubrey faced away from the freezer. He closed his eyes. The phosphenes swirled behind his eyelids. In a few moments, they faded. Only darkness remained. Aubrey turned his head and faced the freezer. He pressed his nose into the metal and centered his head where he remembered Shway Shway to be.

He took a deep breath and bore down with a full chest toward his stomach. Sweat beaded on Aubrey's forehead. Slowly, Shway Shway's form took shape behind Aubrey's eyelids. Suddenly, Shway Shway looked up.

"*Yowaaack!*" Shway Shway screamed.

With his eyes shut, Aubrey watched Shway Shway squall in agony.

"Aubrey!"

Aubrey's eyes snapped open and spun around.

Rodriqa stood next to the poker table, her hands on her hips. "What are you doing?"

Aubrey pushed himself away from the freezer. "Just checking on Shway Shway."

"Why is he screaming?"

Aubrey shrugged and then smiled. "You snuck out."

Rodriqa crossed her arms. "Yeah. Not sure how long I've got."

Aubrey walked up to her. "Remember yesterday when you were on top of Shway Shway and you told me to search him for Solluna?"

Rodriqa nodded, and her beaded braids shook. "Yeah."

Aubrey lowered his voice. "And Shway Shway started shaking?"

"Yeah." Rodriqa rolled her hand in circles, waving for him to get to the point.

"Something happened to you too."

"Yeah. You couldn't see me. You can't see anything in the physical world behind your eyelids. That's nothing new."

"No." Aubrey shook his head. "You disappeared."

"No, I didn't."

Aubrey pulled his inhaler out of his pocket and pressed it in his mouth. "But I could see you behind my eyelids and then when I opened my eyes you were gone."

Rodriqa squinted at him. "I think you were confused...and scared."

Aubrey's head bobbed back and forth, and he turned away. "Look at this." He picked up Mr. Jennings's bulbous lamp on the poker table. "See?" He pointed to the emblem at the lamp's base. "The Circle of Circles."

Rodriqa leaned in to examine it. "So it *is* a lamp."

"Mr. Jennings used it as a lamp." Aubrey popped off the lightbulb and the lampshade. "But it's still a crucible."

Rodriqa examined Mr. Jennings's crucible. "But Ms. Spindergrath's lamp looks different. It has jewels all up and down it."

"But it has a similar shape." Aubrey rubbed its forehead. "And it's just... odd."

Rodriqa nodded. She turned the crucible end up and looked at its bottom.

Aubrey noticed a glint from the bottle's top. "What's that?"

"What's what?" Rodriqa rotated the bottle.

"What's in the top?" Aubrey lifted the top of the crucible and peered inside the round opening. He saw a reflection of his own eye. "It looks like there's a mirror in there."

Rodriqa turned it around and peeked inside. "It's probably part of the setup for the light bulb."

Aubrey scratched his cheek. "But I think Mrs. Gungandeep's bottle did the same thing."

Rodriqa rolled her eyes. "Let's head out." Rodriqa plopped the crucible on the poker table. "We've got a lot to check out, and the sooner I get home, the better."

SIEVESDROPPING

Nose down, cell phone open, Buzz followed the red blinking light representing Magnos on his screen as he walked up Mr. Vandereff's street. Buzz glanced up. He knew Mr. Vandereff's house was around the corner. But Magnos's red dot was scurrying in circles ahead. Buzz stopped in the middle of the road. He surveyed the neighborhood. Magnos was crawling on his stomach through hedges several lawns ahead. Closing his phone, Buzz raced over to the ditch a few yards behind Magnos and dropped to his knees. He scooted over to Magnos.

Magnos raised his head just above the hedge line. He glanced at Buzz and pointed toward Vandereff's house.

Buzz sidled up to Magnos. "What is it?"

"Van Zenny's here." Magnos lowered his head. "He's talking to Vandereff's wife out in her driveway. I couldn't get anywhere near them without being seen."

Buzz examined a distant wedge of yard through which he could see Mrs. Vandereff and Sergeant Van Zenny. They were walking around the grass and shrubbery, searching the ground at their feet. The garage door was open, and Van Zenny's police car was parked in the driveway.

Buzz signaled toward the garage. "Look. It's Mr. Vandereff's Orrery."

Magnos followed Buzz's pointed finger. He saw the tall wooden box with its wires spreading outward from the large light bulb in the middle. "It looks even more torn up than after class on Thursday."

"I wonder what happened." Buzz rubbed his chin. "And why did Mr. Vandereff miss school on Friday?"

Magnos leaned forward and stretched out his neck. "I wish we could hear what they were saying."

Buzz smiled. "Maybe we can." He swung his backpack off his shoulder and rifled through its contents. He pulled out two pairs of trabecular cones with spiral hooks at the end. One set was painted baby blue; the other pair light pink. They reminded Magnos of oddly painted pieces of coral someone might buy at a beachside tourist shop.

Magnos poked one of the cones. It pricked the end of his finger. "What are these?"

"I call them Hearing Combs." Buzz wrapped the hook of one of the pink cylinders around his ear. "They brush up the sounds we want to hear and cut out the rest."

Magnos's cheeks balled up. "They clean our ears?"

"No." Buzz chuckled. "They're made of porous ceramic, which has an internal structure that resonates between approximately 50 and 250 hertz, magnifying any surrounding sounds around those frequencies."

"Huh," grunted Magnos.

"These Hearing Combs are made of materials that naturally amplify sound in the same range as the human voice, allowing us to hear someone speaking from far away without all the background clutter. It's called resonance."

"Oh." Magnos picked up a blue cone and wrapped it around his ear. "So we can hear what Van Zenny and Mrs. Vandereff are saying."

"Yes!"

Magnos grinned. "Why didn't you just say that?"

Buzz shrugged. "I thought you'd want to know how they work."

Magnos nodded and picked up the other blue cone.

"Nope." Buzz yanked the blue cone out of Magnos's hand. "Male and female voices are in different ranges. Blue one for boys' voices. Pink for girls'." Buzz put the blue cone in his unoccupied ear and handed Magnos the remaining pink cone.

Magnos scowled. "I don't want a pink one."

Buzz and Magnos faced Sergeant Van Zenny and Mrs. Vandereff and listened to the distant conversation. "I really wish I had seen more," said Mrs. Vandereff.

"We's gonna figure out what happened," replied Sergeant Van Zenny. "But if ya's could narrow down the description, that'd helps a lot."

"I wish I could." Mrs. Vandereff turned toward the garage. "It happened so fast. He was out working in the garage on that solar system machine. Then all of a sudden, this darkness appeared with green eyes. So many green eyes." Mrs. Vandereff sobbed.

"I's sorry, Sally." The sergeant wrapped his arm around her shoulder. "Can I's asks ya's one more question? Then I'll go."

Mrs. Vandereff sniffled and nodded.

Sergeant Van Zenny pulled a picture out of his front uniform pocket. "Ya's don't happen to have one of these, do ya's?"

Mrs. Vandereff smirked. "Yeah, Edison kept it in the garage. Used it to hold solvents or something. It was some sort of family heirloom. I told him it was too hideous to keep in the house."

"Is it still here?"

Mrs. Vandereff walked over to the garage and scanned the shelving. "Sergeant, I think it's gone."

Buzz pulled out his Hearing Combs. "It's confirmed."

Magnos nodded, then shook his head. "What is?"

Buzz placed the Hearing Combs in his book bag and zipped it closed. "Not only is Aubrey right about the lamps, but there is something, or a bunch of somethings, causing all of this."

THE GHOST THAT
KEEPS ON HAUNTING

"What if nobody's home?" Aubrey swallowed the dry lump in his throat.

"Then we don't have to go inside." Rodriqa nudged him forward. "But how else are we gonna prove your lamp theory if we don't ask?"

Both of them stood at the bottom of the broad stairs, which angled upward to a set of ornately carved doors. Much of the old white paint had peeled away from the walls. Conversion from church to house had rendered the steeple into a miniature watchtower, atop which a murder of crows glared down at Aubrey and Rodriqa.

"Is your raven up there?" whispered Rodriqa.

"I don't know." Aubrey glanced upward. "Do you see one with only one good eye?"

Rodriqa eyed the birds and shrugged. "Not really."

"Then hopefully not."

Rodriqa stepped onto the lowest step of the front porch. The wood creaked. Rodriqa leaned forward, and the step bowed. Quickly, she hopped up to the step above it. Rodriqa looked down at Aubrey. "You'd think they'd maintain this place better since it's a historical site."

Aubrey sighed. "I don't think anyone wants to remember its original owner."

"Hovis Trottle is gone, thanks to us." Rodriqa walked up a few more steps. "Mr. Osterfeld has always been harmless."

Aubrey took a slow step up. "I guess you never forget the first ghost you knock off." He chuckled awkwardly.

Rodriqa rolled her eyes. "Come on, Aub. We're good." She trotted up to the front door.

A chill raced down Aubrey's spine. He decided he didn't want to be at the bottom without Rodriqa next to him. He hastily ran up the steps.

Rodriqa smirked at him. "See, that wasn't so bad."

Suddenly, the front door flung open. Aubrey ducked and covered his face. Rodriqa balled up her fists.

A young woman with blonde, curly hair and large golden hoop earrings peered around the door. "Are you two okay?"

Aubrey sighed and straightened from his squatting position. Rodriqa stiffened her back and scratched her neck.

"He's been a little jumpy lately." Rodriqa nodded toward Aubrey.

"Ah," replied the young woman. "You've been standing outside for a while now. I was wondering if you were coming to visit or just lost."

"We were hoping to find out how Mr. Osterfeld was doing." Rodriqa glanced into the house.

"Phineas is still in the hospital," replied the young woman. "I stopped by to check on a few things."

One of Aubrey's cheeks scrunched up. "Aren't you..." Aubrey stuttered and pointed toward the young woman. "Didn't you win the Paddling Pumpkin Festival one year?"

Rodriqa stared at the young woman. Her jaw dropped. "Yes! You're Kiki Januzweski! I can't believe I didn't recognize you!"

Kiki grinned. "My hair's a little shorter." She stepped into the threshold. "I think I know you two as well."

"You do?" replied Aubrey.

Kiki nodded. "Aren't you in that gang that's been supposedly chasing ghosts?"

Aubrey shoved his hands into his pockets. "It's not a gang."

"We're not as bad as everyone thinks." Rodriqa crossed her arms.

"Oh, no judgments here." Kiki waved her hand. "My uncle is a big fan of yours."

"Really?" Aubrey and Rodriqa looked at each other. "Who's your uncle?"

"Phineas." Kiki took a step back. "And although my uncle is known for being a little...um...eccentric, I think there's a few things he'd like you to know."

MARM ALARM

Dr. Iyashi Gatchiri tersely tapped on her electronic tablet. Profile pictures, brief medical histories, and the current vital signs of the nine active patients in the quarantine bay of Lake Julian Regional Hospital slid into two rows on her screen. She viewed them collectively.

All her patients' heart rates remained between the range of fifty-two and sixty-four beats per minute; their respiratory rates unchanged at eleven breaths per minute. Blood pressures and temperatures were all on the low end of normal, but stable, and oxygen saturations never fell below 93 percent on room air. No medicines. No exceptional support. Each of them had only received maintenance IV fluids. All studies unremarkable. Each of her patients in a coma.

"Torpor," she murmured to herself. "Why are they are in torpor?" With her finger, she slid eliminated categories of possible etiologies off her list of differential diagnoses. Metabolic. Toxicological. Infectious. Every physical cause for her patient's hibernation had been excluded. Then the elevator doors opened. Dr. Gatchiri looked up.

Fully gowned and with his head double-masked, Sergeant Van Zenny marched into the quarantine bay.

Dr. Gatchiri's repaired cleft lip wrinkled. "You can remove your mask, Sergeant." She dropped her tablet to her side. "There are no pathogens here."

Van Zenny walked up to her, leaned down, and whispered. "Then why's everyone in Lake Julian getting sick?"

"Exaggeration." Dr. Gatchiri tapped on her tablet twice. "Only a handful of people are in a coma, and there's no proof it is an illness."

Sergeant pulled his masks off his mouth and peered around the room at the gray-skinned motionless patients. "Then what is it?"

Dr. Gatchiri pursed her lips. "The cause is, as of yet, cryptogenic."

"Speak English, Doctor."

Dr. Gatchiri stared down at her tablet. "I'm not certain at this time. We'll simply have to reschedule another full battery of tests. Sometimes watchful waiting can give us the greatest information."

"Watchful waiting?" Sergeant Van Zenny's forehead crumpled. "What am I's supposed to tell people? Don't worry! We's watchfully waiting?!"

"What any officer of the law should tell their citizenry in a time of crisis. Don't panic."

Van Zenny huffed and pulled his pants up around his pudgy waist.

Dr. Gatchiri walked over to Mr. Osterfeld's bedside and adjusted a section of kinking IV tubing. "Besides, I've already spoken with Mr. Miller twice today. He is aware of my progress."

"Progress." The sergeant chuckled. "Backwards progress."

Dr. Gatchiri shook her head. "Finding the reason for an epidemic takes time, Sergeant."

"An epidemic?" Van Zenny glared at her. "Is that what ya's calling this?"

"Well, what would you call it?"

Suddenly, Dr. Gatchiri's electronic tablet blinked and buzzed. She lifted it up and examined it. One of the patient's vital signs had drastically changed. Heart rate 160. Respiratory rate 32. Blood pressure 160 over 90.

She glanced up at the patient in the far corner.

Elma Jennings stood and pointed to her husband. "Something's happening!"

"Hoaker croaker!" Rodriqa covered her mouth. Her words echoed off a myriad of varnished wooden surfaces, from the renovated vestibule to the split sanctuary of Phineas Osterfeld's church-converted home.

Kiki snickered. "Yeah, it's unusual."

Rodriqa and Aubrey stood in the middle of the long nave of Hovis Trottle's former church. A few of the tall, arching stained-glass windows remained, but many of them had been filled in and stacked with shelves.

"My uncle collects weird things." Kiki raised her hands as the three of them surveyed the nave. Wrought iron chandeliers were suspended from the precipice of the vaulted ceiling. A few worn pews remained in the sanctuary. Except for the area around the altar, which had been converted into a small living area with a kitchenette, a table, and a daybed, most of the floor space held cabinets and display boxes. A spiral metal staircase twisted up from the middle of the nave to the ceiling. Upon the walls hung different types of artifacts. On one section, photographs were posted, from antique to digital, of United States presidents. Another wall held every form of key ever forged, from arm-sized, rust-encrusted skeleton keys to tiny electronic silicon board keys.

"It's like a museum in here." Rodriqa spun in erratic circles, trying to take everything in.

Kiki touched an intact and lidless sphere of clear glass, the size of a basketball that contained a terrarium of tiny plants, peat bog, various insects, and a single tiny frog. Moisture beaded inside its top, and a beetle chewed on a piece of overgrown grass. "My uncle served with the Navy for thirty years. Cryptogenic ops."

"What's cryptogenic ops?" Rodriqa sneered at a moldy jar encasing a five-headed piglet preserved in green liquid.

Kiki walked further down the nave. "Paranormal stuff. He collected the bizarre from all over the world and investigated it for the government. The unexplained was his passion. Unfortunately, so was alcohol, so he never got the credit he deserved."

"Sounds like we're in the same business," mumbled Aubrey. "Without the alcohol."

"What's he do now?" Rodriqa asked. "Besides blow his tugboat horn every night."

"He's retired." Kiki glanced at Aubrey sternly as he touched the tattered rags of a mummified cat, dangling from a miniature gantry.

Aubrey pulled his hand away and coughed. "Are you all from here?"

"No. We're from upstate New York, but I've heard Phineas had had his eye on this area for a while. He always said Lake Julian was a hotspot for the peculiar."

Rodriqa snorted and then scratched her nose.

Aubrey stopped at the base of the stairs and looked up. "What's up here?"

Kiki looked up. "That's the steeple room. I've never been up there."

"I know what these are." Rodriqa pointed to another section where more than a dozen plaster casts of oversized feet peppered the paneling.

"Yeah," sighed Kiki. "Bigfoot prints." She walked further down the nave. "Phineas had been tracking sasquatch in the area last fall until they stopped appearing all of a sudden."

Aubrey and Rodriqa glanced at each other knowingly.

"These are beautiful." Rodriqa nodded at the next section. Along the wall on the left-hand end of the nave, a clump of winding wires twisted into intricate patterns, simulating fractals, nautilus shells, and flowers.

"They're crop circle replicas." Kiki mused at the wall. "Phineas always knew they were fakes, but he thought they were pretty anyway."

"Who knows?" commented Rodriqa. "There's lots in this world that doesn't make sense."

Kiki shrugged her shoulders and nodded.

Honk! Honk!

Aubrey and Rodriqa jerked at the squawking sounds and turned toward the front of the nave.

Waddling from the sanctuary, a lanky-necked goose with dark-green feathers and a navy-blue bill swished its rear from side to side as it hobbled out of the sanctuary.

Rodriqa pointed at the bird. "Who painted that duck?"

"It's a goose." Kiki giggled. "And she's not painted. That's her natural color."

The goose honked again and flapped its wings. In a burst of flight, it launched itself over Aubrey and Rodriqa and landed on the top ledge of an upper window.

Aubrey covered his head. "Why is it inside? Aren't you afraid it'll poop all over the place?"

"Janet doesn't poop." Kiki watched the goose. The bird extended her wings and bathed in the sunlight. "She doesn't eat or drink either."

Rodriqa cocked up an eyebrow. "The goose's name is Janet?"

Kiki smirked and nodded. "Phineas's choice, of course."

Aubrey grimaced. "How can it not eat?"

Kiki pointed toward the bird. "She has chlorophyll in her feathers. Absorbs light, water, and carbon dioxide, and lets out oxygen. No poop."

Aubrey shook his head. "That's crazy."

"Yeah, but kinda sad too." Kiki turned her attention back toward the end of the nave. "Supposedly, she's the only one of her kind, and she's never laid an egg." Kiki walked to the end of the sanctuary and stood beside a table next to the altar. "Oh, here's what I wanted to show you."

Aubrey looked down from Janet. A china hutch grabbed his attention. He saw a bottle, resting in its middle shelf. Running over to the hutch, he shouted, "This is it!"

"What?" asked Rodriqa and Kiki.

Aubrey waved Rodriqa over. She walked toward him. Aubrey opened the hutch and pulled out a multicolored glass jar. Its neck curved upward at right angles. Scenes of winged creatures in battle were painted on the bottle along its base.

"He has a crucible too," whispered Aubrey to Rodriqa.

Mesmerized, both of them turned the crucible around, examining its detail.

Kiki snorted. "My uncle alleges it's an original Aladdin's lamp. Like the whole three wishes thing. It was supposed to contain a being of great power. Now it's just an eyesore." She walked into the kitchen.

"Where did he get it?" asked Aubrey. He peered into the crucible's opening. Aubrey pointed frantically at the bottle's top. "I can see my own eye," he whispered to Rodriqa.

Rodriqa waved him down and stared into the bottle's top. She glanced at Aubrey. "I don't see anything."

Kiki rolled her eyes. "Who knows? He's been all over the world." She walked away from the table with an open book in her hand. "I think you might find this interesting."

Aubrey placed the crucible back in the hutch. Aubrey and Rodriqa walked toward Kiki.

"It's my uncle's journal." Kiki kneeled down on the front pew in the nave. "He had mentioned you in it."

"Really?" asked Rodriqa. She and Aubrey knelt on either side of Kiki.

"Yeah." Kiki flipped through several pages. "He thought you all were ahead of your time."

Aubrey smiled.

Kiki pointed to several lines in her uncle's journal, which mentioned Rodriqa, Aubrey, and Buzz. "He also thought he saw a chupacabra the night before he fell ill." Kiki turned a few more pages toward and pointed to the word *chupacabra*. Rodriqa and Aubrey leaned in and followed Kiki's finger as she and read aloud.

> *Tonight, a plague has settled in Lake Julian...Creatures outside...from the steeple room I can see them roam the banks. Triangular faces, like a cross between a bear and a horse...no fur or hair...round large green eyes....*

Aubrey and Rodriqa glanced at each other. Kiki continued reading.

> *sweeping bat-like wings...tiny forelimbs and hooved hindlimbs...thin spiny tail. Idiogenic lifeform, which certainly is without taxonomic classification. Similar to medieval tales of gargoyles, reminiscent of more recent accounts of the Jersey devil and chupacabra, or the "goat sucker."*

Kiki turned the page.

> *It is possible that these neighborhood children with their enigmatic abilities have brought this creature to our doorstep. However, it is more likely that these creatures are the result of an unauthorized creation, and these children may be our greatest hope to fight such spiritual malady.*

Rodriqa leaned back on her ankles. "Mr. Osterfeld knows more than all of us."

Aubrey stared at Rodriqa and nodded. "He knows what's out there. He knew these creatures were here before anyone else."

Rodriqa thrummed her fingers against her lips. "He must have gone outside to investigate and got more than he bargained for."

"That's when he was attacked and ended up pale and comatose," murmured Aubrey.

Kiki nodded and pointed to the next page. "That's exactly what happened. The last paragraph states he was going to try and capture one."

"Buzz was right." Rodriqa crossed her arms. "These chupacabra are ranching the life out of people."

Rodriqa and Aubrey nodded at each other and stood up quickly. Both of them marched around the pew and down the nave.

Kiki looked up. "Where are you going?"

Rodriqa glanced over her shoulder at Kiki, and Aubrey stepped into the vestibule toward the front door. "Chupacabra hunting," they both replied.

———◆———

Saddled between a crack in a boulder and a pine tree growing out of the rock, Mena Kontrearo aimed her Spooly Pen at Aubrey and Rodriqa as they left Mr. Osterfeld's house. She pressed the blue clicky button several times.

"Gotcha."

The monitors above Elma Jennings flashed red, and the IV tubing running beside her husband jerked violently.

Drenched with sweat and scrambling his arms and legs within his sheets, Mr. Jennings clumsily shoved himself upward. His glassy eyes flashed open. His ruddy cheeks brightened. His chest heaved, and he glared upward.

"Ray!" Mrs. Jennings leaned down and grabbed his shoulders. "Ray, can you hear me?"

Sergeant Van Zenny and Dr. Gatchiri ran over to Mr. Jennings. Dr. Gatchiri tapped her tablet twice and then dropped it on the bed. She opened the top drawer of his bedside cabinet.

"Why's he shaking so bad?" Sergeant Van Zenny glanced between the doctor and Mr. Jennings.

"Is he having a seizure?" cried Mrs. Jennings.

"No." Quickly pulling a vial out of its slot, Dr. Gatchiri flipped off its cap and shoved a needle into its rubber top. She screwed a syringe into the needle and aspirated a clear liquid into the syringe's barrel.

"Then what's going on?" Tears dripped down Mrs. Jennings's cheeks.

Dr. Gatchiri twisted the syringe off the needle and screwed it into a tiny port in Mr. Jennings's IV. She slammed down the plunger. The clear liquid rushed through the tubing and into Mr. Jennings's arm.

Mr. Jennings sighed. His flushed cheeks dulled. His arms and legs relaxed, and slowly, his vital signs normalized. The monitor above his bed stopped flashing.

"Torpor discontinued." Dr. Gatchiri picked up her tablet and typed on its screen.

"What does that mean?" Elma Jennings rubbed her husband's hand.

Dr. Gatchiri gripped Mr. Jennings wrist and read her watch. "It means he's out of his coma."

Van Zenny sat on the bed and looked up at Dr. Gatchiri. "Is he okay?"

Dr. Gatchiri took a step back and typed more on her tablet. "He had a hyperactive sympathetic discharge."

"Wha's that mean?"

"It means his autonomic nervous system had been in a parasympathetic lock, and whatever was causing his torpor finally faded. His sympathetic nervous system rebounded, resulting in a surge of catecholamines. I gave him an intravenous beta blocker to dull the effects."

The sergeant shook his head in bewilderment.

Elma touched Ray's cheek. "It looks like he's coming to."

Sergeant Van Zenny leaned down and examined Mr. Jennings. "Ray Gene? Ya's all right?"

Mr. Jennings cleared his throat, his pupils wavering as he focused on the sergeant's face. "Yeah." He rubbed spittle off his lips. "I think so."

"Ray, I need ya's to listen to me closely and answers me as best ya's can."

Mr. Jennings looked between his wife and the sergeant and nodded.

"What's the last thing you remember?"

Mr. Jennings's eyes darted from side to side. "I was at the store."

"What were ya's doin'?"

Mr. Jennings breathed hard. His tongue rolled in his mouth. "I had left a few things in the basement."

The sergeant nodded. "What attacked you?"

"Attacked?" questioned Elma.

Dr. Gatchiri furrowed her brow.

Mr. Jennings's nostrils flared. "I…"

"Sergeant, my patient is in no condition to be questioned at this time." Dr. Gatchiri tapped her tablet three times.

Van Zenny held up his hand. "Ray Gene, can ya's tell me what attacked you?"

Mr. Jennings grimaced. "I…I don't remember."

Suddenly, Dr. Gatchiri's electronic tablet blinked erratically with multiple red squares flashing across the screen. Van Zenny turned his head. Wide-eyed and radish-red, Mrs. Gungandeep and Mr. Vandereff shook in their beds.

"I don't know what I was thinking." Buzz wiped the sweat off his forehead.

Magnos chuckled. "It's good exercise."

"But we've been walking for miles." Buzz flung droplets of perspiration to the ground. "I think I feel heat exhaustion setting in." Buzz's black curls were limp with sweat, and his T-shirt had soaked through.

"I think we're here." Magnos stopped at the edge of the graveled road and peeked through a break in the forest.

"Good." Buzz stumbled off the road and dropped his rump onto a dead log. Jordana stepped quietly out from a tree next to the log and leaned forward, close to his ear.

"Hey, Buzz," whispered Jordana. Buzz screamed. He jumped off the log. Jordana giggled and waved at him.

Buzz scowled. "You scared the snail shucker out of me."

Magnos grinned. "I doubt that."

Jordana stepped over the log. "Why are you all wet?"

"Because Maggie refused to carry me. I had to walk the entire way from Mr. Vandereff's."

Jordana smiled at Magnos. Magnos pointed to the break in the woods from which Jordana had stepped out. "You found the Crannynook Caves?"

Jordana glanced over her shoulder. "I found the trail that leads to them. I wasn't about to go up there by myself."

"Hey! What did you guys find out?" yelled Rodriqa from several hundred yards down the road.

"Aubrey was right!" hollered Buzz. "Vandereff had a lamp—I mean, a crucible."

"So did Mr. Osterfeld," yelled Aubrey in reply. "You were right too, Buzz!"

Rodriqa trotted forward, closing the gap between them. "Osterfeld saw the creatures before he was attacked! Sounds like he was ranched!"

Aubrey chased after Rodriqa. "And we know what it is!"

Jordana, Magnos, and Buzz walked forward to meet them. "You know what attacked everybody?" asked Buzz.

"Chupacabra," replied Rodriqa as the friends huddled together. "In his diary, Mr. Osterfeld gave a perfect description of a chupacabra."

Aubrey held up his hand and raised a finger with each description. "Triangular head. Hairless skin. Bat wings and hooves. Large green eyes."

Jordana pushed her rose-tinted glasses up her nose. "It kinda sounds like Shway Shway."

"Kinda. Minus the wings." Rodriqa cocked her head to the side. "But Osterfeld didn't describe the ears. How could he miss the ears?"

"But I thought chupacabra only lived in Puerto Rico?" Jordana asked.

"That's where the legends started," replied Buzz. "They've been seen all over the country recently, especially in the south."

Aubrey pointed to Buzz. "And he also mentioned the Jersey devil. Said they were similar legends."

Rodriqa nodded. "Sounds like he considered it a type of chupacabra."

Magnos held out his hands. "Wait."

The other four stared at him with wide eyes.

Magnos furrowed his brow. "What's a...a...chimichanga?"

Buzz guffawed. The other three snickered.

"Chu-pa-cab-ra!" enunciated Rodriqa. "Not a chimichanga."

"A chimichanga is a fried burrito." Buzz wheezed out the words as he doubled over, laughing.

Magnos looked up. "I mean...chu-pa-ca-bra."

Jordana covered her mouth to keep herself from laughing.

Aubrey hit Magnos in the shoulder. "It's okay. It's a hard word to say."

"It's not even English," chuckled Rodriqa. "It's Spanish for goat sucker."

Aubrey smiled at Magnos. "It's this reptile hybrid thingy that drains the blood from livestock."

"Usually sighted around farms and more rural areas," added Rodriqa.

"Of course, a chupacabra." Buzz rubbed his chin. "They're known for hunting all sorts of prey and leaving a bloodless carcass behind. It's probably an erroneous description of how they ranch another being's life force."

"Which is why all the victims are limp and pale," continued Rodriqa.

"But not dead," agreed Aubrey. "The chupacabra are ranching the folks of Lake Julian."

Jordana shook her head. "But why?"

All five of them glanced at each other.

Rodriqa put her hands on her hips. "I may not know why, but I bet Ms. Thistlewood's got something to do with it."

"No doubt," murmured Aubrey. "But what is she doing with a herd of chupacabras?"

The trees behind them rustled. Galloping footsteps plodded down the hidden trail. The friends faced the trailhead and clumped together. They felt the ground pound beneath.

"Get ready." Rodriqa raised her closed fists to her face.

"What is it?" whispered Jordana.

Rodriqa squinted her eyes and took two steps forward. She stared up the hillside. She turned around and shook her head. "Scouts."

With their red ascots bouncing on their necks, three Boy Scouts barreled down the end of the trail, out of the forest, and into the ditch. Stomping into the roadway, they ran past Aubrey, Rodriqa, Buzz, Magnos, and Jordana and headed for the top of the gravel road.

"Don't go up there!" shouted one Scout, pointing his thumb over his shoulder.

"There's monsters in the cave!" squealed another boy, who was kicking gravel out behind his scurrying feet.

All five of the friends looked at each other. "Chupacabra."

SPELUNKERY

Aubrey, Rodriqa, Buzz, Magnos, and Jordana climbed the trail single file, traipsing up the root-lined trench. Occasionally, Aubrey would grab Rodriqa's shirt and close his eyes to look for anything unnatural behind his eyelids, but he never saw anything. Other than a few scurrying squirrels and the knocking of a woodpecker high in the trees, there was little noise from the forest. The sun dipped below the distant mountain peaks. The temperature dropped as they ascended the hillside.

"It's getting awfully late." Jordana brushed trail dust off her tank top and wrapped her arms around her elbows.

"We're almost there." Buzz glanced at his cell phone.

"I hope so," muttered Rodriqa.

At the end of the trail, the five friends stopped at the historical marker. Jordana read the rusting placard. "Do people really vacation here?"

Rodriqa shook her head. "They used to. Too creepy for anybody now."

"Especially if there's chimi—uh, chupacabras here." Magnos popped his neck.

Buzz chortled. Jordana glared at Buzz. Aubrey shut his eyes and scanned the front of the caves.

"See anything?" whispered Rodriqa.

Aubrey shook his head and opened his eyes. "Nope."

"Which one should we go in first?" asked Jordana, counting the dozen small openings in the craggy rock ahead.

"The tall thin one is the entrance to the largest cave." Buzz took a step forward and looked at his watch. "Time isn't our friend today. We should hurry."

Rodriqa nodded and trotted ahead of him. "Let's go."

Magnos sidled up next to Rodriqa. Aubrey and Jordana followed closely behind.

Buzz hobbled after, digging in his backpack. "Here." He passed forward several tiny flashlights. "We'll need these."

"Good thinking." Jordana took a flashlight and handed one to Rodriqa and Magnos.

Aubrey reached for one. Buzz slung his book bag over his shoulder and smirked at him. "Why do you need one?"

"Because." Aubrey frowned at him. "It's dark in caves."

Buzz waved him off. "You're gonna have your eyes closed most of the time anyway."

Rodriqa looked back at both of them. "He's got a point."

Rodriqa tugged Aubrey by his shirt and pulled him to the front of the pack. Two tall stacks of dolomite angled upward, forming a dark crevice in the mountain's face. Tiny plunks of water dripped inside. Several small pebbles crumbled off the edge of the weathered stones. A chill needled down Aubrey's back as an icy breeze blew from the mountain's depths.

Rodriqa angled Aubrey's head toward the darkness of the cave and whispered, "Eyes."

Aubrey sighed. He closed his eyes. Phosphenes swirled behind his eyelids and slowly faded. Only an inky black remained.

Aubrey opened his eyes and glanced at his friends. "Nothing."

Buzz pushed himself to the front and pointed his flashlight into the cave. "Let's check it out."

Magnos and Rodriqa flicked on their flashlights. Three bright cones of light pierced the murk. Magnos and Rodriqa crept forward. Buzz followed closely behind.

Jordana grabbed Aubrey's arm. Aubrey looked at her. She smiled at him. Aubrey's face flushed, and his heart pounded in his chest. They walked into the cave side by side.

The five friends stepped through the opening into the widening chamber. Insects hummed and spun through the flashlight beams. The damp, rocky lining of the cave was peppered with pale-green lichen.

Rodriqa slipped but quickly righted herself. "Be careful. It's wet in here."

"But not as spooky as I thought it'd be." Buzz pushed forward past Magnos and Rodriqa. "Oh, look." Buzz scanned his flashlight along a tiny crevice pooled with stagnant water. A piece of torn coozie bobbed at the water's surface. Broken brown glass and bottle caps were scattered around it.

Magnos looked down over Buzz's shoulder. "Someone's been here."

Rodriqa glanced down and then shined her flashlight further down the cave. "Party, party."

"Litterbugs," grumbled Buzz.

Walking arm in arm, Aubrey and Jordana hobbled up next to Buzz. Jordana flashed her light at the pool. "I wonder if Gaetan's been up here."

Magnos snorted. "Probably, with Fayla."

Magnos walked deeper into the cave. He leaned down as his head grazed the top of the sloping ceiling. "Looks like it's narrowing."

Rodriqa squatted down and sidestepped forward. "There's another room down here." She flashed her light back up the cave. "Aubrey. Eyes."

Squinting, Aubrey held up his hand. "Good thing I didn't need to see with my eyelids open."

"Hurry up," said Rodriqa.

Aubrey and Jordana walked forward, ducking down to avoid the angled ceiling. Aubrey closed his eyes. Jordana gasped. Aubrey felt Jordana pull back on his arm.

Aubrey opened his eyes. "What is it?"

With her eyes closed and nose wrinkled, Jordana pointed down at her feet with her flashlight.

"What's wrong?" asked Buzz, shuffling back to them.

Aubrey looked down. His stomach rolled with nausea. He kicked the muddy floor of the cave. A white jagged object tumbled down the slope ahead.

Buzz leaned over and examined the object. He shrugged. "It's just a bone."

"Is it human?" asked Rodriqa.

Buzz tilted his head. "It's a humerus. Broken midshaft. Looks more animal to me."

"What if you're wrong?" muttered Jordana.

"It could be from anything," added Aubrey.

"But it's most likely from a dead animal," argued Buzz. He kicked it to the side of the cave. "Regardless, it isn't fresh. It's not like we found a decaying carcass hanging from a stalactite. It's a bone."

Jordana grimaced. "Let's keep moving."

Rodriqa took another step into the cave. "Aubrey, do your thing."

Holding onto Jordana, Aubrey scuttled around the spot where the bone had lain and aimed his face down the incline.

The phosphenes dulled, and the darkness pushed in behind his eyes. After a few moments, Aubrey noticed squirming, vertical lines of shimmering light in the distance. Aubrey squeezed his eyelids together and held his breath, but the scintillating image didn't change.

"What do you see?" Buzz stepped up to Aubrey.

Aubrey exhaled loudly, but kept his eyes closed. "I don't know. There's something…" Aubrey waved his hands. "It's just a bunch of shiny lines. I'm not sure if it's anything or not."

"Uh-oh," murmured Rodriqa. She flashed her light ahead.

"What?" asked Jordana and Buzz.

"I *definitely* see something." Rodriqa dropped down into the next chamber and walked forward.

Aubrey opened his eyes. "You do?"

Magnos and Buzz scooted down the incline and hopped down after Rodriqa. Jordana walked past Aubrey and steadied herself on the slippery floor.

Crouching and dipping his head low to look ahead, Aubrey scuffled forward.

"What is *that*?" Jordana took a step back.

"Why is it white?" Magnos's voice echoed.

"I think it's connected to the ceiling," replied Rodriqa distantly.

"Is it a limestone formation?" asked Buzz.

"Nope." Rodriqa crept deeper into the cave. "It's a person."

Aubrey dropped several feet off the incline next to Jordana. Her flashlight's beam diffused through a massive room of rock, the darkness dissolving the light after a hundred yards. Magnos's and Buzz's lights wandered from side to side shortly behind Rodriqa, whose light was fixed on a white oblong object that hung from the top of the chamber.

"Hey, Aubrey! Come here!" hollered Buzz.

Aubrey glanced at Jordana. She nodded at him. Aubrey jogged down the length of the chamber. "Why would a person be down here?"

"I doubt they meant to stay," replied Rodriqa over her shoulder.

"And I think we know them." Buzz shined his light at the bottom of the white object.

Aubrey skidded to a stop.

"Who is that?" Rodriqa asked.

Aubrey raised his pointed finger at the body hanging from the ceiling. "It's Fran Losepkee."

Dressed in a tube top and cut-off jean shorts blotted with mud, the pale, gray, pudgy woman dangled motionless by her feet. Her blonde curls strung wet from the top of her head. Her eyes were closed, but her mouth gaped open.

"Who?" asked Rodriqa.

"One of the Moth-ers," murmured Buzz.

"She looks awful." Aubrey sighed and took a step forward. "She looks just like the others."

Magnos scratched his head with his flashlight. "Then this must be the den of the chupacabra."

"I think we should leave," yelled Jordana from the front of the chamber.

"We have to get her down," replied Aubrey as he walked toward Buzz. He aimed his flashlight toward the top of the cave. "How is she hanging?"

Buzz scooted up to Mrs. Losepkee and examined her feet. They were squeezed between stones and covered with hardened mud and twigs.

Buzz squinted. "Looks like a concretion of some sort. We should be able to pull her down."

Aubrey, Rodriqa, and Buzz turned and looked expectantly at Magnos.

Magnos nodded. He walked over toward Mrs. Losepkee and handed Aubrey his flashlight.

Magnos's hands hesitated as he decided which part of her to grab. Her chest was eye-level to him. He turned his head and wrapped his arms around her trunk. "Sorry, Mrs. Losepkee." He clasped her body tightly and jerked. She didn't move. A few bits of mud flaked off the ceiling and dropped to the ground.

"It's working." Buzz watched a crack form in the concretion at Mrs. Losepkee's feet. "Do it again."

"Whoa!" Magnos jumped back.

"What is it?" Rodriqa tilted her flashlight from side to side.

"Something touched my arm." Magnos brushed off his elbows.

Buzz shook his head. "It was probably just a bug."

"Look!" Rodriqa's flashlight stopped moving. "There's something behind Mrs. Losepkee."

The four of them leaned forward. A long black object hung behind Mrs. Losepkee. A dark, round mound rolled down from the bottom of the object. It was leathery and popped as it moved. Sharp white points flashed at the four friends as the mound continued to roll. Suddenly, large green eyes opened and glared at them.

"Jordana's right," whispered Buzz. "We should go."

The other three nodded and took steps backward. A growl bleated from behind the sharp, white points. The green eyes turned clockwise and bat-like wings unfurled from the object hanging from the ceiling.

"Chupacabra!" Buzz spun around and ran toward the front of the cave. Jordana jerked around and climbed up the drop-off.

The black object twisted and leapt onto the floor, leaving the bald, limp Stan Losepkee hanging behind it. It dug into the dirt with its back hooves and climbed forward on three-fingered hands.

In Aubrey and Rodriqa's flashlight, the creature's triangular head twitched from side to side as it looked at the children. Foamy saliva dribbled off its long canines and plopped onto the rocks beneath it. Its spiny tail whipped in circles, and the pointed spines along its back arched as it growled again.

Rodriqa pushed Aubrey back. "Run!" She stomped her foot on the ground and screamed at the chupacabra. The creature winced and rose back on its hooves. It flapped it wings, beating them against the air. A foul rush of warm rot blew past Rodriqa and Magnos. Aubrey stumbled back and closed his eyes, which stung with the streaming stench. The phosphenes faded quickly, and the squirming lines in the darkness, one by one, were fading away.

Rodriqa felt her fingers tingle. She looked down. Her hands were ghostly white as the spirit of the Tsul'kalu spread up her forearms and across her shoulders.

Magnos lurched forward. He gripped the creature's tiny hand. The chupacabra squealed and snapped at Magnos. He dodged the creature's bite. Magnos anchored one foot next to a rock and spun in a circle, like he was swinging a baseball bat. He flung the chupacabra against the wall of the cave. The creature squalled and crumpled to the floor.

Fully faded into her ghostly form, Rodriqa darted over to the injured chupacabra. Its eyes were closed, and its legs and tail lay limp under its body. Rodriqa pressed her foot against its neck. She glanced over at Magnos. "Grab it!"

Aubrey opened his eyes and pointed toward the back of the chamber. "Guys! I think we're about to have more company!"

Magnos nodded. He charged over and lifted up the creature by its haunches. The chupacabra's eyes snapped open. It twisted in a full circle and launched itself upward. It opened its jaws. Its rows of sharp teeth clamped down on Rodriqa's shoulder.

Rodriqa wailed. She clawed at the creature's leathery skin. The chupacabra grimaced as it fell on top of her. Slowly, the creature's dark muzzle was fading to a ghostly pale as Rodriqa's Tsul'kalu spirit rushed out of her into the creature.

Rodriqa kicked as she screamed. Suddenly, she felt dizzy, and her voice cracked. Her arms dropped limp to her side.

Magnos kicked the creature in its chest. The chupacabra squealed and released Rodriqa. It snapped at Magnos. Aubrey picked up a sharp rock and plunged it into the chupacabra's spiny back. The creature squalled and wrenched its torso upward. Magnos kicked it again, and it rolled to the edge of the cave. Magnos raced over to the creature, lifted a stone the size of a tire, and dropped it on the chupacabra's head.

The creature shuddered. Slowly, its black leathery arms and legs blurred out of focus and evaporated like smoke.

Aubrey fell on his knees next to Rodriqa. "Are you okay?"

Rodriqa nodded limply and grabbed her injured shoulder. Magnos knelt down next to them and pulled the corner of her shirt down. "Look. No blood." Magnos pointed to where there should have been a wound, but her skin was intact.

A rock tumbled in the distant darkness. Aubrey looked up and cast his light toward the end of the chamber. A score of large, green eyes shined across the back of the cave.

Magnos, Aubrey, Jordana, and Buzz ran down the trail below the Crannynook Caves.

"Put me down!" Draped over his shoulder, Rodriqa beat Magnos's back. She no longer twinkled with the spirit of the Tsul'kalu but was pale and mottled.

Magnos bounded over the ditch next to the gravel road and skidded to a stop. He lifted the squirming Rodriqa off his neck and placed her on the ground.

Her arms flailed toward Magnos. "What just happened?" She stopped, and her legs crumpled beneath her. Magnos jumped forward and caught her before her head hit the ground.

Aubrey, Jordana, and Buzz hurried out of the woods and gathered around Rodriqa.

"Are you okay?" Aubrey helped Magnos sit her up on the road.

"She's pale," murmured Buzz. "Just like the others."

Jordana stood next to Magnos with her mouth covered.

Rodriqa strained to keep her eyes open. "That kinda hurt."

"It looked like it hurt," agreed Aubrey.

Rodriqa pointed limply at Jordana. "Why?"

Jordana glanced at Magnos and then looked back at Rodriqa. "Why what?"

Some of Rodriqa's color returned, and her cheeks flushed. "Why did you leave us?" Rodriqa shook her finger at Jordana. "Why did you leave me?"

Jordana squeezed her eyes together. "I couldn't stand to watch anymore."

"That's weak." Rodriqa pushed Aubrey and Magnos away and rocked forward onto her knees.

Jordana scowled and turned away. Buzz looked up at the sky's fading light. "We're outta time." Buzz held up his watch. "It's way late."

"What do we do about the Losepkees?" Aubrey asked.

Buzz looked at his cell phone. "What can we do? We're not prepared to fight."

Jordana rubbed her neck. "We'll just have to come back."

"We could tell Van Zenny," suggested Magnos.

Buzz shook his head. "And then our only ally in the adult world would be chupacabra fodder."

Aubrey pressed his hand against his chest. "We'll come back."

Jordana and Magnos nodded.

Rodriqa squatted upward, then wobbled backward.

Magnos and Aubrey stepped forward to grab her.

Rodriqa stumbled in circles. Slowly, she righted herself and walked forward. She swatted Magnos's beefy hand away. "Don't help me."

<hr />

Lying in a ditch a score of yards up the gravel road from the trailhead, Mena peeked her head above the edge of the road. She watched Aubrey and Magnos shoulder Rodriqa as they scuffled forward.

"*Borracha?*" Mena pulled a twig out of her ponytail and smiled. "Perfect."

Aiming her Spooly Pen at the five friends, she pressed the blue clicky button repeatedly.

"These are not the hardwoods I ordered!" yelled Maximillian Miller at a short, olive-skinned man standing in the Miller home's two-story foyer. The man, who held a plank of beech wood, was shirtless but dressed in denim overalls splattered with white paint.

"But, Mr. Miller," the olive-skinned man flipped the piece of wood, reading the serial numbers on the plank's edges. "This is what the company gave me to put down."

"Manchurian walnut!" The veins on Mr. Miller's bald head pulsated. "I ordered Manchurian Walnut!"

The olive-skinned man shrugged. "I can call the company. Maybe it's all sitting at the warehouse. Maybe it's just a mix-up."

Mr. Miller raised his hands. "Then what are you waiting for?"

The worker stared out the open door at the dusk settling over Mount Camelot. "The warehouse is closed."

Mr. Miller's thin cheeks contracted. "How long will it take you to fix it?"

The olive-skinned man scratched his scalp with the end of the plank of beech wood. "I don't know."

Mr. Miller's shoulders heaved, and he snarled.

The olive-skinned man pointed toward the door. "You have a visitor." Mr. Miller glanced at his front door. Jobe Parotty walked into the house, gazing at the damage to the Miller home as he stepped through the threshold. Mr. Miller sighed quietly and scrunched up his cheeks to present a smile. "Jobe! What a wonderful surprise!" Mr. Miller walked over to Mr. Parotty and thrust out his hand.

Furrowing his brow, Mr. Parotty nodded. "I apologize for the unexpected visit. Looks like I've come at a bad time." He shook Mr. Miller's hand.

"Not at all." Mr. Miller crossed his arms. "Everything is okay at the Rock-U-Quarium, I hope."

"Better than okay." Mr. Parotty grinned. "We're exceeding projections by twenty-five percent."

Mr. Miller nodded. "Wonderful. Wonderful."

Mr. Parotty's smile faded as he looked at the back of the foyer, where several workers hammered planks of beech hardwoods next to a darker wood. "Lake Julian has been the perfect place to begin our venture."

"I am very glad to hear you say that."

Mr. Parotty glanced between the laborers and Mr. Miller, whose face was frozen in a tense smile.

"You do realize…" Mr. Parotty angled his head as he pointed toward the end of the foyer. "Your hardwoods don't match."

Mr. Miller's smile melted. He stepped forward and wrapped his lanky arm around Mr. Parotty, turning him toward the door.

"Hiring someone to fix your home is like giving a chipmunk a latte," murmured Mr. Miller. "The chipmunk acts like he's king while he's drinking, but the rodent completely forgets he'll be chewing on nuts again when he goes home that night."

Mr. Parotty turned his head and and pointed at the chandelier above. "That's really striking! Is it Viennese?"

Mr. Miller looked up. "Etruscan replica. Straight from Rome."

"Ah." Mr. Parotty nodded. "Savoy? Or Jeffersonian?"

Mr. Miller frowned. "Is there something I can do for you?" He glanced around his foyer. "As you can see, I'm a little busy."

"Of course." Mr. Parotty smiled. "I came to ask a favor."

Mr. Miller bowed his head. "Anything."

Mr. Parotty lifted his chin. "I need the five children to attend the Rock-U-Quarium tomorrow."

"Absolutely not!" Mr. Miller reared back.

Mr. Parotty grimaced. "I think it will be good PR. It'll show the community that we are willing to accept even the most outcast of society." Mr. Parotty nudged Mr. Miller in the ribs. "And maybe we can bring them into the fold. They have notoriety. You can't deny that. Your bid for state congressman would be solidified if you befriended them."

Mr. Miller's tightened face relaxed slightly. "Well, maybe." Mr. Miller thought for a moment. His lips pressed together. "No! They are a menace! Lake Julian will be better off once they've been locked up or sent away. All five of them!"

Mr. Parotty lowered his head. "Is there no forgiveness? Why don't we let children be children?"

Mr. Miller scowled. "Because undisciplined children grow into unruly adults."

Mr. Parotty nodded and pursed his lips. "I wish you thought differently."

"I don't." Mr. Miller held up his head. "And I won't. Do not let those children back into your pleasure dome." He raised a pointed index finger to Mr. Parotty's leaning nose. "I'm warning you, Jobe. Those children are trouble. I only have your best interest in mind."

"Hmm." Mr. Parotty stepped away. He shoved his hands into his pockets and stared at the Millers' front door. "That's how you see them? As broken and faulty?"

Mr. Miller glanced between the outside and Mr. Parotty. "Why, yes!"

Mr. Parotty nodded and looked down.

A phone rang from the kitchen.

Mr. Miller sneered. "Excuse me."

Mr. Parotty turned away. "Of course."

Mr. Miller walked into the kitchen and picked up the phone. "Hello."

"Max, I need to ask a favor." The sing-songy tone both soothed his ears and prodded his heart to flutter. Mr. Miller's jaw slowly opened. Sweat beaded on his forehead. He stared into the kitchen wall. Ms. Thistlewood didn't wait for him to reply. "Mr. Parotty will invite the children to the Rock-U-Quarium, with your blessing and insistence."

"Of course," muttered Mr. Miller. His fingers and toes went numb, and his face paled. "Whatever you say."

Mr. Parotty sneered and stepped out the front door. "Eat those nuts, chipmunk."

Aydry Auerbach stepped into her car in the employee's parking lot of the Lake Julian Dam. She closed the door and, glancing out several windows, looked for anyone who might be able to see her. Aydry picked up her cell phone and plugged Buzz's signal amplifier into one of its side ports. Scrolling though her contact list, she tapped on Dan Taylor.

The phone rang. "Hello."

"Dan, it's Aydry."

"Is everything okay?"

"I'm not sure." Mrs. Auerbach bit her lip. "I just got a call from Mr. Miller."

Mr. Taylor mumbled a vivid expletive. "If Aubrey's not home—"

"That's not the problem." Aydry furrowed her brows. "Mr. Miller told me that our kids are expected to attend a private event with Jobe Parotty tomorrow night at the Rock-U-Quarium."

Mr. Taylor chuckled. "I'm sorry, Aydry, I thought you said Mr. Miller wants our kids to go into town tomorrow night."

"That's exactly what I said."

Mr. Taylor paused for a moment. "Why?"

"He listed a slew of reasons. He thought our children should get out more. Maybe keeping them cooped up is worsening their delusions." Mrs. Auerbach thrummed her fingers on the steering wheel. "It almost seemed like he wanted to make up."

Mr. Taylor sighed. "Was he on something?"

Mrs. Auerbach rocked her head. "He sounded a little giddy, for Max, but he was insistent. He said he felt it was important they be there tomorrow no matter what."

"That's really weird. What is up with that guy?"

"I have no idea, but I have a feeling we need to go along with it."

"This seems like trouble."

"We're way past trouble." Mrs. Auerbach scoffed. "I think we're teetering on calamity."

"What do you think Jamison will say?"

Aydry sighed. "I'm not sure, but he's so over Rodriqa's behavior lately, he'll probably tell me to take them."

"I thought Jamison was a stickler for the rules."

"Oh, he is." Mrs. Auerbach lowered her voice. "But I wonder if Mr. Miller is going to try and teach them all a lesson."

"Huh." Mr. Taylor rubbed his chin against his phone's receiver. "You think Max is planning some sort of revenge?"

"I'm not sure, but I wouldn't put it past him."

Mr. Taylor thought for a moment.

Aydry sighed. "So what do you say? Should we let them go?"

Mr. Taylor snorted quietly. "At this point, what do we have to lose?"

TWIST OF THE HEAVY

On the eastern bank of Lake Julian, Buzz ducked down as he raced through the back of the Boy Scout camp. Hidden by twilight and using campfire light to guide his way, he peered through tent netting and over tarps, hunting for Coren.

"You wouldn't believe it even if you'd seen it."

A familiar voice inside a tent caught Buzz's attention. He squatted down and listened.

"It was huge," said another voice.

"Like a bat and a horse and a dog all in one."

"Get off it, dude," replied another voice. "You didn't see anything in those caves." A boy chuckled. "I bet my left shoe is more haunted than that place."

"We're going back tomorrow," said the familiar voice. "Yeah, if you don't believe us, come see for yourself…unless you're scared."

Buzz shook his head and scuttled away from the tent. "Amateurs," he murmured.

Coren Belward rounded the corner and looked down at Buzz, who was on all fours. "What are you doing?"

Buzz crouched back and brushed off his hands. "Looking for you."

Coren's Adam's apple bobbed in his neck. "So's your Dad."

Buzz grimaced. "Did he come looking for me?"

"Oh, yeah." Coren held up his arms. "I told him you were helping rebuild one of our aid stations on the other side of the lake."

"Did he believe you?"

"I think so. He asked when you'd be back. I told him I'd get you back as quick as I could."

"Thanks a lot." Buzz grabbed his hand and shook it. "I owe you one."

Coren smiled and saluted Buzz. "What all did you find out?"

Buzz straightened up. "You wouldn't believe it even if you'd seen it."

Coren grimaced.

"I'll tell you more when I know a little more." Buzz flashed Coren a thumbs-up.

Coren sighed and nodded.

As Buzz approached his tent, he listened to an ongoing conversation inside. Buzz perched his ear next to the front flap.

"I've already cleared it with Sergeant Van Zenny and Mr. Miller."

Mr. Reiselstein cleared his throat. "But he's grounded, and I think it best he learn this lesson sooner rather than later."

"It's only one night, and it's his spring break. He deserves a little fun."

"I don't think he would go alone."

"I've already invited his friends and spoken with their parents as well. Everyone is on board."

Mr. Reiselstein sighed. "I'm just afraid it sends the wrong message."

"I'll be with them the whole time. I won't allow them to get into any more trouble."

"I don't think his mother would approve. She's a bit of a stickler for following through on punishments."

"You can give her my word. One night. A little fun. Maybe some good guidance from an entrepreneur and a former tough guy. And no funny business."

The conversation paused.

"I think we have company," whispered Mr. Reiselstein.

Buzz's eyes widened, and he took several steps away from the tent. The canvas flap opened. Mr. Reiselstein walked out of the tent, holding the flap up with his hand as moved outside.

"Hi, Dad." Buzz waved at his father.

"Hello, son." Mr. Reiselstein had an eyebrow cocked high on his forehead. "Busy day 'repairing an aid station'?"

"Yep." Buzz nodded. "Who you talkin' to?"

Mr. Reiselstein wrinkled his forehead and pointed toward the tent. Jobe Parotty stepped through the flap, his bowl-shaped hair flapping in the cool evening breeze, and his dark mole resting on the tip of his nose.

"Hello, Buzz." Mr. Parotty extended his hand. "I was just asking your father for his permission to invite you to the Rock-U-Quarium for a special event tomorrow."

"Really?" Buzz shook Mr. Parotty's pinky and ring finger. "I'd love to." Buzz scratched the top of his head. "But I'm kind of in trouble."

Mr. Parotty chuckled. "If you weren't in some trouble, you wouldn't be a normal teenager."

Mr. Reiselstein folded his lower lip under his teeth. Buzz laughed awkwardly in reply.

Mr. Parotty bobbed his head back and forth. "So?" He raised his hands. "You in?"

Buzz looked at his dad. Mr. Reiselstein subtly shook his head. Mr. Parotty noticed Buzz's glance and looked over at Mr. Reiselstein. Mr. Reiselstein smiled at Mr. Parotty.

"Sure." Buzz snapped his fingers. "As long as my friends can come too."

———✦———

"I'm fine." Rodriqa pushed Aubrey away as they walked down Dalton Circle with Magnos. Aubrey and Magnos glanced warily at each other. Rodriqa clumsily shuffled several steps ahead through the glow of the streetlights.

"At least she's not pale anymore." Magnos pointed at her head.

Rodriqa glared over her shoulder at Magnos.

Magnos shrugged his shoulders and looked at Aubrey.

"I'm glad you're okay, Rodriqa." Aubrey nodded at Magnos. "If we would have had to take you to the hospital, we'd be shucking snails for sure."

"I'm just glad that chimi—" Magnos scratched his forehead. "Uh, chupacabra didn't kill you."

"I said I'm fine!" Rodriqa stumbled forward.

Magnos held his hands out, ready to catch her.

Aubrey shook his head. "Fine, yes. Well, no." He pointed ahead at Rodriqa's house. "Almost there."

Rodriqa stopped. Her eyes widened. Her hand squeezed her forehead. "Robert."

Aubrey stood next to her. "You'll be okay." Aubrey grabbed her elbow. "But let's hurry."

The three of them sprinted toward Rodriqa's front door. Aubrey and Magnos helped Rodriqa up the steps of her porch as she pulled out her keys. She unlocked the front door, and they ran inside.

Aubrey closed the door. "Anyone home?" His voice echoed through the Auerbach house. No one responded.

"Uh-oh." Magnos peeked outside between the drapes.

"What?" asked Aubrey.

"Robert's home."

Rodriqa stumbled toward the staircase and crawled up the steps on all fours. Magnos and Aubrey rushed behind her and pushed her forward.

At the top of the steps, Magnos picked her up, and Aubrey directed him toward Rodriqa's bedroom.

Downstairs, the front door opened and shut.

Aubrey lifted his index finger to his lips. Rodriqa waddled into bed. Her head dropped to her pillow. Aubrey lifted her covers and draped them over her.

"Rodriqa!" yelled Robert from downstairs.

Magnos glanced around the room. He grabbed Aubrey by the shirt and pulled him over to the bedroom window, which faced Aubrey's bedroom across the yard.

"We're gonna have to jump," whispered Magnos.

Aubrey shook his head. His heart raced, and his palms dampened with sweat.

Magnos quietly slid open Rodriqa's window and pushed out the screen. "I'll catch you." Magnos squeezed over the sill. Aubrey tugged at his shirt. Robert's footsteps pounded up the stairs.

Magnos leapt to the yard. His knees bent as his feet landed firmly on the grass. He looked up and waved at Aubrey.

"Rodriqa! Where are you?" Robert flipped on the hallway light and rounded the top of the stairs.

Aubrey held his breath. He climbed outside. His wet fingers slipped against the wood. He fell out of the window.

Robert marched into Rodriqa's room and stood over her bed. "Rodriqa! Why didn't you answer me?"

Rodriqa snored loudly, her face half-buried in her pillow. A small pool of drool oozed onto her sheets.

Robert frowned. He looked up at her open window. Walking over, he surveyed the outside. He didn't see anything. He stared back at Rodriqa and shook his head.

Hiding in the corner of his back porch and cradled in Magnos's arms, Aubrey peered up at Rodriqa's window. He could see Robert shaking his head.

"That was close." Aubrey looked up at Magnos.

"Too close," agreed Magnos.

Aubrey glanced down. "I think you can put me down now."

Magnos nodded. Window screen in hand, Magnos planted Aubrey on the porch and rested the screen against the railing.

Aubrey gazed up at the window again, trying to see what was happening in Rodriqa's room. "I hope she's okay."

Magnos lowered his head. "Me too."

⊰⊱

Mona Kontrearo rapped on the foggy glass of a door with the word *Editor* stenciled into it.

With his black, untied bowtie dangling around his neck, Fagan McElory opened the door and gazed down at Mena. "Yes?" he grumbled.

Mena scratched her scalp underneath her ponytail. "Mr. McElory! I've got pictures!"

Mr. McElory frowned, his thick, black mustache fanning forward. "Of what?"

Mena leaned toward him. "The NeighborGhoul Watch."

Mr. McElory waved her toward him. His voice softened. "Show me."

Mena pulled her laptop out of the book bag. She propped it open in her elbow, and the screen booted up. Lifting her purple Spooly Pen from her pocket, she gripped the end of it with her teeth and pulled off the bottom, revealing a USB plug. Mena shoved the plug into a port on the side of her laptop. Pictures flashed across the screen. "These are some *niños malos*."

Mr. McElory scrunched up his cheek as he viewed her laptop. "So what?"

Mena cocked her head to the side. "They're supposed to be on house arrest."

Mr. McElory shrugged. "They broke curfew. Who cares? Everyone already knows they're bad." He tightened his fist and shook it in front of his face. "I need news. Something gritty. Something hardcore. You got me?"

"But..." Mena shifted her weight. "This is what everyone wants to know."

"Everyone wants to know *why* they're bad and what they're up to next. Not that they're on a house-hopping tour."

Mena crumpled her lips together.

Mr. McElory backed up and closed his door. "Don't bother me until you've got some meat."

"How many were killed?"

Matsinstrus cowered at the top of the double-spiral stairs with one skeletal hand on the bannister. "Only one."

In front of the fireplace, Magnolia Thistlewood balled up her fists. "Were any of the children ranched?"

Matsinstrus held up a bony finger. "I know at least one keeper tried."

"Then how did the children escape?"

Matsinstrus bowed his head. "I'm not sure." He choked on the fumes seeping up from his ribcage. "I think most of the keepers were sleeping."

Ms. Thistlewood turned away and stared into the flames. The orange-yellow fire glinted off her pale-green eyes and brightened her long red hair.

Matsinstrus took a step down. "Should I move the keepers?"

Ms. Thistlewood thought for a moment. "Keep a quarter of them in the caves. Take the rest to the gorge below the dam." Ms. Thistlewood glared at Matsinstrus. "And don't leave them unguarded again."

Matsinstrus nodded. "But what about tomorrow night?"

Ms. Thistlewood marched over to the window atop the massive oak tree. Night had blanketed the valley, and she squinted to see the two forms, standing guard among the tall grass below. "Send the Kluggards. They can help you move them."

"Yes, my queen." Matsinstrus turned to walk down the steps.

Ms. Thistlewood noted a cloaked figure walking toward the front door of the oak tree. "Oh and, Matsinstrus?"

Matsinstrus stopped and looked over his shoulder. "Yes."

"Tomorrow night had better go well. If it doesn't, it looks like I've already found your replacement."

Matsinstrus turned and plodded down the stairs.

Ms. Thistlewood walked briskly to the other side of the spiral staircase and hurried to the bottom level.

The red front door opened. With only fingers and boots exposed, the hooded, cloaked figure walked inside. Ms. Thistlewood stopped at the last step and flipped her hair behind her shoulders.

The visitor held up a small, round voice modulator and spoke through electronic tones, "Your thugs wouldn't let me in."

Ms. Thistlewood crossed her arms. "They weren't supposed to."

The figure squeezed the modulator. "Fortunately, they were easy to convince otherwise."

Ms. Thistlewood tapped her tongue on the roof of her mouth. "Why are you here?"

"I did what you asked."

Ms. Thistlewood laughed. "That I know, obviously."

The visitor's head cocked to one side. "Then obviously you know why I've come."

Ms. Thistlewood crossed her arms. "Do you think I give my gifts so freely?"

The visitor shook their head. "I've done what you've asked. What more do you want?"

"Obedience."

The visitor walked forward. "Done."

Ms. Thistlewood faced the visitor. "Unquestioning, unwavering, unrelenting obedience."

The visitor knelt before Ms. Thistlewood. "Done."

Ms. Thistlewood peered at the skin under the cloak. "Do you give away your freedom so lightly?"

The visitor laughed. "Who needs freedom when you can have power?"

Ms. Thistlewood nodded. She stretched out her arm and with her opposite hand turned the dial on her sandstone watch. The phylactery hissed, and its top plate snapped upward.

"Take my hand." Ms. Thistlewood reached for the visitor.

The visitor's slender fingers slid out from the cloak. Ms. Thistlewood grasped her wrist.

Shimmering, black spirit shards spewed from Ms. Thistlewood's phylactery. Rings of sharp teeth bit at the air.

The visitor pulled back. Ms. Thistlewood held up her other hand. "Ah ah ah. Remember, you asked for this."

The spirit shards jumped from the sandstone watch and latched themselves onto the visitor's arm, chewing at her skin as they squirmed and spiraled up it.

The voice modulator dropped to the ground. The visitor fell backward. She shook her hand erratically, trying to fling off the shadowy serpents. She looked at the tips of her fingers. Only charred skeleton remained.

"What...what have you done to me?"

Ms. Thistlewood smiled. "I've given you the greatest gift you could ever imagine, my dear sweet Icharida."

Tuesday.

"I can't believe you're letting him go."

Gaetan's voice from downstairs roused Aubrey from sleep. He yawned, stretched out his arms, and listened.

"I was asked by the owner to let him go," replied Aubrey's father. Cabinet doors banged and dishes clashed in the sink.

"But he's in trouble!"

"I know that."

"Then why don't you be his dad and man up!"

Aubrey scooted up in his bed. There was a long stretch of silence. "Why does he get to go to back to the Rock-U-Quarium? Why am I stuck in Lake Julian for spring break when I haven't done anything wrong?"

Mr. Taylor marched through the living room. "I'm sorry you didn't get to go to Florida with your friends, but Daytona is no place for a teenager. Besides, you know money is short right now."

"You just don't trust me!" There was a loud clang in the living room. "And I'm not the son you shouldn't trust!" The front door slammed shut.

Aubrey could hear his dad stomp up the stairs. He lay back and looked away from the doorless threshold of his bedroom.

Mr. Taylor leaned his head into the room from the hallway, his eyebrows furrowed. "Mrs. Auerbach is taking you and your friends to the Rock-U-Quarium this evening." Aubrey looked at him and nodded. "She will pick you up shortly after. You're to go there and come straight home. This is not a play date. Understand me?"

"Yes, sir."

Mr. Taylor pulled back into the hallway and leaned in again. "Another thing."

Aubrey nodded.

"Don't act up."

"Yes, sir."

Mr. Taylor stomped back down the stairs and left through the back door.

Aubrey sat up in bed and looked at his cell phone. It was blinking red. He flipped it open and tapped on Cliqcom. He had six new messages.

B: (Buzz Reiselstein): Mr. Parotty asked for us! Can you believe it? This is perfect! :D

J: (Jordana Galilahi): Uncle told me this morning. He wasn't happy.

B: Who cares? When has your uncle ever been happy. This is awesome news!

M: (Magnos Strumgarten): I'm excited. Fayla was ticked.

J: I think it's a trap.

B: Why would it be a trap? Mr. Parotty is an entrepreneur, not a specter

Aubrey typed in Cliqcom.

A: (Aubrey Taylor): Jordana might be right. Mr. Parotty has been asking me for my help.

B: What? Why didn't you tell us?

J: I told you something was funny about this.

B: Funny? We could have been going to the Rock-U-Quarium every day this week.

J: Oh yeah, except we're wanted criminals on house arrest :(

M: LOL :(

B: Whatevs. This is perfect. We can hang at the Rock-U-Quarium for a bit, and then we can sneak out and do some more investigating.

J: NO! We were already out too late yesterday!

B: But we've gotta get the Losepkees out of the caves

M: I heard there were ten more people admitted to the hospital yesterday.

A: Really?

M: I overheard Fayla talking about it on the phone. Andy Anacker's mom was attacked on her way to the million moth metamorphosis.

B: If we don't do something, we're all gonna be hanging up in that cave or comatose in the hospital.

A few moments passed.

B: Plus, if we help out Mr. Parotty, we would have a HUGE ally, especially since he knows Mr. Miller.

A: True.

M: We need a plan.

B: Problem is we had trouble killing one. And there was a whole bunch more behind it. How do we kill a herd of chupacabras?

A: Hey, why isn't Rodriqa texting?

Aubrey rested his cell phone on his nightstand and looked out his bedroom window. Rodriqa's window was directly across the yard. Her room was dark, and her window was still open.

Aubrey rushed over to his window and opened it.

"Rodriqa!" he yelled across the yard. "Are you up?"

Mrs. Auerbach approached her sill. "She's still sleeping. I don't think she feels well."

Aubrey frowned. "Can I come over?"

"I don't think that's a good idea." Mrs. Auerbach's hands grabbed the top of the window. "I'll see you tonight." She slid it closed.

Aubrey took a couple of steps back. Should he run over and tell Mrs. Auerbach to take her to the hospital? Should he tell her what happened? But then he'd run the risk of never hanging out with Rodriqa again. What if she had been ranched? When would she wake up? Aubrey paced in his room, considering his options. Maybe he could find the old widow and ask her what to do, but usually her cryptic responses weren't helpful. He could talk to Griggs, but he'd been grumpy lately, and if he had to tell Griggs he lost Solluna, who knows what would happen?

That's it! Aubrey thought to himself. He rummaged through his closet and changed out of his pajamas. He combed his messy red hair with his fingers and ran out of his room.

⋯⊰⊱⋯

In the Smart Mart & Finer Diner basement, Aubrey warily approached the poker table where Mr. Jennings's crucible rested. He looked into its round opening. He saw the reflection of his own eye again.

Pressing against the outside of the colorful lamp, he noticed how hard the glass felt, yet how smoothly finished its glaze was, despite the Circle of Circles depicted around its surface. Aubrey eyed the edge of the opening. It was very thin. He flicked it. His nail thudded against the glass.

"Come to torture me again, Seer?" The inward wheeze, muffled by the thickness of a stainless steel door, echoed from the freezer ahead. Aubrey looked up. Shway Shway's round, green eye stared back at him through the slender window.

"I don't want to hurt you." Aubrey pulled out his inhaler and pressed it in his mouth. "Do you want to hurt me?"

"I have no love for puds." The creature breathed in as it spoke. "But I need to attend to my master. So if you will let me out, I will not touch you."

Aubrey took a step forward. Sweat beaded on his upper lip. "Then I need Solluna back."

The pale, reptilian-skinned creature laughed. "You cannot have it."

Aubrey took another step forward. "Why?"

Shway Shway walked away from the door.

Aubrey trotted up to the window and looked inside. Wrapped in his oversized Elemag suit, Shway Shway stood with his back to the door several yards ahead. The ice-laden room was now bare except for a towering pile of metal bits, cardboard shreds, and meat stuffs heaped in the middle of the freezer.

"Are you responsible for all the people who have been attacked?"

"How would I know?" Shway Shway growled. "I've been trapped in here."

"Can you get out of here?" Aubrey asked.

Shway Shway spun on his hooves and launched himself at the door. The door shuddered. Shway Shway rattled it violently and inhaled a scream. "What do you think?"

Aubrey jumped back. The stainless steel convulsed under the creature's attack but held firm. Aubrey didn't know what to do. A metal hinge moaned. Aubrey decided to bargain. "I'll let you out!"

The door stopped shaking.

"But I need something in return," added Aubrey.

Shway Shway hissed. "What do you want?"

Aubrey searched his mind. He wanted to get Solluna back, but he couldn't think of a good plan to trick the creature. Aubrey squeaked out the only word that pressed o the forefront of his mind. "Knowledge."

Shway Shway hopped off the door. "Of course, you do, Seer." The creature walked back into the middle of the freezer. "But first I need you to make a covenant with me."

"A what?" Aubrey took several steps forward.

"A covenant!" Shway Shway looked over his shoulder. "I think you puds call it a promise."

Aubrey looked inside the freezer. "What kind of promise?"

"If you lie to me, then you will die."

Aubrey scrunched up his face. "What?"

Shway Shway turned and stormed toward the door. "If you lie, then you die!"

"Why would I lie to you?"

"I know puds, and I know seers." Shway Shway snarled. "Either we have a covenant, or we have nothing."

Aubrey thought about what he said. He wasn't sure why the creature wanted such a promise, but it wasn't a big deal as long as Aubrey made sure he told the creature the truth. He decided it was a fair trade for some answers, but he needed more.

Aubrey sighed. "If I have to promise that, then I want Solluna too."

Shway Shway walked away. "Take your trinket." Foam seeped between his sharp teeth. "You'll only get it stolen from you again." Shway Shway's stomach lurched. His large green eyes rolled in their sockets. His chest heaved, and he spit repeatedly. Finally, in a large wretch, Shway Shway regurgitated Solluna onto the icy ground. He kicked it. The smoky-colored pyramid tumbled to the other side of the room.

"Okay." Aubrey bit his lip. "I promise."

Shway Shway wiped his thin lips with the sleeve of his suit. "If you want your toy, you'll have to come get it."

Aubrey lowered his head and swallowed hard.

Shway Shway squatted. "I will not yell what you want to know through my prison door." Shway Shway clawed at the ice beneath him. "Come in, or go away."

"You might hurt me again," said Aubrey. "I remember how it felt when—"

"How am I any danger to you?" Shway Shway dug at his suit. "You know how to harm me. You have beaten me. You have the advantage. I ask for fairness in return."

Aubrey studied the creature. "And you'll tell me what I want to know?" Shway Shway nodded. Aubrey took a deep breath. He steadied his hands against the door handle. Quickly, he opened the door, slipped into the freezer, and pulled it shut.

His stomach sank. Suddenly, he remembered it only opened from the outside. He was locked inside.

Shway Shway stared at Aubrey with a ragged grin, exposing his razorous teeth. "Seer is brave without his guardian."

Aubrey slid his hand into his pocket and pulled out his cell phone. He flipped it open. Aubrey trembled. His phone had no signal inside the freezer.

Shway Shway jumped up and trotted toward Aubrey. "That is dangerous to be away from her. I've known four seers. They were all killed without their guardian."

"Help!" Aubrey shook the freezer door. The chill of the room stung his skin.

Shway Shway grabbed Aubrey by his shirt and spun him around. Aubrey raised his hands to cover his face. Shway Shway clasped Aubrey's wrists and dragged him in.

Aubrey scuffed his feet against the frozen metal, stumbling on the ice.

In the middle of the room, Shway Shway released Aubrey and squatted again in front of the pile of torn debris. Shway Shway extended one of his clawed fingers. Into the ice of the floor, he scratched four detached lines in the shape of a diamond.

Aubrey stood over Shway Shway and watched. "What are you doing?"

Shway Shway didn't look up. "Knowledge."

Aubrey replaced his phone in his pocket. A thousand questions raced through his mind. "Why are the chupacabra here? Where did they come from? How do we stop them?"

Shway Shway held up his other hand. "No questions."

Aubrey sputtered, "But, then how—"

Shway Shway smacked his fist into the metal floor and growled. "I already know what you need to know, Seer." Shway Shway squiggled a tiny divot in the middle of the lines of the detached diamond. Inside the diamond, he scratched four lines east, west, north, and south, then cut two semicircles of different sizes on either side of the diamond. Shway Shway stared up at Aubrey. "In the beginning…"

"There are way too many people here." Fayla's silvery-blonde hair rustled around her long neck as she glanced at the crowds along Lake Julian's banks.

Gaetan nodded. He grabbed Fayla's hand and pulled her out of the way of a train of young children dressed in brightly colored moth costumes rushing past them. "Why is a bunch of mating moths so exciting anyway?"

"Seriously." Fayla gazed at the detail of the costumes' wings. One of the straggler moths with green wings and purple polka dots squirmed in her outfit and traced awkward paths through the onlookers. "They mate, then they die. What a boring life."

Gaetan smirked. "At least it's exciting."

Fayla laughed at him. "Exciting for them. Annoying for us."

"Totally." Gaetan scuffed his feet through the grass. "I can't believe we're stuck here for spring break."

"My mom owes me big time for leaving town again." Fayla sidestepped a Boy Scout who weaved between a hot dog concessioner and the green-and-purple-polka-dotted moth. "I think I'm gonna try to guilt her into buying me a new car."

"That'd be sweet." Gaetan ducked as the edge of a plastic banner swung toward his face. "You should get something fast and fun."

Fayla's lip curved upward slightly, and she looked away. "I wish we could *do* something fast and fun."

"Wanna go to the mall?"

"Nah, we've been twice already this week." Fayla pulled Gaetan toward her. "We could go hang at my place."

Gaetan looked upward as he thought. "But isn't Magnos stuck at home, just like Aubrey?"

Fayla leaned in and whispered, "Not tonight."

Suddenly, Gaetan realized what Fayla was saying. His mouth gaped open as he sputtered, "That's right. Magnos will be with Aubrey at the Rock-U-Quarium."

Fayla raised her eyebrows. She released his hand and walked into the crowd.

"Perfect." Gaetan chased after her.

The green-and-purple-polka-dotted moth stopped abruptly in the middle of folks walking to and fro. She shifted her bobbing antennae back off her head and stood up straight.

Mena Kontrearo smiled widely. She knew exactly where she needed to be tonight.

Under the overpass near the top of Dalton Circle, Old Widow Wizenblatt sat on a stump between her wood-fired oven and her doorless refrigerator. Splattered with dirt and lying on its back, the refrigerator held a muddy pool of stagnant water and decaying sticks. A mallard swam lazily atop its dingy surface. The oven crackled with flames that licked up through empty burner holes, heating a cast iron pot on top of the stove. From a concrete abutment above the stove hung a wind chime of hollow steel rods and glass trinkets. The widow rubbed one of the dented aluminum legs of her walker with a rag. One scratch wouldn't go away. She spit on the rag and rubbed harder.

The pot on the stove boiled. The widow rested the walker upright on a log in front of her and pushed herself up. Her knees and hips cracked, and she grabbed her back as she straightened.

She waddled over to the stove. Picking up a ladle, the widow stirred the steamy, yellow broth in the pot. She scooped up a small dollop and tasted it. Grimacing, she stirred the broth some more.

The wind chimes clinked and spun above her head. Mrs. Wizenblatt looked up. There was no breeze. Someone was there.

In an instant, she grabbed her oven by the sides, lifted it over her head, spun around, and launched it toward the three tall, gray-skinned figures standing behind her. The mallard erupted into flight and soared from underneath the overpass.

The oven tumbled through the air toward the figures, then slowed and hovered several feet above the ground.

Angling his bald head, Thalazzaran held his hands up and squinted his eyes. A sliver of a smile curved his lips. He rotated his hand. The oven spun, following the Graviteer's command.

"There's no need to play." Gaspian waved his hand. Bits of the stove flitted to the ground in tiny grains transforming into a pile of sand.

Old Widow Wizenblatt's jaw dropped. She bowed on one knee but kept her head up. "Master Magi."

Electric sparks cracked between the frizzy hair of Melkyor's beard. "Finally, someone treats us with respect."

"Of course, it would be a slave," mumbled Gaspian as he morphed his leather jacket from a rough brown to a black duster.

The Widow stood up. "If you're here, then you must be worried." She chuckled quietly as she hopped in place.

Thalazzaran crossed his arms as bits of rock floated in orbit around his shoulders. "We know the seer is here."

Mrs. Wizenblatt held up her finger. "But not just any seer. The last one."

"The Terminal Prophecy isn't real!" A wide electric arc sparked from Melkyor's head to his legs.

Gaspian took a step forward. "Has anyone told the prophecy to the puds?"

"I'm not sure," replied the widow. "I know Magnolia Thistlewood has done everything in her power to prevent the seer from finding out."

Thalazzaran nodded. "That is another reason we're here."

Melkyor frowned. "We have seen the witch's power grow."

"She has accumulated too many divinoi," added Gaspian.

"She threatens the balance," continued Melkyor.

"And we have come to restore it." Thalazzaran waved the widow toward him. "Come here, cherub."

Mrs. Wizenblatt took several steps forward. Thalazzaran clenched his hand and lifted it upward. In a single undulating block, the brown, stagnant water in the refrigerator rose out of its container and hovered in the air. Thalazzaran nodded at Gaspian. Gaspian grinned and wiggled his fingers. The murky water solidified into a firm slab of lead.

Thalazzaran swung his arms forward. The lead flew at the widow. She slapped her hands together and then pulled them apart. The ether around her warped, and the air under the overpass rippled. As the lead slab approached her, it ripped in half. Each section hurdled past her into the valley below.

"So it is true." Thalazzaran laughed. "You are a Graviteer."

Melkyor pointed at the widow. "Not many of you have mastered a divinoi."

"How did you learn this?" questioned Gaspian.

"Talent and hard work," the widow heaved, nearly out of breath. "As the Clockmaker wills."

"Truly." Thalazzaran bowed slightly. "We have brought you a gift." He turned his hand over. A small ball of sand rose from the pile that used to be the oven and spun in a circle.

"A way to restore the balance." Melkyor giggled manically. He shocked the ball of sand with light from his fingernails. The sand melted into glass and spun faster.

"Tonight, the seer is threatened." Gaspian waved his hand over the ball of sand. It blackened and spun even faster.

"You can save him if you choose." Thalazzaran tightened his fist. The air around the black ball bent as its gravity grew. "And curtail the witch's largesse."

FIGHT OF THE WOUNDED GUARDIAN

A blurry light flashed across Rodriqa's sight. Her eyelids opened slightly. The ivory haze was dotted with several drably colored bobbles. She concentrated. The white light burned her brain, and her eyes strained to hold open. The words mumbling around her slowly focused into intelligible conversation. Her eyes cleared. Four figures stood over her.

Mrs. Auerbach sat at the edge of Rodriqa's bed. Caressing her daughter's limp hand, she watched her breathe deeply. Mrs. Auerbach looked up at Magnos, Jordana, and Buzz, who were standing close by. "She's in no shape to go."

"But we need her." Buzz straightened his blue paisley bowtie. "Mr. Parotty specifically asked for all of us to come to the Rock-U-Quarium."

"I know," replied Mrs. Auerbach, "but she's not herself."

"We shouldn't go without her." Jordana bit her lip.

Magnos arched his eyebrows. "Maybe she should go to the doctor."

"Maybe. I know she's not been resting well lately." Mrs. Auerbach looked back at her daughter. "Did you find Aubrey?"

Buzz shook his head. He pulled out his cell phone and flipped it open. "He won't answer his texts, and I can't locate him on our GPS."

Magnos opened his cell phone. "Do you think his dad decided he couldn't go?"

Mrs. Auerbach patted Rodriqa on the cheek. "No, Dan said I was supposed to take him and bring him straight home."

"What if he's in trouble?" said Jordana.

Magnos sighed. "It's not like him to be out of touch."

Mrs. Auerbach stood up. "I'm going to take Rodriqa to the hospital. Something's not right. You all can go with me, or I'll take you home."

"Hospital," agreed Jordana.

"Yep," said Magnos. "Hospital."

Buzz sighed and nodded.

Mrs. Auerbach walked over to Rodriqa's dresser. "Magnos, would you mind picking her up?"

Magnos nodded and leaned down.

"I'm not going to the hospital." Rodriqa lurched her head forward and scooted up on her elbows.

Buzz grinned. "There she is."

"Thank goodness." Mrs. Auerbach walked back over to Rodriqa's bed. "Are you okay?"

Rodriqa frowned and nodded. "What's wrong with Aubrey?"

"We can't find him." Jordana raised her hands. "He was supposed to meet us here, but we haven't heard from him since this morning."

Rodriqa shook her head and pulled herself to the side of her bed. "What time is it?"

Buzz glanced at his phone. "It's seven forty-three."

Rodriqa frowned and rubbed her shoulder. "So I've slept all day."

Mrs. Auerbach reached down to touch her forehead and nodded. "Do you need to sleep more?"

"I'm fine. I just haven't been getting enough rest." Rodriqa pushed her hand away. "Why are you all here?"

Buzz shimmied his shoulders. "We're going to the Rock-U-Quarium!"

Rodriqa leaned forward. "Why?"

"Mr. Parotty invited us for a special night out." Buzz tapped on his rectangular silver belt buckle. "Your mom is taking us there."

Rodriqa grimaced. "Sounds suspicious."

"That's what I said," murmured Jordana.

"Why is it suspicious?" Mrs. Auerbach glanced between Rodriqa and Jordana.

Rodriqa waved her off. "Where's Aubrey, again?"

Jordana wrinkled her eyebrows. "We can't find him."

"He was supposed to meet us here," added Buzz.

Rodriqa pulled her legs to the side of the bed. She thought for a moment. Her eyes widened as her memories fell into place. "I know where he is."

Rodriqa bounded down the stairs in Mr. Jennings's Smart Mart & Finer Diner. Magnos, Jordana, and Buzz followed slowly behind.

"Are you sure you're okay?" asked Jordana.

"I'm fine," scoffed Rodriqa.

"I don't know," mumbled Buzz. "You were out like a trout."

"Hurry up," said Rodriqa, waving her friends off. "My mom won't stay in her car long."

"Shew!" Jordana clamped off her nose as she stepped down into the basement. "This place stinks."

"If he's not here, we need to hurry and go. We're gonna be late," said Buzz.

"We can't go without him." Magnos pushed Buzz down the last step and walked around him.

Rodriqa trotted past the poker table and peered through the small glass window into the freezer. "Yep. He's here." She tapped on the glass. "Aubrey! What are you doing?"

In his blue-and-silver-stripped Elemag suit, Shway Shway leaned against the wall, carving unusual glyphs into the ice. He stepped to his right and drew a large rhombus. Nearly every surface of the freezer had been scrawled with unusual symbols, like a glacial geometry textbook. Circles, lines, crosses, curlicues, pictograms.

Shivering, with his arms wrapped around his chest, Aubrey sat on the edge of the towering mound of scrapped metal, cardboard, and frozen meat staring at Shway Shway.

"Aubrey!" Rodriqa pressed on the freezer door's handle, and it swooshed open.

Aubrey turned toward the door. He stood up. "Hey!"

Rodriqa ran inside. Aubrey walked toward her. She hugged him. "You're freezing! What are you doing in here?"

Aubrey trembled and looked at Rodriqa. "Learning." A smile creased his lips.

Magnos and Buzz ran inside. Magnos headed for Shway Shway. Shway Shway squawked and cowered into the corner.

"Are you okay?" asked Buzz. Aubrey nodded.

Jordana stood in the threshold, holding the door. "Why didn't you tell us you were coming down here?"

Aubrey snickered. "I didn't plan on getting stuck in here."

Buzz frowned at him. "You could have answered our texts."

"No signal." Aubrey waved his cell phone at them. "What time is it?"

"Past time for us to leave for the Rock-U-Quarium." Rodriqa grabbed Aubrey's hand and walked toward the door, pulling him outside. Buzz followed. Magnos crept backward, watching Shway Shway, who crouched, covering his head. The five of them left the freezer, and Magnos closed the door.

"Wait!" Aubrey struggled against Rodriqa, who had already dragged him to the poker table. "I need Solluna. It's on the floor."

Rodriqa stopped and rolled her eyes. "You've got to be kidding me."

"I see it." Magnos glanced through the window. "I'll grab it." He opened the door and rushed inside.

Aubrey pointed to the crucible. "I think I know what's in here."

Buzz closed his right eye and looked into the bottle with his left. "It's empty."

"We can't see it. We have to get inside."

"You might fit in the lamp," said Rodriqa. "But I doubt Buzz will."

Buzz feigned a laugh and then rolled his eyes.

"But I might stuff you in it," Rodriqa said to Aubrey. "If you lock yourself in the freezer with that creature again."

"Seriously." Aubrey pulled his inhaler out of his pocket and pressed it to his lips. "We have to get inside before the chupacabras do. That's what they're after. Whatever is in here."

"Are you sure?" asked Jordana.

Aubrey nodded.

Magnos walked out of the freezer and closed the door. "It looks different." He held up the crystal pyramid, which was smoky gray. "And it has writing on it."

"Exactly." Aubrey trotted over to Magnos. Magnos handed him Solluna. Aubrey held it up and scanned each word written on the four faces of the pyramid.

Buzz scooted next to Aubrey and examined Solluna. "What does it mean?"

"At first it said, 'To open the sealed.' Then it read, 'To seal the opened.' Now it says, 'Eye for an eye.'" Aubrey grabbed the crucible and brought Solluna and the multicolored lamp together. "It's telling us how to get inside."

A small rounded pedestal as thick as a coin slid out from the bottom of Solluna. The words "Eye for an eye" faded from its faces. Aubrey raised the pyramid and the crucible to eye level. Magnos, Rodriqa, Jordana, and Buzz leaned in. The size of the pedestal exactly matched the size of the crucible's opening. Aubrey hovered Solluna over the crucible. Suddenly, with a gust of air, Solluna's pedestal was pulled into the crucible. Aubrey tugged on Solluna. It wouldn't move. Magnos gripped the pyramid and yanked on it. It remained firmly fixed in the crucible with its pyramid fully exposed.

"See?" said Aubrey. "Solluna was leading us to crucible the whole time."

"That's perfect," replied Rodriqa. "But how does *that* get us inside?"

Aubrey shook the crucible. "I don't know." He set it on the poker table and grimaced.

Buzz shook his head. "It's just another trick, Aubrey. That's what Solluna does. Griggs told you that."

"But, it…it should work. We have to get inside."

"No, we have to leave." Rodriqa glanced toward the stairs. "My mom will be down here any second."

The freezer door shook violently. The five friends turned toward the back of the basement. One of Shway Shway's large green eyes peered through the window.

Aubrey took a step forward. "We have to let Shway Shway out."

Buzz took a step back. "No can do."

"But I promised." Aubrey looked at Rodriqa.

Rodriqa frowned at him. "You promised. I didn't." She grabbed Aubrey's hand and pulled him toward the stairs. "Let's go."

"You look like you feel better." Aubrey tightened his belt around his loose pants.

"Yeah." Rodriqa waved to her mom as Mrs. Auerbach drove down Lake Julian Square.

Buzz scoffed. "You were somethin' else."

Rodriqa cocked an eyebrow upward. "You take a bite from a chupacabra and see how you feel." She rubbed her shoulder.

"We were worried about you." Jordana touched her arm.

Rodriqa pulled away. "Thanks, but I'm fine." She walked away from the curb toward the entrance to the Rock-U-Quarium. The sign trembled and blinked. Loud music blared from the speakers behind it.

Aubrey trotted up behind her. "Hey! Look!" He pointed toward the podium near the darkened bank of glass doors. "The Kluggards aren't here."

"Good," grunted Magnos.

"Yeah! Maybe that's a good omen," agreed Buzz.

"Hope so," mumbled Rodriqa in a sing-songy tone.

The five friends filed into the end of the line. Quickly, they moved forward and entered the building. They stopped at the box office, which had replaced the counter at the bottom of the marble staircase.

Buzz leaned his elbows on the counter and spoke into the round, silver voice conduit. "Mr. Parotty is expecting us."

The woman inside the box office nodded and picked up a red phone in the booth. "Head on in."

"Thanks." Buzz feigned shooting at the woman with his pointed index finger and cocked thumb and made a clicking noise with his tongue as he winked.

Rodriqa pushed him forward. "Why did you wear your 'white man's best friend' if Mr. Parotty asked to see us?"

"Because you never know when there's gonna be a spontaneous 'party-splosion.'" Buzz pulled one of the retractable wires from his bulky belt buckle and released it. Rodriqa cocked her head, tossing her beaded braids around her neck. "Are we here to party, or is this official NGW business?"

Buzz and Magnos said, "Party," and Aubrey and Jordana said, "Business."

Rodriqa stood at the bottom of the marble stairs. She pursed her lips and glanced at each of her friends.

Buzz walked up several steps. "Mr. Parotty wants us to have some fun. I think he realizes we're important to Lake Julian and that we've been given a raw deal. Why else would we have gotten an invitation to the grand opening?"

Rodriqa raised her hands. "But what about those people in the cave?" Her voice echoed in the foyer. Several patrons at the box office glanced toward her.

Scurrying around Rodriqa and quietly hushing her, Magnos, Jordana, and Aubrey pushed her up the stairs.

"As soon as we can, we'll get out of here and go back to the cave," whispered Aubrey.

Jordana nodded. "That's the plan. The quicker we can get out of here, the better."

Buzz leaned down as his friends reached him at the top of the stairs. "And if we can make a friend out of Mr. Parotty, he'll be a powerful ally against Mr. Miller."

"Crazy." Rodriqa stopped at the top of the stairs. "You're all crazy, but since I'm in no mood to fight—"

"Good." Buzz bobbed his chin. "Now let's check things out." The five friends walked through the spacious main ballroom. Sitting at the scattering of oddly shaped tables, teenagers and adults, attired in everything from gym shorts and tank tops to jeans and T-shirts to formal wear, ate and spoke and gazed at the electronic banners and marquees streaming around them. Aubrey leaned toward Magnos and pointed at the multitude of wind chime-like chandeliers dotting the ceiling. "Those still creep me out."

Magnos glanced up. "Yep."

"Anyone see Mr. Parotty?" Buzz walked in front of the group, popping up on his tiptoes to scan the crowd.

"Not yet," said Rodriqa.

"Let's head over there." Buzz pointed toward the curved dark hallway to their right. The other four followed Buzz.

Aubrey sidled up next to Rodriqa. "I can't believe that chupacabra bit you. Did it leave a mark?"

"Not on the outside." Rodriqa stretched out her shoulder.

"When it bit you, did it just hurt, or did it feel different?"

Rodriqa twisted her lips. "It felt like I was dying."

Aubrey looked down. "I think it ranched you."

Rodriqa frowned at him. "Why do you say that?"

"Because its head faded out when it bit you," said Aubrey. "Its face looked like you do when you have the spirit of the Tsul'kalu." Rodriqa scrunched up her face and stared at the ground.

The five of them wormed their way through the droves of people walking along the hallway. Bright florescent lights from Gymanergy spread around the corner.

Buzz stopped in front of the transparent wall and gawked. The spinning wheels of dozens of stationary bikes and the pumping hydraulics of exercise equipment hummed as nearly every pedal, seat, and flange moved in the two-story fitness center.

"Look who's here." Rodriqa nodded toward a row of ellipticals at the side of the room. "The flack pack."

The friends followed Rodriqa's finger. Pam Trank, Mesilla Uztek, Zaniah Jones, and the bruised and swollen Jon Harney dripped with sweat as their legs spun on their machines.

"Hey! Have y'all seen McCrayden?" said a cloyingly southern drawl next to them.

The friends turned around. Vidalia Arsvine was dabbing her cheeks with a pink towel.

"Why would we have seen McCrayden?" replied Rodriqa.

Vidalia batted hereyelashes as she smiled. "We haven't seen her for a few days. Thought she might have defected to the misfits."

"What do you mean?" Buzz concentrated on her eyelashes so as not to stare at her sweat-soaked top.

"Nothing, sugar." Vidalia poked his silver, belt buckle. "I was just making sure she wasn't keepin' poor company."

Rodriqa crossed her arms. "Excuse me?"

"Don't get in a tizzy." Vidalia walked away toward the entrance to Gymanergy. "I know my place. Remember yours."

"I'm really getting tired of being the butt around here," said Rodriqa.

"Eh," said Buzz. He stared at Vidalia who climbed onto the unwinding plates of a stair stepper, next to Jon Harney. "They're rowdies. That's how they've always been."

Rodriqa nudged Buzz with her shoulder. "That doesn't make it right."

Aubrey grinned at Rodriqa. "Good thing we know our place."

Rodriqa pressed her lips together and tried not to smile.

Buzz flapped his hands. "Let's go check out the Re-Reality Room. Can't wait to master one of those Cyber Rudders."

Mr. Parotty walked up behind Aubrey. "Maybe later you all can have the place to yourselves."

Buzz's eyes widened. "That would be awesome!" He hopped forward and shook Mr. Parotty's hand.

Mr. Parotty grinned and nodded at them. "I'm so glad you all could join me this evening. I'm sorry I haven't had a chance to entertain you sooner." Brushing his bowl-shaped, salt-and-pepper hair off the middle of his forehead, he reached out for Aubrey's hand.

Aubrey forced himself to smile and shook his hand. He noticed Mr. Parotty's mole was now on his right ear lobe.

"We appreciated the invitations to the grand opening, but I'm gonna cut to the chase." Rodriqa stared at Mr. Parotty. "Why us? We're on most people's bad list. Why would you want us here twice in less than a week?"

Mr. Parotty chuckled. "Because you all are special, even if no one in this tiny little town recognizes it."

Rodriqa raised an eyebrow. "And by special, you mean…"

Mr. Parotty nodded and glanced down at the floor. He looked around at the patrons passing by and waved everyone closer into him. The friends looked at each other warily and then huddled around Mr. Parotty.

"I need your help, and I've heard that you all have a special expertise regarding a few issues that have been a thorn in my proverbial side."

"You have a ghost?" asked Buzz.

Mr. Parotty grinned. "Something like that."

CLASH OF THE TIGHTENED, PART 2

"I bet she's been following us the whole time," Rodriqa whispered to Aubrey.

Aubrey rubbed his chin against his shoulder, glancing behind him. A short Latin female with a peeling glue-on mustache and an Afro was following the friends as they followed Mr. Parotty. Mr. Parotty hurried around the curved corridor, past the Parkourium and the Re-Reality Room and hugged the left-hand rounded wall. Dance music echoed down the hallway, and dazzles of various colors flashed ahead.

Mr. Parotty stopped at the edge of the entrance to the dance floor. A taper-chested bartender with a fauxhawk hopped off the rotating bar and walked across the Break-n-Shake up to Mr. Parotty. The bartender fished his pockets and then handed his boss a ring of keys.

Mr. Parotty nodded. "Thanks." He flipped through several metal keys and singled out a black plastic one. He pressed it into a hole in the wall and turned it. A small section of the rounded wall opened, like a door. Mr. Parotty pocketed the keys and waved the children forward. One by one, they rounded the concave door and walked into the opening. A metal-lined hallway, only a few yards in length and width, ended in a stainless steel elevator door.

"Cool!" muttered Buzz. "Are we gonna see all the behind-the-scenes stuff?"

Mr. Parotty slipped in behind them. "Absolutely."

Jordana frowned and pulled her rose-tinted glasses down her nose. "Where are we?"

Mr. Parotty walked around the friends toward the elevator. "We're heading to the source of the problem."

Rodriqa scowled. "And where is that?"

Mr. Parotty pressed a button next to the elevator, which chimed as it alighted. Slowly facing the children, he steadily raised his arm toward the opening door and smiled. "My office."

Buzz trotted forward. "Is that where the ghost is?" The other four stood in place and stared at Buzz.

Mr. Parotty waved them all forward. "We should hurry. Don't want to keep you past your curfew."

Buzz ran into the elevator and marveled at its leather bench and wood paneling.

Jordana and Magnos slowly followed. Rodriqa and Aubrey sighed and walked into the elevator after them.

Thud!

Aubrey and Rodriqa looked over their shoulders. A shoe was jamming the concave door open.

"Let me in!" insisted a voice from the other side. Fingers curled around the door's edge through its crack.

Mena Kontrearo yanked on the door as the bartender attempted to squeeze it shut. Waves of scintillating lights from the Break-n-Shake squirreled into the hallway as the parabolic door swung in and out. Mena's head bobbed forward. Her wig was riding down the back of her scalp, and her fake mustache clung to her upper lip by only a few gummy fibers.

"This is a restricted area," grunted the bartender.

"*Ave sucia!*" Mena head butted the bartender in the stomach. "You're just as rude as the red-haired lady out front. Does everyone who works here have an attitude problem?"

With the NGW in the elevator, Mr. Parotty stepped inside and pushed the Close button. "So many fans." He snickered awkwardly. "We can't let everyone see everything." The elevator door closed.

Magnos sighed. "What's she up to?"

"Nothing good." Rodriqa chuckled. Aubrey furrowed his brow. Something wasn't right.

Buzz pushed his friends aside and sidled up next to Mr. Parotty. "Oh, it's just Mena. She's a little…" He twirled his fingers next to his temples. "If you know what I mean."

Mr. Parotty laughed and threaded his tie into his sports coat. "I don't disagree."

Aubrey closed his mind to the conversation. Mena's words spun in his mind, like an MP3 clip repeating itself.

Buzz crossed his arms. "Mr. Parotty, I need to be honest here."

Mr. Parotty stared at Buzz. "Please do."

A fog settled over Aubrey's mind. Mena's words slowed and quickened. He couldn't focus on anything else.

Buzz looked down. "We don't have any of our equipment. I don't think we're prepared to tackle anything too supernatural tonight."

A glint of a smile snaked across Mr. Parotty's lips. He grabbed Buzz's shoulder. "I'm sure you're exactly in the state I need you."

A bell chimed overhead. The elevator door opened. Buzz and Mr. Parotty stepped out of the elevator, and Jordana, Magnos, and Rodriqa followed them. Aubrey stood in the elevator holding his head.

Aubrey's friends stepped into a long metal-lined hallway, similar to the elevator's anteroom. Cooled air spilled into the corridor through large metal grates on either side. A glass-faced, red fire alarm jutted out from the right wall, the only decoration the entire length of the hallway.

"My office is around the corner." Mr. Parotty pointed toward the corridor's end. "I need you to help me figure something out."

"What exactly?" asked Rodriqa.

"You'll understand better if I showed you."

Then suddenly, everything connected for Aubrey, like waking from a dream and understanding exactly what it meant. Aubrey knew whom Mena had seen, and if she was here, they were in trouble. Aubrey looked up. His friends followed Mr. Parotty into his office.

Aubrey bolted down the hallway. He gripped the corner as he rounded it. Mr. Parotty's office was also metal-lined, ceiling to floor, with a few varnished shelves bolted into the sidewalls. Four rows of five security TV screens filled the wall behind his glass desk, displaying action in various corners of the Rock-U-Quarium. Aubrey's friends gathered around the front of the desk.

Aubrey trotted several steps inside. It smelled like charcoal. Mr. Parotty stooped over a safe beside his desk and turned its combination lock. Aubrey stared at Mr. Parotty and closed his eyes. Red and green phosphenes swirled behind his eyelids. Darkness pressed in from the boundaries of his sight. A skeletal figure, shimmering in green, appeared only a few yards away, stooped over in the darkness.

Aubrey gasped quietly. In his dark sight, he saw three more shapes to his left. Highlighted in gleaming green, a curvy figure walked toward him with two forms, scuttling on tiny forehands and back hooves beside the figure.

"Aha!"The safe clicked. Mr. Parotty turned its handle, and its door opened.

Aubrey snapped opened his eyes. His four friends huddled around Mr. Parotty's desk, looking toward the safe on the floor.

Aubrey ran up to Rodriqa. Covering his mouth with his hand, he leaned toward her ear. "Scream," he whispered.

Rodriqa turned and pulled away. "Why would I do that?"

Aubrey pointed behind Magnos toward Mr. Parotty. "Chupacabra."

Rodriqa glanced between Mr. Parotty and Aubrey. "What?"

"Here we go." Mr. Parotty pulled an object out of the safe. "I trust you can enlighten me regarding this." He straightened up and, cupping his hands, laid Ms. Spindergrath's crucible on his desk.

Rodriqa eyes widened. She stared at Aubrey. Aubrey nodded. Rodriqa shoved herself between Magnos and Jordana. She inhaled a chest-full of air and shrieked.

CLASH OF THE TIGHTENED, PART 3

"*Aeyayay!*" After squeezing every ounce of air out of her lungs, Rodriqa inhaled and screamed again. The tip of her nose sparkled and faded to a ghostly white as the spirit of the Tsul'kalu spread across her face.

Jordana and Magnos stepped back and watched her warily. Buzz covered his ears and stumbled against Mr. Parotty's glass desk. "What are you doing?"

"That!" Aubrey leaned forward and pointed toward Mr. Parotty.

Two large spirit shards plopped onto the metal floor. In their shimmering blackness, they writhed and squalled, flashing rings of sharp teeth.

Jobe Parotty fell back against the bank of security TVs, which flashed with snow.

Where flesh had been, Jobe Parotty's right hand and forearm were now charred bones. The left side of his face congealed with wriggling shadow, exposing a blackened maxilla and mandible. Mr. Parotty reached up with his left hand and covered the exposed area of his face.

Jordana ran out into the hallway.

"What the..." Magnos looked away.

"No way!" Buzz leaned in to examine the missing parts of Mr. Parotty.

Rodriqa lost her breath. She inhaled and screamed again. Another spirit shard dropped from Mr. Parotty's left arm and writhed on the floor. Both of Mr. Parotty's hands and forearms were now only dark bones.

Aubrey pulled on Buzz and Magnos. "He's not alone!" A door next to the far left corner swung open. Flanked by two chupacabras, bearing their glistening fangs, Magnolia Thistlewood charged into the room.

The red-haired, green-eyed woman glowered at the scene. She pointed at Rodriqa and Aubrey. "Get them!"

The chupacabra lunged forward. Magnos reached underneath the glass desk and, with a single grunt, wrenched up the desk. The desk twisted skyward, flipped over, and landed on top of both chupacabra. The glass desk shattered. The chupacabras squealed as they were dashed against the metal floor. Ms. Thistlewood raised her hands to her face. The chupacabras whimpered backward. Ms. Thistlewood swung her hands down. The shrapnel of glass shards dropped toward the metal floor. In midair, they liquefied into water and fell like rain, splashing against the metal.

Buzz scurried behind Rodriqa. He looked at Magnos. "You learned that trick in detention!"

The three spirit shards on the floor writhed toward Magnos, snapping at his leg. Magnos reared up his left leg. "Not learned." His size-16 foot slammed against the three spirit shards. A chorus of moans squawked from underneath his sole. The flailing shadows evaporated into dark ash. "Mastered."

Rodriqa heaved haggard breaths. "Time...to...go."

Rodriqa, Buzz, Aubrey, and Magnos rushed into the hallway.

Ms. Thistlewood hurried over to Mr. Parotty. With a curled lip, she examined him. "What happened?"

"I..." Mr. Parotty pulled his hands away from his face and gazed at his mismatched self, the physical and spectral parts writhing, unable to form a coherent whole. "Don't know."

"I warned you, Matsinstrus." She grabbed his skeletal wrist. "Never underestimate these children." She ripped his brown sandstone phylactery off his wrist. Quickly, she turned the dial. The remaining spirit shards enwrapping Mr. Parotty's body squirmed off of him and squeezed into the phylactery.

Fully a charred skeleton, Matsinstrus bowed and backed away from her.

Ms. Thistlewood stormed over to the two wounded chupacabras. "Stay close but out of sight!" Matsinstrus nodded, yellow smoke seeping from his ribcage. Grabbing both of the beasts by the scruff of their necks, Ms. Thistlewood pulled them toward the door. They reared back and whined. "I've got a bone to pick."

Rodriqa, Buzz, Aubrey, and Magnos rounded out of Mr. Parotty's office and headed toward Jordana at the end of the corridor, who was repeatedly pressing the glowing elevator button.

"Not that way!" hollered Buzz. "Elevators are always traps in an emergency situation."

"Then where?" Jordana beat her fist against the elevator door.

Buzz skidded to a stop. "There!" He pointed to the air duct grates.

Magnos nodded. He rushed over to the wall and pressed his fingertips into one of the grate's tines. The metal bent, opening spaces for his fingers, and he flexed them. Magnos yanked the grate out of the wall.

"Go!" Rodriqa shoved Aubrey toward the open duct. Aubrey climbed inside. Rodriqa followed him.

"Oh!" Buzz pointed to the fire alarm. "I have *always* wanted to do this!"

Buzz slammed his elbow into the safety glass. The glass didn't break. Throbbing pains seared up Buzz's elbow, and he doubled over in agony.

"Hurry up!" Magnos glanced at Buzz and Jordana.

Jordana ran over to Magnos. He pulled the opposite grate off the wall and helped Jordana inside.

Buzz straightened up. "We've gotta set this off!" Buzz threw his open palm into the fire alarm's safety glass. The glass remained intact. Buzz shook his hand. Magnos took a single step back. Closing his hand and swinging his shoulder, he shattered the safety glass with his meaty fist. Magnos pulled down on the white lever in the middle of the red alarm. Sirens squealed overhead. Orange lights flashed along the metal walls. Sprays of water rained down from recessed sprinklers in the ceiling.

"Come on!" shouted Magnos. He dragged Buzz by his shirt across the hallway.

"Show off." Buzz climbed into the air duct.

With a chupacabra on either side of her, Ms. Thistlewood stepped into the hallway and glowered at Magnos, jets of water drenching her bright red hair. Magnos shoved Buzz deeper into the duct and then dove in after him.

Several yards into the duct system, the aluminum conduits forked. Buzz pulled himself forward, and he crawled into the left duct. Magnos scrambled against the metal, denting it. He followed Jordana through the right duct.

Buzz hobbled up and down in the narrowing duct, his belly bouncing against the metal. He felt a support around the duct loosen as the airshaft bobbed further with each motion forward. Buzz shimmied, shortening each movement. He crept ahead on his stomach, inches at a time.

The metal ahead wrenched with a screech. Buzz stopped. A rivet popped out of its hole. A seam separated. The duct broke apart and sagged downward. Buzz clambered to hold himself in place. He slid backward against the slick aluminum. The airshaft swung down. Buzz fell out of the open end of the duct. With a hard thud, he landed on his rump several feet below. He bit his lip and squeezed his eyelids together to keep from crying.

He heard people shouting below him. Buzz looked up. The orange fire alarms were blinking, but there were no sprinklers spraying water. Every surface was painted black. He rolled over onto his side and gazed at the floor below.

Buzz grinned. "Ah, yeah."

<hr/>

Squirming through the ducts, Magnos struggled to keep pace with Jordana. They snaked around several more corners. Jordana stopped at a grate and peeped through its slits.

"Look," she whispered to Magnos. "It's the Parkourium."

Magnos angled his head and, with one eye, looked out.

"Maybe we can get out this way." Jordana tugged on the grate.

Magnos nodded. He freed his right hand from under his chest and batted at the grate. With the third smack, it popped off and dropped several stories below. Magnos scooted his head out of the opening. Like a rainstorm, water spewed from spouts overhead. Several people slipped down the bottom portions of the Parkourium's obstacles, stripped off their padded body suits and rushed out the door.

Magnos looked at Jordana. "Do you trust me?"

Jordana pressed her glasses to the top of her nose and nodded weakly.

Pulling his hands from next to his body, he reached around to the opposite wall from the duct and gripped a wet ledge. Carefully, he slipped his torso and legs through the opening and swung underneath the duct. Jordana peered from the opening. Several poles and ledges crisscrossed below. Magnos reached forward with his right hand and grabbed the inside of the duct underneath Jordana. He swung forward, released the ledge, and clutched the inside of the duct with his left hand.

"Climb down!" shouted Magnos over the din of the falling water.

"You're not Tarzan!" yelled Jordana.

"That's okay," said Magnos. "You're not Jane."

Jordana glanced at him sternly. He smiled glibly back. She pulled her glasses off her nose, closed the arms, and pocketed them. She turned around and backed out of the vent feet first. Apprehensively, her slender legs stepped onto Magnos's shoulders, and she slid down his torso, clenching her arms around his. She wrapped her feet around his back.

"This is *not* my idea of fun!" said Jordana.

"No, but it's about to be!" Magnos swung his legs back and forth, and the two of them rocked like a pendulum. "Hold on!"

Drenched, Jordana closed her eyes and pulled him tighter. With a final kick, Magnos jerked forward and let go of the duct. Jordana screamed. Together they fell forward. Several yards below, Magnos caught a round bar, which held the lines for the body suits. Using the momentum from the previous fall, Magnos kicked his legs again and released the bar.

Rodriqa and Aubrey scurried around the system of ducts, rounding corners and crawling down as the venting system angled through the building.

Now fully ghostly, Rodriqa stopped at a vent and looked down through the slits. "We're at the top of Gymanergy."

Aubrey sidled up next to her. "Hurry." Through the grating, he could see ferns and banana leaves being pelted by water from the sprinklers. "Let's get out of here."

Rodriqa rocked back on her arms and raised her feet up. She cocked her legs back, then kicked out. The grate popped off. Aubrey and Rodriqa jumped down into a muddy mound of potting soil.

They ran over to the edge of the catwalk and looked below to the fitness center. A few stragglers raced out into the curved hallway.

"Come on!" Rodriqa pulled Aubrey toward a set of stairs. They hurried down, stepped across the puddle-laden tile of the fitness area, and ran out into the corridor.

A few soaked patrons bolted from the end of the hallway toward the main ballroom. Harried yelling echoed from both ends of the curved corridor. Rodriqa and Aubrey turned toward the main ballroom.

"At least there's no water out here," said Aubrey.

Suddenly, Magnolia Thistlewood rounded the corner, walking in long, careful strides. The barb of her high-heel shoes struck the floor rhythmically. Her fitted blouse and knee-length skirt clung to the curves of her soaked skin, and she wrung the water out of her bright red hair.

Aubrey and Rodriqa skidded to a stop. Rodriqa placed her hand in front of Aubrey and waved him back.

Ms. Thistlewood's pale eyes quivered. "You've made a mess." She waved her hand over the water on the floor. It ran together and rolled into a single cylinder, billowing up. "This is what happens when children lack direction. They destroy things that don't belong to them!" She flipped her hand over. The water congealed into an iron spike. In a single motion, she swung her arm low, grabbed the iron spike, and flung it at Aubrey and Rodriqa.

Rodriqa turned and huddled over Aubrey, and they both ducked. The iron spike soared past them and pierced the curved transparent wall behind them. Jagged cracks split out from its point of impact.

"Run!" Rodriqa grabbed Aubrey's arm. They both sprinted away from Ms. Thistlewood. Aubrey and Rodriqa rounded the corridor. They collided into the water-soaked Jordana and Magnos, who were rushing out of the Parkourium.

"Are you okay?" asked Rodriqa, scanning Magnos and Jordana.

Jordana's head more shivered than nodded. She spread apart her saturated bangs and slipped her glasses on her nose.

"We're good." Magnos shook his wet blond hair. "We've just had the ride of a lifetime. Where's Buzz?"

"I don't know." Rodriqa pulled at Magnos and Jordana. "But we need to run!"

All four of them ran a few yards. Rodriqa skidded to a stop, with Jordana, Magnos, and Aubrey halting closely behind her.

The animated, blackened skeleton of Matsinstrus walked toward them from the Break-n-Shake, flanked by two chupacabras. The beasts gripped the floor with their small, three-fingered forelimbs as their hind hooves slipped along the floor. Their large, green eyes focused on the friends as they extended their bat-like wings and hissed.

"There is no escape." Yellow fumes seeped out from Matsinstrus's eye sockets. "You will give us what we want."

"What do you want?" Aubrey's voice cracked.

"So many secrets. So much you don't know." Matsinstrus stretched out his bony arm. "Join us!"

"You can't kill us," challenged Rodriqa. "Everyone would know who did it."

"Mr. Parotty is prepared to take the fall," said Ms. Thistlewood from behind them.

"Besides what's a hundred years in prison," added Matsinstrus, "when you can't die?"

Ms. Thistlewood chuckled and wiped water from her forehead. "Give me Solluna."

"I don't have it," said Aubrey.

"I know it's not *on* you. Where is it?"

Aubrey swallowed hard against his tightening throat. "It's in the basement of the Smart Mart & Finer Diner."

"Good try." Magnolia Thistlewood stopped and twirled water between her fingers on her right hand. The water thickened to a slimy goo. "Whimperfidget already searched the Jennings's store. It's not there."

Aubrey looked at Rodriqa, Jordana, and Magnos. Magnos was pale and stood rigidly still. Rodriqa shook her head almost imperceptibly. Jordana nodded at Aubrey and slid her rose-tinted glasses off her nose.

Jordana stared at Ms. Thistlewood. "Let us go."

Ms. Thistlewood shielded her eyes with her left hand. "Oh no, you don't." With her right hand, she flung the now tarry taff between her fingers at Jordana.

The sludge splatted against Jordana's eyes. She screamed and doubled over. Raking at her face, Jordana dropped her glasses.

Bam!

The door to the Re-Reality Room flew off its hinges and smacked against the opposite wall. One by one, three eight-foot tall husky-torsoed Cyber Rudders stormed into the curved corridor. The first one turned toward Ms. Thistlewood, the second toward Mr. Parotty, and the third one also toward Ms. Thistlewood. More Cyber Rudders followed. Within moments, the corridor was full of a robotic army. Their fighter pilot helmets turned back and forth, and their polyvinyl arms swung side to side as they advanced.

Their synchronized pace filled the area with rhythmic stomps. The friends huddled back against the far wall and covered their ears as they watched the Cyber Rudders march.

Ms. Thistlewood took a couple of steps back and held her hand out toward the closest Cyber Rudder. In an instant, it transformed to stone, frozen in midstride. Two more Cyber Rudders marched in angles around their petrified comrade and swung at Ms. Thistlewood. Ms. Thistlewood ducked and touched the Cyber Rudder to her left. It melted into a large glop of plastic onto the floor. The other Cyber Rudder struck her in the temple. She toppled backward. She waved her hand. The attacking Cyber Rudder's skin slowly steamed, evaporating a bit at a time into the air. Four more Cyber Rudders wound around the injured robots and pressed Ms. Thistlewood further into the corridor.

On the other end, the two chupacabras pounced on the nearest Cyber Rudder. White teeth flashed in front of dark wings with gripping claws and scraping hooves. The first Cyber Rudder crumpled to pieces. From behind, two more Cyber Rudders swiped at the chupacabras. The beasts charged the robotic suits, forcing them to the floor. Four more Cyber Rudders marched forward, swatting at the chupacabras. One chupacabra took a hit to its eye and whimpered backward.

After scores of Cyber Rudders had exited the Re-Reality Room, Buzz jumped out from behind the last one.

"Dat-tada-da!" Buzz ran forward to his friends, picked Jordana's glasses off the floor and, with arms as wide as his smile, shouted, "Reiselstein to the rescue!"

Aubrey and Rodriqa jumped forward and squeezed Buzz in a double bear hug.

"You did this?" asked Aubrey.

Buzz looked up and down both ends of the corridor. Ms. Thistlewood was trapped in a cage of Cyber Rudders, and the two chupacabras had been backed into a corner by the Break-n-Shake, with Mr. Parotty futilely clawing at the onslaught.

Buzz pumped his fist. "Let's see Bates Hindenberg edit a million lines of code in less than five minutes!"

Rodriqa hugged him again. "You're a genius!"

Jordana cleaned the remaining goop from around her eyes, her face now sunburn red. She took her glasses from Buzz, slid them on her nose, and hugged him.

Magnos stepped forward. "Dude, no doubt you're awesome! But we should go while we still can."

Buzz held up his index finger. "Point taken."

The five of them raced down the corridor. Matsinstrus charged the group. Magnos swung his meaty closed fist toward the rushing charred skeleton and hit him in the jaw. Matsinstrus collapsed.

The friends ran past the rotating bar with Magnos. They wound between the oddly shaped tables, glancing up at the glass and metal chandeliers, which were dripping with water.

"Wait!" yelled Jordana.

The other four turned. A clover-shaped plastic table was unraveling into long strips from its granite edges. Several of the strips curled around Jordana's legs and arms.

"Jordana!" hollered Aubrey. He raced toward her. Magnos, Rodriqa, and Buzz followed him.

"Where are you going?" Magnolia Thistlewood strutted into the main ballroom from the opposite entrance. Bits of broken Cyber Rudder tumbled out of the curved corridor as she brushed plastic crumbs off her arms. "It's rude to leave without saying good-bye." She whipped her hands in circles. Jordana was lifted up by the winding strips. Jordana hung in the strips' grasp, facing away from the corridor. She struggled against the plastic, but it wouldn't budge.

Evaporating in a large blast of smoke, a hole gaped open in the floor beneath Rodriqa as she ran toward Jordana. Still in her ghostly form, Rodriqa dropped into the dark hole and yelped as she hit the bottom seven feet below.

Ms. Thistlewood waved her hand. The tile at the hole's brim bubbled and stretched across the opening in the floor, coalescing over it and sealing Rodriqa inside.

Ms. Thistlewood's lip curled. "Let's see if the spirit of the Tsul'kalu helps her breathe."

Magnos raced for Rodriqa. Buzz stopped where Rodriqa had fallen and pounded his foot against the hole's covering. Aubrey took several steps toward Jordana then stumbled back to Rodriqa, wavering between them.

Ms. Thistlewood twisted her fingers in circles. Three oddly shaped tables in the middle of the ballroom wrenched pieces from their tops. Malleable arms of granite grabbed each of the four friends and lifted them off the ground, wrapping stony tendrils tightly around their extremities. Everyone faced a different direction.

"What's going on?" shouted Buzz.

"Thistlewood's using her divinoi to manipulate matter!" shouted Jordana.

"Very good," replied Ms. Thistlewood. "Someone's done their home-work." She walked into the middle of the ballroom with the four children suspended around her.

Magnos broke his right arm free, and granite crumbled to the ground. Magnos grunted and twisted his torso. His left leg cracked the granite encasing it. Magnos swung at Ms. Thistlewood.

"Ah-ah-ah." Ms. Thistlewood dodged the blow. "Let me show you another trick I've recently learned."

Ms. Thistlewood sighed and brought her hands together. She closed her eyes. Her forehead crumpled, and her arms trembled. Slowly, the broken granite around the flailing Magnos grew up around him like rocky tendrils. Magnos punched at it and cracked off another piece. Then the portions of granite faded to a dull white. It jumped toward Magnos's free arm and leg. The dull white, shiny marble substance encased his limbs and solidified. Magnos struggled. The new dull white matter didn't move or shimmy.

"I'm stuck," groaned Magnos.

"Anyone know what I just did?" Ms. Thistlewood looked around at the children.

Continuing to pull against their stony bonds, each of them glanced between Magnos and their own makeshift manacles.

Ms. Thistlewood clicked her tongue against the roof of her mouth. "Pity."

"What do you want from us?" screamed Jordana.

Ms. Thistlewood faced Jordana. "To go away." Ms. Thistlewood pulled her bright red hair off her shoulders and held up her chin. "But before you go, there's something I need." With her index finger to her lips, she strutted past Magnos and Buzz, examining them with squinted eyes. "I have your divinoi. A wonderful gift from our last encounter."

Ms. Thistlewood glanced over her shoulder at Jordana. "Yours I don't need." She walked over to the middle of the ballroom and stood over the spot where Rodriqa was confined. Rodriqa's muffled screams echoed from underneath the newly formed tile. Looking at the floor, Ms. Thistlewood shook her head. "Bless her. What a useless ability."

Ms. Thistlewood glared up at Aubrey, who, strung up in twines of granite, was pale and sweating. "But you. You are unique." She walked over toward him. "There hasn't been a seer in many years." With her outstretched fingers, she caressed the snaked granite that held him. "But I knew where the next seer would appear.

"I have often wondered what would happen if I ranched a seer. I'm so grateful you'll help me find out." Magnolia Thistlewood held up her hand. The spirit shard covering it wriggled back onto to her forearm, revealing a charred bony hand, which glowed a shimmering green.

Jordana inhaled a sob and sighed deeply. Her head turned to the side as she stared outside. "What's that?" she asked in a calm voice.

"Hah!" Ms. Thistlewood glared at her. "Try harder."

"What *is* that?" Magnos stopped struggling as he followed Jordana's gaze. On the opposite side of darkened glass doors, something was moving rapidly toward the Rock-U-Quarium, separating the crowds gathered out front.

Buzz turned his head toward the entrance. He grimaced. "Oh, great. Just what we don't need."

Ms. Thistlewood snapped her head toward the entrance of the Rock-U-Quarium.

With her walker held high overhead, Old Widow Wizenblatt raced toward the front doors. Her bare feet pounded the pavement. Her tattered floral dress and disheveled white curls flittered in the wind. Passers-by gawked and grimaced at the unusual sight.

Mrs. Wizenblatt leapt onto the sidewalk from the cobblestone street and, in a single swing, flung her walker at the tinted glass. The glass shattered into a bloom of shards. She bounded twice, leaping into the foyer and then jumping again into the main ballroom.

Ms. Thistlewood backed away.

The widow slipped along the wet floor and, in an instant, vanished from sight, as if her body had evaporated.

"No!" Ms. Thistlewood held her hands to her face.

"Where did she go?" asked Aubrey.

Broken glass tinkled in the foyer, and Rodriqa's faint screams reverberated from below the tile.

Suddenly, a blinding crack of white light split the air in front of Magnolia Thistlewood. As if space had been cut and peeled upon itself, the brightening blaze tore a hole in the air, and the Widow jumped out from it. Wings as broad and tall as a house expanded outward from her back, knocking over tables and downing chandeliers. Plumes of steam rolled off of them like bushy white feathers. Ringed chains, partially embedded in her skin, reflected light like milk glass and wound around her arms and legs. Her hair, coifed with sculpted ringlets, spiraled around the crown of her head like carved stone. Pupilless, her eyes glowed like gems sparkling in the sunlight. Her tattered, water-stained floral dress had been transformed into a tunic of white linen.

Magnolia Thistlewood stepped backward. Old Widow Wizenblatt flapped her wings once. Ms. Thistlewood fell onto the floor. She crawled away from the widow on her elbows and heels.

Mrs. Wizenblatt pointed at Ms. Thistlewood. "You have overstepped your bounds, witch."

Ms. Thistlewood held out her shimmering green, skeletal hand. "And you have forgotten your place, slave!" She swiped her bony hand at the widow's legs.

Mrs. Wizenblatt stepped back. "This will not continue. You cannot interrupt what the Clockmaker has decided."

"I have grown nearly as powerful as the Clockmaker." Ms. Thistlewood scrambled away toward the reconfigured table that trapped Magnos. She pulled herself up to her feet. "Soon he will answer to me."

Mrs. Wizenblatt cackled. "Having the power of the Clockmaker does not make you able to take his place."

Ms. Thistlewood caressed the crystalline marble holding Magnos. "Do you like?" She eyed the widow. "I know it's familiar."

The widow scowled at the Magnolia. "Mock my chains, will you?" She flexed her back, and her wings stretched outward. "Whose life did you sacrifice for such an ornament?"

"It is no ornament." Magnolia's pale green eyes quivered. "I created it."

The widow shook her head. "Not possible."

"Oh really?" She closed her eyes, and her eyebrows and cheeks furrowed.

The tile at the widow's feet bubbled like boiling soup. A single tine of ceramic reached upward and froze. It melded into a cast of crystalline marble.

The widow stepped forward. She leaned down and grasped the spike of crystalline marble sticking up from the floor. It didn't move. She jerked her arm. Nothing happened. She glared at Ms. Thistlewood. "Nice trick."

Ms. Thistlewood chuckled, and her bright red hair fell forward. "It is no trick. It's fundamentium. As the Clockmaker creates, so do I."

"Creating the universe's building block does not make you equal to the Clockmaker." The widow straightened herself. "This will not work."

"For millennia, the Clockmaker has tortured me. It is time he knew disappointment."

The widow flexed her wings again. "Rebellion does not work."

"Every rebellion works. Some are simply more productive than others." Ms. Thistlewood stepped behind Magnos and stared at the widow through his bound legs. "And once the Terminal Prophecy is wiped from the minds of all his children, everyone will know that the Clockmaker is nothing more than the greatest fraud of eternity." Ms. Thistlewood closed her eyes. The tile underneath the widow's bare feet boiled and wrenched upward toward her ankles. Melding into crystalline marble, blobs of tile snaked around the widow's chains and solidified.

Mrs. Wizenblatt flapped her wings and floated upward. The spiking crags of fundamentium held her tautly to the floor.

Ms. Thistlewood chuckled. "A slave again, as you have always been. There's nothing more pathetic than a trapped angel."

The widow struggled against the crystalline marble holding her in place. Slowly, she folded her wings behind her back. "Funny." She cupped her hands together. "I've learned a new trick as well."

Ms. Thistlewood trotted over toward Aubrey. "It is exceptional a cherub has learned a divinoi." She stretched out her green, skeletal hand. "And honestly, I've coveted the power of the Graviteer for quite some time. But not all divinoi were created equal." Ms. Thistlewood pulled her bony hand in toward Aubrey's skin.

"Maybe not equal." Mrs. Wizenblatt flexed her fingers, and the crystalline marble at her ankle shattered. "But just as scary." The bits of broken fundamentium floated upward and whirred in front of her, congealing into a spinning black sphere.

Ms. Thistlewood gazed at the whirling round stone. "No," she murmured. "You can't..."

The widow arched her back. Space warped around her, and every item with mass in the main ballroom shifted toward the spinning, dark sphere. "Yes, I can."

The widow pressed her arms forward. The sphere floated upward toward Magnos. Flecks of his crystalline marble shackles broke off and flew into the sphere. The turning ball grew in size.

Ms. Thistlewood stumbled backward. The air around the spinning ball was drawn into it as its gravity grew. Tables scooted toward it, and chandeliers swung in its direction, dragged by its unseen tow. The widow grunted as she pressed her hands out. The ball moved forward.

"How could you learn this?" Ms. Thistlewood backed away as the ball approached her.

The widow took a step forward. When the ball passed by Magnos, he strained as it pulled him against his cage of fundamentium. Flecks of the crystalline marble broke off and flew into the sphere. The ball grew larger. Most of Magnos's bonds split into small pieces.

Aubrey glanced around. Tiny bits of glass and dirt soared across the room, disappearing as they were siphoned into the sphere. Peeking at the action from the corners of their eyes, Buzz and Jordana held their heads down as debris jetted past them. Aubrey closed his eyes. The phosphenes spun and faded, but instead of darkness, the brilliant white shape of Mrs.

Wizenblatt filled his vision and seared his mind. He opened his eyes and held his breath.

The walls of the main ballroom moaned as they leaned inward. Outside air from the broken doors whooshed inside. The crowds scurried away from the sidewalk.

The turning black orb was now the size of a bowling ball. Mrs. Wizenblatt treaded forward, straining to hold the ball away from her. Ms. Thistlewood turned and tried to run, the gravity from the ball towing her backward that she appeared to be moving in slow motion.

Mrs. Wizenblatt gritted her teeth and flung the ball toward Ms. Thistlewood. As the spinning sphere contacted her back, the witch's body contorted and swirled. In an instant, Magnolia Thistlewood was drawn into the black ball and disappeared.

"That was awesome!" screamed Buzz. "You made a singularity!"

"It's a pseudosingularity!" exclaimed the widow, struggling to control the orb at the back of the ballroom. "Which means, when I let go, everything inside of it comes spewing back out!"

"Hoaker croaker!" Buzz shimmied his body, trying to free himself.

"Get out now!" shouted the widow.

"What's a singularity?" hollered Aubrey.

"Black hole!" Buzz shook his head. "She created a temporary black hole!"

Aubrey and Jordana glanced at each other with wide eyes and then jerked their still-trapped bodies in the granite.

Magnos arched his back and heaved his shoulders outward. The crystalline marble trembled. In a final snap, his cage of fundamentium exploded. The free fragments hurdled through the room into the pseudosingularity.

Magnos hopped down and shouted into the floor, "Rodriqa, get low!" He raised his knee and slammed the tile over her with his size-16 foot. The tile cracked. He jumped up high in the air and stomped with both of his feet against the crack's edge. The tile crumbled into the hole. Reaching down, Magnos pulled the ghostly Rodriqa onto the floor.

"Hurry!" The widow's hands trembled as she pressed them toward each other. Growing and spinning, the pseudosingularity was now more than a yard wide.

Magnos jumped toward Jordana and wrenched apart the granite holding her. Broken stone fell to the floor and scooted toward the pseudosingularity. Rodriqa raced over to Aubrey, and with a single swing of her white sparkling arm, shattered the granite around him.

"Go!" Magnos pointed toward the front doors. Aubrey and Jordana climbed down and pushed themselves forward.

"Faster!" shouted the widow, her wings unfolding forward from the pull of the black globe.

Magnos and Rodriqa ran to Buzz and slammed their fists into his rocky shackles. The stone split, and Buzz fell out of his cage and landed on top of them, knocking them both to the floor.

"Run!" The widow's eyes darkened, and hot steam poured off her wings toward the pseudosingularity. Buzz, Magnos, and Rodriqa stumbled over each other to gain their feet. "Run now!" The widow turned her head toward them. Her eyes flashed a golden green, and her spiral hair spiked with a yellow brilliance.

Magnos bench-pressed Rodriqa and Buzz forward. Rodriqa leapt up, grabbed Buzz's arms, and catapulted him toward the exit. Magnos climbed to his feet.

All five of them clambered, scraped, and squirmed toward the doors, shielding their faces from the rushing wind and debris.

Magnos dropped into the foyer first and pulled his friends down the short marble stairs. They huddled together, and with the gale squeezing in, the NGW scrambled out of the Rock-U-Quarium and dashed across the cobblestone street.

Mrs. Wizenblatt watched the five children leave the building. She turned toward the pseudosingularity, which was now as wide as she was tall.

Relaxing her arms and wings, Old Widow Wizenblatt sighed. Her shoulders dropped. Her glowing eyes faded. She vanished into the ether. With the spark of a star, the pseudosingularity dissolved, releasing all its absorbed contents in a single, massive explosion.

BALLISTIC

Standing in the midst of a small crowd at the end of Lake Julian Square, Mena Kontrearo steadied herself behind a parked car, aimed her Spooly Pen at the shattered glass doors of the Rock-U-Quarium, and pressed its blue clicky button several times. The building's sign no longer blinked, but the streetlights flickered, and a howling whoosh of air echoed down the dark cobblestone street.

Magnos, Rodriqa, Jordana, Aubrey, and Buzz raced out of the front doors and up the street away from the crowd. Mena clicked her pen repeatedly. Abruptly, her thumb spasmed. Pulling her Spooly Pen away from her eye, she stared down the street. Mena watched Rodriqa's sparkling white color fade.

Shivering in her damp gym clothes, Vidalia Arsvine rubbed her hands against her arms and walked up to Mena. Vidalia stared over Mena's shoulder down Lake Julian Square. "Was Rodriqa Auerbach glowing?" asked Vidalia.

Mena nodded. She pulled the Spooly Pen back to her eye and pressed the blue clicky button several more times. "*Espiritu traviesa*," she murmured.

The five friends turned a distant corner. Suddenly, the whooshing sound stopped. The air stilled. The streetlights glowed brightly. A murmur rushed through the crowd as the onlookers gazed at the building. Several people slowly walked down the square. Suddenly, the Rock-U-Quarium exploded, and shrapnel of fragmented brick and rendered steel shot across the street and into the sky. A mushroom cloud of dust billowed upward. A spray of industrial flotsam flew out from the collapsing building and collided against the State of the Mart.

People in the crowd ducked and screamed. Mena and Vidalia fell behind the car. The face of the State of the Mart imploded from the blast, its stone and metal exterior crumpling into rubble.

Screeching sirens blared from around a distant corner as flashing red and blue lights gleamed off buildings and lit up the night sky. Two fire trucks and several police cars turned into the square and barreled toward the destruction.

Falling chunks of concrete and twisted metal pelted the cobblestone and sidewalks. A lingering smog of dust filtered through the air, spreading out along the street. Small flames sprouted in the settling dross.

With covered mouths and widened eyes, the onlookers stood up and backed away. Next to them, a black Fisker drove through a side alleyway and onto the cobblestone road; the car's blue-tinged headlights shone against the scattering crowd.

The Fisker braked in the middle of the street. Its headlights on and motor running, the driver side door opened, and a tall, bald-headed man, dressed in a suit, stepped out. Mena stopped and eyed the sleek sports car. Five bedraggled teenagers broke away from the crowd and trotted toward the driver.

Next to his Fisker, Mr. Miller swiveled his head, glancing between the teenagers. "Where's McCrayden?"

Vidalia shrugged. "We haven't seen her."

Mr. Miller's voice turned raspy. "Was she inside?"

Pam Trank shook her head. "No, sir."

Mr. Miller relaxed. He watched firemen race into the destruction. "What happened?"

Trembling, Vidalia Arsvine sidled next to Mr. Miller. "It was so awful."

"The fire alarm went off, and we all ran out." Zaniah Jones pointed toward the remains of the Rock-u-Quarium.

Pam Trank held her head down and wrapped her arms around her elbows. "Then there was all this banging and yelling."

"After that, the whole place went blew-ey." Mesilla Uztek flailed her arms about.

"And you'll never guess who we saw leaving just before it exploded," murmured Jon Harney.

Mr. Miller pulled off his suit coat and draped it around Vidalia, Zaniah, and Pam, who were huddling together. "Who?"

The five teenagers eyed Mr. Miller warily.

Mr. Miller clenched his jaw. "Who?!"

"We're afraid to say." Jon Harney stared at the cobblestone and straightened his lips to keep his grin from creasing through.

"I've got better than that!" shouted Mena from several yards away. She ran over to Mr. Miller and the rowdies and held up her Spooly Pen. "I've got proof."

Mr. Miller crinkled an eyebrow. "Proof? In your pen?"

"Yes, sir." Mena nodded fervently. "All I need is a computer." She pulled off the bottom of her pen, exposing its USB port.

Mr. Miller scowled. Leaning down into his Fisker, he reached inside and pulled out his laptop. He snapped it open and waved Mena forward.

Mena rushed over to him. She plugged her pen into his computer. The pen's flash drive popped up on the screen. Mena scrolled through her files.

With each picture flashing by, Mr. Miller's brow furrowed more tightly.

"Ya'll okay?" The beam of a bright flashlight panned from building to street to the dispersing crowd, then back again.

"Alec? Is that you?" shouted Mr. Miller.

Sergeant Van Zenny hobbled forward and squinted through the dust dancing in the Fisker's headlights. "Mr. Miller?"

"Yeah." Mr. Miller cleared his throat and placed his computer on the top of his car. "Come here. I need to show you something."

Van Zenny hurried over to Mr. Miller. He scanned everyone quickly with his flashlight. "Anyone hurt?"

The teenagers shook their heads and backed away.

Mr. Miller grabbed Van Zenny's flashlight and shined it up into the officer's face. "Do you know what's happened?"

The sergeant shook his head. The fat under his chin wobbled.

Mr. Miller yanked the flashlight toward his computer. "The two newest and greatest business ventures of Lake Julian have just been destroyed. And any guess as to whom is responsible?"

The sergeant stared at Mr. Miller's laptop. His eyes quivered as image after image of the five friends crossed the screen.

Mr. Miller slammed his laptop close and jerked the flashlight upward into Van Zenny's eyes. "I want them stopped. I want them in jail. And I want it now!" Mr. Miller leaned down and pressed his face close to the sergeant's. "Do you understand me?"

Van Zenny closed his eyes. "Ya'sir."

Quickly donning yellow suits and oxygen masks, a score of firefighters pulled ribbons of hoses from their trucks and clamped them to the hydrants close by. The air thickened as flourishing fires churned the foggy soot.

Within the State of the Mart, several boulders of fractured concrete tumbled down a precipice of bent steel and split wood. A few smaller pebbles warbled and evaporated into dust. The dust separated, and the air cleared above a crevice in the destruction. A blackened skeletal hand stretched out from underneath. The concrete around the bony forearm melted into water. Another skeletal hand emerged and turned the dial on the brown sandstone watch on its wrist.

Stomping through waist-high grass, Magnolia Thistlewood trudged up to her massive oak tree in the meadow below Mount Camelot. Her curvy figure congealed around her chest and hips as her bright red hair cascaded down from her skull and around her shoulders.

Firelight glowed from the oak's windows. A soft breeze wafted through the tall weeds. Several chupacabras bowed as she approached. A line of light shone from a thin crease between the door and its frame. Ms. Thistlewood peered inside.

Standing with outstretched hands, Zaks stood in the middle of the first level, his head raised and eyes squeezed shut. His gray skin partially reflected the light flickering from the fireplace behind him. The air warped around his torn cloth tunic and his arms trembled as he pressed gravity downward.

Ms. Thistlewood's jaw clenched. She glanced down at his feet. Zaks hovered several inches off the wooden floor. The obese Ned and the lanky Fred Kluggard, along with the charred skeleton Matsinstrus, lay prone against the floor, groaning under the pressure squeezing down on them.

Ms. Thistlewood stepped inside. "You shouldn't play with stuff that doesn't belong to you." In the firelight, both parts of her form were clearly visible. Her hips and chest appeared human, but her jaw and limbs were a blackened skeleton and fumed a yellow haze.

Zaks opened his good left eye. The black oval glared at her. "You have gone too far."

Ms. Thistlewood wagged a bony finger at him. "Be careful, Magi. You wouldn't want to upset the balance."

"I am restoring it." Zaks moved his hands down. Matsinstrus moaned. Ned squealed. "Insanity needs limits."

She crossed her arms. "What a shame you've forgotten who made you choose between right and wrong." She shook her head. "What a shame you lack the vision to fight against our real enemy."

Zaks's lips tightened. "You killed Tartan."

Ms. Thistlewood scrunched her forehead. "Who?"

"One of my keepers." Zaks's lower lip trembled. "You took him to create your army of aberrations."

Ms. Thistlewood chuckled. "The creature was put to good use."

Zaks flexed his arms. The interior walls of the massive oak creaked as they bowed inward. "I am not some expendable waif of scrap, Magnolia. And I am not part of your plan either."

Ms. Thistlewood walked over to a small table adorned with several small jars. She lifted the lid of the closest jar. Several shimmering black spirit shards escaped, crawled up her arm and settled around her lower face. Her jaw and nose transformed into pale flesh. "You were always part of my plan, Magi, whether you are with me or against me."

A thin smile creased across Zaks's face. "If you cannot best the widow, how can you expect to beat the Clockmaker?"

Ms. Thistlewood waved him off. "Once my army has matured, she won't matter."

Zaks nodded. "Did you know your deviant army has created unintended consequences?"

"Really?" She opened another jar. Spirit shards wrapped around her arms and congealed into skin. "How perfectly wonderful."

"The Master Magi are here."

Ms. Thistlewood stared at Zaks. She smiled. "Better than wonderful."

"But they are not here for you." Zaks lifted his chin. "They came for the seer."

Ms. Thistlewood's lip curled. "No matter. They are here. The more Magi, the better." She opened two more jars, and two spirit shards seeped out and clung to her legs.

Zaks squinted his black eye. "This will not work. There's one thing you've forgotten."

"What is that?" She opened the last jar and turned the dial on her brown sandstone watch. Spirit shards fumed from the jar and were sucked under the dial. Magnolia Thistlewood raised her hands and closed her eyes. The crystalline marble of the hearth behind Zaks shuddered. Two molten cords of fundamentium reached out from the mantle.

Zaks tumbled forward. "The Bloodrunner anathem." He closed his eyes and inhaled deeply. Bits of dirt, dust, and stone swirled in orbit around him. Quickly, his form shrank, and the raven burst through the spinning soot. Zaks flew up the spiral staircase and escaped out the upstairs window.

The massive oak's walls settled, and the three henchmen on the ground inhaled deeply as the gravity in the room returned to normal.

"Get up!" yelled Ms. Thistlewood, now fully human in appearance. She kicked at Fred as he rolled away. "Why did you let him in?"

"We didn't exactly have another option." Ned flopped over onto his back and sat up.

"We need to learn how to control gravity," added Matsinstrus.

She scowled at the charred skeleton, who was rocking back onto his legs. "Trust me. I've tried."

"We need more help." Ned grunted, regaining his feet. "Moving all those keepers to the gorge below the dam was nearly impossible." He rubbed his left forearm, where a tear in his uniform shirt gapped open. "They bite now."

Ms. Thistlewood grinned. "Then more help is exactly what you'll have." She walked over to the back of the room, beyond the hearth, and opened a small closet door. A wedge of light from the fireplace swept inside.

"Icharida?" She peered inside. "How is my sweet Icharida?"

Shivering in the closet with her knees to her chest, the dark form huddled with her head down as squirming, shimmering spirit shards writhed over her shoulders and down her flanks.

Ms. Thistlewood waved her forward. "How do you feel?"

Icharida squeaked and grunted, but she couldn't speak.

Ms. Thistlewood glanced over at Matsinstrus. "Your replacement—I mean your help is coming along nicely." She turned back to Icharida. "Don't worry, dear. It will be over soon."

Icharida reached for Ms. Thistlewood. Bubbling skin slid off her arm and plopped onto the floor, revealing a charred, simmering skeleton underneath.

"Very soon." Ms. Thistlewood closed the closet door.

Whimperfidget dug feverishly at the gravel in the parking lot behind Mr. Jennings's Smart Mart & Finer Diner. The dark night air was still, and plumes of dust spewed from the pit as the cat's sharp claws burrowed deeper into the dirt.

A bright light pierced the darkness from behind the store. Whimperfidget stopped digging. His red eyes glowed brighter, and the tangled mats of hair on his back hunched upward. The cat leapt up to the edge of the pit and growled.

A hundred feet away, Old Widow Wizenblatt stepped forward from a patch of dense woods, her wings unfurling with rolling white steam. Her eyes gleamed, and she stretched out her hands. "Careful, kitty. I'm here to help."

Whimperfidget screeched a stinging hiss and scratched manically at the gravel.

The widow closed her eyes and recited the Bloodrunner anathem.

> You should not exist,
> Lest death never desist.

Whimperfidget's whiskers twisted in knots, and he snorted snot from his nose. The widow continued chanting.

> By All Law, be dismissed,
> Or else as a slave persist.

Whimperfidget howled and sprinted toward the widow.

> In suffering, you shall subsist,
> Rended will, from freedom's twist.

With claws extended, Whimperfidget leapt toward the widow. The widow grabbed her wings and quickly finished the anathem's final phrase.

> Through my gift and by this curse,
> May your soul never resist.

Whimperfidget crumpled into a limp ball of cream-and-charcoal-colored hair and fell at the feet of the widow. The cat's red eyes dimmed, and its claws slowly retracted. The widow's wings faded from view, but she remained in her angelic form. She leaned down and stroked the cat's head. Whimperfidget trembled.

"Don't you worry, little one." She scratched his ear. "Rodriqa Auerbach is gonna take good care of you."

LAST CALL

Aydry Auerbach sat in her car at the end of Lake Julian Square, watching the firemen spraying water into the smoldering blazes that fumed amid the rubble where two massive buildings once stood. Picking up her cell phone, she scrolled down to Dan Taylor in her contact list and pressed his name. The phone rang.

"Hello."

"Dan, we have a problem."

"Aydry?" Shuffling noises scratched across her receiver. "What's wrong?"

"I went to go pick up our kids, but they're not here."

"What? Where are they?"

"I'm...I'm not sure," replied Mrs. Auerbach.

"Are they okay?"

Mrs. Auerbach sighed. "I'm not sure of that either."

"What happened?"

Mrs. Auerbach closed her eyes. "They may be responsible for blowing up the Rock-U-Quarium."

"What?"

"It's a little unclear, but from what Sergeant Van Zenny has told me, there are pictures of them leaving the building before it...it exploded."

"Oh no," murmured Mr. Taylor.

Refocusing her thoughts, Mrs. Auerbach shook her head and opened her eyes. "Do you have any idea where they might have gone?"

"Umm, maybe," said Mr. Taylor. "I can think of a few places. Have you called anyone else?"

"No, not yet."

Mr. Taylor paused for a moment. "I'll call Arvel and Ragna Strumgarten. Can you call Principal Lequoia and let him and Jordana's dad know what's going on?"

"Okay, but, Dan, there's another problem."

"What's that?" said Mr. Taylor.

"The police have issued warrants for their arrest. Sergeant Van Zenny has every available cop in Poage County hunting for them right now."

Mr. Taylor sighed. "I'll be there as soon as I can."

Wednesday.

"We're going to jail. We're going to jail. It's only a matter of time till the police find us! We're going to jail!" Jordana wrung her hands as she paced next to a single candle from an electric menorah, which glowed dimly in the loft of the Screever's Lair.

Buzz hammered the granite hoops binding Aubrey's wrist against a tiny metal anvil. The stone cracked, and Aubrey brushed bits of rubble off his hands and rubbed his wrists. "Old Widow Wizenblatt is an angel. All this time, we thought she was some beggar woman who had it in for us, but she's an angel."

"An angel who can make black holes!" exclaimed Buzz. "It doesn't get any cooler than that!"

Sitting cross-legged in front of the candle, Rodriqa snorted. "Except we're gonna take the hit for all the damage that she and Ms. Thunderwhoopin' did tonight."

"You mean Ms. Thistlewood?" asked Magnos, who was sitting on a mattress in the corner.

Rodriqa nodded. Aubrey stared into the dark rafters of the Screever's Lair. "That's what we've been fighting between all this time. Angels and demons. We're in the middle of a war between angels and demons."

"Who cares about angels and demons?" Jordana shook her head. "We were already in trouble, now they're gonna take us to jail and keep us there."

"We care!" Buzz stood over the candle.

Jordana glared at Buzz. "But we're the bad guys now!"

Buzz shook his head. "No, we're not. We're the good guys. We've been fighting these battles since last fall. Not because we're righteous or special or even good, but because we were here and we had to."

Jordana looked away, her curtain of dark hair concealing her face. "And look what doing the right thing has gotten us. We're felons."

Rodriqa pressed herself up to standing. "Jordana's right." She looked at Buzz sternly. "We've been trying to do what's right, but now there's a crowd of folks who saw us leaving the Rock-U-Quarium right before it exploded." She pushed Buzz away from the candle. "We're toast."

Aubrey walked between Rodriqa and Buzz and looked at her. "But what about the ghosts? What about everything we've fought? We can't forget about that."

"But no one believes us." Rodriqa rested her hands on her hips "All the police will believe is what people tell them. And after tonight, Mr. Miller will have all the evidence he needs to put us away for a long time."

Buzz raised a pointed finger. "Only if he finds us."

Rodriqa scowled. "It won't be long till they figure out where we are."

Magnos looked up at his friends. "Then maybe we should run away." Rodriqa and Aubrey sighed. Buzz continued to hold his finger up, thinking.

"Maybe." Jordana walked over to Magnos, sat down, and leaned into him.

Aubrey turned around. "But what about the chupacabras? We're the only ones who know what they're doing." He glanced over his shoulder at Rodriqa. "We saw what one chupacabra did to you when you were in your Tsul'kalu form. It's no wonder so many people have fallen ill. We can't let this go on."

"Which is why Ms. Thistlewood set a trap for us." Buzz lowered his finger and pointed at Aubrey. "She doesn't want us interfering with her army." Everyone looked at Buzz with puzzled faces. Buzz waved his hands. "Last fall, she tried to open the Tomb of Enoch to get *all* the Watchers out. We stopped her. Now she's made an army of these creatures that can subdue everyone who gets in her way, except us."

"But she failed," said Rodriqa. "She's dead now. She got sucked into that black hole."

"Doubtful," said Buzz. "She survived a burning house on Dalton Circle eight months ago. Remember what the widow said? It was a *pseudo*singularity. Whatever went into that black hole came back out in the explosion."

Aubrey plopped his hands on top of his head. "Buzz, you're a genius."

Buzz crossed his arms and smiled. "Clearly."

Aubrey turned around. "This is not about us. It's not even about Lake Julian. Ms. Thistlewood is planning something. Something big!"

Jordana choked back a sob. "But what would someone want with an army?"

Buzz rubbed his belly. "What does any general plan with an army?"

Aubrey rubbed his chin. "Conquest."

Rodriqa raised her head and bit her lip. "We need to go get the Losepkees out of the Crannynook Caves."

Aubrey smiled at her. "Yes, but we also need to get the crucible in Mr. Jennings's store basement. The chupacabras are after the lamps, and we need to get to whatever Ms. Thistlewood is after before she does."

"Not the lamps again," moaned Rodriqa.

Buzz stepped forward. "I think Aubrey has a point."

"If we go anywhere near anything, we're gonna be seen and arrested," said Jordana.

"Not if we're smart," replied Buzz. "We know Lake Julian well. We can get around town without being seen."

"Not while there's thousands of people here for the million moth meta-morphosis," agreed Rodriqa. "Besides, if we don't do something fast, our parents will find us. They know where we hang out."

"Mostly." Buzz flashed a wily grin. "We just need to figure out the best thing to do."

Rodriqa crossed her arms. Buzz looked up at the ceiling and murmured to himself. Aubrey walked in circles around the candle. Magnos chuckled. The other four looked at him.

"Sorry." Magnos planted his feet on the floor. "I still can't get over how the widow kicked Ms. Thistlewood's wompus."

Buzz laughed and flexed his arms, hands, and fingers in the air, mim-icking the widow. "It was so incredible. She manipulated gravity like it was putty. Unspittin'-believable!"

"How is that possible?" Rodriqa asked.

Buzz snorted. "How is it possible that Aubrey sees through the dark-ness? Or you turn into a ghost?" He waved at Rodriqa. "Or Jordana does her eye thingy?"

Jordana glared up at him. "Don't talk about me like that."

"He's right." Magnos nudged Jordana softly. "We're all sorta special."

Aubrey walked over to Jordana. "Very special."

Jordana grinned and wiped her face. "Guess you're right." She pulled her cell phone out of her pocket. "I think I found something that talks about us."

"Uh-huh." Rodriqa smiled.

Magnos and Aubrey leaned in as Buzz walked over. Jordana opened her phone. "Remember the book that Hovis Trottle had in his library under the cemetery? The one with the leather pages and all the ornate stenciling?"

A shiver rifled down Aubrey's spine. "Yeah."

"It was called *Anathagraphia*," said Rodriqa.

"Yep, that was it," replied Jordana, eyeing Rodriqa. "My uncle has one in his library, but he's forbidden me to read it."

"Really?" Buzz's eyes widened. "Can you get ahold of it?"

Jordana shrugged her shoulders. "I've been sneaking into his office and reading it some."

Rodriqa's arms dropped limply. "Why didn't you tell us?"

Jordana shrugged. "I was afraid to say too much. I figured someone might try to steal it." She glanced at Buzz. "It's an old tribal artifact. No one is supposed to look at it, but since I had already seen it in Hovis Trottle's house, I thought it would be okay."

Aubrey nodded. "That sounds reasonable."

Jordana shook her head. "Not according to Uncle. After he caught me reading it, he's hidden it someplace else, and I can't find it."

"Bummer," sighed Buzz.

Jordana held up her phone. "But that wasn't before I had a chance to take pictures of a few pages."

Magnos squinted as he read her phone. "So cool."

Rodriqa, Buzz, and Aubrey huddled around Jordana on the mattress. "So that's how you know so much about the Bloodrunner anathem," concluded Rodriqa.

"Uh-huh." Jordana pointed to her phone. "This page tells about the divinoi."

> **Seeing** is the most rare of all divinoi. A seer not only perceives both physical and spiritual realms but also pierces the membrane between them, exposing the hidden nature of one world to the other and translating supernatural elements to mundane constituents. A seer can also peel time from space and view events from past and future. However, as knowing space without its time disrupts the existential fabric and unravels the mortal mind, seeing in the absence of meter must only occur by dispensation of the Clockmaker. Uninvited engagement into extrapresent events results in the transformation of the individual into a guer-seer, whereas the bearer recalls and predicts with impeccable precision what is to come, yet without recognition of perspective, plan, or purpose.
>
> **Might** brings strife. Such is the life of the Nazirite if this divinoi benefits friend or foe. But whether employed for self and soul or bargained by for the seat of a hero, tyranny takes hold and, in place, a Giborite brands a martyr's mold. Bending the physical will of all objects, inanimate, enspirited, or languished grants the bearer of this divinoi formidable strength and agility.

Healing accelerates innate recovery of an entity during a state of malady, dysfunction, or disrepair. The degree of healing is proportionately commensurate with the compassion felt by the healer toward the recipient. Contrary to healing, ranching extracts the psychoplasm out of another being, empowering the offender with the victim's abilities and vigor. The basest form of evil, the transcendent thievery of ranching, provides monumental opportunity, but poisons the soul of the wielder with each attempt.

Protection endows an individual to exact guardianship over another being's welfare. For the guardian, when violence erupts, fortitude resolves to potency. When character fails, fear melds hope. When the object of protection is threatened, the guardian is imbued with superior resilience and fortitude, matching the aptitude of the bearer's opponent. Twisting the talents imbued to hunt or slay a discrete target ravishes the heart, rending compassion and mercy from judgment. The executor's venery becomes insatiable, and thus abasement of this divinoi is irrevocable.

Confession draws emotion, experienced by another, to the surface, exposing an inner truth. The confessor concentrates their emotion and channels that passion to the receptive entity, igniting a reactive catharsis. The abuse of this ability, whereby the confessor compels another individual to feel something unnatural to their subconscious, is termed *coercion*. The nefarious and unbridled employment of coercion can place the user at risk of anathema and can alter how a coercing individual manifests their divinoi.

"Each divinoi has a good and a bad side," remarked Aubrey.

Rodriqa nodded. "And apparently, if you don't walk the straight and narrow, the consequences aren't pretty."

"Hey!" Buzz ran his finger down Jordana's phone. "Where's mine?"

"Sorry, Buzz." Jordana wrinkled her eyebrows. "I didn't have a chance to take a picture of the next page."

Buzz frowned. "But all your divinoi are on here. What about me? Does that mean I'm a healer?"

Rodriqa snorted. "Doubtful."

Aubrey reached up and squeezed Buzz's shoulder. "Don't worry. We'll figure it out," he looked at Jordana, "once we find the book."

Bang! Bang! Bang! The metal warehouse shook with a knock at the door downstairs. "Flustered mustard." Rodriqa covered her mouth with her hands.

"Game over," murmured Magnos.

"The game's not over till I say it's over." Buzz trotted over to the back of the loft. He picked up a metal hemisphere adorned with scores of tiny, pointy knobs, each attached to a small fan blade. He pulled the hemisphere's antenna and grabbed a joystick next to it. Buzz marched over to the edge of the loft and threw the hemisphere into the lower level of the Screever's Lair. The hemisphere popped as it landed on the dirt floor. Buzz bounded back to the corner and grabbed a plastic grocery bag. He pulled out a small thread spool, which was wrapped with a copper wire. On one end of the spool, Velcro was glued; at the other end, a watch battery was connected to the ends of the copper wire. Buzz slapped the wire-wrapped spool against his chest. Its Velcro stuck to his shirt.

Buzz held up the joystick and extended its antenna. "If they want us, they'll have to make it through the Taser bomb."

"What's a Taser bomb?" asked Rodriqa.

"Is that a Taser bomb?" Aubrey peered over the ledge at the contraption.

Magnos stood up. "I don't think tasering the police is a good idea right now."

Bang! Bang! Bang!

Buzz handed Aubrey the plastic grocery bag. After climbing down the ladder to the lower level, Buzz tiptoed across the dirt toward the entrance. He peered through a peephole next to the sliding front door. "It's Coren Belward!"

Rodriqa leaned over the edge of the loft. "The Scout leader?"

"Yeah!" Buzz unlocked the door and slid it open.

Rodriqa looked at Aubrey. "What's he doin' here?"

Aubrey shrugged.

Buzz waved his hand at Coren, who stepped into the Screever's Lair. Gawking at the interior, Coren's Adam's apple bobbed up and down. "You live here?"

Buzz chuckled. "No, this is where I do all my inventing."

"Oh." Coren's eyes danced between the metallic Vitruvian man and the hippie mural.

He looked up at Buzz's four friends, who were perched at the edge of the loft. Coren saluted them. They waved at him warily.

Coren turned to Buzz. "What have you found out?"

"A ton. You won't believe what's going on."

Rodriqa cleared her throat from above.

Buzz shook his head. "What are you doing here?"

Coren looked up at the loft. "Everyone already knows you all demolished the Rock-U-Quarium."

Aubrey's and Jordana's shoulders slumped.

Rodriqa crossed her arms. "How did you find out so fast?"

Coren ran his hand over his high-and-tight hair. "The explosion rocked the valley. Folks from the million moth metamorphosis were up at the Square and ran back. Word spread quickly."

"How did you know we were here?" Buzz asked.

Coren looked at Buzz. "I asked your dad. He guessed you would be here."

"I can't believe your dad sold us out," said Rodriqa. "No need to run now. The police will be here any minute."

Coren wagged his head. "No. No one else knows you're here." He walked over to the ladder. "I need your help."

"Since when does a Boy Scout need help?" Rodriqa asked. "I thought it was supposed to be the other way around."

Coren looked down at the dirt. "All my Scouts are gone."

Aubrey crouched down on the ledge. "You mean they went home?"

"Nope." Coren shook his head. "I don't know where they went."

Buzz walked over to Coren. "You mean they're missing?"

Coren nodded. "Except for Maulden, who's in the hospital, they've all disappeared."

Buzz rubbed his chin. "Disappeared?"

Magnos spun onto the top of the ladder and, in a second, slid to the bottom of the Screever's Lair. He turned toward Buzz. "Just like the Losepkees."

Buzz's eyes slowly widened. He punched Magnos in the elbow. "Now you're the genius!"

"Oh no," murmured Jordana. "That means…"

"They're in the Crannynook Caves," said Aubrey.

Coren cocked his head to the side. "I don't think they would have all gone there this late at night."

Aubrey climbed onto the ladder. "I don't think they're staying there because they want to."

Buzz ran over, picked up his Taser bomb and carried it out the sliding door. Parked out front, Coren's four-wheeler and trailer rested a few yards from the Screever's Lair. Buzz threw the Taser bomb on the trailer bed and ran back inside.

"Come on!" Buzz waved his friends down. "We need to go!"

HUNGRY CAVE

Loaded with a ladder and the Taser bomb, Coren Belward's four-wheeler rumbled up the steep trail leading to the Crannynook Caves, while Aubrey, Rodriqa, Buzz, Magnos, and Jordana clung to its rails. The four-wheeler's headlights bleached the darkness with a bright path. The wooden trailer bed rocked and creaked, its wheels heaving upward and then spinning out before lurching forward again.

From behind the mountain above, the heralding glow of sunrise faintly warmed the fading night under the tiring stars. A brisk breeze slipped through the trees, damp from dews' demise.

At the trailhead, Coren stopped and shut off the four-wheeler but left the headlights shining. He jumped from the seat and faced the friends lying in the trailer bed. "Tell me again why we need a ladder in a cave?"

Buzz brushed twigs and mud out of his curly, black hair. He slid out of the trailer bed, holding the Taser bomb under his arm. "You'll see."

Rodriqa popped her knuckles and shook out her hands. "I think I lost most of my teeth along the trail."

Aubrey held up his pale hands. "My fingers are numb."

Jordana spat strands of her black hair out of her mouth as she unhinged herself off Magnos's back. "I hope your Scouts are here," she muttered.

Magnos stood up and jumped off the trailer bed. Hoisting the ladder onto his shoulder, he searched the trail behind them. "I don't think we were followed."

"It wouldn't have been hard." Rodriqa picked bits of dirt out of her beaded braids. "It's not like we're exactly covert."

Buzz picked up several flashlights and tossed them to his friends. He marched up to Coren, who had pulled a tiny flashlight off his belt. "Let's find your boys." Buzz patted Coren on the shoulder.

Coren and Buzz walked up to the mouth of the cave. They shined their flashlights inside and stepped down into the damp darkness.

A dozen boys of various ages, each dressed in their tan button-down shirts and green shorts, hung by their feet from the ceiling, their arms dangling down from their shoulders, their eyes closed, their skin pale, and their bodies limp.

Coren's eyes widened. "So this is why we need the ladder."

"Yep." Buzz angled his light in various directions, illuminating the faces of several Scouts. Buzz shouted over his shoulder, "Found 'em!"

Aubrey, Rodriqa, Jordana, and Magnos huddled up behind Buzz and examined the craggy chamber. "Is this the same cave we went into before?" Jordana asked.

Buzz nodded. "Pretty sure."

Jordana turned her head sideways. "It looks different."

"She's right." Rodriqa stepped forward and aimed her flashlight toward the end. "The ledge is gone, and the slope is more even."

Aubrey followed Rodriqa's light. "The chupacabras must have dug it out."

With flashlight in hand, Magnos stretched his arm between Coren and Buzz and directed his light at the two adults hanging deep inside the cave. "And we can see the Losepkees from here. Hopefully there isn't a secret something hiding behind them this time."

Coren looked at Magnos. "What…what do you mean?"

Buzz took a step down. "We know what's doing this to your Scouts." Pebbles tumbled under each step. "And they aren't pretty." He threw the Taser bomb into the middle of the large chamber. "Aubrey. Eyes."

Aubrey pulled his inhaler out of his pants pocket and pressed it into his mouth. After discharging the tiny canister, he repocketed his asthma medicine and closed his eyes.

The phosphenes swirled behind his eyelids and slowly faded. The distant shimmering lights hung in the background, like a scrim.

"Same as before." Aubrey angled his head for a different view, but what he could see didn't change. "Lots of squiggly stuff far away. Nothing close."

"Let's get everyone out." Buzz leaned down and flipped a switch underneath the hemispheric chassis of the Taser bomb. "Everyone keep your eyes open, except for Aubrey."

Rodriqa grabbed Aubrey's hand and led him into the cave toward Buzz.

Magnos trotted forward and set up the ladder next to the nearest Scout. Coren and Jordana followed behind him. Clenching his flashlight between his teeth, Magnos climbed the ladder and gripped the boy by his ankles. With a quick jerk, he pulled downward. The stone at the Scout's feet cracked, and he dropped a foot before Magnos's arms tightened, holding him in midair. Coren and Jordana reached up for the Scout, and as Magnos descended the ladder, the three gently laid the boy on the rocky, wet cave floor.

Rodriqa redirected Aubrey toward the end of the cave, aiming his supernatural vision toward the darkness. "You okay?"

Aubrey nodded. "I still only see a bunch of shiny lines."

Rodriqa squeezed his arm. "I'm gonna help the others."

"Okay."

Buzz untied the plastic grocery bag from around a belt loop at his hip. He opened it and threw a copper-wound spool connected to a watch battery at Rodriqa. "Put this on."

Rodriqa caught it. She turned the cooper-wound spool over and examined it. "What's this?"

Buzz tossed three more spools to Magnos, Coren, and Jordana. "It emits a specific frequency that signals the Taser bomb not to taze you."

"Great." Rodriqa rolled her eyes and slapped the Velcro on the watch battery against her shirt.

Buzz threw another one to Rodriqa. "Put one on Aubrey too."

Rodriqa snatched it out of the air and slapped it on Aubrey's chest. Magnos and Jordana velcroed their copper-wound spools to their shoulders. Still standing on the ladder, Magnos reached over to the next Scout and pulled his feet free from the ceiling. Jordana helped Magnos lower the limp boy to the ground. Magnos gripped the top metal rung and hopped the ladder, like a metal grasshopper, several yards over to the next dangling Scout. Jordana and Rodriqa followed.

"Make sure you look close behind each Scout," hollered Rodriqa into the cave. Her voice echoed off the ragged rock walls.

Coren slipped his copper-wound spool in his uniform shirt pocket and leaned over the first Scout, who remained motionless on the cave's muddy floor. He leaned down and listened over the boy's nose and palpated the side of his neck. "His pulse is good, and he's still breathing."

"Just like everyone in the hospital," murmured Buzz. He adjusted several pointy knobs on the Taser bomb.

Gently smacking the Scout on the cheek with the back of his hand, Coren spoke with a cracked voice, "Dylan? Dylan! Wake up!"

Aubrey held up his hands. "I see something!" Behind his eyelids, tiny white sparks flashed in the corner of his sight.

Magnos yanked down on another Scout and searched the end of the cave with the flashlight in his mouth. Rodriqa caught the Scout, and Jordana helped her lower the Scout to the ground as Magnos moved on.

Buzz stood up and extended the antenna from his joystick. "Where?"

"Over there." Aubrey pointed to his right but kept his head forward. "Wait." Aubrey cocked his head to the side. "It's gone."

Buzz, Magnos, and Rodriqa all sighed deeply.

"What was it?" asked Buzz.

Aubrey shrugged.

"He's awake!" shouted Coren. Everyone glanced over toward him.

Dylan coughed and sputtered as his eyes opened. He pushed himself up as a peachy color returned to his face. "What…what happened?"

Coren lifted him forward. "Just rest. We're gonna get you out of here."

"Who's awake?" asked Aubrey as he watched the dark, shimmering lines in his vision.

"One of the Scouts is up," replied Buzz. He walked over to the Scout and stood over him. "What do you remember?"

Dylan rubbed his forehead and grimaced. "Monsters." Tears filled his reddened eyelids. "Lots of monsters."

"It's gonna be okay." Coren rubbed his shoulder. He looked around at the other Scouts lying limp on the ground. He hopped up and rushed over to the nearest boy.

"I see it again," said Aubrey.

"What?" asked Buzz.

"It's a tiny flashing light." Aubrey pointed deeper into the cave. "But now it's gone again." Aubrey took a step forward. "There it is!" He pointed to another spot on the opposite end of the cave. "It's moving."

Buzz swiveled his flashlight, searching where Aubrey pointed. "I don't see anything."

"The last of the Scouts are down!" shouted Rodriqa from deep inside the cave. "No chupacabras yet. We're getting the Losepkees. We need to get everyone out!"

"No problem," replied Coren. "The Scouts are here to help."

Magnos hopped toward the Losepkees on the ladder. He shined his light back up through the cave. His eyes widened. "Look," he murmured to Rodriqa and Jordana as he nodded toward the mouth of the cave.

Four Scouts were standing, and three were helping several other Scouts who were waking up and pushing themselves off the ground. Coren trotted over to the last two Scouts, who were lying motionless.

"How did that happen?" asked Rodriqa.

Magnos shrugged and reached for Stan Losepkee. He heaved down on his ankles. "Grab him. He's heavy."

"Guys!" shouted Aubrey. "Something's happening!"

Buzz shined his light at Aubrey's eyes. "I think you're just seeing the flashlights."

Aubrey winced and held up his hands, opening his eyes. "No. All the shimmering lines just disappeared."

"Uh-oh." Buzz angled his flashlight toward the end of the cave.

"Okay!" Rodriqa lowered Fran Losepkee to the ground. "Everyone's down! Get everyone out!"

The last two Scouts stood up, and Coren ushered them forward. All the Scouts huddled together in the middle of the cave, muttering to each other.

"Scouts! Head outside!" Coren walked over to the Losepkees and leaned down to examine them. He felt both of their wrists for pulses.

Ayck!

Everyone in the cave jumped. Fran Losepkee sat up and screamed. Bits of dirt from her wet curly hair pitched forward. Coren fell onto Stan Losepkee's chest. Mr. Losepkee's eyes snapped open, and he raked his hands at Coren.

Fran turned to her side and shoved Coren off Mr. Losepkee. "Stan!" she shouted. "Get off your keister!" She pulled him up by his arm. "The Jersey devils are after us!"

Stan leaned forward onto his knees and held his head. "Don't yell at me! My katzenjammer is kicking my wompus!"

Fran rolled up to her feet and smacked Mr. Losepkee at the back of his head.

"Ow!" Mr. Losepkee pushed himself up. "You're killin' me, Franny!"

The two of them staggered toward the glowing sunrise at the cave's mouth. The Scouts and the five friends quietly watched them leave.

Jordana squealed and jumped back. Two round green eyes broke through the darkness at the end of the cave. Magnos pulled Jordana back and grabbed the ladder. Another pair of eyes peered out of the darkness.

Rodriqa turned and saw the chupacabras. She felt her skin tingle. Her fingers faded into her ghostly, sparkling form. "Run!" she shouted.

Coren raced toward his Scouts and shoved them toward the mouth of the cave. Aubrey shuffled into the cave. Jordana stumbled backward.

Buzz ran over to the Taser bomb and waved at the Scouts, "Get out!"

The triangular heads of two chupacabra peered at Magnos as they crawled into the chamber. Both of them growled, exposing their long sharp teeth. Drool dripped over their jaws' reptilian skin and plopped on the cave floor. They stepped forward on their hooves and spread their three-fingered hands wide.

With her neck, arms, and face now ghostly white, Rodriqa held up her hands. "Buzz! Now would be a good time for your Taser bomb!"

"Not yet!" Buzz held up his joystick. "Bring them closer!"

Magnos lifted the ladder in his right hand. "They're not going any-where." He swung it.

The two chupacabras lurched back and hissed, unfurling their bat like wings from their spiny backs.

"Separate them." Magnos jabbed the ladder at the creatures. Their heads dodged as their green eyes lobbed back and forth.

"Heyah! Heyah!" Rodriqa lunged at the left-hand chupacabra with her fists up. It snapped its jowls and shuffled toward her.

Magnos spun the ladder on its edge and slapped the chupacabra on his right in the neck. The creature grunted, and its head scuffed the muddy ground. It wagged its flap-like ears and stumbled. Magnos leapt forward and turned to his left. He braced his feet against a rock and, with the lad-der legs forward, he charged. Both chupacabras were caught in the ladder's path. They squalled as Magnos pressed them into the cave wall, pinning them against each other.

Rodriqa kicked the end of a stalagmite, and its tip broke off. She rammed the rocky point into the chest of one chupacabra. The point ran through to the other's head. Both creatures evaporated into black smoke.

"Good show." Magnos high-fived Rodriqa.

More growls echoed from the darkness of the cave. Four more pairs of large green eyes emerged into the chamber.

After escorting his scouts outside, Coren trotted back into the cave and ran over to Buzz and Aubrey. He furrowed his brow at the creatures deep in the cave. "What are those things?"

"Chupacabra," said Buzz.

"We've been tracking them all week," added Aubrey.

"Taser bomb!" shouted Rodriqa, backing up.

Two more pairs of eyes appeared on either side of the cave, pressing Magnos and Rodriqa away from the walls.

"I think we need more than a Taser." Magnos held up his hands.

"Watch out!" yelled Jordana.

Rodriqa and Magnos turned toward the mouth of the cave. Another chupacabra flapped its wings and bounded over the others, slamming down onto Magnos. Magnos fell face down. The chupacabra snapped at his head and raked the back of his shirt.

Rodriqa jumped to them. She grabbed the chupacabra's wing and spun away from it. The wing snapped off. The creature squalled. Magnos reared backward and bucked it off of him and then regained his feet.

"Buzz! Now!" hollered Rodriqa.

Buzz kicked the Taser bomb. It skidded several yards forward along the rocks. He held up his joystick and pressed its red button.

A swoosh sizzled up from under the hemispheric chassis of the Taser bomb. It popped up in the air and then fizzled. Aubrey and Coren stared at Buzz. Buzz pumped the red button with his thumb. Nothing happened.

Two chupacabras charged Rodriqa. She swung the torn wing, swatting them away. Buzz scuttled forward and dropped to his knees. He lifted the Taser bomb and examined the tangle of wires underneath its chassis. "The propellant cartridge is jammed."

"Fix it!" Jordana raised her hands to her mouth while she watched six more chupacabra emerge from the darkness of the cave.

Magnos yanked one chupacabra by the tail and flung it against three other chupacabras.

"We've gotta go," said Coren. "There's too many."

"We gotta get everybody out!" Aubrey ran up behind Buzz. "Can you fix it?"

Buzz pulled on a tiny cylinder under the lip at the hemisphere's edge. "I'm trying!"

A chupacabra bit into the wing Rodriqa was wielding and tore it in two. Another chupacabra pounced on Rodriqa, knocking her to the floor. Rodriqa punched the creature on top of her, and it yelped. The other chupacabra snapped at Rodriqa's head.

"Hurry!" Jordana trembled, glancing between Buzz and the end of the cave.

"I'm hurrying!" Buzz flipped the Taser bomb over.

Rodriqa ducked. The two chupacabras above her lurched forward and bit at her face and shoulders. Another chupacabra rushed up and clamped down on Rodriqa's foot with its teeth. Rodriqa screamed. The chupacabra pulled Rodriqa back into the darkness. Her scream was quickly muffled, and she disappeared.

Jordana screamed. "They got Rodriqa!"

Aubrey and Coren leapt forward and tripped against the other. Both landed face down in the mud.

Magnos swung his closed fists at five chupacabras bearing down on him. He knocked two to the side. One bit his elbow, and he wrenched himself free. Another chupacabra kicked its hoof against Magnos's ankle. Magnos fell to the ground.

Jordana bit her lip. A single tear streamed down her cheek. She closed her eyes and pulled her rose-tinted glasses off her face. She pressed all her fear, anger, and despair into her stomach. She felt her eyes burn. She sighed deeply and opened her eyes. Pupilless, they glowed white. Jordana marched forward.

She waved her hands and shouted at the chupacabra. The three standing over Magnos looked up at her and hissed. Suddenly their large green eyes narrowed. The creatures bowed and scuffled backward.

Magnos flipped himself over and glanced at Jordana.

"Don't look at me!"

Gaining his feet, Magnos looked away.

"Get Rodriqua!" shouted Jordana.

Jordana angled her head to the opposite side of the cave where a small horde of chupacabra were scampering toward her. As they looked at her, their eyes narrowed. They bowed and stepped back.

From the side, two chupacabras raced toward Magnos. Magnos hunkered down, bracing for the attack. Jordana turned and glared at the two chupacabras. They whimpered as they saw her eyes and scuttled back into the darkness.

Nearly twenty chupacabra now stood in straight rows at the back of the cave, eyes squinting, heads lowered.

Magnos bent down and picked up a flashlight. He searched between the legs of the chupacabras.

"I don't know how long I can keep doing this!" Jordana's head and body quavered.

"What is she doing?" asked Coren. He helped Aubrey up.

Aubrey gazed at her. "Something amazing."

"Found her!" shouted Magnos. He dove between two chupacabra, grabbed Rodriqa, and pulled her limp body into the glow of the flashlights.

"Get everybody out!" Jordana clutched her legs to steady herself.

Magnos cradled Rodriqa in his arms and ran toward the mouth of the cave. Once he reached Aubrey and Coren, he nodded at them. "Come on! Let's go! Get Buzz!"

Buzz lay on his back with the Taser bomb resting on his knees. He plucked mud out of the gears underneath it. "It's almost ready."

Aubrey and Coren followed Magnos out. All the scouts huddled around Coren's four-wheeler. Magnos rested Rodriqa's pale, gray body on the ground. Coren and Aubrey knelt beside her.

Magnos ran back inside.

"Got it!" Buzz rolled over and dropped the Taser bomb on the floor. He held up the joystick and pressed its red button.

The Taser bomb hummed. The individual fan blades behind the hundred pointy knobs mounted on the hemisphere, whirred furiously. In a massive spray of shiny metal and tiny sparks, the pointy knobs launched from the hemisphere and flew around the cave, like a colony of mechanical flies. They buzzed through the air, searching for a target.

Magnos frowned as he dodged several tiny pointy knobs that diverted when they neared him.

Magnos yanked Buzz up by the neck of his shirt. "Leave!"

Buzz hobbled out through the mouth of the cave.

Magnos looked up. Jordana was on her hands and knees, shivering, with her head facing the chupacabra.

Magnos rushed up to her and placed his hands under her shoulders. "It's me."

"I can't...I can't do this." Spittle dripped over Jordana's lips and down her chin.

"You don't have to anymore." Magnos picked her up. Jordana exhaled and passed out. The chupacabras eyes widened. A few growled. Several raised their heads, and two stumbled toward Magnos.

Magnos hurled out of the cave mouth. "Run!" Carrying Jordana in his arms, he bounded down the trail.

"Why?" Buzz held up his hands. "Didn't the Taser bomb work?"

A blinding series of blue flashes erupted from the cave. Like a lightning storm, sparks of jagged glints shot out from the cave. Moaning and grunting echoed from within.

"Ah, yeah." Buzz smiled. "It worked."

Magnos skidded to a stop and watched the lightworks display. Jordana slowly roused and squirmed out of Magnos's arms.

"Are you okay?" Magnos asked.

Jordana brushed the damp hair off her face and nodded.

"That's incredible." Coren rubbed his scalp. "How did you do that?"

Buzz turned his hands slowly in the air. "Well, it really comes down to impeding the charge escape velocity in a capacitor, which only uses a dielectric—"

"Later." Rodriqa stood up from a crouching position. "Coren, get your Scouts someplace safe." She pointed to Aubrey and Buzz. "We have a witch to take care of."

Coren nodded. Magnos stared at Rodriqa. "Driqa, aren't you hurt?"

Rodriqa shook her head. "I'm fine."

Magnos furrowed his eyebrows and looked at Aubrey. "How are you fine?"

Aubrey shrugged. "She got up shortly after Coren and I knelt down next to her."

"I'm great." Rodriqa rested her hands on her hips. "We've bested Ms. Thistlewood's army. Now it's time for us to dethrone the general."

"I agree." Buzz pumped his fist.

"Sounds good to me," replied Magnos.

Jordana nodded and placed her glasses on her nose. "I'm ready."

Aubrey nodded and smiled. He winced at a bright light that shone in the corner of his eye. He held up his hand as the rising morning sun peeked over the top of the mountain. Suddenly, he remembered something he had forgotten. A trick he had tried before, and it had worked. "Wait," said Aubrey. "There's another stop I need to make first."

Hoodie up and sunglasses low, Mena Kontrearo walked up to the visitor's entrance of the Lake Julian Dam. The sunlight from behind her reflected off the bleached sandstone walls and steel-trimmed glass doors. Mena squinted and held her head down.

Wearing a security guard uniform, Charlie Buckswaine stood with crossed arms in front of the doors, watching tourists mill about the courtyard. Mena attempted to walk through the door next to him. Charlie held out his hand and redirected her to the door to his right. "Tourists can only enter the visitor's gallery through the security scanner."

Mena slid her hoodie down. The flattened ponytail on the side of her head sprung out. She peered through the glass door. "Since when did the dam have a security scanner?"

"Since now."

"But I'm not a tourist. I'm a journalist." Mena flashed Charlie her *Lake Julian Mountain Lyre* press badge.

Charlie scowled. "Perhaps you should go through the scanner twice."

Mena huffed and murmured quietly as she walked through the door. She emptied her pockets and dropped a set of keys, a small wallet, and her purple Spooly Pen into a plastic bowl, which she then placed on the scanner's conveyor belt. Once she passed through the metal detector, she gathered her things and searched the gallery.

Throughout the long room, several security guards were stationed at regular points. Mena saw her brother behind the security desk and walked toward him.

Jaime glanced up from the monitor, which depicted camera displays from various corners in the dam. "What are you doing here?"

"Did you hear about what happened?"

"Of course. Everyone is talking about it." Jaime looked up and down the visitor's gallery. "Why do you think there are so many guards on post? They're searching for those brats."

Mena shook her head. "I think Aubrey and his friends might be onto something." Jaime cocked up an eyebrow. Mena hopped up and landed with her torso on the countertop.

"*Chiquita*! Stop!" Jaime reached for her shoulder.

Mena batted his hands away. "Let me show you something, *tarado*." She unsheathed her Spooly Pen and shoved its USB port into the back of the monitor. She tapped on the keyboard's return key. "Look at these." She looked over the top of the monitor. "They're pictures from the explosion at the Rock-U-Quarium."

"Good for you." Jamie scrunched his forehead, seeing the images of dust and rubble flash across the screen. "You finally got your story. Now leave me alone."

"No! Look!" Mena magnified the lower right-hand corner of the screen. The five friends fleeing from the broken front doors pixelated into view.

"Finally." Jaime scoffed. "Now there's no doubt they're full of it."

"No." Mena enlarged the screen in the next picture. "Look at Rodriqa."

Jaime leaned toward the screen and squinted his eyes. "So what? It looks like there's a glare from your flash."

Mena shook her head. "It was dark."

Jaime shrugged. "It's probably just a smudge on your lens."

Mena pulled herself toward his face. "No, *tonto*! That's how she looked in real life too. Like a ghost. Like a living, breathing, running specter."

"Whatever." Jaime pulled the Spooly Pen out of the USB port and handed it to Mena.

Mena grabbed her pen and recapped it. "I need to know where they are. I need to talk to them."

Jaime rolled his eyes. "I'm sure the police already have them in custody."

"Then why are they still looking for them all over town?" Mena dropped from the counter onto the floor. "I've been listening to the police scanners all night. Even their parents don't know where they are." She scratched her scalp under her ponytail. "I need your help. I need to find out what's going on before the police find them. I could win a Pulitzer for this kind of story."

"You can't be serious." Jaime sighed. "You need to stay out of it and let the police do their job."

Mena scowled at him and lifted her hoodie over her head. "I'll find them without your help then. And I'm telling Mom about how you stole her and dad's tickets to the Rock-U-Quarium last week." She stormed away from the counter.

Jaime stood up from his chair. "Mena, come back here."

Mena stopped and leaned back. Jaime waved her toward him. She tip-toed backward.

Jaime lowered his voice. "The police have spoken with each of the parents, but the one most likely to help you is staying near the lake."

"Arvel Reiselstein?" asked Mena.

Jaime nodded. "He's staying along the east shore close to the southern-most parking area."

"I'll make sure to include you in my acceptance speech at the Pulitzer Award banquet." Mena trotted toward the front doors.

Jaime rolled his eyes.

Rubbing his stubbly jaw, Arvel Reiselstein sat on his cooler in the Mole-Pole tent. His eyebrows balled together, and he flattened his lips. The Superterrestrial Solar Panel and ESAU lay in the corner of the tent. The remote controls and smaller plastic satellite dish of ESAU rested against the crumpled panels of the solar panel. There was an item missing, but Mr. Reiselstein couldn't figure out what it was. He sighed and crossed his legs.

Mr. Reiselstein bit his lip, intently concerned about his son's recent behavior. *How could Buzz be so reckless?* he thought to himself. *Buzz was, at times, impulsive, but always in an energetic way. He had never been destructive, at least not directly, and Buzz had always been so well-intentioned.*

Suddenly, a side section in the underbelly of the solar panel dropped open, exposing its wiring.

Mr. Reiselstein tilted his head. "Wait a sec." He leaned down to the solar panel and picked up ESAU. He pulled an all-purpose knife from his back pocket and spliced together several wires on both contraptions.

"Mr. Reiselstein? Can I ask you a question?" The sweet sing-songy tone drifted from outside.

Mr. Reiselstein glanced at the tent's flap. "I've already spoken to the police three times this morning. I'm not answering anymore questions right now."

A shadow was cast on the grass outside the flap. There was no reply. Shoes scuffed against the ground.

Mr. Reiselstein rubbed the back of his neck. "I'm not trying to be difficult. I'm just worried about my son." He looked at his watch and then glanced back at the ground outside the flap, where the shadow hovered. "Have a good day." Mr. Reiselstein turned back to the solar panel.

"I'm concerned about your son as well."

Mr. Reiselstein dropped his knife and shook his head. "As concerned as I am?"

A cloud passed overhead. The shadow faded.

Mr. Reiselstein sighed. "Didn't think so."

The flap slid back. "Buzz has always been special to me." Magnolia Thistlewood knelt down into the tent. Her short, knit skirt crumpled up her thighs. She rested her hands on her lap and leaned forward, her bright red hair rolling down her shoulders. "How could anyone not realize how unique he is?"

Mr. Reiselsteingazed at her pale green eyes. "Thank you."

Ms. Thistlewood grinned. "For what?"

Mr. Reiselstein swallowed. "For your kindness."

Ms. Thistlewood nodded. "That's why I'm here." She scooted forward on her knees. "Not to harass you for answers, which you do not have." She bent forward and slid onto the cooler. "But simply to offer your talented son my assistance."

"Are you a lawyer?" Mr. Reiselstein chuckled darkly.

"I'm better than that."

Mr. Reiselstein wrinkled his nose. "What?"

"I can rescue your son and his friends from their fate."

"I don't understand."

"You don't need to. All I need to know is where they are."

Mr. Reiselstein's head dropped. "I wish I knew. None of his friends' parents know where he is. Thought he would return to the Screever's Lair, but the police searched there this morning."

"Now, you must think." Ms. Thistlewood clasped her hands together. "You must try harder if you want me to help your son."

Mr. Reiselstein looked down. "I don't know."

Ms. Thistlewood angled her head. "Is there really nowhere else you think he could be?"

Mr. Reiselstein raised his hands. "Not anywhere the police haven't already looked."

"I see." Ms. Thistlewood gazed at her hands in her lap. "Then perhaps you need more incentive."

"What do you mean?"

Ms. Thistlewood stood up. She held out her left arm and turned the brown sandstone phylactery on her right wrist.

Mr. Reiselstein watched her, intrigued by the woman's odd behavior. A rumbling motor reverberated from outside. The ground trembled. A diesel roar quickly crescendoed.

Suddenly, the side of tent collapsed and swung toward Ms. Thistlewood, knocking her down. The Mole-Pole tent was drug to the ground. The engine outside stalled and then puttered out.

Arms and legs flailing, Mr. Reiselstein and Ms. Thistlewood swam in flaps of canvas.

The door to the Losepkee's RV slammed shut.

"Frannie! Look what you did!" Stan Losepkee marched around the front of the RV and pointed at the downed Mole-Pole tent. "You killed our neighbors!"

Mr. Reiselstein's head popped out from under the tent. "No harm done!"

Running over, Coren Belward leaned down and grabbed Mr. Reiselstein's hands. "I've got ya, sir." He pulled Mr. Reiselstein out from under the canvas.

Fran Losepkee opened the door to the RV. "Get back in here and get us home!"

Stan trotted back into the RV and shut the door. The camper's engine sputtered, and the Losepkees drove away.

Mr. Reiselstein pushed himself to his knees and brushed off his hands. He looked up at Coren and saluted him with three fingers. "Thank you, sir scout."

Coren Belward saluted him back. "Are you okay?"

Mr. Reiselstein nodded. "Yep, but I'm not so sure about my company." He looked back over the downed tent. The canvas didn't move.

Coren stepped lightly onto the tent, searching wrinkles in the material and pressing down with his feet for lumps. A few strands of bright red hair caught his eye. Coren bounded over and peeled back the flap.

Ms. Thistlewood lay on the ground with her face down, her arms limp at her sides.

"Ma'am? Are you okay?" Coren dropped to his knees and shook her shoulder. Sparks jolted between Coren's hands and Ms. Thistlewood's upper arm. Shocked, Coren fell backward.

Ms. Thistlewood turned her head and snarled at Coren. She scrambled away from him and rolled off the tent. Sitting up, she straightened her shirt. "I'm fine."

Mr. Reiselstein walked toward her. "Are you sure?"

Ms. Thistlewood rolled forward and stood up. "Yes." She tugged her skirt down and marched away.

With widened eyes, Coren looked at his hands. Lifting up his head, he watched Ms. Thistlewood leaving. Coren chased after her.

"Excuse me, ma'am."

"I said I'm fine." Ms. Thistlewood quickened her pace.

Coren trotted next to her. "I apologize for eavesdropping, but are you really trying to help out Buzz and his friends?"

Suddenly, Ms. Thistlewood stopped. She glared at Coren, examining him from his head to his feet. Slowly, her lips softened, and she smiled. "Most assuredly. Finding them and saving them from the horrors they might face is my only concern."

Coren rubbed his bulbous larynx. "Then I might be able to help you."

She reached out to touch his arm, then stopped short and smiled wider. "It would mean the world to me."

"I was with them this morning."

"Really? Where?"

"It's not important." Coren looked around for anyone who might be listening. "But before we separated, they mentioned where they were headed."

"Tell me." Ms. Thistlewood's smile flattened. "Tell me now."

Coren leaned in toward her. "Do you know a Mr. Jennings?"

⚜

Mena Kontrearo's lopsided ponytail peeked over the top of a tent in the scout camp several yards away from Coren and Ms. Thistlewood. She grinned and snapped a picture with her Spooly Pen. "Mr. Jennings," she murmured to herself. "I should have known that *viejo pedorro* was in on all this."

"Whatchya doin'?" whispered a voice next to Mena.

Mena jumped sideways and covered her pen with her hands. She looked at the short, plump, brown-freckled boy dressed in his tan and green scout uniform, standing next to her.

Mena cleared her throat and scratched her scalp under her ponytail. "I'm a journalist. I'm covering a story."

"Really?" The young scout's eyes widened. "Then I've got a story for you."

Rodriqa yawned. Her eyes burned as she looked up at the sun, glowing in the summit of the sky. She dropped her head. Crouching in a muddy ditch along the Asheville Highway, Rodriqa rubbed her face. "I'm so tired."

Jordana smacked her lips and wiped their corners. "I feel like there's a skunk sitting in my mouth."

Magnos slapped himself in the face. "I thought the fugitive's adrenaline rush would keep us awake."

"Adrenaline ran out a long time ago," murmured Aubrey.

Jordana squatted above the grass behind the ditch. "There's no way we can beat Ms. Thistlewood like this."

Aubrey looked up and down the road. "I think we'll know a lot more once I get Solluna back in the sunlight."

"We better." Rodriqa held her sides. "I'm gonna be upset if we just slinked across Lake Julian, dodging police and tourists for nothin'."

With his chunky flab bouncing as he raced across Asheville Highway, Buzz slid into the ditch next to them. "Mr. Jennings's parking lot is empty." He held up his hands. "There are no cars along the street. Let's go!"

Aubrey nodded and jumped forward. Jordana leaned up and teetered out of the ditch. Rodriqa stretched upward, arching her back. The friends hurried across the road and rounded the corner of Mr. Jennings's Smart Mart & Finer Diner.

Aubrey pulled out his key to the store. The other four huddled around him and watched for traffic. Aubrey slid the key into the lock, and the door opened. Aubrey pushed away from the door, closing it. "It's unlocked."

"Of course, it is." Buzz turned around and grabbed the handle. "You unlocked it."

Aubrey shook his head. "No, I didn't. I never turned the key."

Jordana peered through the glass door. "Do you think Shway Shway got out?"

Rodriqa jerked open the door. "Just get inside." She pushed everyone in.

An electronic chime dinged overhead.

Instantly, they stopped. The door closed behind them.

"Good morning!" Mr. Jennings stood up from behind the wooden counter. He pressed several buttons on the cash register, and glanced at his watch. "Excuse me. Good afternoon."

The friends stared at Mr. Jennings. Rodriqa shoved Aubrey. He stumbled forward. Mr. Jennings grinned at him.

Aubrey glanced up at the shelves. Although mostly bare, several rows of metal racks had been filled with candy bars, chips, and other new merchandise. Aubrey glanced between the shelving and the counter. "You—you're back."

"Seems so." Mr. Jennings lifted his royal blue ball cap and brushed a few sprigs of gray hair underneath it. "Haven't you heard? State of the Mart is out of business. Some sort of explosion nearly destroyed the place. I can reopen the store. I've already had five customers this morning."

"No, I mean…" Aubrey swallowed the rising lump in his throat. "You're back. You're out of the hospital."

Mr. Jennings drummed his chest with his fist. "Fit as always."

With his arms wrapped around his belly, Buzz rushed forward to the rack of candy bars. "Food!" He pulled the wrappers off two chocolate bars and shoved them both in his mouth. "Can I pay you back, Mr. Jennings? I'm so hungry. I feel like I haven't eaten in years." Flecks of moist nougat and chewy marshmallow sprayed out of Buzz's mouth.

Rodriqa and Jordana scrunched up their cheeks and looked away.

Mr. Jennings chuckled. "Have all you want. I'll put it on your tab."

Magnos smiled and stretched his hand out, stepping up next to Buzz. "Can I?"

Mr. Jennings nodded. "Help your self."

Magnos ripped open a wrapper and jammed it in his mouth. He chomped twice and swallowed it.

Buzz scooped an armful of candy bars and handed them out to Aubrey, Rodriqa, and Jordana. Everyone took a moment to eat.

Aubrey stepped toward the counter. Mr. Jennings appeared well. He was no longer pale gray, still wrinkly, but his color had returned. "What did the doctors say?"

Mr. Jennings snorted. "Lots of fancy words, but not a bit of it makes any sense."

"Didn't they give you a diagnosis or any medicine?"

"Not really." Mr. Jennings shrugged. "They kept using some funny word over and over again. I think they just made it up."

Aubrey squinted. "What word?"

Mr. Jennings frowned. "*Twirp*? No. *Teeper*? That wasn't it."

"Twitter?" asked Jordana.

Mr. Jennings shook his head. "It was more like *tordor*."

Buzz stepped forward and stopped chewing. "Torpor?"

Mr. Jennings raised his finger to his nose. "That's it."

Buzz rubbed his chin and tossed eight candy wrappers in the garbage bin.

Mr. Jennings closed the register. "I have to say, I really appreciate all you've done."

Aubrey's eyebrows bunched together. "What?"

"Looking after the store and all while I was sick."

Aubrey's heart pounded. "Have you been to the basement yet?"

"Haven't had time. Was about to head down there now."

Aubrey held up his hands. "Don't…"

Rodriqa nudged Aubrey in the ribs. "Aubrey left something down there." Rodriqa glanced at Aubrey sternly. "Would it be okay if we went and got it?"

Mr. Jennings tilted his head to the side. "Make yourself at home."

Buzz stumbled at the bottom of the stairs in the basement of Mr. Jennings's Smart Mart & Finer Diner. "Mr. Jennings was ranched!"

"How do you know?" Rodriqa held her nose and stepped onto the shaggy carpet.

"Torpor." Buzz held up his finger. "It's like hibernation, but humans don't hibernate. Leaving only one explanation. Something drew the life out of him."

Magnos walked toward the freezer. "Chupacabra?"

Buzz nodded. "Exactly."

Jordana stayed atop the bottom step. "But how did he get better?"

Buzz shrugged. "Maybe he healed with time. Just like any other illness."

"That leaves a question." Aubrey trotted over to the poker table and picked up Mr. Jennings's crucible. Tipping the pyramid of Solluna attached to the bottle's opening, Aubrey aimed its precipice at the window in the freezer door. "Is Shway Shway a chupacabra?" The creature's round green eye rolled in the window.

Magnos stepped in front of the window. "He looks more like a rat than a chupacabra."

Shway Shway growled and stepped back. "Seer! Seer! You must keep your promise." The creature inhaled as he spoke.

"He's right," said Aubrey. "We have to let him out now."

Buzz nodded. "Mr. Jennings might stroke if he sees him."

Rodriqa walked up behind Magnos and looked through the window. "He'll probably stroke after he sees his freezer."

"But how do we get Shway Shway out?" asked Jordana.

"And where do we put him?" added Rodriqa.

Magnos walked over to the corner. "I have an idea."

Jordana, Buzz, and Aubrey raced up from the basement. Buzz looked around and then stood in front of the glass front doors. "All clear."

Aubrey and Jordana peered down the stairs. Leaning forward, Rodriqa slowly backed up the stairs. She clutched a shivering wooden chest that Magnos carried a few steps behind her. Topping the stairs, Magnos and Rodriqa scuttled through the front part of the store. The chest shook, and a hiss echoed from within. Buzz opened the front door. The electronic chime dinged. Magnos, Rodriqa, and Buzz rushed outside. Aubrey and Jordana followed after them.

"Aubrey? What is that?" asked Mr. Jennings from the frozen-aisle section.

Jordana ran outside and held the door open for Aubrey. She waved him out.

"Ummm." Holding the crucible and Solluna behind his back, Aubrey looked back and forth between Jordana and Mr. Jennings. "I'll explain everything later, I promise. I'm really sorry about your freezer downstairs. I'll clean it up. I'm glad you're feeling better." Aubrey ran outside.

Magnos and Rodriqa scurried around the corner with the wobbling chest between them. Buzz, Jordana, and Aubrey chased after them. At the back of the corner store, next to a brown dumpster, Magnos and Rodriqa placed the chest on the gravel. The chest bounced and shimmied.

Rodriqa squatted down and gripped the iron lock on the chest. "This isn't gonna hold long."

"Maybe we won't need it to." Aubrey was holding the crucible capped with Solluna above his head. The bottle's figures and Circle of Circles emblems twinkled in the sunlight. Slowly, the smoky dark inner portion of the pyramid faded. Solluna returned to its crystal clear appearance.

"Whoa," said Buzz.

"What's it doing?" asked Jordana.

"I'm afraid we're about to find out." Rodriqa stood up.

Cursive letters scrawled across each of the four faces of the pyramid. Aubrey turned the crucible to reveal each face. The etchings read, "To open the sealed."

"What does that mean?" mumbled Buzz.

Aubrey shook his head. He smiled, marveling at the beauty of the crucible and Solluna in the open daylight.

"Look." Magnos pointed at the parking lot. Spots of light glowed on the gravel as rays of sun passed through the glass pyramid and shone on the ground. The areas of light expanded, and the entire back wall of the corner store glowed.

"What's happening?" Jordana stepped backward, but the air was thick as mud.

"I can't move!" Rodriqa jerked her leg, trying to lift her foot.

The light flashed blinding white. The five friends dissolved within the brightness. The light faded. Solluna and the crucible dropped to the gravel. Except for the chest and the dumpster, the parking lot was empty.

ONE ARABIAN NIGHT

Thud! Thud-dud-dud! Thud! The sounds of bodies landing ricocheted off slick walls in total darkness.

"Ow!"

"Why is it so dark?"

"What the..."

"Who's sitting on me?"

"What happened?"

Grunts and groans sputtered and spewed from the heap of teenagers.

"I'm blind!" shouted Buzz.

"I think it's just dark," said Magnos.

"How can you be sure?"

"I don't know," mumbled Magnos. "Can anyone else see?"

An array of nettling no's echoed from each of the friends.

"See," said Magnos. "It's dark."

"What if we're all blind?" questioned Buzz.

"Is there hay on the floor?" asked Aubrey.

"Get your hand out of my hair," squealed Rodriqa.

"Where are we?" Jordana asked.

"I think we're in the lamp," said Aubrey.

"You mean the bottle," corrected Rodriqa.

"The crucible," said Jordana.

"Yeah, that," murmured Aubrey.

"How did we get in here?" asked Magnos.

"Solluna," replied Aubrey. "'To open the sealed.' The sun pulled us into the lamp through Solluna."

"That's not possible," said Rodriqa.

"Are we really gonna argue about what's not possible right now?" grumbled Aubrey.

"Does anyone have a flashlight?" asked Jordana.

From the floor, a dull, orange glow slowly encircled the edges of a round room revealing a black curving wall along the outer edge. Climbing over each other, the five friends watched the racing gleam as it traced a perfect circle a hundred feet in diameter around them.

Aubrey looked up. He could see a small round hole in the ceiling several stories above them.

"I told you, you weren't blind." Magnos lifted Buzz's rump off Jordana's ankle.

"I think we *are* in the bottle." Buzz surveyed the room and watched the light burn brighter.

"Great!" Rodriqa brushed her beaded hair in place with her fingers. "Now how do we get out?"

"I don't see an exit." Jordana looked up at the rounded ceiling. The bright light slid around the floor, tracing circles toward them.

Magnos pounded his fist against the floor. "Sounds pretty solid."

"I think I know where we are," whispered Buzz.

"Where?" asked Jordana, Rodriqa, and Magnos simultaneously.

"We're in a genie's lamp," replied Buzz.

Jordana and Rodriqa looked at each other and shook their heads. The bright light on the floor raced past Magnos, singeing his shoe.

"Seriously," insisted Buzz.

"What do you mean?" Magnos stood up with his arms close to his sides.

"*Genie* is derived from *djinn*, an Arabic term meaning hidden. This bottle has the Circle of Circles emblem on it, which means something at some point was trying to keep whatever is in here hidden for good."

"Uh-oh." Aubrey sidled up close to Magnos. "Look at the light."

Buzz, Jordana, and Rodriqa stood and watched it squiggle more closely to them.

"Buzz might be right." Aubrey traced where the light had traveled. "It's making a Circle of Circles on the floor."

Rodriqa held up a foot and the light burned underneath her. "And it looks like it's almost done."

Suddenly, the light fizzled into darkness. Small panels of the floor dropped out of sight, revealing a dull blue light below.

A small curved section fell out of the floor next to Aubrey. He scooted sideways and peered down the hole. He scrunched up his face at the clear blue liquid below. "It looks like water."

A section under Buzz dropped. Buzz fell through the floor. Magnos reached for him, but Buzz slipped away too quickly. Buzz fell for several seconds and then a splash echoed distantly. Buzz disappeared into the blue liquid below.

"Buzz!" shouted Rodriqa and Aubrey. They steadied themselves over the holes and gazed down.

More portions of the floor fell. Two sections dropped, and Magnos and Jordana fell.

Rodriqa reached for Aubrey. "Grab my hand!"

Aubrey raised his arm but missed Rodriqa. She dropped with part of the floor beneath her. Aubrey watched his four friends fade into the mired blue far below. He reached down and gripped the edge under him. A small section of floor behind him dropped. Aubrey scuttled his feet forward, but he couldn't gain enough friction. His feet slipped backward. Aubrey swung below the broken floor, his hands wrapped around a section above his head.

Aubrey could feel his fingers sting as the muscles in each digit tightened, squeezing the blood out of them. Warm moist air floated upward around him. He rotated his hands forward to gain a better grip. His fingers stiffened. His hands slid off the edge.

Aubrey fell. Each moment stretched into an age. He lost his breath as his stomach winced at his quickening descent. The undulating blueness beneath sloshed toward him.

He splashed into the waves. He could taste the hot, briny water fill his mouth and sting the inside of his nose. He forced open his eyes. Bubbles swarmed around him. Aubrey flailed to swim, grasping for the air above, but the current was too strong. Aubrey fell through the water. He struggled to hold his breath against his diaphragm, which cinched to draw in air. Suddenly, his feet lightened. His legs kicked easily. His torso was free. A breeze dried his face. He gasped violently and then fell another twenty feet through the air. He splashed again into a tumbling pool of water.

Magnos reached out and grabbed Aubrey by the shoulder. Magnos pulled him to the water's surface and drug him to a round, pumice-like pedestal, where Magnos and the others clung. A bright light shone from the top of the pedestal, illuminating the churning waters above and below.

"Is he okay?" Rodriqa wiped her face.

"I'm okay." Aubrey spit out his words along with some water.

Jordana parted her wet hair from her face. "Where are we?"

"Look!" Buzz bobbed up and down as he pointed to the water above them. "It's raining both ways!"

Rodriqa looked around. She noticed droplets falling up and down.

"Water above and water below," shouted Buzz. "Just like the second day of the Torah."

"Weird." Aubrey leaned upward onto the edge of the pedestal. A white light glowed from its middle. However, just above the light, several thin metal bars and two semicircles lay in disarray. Open clips were attached to its edges.

Aubrey tilted his head and gazed into the light. "Hey! This looks familiar!"

Buzz pushed his head atop the pedestal. "Just looks like a broken grate for the light to me."

"No! It's more." Aubrey tugged at Magnos. "Push me up."

Magnos thrust Aubrey up by his rear. Aubrey gained his feet, steadying himself on opposite sides of the pedestal's edge. His drenched clothes dribbled water onto the light. He wiped his face and leaned over the metal pieces.

"What are you doing?" asked Rodriqa.

"Shway Shway showed me this." Aubrey reached down and dragged one of the metal bars into a different position. "It's not just a random pattern. It's the Clockmaker's Mark."

His four friends pulled themselves up and watched the pattern emerge as Aubrey shifted more of the thin metal.

"Whoa," Buzz murmured when the final piece was relocated. The pedestal shook, and the light brightened. Aubrey covered his face and toppled backward into the water. Jordana slipped off the edge of the pedestal. Aubrey resurfaced and slapped his hands on top of the swirling water.

Rodriqa's fingers slipped down the pedestal's rocky side. "What's happening?!"

"The water's dropping!" Buzz swam toward the pedestal, but the current pulled him away.

Quickly, the pedestal rose above them as the water level fell. The pressure dragged Aubrey, Rodriqa, and Jordana in circles. Magnos hugged the pedestal. Like a whirlpool, the water coned inward. Buzz and Aubrey dropped under the water.

"Aubrey?" Mr. Jennings rounded the corner of his store toward the back gravel lot. "Aubrey!" He dropped his head, and the bill of his royal blue ball cap shielded his eyes from the afternoon sun.

Mr. Jennings's eyes widened. A wooden chest hopped across the gravel. He noticed the crucible, attached to the crystal pyramid, lying on its side. Mr. Jennings shuffled over and picked up his wife's lamp.

The chest cracked. Mr. Jennings scuttled backward. The chest scooted sideways in the gravel. Three scaly fingers slid out of a ragged hole in the wood.

Mr. Jennings jumped back and hurried around the corner, back into his store. Once inside, the electronic chime dinged overhead. Rushing behind the counter, he placed Solluna and the crucible next to the register and picked up his rotary phone.

Mr. Jennings dialed. A feminine voiced answered. He cut her off. "Mr. Poschyev, please."

"I'll connect you to his extension."

"Hallo."

"Simon?" asked Mr. Jennings.

"Yes," replied the animal control officer in his Slovakian accent

"This is Ray Gene Jennings, down off Dalton Circle. I've got something you need to see."

"What do you have?"

"There's some sort of reptile in a chest behind my store. It's locked up, but it'll be out any minute now."

Mr. Poschyev dropped his phone. Scrambling noises shuffled across the receiver. "I'll be there right away."

Mr. Jennings hung up the phone. The electronic chime dinged overhead again. He turned around. The door was closed, and he couldn't see anyone near the front. Mr. Jennings furrowed his brow and looked around.

"May I ask you a question?" Ms. Thistlewood stood next to him behind the counter with her pale hand gripping the neck of Mr. Jennings's lamp.

"Oh!" Mr. Jennings jumped to the side and knocked his phone off its ringer. "Uh, where did you come from?"

Ms. Thistlewood smiled. "I apologize. Sometimes subtlety eludes me."

Mr. Jennings nodded. Reaching down and replacing the phone, he straightened up and pointed a finger at her. "Do I know you?"

"Not really." Ms. Thistlewood narrowed her eyes. She nodded toward the crucible. "Aubrey left this here. He sent me to fetch it."

Mr. Jennings glanced between her and his lamp. "Where is Aubrey?"

"He's busy at the moment. Another ghost to chase."

Mr. Jennings twisted his lips. "But this belongs to my wife."

Ms. Thistlewood scowled. "Are you sure she wants it?"

"Not—not really." Mr. Jennings chuckled. He pointed to the crystal pyramid connected to the top. "What's that?"

"A toy." Ms. Thistlewood flattened her lips. "I'll pay you for it."

Mr. Jennings waved her off. "Don't bother. If Aubrey needs it, then give it to him."

"Very wise." She clutched the crucible to her chest, turned, and walked outside, the click of her high heels tapping as she exited. She traipsed across the gravel, and her shoes slowly melted into the dirt. Barefooted, Ms. Thistlewood turned up the highway and glanced back at the corner store. The wooden chest in the back parking lot lay in shattered pieces along the gravel. The creature it had contained was gone.

Hisss!

Ms. Thistlewood turned toward the road. Whimperfidget, with his matted cream-and-charcoal-colored, fur twisted, hunched his back, and raked the asphalt, glaring at her with his red eyes.

Ms. Thistlewood smiled and stepped forward. "There's my precious little one." She leaned down to pet him. "No worries. Your job is done."

Whimperfidget bit at her fingers.

Ms. Thistlewood retracted her hand and scowled. "Bad kitty." Whimperfidget hissed again. She raised her hand over him and spread wide her fingers. The asphalt underneath the cat reached up around him and solidified, forming a cage of craggy pitch.

Whimperfidget squalled and batted at the cage with his claws.

"Time to go home." Ms. Thistlewood grabbed the top of the cage and walked away.

Magnolia Thistlewood carried the caged Whimperfidget and Mr. Jennings's crucible, coupled with Solluna, up the double spiral staircase in her tree house. Whimperfidget growled and swiped his claws at the edges of his bituminous entrapment.

Ms. Thistlewood stepped onto the top level. She marched to the arched window and sat Whimperfidget next to the fundamentium hearth as she passed by the fireplace.

Tracing her fingers along the words "To open the sealed" etched in the faces of the clear pyramid, the red-haired woman giggled at the tingle of the crystal. She knew what Solluna had done in the sun, and she was excited to see what would happen under the moon.

"Is that what that golden book used to be?" Holding his belly, Ned Kluggard hobbled up the last few stairs and peered around the railings.

Magnolia Thistlewood smiled. "Beautiful, isn't it?" She took a step back and marveled at the orange glow of sunset glinting off the multicolored lamp and its transparent adornment. "It was once a bonded gift between two friends. It's incredible how it retains its ability to serve two masters."

Ned sneered. "But why is it stuck in that lamp?" The lanky Fred wandered up behind Ned, nodding at the question.

"Because that's where our Magi and the seer are trapped." Matsinstrus walked up behind the Kluggards, a yellow haze wheezing from his charred skeletal chest.

"What?" Ned jerked his head between Matsinstrus and Ms. Thistlewood. "Both of them?"

Matsinstrus nodded as he walked past Ned and Fred. "Yes. And all due to the greatness of our majestic queen." Matsinstrus kneeled to the side of Ms. Thistlewood and leaned his skull to her fingers.

"Not yet." Ms. Thistlewood's lips creased with a faint smile. "Not until the moonlight fills Solluna."

"When will that be?" asked Ned.

Ms. Thistlewood faced Ned and Fred. She raised her hand toward Solluna. The letters etched in its face were fading. A gray film hovered inside it.

"Soon." Ms. Thistlewood looked down at Matsinstrus. "Which means our army will have no resistance, our plans will advance as expected, and the world will see my might." She stepped back and sat in her rocking chair. "Tonight, Lake Julian. Tomorrow, the universe."

"I'm so excited, I'm starved!" Ned danced a jig forward.

Ms. Thistlewood held up her hand. "Celebrate later." She glared at Matsinstrus. "Prepare the keepers in the gorge below the dam. Make sure they are ready to devastate everything they touch. Take the Kluggards with you. My growing army may be more than one person can control."

"What about the keepers in the caves?" asked Matsinstrus.

Ms. Thistlewood thought for a moment. "Let them rest for the next battle."

"Yes, my queen." Matsinstrus stood up and waved the Kluggards away. They turned and shuffled down the stairs. Matsinstrus followed.

Ms. Thistlewood gazed out the window. The sun had faded below the tree-topped skyline, and the first bright stars of evening pierced dusk's navy-blue veil. Within the hour, all her obstacles would be contained. Within a day, she would prove to Azrynon her strength. She cheerfully mused at what was possible within a year. The vision of a repentant Clockmaker, in despair from defeat, filled her heart with hubris-rich joy.

Yet she knew she would need Solluna to complete her plans. And now Solluna was trapped containing her enemies. At some point, she would need to remove Solluna from the crucible and defeat those inside. But only if she had someone she could trust. Someone strong enough to complete the task.

Ms. Thistlewood turned and called down the stairs. "Icharida? Icharida! How are you feeling?" She angled her head and listened for a reply. Everything was quiet.

She stepped over to the top of the double staircase and leaned down. "Icharida! Come up here! I want to show you something!"

The closet door downstairs clicked open. Ms. Thistlewood smiled. She straightened her shoulders and watched her new apprentice emerge.

The charred skeleton of Icharida plodded forward, her bony feet slapping against the wood. A yellow haze seeped from between her ribs and out of her nose. Her skull slumped forward, staring at the steps. Slowly shifting her pelvis forward, her legs craned up one step at a time in a lumbering jerk.

Once Icharida was only a few steps out of reach, Ms. Thistlewood grabbed her by her wrist and pulled her up to the floor. Ms. Thistlewood hovered inches from her skeletal face, peering at every detail. "How do you feel?"

Icharida cleared her throat. "So tired…and so strong."

"Good." Ms. Thistlewood grinned. "Very good. The polarity of power you feel will grow and give you a reserve of rage, which will allow you to do unimaginable things."

Icharida nodded. "I want to sleep."

"Fight it." Ms. Thistlewood held her palm up and intertwined Icahrdia's bony fingers with her own fleshy hand. "Let me give you your first lesson."

"What?" A yellow light glowed in Icharida's eye sockets.

"The first divinoi you need to obtain all the others. Ranching." Ms. Thistlewood closed her eyes and inhaled deeply. "When you can ranch, you can take whatever you want from whomever you want, except a healer." Ms. Thistlewood clenched Icharida's hand. "Never touch a healer."

Icharida winced. "Okay."

The skin, muscle, and blood from Ms. Thistlewood's fingers retreated. A green glow gleamed from the remaining charred bones.

Icharida gasped. Yellow smoke poured from her jaw. The glow in her eye sockets brightened.

"This is my second gift." Ms. Thistlewood grinned.

Aubrey's eyes burned. He squinted them open and held up his hand. A sliver of white light split the darkness several yards away from him.

He grunted. His body ached. Looking down, Aubrey noticed he lay face down on gravel. Rubbing the dirt off his cheek, he glanced around. His four friends were quiet and still next to him on the gravel.

The bright light in front of Aubrey widened. He pressed himself onto his knees and scooted over to Buzz. Aubrey shook Buzz's leg. Buzz's head snapped up.

He stared at Aubrey.

"Are you okay?"

Buzz looked over his belly at his feet and nodded. He rolled toward the light and covered his face with his hand. "How long was I out?"

"I'm not sure." Aubrey kneeled forward, but the gravel pricked his skin. He reached for Jordana and jostled her foot. "Are you hurt?"

Jordana turned her head. Her rose-tinted glasses were next to her. She lifted them from the gravel and rested them on her nose. "Are we still in the crucible?"

"I think so." Buzz gazed at the light through his fingers.

Rodriqa rubbed her forehead and she sat up. Magnos rolled over and popped his neck.

The white light brightened again and widened into the rectangular shape of a door.

"What is that?" Buzz stood up and squinted at the light.

Jordana covered her eyes. "It hurts."

Magnos stood and walked over to Buzz. Magnos pointed at the ground. "Look at that."

Buzz glanced down. A patch of gravel at their feet was tumbling along the ground toward the light. "Crazy," Buzz murmured. He kicked the ground. Several small rocks skidded ahead and disappeared into the light.

Jordana pushed herself up on her elbows. "What's going on?"

Magnos rocked back and looked around. "All the gravel is moving."

Buzz stepped forward and held out his hand, trying to feel the light. "It's not just the gravel."

"What do you mean?" Rodriqa jumped up beside Magnos and stepped on her tiptoes, avoiding the moving gravel.

"It's gravity. The light has gravity." Buzz pressed both feet against the ground and locked his knees, but he continued to slide forward.

"I don't think getting too close to that light is a good idea." Aubrey stood up and offered a hand to Jordana. Jordana grabbed his arm, and he pulled her clumsily to her feet.

Buzz lurched forward. He turned and stepped away. His foot slipped out from underneath him. Buzz dropped forward. "Too late!" Quickly, he skimmed along the gravel and disappeared into the rectangular light.

"Buzz!" Magnos and Rodriqa leapt forward and reached for Buzz, but he was already gone.

Magnos spun and reached for Rodriqa. They both fell and disappeared.

"Mag!" Jordana ran after him.

Aubrey stepped forward and reached for Jordana. She got too close to the light. Suddenly, she slid and vanished through it.

Aubrey felt the tug on his clothes. The gravel under his feet scooted forward. Aubrey fell backward. The light blinded him. Aubrey closed his eyes and concentrated. The phosphenes swirled, but the light brightened his view behind his eyelids. Aubrey felt warm. He slipped off the edge of the ground and floated forward.

Several dark dots appeared in his vision. He tried to open his eyes, but the light was still too bright.

Aubrey heard Buzz yelp in the distance. Swinging his arms and legs, Aubrey tried to move forward faster. More spots popped up in his dark sight, like a pixelated view of shadows drifting toward him.

Suddenly, he felt several small pricks to his face. He wiped his cheeks. Aubrey could feel dirt on his fingers. The light dimmed. He opened his eyes. He gasped. He was floating forward through a massive expanse of darkness. Tiny lights, like stars, twinkled all around in the distance. A yellow orb glowed far away. And spinning slowly, yet orbiting the blazing yellow glow, the planets of the solar system gleamed in their range of colors.

"I just bounced off Jupiter!" Buzz twirled in the darkness, holding his gut and chortling.

Magnos held out his hand to touch Saturn's rings. They tickled his skin, and he let out a tiny giggle but quickly retracted his hand. "They're cold!"

"Ack!" Jordana waved her hands through her straight hair. "There's something in my ear!"

Gleefully, Buzz spun and pointed. "No! It's Halley's Comet!"

Magnos and Rodriqa laughed as they watched a glowing cratered rock flying past her.

"This is incredible!" shouted Aubrey. "It's like Mr. Vandereff's orrery! Only bigger!" He held out a finger and ran it through the bright blue upper atmosphere of Neptune.

"Much bigger." Rodriqa echoed. She writhed her torso to avoid several of Saturn's moons.

"Ouch! Ouch! Ouch! Ouch! Ouch!" Buzz curled himself into a ball.

"What's wrong?" shouted Rodriqa.

"Asteroid belt." Buzz sighed, a final tiny pebble scrapping his skin.

"Look!" hollered Magnos. "It's Earth!"

Everyone turned where Magnos was pointing. There, only a few yards away from the yellow orb in the center, was a greenish-blue, white-capped sphere. So very small. So easily ignored. So distinctly home.

Rodriqa glanced between Aubrey at the end of the pack and Buzz up front and noted how the five of them were essentially following a similar path. "Where are we going?"

Buzz looked up from dabbing his finger at Phobos and Deimos, spinning around Mars. He held out his hand toward the yellow orb in the center. His palm warmed. "Uh, I think we're heading for the sun. And it's hot."

"Uh-oh." Magnos stiffened.

"What?" asked Rodriqa and Buzz.

Magnos gaze was fixed downward. "Remember Aubrey's raven?"

"Yeah," replied Rodriqa.

"He's here." Magnos pointed down, below the sun. The sable raven stood on a solid black surface that twinkled with stars. The bird's wings were folded, and it glared at them with its black left eye.

"Hot! Hot! Hot!" Buzz arched his back and spun away from the sun as he approached. Slowly, he drifted downward and came to rest at a standing position in front of the raven. One by one, the other four friends followed his course through space, landing on solid darkness. The five of them huddled together.

The raven cawed loudly and flapped its wings. The friends jumped. Suddenly, strands of the raven's long, ebony plumage spewed away from its body and whipped around its head and talons like a feathery black hurricane. The dark, rotating mass enlarged into a rotating whirlwind of debris.

Finally, the wind relented. The swirling matter materialized into a gray-skinned humanoid with long spindly arms and a bald head who was clothed in a gray tunic. His opaque right eye sat stagnant as he gazed at the children with his black left eye. "Nawbey."

Aubrey's throat tightened. He had heard spirits call him that before, and it was usually the bad ones.

Rodriqa stepped in front of Aubrey.

Buzz snapped his fingers. "Genie!"

The man didn't move.

Buzz took a step back. "I mean…Djinn?"

The gray man nodded. "Genie. Djinn. I have been called by those names. Originally, I am a Magi. But my name is Zaks."

With her hoodie up, Mena dashed across the parking lot of Mr. Jennings's Smart Mart & Finer Diner. Out of the corner of her eye, she noticed a quick sweep of movement from behind the store. She stopped and looked again. But there was nothing there.

Under the glow of the store's neon lights, Mena ran up to the front doors and pulled on the handle. It didn't move. She placed her face against the glass. Inside, it was dark, and she couldn't see anyone. Slowly, she sidled up next to the building's outer wall and tiptoed around two corners to the back. Pulling her hoodie off her head, she peeked around the edge of the building.

Crouching down between the wall and the brown dumpster, Shway Shway, still festooned in the Elemag suit, raked his hands against the gravel. His triangular, reptilian-skinned head glistened in the last rays of twilight, and his large, round, green eyes peered at the ground. His head rolled backward, and his flap-like ears unfurled. Then he looked at Mena.

Mena gasped. She pulled her head back behind the corner. Her heart sputtered rapidly in her chest. She heard gravel tumble around the corner. Mena pulled her Spooly Pen out of her pocket. She held it up, squeezed her eyelids together and tightened her stomach. Pushing herself off the wall, Mena jumped to the side and pressed the blue clicky button several times.

She opened her eyes. The creature was gone. She took a step forward and leaned down. Mena couldn't see any movement under the dumpster. She stepped lightly forward and peered over the lip of the dumpster. Inside, there was nothing but trash.

Mena felt a tug at her hand. Shway Shway stood next to her.

"Free me!" The creature inhaled as it spoke.

"*Socorro!*" Mena screamed and spun around, backing against the dumpster. "What are you?"

"Shway Shway." He lowered his head and held up his hands. "Free me."

"Sh-sh-sh-shuck sheer?"

"Shway Shway," he grumbled. "Let me go!"

Mena edged herself toward the side of the dumpster. "You're already free."

Shway Shway shook his arms. "Take me out of this."

"You want me to undress you?" Mena snarled.

Shway Shway growled and then turned around. "Take this off." He shoved the black battery pack at her.

Mena looked at the battery. She glanced over his head. There was no one around. She clawed clumsily at the battery.

Shway Shway shook his head and hissed over his shoulder. "No! You must press the levers and pull out the battery."

Mena took a second look. Her mind focused. "Wait a second."

She slipped away from the dumpster. "That's an Elemag suit." She pointed accusingly at Shway Shway with her Spooly Pen. "That belongs to the NGW, and wearing it is illegal."

Shway Shway turned and exposed his fangs.

"You can't hurt me in that, can you?" Mena examined him from several angles. "You're trapped in that suit."

Shway Shway plopped his rump on the ground. Closing his eyes, he clawed at his head.

Mena smiled and stepped forward. She tapped the Spooly Pen on her chin. "Do you know where Aubrey is?"

Shway Shway stopped moving. His large, green eyes rolled up at her. "I know exactly where he is."

"Can you take me to him?"

Shway Shway jumped onto his hooves. "Yes, if you free me."

Mena bunched her lips together. "That's no good."

Shway Shway growled. "Why not?"

Mena raised an eyebrow. "Because if I let you go, you'll just leave. Or worse, bite me."

"Yuck." Shway Shway's upper lip curled. "I promise, if you free me, I'll take you to Aubrey Taylor."

Mena scoffed. "What's a promise to something like you? I don't even know what you are."

Shway Shway bowed his head. "I am a keeper. And I know where the seer is."

Mena's eyes widened. She pocketed her Spooly Pen and twirled her index finger. "Turn around."

Shway Shway clomped his body around. Arching his back, he offered the battery to Mena. Mena examined the battery pack. She placed both her thumbs on the levers and pressed down firmly. The battery popped out of its holder.

The suit sizzled. The battery dropped to the gravel. Shway Shway sighed. Falling to his hands, Shway Shway raced away on all fours. Within a few leaps, he was speeding down Asheville Highway.

Mena clenched her fists. "Wait!" She chased after him. "You promised!"

Shway Shway glanced over his shoulder and grinned. Instantly, he vanished, and the Elemag suit dropped to the asphalt.

"*Mentiroso!*" Mena stomped her feet against the ground.

A gust of wind blew across the highway. The Elemag suit flopped and tumbled into the ditch.

Suddenly, a pair of large, round green eyes appeared on the highway, staring at Mena and bouncing as they sped toward her. Coalescing around the eyes, a large glossy-skinned creature, the size of a horse with bat-like wings galloped toward her on three-fingered foreclaws and hind hooves.

Screaming, Mena spun and ran back through the parking lot. In seconds, the transformed Shway Shway was directly behind her, snapping at Mena's head with sharp fangs. Shway Shway clamped down on her hoodie and wrenched his head upward. In an overhead flip, Mena toppled over backward in the air and landed on Shway Shway's spiny back. Shway Shway beat his wings furiously, launching into flight. Mena clamped down on his reptilian neck with both arms. Stunned by her aerial somersault, she lost her breath and her chest heaved, hungry for air.

Shway Shway pitched to the side. Rapidly gaining altitude, they flew over Mr. Jennings's store, clearing the neon sign. Within a few moments, Shway Shway and Mena were soaring over the Lake Julian Dam. Mena looked up. The house lights from Mount Camelot twinkled in the distance, and the skyline from Asheville glowed along the horizon. They flew through one of the bright beams of light from the dam's observation tower. She heard the murmur from crowds of Moth-ers along the lake's banks.

Mena reared up and waved her right arm at the crowds. "Help! Help!"

Shway Shway growled. He reached back around his neck with his three-fingered claws, gripped her hands, and pulled her tightly against his back. His wings beat with tempest vigor. They burst through the thin layer of clouds overhead, lifting through thousands of feet over Lake Julian.

With his hand on his shaven head, Coren Belward stood in the middle of the deconstructed scout camp, watching as parents helped their children gather their belongings and haul mounds of equipment to the parking lot along the eastern bank of Lake Julian.

In the distance, from the fog of noise surrounding him, Coren heard a frightful screech. He searched the sky. He focused on a moving dot above the lake. Suddenly, as the object disappeared, he recognized what he saw. "Chupacabra," he murmured. "The chupacabra are winning."

Coren ran over to his four-wheeler and cranked down on the starter. The engine sputtered to life. He pressed the accelerator and ripped through the camp.

"Hey, Coren!" shouted one of the scouts. "Where are you going?"

"To help some friends!"

"You're the raven?" Rodriqa pointed at Zaks.

Zaks nodded his bald gray head.

Rodriqa scrunched up her forehead. "Why have you been following us?"

Zaks raised the thin eyebrow over his black eye. "You know the answer to that question."

"Because we're different," mumbled Jordana.

"Not different." Zaks shook his head. "Every child of the Clockmaker innately controls a divinoi. Some choose to use it. Many do not. You each are quite adept at using yours. Unfortunately, your predilection for stumbling into misfortune is also quite astounding."

Magnos held up his hands. "So we have gifts from the Clockmaker?"

"Some more finely tuned than others." Zaks stared at Jordana.

Jordana hung her head, her hair spreading down like a curtain in front of her face.

Zaks bowed his head. "After the second rebellion, when the Watchers taught humans how to manipulate their divinoi at the expense of the Magi, many of the Clockmaker's children contended that the Clockmaker had allowed humans to become too powerful."

Rodriqa shook her head. "What other children?"

Zaks raised his hands. "Shinar. Spirits. Angels and demons, you call them."

Glancing at Aubrey, Rodriqa's mouth rounded with enlightenment.

"The baby of creation, the favorite of the universe, the last of the molded clay, had been imbued with just as much will and potency as the Potter. And many were jealous." Zaks folded his long arms. "When Noah's flood came and the Watchers were entombed, the Clockmaker divided his divinoi amongst the remaining humans into twelve parts, so no one person would have all the Clockmaker's abilities."

"So there's twelve different divinoi?" asked Buzz.

"And we each have one?" asked Rodriqa.

Zaks nodded.

"Not me," murmured Buzz.

"Wait!" Rodriqa frowned. "You said that was the second rebellion. What was the first?"

Zaks lifted his head. "When Tavekashaban threatened the Clockmaker's son." Zaks squinted his black eye. "It began with a meager argument over the speed of want versus the speed of need and blossomed into the war in which we are all enmeshed today."

"Speed of want?" questioned Buzz.

"Speed of need?" asked Rodriqa.

Zaks sighed. "Very early on, the Clockmaker decided how quickly his children would move from place to place. One shinar might trek slowly across a world. A Watcher may fly a few hundred cubits in the blink of an eye."

"I thought angels traveled as fast as light," said Magnos.

"Not shinar," replied Zaks. "It remains the Clockmaker's discretion how quickly they move. Most accepted his sovereignty. Others disagreed and wanted the freedom to choose how quickly they traversed the universe. Will drove want, and a few felt it was their obligation to argue with the Clockmaker and prove him wrong."

"So they rose up against him?" asked Aubrey.

Zaks nodded. "Arguments bore protests. Protests fueled dissension. Dissension fractured the hearts of all the Clockmaker's children, and the first battle for shamayim erupted from rebellion."

"Shamayim?" asked Aubrey.

"Paradise," replied Zaks. "When the first battle was over, the Clockmaker punished the leader of the rebellion the harshest. Tavekashaban was the first cast from shamayim. Ultimately, everyone was asked to choose a side. Either we would obey the Clockmaker or follow another path."

Rodriqa glared at Zaks. "You chose Tavekashaban's side."

"Not exactly." Zaks shook his head. "The Clockmaker was the architect of the universe, but the Magi were his engineers." Zaks held up his hands. "Each of us was imbued with the ability to manipulate the physical laws, which the Clockmaker had constructed. Quarkherders brewed matter from cosmic clouds of gas. Graviteers set planets and galaxies into motion, and Magnelecticists energized it all. We were very close to the Clockmaker for eons, shaping his creation as he directed."

"Different Magi to control the four fundamental forces of nature," said Buzz. "That's so cool!"

"There are only three kinds of Magi," scoffed Rodriqa.

"Quarkherders can bend both the strong and weak nuclear force as you call it." Zaks watched Buzz from the corner of his eye.

Buzz smiled.

Rodriqa rolled her eyes.

"Which one are you?" asked Aubrey to Zaks.

Zaks held up an index finger. "Graviteer." The space around his finger warped, and each of the friends felt an invisible tug pulling them forward. "And your solar system was one of my finest accomplishments." Zaks held up his hand to the glowing yellow sun and orbiting planets above them.

"So why are you not in shamayim?" asked Buzz.

Zaks lowered his arms. "Seeing prudence in both sides of the rebellion, the Magi collectively asked to remain nonpartisan at the conclusion of the first rebellion. After much conversation, the Clockmaker agreed, provisionally."

Rodriqa crossed her arms. "So you're not bad, but you're not good?"

Zaks thought for a moment. "The Magi are expected to remain neutral for eternity. We shall never aid either side, nor allow either to prevail. So we have made it our mission to maintain the balance."

"Isn't that impossible?" asked Aubrey.

Zaks lifted his chin. "I am detached and dispassionate as my order expects."

"But you destroyed Mayree Krouse," replied Aubrey.

"Exactly." Zaks angled his head. "I tipped the scale back into balance."

Aubrey shook his head. "But how did you stop time? To talk to me?"

Aubrey's friends eyed him warily.

"I did not stop time." Zaks wiggled his index finger. "I slowed it. Time is a function of gravity."

"So did you create the chupacabra?" asked Rodriqa. "You know, to maintain the balance?"

Zaks frowned. "Chupacabra?"

"The horse-reptile-bat creatures with, big green eyes that keep attacking townies," added Magnos.

"Oh." Zaks smiled. "They're not chupacabra. The hordes roaming around town are aberrant keepers. And no, I did not create them. But I think you know who did."

"Magnolia Thistlewood," murmured Rodriqa.

Zaks nodded.

"Where did they all come from?" asked Jordana.

Zaks looked down. "She sacrificed one of my keepers to create her army of aberrations."

"Keeper?" questioned Rodriqa.

Zaks furrowed his brow. "My protectors, Tartan and Shway Shway. I have lost both of them."

"Shway Shway?" asked Rodriqa. "Seriously? That nasty thing protects you?"

"We know where he is," said Buzz and Magnos.

"Where?" asked Zaks.

Magnos and Buzz pointed upward awkwardly.

"Outside of here," replied Rodriqa.

Suddenly, the floor and walls trembled. From above, Neptune flew out of its orbit and dipped down, bouncing along the floor. A white light dulled the darkness of the surrounding space. Zaks held up his hands. The ether moved, and the five children felt the air squeeze in around them. Zaks flexed his wiry arms. The floor shook. The friends were pressed together, and they groaned under the invisible strain.

Zaks relaxed, and his arms flopped to his sides. "We are trapped."

Whimperfidget howled in his asphalt cage.

"Hush," insisted Ms. Thistlewood. She crouched before the window and cradled her hands around the bottom of the crucible. "It's happening."

Icharida stood behind her, peering over her shoulder.

The full moon crested above the treetops. The sunlight faded, and stars glinted in the shadowy sky overhead.

Fastened to the top of the multicolored crucible, Solluna darkened, and slowly, lines etched in the pyramid's face.

"What's happening?" Ichardia leaned forward. Yellow vapor oozed from between her blackened skeletal ribs.

"Victory," murmured Ms. Thistlewood.

The crucible trembled on the windowsill. A heavy clunk shook the side of the tree house.

Ms. Thistlewood stood up and peered at the four sides of the pyramid. She turned to Icharida. "Tonight, we have dealt the Clockmaker a serious blow. My climb toward supremacy has begun." She walked over toward the fundamentium hearth and wrapped her arms around herself.

Icharida bowed and looked over her shoulder. Ms. Thistlewood stood away from her, staring into the fire. A single tear dripped down her pale cheek.

Icharida stepped forward and gazed at Solluna. She read the words etched into the pyramid.

"To seal the opened."

Icharida stretched out her boney fingers and felt the pyramid's edge. An ecstatic tingle, much like touching your tongue to a nine-volt battery, wisped up her arm.

"What's happening?" Jordana tried to push herself off Buzz. The five friends were pressed into a huddle against one another.

"Someone has found a way to imprison me in my crucible again." Zaks flexed his arms outward.

"Could you stop squeezing us?" Rodriqa freed her hand from between Magnos and Aubrey and waved it above her head.

Zaks relaxed his arms. The friends fell in a clump onto the black, starry floor.

"What do you mean imprisoned?" Buzz climbed over Magnos to his feet.

"Is he saying we're stuck in here?" Jordana squirmed out from under Rodriqa.

Zaks pressed his palms toward the floor. The floor quaked. Buzz fell on top of Magnos's back. Magnos grunted.

Zaks knelt to the floor, shaking his head. "Not again."

Rodriqa pushed herself to her knees and faced Zaks. "What's going on?"

"The crucible is closed. Nothing can leave or enter."

Rodriqa stood up and pulled Aubrey to his feet. "What?"

Zaks chuckled darkly. "After all, that is what a crucible is."

"A prison." Aubrey stared at Zaks. "A prison for the Magi."

Zaks glanced at Aubrey and nodded.

Rodriqa sneered at Aubrey. Magnos helped Jordana stand. Buzz scooted up next to Aubrey. "How do you know?"

Aubrey rubbed his forehead with his forearm. "Before Noah's flood, the Watchers accused the Magi of being a threat to humans, and the Watchers imprisoned the Magi in these bottles."

Zaks looked up at Aubrey with a tense black eye. "So the seer has a teacher."

Aubrey nodded. "It didn't make sense to me before. But it does now."

Aubrey looked around at his friends. "The Watchers used some of their children as guards to make sure the Magi weren't freed. That's where the chupacabra came from—I mean, the keepers." Zaks stood up and folded his arms.

Aubrey took a step toward Zaks. "After the Watchers were placed in Enoch's tomb, the Magi bound the keepers with the Bloodrunner anathem, making protectors out of them, forcing them into eternal servitude."

Zaks nodded. "And we kept our crucibles as a symbol of our unjusti-fied imprisonment."

"But the Watchers are all buried and gone," said Buzz, sitting on the floor. "Who could trap us in here?"

"Magnolia Thistlewood," grumbled Rodriqa.

"How do we get out?" Jordana wrung her hands.

"Someone from the outside must free us," replied Zaks.

Jordana trembled. "Well, how long were you in here the last time?"

Zaks hung his head. "Ten thousand years."

Jordana's mouth opened widely.

Aubrey scratched his cheek. "But Shway Shway is free. Won't he come looking for you?"

Zaks nodded. "He may be our only way out."

"No." Aubrey shook his head and gazed at his friends. "There are too many people looking for us."

THE WIDOW, THE WITCH, AND THE CRUCIBLE

"Icharida." Magnolia Thistlewood turned toward the window. "Don't touch that."

Icharida glanced over her shoulder and slunk away from Solluna and the crucible.

Ms. Thistlewood stepped over to Icharida and placed her fingers under her mandible. "I need you to take the keepers from the caves and lead them toward the lake to feed. Can you do that for me?"

Icharida nodded.

Tap! Tap! Tap!

A knocking sound resounded from the front door downstairs. Ms. Thistlewood straightened up and walked over to the window. She viewed the dark grounds outside. She couldn't see anything.

Tap! Tap! Tap!

Scowling, Ms. Thistlewood stomped past Icharida and marched down one side of the double spiral staircase. Icharida followed but took the opposite set of stairs and hurried out the back door.

Once downstairs, Ms. Thistlewood strode toward the red front door and opened it.

With her hands raised, Old Widow Wizenblatt's eyes glowed white as she glared at Ms. Thistlewood. Missing her wings, her sculpted hair wrapped around her head like carved stone, and strands of her tunic flitted in the breeze.

Hovering in the air with arms and legs flailing, Ned and Fred Kluggard hung above the widow like flies caught in an invisible web.

The widow lifted her arms, and Ned and Fred rose higher. "You shouldn't leave your trash on the lawn."

Ms. Thistlewood crushed the door handle. The door melted and congealed into a long black spear. "This ends tonight."

The widow chuckled. "You bet your sweet bippy it does." She curled her finger. The end of the spear bent back toward Ms. Thistlewood.

Crash!

The upper side of the oak tree exploded. Splinters of wood and furniture rained down onto the grass outside. Ms. Thistlewood ducked.

The widow leaned inside and screamed toward the upstairs. "Grab the bottle with the pyramid on top of it, and smash it!"

Ms. Thistlewood turned and fled for the stairs. The widow raised her arms and crumpled her fingers together. Fred and Ned dropped to the grass and scrambled away on their hands and feet. The widow flexed her shoulders. The walls of the oak tree groaned. Grappled by unseen force, Ms. Thistlewood dropped to the floor and slid backward. She wrapped her body around the bottom bannister of the stairs. Her legs lifted off the ground, drawn toward the widow.

Upstairs, curled in a ball with his wings folded, Shway Shway lay against the hearth among wooden debris. Slowly, Mena peeled Shway Shway's limbs away from her and stood up. She looked down at him. The creature evaporated into the ether.

Glancing at the broken room around her, Mena shook her head and rubbed the scalp under her ponytail. "*Atascadero.*" She walked over to the splintered hole at the edge of the room and called out to the widow, "What?"

Outside, the widow took several steps back and looked up at Mena. "Smash the bottle with the pyramid!" The widow looked back at Ms. Thistlewood. Stripping off her own skin, she hurled several spirit shards at the widow. The widow pressed her thumb and index fingers together. The black shimmering worms screeched in midair and disappeared.

Mena frowned. "Why?"

The widow concentrated on Ms. Thistlewood. "Because that's where Aubrey Taylor is!"

Mena scrunched up her cheeks.

The widow glanced back at Mena. "Now!"

Mena took a step back and looked around. A settling dust hovered over cracked lumber and shattered stone. In the corner, next to the crystalline marble hearth, stood Shway Shway, a little more than three feet tall, with his triangular head down and his arms behind his back.

Mena walked forward and held out her hands. "Give it to me, please."

Downstairs, the widow dodged several bannister rails, which transformed in flight toward her into sharp metal lances. Now appearing more like a charred skeleton, Ms. Thistlewood stretched her arms upward, pulling herself onto the stairs.

"Fred! Ned!" Ms. Thistlewood shouted. "Protect Solluna!"

The widow reared back her arms, and Ms. Thistlewood slipped down a step from the stairs. She pulled a strip of wood from the floor and flung it at the widow. The wood transformed into a boulder. The widow dropped her hands and stepped several feet to her left. The rock blasted through the wall. The oak shuddered. Ms. Thistlewood scampered up several steps before the invisible pull on her skeleton returned, and she hung onto the bannister again. The widow stepped back into the threshold, her arms and hands flexed.

Ned and Fred ran through the back door and raced up the back of the double staircase, skipping steps to escape the widow's hold.

Upstairs, Shway Shway hopped from hoof to hoof and dodged Mena as she reached for the crucible and Solluna. Huffing through rapid, shallow breaths, Ned climbed up to the landing. Pulling his pants over his flub, he pointed at Mena and Shway Shway. "Play time is over, kiddies!" The lanky Fred sidled up behind Ned.

Mena turned around and sighed. "*Gracias a Dios!*" She pointed at Shway Shway. "Help me get that bottle away from that *criatura!*"

Ned grinned. "Certainly."

Ned hobbled forward and knocked Mena to the floor. Fred rushed around Ned toward Shway Shway. Shway Shway grimaced and disappeared. The crucible and Solluna fell to the floor. Fred scooped up the crucible, turned around, and ran back toward the stairs.

"*Tacaño!*" Mena pushed herself up.

Ned chuckled and shuffled toward the staircase.

Suddenly, Shway Shway reappeared next to the stairs, his wings open and his horse-sized, reptilian body looming over Fred. Shway Shway growled.

Fred yelped and jumped onto the staircase.

With his jaws, Shway Shway clamped down on the crucible and yanked it away. The crucible and Solluna skidded back across the wooden floor.

Fred scurried down the stairs. Shway Shway chased after him. The bannister cracked as Shway Shway pushed his wings and torso down.

Mena dove for the crucible. Grunting, Ned leaned over and picked it off the floor before Mena could grab it. Ned laughed and turned away.

Mena scowled at him. "Give it back!"

With his back to her, Ned twirled the crucible over his head and laughed.

Mena stood up and rushed at Ned. She clasped her arms around his globular waist and wrenched back.

Ned stopped. He spun around and pushed Mena away. Mena tumbled against the floor.

Ned spit at her. "You have no idea what you're messing with." He turned away and walked toward the stairs.

Mena curled her lip. Pulling her Spooly Pen out of her pocket, she held it over her head and pressed the black clicky button. Two tiny prongs jutted out from its end, and electric sparks jolted between them. She stood up and ran toward Ned.

Mena jabbed the Spooly Pen at Ned. Ned screeched and jumped into the air, thousands of volts surging through him.

He turned around. "Why you…" He swung the crucible at Mena's head. Mena ducked and jabbed his leg with the Spooly Pen.

Ned jerked. Howling, he swung the crucible again. Mena leaned to the side and pressed the Spooly Pen into his arm.

Ned screamed and took several steps back. Shivering, he held the crucible overhead in both hands. He took a step forward but was pulled back by the crucible. Ned looked up. Shway Shway had the end of the bottle in his jaws. Ned released the crucible and stepped away.

Shway Shway slapped his wings downward, smacking Ned between them. Ned's eyes rolled back into his head, and he slumped to the floor.

Shway Shway disappeared. The crucible, still with Solluna attached to its top, dropped next to the incapacitated Ned. Mena unclicked her pen and slid it into her pocket. She reached forward and lifted the crucible from the floor. She smacked it against the wooden floor, and the floor shook with a thud. Mena stood up and hit the wooden slats again. The crucible and Solluna remained as they were.

Mena trotted over to the hole where the window used to be. She held up the crucible and shouted at Mrs. Wizenblatt below. "It won't break!"

The widow thrust her hands forward. Ms. Thistlewood blasted through the stairs and out the back of the tree house, hurtling across the field. "Hit it against the hearth!" Strutting through the bottom floor of the oak tree, she ran out the back side toward Ms. Thistlewood.

Mena turned around and stared at the crystalline, marble fireplace. She walked over to it and swung the crucible at its edge.

Crack!

Mena examined the crucible. A crevice snaked down its side. Mena took a deep breath and spun in circles. She slammed the bottle into the hearth. The crucible split into three pieces.

Suddenly, a mighty wind spun throughout the room.

Mena stepped away from the hearth. A shard of the crucible rolled across the wooden floor, and she stumbled over it. A hurricane of debris and mist spun at the edges of the room. Mena covered her face, watching and breathing through her fingers.

Mena gasped. Materializing from the swirling smog of dirt, wood, and vapor, Aubrey's red hair and brace-beset teeth focused in front of her out of the blurry gale. She turned. More figures condensed in the mist: Buzz's chunky frame and his dark curly hair, Jordana's long black hair and rose-tinted glasses. Slowly, the wind subsided, and the fog lifted. All five friends stood in a circle around Mena, examining their fully corporeal hands and bodies and staring at the cluttered room around them.

"Thank you." From behind Mena, the words pricked her out of her shock.

Mena spun around. A tall, gray-skinned, bald-headed man bowed in front of the hearth.

"You freed us." Zaks inhaled and looked at Mena with his left black eye.

Mena's jaw dropped as she stared at the Magi.

"Where are we?" Rodriqa kicked a piece of splintered lumber next to her foot. Behind the wood, an asphalt cage rested on its edge, enclosing a shivering cat with matted fur.

Rodriqa's mouth rounded, and she knelt to the ground. "Whimperfidget!"

The disheveled cat in the cage reared its head and pawed at the bars.

Rodriqa grabbed the asphalt bars and pulled. They didn't move. She looked over at Magnos. "Help me get him out!"

Magnos walked over to Rodriqa. He leaned over and grabbed the cage. With a snap, he broke two of the asphalt bars. Whimperfidget leapt out of the cage onto Rodriqa's shoulders, purring and nuzzling her neck.

Rodriqa scratched Whimperfidget's head. "It's okay. You're safe now."

Zaks glanced around. "We are in Magnolia Thistlewood's tree house."

Mena scrambled through her pocket. She pulled out her Spooly Pen and, aiming it at Zaks, pressed the blue clicky button.

"The big tree below Mount Camelot?" asked Buzz.

Zaks nodded.

Buzz and Jordana looked out the hole in the side of the room up at the houses lining Mount Camelot's forested summit.

Mena spun around and took more pictures.

"Uh, guys." Magnos stared out the gaping hole where the window used to be. "The chupacabras are coming."

His friends stood behind Magnos and looked outside.

From the ridge above the Crannynook Caves, a dozen winged keepers charged down the mountainside toward the tree house. Mena scuttled forward and took pictures of them.

"Let's go!" Buzz turned and ran for the stairs.

Aubrey turned around. Shway Shway, now in his humanoid form, gathered the three broken pieces of the crucible at Zaks's feet. Solluna was still attached to the top portion of the bottle. Shway Shway bowed before his master and inhaled as he spoke, "I'm sorry."

Aubrey ran over to Shway Shway and Zaks. He looked at Shway Shway. "I'm glad you're free."

Shway Shway curled his lip and hopped up to Zaks, who cradled him in his arms.

Aubrey looked up at Zaks. "I'm sorry about your crucible."

Zaks glanced down at the broken bottle. "Take it. Solluna belongs to you, and the pieces of the crucible can be of use."

Aubrey nodded. He leaned down and scooped up the three pieces. He followed after Magnos, Rodriqa, and Jordana, who were running down the steps.

Downstairs, the friends ogled the splintered destruction and the two gaping holes in either side of the bottom level of the tree.

Rodriqa shook her head. "Looks like a war went on in here."

"I wonder what happened," added Aubrey.

"Look!" Jordana pointed out the hole next to the front door. "Ms. Thistlewood and the old widow are fighting!"

A hundred yards in the distance, the widow and the partly skeletal Ms. Thistlewood shouted at each other. Grasses flattened around the widow. Ms. Thistlewood drew stones from the ground and hurled them at her opponent as they transformed in midair into machetes and axes.

"Good." Buzz stepped outside. "Let those two duke it out. We've got bigger snails to shuck."

The friends slunk out of the tree house and wheeled toward the oncoming group of keepers. Mena ran from behind them toward the widow and Ms. Thistlewood, feverishly snapping pictures.

Magnos, Rodriqa, Buzz, Jordana, and Aubrey ran into the field down from Mount Camelot.

"I don't think they're coming this way," said Rodriqa, with Whimperfidget clinging to her shoulders.

In the distance, a stampede of a dozen winged keepers bounded down the mountainside from the Crannynook Caves and shifted away from the tree house. Aubrey stopped and glanced between the keepers and the direction they were heading. "Oh no." Aubrey chased after his friends. "They're going for the lake!"

Buzz stopped and pointed toward a flattening area of grass ahead. "There's something coming from the other direction."

Magnos, Jordana, and Rodriqa watched the approaching figure in the field.

"Do you hear that?" Buzz turned his ear toward the sound.

They each listened.

"It's buzzing," replied Jordana.

Buzz smiled. "No, it's a motor."

The form came into view and stopped a few yards ahead.

Buzz ran up to Coren Belward, who hopped off his four-wheeler. "What are you doing here?"

Coren saluted Buzz. "I saw one of the chupacabras flying this way. I figured you might need some help." Coren surveyed the dozen keepers racing across the field. "Looks like we need more people."

"We gotta stop them!" Aubrey shouted. "They're heading for the Moth-ers!"

"Aubrey's right!" Rodriqa pointed at Magnos and Jordana. "The three of us up front. Everyone else stay back." She glanced over her shoulder. "Aubrey, eyes."

Aubrey nodded. He aimed his face toward the keepers and closed his eyes. The phosphenes swirled and faded behind his eyelids. Darkness filled his vision. A green wispy light appeared in the middle of the herd of keepers.

Aubrey opened his eyes. "There's a skeleton riding one of the keepers."

Rodriqa squinted, gazing at the oncoming herd. She nodded as she saw the charred skeleton.

"What am I gonna fight with?" Buzz held up his hands. "I don't have my stuff."

Rodriqa looked around. She noticed the crucible shards in Aubrey's hands. She grabbed a spiral-shaped shard from the crucible and threw it at Buzz. "Use this." The broken bottle piece hit Buzz's gut and bounced down to his feet.

Rodriqa took another look at Aubrey's hands. She grabbed another broken portion. "Actually, I'll take one myself."

Aubrey looked down at the darkened pyramid attached to the top of the shattered crucible. He sighed. "At least I got Solluna back."

Coren pulled out a Swiss army knife and flipped it open. "I'm ready."

Magnos wrapped his right arm around Jordana's back. Jordana looked down and bit her lip. Reaching around with her left arm, she threaded her slender fingers through to his meaty palm on her hip. The two of them and Rodriqa marched toward the oncoming keepers. Aubrey, Buzz, and Coren followed behind.

Magnolia Thistlewood picked up a rock and lobbed it at the widow. Twisting and rolling her fingers, Ms. Thistlewood concentrated on the sailing rock. It popped loudly and cracked down its center. Smoldering to a glowing red, the rock dropped toward Mrs. Wizenblatt. The widow jumped backward, dodging the molten shrapnel that splattered and scorched the grass and ground.

Mena ran several steps forward, clicking pictures of the scene.

Glancing between the advancing keepers and the ongoing fight between Ms. Thistlewood and the widow, Zaks hovered out of the maimed tree house, cradling Shway Shway in his left arm. He raised his hand toward Mena. "Stop!"

Ms. Thistlewood looked over at Mena. She grimaced and pulled several sheaths of long grass out of the ground. The clumps of root balls melded into spiked, iron mace balls, and the sheaths transformed into chains. Ms. Thistlewood hurled the nest of flails at Mena.

Mena clicked pictures of the spiked balls hurtling toward her.

The widow pushed her arm outward. Zaks moved his arm to the side. Caught between the invisible forces of the two Graviteers, Mena rose off the ground and flew through the air. With a grunt, she landed on her side a hundred yards away. Mena sat up and then passed out.

———❧———

Rodriqa held her arms up. "Spread out."

Whimperfidget hopped off Rodriqa's shoulders onto the ground. He raked his claws into the dirt and, facing the keepers, hissed with his back arched and his tail straight up.

Hunkering their triangular heads down and bearing racks of sharp fangs, the dozen keepers changed direction and galloped toward them.

Magnos and Jordana let each other go and took several steps apart. Rodriqa tied her beaded braids in a knot. She popped her neck and eyed the keepers charging toward her. Feeling her fingers tingle, Rodriqa jogged in place as the spirit of the Tsul'kalu spread up her extremities and into her trunk. Magnos cracked his knuckles. Jordana closed her eyes and slipped off her rosy-tinted glasses. Inhaling deeply and centering her pain in her heart, Jordana opened her eyes and glared at the charging reptilian-skinned beasts.

Riding atop the bony spine of one of the middle keepers, Icharida kicked her charred skeletal heels into the creature's haunches. The keeper reared its head backward and screeched. Flapping its wings, Icharida's keeper along with two flanking keepers, lifted upward and leapt over Jordana.

Aubrey watched the flying keeper's arc overhead and then land in the grass in front of him.

Aubrey stumbled backward. Coren jabbed his knife at the keepers. Their large, round eyes followed the shiny tip of the knife as they growled at Coren.

"Come on!" Buzz stepped forward and swung the bottle shard. "Bring it!"

Rodriqa glanced back at Aubrey. Two keepers from the rest of the pack lunged at her. She dodged them as Whimperfidget pounced on the hind leg of one and bit its sinewy calf. The keeper growled and kicked the cat off. Whimperfidget rolled away in the grass.

Three other keepers raced at Magnos. Magnos bounded forward and spun around, kicking one keeper in the face and pounding another in the jaw with his fist. He ducked as a third keeper snapped at him, and then he head butted it from underneath. The keeper fell back on its rump, dazed.

Jordana glared at a keeper in front of her. The keeper's green eyes widened, and it bowed its head. Suddenly, it chomped down on a keeper close to Rodriqa. It kicked its hoof, then turned and growled at its attacking companion. The keeper under Jordana's control leapt onto the nearest keeper's back, pinning it to the ground.

Rodriqa grabbed the wing of the other keeper lunging at her and snapped it forward. The keeper squalled. Rodriqa folded its wing on its neck and pressed it to the ground.

Icharida glanced between Aubrey and Jordana. The charred skeleton gripped her keeper's ears and twisted them sharply. It screeched, flattened out its wings, and spun in circles. Its wings knocked Jordana to the ground and undercut Aubrey's legs. Jordana fell into the grass. Aubrey dropped onto his back, flinging Solluna into the air. Icharida caught Solluna. She kicked her keeper in the sides, and they galloped away.

The keepers attacking Buzz and Coren bit and clawed at the two boys, pressing them away from Aubrey, who scrambled to regain his feet.

Now free of Jordana's coercion, the bewitched keeper bounded off his companion toward Rodriqa, knocking her to the ground and away from the wounded keeper.

Magnos jumped up, twirled in the air, and beat two of the keepers next to him with his fists. They yelped and ran toward Rodriqa.

Whimperfidget scurried through the grass and leapt into the air. His teeth clamped down on the nearest keeper's ear. The keeper raked at its head. Whimperfidget growled and clamped down more tightly. The keeper winced and slapped its ear to the ground. Whimperfidget moaned but didn't release his grip. Another keeper chomped down on Whimperfidget's back, and Whimperfidget squealed. The keeper shook his head and flung the cat into the meadow.

Four keepers pressed in on Rodriqa. She swung her arms and screamed at them. They surrounded her. She dodged snapping jowls and scraping claws, jabbing a keeper's eye and elbowing a chin.

Magnos ran over to Jordana and helped her up. Jordana was trying to catch an eye of one of the keepers circling Rodriqa.

Whimperfidget jumped onto the back of one of the keepers around Rodriqa. Its neighbor flapped its wing, swiping the cat into the field.

A keeper kicked Rodriqa in the back, knocking her to the ground. The other three keepers pounced on top of her. Rodriqa clawed at the dirt, trying to pull away. A keeper bit her leg. Another clamped down on her shoulder. Rodriqa screamed. Slowly, the keepers, chewing on Rodriqa, twinkled and faded translucent, ranching the spirit of the Tsul'kalu out of her.

"Rodriqa!" Aubrey screamed, running toward her.

Magnos jumped toward the keepers surrounding Rodriqa.

Suddenly, Magnos and Aubrey were lifted off the ground, and they hovered upward, their legs cycling wildly.

"No!" Aubrey tore at the air, but he didn't move. He shifted his weight and looked around.

With Shway Shway clinging to his legs, Zaks stood near Aubrey, Buzz, and Coren, with two fingers extended and his left black eye staring at Aubrey.

"What are you doing?" shouted Aubrey. "Let us go!"

The keeper that had knocked Rodriqa to the ground, gripped her trunk with its teeth, and lifted her, pulling her away from the other keepers. With Rodriqa hanging limply in its jaws, it galloped away. The other three keepers chased after. Swollen and bleeding, Whimperfidget leapt onto the head of the keeper carrying Rodriqa and clawed at its large, green eyes, but the keeper shook him off. Whimperfidget fell forward. The keeper trampled Whimperfidget with its hooves. Whimperfidget groaned. Suddenly, his paws expanded. His tail lengthened. His head grew in size, and giant feathery wings erupted from his back.

In an instant, a reborn Whimperfidget leapt out of his skin. His head crowned in a plush, brown mane and his body gleaming with a glossy golden coat, Whimperfidget the lion unfurled his smoldering angel's wings and stood on the grassy meadow, roaring at the fleeing keepers. The keepers ran faster away. The lion Whimperfidget charged after them.

———✦———

Zaks raised three more fingers on his right hand. "I will not let that witch have Solluna." Coren, Buzz, and Jordana floated into the air, joining Aubrey and Magnos. "And there's only one way to destroy all of these aberrations at once."

With the children orbiting in a ring above Zaks, he held up his left hand. Wind rushed across the field, blasting the grass to the ground. The earth quaked, and the ether around them shuddered. Zaks pressed his left hand skyward, and his lanky limbs trembled. Shway Shway pulled himself between Zaks's legs.

A rock pierced the soil at Zaks's feet. Dirt crumbled away from it as the rock emerged from the ground. Within moments, a mountain of bedrock rose skyward from the loamy earth beneath Zaks. He stood on the rock's pinnacle as the craggy behemoth jutted upward hundreds of yards. The children hanging in the air above Zaks gained altitude with him. They stared wide-eyed at the summit protruding out of the ground and the distant site of the Lake Julian Dam and Mount Camelot, which were now lower in elevation than they were. At the base of the growing mountain, dirt fell into the empty crevice created. Rapidly, the spreading sinkhole engulfed the entire meadow around them. Ms. Thistlewood's battered tree house creaked as it dropped into the hole. The keepers that were hurrying away fell one by one into the earth. Icharida clambered to escape the swiftly approaching wave of falling land, but she too was lost in the depths.

Sighing deeply, Zaks dropped his left hand. The mountain of rock, floating above the meadow, plunged into the ground. A cloud of dust burst around them. A ten-foot tall hill of stone stood where the meadow once was. Zaks slowly clenched the fingers of his right hand. The five children floated to the ground.

Shway Shway leapt into Zaks's arms, and the two of them faded away in the loamy soot.

Aubrey plopped onto the crumbled soil and sprung to his feet. "Where's Rodriqa?" He batted away the dust.

"Who was that?" asked Coren. "What just happened?"

"It's complicated." Buzz cleared the gritty grime off his glasses. "I'll explain later." He hurried toward Aubrey, who started searching for Rodriqa.

Through the dusty cloud, a form walked on all fours toward them. Wings folded, the lion Whimperfidget held the limp and pale Rodriqa in his massive jaws. Approaching Aubrey, Whimperfidget laid Rodriqa at Aubrey's feet. He nudged her with his massive muzzle. She didn't move. The lion lowered his head and whined.

"Oh no." Aubrey leaned down and shook her by the shoulders. "Rodriqa! Wake up!" Her eyes were closed. Her limbs were flaccid.

Magnos, Jordana, and Buzz rushed over behind Aubrey.

Jordana covered her mouth. "Is she okay?"

Aubrey pinched her arm. Nothing happened. "She won't wake up."

"Is she alive?" Buzz squatted down and felt her neck. He looked up at Magnos. "She doesn't have a pulse."

"Is she breathing?" asked Aubrey.

Buzz leaned his ear next to her mouth. He listened for a moment. He looked up at Aubrey and shook his head.

"She needs CPR!" Coren loped up behind the four friends, who were hovering over Rodriqa's lifeless body. "Who else knows CPR?"

Aubrey pulled away from Rodriqa and stared at her ashen skin.

Magnos nodded. He squatted above Rodriqa with a knee planted on either side of her. "We learned CPR in Mr. Vandereff's class from that doctor lady." Magnos pointed at Buzz. "Give the rescue breaths."

Buzz shuddered. He glanced between Rodriqa's gaping mouth and Magnos.

Magnos furrowed his brow, glaring at Buzz. "Now." He wrapped one hand on top of another and rested the pair on the middle of Rodriqa's chest. Magnos pressed down, counting, "One, two, three." At the side of Rodriqa, the lion Whimperfidget covered his face with his bulky paws.

Buzz scooted up to Rodriqa's head. He cradled it between his hands and angled her jaw outward. Leaning down with his face inches from Rodriqa's, Buzz listened to Magnos's count. Rodriqa's limp body lurched up and down with each of Magnos's compressions.

Jordana grimaced. Her stomach lurched forward, and hot, sour bile burned the back of her throat. "9-1-1," murmured Jordana as she stepped away. "Someone needs to call 9-1-1!"

"Right," replied Aubrey. He stood up and pulled his cell phone out of his pocket. He smacked the side of his screen several times and looked up at Jordana. "I don't have a signal."

Coren dug into his pocket and pulled out his phone. With his lanky arms, he held it above his head. "I don't either."

Magnos heaved downward against Rodriqa's chest. "Twenty-eight, twenty-nine, thirty." Magnos glanced up at Buzz. "Breathe."

Buzz pursed his lips and inhaled deeply. Closing his eyes, he cupped his mouth over Rodriqa's and pushed a chestful of air past her teeth. Then he took another deep breath and did it again.

Buzz sat up and wiped his mouth against his shoulder. Teetering forward on his knees, Magnos thrust his entwined hands against Rodriqa's chest again.

Jordana pulled at Aubrey's arm, turning him toward her. "What are we gonna do?"

Aubrey kept his head down, focusing on his phone, as his mind fogged over.

"Aubrey!" Jordana shook Aubrey's arm. "You need to do something!"

Aubrey crumpled up his forehead. He looked at Jordana. For a moment, clarity brightened his thoughts as the events of the past week barreling round in his brain sifted to the last time they had seen Coren. "No, I don't."

"What?" A tear fell from Jordana's eyelid.

"Coren." Aubrey turned around and looked at the tall Boy Scout standing behind them. "Coren needs to do something."

Coren's Adam's apple bobbed in his throat. "You're right." He raised his finger and shook it at Aubrey. "I can relieve Magnos." Coren took a step toward Rodriqa.

Aubrey lifted up his arm, stopping Coren. "No, you don't." Aubrey raised his chin and faced Coren. "You know what you need to do."

Coren shook his head and scrunched up one eyebrow. "I can drive back to town and get help?"

"No." Aubrey grabbed Coren's wrist. "You're a healer." Aubrey pulled Coren's hand in front of his face. "You heal her."

"But...but...but I don't have any medical supplies." Coren glanced between Aubrey and Rodriqa. "Let me run back to the camp."

"Breathe." Magnos reared back and wiped sweat off his forehead. Buzz leaned down and heaved two more breaths into Rodriqa's mouth.

"That'll take too long." Aubrey looked down at Rodriqa. "It's already late." Aubrey stretched Coren's hand outward toward Rodriqa "Besides, you don't need medical supplies."

Jordana stepped forward and faced Aubrey. "What are you doing? Let him go get help!"

Aubrey shook his head. "Don't you see? He's all the help we need."

"Exactly!" Jordana shouted. "Let him go back to town!"

Aubrey curled his lip at Jordana. "Then Rodriqa will die."

"Somebody go get help!" Magnos yelled.

Aubrey dropped Coren's arm and raised both of his hands. "The cave! He saved his scouts in the cave!"

"No, I did that!" Jordana looked away.

Aubrey smiled and closed his eyes. "You kept the chupacabras away. But who woke up the sleeping scouts? Mr. Vandereff, Mrs. Gungandeep, Mr. Jennings were all asleep for days. The scouts were gone for less than a day, and once Coren touched them, they woke up."

Jordana opened her mouth to say something. Then she closed it and bit her lip.

Coren turned his head between Aubrey and Jordana, who were now both staring at him. "I-I don't know what you mean."

Aubrey balled his hands into fists. "'Everything has a point. Everything has a purpose. There is no coincidence. Everything has a reason.' Old Widow Wizenblatt told me that. And it's true. You are here because you were meant to be here."

Coren's larynx pulsed in his throat as he wagged his head.

Aubrey leaned in toward Coren. "Deep down, you know what I'm talking about. You know you can do it." Aubrey tapped his own temple. "You've helped someone in the past, and you didn't know how or why. You felt a charge of life between you and another person, and they were better. An elderly woman. An injured child. You've healed them before. It was completely clear, but it wasn't obvious. But you know you did something." Aubrey looked down at Rodriqa. "And now I'm asking you to heal my friend."

Coren stared at Rodriqa.

Jordana tugged at Coren's arm. "Do you know what he's talking about?"

Coren's eyes flitted. "I do." He wrung his hands. "I mean...I think I do."

Aubrey nodded. "Then do what you can for Rodriqa."

Coren gazed at the limp Rodriqa, trying to escape Aubrey and Jordana's persistent stares.

A ring of sweat dotted the neck of Buzz's shirt. Magnos grunted with each compression that struck Rodriqa's chest.

Coren gritted his teeth. He knelt down at the side of Rodriqa, flanking Magnos.

"Breathe!" yelled Magnos as he stretched out his hands.

Buzz leaned in toward Rodriqa.

Coren lifted Rodriqa's wrist. He clasped her palm between his two hands and bowed his head.

Aubrey closed his eyes. The phosphenes faded, and a blinding light filled his dark sight.

Only an inch away, Buzz's puckered lips hovered over Rodriqa's mouth. Rodriqa's eyes snapped open. Buzz blinked at her. Rodriqa screamed.

Rodriqa shoved Buzz up by the shoulders. "What are you toad throwers doing to me?" Buzz toppled backward.

Straddling Rodriqa, Magnos's eyes widened. He held up his hands.

Rodriqa jerked her hand out from between Coren's and rose onto her elbows.

"We…we thought you were dead," stuttered Magnos.

Coren reared back on his feet and sprung up.

Jordana gasped.

Aubrey quietly smiled.

Rodriqa wriggled out from underneath Magnos. "What?"

Buzz rolled over onto this belly and pushed himself up. "You didn't have a pulse, and you weren't breathing!"

Rodriqa dusted her shirt off and pushed herself up. "What are you talking about?"

Jordana stepped forward. "Don't you remember what just happened?"

Panting, the lion Whimperfidget leapt to his feet. His wings unfurled. He pounced toward Rodriqa and licked her with his rough, wide tongue.

Rodriqa shielded her face with her forearms and pushed Whimperfidget away. "Why does everybody want to kiss me all of a sudden?"

Buzz stepped forward and pointed at the lion. "Is that…"

"Whimperfidget, sit!" commanded Rodriqa.

The lion folded its wings. The ground thudded as his rear dropped.

Rodriqa took a step forward and scratched his mane. "He helped me fight off the chupacabras." Whimperfidget purred so loudly the air around him vibrated.

"He didn't help you as much as you think," mumbled Buzz.

"Who hit me?" wafted a voice out of the dust.

The children turned around.

Rubbing her scalp, Mena wandered around the stone protruding out of the dirt. Her elastic band had loosened, and her ponytail ballooned out from her head.

Jordana grimaced as she looked Mena up and down. She was caked with dirt and her shirt was torn. "Are you okay?"

Mena nodded and then shook her head. "I don't know."

A string of red and blue flashing lights flickered along the road, leading down from Mount Camelot.

"Oh no," murmured Aubrey. He rubbed his eyes and strained to see through the dust. "The police are coming."

"No surprise, with the commotion we just made," said Jordana.

Zaks floated out of the ether toward the friends. He held Shway Shway in his right arm, and the crystal pyramid Solluna twirled above his open palm. "Quickly. You have to leave."

"You think?" murmured Rodriqa.

Jordana stared blankly at the series of oncoming police cars. "Maybe we should give ourselves up."

"Why?" asked Buzz "So they can lock us up forever?"

Jordana shrugged. "At least we'd be safe."

"No. There are more keepers." Zaks dropped his left hand. Solluna floated through the air to Aubrey. Aubrey caught it and pushed it into his pocket. "Ms. Thistlewood only had a tiny fraction of her army hidden in the caves. She knew you were a threat. Hundreds of them have been placed in the gorge below the dam."

"They'll be after the tourists at the lake," murmured Magnos.

Zaks nodded. "Only you can stop them."

Jordana shook her head and chuckled. "There is no way we can get there. The police will be here in a few minutes." Jordana looked up at Zaks. "This is over."

Zaks glanced at Shway Shway. Shway Shway nodded. He leapt out of Zaks's arms and disappeared. Then he reappeared in his quadruped form. Shway Shway closed his large green eyes, bowed his triangular head, and folded his bat-like wings. His thin tail swished behind him. Lowering his trunk, Shway Shway offered Aubrey his spiny back. Aubrey turned and stared at Zaks.

Zaks pointed toward the dam. "Take my keeper and the danielion. The two of them can get the five of you to the gorge safely."

"Danielion?" questioned Aubrey.

Shway Shway turned his head toward Whimperfidget and hissed. Whimperfidget growled.

Buzz's eyes widened. "You mean?"

Zaks folded his arms. "You fly there. It will be the fastest way, and you will avoid the authorities."

Buzz looked at Aubrey and grinned. "This is gonna be so awesome." Buzz ran to Shway Shway and hopped onto his back. Shway Shway grunted under the weight.

Thoughts sped through Aubrey's mind. Like the clicking of a clock, ideas presented themselves in succession. "Right." Aubrey pointed to Coren. "Take Mena back to Lake Julian. Get her help."

"Tell my dad to grab my stuff and come to the gorge." Buzz steadied himself on Shway Shway's back. "He'll know what to do."

Coren saluted Aubrey and Buzz. "Will do." He turned and helped Mena to his four-wheeler.

Aubrey pointed to Magnos. "Grab Jordana. You two and Rodriqa ride Whimperfidget. Let us know when you get there."

Rodriqa snorted. "Get there?" She petted Whimperfidget. "I doubt your chimichanga can keep up."

LET US PREY

Shway Shway and Whimperfidget soared down into the gorge below the Lake Julian Dam and, flapping to a stop, landed with the five friends on an island in the middle of the gully's river. Bright fluorescent lights illuminated the bottom of the gorge, which was showered in a damp spray floating up from the lake water cascading out of the bottom of the dam. Budding trees and sprouting grasses layered the gorge's steep walls, and tightly cornered switchback trails angled upward through the scant foliage.

Buzz tumbled off Shway Shway's spiny back. "Hoaker croaker!" Buzz steadied himself up and wagged his head.

Shway Shway lowered his neck, and Aubrey scuttled to the ground. He held his stomach and pursed his lips, trying not to vomit.

Magnos helped Jordana off Whimperfidget and jumped next to her. Her hair was now a frizzy mat of black tangles. Rodriqa slid off Whimperfidget. The lion turned and nuzzled her neck with his stiff-whiskered muzzle.

Magnos stared down into the darkness of the gorge. The waters raced down shallow rapids into the night. He squinted. "What's that?" He pointed down the river. Shway Shway faded and disappeared.

Rodriqa pulled her sharp crucible shard out of her pocket and held it up like a knife. "Where?"

Buzz pulled out his cell phone. He tapped its screen three times. A bright light shone from its face. Buzz held his cell phone out in front of him. The light illuminated the gorge.

The shine from a hundred large, round green eyes flickered from the rushing waters, from the embankments, and from the end of the island ahead.

Lowering his head, Whimperfidget growled.

"Uh-oh," murmured Magnos.

Her eyes wide, Jordana shook her head and took a step back. "Is this a trap?"

"I think this is more than we can handle." A ghostly white spread up Rodriqa's fingers.

Aubrey swallowed against his drying throat. Closing his eyes, he viewed the gorge from behind his eyelids. The phosphenes swirled and faded. Darkness was all that remained. "I don't see anything else. It's just them."

"All of them," muttered Buzz. He angled his phone to take a greater look at the gorge's walls.

Tree limbs snapped. Water splashed in the rapids. Distant growling and hissing echoed from the edge of the island.

Leaning over, Buzz propped his cell phone on a rock so its light shone forward. "Get ready." Buzz pulled a broken shard of crucible out of his pocket and held it up.

Magnos stepped forward. He wiped the sweat from his forehead and balled up his fists.

Now fully veiled in the spirit of the Tsul'kalu, Rodriqa stepped up between Magnos and Buzz. "Hold onto your toad throwers."

"We can't beat them!" Jordana cried. "There were only twelve last time, and we would have died without Zaks and Coren!"

Aubrey nodded. Licking his dry lips, he glanced between Rodriqa and the oncoming herd of chupacabras. "She's right. We need help."

Rodriqa frowned at Aubrey. "From where? You think the police can handle this?"

"Maybe we should let them try!" squealed Jordana.

Rodriqa's shoulders slumped, and she rolled her eyes. "Sure, they can try." She pointed to the cell phone on the ground. "Buzz, call 9-1-1."

Furrowing his brow, Buzz looked at Rodriqa.

"There is no one else!" Rodriqa raised her arms. "We're it! Don't you get it?" She turned around and stared at her friends. "This is why we are here! This is why all this has happened. We have to beat them, or else they'll hurt everyone we care about!" Rodriqa straightened her shoulders and cracked her neck. "Now is our time! Our time to be brave! Time to prove we're good and not bad! And show the universe we're not to be messed with!"

The friends looked at each other with stolid faces.

Aubrey nodded. "You're right." He looked at Jordana. "We need to finish this, for better or for worse."

Jordana looked down and shook her head.

Aubrey stretched out his hand to Jordana. "We need you. You're the strongest of us all."

Jordana bit her lip and whispered, "You're wrong."

"Pretty speech for a dainty pud." A crisp, screechy voice echoed from over head. The friends jerked around to search for the speaker.

Four figures floated down from the dam's face behind the children. They recognized Zaks, hovering below the other three, but it was not Zaks who had spoken. An elderly man with a scraggly hair and beard, who had sparks arcing off his shoulders, was snickering at them. He was accompanied by a tall baldheaded man adorned in a torn tunic, and a smooth-skinned man with thin eyes and black spiky hair.

The four gray forms glided through the air over the sprays of water gushing from the dam. Rocks orbited around the baldheaded man. And the smooth-skinned man's clothes transformed from a jacket and khaki pants into a copper-trimmed purple robe.

"More Magi," mumbled Aubrey.

The friends and Whimperfidget huddled together and watched the Magi as they approached.

The baldheaded Thalazzaran looked over the friends' heads at the gorge beyond. "Zaks, remove the aberrations." His deep voice vibrated the ground beneath the children.

Zaks nodded. He closed his left black eye and held out his hands. "You should not exist, lest death never desist. By All Law, be dismissed." His arms trembled.

Wails and shrieks of a hundred dying creatures suffused the gorge. Scores of green eyes flashed brightly before they darkened. Bat-like wings, hooves, and reptilian skin melted into bubbling mounds of tarry, dull embers. Within a few moments, all the chupacabra had dissolved into the darkness.

"You've got to be kidding me." Rodriqa looked back and forth between the gorge behind them and Zaks. "You mean to tell me you could have killed all these things at any time?"

Zaks looked away. "It is not my place to interfere."

Aubrey stepped toward Zaks and wrung his hands. "I'm so glad you're here."

Zaks pursed his lips. "You won't be."

FATHER KNOWS PEST

The bright headlights from Coren's four-wheeler split the night as he drove through camps and past RVs on the eastern bank of Lake Julian. In the seat behind him, Mena buried her head into Coren's back, gripping him tightly around the waist.

At the Mole-Pole tent, Coren stopped and hopped off his four-wheeler. He glanced at the patch of empty grass where his scout camp had been and pressed his lips together.

Mr. Reiselstein stepped out of the tent. He walked up to Coren and stood close to him, whispering, "Is Buzz okay?"

Coren nodded. "He needs your help. He said to bring his stuff to the gorge below the dam. He'll meet you there."

Mr. Reiselstein furrowed his brow. "Why?"

Coren looked around, searching for eavesdroppers. "I'm not exactly sure, but I can tell you that he and his friends are fighting things I've never seen before."

Mr. Reiselstein took a step back. "There are monsters in Lake Julian?"

Coren nodded and looked away. Mena stumbled up to them, rubbing her scalp. "Lots of monsters."

Mr. Reiselstein frowned. "Mena Kontrearo? Are you okay?"

She nodded quietly; then she shook her head and leaned against Coren.

Coren held her up. "I need to get her to the hospital."

"Right." Mr. Reiselstein scratched his chin. He glanced between the tent and the four-wheeler. "Coren, I need to ask you a favor."

"Anything, sir."

Mr. Reiselstein turned and walked into the tent. Within a few seconds, he ran back out with a steel-mesh sack in his hand. Mr. Reiselstein reached in his pocket. "Here are the keys to my car." He handed the keys to Coren and pointed to his right. "It's a jeep with its top off in the lot over there. You can drive Mena to the hospital in my jeep if I can borrow your four-wheeler." Mr. Reiselstein trotted over to the four-wheeler's trailer bed and dropped the sack in it.

Coren frowned. "Are you sure?"

Mr. Reiselstein ran back into the tent and came out again, cradling the Superterrestrial Solar Panel and ESAU. "Yes. It'll be the easiest way for me to avoid the police." He slid Buzz's inventions into the trailer.

Coren nodded. "Be prepared, sir. You won't believe what you're gonna see."

Mr. Reiselstein searched Coren's face and nodded.

With his arm around Mena, Coren walked toward the parking lot. A few tiny dots of light over the tip of Lake Julian, where Wontawanna Creek emptied, caught Coren's attention. Coren stopped and pointed. "Look! The moths are hatching from their pupas!"

Mr. Reiselstein looked up and narrowed his eyes. "I guess so."

A flurry of tiny pink, blue, and green lights flitted through the air. Mr. Reiselstein climbed onto the four-wheeler and cranked the starter. "Hopefully that's a good omen."

"There is another aberration that has lost its way," Thalazzaran announced in his deep voice.

"Where is the walking Hadean?" screeched Melkyor.

Zaks hovered forward. He swung his arm outward. Matsinstrus, half-skeleton and half-human, flew out of the torrent of water churning at the bottom of the dam and floated in the air. Zaks suspended Matsinstrus in front of the other Magi.

"It's Mr. Parotty," remarked Buzz.

Jordana grimaced. "I wonder what they're going to do to him."

"You should not be here." Thalazzaran raised his pointed index finger at Matsinstrus. "You violate All Law."

"Because of your curse, you cannot be killed." Melkyor raised his fingers and wiggled them. "But you can be locked away."

Thalazzaran raised a mound of dirt and rock from the island below. Gaspian bowed his head and flexed his hands. The floating mound separated into three portions. The first portion expanded into sand. The second section of rock congealed together into a hollow ball. The remaining bits of earth transformed into a hundred spikes of quartz.

Zaks twisted his hand. Matsinstrus was shoved into the hollow ball of rock. Sand filled in its edges. The spikes of quartz pierced the rock, leaving only their tips exposed to the air. Streams of jagged electricity jolted from Melkyor and shocked the rock, melting it shut.

"The Tomb of Enoch isn't just for Watchers," snickered Gaspian.

Zaks opened up a rift in the ground. Thalazzaran thrust his arms downward. The Tomb of Enoch dropped deep into the earth.

"There are always ways of dealing with deviants." Thalazzaran looked at the children.

Jordana, Magnos, and Buzz trembled. Aubrey held Rodriqa's hand.

"Is this the seer?" Melkyor stretched out his hand, pointing to Magnos.

Zaks hovered forward and shook his head. He pointed to Aubrey. "This one."

Thalazzaran squinted his eyes as he examined Aubrey. "Ah, yes. The Clockmaker has attempted to remind us of his cleverness. He likes to place souls of great power in diminutive vessels." Thalazzaran turned to Zaks. "You have done well, Graviteer. For bringing the seer to us, your past indiscretions shall be forgotten."

"What?" said Rodriqa as her ghostly form faded. She pointed to Zaks. "You brought them here? To us?"

"They arrived of their own volition." Zaks didn't look at Rodriqa. "I did as I was commanded."

"Who are these people?" Rodriqa crossed her arms.

Aubrey took a step forward. "Melkyor. Thalazzaran. Gaspian. The Master Magi."

Gaspian's eyes widened, and he stared at Zaks. "How did he know that?"

Thalazzaran chuckled. "Clearly, the seer has a teacher." Thalazzaran stepped onto the ground and walked toward Aubrey. He kneeled down. "Tell me, little one. Who is your teacher?"

Aubrey glanced between Zaks and Thalazzaran. Zaks's head was down. Aubrey looked straight at Thalazzaran. "Shway Shway."

"What?" asked Thalazzaran. "What is Shway Shway?"

Zaks frowned at Aubrey. "Shway Shway is my keeper." Zaks flexed his right arm. The ether warped, and the wind blew. Shway Shway yelped as he appeared in his bipedal form at Zaks's feet. The creature dropped to his backward-bent knees, the invisible pressure from his master knocking him to the ground.

"Your keeper needs discipline." Melkyor tapped his fingers together. Electricity jolted between them. "Perhaps he needs a master's touch."

Thalazzaran waved Melkyor off. "The seer has passed the first test. He has a teacher." Thalazzaran leaned in toward Aubrey. "Now for the second test. Does he have a guardian?"

Rodriqa cleared her throat. Thalazzaran turned toward Rodriqa and smirked.

Thalazzaran raised his arm and swung at Aubrey. In an instant, Rodriqa flashed a ghostly white and jumped in front of Aubrey, knocking him to the ground and catching Thalazzaran's huge hand in hers.

Thalazzaran stood up and chortled, brushing Rodriqa away. "Very good." He hovered up, rejoining his compatriots. "The guardian knows her place."

"One more test," grumbled Gaspian.

"Yes! A final test!" Melkyor snapped his fingers.

"Bind his friends."

"No one can help him."

"Agreed," replied Thalazzaran. He raised his right hand and flexed his fingers. Magnos, Rodriqa, Buzz, Jordana, and the lion Whimperfidget floated into the air several yards above Aubrey.

Magnos twisted his shoulders. "What the…?"

Jordana screamed.

"Let go of me!" yelled Rodriqa, her legs kicking beneath her.

"Hey! I can't move my arms." Buzz looked straight at the ground, dropping below him.

Whimperfidget roared, twitching his tail through the air.

Arvel Reiselstein careened Coren's four-wheeler down into the gorge, navigating the tight switchback curves of the trail. A few hundred yards from the rapids below, Mr. Reiselstein looked up and pressed hard on the brake. Quickly, he turned off the motor and headlight.

In the distance, Mr. Reiselstein saw the four gray-skinned Magi hovering at the bottom of the dam, and the five children huddled together on an island in the middle of the gorge.

Mr. Reiselstein slid off the four-wheeler and gathered Buzz's inventions in the steel-mesh sack. Flinging the bag over his shoulder, Mr. Reiselstein grunted under its weight and stumbled down the trail.

Thalazzaran hovered a few yards closer to Aubrey. "If you are a seer, then fending off a few minor shade will be no challenge for you." Thalazzaran glanced over his shoulder. "Keepers, show yourselves."

Below the Master Magi, five reptilian-skinned creatures with flap-like ears and three-fingered hands appeared, each with distinct features. One had blonde hair, another sparse black hair. One had metallic hands, another long pointy canines, and the last had bushy green braided hair.

Thalazzaran waved his hand. An invisible force shoved the keepers forward. "Keepers, attack the seer."

The blonde keeper raked the ground with its hooves. The one with metallic hands clacked its fingers together.

Each of them grinned, exposing their racks of razorous teeth. They faded away, vanishing from sight.

"Leave Aubrey alone!" shouted Rodriqa above Aubrey.

"Jordana, can you try to coerce them?" asked Buzz, his voice an octave higher than usual.

"I can't even see them. How am I supposed to coerce them?" whined Jordana.

Aubrey stumbled backward. He closed his eyes, but he tripped and landed on a stone. Sharp pains shot up his back. He opened his eyes and rubbed his rear.

"Get up!" yelled Rodriqa.

"Aubrey! Here!" shouted a voice from the edge of the island. His shirt and cut-off carpenter shorts soaked with water, Mr. Reiselstein threw a battle prod at Aubrey. "Use this!"

The battle prod, modified with a computer motherboard at its handle, tumbled through the air and bounced next to Aubrey.

"No interference!" demanded Melkyor. Out of the Magi's eyes, a flash of lightning sparked across the island, shocking Mr. Reiselstein. Arvel dropped to the ground, with the steel-mesh sack on his back.

"Dad! No!" Buzz screamed.

"Silence!" commanded Thalazzaran. He pinched his thumb and index finger together, clamping Buzz's mouth shut. Buzz squirmed and grunted.

Aubrey picked up the battle prod and clicked it on. The end of the battle prod sizzled. Aubrey pushed himself up and closed his eyes. The phosphenes swirled behind his eyelids and faded. The five keepers came into view. With their hands extended, each approached him from a different angle, making a semicircle in front of him.

Aubrey waved the battle prod. The bushy green-haired keeper jumped back. Suddenly, the words of his father slammed into Aubrey's mind. *Spread your feet shoulder width apart. Bend your knees a little bit. Grip the bat with both hands and hold it just out from your ear.*

Aubrey turned his hip toward the keepers. He held up the battle prod like a bat and loosened his shoulders. The keepers inched closer. Aubrey opened his eyes. The five keepers flashed into view. Aubrey swung. The battle prod smacked three of the keepers in the face, zapping them with a hundred thousand volts. They dropped to the ground and screamed. The other two growled, stepped back, and disappeared again. Aubrey pressed the battle prod against the right hoof of the keeper with metallic hands. The keeper trembled and then evaporated into a cloud of foamy black smoke.

An invisible hand grabbed Aubrey's ankle and yanked his foot upward. Aubrey fell back onto his flank. He waved the battle prod around him. As he closed his eyes, Aubrey scooted up onto his knees and looked around. In his dark sight, he could see two keepers bite at his head. Aubrey opened his eyes. The blonde keeper and the one with long, pointy canines stood over him. Aubrey swung the battle prod. He slapped the blonde keeper, who screeched and fell backward. The other keeper chomped down on Aubrey's arm.

Aubrey screamed and dropped the battle prod. The other three keepers laughed and crawled toward Aubrey. The blonde keeper bit his ankle. The bushy green-haired keeper chewed his fingers.

Aubrey writhed and screamed. Tingling numbness seeped up his extremities. Quickly, his strength waned, and even though his eyes were open, darkness curled in from the edges of his sight.

Shway Shway pushed himself out from underneath Zaks's invisible grip. He exhaled and then inhaled as he yelled, "Eyes, Nawbey! Eyes!"

Zaks pulled Shway Shway up by his neck and squeezed it. Shway Shway choked.

"You need to train your keeper," hissed Gaspian.

Aubrey heard Shway Shway distantly, but as the four keepers around him crunched on his flesh, his hearing dulled. The name of the creature, who had taught him so much, flitted through his mind. *Shway Shway. Shway Shway.*

Suddenly, Aubrey knew what Shway Shway was trying to tell him. If he could hurt Shway Shway with his dark sight, why not the other keepers? Aubrey squeezed his eyelids together. He focused his thoughts and tightened his stomach.

The blonde keeper stood up and moaned. She stumbled backward and convulsed. The keeper with long, pointy canines released Aubrey and rolled over. His head and trunk shook violently. The other two fell backward and quivered stiffly.

Aubrey groaned. His strength returned. He balled his fists and pulled his knees into his stomach, concentrating on the seizing keepers in his dark sight.

The Master Magi frowned as, one by one, their keepers boiled away into blackness.

Once the last keeper had faded, Aubrey sat up. He grabbed his stomach and vomited on the ground beside him.

"Yes!" shouted Rodriqa. "That's my Aub!"

"Woohoo!" crowed Magnos.

The Master Magi dropped to the ground. Thalazzaran stepped up to Aubrey and kneeled in front of him. "You are the last seer. The rumors are true."

"Great," mumbled Aubrey as he wiped off his mouth. "Does that mean we can go home?"

Thalazzaran chuckled. "I have a better offer than that." He snapped his fingers. Melkyor and Gaspian nodded. They waved their hands over the ground.

Below Thalazzaran, a pile of shiny, gold bars congealed out of the mud. Underneath Gaspian, a dead tree to his left transformed into a ten-foot tall cabinet full of perfume, incense, and medicine. Behind Melkyor, a rack of designer clothes and a Bentley convertible swirled together in a storm of sparks and flashing lights.

Another golden bar congealed out of the mud every second. The mound of gleaming gold piled up to the height of Aubrey's eyes. Three bars tumbled down to Aubrey's feet. He reached down and felt the slick, hard surface of the metal. He knew a single gold bar would change his life forever.

The cool evening breeze chilled Aubrey's nose. From the cabinet of incense, one by one, familiar scents drifted by him. He stood up and inhaled deeply. Lavender. Watermelon. Freshly baked chocolate chip cookies. Grilled steak. Nutmeg. Aubrey's empty stomach twisted and gurgled at the wave of enticing smells.

Thalazzaran smiled as he watched Aubrey enjoy the gifts. The Magi pointed to the rack of clothes. "All tailor-made. Just for you."

"Whoa," murmured Magnos.

"Is that a Bentley?" asked Jordana.

Melkyor grinned and nodded.

"We have come to offer you an eternity of health, wealth, and prosperity." Thalazzaran stood up and raised his hands. "You will never know pain or suffering. You will forever be happy and lack nothing. Your life will be full and rich as you deserve."

"Really?" Aubrey shook his head in disbelief.

Thalazzaran nodded. "Yes. Anything. Everything. All things which you desire will be yours forever." Thalazzaran leaned down and faced Aubrey. "All that we ask is that you never use your divinoi ever again."

Aubrey cocked his head to the side. "What?"

Thalazzaran's lips curled. "You are never, under any circumstance, to use your ability to see the spiritual world or bring spirits into natural view ever again." Thalazzaran raised his hand over Aubrey. "Have I made myself clear?"

Aubrey glanced between the gold and Thalazzaran and then up to his friends, who gazed down at him. Rodriqa shook her head slightly.

Aubrey cleared his throat. "Master Magi, your offer is ridiculously generous. Anyone would be a fool to turn you down, but…" Aubrey sighed as he looked up at Rodriqa. She smiled at him. "But I think what I have already, my divinoi, is a gift. A gift given with expectation. So I don't think I can trade something bestowed upon me for something I have not earned."

Thalazzaran lifted his chin. "Are you certain?" The Magi's lips tightened. "Do you understand what is being offered? I am handing you a life free of discomfort, a life like no other—"

Aubrey held up his hand and interrupted the Magi. "I understand. And it's great and wonderful of you to offer, but I don't think it's a good idea for me to take these things from you."

"You cannot refuse," growled Gaspian.

"But he did." Zaks floated down to Aubrey and stood beside him. "And now you must respect his decision."

Thalazzaran turned around and waved his hand. Each of the gifts was pressed into the ground. The island shuddered. "Unacceptable." Aubrey's four friends and the lion Whimperfidget dropped to the dirt.

"You have no choice." Zaks tossed Shway Shway to the ground. "The seer has made his decision. Now you must maintain the balance." Shway Shway sidled up next to Aubrey.

"No." Thalazzaran flexed his arms. "The last seer upsets the balance. He must not be allowed to live."

"Are you challenging me, Zaks?" bellowed Thalazzaran.

Zaks lifted his chin and stepped forward. "Yes."

Thalazzaran chuckled. "Good." Thalazzaran gripped the air with his left hand and pulled back. Buzz skidded forward along the ground.

"Hey!" shouted Buzz as he rolled to a stop. The shard of crucible in Buzz's hand floated up and snapped in half. Half of it hovered to Zaks, and the other piece went to Thalazzaran.

Buzz pushed himself up and ran over to his dad. Arvel Reiselstein lay on his side in the mud, with the steel-mesh sack full of Buzz's inventions draped over his torso.

Buzz shook his father's shoulder. "Are you okay?" Buzz put his hand on his father's chest. He could feel him breathing. "Dad?" Buzz shook him harder. "Can you hear me?"

Arvel Reiselstein coughed, and his eyes rolled open toward Buzz. "That's one mean monster."

Buzz flashed a grin and then looked his father over. "Where are you hurt?"

Mr. Reiselstein shook his head. "I'm okay." Grunting, he rolled the steel-mesh sack off him. "What are those things?"

Buzz shook his head. "It's a long story. Let's get you to the hospital."

"Are these the monsters you've been fighting?"

Furrowing his brow, Buzz looked down. "Sort of."

"Then go help your friends." Mr. Reiselstein patted his son on the shoulder.

Buzz glanced over at Aubrey and then back to his dad. "They'll be fine without me."

"I'm proud of you, son." Arvel gripped his son's cheek. "Not many kids can stand up to monsters."

Buzz rubbed his forehead.

"Go." Mr. Reiselstein held up a clenched fist. "Beat the monster."

Buzz looked back at Melkyor and frowned. He leaned over and opened the steel-mesh sack. His eyes widened at what he saw. "Dad, you rock!"

Zaks and Thalazzaran held both hands up, mirroring each other. Their right hands were open. Their left hands were cupped near their chests. Above their left hands, each piece of crucible squeezed down into a black sphere, which spun feverishly. These singularities pulled the Graviteers toward each other, while they pushed each other away with their right hands. The trees creaked and groaned under the escaping force. Melkyor and Gaspian bowed and floated a few yards further away.

"We've got your back, Zaks." Rodriqa held up her crucible shard and ran toward Thalazzaran.

"No!" Thalazzaran nodded his head. A blast of force blew the four friends, Whimperfidget, and Shway Shway to the ground. "No one interferes!"

Magnos caught Jordana in midair, and they tumbled backward across the dirt.

"I'm gettin' real tired of them pushin' us around," grumbled Magnos as he stood up.

Rodriqa groaned, pushing herself onto her elbows. She looked at Shway Shway, who hopped up onto his hind hooves.

"What's going on?" asked Rodriqa.

Shway Shway glanced between Zaks and Thalazzaran. "It is a Graviteer's duel." He breathed in as he spoke. "If Zaks wins, he would take the Master Magi's position."

"If he loses?" Rodriqa sat forward.

Shway Shway's large green eyes rolled. "He will be trapped in a realm of eternal torment."

"What would happen to you if that happens?" Aubrey brushed himself off as he stood up.

"I would cease to exist." Shway Shway crouched down. "The Bloodrunner anathem would be broken."

The lion Whimperfidget rolled off his back and leapt to his feet. Unfurling his wings, he roared at Thalazzaran.

"Silence!" seethed Melkyor. A quick, blue snap left his hand and zapped Whimperfidget. The lion whimpered and dropped onto his stomach, shrinking into his domestic cat form. Dashing off the island, Whimperfidget hopped through rapids and disappeared into the bushes lining the riverbank.

"Hey!" shouted Rodriqa, taking a step toward Melkyor. "Stop that!"

Melkyor snickered. An arc of electricity cracked from his beard toward Rodriqa. Aubrey, Rodriqa, and Shway Shway jumped out of its path onto the mud.

Rodriqa spit dirt from her mouth as she pushed herself up. "You toad thrower!"

"Don't worry." Buzz walked toward Melkyor. "I've got this." The Superterrestrial Solar Panel was strapped to his back and the satellite dish-gun from ESAU, secured to his belly, pointed at Melkyor. Electrical cords ran around Buzz's flanks, connecting his two inventions. Buzz pulled a strap next to his arm. "Nobody hurts my dad." The curved wires from the solar panel snapped outward, creating a halo of metal prongs around his body.

"Huzzah." Buzz smirked at Melkyor.

Thalazzaran and Zaks hovered closer together, the push and pull of gravity locking them in orbit. The two Magi spun around each other and lifted higher into the sky.

Gaspian floated toward Aubrey and raised his hand. Aubrey lowered his head. His chest and stomach trembled. He tried to think of a quick way to escape. Closing his eyes, Gaspian smelled the air above Aubrey. The Quarkherder scowled at Aubrey. "You have something that doesn't belong to you, pud." Gaspian pointed at Aubrey's right pant's pocket. The fabric melted into water, dripping down his leg. Solluna tumbled onto the ground.

Seeing that there was a hole on the side of his pants, Aubrey scooted away from Gaspian. Gaspian leaned down and picked up Solluna. "Why do you have Tavekashaban's toy?"

"I...I...I don't know." Aubrey wiped the water off his leg.

Gaspian curled his lips. "This is not a child's plaything." He wrapped his fingers around Solluna. The crystal pyramid cracked, and sparks jumped from the edges. The pyramid crumbled into a mound of dust. Pursing his lips, Gaspian blew the dust away. A tangled silver bracelet embedded with an assortment of precious gems remained in his palm.

"Ha." Gaspian shook his head. "Always the trickster." He tossed the bracelet far over his head, launching it over the dam.

Gaspian looked back down at Aubrey. "This seer doesn't obey the rules." He stepped toward Aubrey and reached down for him. "A seer should never steal."

"Leave him alone!" Jordana stood a few yards behind Aubrey. Her glasses were off. She was glaring at Gaspian.

His eyes widening, Gaspian choked on the air. Guttural grunts eked out from his throat as his arms drifted down to his sides. His purple gown faded to a dull pink.

Jordana took a step forward, her eyes quivering as she kept her stare locked on the Magi. Magnos sidled up next to her and watched her closely, ready to catch her.

"Go, Jordana!" Rodriqa hopped up and pulled Aubrey to a stand. "We gotta help Zaks."

Aubrey furrowed his brow. "Yeah, but how?" He looked up. "They're way up there."

Rodriqa smiled. She glanced over her shoulder at Jordana and Magnos. "You two got the Magi in the dress?"

Magnos nodded and gently wrapped an arm around Jordana.

Rodriqa looked back at Aubrey. "I've got a plan. Just be ready to do your eye thing."

Aubrey winced. "Okay."

Rodriqa turned to Shway Shway, who was crouched behind her. "Giddy-up, little man. It's time to help your master."

Shway Shway straightened his backward-bent knees, his ears flapping as he stared at Rodriqa.

"Can you fly us both up to the dueling Magi?"

Shway Shway nodded. "I am strong."

"Okay." Rodriqa twirled her index finger. "Take your chupacabra form, and let's go." She pointed to the sky.

Shway Shway shook his head. "You cannot beat Thalazzaran."

Rodriqa pressed her thumb into her chest and leaned down to Shway Shway. "Honey, he's never met *this* guardian before." She turned up to Aubrey. "Keep your eyes on the Thalazzaran dude. I'll let you know when to open and close your eyes."

Aubrey nodded.

Rodriqa turned and waited for Shway Shway.

"Impossible puds," grumbled Shway Shway. He faded away and, a few seconds later, reappeared next to Aubrey in his larger form, his wings down and his bony haunches to the ground. Aubrey and Rodriqa climbed onto Shway Shway's back.

"Hiya!" Rodriqa slapped Shway Shway on the rear. Shway Shway growled and, flapping his wings, leapt into the air. Within seconds, Shway Shway was soaring high above the gorge.

<hr />

"Do not approach me!" shrieked Melkyor. He raised his hands. Sparks fired from his fingertips and sizzled down his long beard.

Buzz marched toward Melkyor, his fused contraptions aimed at him. Pumping a small squeeze handle, Buzz filled the trash bags between the wires with his customized silicon gel. He dropped the pump and glanced down at ESAU's electric dial. It read fifteen millimeters wavelength.

"Do not approach me!" Melkyor reared back his head. Bolts of electricity fanned out from his body.

"I may not have a divinoi," Buzz strode toward Melkyor. "But I can still teach a bully a lesson."

"You do not have permission to address me!" yelled Melkyor. An array of jagged arcs of lightning burst from around Melkyor and streamed toward Buzz. Waves of colossal current slammed into Buzz and the solar panels. His hair stood on end. The heat cracked the lenses in his glasses. Digging his heels into the dirt, Buzz leaned into the megavolts of energy flushing through him. His muscles contracted, but he forced himself to breathe. His heart pounded feverishly, the thunderous amperage from the electrical onslaught invigorating, not denaturing, every peptide within him. Buzz felt like he was having the worst seizure of his life.

The wires and trash bags from the solar panel crackled and hummed. The conversion of the electricity to potential energy flooded the invention's battery, and its meter jumped from red to yellow as it filled. Another wave of energy pulsated out from Melkyor. Jordana and Magnos were knocked off their feet.

Released from Jordana's gaze, Gaspian sighed and leaned over. His eyes focused, his mind returning to him. The Magi straightened himself and waved his hand. "There are penalties for those who defy us."

Magnos scrambled onto his knees and reached for Jordana. Suddenly, their clothes transformed into sheets of steel. Jordana lay prostrate in her skirt and tank top, cocooned in her metal clothes. Magnos heaved himself toward Jordana, slowly bending the metal his jeans and T-shirt had become.

Gaspian hovered toward them. "Now you will suffer, like puds should."

A mile above Lake Julian, Shway Shway flapped feverishly as he gained altitude with Aubrey and Rodriqa clinging to his back. Rodriqa looked down to see the curvature of the earth bend below her and Lake Julian shrink to a small swathe of lights and lines on the distant ground. Glancing at her, she noted him tensing to hold onto the keeper as his red hair shifted in the wind.

"There they are!" Aubrey lifted his arm next to Shway Shway's neck, pointing ahead at Zaks and Thalazzaran.

Thalazzaran glanced at Aubrey and Rodriqa riding on Shway Shway. He bent his thumb on his outstretched hand. A wave of force blasted toward Shway Shway. The keeper's wings crumpled, and Shway Shway dropped a hundred feet. Aubrey and Rodriqa screamed and gripped the creature's back tightly. Shway Shway's wings snapped open. Beating them against the wind, they gained altitude again.

"We have to get closer!" shouted Rodriqa.

Shway Shway wagged his head. "Thalazzaran is too powerful."

Rodriqa thought for a moment as they flew around the Magi. She glanced down and tightened her lips. "Then you'll just have to throw me to them!"

Aubrey shook his head. "What?"

Rodriqa slid down Shway Shway's back and clutched his spiny tail. Shway Shway pitched his wings to account for the shift in his center of gravity.

"What are you doing?" yelled Aubrey looking down at Rodriqa, dangling behind him.

"Close your eyes!" Rodriqa faded into her spirit of the Tsul'kalu.

Aubrey sighed and closed his eyes. The phosphenes swirled behind his eyelids and faded. In his dark sight, Aubrey could see Rodriqa twinkling below him and the Magi orbiting each other in the distance.

Rodriqa gazed at the Magi and then looked up at Aubrey. "Can you see me?"

"Yes!" Aubrey shouted.

"After Shway Shway throws me, count to three, then open your eyes!"

"No!" Aubrey shook his head.

"Just do it!"

Aubrey sighed.

Slipping one hand off Shway Shway's tail, Rodriqa pulled the crucible shard from her pocket. "Throw me!"

Shway Shway snorted and wagged his head.

Rodriqa squeezed his tail with all her strength. "Shway Shway, throw me!"

Shway Shway squalled. Wrenching his body forward, he flipped Rodriqa off his tail with the snap of a whip.

Rodriqa soared through the air toward the Magi, her arms and legs cycling as she pitched in an arc through the sky.

Aubrey counted quickly. "One, two, three." He opened his eyes and looked up for Rodriqa. She had disappeared.

Suddenly, Aubrey gasped. His stomach lurched upward. His arms and legs scrambled wildly as he grasped the air. He was falling quickly. Shway Shway had also disappeared.

<hr/>

Jordana turned her head to the side and looked for Gaspian. Gaspian held up his hand, shielding his eye. "Oh no, Coercer. That was the only opportunity you'll get to control me."

Jordana grunted, trying to move in her steel clothes.

Magnos thrust down his chest in a mighty sit up. The bottom of his steel shirt split. He reached down for Jordana and turned her over, so she could face him.

Jordana closed her eyes. "Get me closer to him," she whispered to Magnos.

"Working…on…it," grunted Magnos, straightening his legs. His steel jeans ripped at the waist and ankles. Magnos stood up, looking like a man in tin clothes. He leaned down and pulled Jordana upright.

"Stop!" shouted Gaspian. He pointed at Magnos. Magnos's metal clothes transformed into plates of slate.

A tide of blue jolts continued to stream out from Melkyor into Buzz and his solar panel. Buzz shuddered as the energy coursed around him. The solar panel's battery meter was now registering to the highest green bar.

With a hollow groan, Melkyor's hands dropped to his sides. The barrage of electricity stopped.

Smoke rose off Buzz. His solar panel whined, overloaded with gigajoules of energy. Buzz popped his neck. "That…that…that all you go-got?"

Melkyor grinned. Sparks arced across his fingers. "That's why puds were never meant to last." He raised his hands and pointed them at Buzz. "Their children are so foolish."

"Except we've learned about the Clockmaker's universe"—coughing, Buzz adjusted the dial on his meter to sixteen millimeters wavelength—"instead of just playing with it." Buzz reached behind him and pulled down a lever connected to the solar panel's battery.

Waves of electricity blasted out from the solar panels. Melkyor screeched. His form blurred as clouds of black smoke billowed up from his head and beard. The copper and gold seams of his tunic melted and dripped to the ground. The Magi faded. In a single blast, the scorched Magneleckticist burst into dollops of muddy pitch that scattered across the island.

Buzz pulled up on the lever, and the solar panel sizzled out.

"No!" shouted Gaspian. "You cannot kill a Magi!"

Buzz turned toward Gaspian, aiming ESAU's satellite dish at him. "Dissonance is a snail shucker, isn't it?" Buzz pulled the battery's lever back down.

A mile above Lake Julian, Zaks and Thalazzaran pushed and pulled against one another, each controlling their own black hole as they spun in the sky.

Dazzling in her ghostly transparent form, Rodriqa soared through the air and appeared next to Thalazzaran out of the ether. With crucible shard in hand, she landed on Thalazzaran's back and wrapped her arms around his neck.

Rodriqa raked the sharp edge of the crucible down his chest. A blinding white light sprayed from his splitting skin.

"Show's over!" shouted Rodriqa.

"Nooooo!" Thalazzaran reared backward. His arms flailed outward. Losing control of gravity, Thalazzaran's black hole flew forward into Zaks's singularity and was instantly absorbed. Zaks's spinning black orb doubled in size.

Zaks leaned forward and pressed his fingers closer to his singularity.

Thalazzaran and Rodriqa were yanked toward Zaks. He reached forward with his right hand and grabbed Rodriqa, her feet dangling inches above the black hole.

His form contorting and rippling, Thalazzaran stretched into a spinning whirlpool around the black hole and was devoured by its gravity. The Magi screamed. His voice suddenly stopped as his spirit was crushed into a single tiny point of matter.

Zaks closed his left hand. The singularity dissolved into the ether. The air calmed around them.

Zaks cradled Rodriqa in his right arm. "Very good, little guardian." He looked at her and grinned.

Rodriqa lurched her head around Zaks's torso. She pointed at the ground. "Aubrey!"

Aubrey dropped toward the earth, Lake Julian and its dam hurriedly growing in size as he rushed toward the ground. He churned in the air, looking for a way to slow himself down. He glanced up against the pressure of the rushing air. Shway Shway had reappeared a hundred yards above. Flapping in a nosedive toward Aubrey, the keeper held his green eyes open, focused on the falling seer.

Aubrey reached up toward Shway Shway. The wind pushed Aubrey, and he turned flips in the battering air. The earth and sky twirled around him. His stomach lurched sour bile into his throat. At the edge of his vision, he could see the top of the gorge pass him. The ground was only a few hundred feet below. He took a deep breath, hoping it would be over soon.

THE NEW QUEEN

In the soil-torn meadow below Mount Camelot, a charred skeletal hand stretched out of the dirt a few yards away from the newly planted, ten-foot scarp of bedrock protruding from the ground. The skeleton's phalanges seemed to dance in the crumbling earth. The hand searched for something solid to grasp.

Slowly, the newest walking Hadean, Icharida, pulled herself out of her loamy fetters and heaved her ribcage and legs from the dirt. With a sigh, she lay prostrate, a yellow haze seeping from between her ribs. She rolled over and stared at the moonlit sky above.

Her mind spun with all the events that had taken place over the past few days. She held her bony hand in front of her face. She wanted to cry at her lost beauty, but her dry skull held no tears. Sadness was a fleeting thought tonight. The pulse of power that she had gained in return for the monster she had become quelled her anguish.

She dropped her hand to her side. She considered what she should do next. She couldn't be seen in Lake Julian like this. But where could she go? Somehow, Magnolia Thistlewood had remastered her own flesh. Icharida knew she could learn to do the same.

A familiar tingle tickled her right hand. She jerked away and sat up. On the ground next to her a tangled silver bracelet, embedded with an assortment of precious gems, snaked toward her on the ground, its links squirming like scales across the soil.

Icharida angled her head to the side. The electric tingle was familiar, but the object had changed. She held out her hand toward the bracelet. The bracelet crawled up her fingers and wound itself around her wrist.

Icharida gasped. She could feel her hand and forearm warming. Slowly, flesh congealed over her blackened bones.

Solluna had found its new master.

"Got ya!"

Aubrey grunted as he landed in Griggs's arms. The janitor was no longer dressed in his forest-green, button-down uniform; instead he wore a white, button-down tunic. Ringed chains, partially embedded in his skin, reflected light like milk glass. His white wooly worm eyebrows were now sculpted marble, and at his back, a pair of wings, with steam rolling off of them, flapped gently, carrying the angel and Aubrey to the island below.

Aubrey heaved deep breaths. "You're…you're…you're an—"

Griggs grinned and nodded. "Yep."

Buzz, Magnos, and Jordana stared upward as Griggs and Zaks, carrying Aubrey and Rodriqa, drifted down through the gorge. Shway Shway flew circles around them and then disappeared in midflight. A few moments later, he reappeared in his bipedal form next to Magnos and Jordana on the ground.

Buzz stumbled forward. Sparks flickered between spiky twirls of his hair. The solar panel's wires had melted and curled inward. The trash bags leaked silicon gel from gaping tears, and the clear plastic of ESAU's satellite dish had been scorched brown.

Buzz unsnapped the two inventions from around him. The Superterrestrial Solar Panel and ESAU tumbled to the ground into pieces. His limbs trembling, Buzz took a couple of steps forward and dropped to his knees. He pulled off his glasses and examined their cracked lenses. He wiped a smudge off and reset his spectacles on his face.

Zaks hovered within a foot off the ground and placed Rodriqa down on her feet. Shway Shway ran over to Zaks and hopped into his arms.

Zaks looked around. "Where are Gaspian and Melkyor?"

Jordana, still confined within her metal clothes, and Magnos, trapped in slate, looked at Buzz.

Buzz smiled and dusted a fine layer of black dust off his hands.

Griggs rested Aubrey on the ground. "The Master Magi have all been defeated." The angel floated over to Jordana and Magnos. "The Terminal Prophecy is at hand."

Rodriqa sheathed the crucible shard in her pants pocket. "What is this Terminal Prophecy we keep hearing about?"

Griggs glanced at Rodriqa and smiled. "Oh, you'll figure it out, eventually." He examined Jordana and Magnos. "Now you two are in quite the pickle, aren't ya?"

Jordana looked down at her metal clothes and blushed.

Griggs looked around at the others. "Anyone have some extra clothes?"

Mr. Reiselstein limped forward. "Jordana can have my shirt." He unsnapped his plaid button-down and handed it to Griggs.

Jordana reared backward in her confines. "Can't you just turn our clothes back to the way they were?"

"Sorry." Griggs raised his hands. "Not my divinoi." Slowly, the angel shrank, and his wings folded into his back. Griggs transformed into his fleshly form, dressed in his forest-green uniform.

"Everyone look away." Griggs stared at Magnos. Magnos nodded and angled his head upward.

Turning his head away, Griggs ripped open Jordana's metal clothing and handed her Mr. Reiselstein's shirt. Then he unbuttoned his shirt, revealing his white T-shirt underneath. Griggs broke the slate around Magnos and handed him the top of his uniform.

Mr. Reiselstein limped toward Buzz. Buzz smiled and waddled over to his father. They met in an embrace. Mr. Reiselstein kissed his son's forehead. He got a small shock. Mr. Reiselstein reared back and laughed. He brushed down his son's hair and whispered to him, "I always knew you were something special."

Buzz looked up at his dad and hugged him harder.

Staring at Zaks, Aubrey rubbed his eyes. He pointed at the gray-skinned, baldheaded Magi. "What's happening?"

Everyone turned and stared at Zaks. Emanating from his fingers and shoulders, a flurry of tiny pink, blue, and green lights flitted through the air. Slowly, his digits and skin from his chest peeled away and floated upward, glowing in pastel colors. The trees and brush around them erupted in a similar flurry of tiny lights as reborn caterpillars broke free from their chrysalides.

Mr. Reiselstein marveled at the display. "Looks like the million moth metamorphosis is finally here."

Zaks lowered his head. Shway Shway hopped down and grabbed his master's legs, sobbing. Large tears plopped onto the dirt of the island.

"What's going on?" Rodriqa ran toward Zaks and gazed at him.

"The Magi chose a side." Griggs cleared his throat. "He broke the covenant that all Magi share with the Clockmaker."

"Griggs is correct." replied Zaks.

"Is he dying?" Aubrey's voice cracked.

Griggs shook his head. "The Magi is no longer neutral. He returns to the side he chose."

"What happens to Shway Shway?" Aubrey asked.

"The Bloodrunner anathem is broken." Griggs looked away. "He will be no more."

Shway Shway inhaled through snivels. "I'll go wherever you go, Master."

Zaks bent over and stared at his keeper. The Magi's left black eye closed. "No. You are the seer's teacher. You must stay with him."

"No!" Shway Shway wagged his head.

Zaks grasped Shway Shway by the scruff of his neck and pulled him into the air.

"No, Master!" Shway Shway writhed in the air.

"Enough." Zaks opened his black eye and glared at Shway Shway.

Shway Shway looked down, and his limbs dropped limply next to him.

Zaks sighed. "I have one gift left to offer." He plunged his free hand into his own chest. Light streamed outward from the edges of the hole. Through coughs and sputters, Zaks recited the Bloodrunner anathem.

Grunting, Zaks pulled his hand out of his chest. In his hand, the Magi's white stone, orbited by an orange light, glowed and then faded until it vanished.

Zaks's black eye dimmed. "Aubrey Taylor, Shway Shway is your keeper now."

The Magi stiffened. His skin blanched white. The remaining portions of Zaks's form transformed into a crumbling pillar of salt.

Shway Shway dropped to the ground. His backward-bent legs crumpled underneath him. He held his three-fingered hands over his large, green eyes and cried.

Numb, Aubrey stood still, staring at Shway Shway.

Rodriqa walked over to the keeper and squatted next to him. "You're gonna be okay." She rubbed his reptilian-skinned scalp.

Shway Shway looked up through his fingers. He wiped his face and nodded. "Yes, but you are not." Shway Shway pointed over Rodriqa's shoulder to the bank on the other side of the island.

Rodriqa turned around. Her friends, Mr. Reiselstein, and Griggs followed Shway Shway's finger.

"Mr. Reiselstein and Mr. Griggs! Back aways from the children!" With his gun aimed at the ground, Sergeant Van Zenny tromped through the dirt toward the five friends. Six other officers with their hands on their unsnapped holsters surrounded the sergeant.

Rodriqa stood up. "Flustered mustard."

Shway Shway disappeared.

Friday.

Materializing from the ether, Shway Shway slunk across the roof of the Lake Julian's City Hall. The setting sun cast a long shadow along the metal as he twisted his head from side to side, searching for anyone watching him.

Quickly, he scampered to the edge and crawled, head first, down the brick wall. Shway Shway peeked over the top edge of several windows until he stopped at a window on the first floor. From a glancing view, he could see a council room full of people with two banks of chairs occupying most of the back and middle. A podium and a long cherry wood council table were set near the front.

A head of red hair caught Shway Shway's attention. Aubrey, who was sitting in front between his father and Magnos on the left-hand side. Buzz and Mr. Reiselstein were to the right of Mr. Taylor. A row behind them, Aydria and Jamison Auerbach sat on either side of Rodriqa, and Principal Lequoia was beside Jordana, sitting in an aisle seat, so she could sit next to her father, Arturo, whose wheelchair was parked in the aisle. All of them stared quietly toward the front.

A growl echoed down the alleyway. Shway Shway turned toward the noise. A charcoal-and-cream-colored cat, its fur matted and twisted, bounded down the street and hopped onto the window ledge. Whimperfidget and Shway Shway glared at each other and then looked through the window.

Sitting behind the council table, Maximillian Miller shuffled through a pile of papers as Mayor Brackenwright and Judge Arsvine stood behind him, reading over his shoulder. The other town council members—Freyma Spindergrath, Earlyan Gungandeep, and Cyrus Harney—sat beside Mr. Miller. Mrs. Spindergrath was reading the front page of *The Lake Julian Mountain Lyre*, whose headline read, Town Council Meets, Decides Fate of NGW, above an enlarged photo of the friends escaping the shattered doors of the Rock-U-Quarium.

Behind Aubrey and his friends sat Ray and Elma Jennings. Elma tugged at Ray's shirtsleeve and pointed at his head. Ray slipped off his royal blue ball cap and combed a few sprigs of white hair forward with his fingers.

On the right-hand side, Dr. Gatchiri, Sergeant Van Zenny, and several of his deputies occupied the front row. Behind them sat Gaetan Taylor and Fayla Strumgarten among several rows of joxsters and rowdies from the high school, who were talking and giggling. Scores of parents and small business owners filled the rest of the seats on both sides of the aisle.

Jafar huddled up next to his mother, Brandy Gungandeep, in a couple of chairs at the back right corner.

Councilman Gungandeep looked at his wife, but her eyes stared past the council table. He licked his lips and leaned toward Mr. Harney. "I've never seen this many people at a town council meeting before." Mr. Gungandeep counted the number of people standing at the back of the room. "We might be exceeding fire capacity."

Mr. Harney glanced over his glasses at his fellow councilman. "Good. That will give us a good reason to ask folks to leave if they start acting up."

Weaving her way through the crowd, McCrayden Miller strode into the council room, her golden curls bouncing against her cashmere cardigan, and rouge blushing her pale cheeks. She pushed her way toward the front and sat down casually next to Vidalia Arsvine.

Vidalia turned toward McCrayden and looked her up and down. "There she is. It's about time you showed up."

McCrayden kept her face forward, watching her father and the mayor speak to each other. "Oh, I wouldn't miss this for anything."

Pam Trank leaned forward in her seat, trying to get McCrayden to look at her. "Cray, where have you been?"

Shrugging her shoulders, McCrayden glanced at Pam. "I've been around."

Vidalia chuckled. "No, you haven't. We've been trying to find you all week."

"Glamor glitch much?" McCrayden flipped her hair and looked away. "It was my spring break. I wanted to have a little fun."

"Fun, huh?" Jon Harney pushed up his fedora, revealing the greenish yellow hues of healing bruises under his eyes. "What kind of fun?"

"I never reveal all my secrets." McCrayden twisted a silver bracelet, embedded with an assortment of precious gems, on her wrist. "It adds to my mystery."

"Your dad has been worried sick about you," accused Mesilla.

"Yeah, he's been bugging us for days," agreed Zaniah.

McCrayden sighed. "Daddy's fine. He was a little upset with me at first, but I told him I'd been with my Aunt Sally, and he calmed down. I made him his favorite sweet potato waffles, and he had to forgive me for being gone."

"Were you with your Aunt Sally?" asked Jon.

With a flinch to her brow, McCrayden scoffed. "No, but she always covers for me."

"Have you heard about everything that's happened?" asked Vidalia. McCrayden nodded.

"It's crazy." Pam Trank shook her head. "Those misfits destroyed two buildings and made like fifty people sick."

Vidalia sat up straight. "Your dad and my dad are gonna make sure those yobs are locked up for life."

"One can only hope." McCrayden glared across the room at Aubrey.

Aubrey glanced over his shoulder. His and McCrayden's eyes met. She was smiling at him, but her brow quivered with rage. A cold shiver raced across his shoulders.

Aubrey looked forward and slumped down in his chair. "Everyone in town is here."

Mr. Taylor glanced over his shoulder. "Almost."

"What does Mom think about all of this?"

"I hadn't told her." Mr. Taylor pinched his lips together. "I don't think she could handle it."

Aubrey nodded and looked down.

With a series of loud raps, Mr. Miller banged his gavel. The rustling din of the crowd quieted, and every eye focused toward the front of the room. Judge Arsvine stepped away from the table and sat in a pair of chairs to Mr. Miller's left.

Mayor Brackenwright walked to the front of the council table and held up his hands.

"I call this meeting of the Lake Julian Town Council to order on this twenty-third day of April, at…" the mayor glanced down at his watch, "…6:10 p.m." He glanced to his left. "Mr. Harney, have you taken roll?"

Mr. Harney nodded. "All members of the town council are present."

"Representing the town of Lake Julian as counsel, we also have Judge Rakeman Arsvine present this evening." Mayor Brackenwright raised his hand toward the judge. "Please make note of it."

"Yes, sir." Mr. Harney scratched a small scribble on the paper in front of him.

The mayor lowered his hands. "I am very sad we are meeting like this today. I have always seen it as my duty to be a protector of children, not their accuser." The mayor took a step forward. "However, this week, Lake Julian has been seriously injured. As head steward of our community, it is my job to protect our well-being in every regard, no matter how distasteful it may seem."

The mayor raised his hands toward the five friends and their families. "Because of the allegations these children face and the seriousness of their consequences, I felt it appropriate for our town to contribute to either their innocence or their guilt before proceeding further with formal charges." The mayor nodded toward the judge. "As the children are present at the discretion of the city administration and do not currently have counsel, they and their families have been instructed by Judge Arsvine that is in their best interest to remain quiet at this time." The mayor turned toward the council table. "Councilman Miller, the floor is yours." The mayor took a seat next to the judge.

Mr. Miller stood up and turned toward the American flag in the back corner. "Thank you, Mayor. Now, if everyone will please stand for the Pledge of Allegiance."

Scoots and shuffles echoed throughout the room as everyone not already standing stood up. Most placed their right hands over their chests.

Buzz leaned up to his dad. "Do you think they'll take us back to jail tonight?"

Mr. Reiselstein grimaced. "I hope not."

Tears swelled in Buzz's lower eyelids. "I can't stay in there another night."

Mr. Reiselstein wrapped his arm around his son's shoulders. "We'll figure something out." Mr. Reiselstein looked down at Magnos. "I thought Ragna Strumgarten would be here. I called her." Mr. Reiselstein glanced around the back of the room. "I thought for sure she would show up." Magnos leaned against the chair in front of him and stared at the floor.

Everyone recited the Pledge of Allegiance. The tone of many of the voices was dull and somber, more like a funeral prayer than an assertion of loyalty.

Mr. Miller waved his hands down. "Please take your seats." He sat down, and everyone who had a chair followed suit. Mr. Miller moved several stacks of papers around in front of him. "Today's meeting will be focused on a single agenda item. This will be a public forum to obtain information from our community to determine the culpability of Aubrey Taylor, Rodriqa Auerbach, Virgil Reiselstein, Magnos Strumgarten, and Jordana Galilahi in recent untoward events that have adversely affected the prosperity of Lake Julian and its citizens." Mr. Miller glared at the front row. "These aforementioned five minors are allegedly responsible for afflicting more than fifty individuals with a debilitating illness, the flagrant destruction of local properties, and propagating deception regarding the nature of their furtive activities.

"As we have been unable to locate Mr. Jobe Parotty…"

Buzz leaned forward and, with raised eyebrows, stared at his father and Aubrey. Keeping his gaze on Mr. Miller, Mr. Reiselstein slid his hand onto Buzz's chest and pressed him back into his chair.

"...I will represent the State of the Mart Corporation as a member of its board." Mr. Miller rested his hand on one of the stacks of papers. "Insurance adjustors and forensic engineers have evaluated both disaster sites. In short, these documents clearly state that the destruction of the two establishments was due to an explosion from an incendiary or chemical device, most likely of amateur construction, and the approximate cost of repairs is estimated at forty-three million dollars."

Mr. Jennings whistled loudly. An angry murmur rippled through the crowd. Rodriqa's eyes widened. She crossed her arms and dropped her chin. Jordana slid in her seat closer to her uncle.

Mr. Miller banged his gavel. "Our first witnesses are—" he read another sheet of paper. "—Mr. Ned and Fred Kluggard."

Dressed in matching gray security guard uniforms, the rotund Ned and the lanky Fred walked down the aisle. Ned stopped in front of the microphone on the podium and pulled it down by its adjustable neck. Fred stood limply beside him.

"Thank you for hearing us, sir." Ned grinned.

Mr. Miller's eyes shifted between the two men. "What do you have to share with the city council?"

Ned stepped closer to the mic. "We have had several run-ins with these children since last fall. Every instance where these delinquents were involved, either something was destroyed or someone was killed."

Several members of the audience clapped. Many others groaned angrily.

"We won't say more without a lawyer present, but there is nothing good about any of these kids." Ned turned his head and glared at Aubrey. "And they deserve to be punished."

Aubrey gritted his teeth. Hoping to disappear, he closed his eyes.

Ned's eyes widened. He faced Mr. Miller. "That's all we have to say for now." Quickly, he grabbed Fred by the arm, and the two of them shuffled out of the council room.

"Okay." Mr. Miller frowned and looked down at his paper. "Next, we have Stanley and Francine Losepkee from Wassahatchet, New Jersey. Reportedly, they were tourists visiting Lake Julian for the million moth metamorphosis."

"That's right!" Fran Losepkee stood up at the back. Her blonde hair was curled, and the dark roots were teased out at her temples. Her bright red lipstick matched her miniskirt, and her sleeveless white blouse exposed rolls of fat under her arms. "Come on, Stan!" She smacked her husband on the shoulder. Fran marched up to the podium. Stan followed behind her with his head down. He wore a green long-sleeved shirt, two sizes too small, causing the material to stretch at the buttons.

Fran winked at Mr. Miller, and she leaned into the microphone. Her smile wrinkled into a frown as she gazed at Aubrey. "These children are a menace! They drugged me and my husband, carried us to the caves, and kept us there for days." Fran turned and faced the audience. "One can only imagine what they had in store for us."

Buzz smacked his fist into his thigh. Rodriqa squeezed her heels and toes together, trying to keep herself from saying anything.

"That's terrible, Mrs. Losepkee." Mr. Miller scribbled on his paper. "Perhaps we should add kidnapping and unlawful imprisonment to their charges."

"I think you should," barked Fran. "And this one is sicko fresh." She pointed to Magnos. "He tried to grab my..." She pointed to her chest. "I can only guess the nasty thoughts running through his mind."

A couple of gasps escaped the crowd, followed by a few snickers. Magnos blushed and shook his head.

"Ah, yes." Mr. Miller nodded and twisted his lips. "Thank you very much, Mr. and Mrs. Losepkee. Sergeant Van Zenny will be available to take your statement after the proceedings."

"Thank you, sir." Fran smiled widely at Mr. Miller. Stan glared at Fran. She grabbed his arm and pulled him toward the back of the room.

Mr. Miller shook his head. "Now, Dr. Iyashi Gatchiri will speak on behalf of the those afflicted with the illness in question this week." Mr. Miller glanced at the short Japanese woman with white hair who sat in the front row. "Doctor."

Rodriqa grunted. Aydria Auerbach's head snapped toward her daughter, her nose and forehead wrinkled. Rodriqa sank in her chair.

Dr. Gatchiri stood up and pulled her electronic tablet from her satchel at the foot of her chair. She straightened the jacket of her black pantsuit and strode toward the podium.

Mr. Miller smiled. "We are grateful for the input and direction of the I-5, in our community's hour of need."

Dr. Gatchiri pulled the adjustable microphone all the way down and rested her tablet on the podium. "As always, the Institute prides itself in recognizing and treating disease and investigating maladies that are difficult to explain from a pathological perspective."

"Thank you for your time, Doctor." Mr. Miller leaned back in his chair. "What do you have to share with the town council this evening?"

Dr. Gatchiri tapped her tablet and the liquid crystal illuminated. "We have concluded our evaluation of the fifty-three patients who suffered from a series of similar symptoms, including catatonia, pallor, and autonomic dysregulation. I have discussed our findings with my superiors, and after consultations with the highest experts, we are happy with our final conclusion."

"Wonderful, Doctor." Mr. Miller rolled his neck.

Dr. Gatchiri crinkled her lip, and her scar wrinkled. "Have you ever heard of *folie à deux*?"

"No, Doctor. Please enlighten us."

"It is extremely rare, and potentially debilitating to all parties involved, regardless of prior medical history."

Mr. Miller rested his chin against his hand. "Go on."

"Folie *à deux* is a shared psychotic disorder where one person's hallucinations are so compelling that it essentially 'infects' another person's mind, resulting in the sharing of psychosis between individuals."

Mr. Miller's mouth hung open. "You can't be serious."

"Absolutely," continued Dr. Gatchiri. "There have been a few reported cases of *folie a trois* and even *folie a famille*. But this may be the first documented case of *folie a petite ville*."

"What?" Mr. Miller leaned forward in his chair and raised his hand at Aubrey. "But you told me these children created this plague."

"You asked me if these suspected children could be responsible for the illness, and I told you, 'In a sense, yes.'" Dr. Gatchiri held up her finger. "Their delusion has become a shared delusion. Therefore, they are the index cases of this illness. But they are no more responsible for spreading psychosis than a person with a cold is responsible for causing an influenza pandemic."

Rodriqa raised her hand and clenched her fist. Buzz kicked the legs of his chair in a flurry of tiny knocks.

Mr. Miller furrowed his brow. "Then are you accusing all the people in our town of being crazy?"

"No." Dr. Gatchiri raised her chin. "But it seems this plague was all supratentorial."

"Excuse me?" growled Mr. Miller.

Dr. Gatchiri pointed to her temple.

"That's your official conclusion," huffed Mr. Miller.

"It is." Dr. Gatchiri tapped her tablet. It turned off. "You will have my complete report in six to eight weeks." The doctor turned, walked down the aisle and out of the council room.

Mr. Miller rubbed his bald head. "Not withstanding this new information, we have accumulated the necessary evidence to press charges." Mr. Miller glanced at his paper. "As there are no further witnesses to the delinquency in question, I move to adjourn this meeting."

"Excuse me." A shrill voice echoed from the back of the room. Mr. Miller looked up and curled his lip. Everyone turned around to see who had spoken.

Standing in the middle of the aisle, a few steps in front of the crowd, Ragna Strumgarten, dressed in her Marine blue dress uniform and white cap, stood with her feet apart and her hands clasped at her waist. The light from the ceiling glinted off the dozen gold and silver medals hanging next to her lapel.

She stared at Mr. Miller. "I apologize for my tardiness. The world is a dangerous place."

"Even more so in Lake Julian," replied Mr. Miller.

"So it seems." Ragna Strumgarten walked down the aisle toward the podium.

Magnos stood up. "Mom?" he whispered. She was half of his height. Raising her hand, she nodded toward her son's chair. Magnos sat back down.

Mr. Miller slid his piles of papers together. "What can I do for you, Colonel?"

Colonel Strumgarten spoke into the microphone. "I met several individuals outside, who said they weren't allowed to attend tonight's town council meeting, even though they had something to share. As it has been my duty to protect our freedoms for more than thirty years, I didn't think you would object to me letting them in." The colonel turned around and waved a small group forward.

Mr. Miller hung his head.

Emerging from the standing crowd, Coren Belward and five young Boy Scouts, each dressed in their uniforms, shuffled toward the podium.

The colonel stepped aside and looked at Coren. "Tell them what you told me outside."

Coren's Adam's apple bobbed in his throat. He pulled the adjustable microphone up to his mouth. "Lake Julian was attacked by monsters."

Chuckles trilled throughout the room.

A scout next to Coren grabbed the microphone. "He's serious. Your town is infested with these…these chupacabras."

Guffaws and cackles roared in the council room. Mr. Miller looked up and smiled.

Another scout leaned into the mic. "They attacked all of us. We saw it."

The laughter continued. Mr. Vandereff, Brandy Gungandeep, and Elma and Ray Gene Jennings stared at the floor.

"Laugh all you want." Coren's voice cracked. "But if it wasn't for the bravery and determination of Aubrey Taylor and his friends, my scouts wouldn't be alive today."

Wiping a gleeful tear from his eye, Mr. Miller pointed at the podium. "What's your name again?"

"Coren Belward, sir," replied the scout leader.

"And what troop is this?"

"Troop 254, St. Pinnetakwah Council of northeast Georgia."

"And why were you visiting Lake Julian?"

"My Eagle Scout project was to provide basic medical care to those visiting the million moth metamorphosis."

"Really?" Mr. Miller chuckled. "Perhaps you've snorted a few too many of your Epsom salts then."

Colonel Strumgarten stepped up to the podium. "Mr. Miller, your tone is highly inappropriate—"

"The good doctor has already determined there was no real plague, ergo no monsters." Mr. Miller waved the colonel off. "The children of the NGW will still be held liable for the massive destruction of property in Lake Julian. Now I move to adjourn this meeting."

Coren and his scouts skulked away from the podium.

"Wait!" The colonel stepped around the podium. "There is someone else who wants to speak."

Mr. Miller turned to the Mayor. "How much more of this foolishness do we have to listen to?"

Mayor Brackenwright stood up with his hands raised.

"I have something you may want to see." Standing at the podium holding a CD, Griggs wrapped his arm around Mena Kontrearo. Her head was wrapped with a thick cotton bandage, and she carried a laptop under her arm.

"Now I have to listen to the high school janitor?" scoffed Mr. Miller.

Griggs handed Mena the CD. Gently, he pushed her forward. Mena strode up to the council table and placed her laptop in front of Mr. Miller. Mr. Miller rolled his eyes and leaned back in his chair. Mena opened the laptop and turned it so the monitor faced him. She inserted the CD and hit the Enter key. "Watch this."

Black and white video flashed across the screen. Freyma Spindergrath, Earlyan Gungandeep, and Cyrus Harney leaned toward Mr. Miller to watch. Mayor Brackenwright and Judge Arsvine walked over and stood behind Mr. Miller.

Griggs stepped forward. "This is a security CD retrieved from the cleanup site at the Rock-U-Quarium. It shows the final minutes inside."

Buzz and Rodriqa jumped out of their seats and ran up to the council table. Aydria and Arvel grabbed at their children, but they slipped out of their grasps.

Buzz and Rodriqa stood next to Mena, leaning over to see the screen.

The video replayed several short segments, each lasting only a few seconds as it flipped between cameras. In each segment, a curvy woman with soaking wet hair destroyed Cyber Rudders outside of the Re-Reality Room and ripped apart tables in the main ballroom. Mr. Miller crossed his arms as he watched Magnolia Thistlewood demolish the insides of the Rock-u-Quarium.

"Yes!" shouted Rodriqa. "Now you know who the real enemy is!"

Buzz turned the screen around to face the podium. He waved everyone forward. Aubrey, Jordana, and Magnos ran up to the table. Most of the seated adults stood up and, threading through folks meandering from the back, walked toward the council table.

Rodriqa leaned down to Mena's ear and whispered, "You're our hero!"

Mena grinned broadly.

Jordana smiled as she watched the video. She tapped Mena on the shoulder. Mena turned around, and Jordana hugged her.

Mr. Miller banged his gavel. "Everyone back off! This video doesn't prove anything!"

Judge Asrvine leaned over the council table. "Actually, it proves everything."

Mayor Brackenwright nodded. "This woman is who we need to prosecute."

Mr. Miller stood up. "But...but we can't forget..."

"Max, forget the kids," interrupted the judge. "We have bigger snails to shuck."

"I'm so glad you came." Wrapping his arms around his much smaller mother, Magnos hugged the colonel tightly among the murmuring and departing crowd.

The colonel squeezed him back. "Clearly, I need to be home more often." She pulled back and reached up, holding her son's face in her hands. "I need to get a closer assignment."

Grinning, Magnos nodded and looked down. "That would be nice."

From the rooftop, Shway Shway and Whimperfidget stared at the crowds leaving through the front doors of Lake Julian's City Hall. Both creatures craned their necks, hunting for their new masters.

"Hoaker croaker! You are amazing!" Buzz hugged Mena's neck. "Where did you find it?" Aubrey, Rodriqa, Jordana, Buzz, and Mena stepped down the front steps of City Hall into the cool night air.

Mena grunted under Buzz's squeeze. "After I left the hospital the other night, I decided to head back to the scene of the crime." Mena looked Rodriqa up and down. "Especially after seeing Rodriqa's ghost form in action. I ran into Griggs there. He showed me where to find the CD. It was under a pile of rubble, completely untarnished. I couldn't believe it."

"That's so awesome." Aubrey chuckled.

Mena looked behind them. "Where is Griggs?"

"Oh, he'll show up...sometime." Buzz nudged Aubrey. "Hey! Look!" Rodriqa pointed down the sidewalk. "There's Coren!"

They hurried down Lake Julian Square.

Coren saluted them. He reached out and air-rubbed Mena's head. "How's the wound, X?"

"I'm on the mend." Mena hugged Coren at the waist.

"X?" Rodriqa scrunched her cheeks. "Who's X?"

Coren rested his chin gently on Mena's head. "Her real name is Xiomena. I found that out when I checked her into the hospital. So I started calling her X."

Mena stepped back and arched her back. "I like it. Makes me feel kinda thug."

Rodriqa and Buzz glanced at each other with uplifted brows.

"So what about all the chupacabras?" asked Coren. "How many more are there? Where did they come from? Did you figure out how to kill them?"

Buzz chortled, pulling out his cell phone. "Give me your number. I'll text you the story sometime."

Jamison Auerbach walked up behind his daughter and placed his hand on her shoulder. "This is it for the shenanigans. No more. Do you understand me?"

Rodriqa turned around, out of her father's grip, and raised her chin. "But we don't find trouble..." Suddenly, Rodriqa saw something cream-and-charcoal-colored flash above her father. Quickly, she shoved her father back and held out her arms. Whimperfidget jumped onto her chest. and nuzzled her neck. "It finds us."

Mr. Auerbach's head twisted as he glanced between the sky and his daughter.

Aydria Auerbach laughed, walking up to her husband and looping her arm around his elbow. "Obstinacy is a family trait." She leaned into his ear. "I don't think you'll win this battle tonight, honey."

"I'd listen to Aydry on this one." Dan Taylor walked up to Aubrey and ruffled his son's hair. "I learned the hard way."

Aubrey smiled. Combing his stringy red hair with his fingers, he leaned into his dad. Jordana wrapped her arms around Aubrey's elbow. She smiled at him. Aubrey's heart pounded feverishly as his cheeks flushed.

"And I've learned that sometimes a little faith in your child goes a long way." Arvel Reiselstein walked up behind Buzz and rubbed his fist into his son's scalp. Buzz shook his head and tussled with his father.

Mr. Auerbach curled his lip. "Well, we're not keeping the cat."

Purring loudly, Whimperfidget crawled onto Rodriqa's shoulders and then slipped back down into her arms.

Rodriqa kissed Whimperfidget's ear. "But he won't leave me alone."

Sighing, Mrs. Auerbach shrugged her shoulders. "A pet is better than a monster, I suppose."

Shway Shway leapt from the top of the City Hall building and landed in the middle of the huddle.

Hopping away, Mrs. Auerbach shrieked. The three fathers furrowed their brows and took a step back.

Shway Shway turned in circles, looking up at everyone around him with his large, round green eyes. His flap-like ears drooped against his reptilian skin. He raked the sidewalk with his hooves and then hopped into Aubrey's arms.

Aubrey caught him, teetering sideways to maintain his balance. "Bad news, Dad. I've got my own monster."

"What is that thing?" asked Mrs. Auerbach.

"It's a chupacabra." Mena stepped forward and reached out to scratch Shway Shway's ear.

Shway Shway growled, "Not a chupacabra. A keeper." The creature slapped Aubrey's chest. "Aubrey's keeper."

Aubrey winced and nodded.

Coren pointed at Shway Shway. "Isn't that the enemy?!"

Buzz waved Coren off. "It's complicated."

"I can't believe this." Mr. Miller threw a pile of papers in a trashcan as he stormed out of city hall. "McCrayden, mark my words. A pig rots from the snout out. Once society loosens its hold on indiscretions, it gives the rest of the swine a green light to tap the glutton button."

"You are so right, Daddy." McCrayden grabbed his arm and walked next to him. "You'll have another chance. You know they won't stay out of trouble for long."

Mr. Miller snorted. "Right you are."

The rowdies and joxsters raced up behind McCrayden and Mr. Miller as they marched down the sidewalk.

Mr. Miller squeezed his daughter's hand. "Aubrey Taylor is officially on my Git List."

McCrayden chuckled. "I'm with you on that one."

"He's a total toad thrower, Mr. Miller." Gaetan Taylor trotted up next to him. "I know. I've had to live with him for fifteen years."

"I can't believe my mother." Fayla held onto Gaetan's arm. "She's never home. Why tonight? She had to show up tonight, of all nights."

Mr. Miller stopped suddenly. He stared down the sidewalk. Everyone else slowed and huddled around him.

"What's wrong?" asked Gaetan.

Mr. Miller pushed Gaetan aside and took several steps forward. "Aubrey Taylor!"

Aubrey, his friends, and their parents turned toward Mr. Miller, who was twenty yards down the square. Aubrey handed Shway Shway to Buzz and stepped out from their circle. Mr. Taylor reached for Aubrey, but Aubrey slipped out of his grasp.

Shway Shway moaned and pressed his three-fingered hands against Buzz's face. Buzz gripped the creature around his thin torso and struggled to hide him.

"Yes?" Aubrey held up his chin and glared at Mr. Miller.

"Aubrey Taylor." Mr. Miller held out a pointed finger. "I'll have my eyes on you." Aubrey pressed his lips together. There was so much he wanted to say, but he knew tonight he had won, and he wouldn't do or say anything to ruin that victory for himself or his friends.

Shway Shway clacked his hooves together and pinched Buzz's belly.

"Ouch!" grunted Buzz. He dropped Shway Shway.

The creature bounded out of the circle, over Aubrey's head, and landed a few feet in front of Aubrey. Shway Shway inhaled as he spoke. "And Aubrey Taylor will have his eyes on you!" His large, green eyes peered at Mr. Miller, and he exposed the tips of his sharp teeth.

Aubrey picked up Shway Shway and ran back toward his father. Quickly, the entire circle of Aubrey's friends and their parents shifted forward. Mr. Miller gasped and hurriedly walked away.

"Ew!" Fayla shuddered. "What was that?"

"Freaks," muttered Gaetan. He shook his head.

The circle of friends and parents around Aubrey glided down the sidewalk away from Mr. Miller.

The teens around Mr. Miller sneered at Aubrey, following the councilman up Lake Julian Square. All except McCrayden. McCrayden stood in the middle of the sidewalk, rubbing her silver bracelet and staring at Aubrey. Just staring.